The Second Book of
# Ayesha

The Second Book of
# Ayesha

She and Allan

★

Wisdom's Daughter

## H. Rider Haggard

LEONAUR

*The Second Book of Ayesha—She and Allan & Wisdom's Daughter*
by H. Rider Haggard

Leonaur is an imprint of Oakpast Ltd

Material original to this edition and
presentation of the text in this form
copyright © 2009 Oakpast Ltd

ISBN: 978-1-84677-724-0 (hardcover)
ISBN: 978-1-84677-723-3 (softcover)

**http://www.leonaur.com**

**Publisher's Notes**

The views expressed in this book are not necessarily
those of the publisher.

# Contents

# She and Allan

# Note by the Late
# Mr. Allan Quatermain

My friend, into whose hands I hope that all these manuscripts of mine will pass one day, of this one I have something to say to you.

A long while ago I jotted down in it the history of the events that it details with more or less completeness. This I did for my own satisfaction. You will have noted how memory fails us as we advance in years; we recollect, with an almost painful exactitude, what we experienced and saw in our youth, but the happenings of our middle life slip away from us or become blurred, like a stretch of low-lying landscape overflowed by grey and nebulous mist. Far off the sun still seems to shine upon the plains and hills of adolescence and early manhood, as yet it shines about us in the fleeting hours of our age, that ground on which we stand today, but the valley between is filled with fog. Yes, even its prominences, which symbolise the more startling events of that past, often are lost in this confusing fog.

It was an appreciation of these truths which led me to set down the following details (though of course much is omitted) of my brief intercourse with the strange and splendid creature whom I knew under the names of *Ayesha*, or *Híya*, or *She-who-commands*; not indeed with any view to their publication, but before I forgot them that, if I wished to do so, I might re-peruse them in the evening of old age to which I hope to attain.

Indeed, at the time the last thing I intended was that they should be given to the world even after my own death, because they, or many of them, are so unusual that I feared lest they should cause smiles and in a way cast a slur upon my memory and truthfulness. Also, as you will read, as to this matter I made a promise and I have always tried to keep my promises and to guard the secrets of others. For these reasons I proposed, in case I neglected or forgot to destroy them myself, to

9

leave a direction that this should be done by my executors. Further, I have been careful to make no allusion *whatever* to them either in casual conversation or in anything else that I may have written, my desire being that this page of my life should be kept quite private, something known only to myself. Therefore, too, I never so much as hinted of them to anyone, not even to yourself to whom I have told so much.

Well, I recorded the main facts concerning this expedition and its issues, simply and with as much exactness as I could, and laid them aside. I do not say that I never thought of them again, since amongst them were some which, together with the problems they suggested, proved to be of an unforgettable nature.

Also, whenever any of Ayesha's sayings or stories which are not preserved in these pages came back to me, as has happened from time to time, I jotted them down and put them away with this manuscript. Thus among these notes you will find a history of the city of Kôr as she told it to me, which I have omitted here. Still, many of these remarkable events did more or less fade from my mind, as the image does from an unfixed photograph, till only their outlines remained, faint if distinguishable.

To tell the truth, I was rather ashamed of the whole story in which I cut so poor a figure. On reflection it was obvious to me, although honesty had compelled me to set out all that is essential exactly as it occurred, adding nothing and taking nothing away, that I had been the victim of very gross deceit. This strange woman, whom I had met in the ruins of a place called Kôr, without any doubt had thrown a glamour over my senses and at the moment almost caused me to believe much that is quite unbelievable.

For instance, she had told me ridiculous stories as to interviews between herself and certain heathen goddesses, though it is true that, almost with her next breath, these she qualified or contradicted. Also, she had suggested that her life had been prolonged far beyond our mortal span, for hundreds and hundreds of years, indeed; which, as Euclid says, is absurd, and had pretended to supernatural powers, which is still more absurd. Moreover, by a clever use of some hypnotic or mesmeric power, she had feigned to transport me to some place beyond the earth and in the Halls of Hades to show me what is veiled from the eyes of man, and not only me, but the savage warrior Umhlopekazi, commonly called Umslopogaas of the Axe, who, with Hans, a Hottentot, was my companion upon that adventure. There were like things equally incredible, such as her appearance, when all seemed lost, in the battle with the troll-like Rezu. To omit these, the sum of it was that I had been shamefully duped, and if anyone finds himself in that position, as most people have at one time or another in their lives, Wisdom suggests that he had better keep the circumstances to himself.

Well, so the matter stood, or rather lay in the recesses of my mind—and in the cupboard where I hide my papers—when one evening someone, as a matter of fact it was Captain Good, an individual of romantic tendencies who is fond, sometimes I think too fond, of fiction, brought a book to this house which he insisted over and over again really I must peruse.

Ascertaining that it was a novel I declined, for to tell the truth I am not fond of romance in any shape, being a person who has found the hard facts of life of sufficient interest as they stand.

Reading I admit I like, but in this matter, as in everything else, my range is limited. I study the Bible, especially the Old Testament, both because of its sacred lessons and of the majesty of the language of its inspired translators; whereof that of Ayesha, which I render so poorly from her flowing and melodious Arabic, reminded me. For poetry I turn to Shakespeare, and, at the other end of the scale, to the *Ingoldsby Legends*, many of which I know almost by heart, while for current affairs I content myself with the newspapers.

For the rest I peruse anything to do with ancient Egypt that I happen to come across, because this land and its history have a queer fascination for me, that perhaps has its roots in occurrences or dreams of which this is not the place to speak. Lastly now and again I read one of the Latin or Greek authors in a translation, since I regret to say that my lack of education does not enable me to do so in the original. But for modern fiction I have no taste, although from time to time I sample it in a railway train and occasionally am amused by such excursions into the poetic and unreal.

So it came about that the more Good bothered me to read this particular romance, the more I determined that I would do nothing of the sort. Being a persistent person, however, when he went away about ten o'clock at night, he deposited it by my side, under my nose indeed, so that it might not be overlooked. Thus it came about that I could not help seeing some Egyptian hieroglyphics in an oval on the cover, also the title, and underneath it your own name, my friend, all of which excited my curiosity, especially the title, which was brief and enigmatic, consisting indeed of one word, "*She*."

I took up the work and on opening it the first thing my eye fell upon was a picture of a veiled woman, the sight of which made my heart stand still, so painfully did it remind me of a certain veiled woman whom once it had been my fortune to meet. Glancing from it to the printed page one word seemed to leap at me. It was *Kôr*! Now of veiled women there are plenty in the world, but were there also two Kôrs?

Then I turned to the beginning and began to read. This happened in the autumn when the sun does not rise till about six, but it was broad daylight before I ceased from reading, or rather rushing through that book.

Oh! what was I to make of it? For here in its pages (to say nothing of old Billali, who, by the way lied, probably to order, when he told Mr. Holly that no white man had visited his country for many generations, and those gloomy, man-eating Amahagger scoundrels) once again I found myself face to face with *She-who-commands*, now rendered as *She-who-must-be-obeyed*, which means much the same thing—in her case at least; yes, with Ayesha the lovely, the mystic, the changeful and the imperious.

Moreover the history filled up many gaps in my own limited experiences of that enigmatical being who was half divine (though, I think, rather wicked or at any rate unmoral in her way) and yet all woman. It is true that it showed her in lights very different from and higher than those in which she had presented herself to me. Yet the substratum of her character was the same, or rather of her characters, for of these she seemed to have several in a single body, being, as she said of herself to me, "not *one* but *many* and not *here* but *everywhere*."

Further, I found the story of Kallikrates, which I had set down as a mere falsehood invented for my bewilderment, expanded and explained. Or rather not explained, since, perhaps that she might deceive, to me she had spoken of this murdered Kallikrates without enthusiasm, as a handsome person to whom, because of an indiscretion of her youth, she was bound by destiny and whose return—somewhat to her sorrow—she must wait. At least she did so at first, though in the end when she bared her heart at the moment of our farewell, she vowed she loved him only and was "appointed" to him "by a divine decree."

Also I found other things of which I knew nothing, such as the Fire of Life with its fatal gift of indefinite existence, although I remember that like the giant Rezu whom Umslopogaas defeated, she did talk of a "Cup of Life" of which she had drunk, that might have been offered to my lips, had I been politic, bowed the knee and shown more faith in her and her supernatural pretensions.

Lastly I saw the story of her end, and as I read it I wept, yes, I confess I wept, although I feel sure that she will return again. Now I understood why she had quailed and even seemed to shrivel when, in my last interview with her, stung beyond endurance by her witcheries and sarcasms, I had suggested that even for her with all her powers, Fate might reserve one of its shrewdest blows. Some prescience had told her that if the words seemed random, Truth spoke through my lips, although, and this was the worst of it, she did not know what weapon would deal the stroke or when and where it was doomed to fall.

I was amazed, I was overcome, but as I closed that book I made up my mind, first that I would continue to preserve absolute silence as to Ayesha and my dealings with her, as, during my life, I was bound by oath to do, and secondly that I would *not* cause my manuscript to be destroyed. I did not feel that I had any right to do so in view of what already had been published to the world. There let it lie to appear one day, or not to appear, as might be fated. Meanwhile my lips were sealed. I would give Good back his book without comment and—buy another copy!

One more word. It is clear that I did not touch more than the fringe of the real Ayesha. In a thousand ways she bewitched and deceived me so that I never plumbed her nature's depths. Perhaps this was my own fault because from the first I showed a lack of faith in her and she wished to pay me back in her own fashion, or perhaps she had other private reasons for her secrecy. Certainly the character she discovered to me differed in many ways from that which she revealed to Mr. Holly and to Leo Vincey, or Kallikrates, whom, it seems, once she slew in her jealousy and rage.

She told me as much as she thought it fit that I should know, and no more!

*Allan Quatermain*
The Grange
Yorkshire

## CHAPTER 1

# The Talisman

I believe it was the old Egyptians, a very wise people, probably indeed much wiser than we know, for in the leisure of their ample centuries they had time to think out things, who declared that each individual personality is made up of six or seven different elements, although the Bible only allows us three, namely, body, soul, and spirit. The body that the man or woman wore, if I understand their theory aright which perhaps I, an ignorant person, do not, was but a kind of sack or fleshly covering containing these different principles. Or mayhap it did not contain them all, but was simply a house as it were, in which they lived from time to time and seldom all together, although one or more of them was present continually, as though to keep the place warmed and aired.

This is but a casual illustrative suggestion, for what right have I, Allan Quatermain, out of my little reading and probably erroneous deductions, to form any judgment as to the theories of the old Egyptians? Still these, as I understand them, suffice to furnish me with the text that man is not one, but many, in which connection it may be remembered that often in Scripture he is spoken of as being the home of many demons, seven, I think. Also, to come to another far-off example, the Zulus talk of their witch-doctors as being inhabited by "a multitude of spirits."

Anyhow of one thing I am quite sure, we are not always the same. Different personalities actuate us at different times. In one hour passion of this sort or the other is our lord; in another we are reason itself. In one hour we follow the basest appetites; in another we hate them and the spirit arising through our mortal murk shines within or above us like a star. In one hour our desire is to kill and spare not; in another we are filled with the holiest compassion even towards an insect or a snake, and are ready to forgive like a god. Everything rules us in turn, to such an extent indeed, that sometimes one begins to wonder whether we really rule anything.

Now the reason of all this homily is that I, Allan, the most practical and unimaginative of persons, just a homely, half-educated hunter and trader who chances to have seen a good deal of the particular little world in which his lot was cast, at one period of my life became the victim of spiritual longings.

I am a man who has suffered great bereavements in my time such as have seared my soul, since, perhaps because of my rather primitive and simple nature, my affections are very strong. By day or night I can never forget those whom I have loved and whom I believe to have loved me.

For you know, in our vanity some of us are apt to hold that certain people with whom we have been intimate upon the earth, really did care for us and, in our still greater vanity—or should it be called madness?—to imagine that they still care for us after they have left the earth and entered on some new state of society and surroundings which, if they exist, inferentially are much more congenial than any they can have experienced here. At times, however, cold doubts strike us as to this matter, of which we long to know the truth. Also behind looms a still blacker doubt, namely whether they live at all.

For some years of my lonely existence these problems haunted me day by day, till at length I desired above everything on earth to lay them at rest in one way or another. Once, at Durban, I met a man who was a spiritualist to whom I confided a little of my perplexities. He laughed at me and said that they could be settled with the greatest ease. All I had to do was to visit a certain local medium who for a fee of one guinea would tell me everything I wanted to know. Although I rather grudged the guinea, being more than usually hard up at the time, I called upon this person, but over the results of that visit, or rather the lack of them, I draw a veil.

My queer and perhaps unwholesome longing, however, remained with me and would not be abated. I consulted a clergyman of my acquaintance, a good and spiritually-minded man, but he could only shrug his shoulders and refer me to the Bible, saying, quite rightly I doubt not, that with what it reveals I ought to be contented. Then I read certain mystical books which were recommended to me. These were full of fine words, undiscoverable in a pocket dictionary, but really took me no forwarder, since in them I found nothing that I could not have invented myself, although while I was actually studying them, they seemed to convince me. I even tackled Swedenborg, or rather samples of him, for he is very copious, but without satisfactory results.

Then I gave up the business.

********

Some months later I was in Zululand and being near the Black Kloof where he dwelt, I paid a visit to my acquaintance of whom I have written elsewhere, the wonderful and ancient dwarf, Zikali, known as *The-Thing-that-should-never-have-been-born*, also more universally among the Zulus as *Opener-of-Roads*. When we had talked of many things connected with the state of Zululand and its politics, I rose to leave for my wagon, since I never cared for sleeping in the Black Kloof if it could be avoided.

"Is there nothing else that you want to ask me, Macumazahn?" asked the old dwarf, tossing back his long hair and looking at—I had almost written through—me.

I shook my head.

"That is strange, Macumazahn, for I seem to see something written on your mind—something to do with spirits."

Then I remembered all the problems that had been troubling me, although in truth I had never thought of propounding them to Zikali.

"Ah! it comes back, does it?" he exclaimed, reading my thought. "Out with it, then, Macumazahn, while I am in a mood to answer, and before I grow tired, for you are an old friend of mine and will so remain till the end, many years hence, and if I can serve you, I will."

I filled my pipe and sat down again upon the stool of carved redwood which had been brought for me.

"You are named 'Opener-of-Roads,' are you not, Zikali?" I said.

"Yes, the Zulus have always called me that, since before the days of Chaka. But what of names, which often enough mean nothing at all?"

"Only that *I* want to open a road, Zikali, that which runs across the River of Death."

"Oho!" he laughed, "it is very easy," and snatching up a little assegai that lay beside him, he proffered it to me, adding, "Be brave now and fall on that. Then before I have counted sixty the road will be wide open, but whether you will see anything on it I cannot tell you."

Again I shook my head and answered, "It is against our law. Also while I still live I desire to know whether I shall meet certain others on that road after my time has come to cross the River. Perhaps you who deal with spirits, can prove the matter to me, which no one else seems able to do."

"Oho!" laughed Zikali again. "What do my ears hear? Am I, the poor Zulu cheat, as you will remember once you called me, Macumazahn, asked to show that which is hidden from all the wisdom of the great White People?"

"The question is," I answered with irritation, "not what you are asked to do, but what you can do."

"That I do not know yet, Macumazahn. Whose spirits do you desire to see? If that of a woman called Mameena is one of them, I think that perhaps I whom she loved——"[1]

"She is *not* one of them, Zikali. Moreover, if she loved you, you paid back her love with death."

"Which perhaps was the kindest thing I could do, Macumazahn, for reasons that you may be able to guess, and others with which I will not trouble you. But if not hers, whose? Let me look, let me look! Why, there seems to be two of them, head-wives, I mean, and I thought that white men only took one wife. Also a multitude of others; their faces float up in the water of your mind. An old man with grey hair, little children, perhaps they were brothers and sisters, and some who may be friends. Also very clear indeed that Mameena whom you do not wish to see. Well, Macumazahn, this is unfortunate, since she is the only one whom I can show you, or rather put you in the way of finding. Unless indeed there are other *Kaffir* women——"

"What do you mean?" I asked.

"I mean, Macumazahn, that only black feet travel on the road which I can open; over those in which ran white blood I have no power."

"Then it is finished," I said, rising again and taking a step or two towards the gate.

"Come back and sit down, Macumazahn. I did not say so. Am I the only ruler of magic in Africa, which I am told is a big country?"

I came back and sat down, for my curiosity, a great failing with me, was excited.

"Thank you, Zikali," I said, "but I will have no dealings with more of your witch-doctors."

"No, no, because you are afraid of them; quite without reason, Macumazahn, seeing that they are all cheats except myself. I am the last child of wisdom, the rest are stuffed with lies, as Chaka found out when he killed every one of them whom he could catch. But perhaps there might be a white doctor who would have rule over white spirits."

"If you mean missionaries——" I began hastily.

1. For the history of Mameena see the book called *Child of Storm.*—Editor

"No, Macumazahn, I do not mean your praying men who are cast in one mould and measured with one rule, and say what they are taught to say, not thinking for themselves."

"Some of them think, Zikali."

"Yes, and then the others fall on them with big sticks. The real priest is he to whom the Spirit comes, not he who feeds upon its wrappings, and speaks through a mask carved by his father's fathers. I am a priest like that, which is why all my fellowship have hated me."

"If so, you have paid back their hate, Zikali, but cease to cast round the lion, like a timid hound, and tell me what you mean. Of whom do you speak?"

"That is the trouble, Macumazahn. I do not know. This lion, or rather lioness, lies hid in the caves of a very distant mountain and I have never seen her—in the flesh."

"Then how can you talk of what you have never seen?"

"In the same way, Macumazahn, that your priests talk of what they have never seen, because they, or a few of them, have knowledge of it. I will tell you a secret. All seers who live at the same time, if they are great, commune with each other because they are akin and their spirits meet in sleep or dreams. Therefore I know of a mistress of our craft, a very lioness among jackals, who for thousands of years has lain sleeping in the northern caves and, humble though I am, she knows of me."

"Quite so," I said, yawning, "but perhaps, Zikali, you will come to the point of the spear. What of her? How is she named, and if she exists will she help me?"

"I will answer your question backwards, Macumazahn. I think that she will help you if you help her, in what way I do not know, because although witch-doctors sometimes work without pay, as I am doing now, Macumazahn, witch-doctoresses never do. As for her name, the only one that she has among our company is 'Queen,' because she is the first of all of them and the most beauteous among women. For the rest I can tell you nothing, except that she has always been and I suppose, in this shape or in that, will always be while the world lasts, because she has found the secret of life unending."

"You mean that she is immortal, Zikali," I answered with a smile.

"I do not say that, Macumazahn, because my little mind cannot shape the thought of immortality. But when I was a babe, which is far ago, she had lived so long that scarce would she knew the difference between then and now, and already in her breast was all wisdom gathered. I know it, because although, as I have said, we have never seen each other, at times we walk together in our sleep, for thus she shares her loneliness, and I think, though this may be but a dream, that last night she told me to send you on to her to seek an answer to certain questions which you would put to me today. Also to me she seemed to desire that you should do her a service; I know not what service."

Now I grew angry and asked, "Why does it please you to fool me, Zikali, with such talk as this? If there is any truth in it, show me where the woman called *Queen* lives and how I am to come to her."

The old wizard took up the little assegai which he had offered to me and with its blade raked our ashes from the fire that always burnt in front of him. While he did so, he talked to me, as I thought in a random fashion, perhaps to distract my attention, of a certain white man whom he said I should meet upon my journey and of his affairs, also of other matters, none of which interested me much at the time. These ashes he patted down flat and then on them drew a map with the point of his spear, making grooves for streams, certain marks for bush and forest, wavy lines for water and swamps and little heaps for hills.

When he had finished it all he bade me come round the fire and study the picture across which by an after-thought he drew a wandering furrow with the edge of the assegai to represent a river, and gathered the ashes in a lump at the northern end to signify a large mountain.

"Look at it well, Macumazahn," he said, "and forget nothing, since if you make this journey and forget, you die. Nay, no need to copy it in that book of yours, for see, I will stamp it on your mind."

Then suddenly he gathered up the warm ashes in a double handful and threw them into my face, muttering something as he did so and adding aloud, "There, now you will remember."

"Certainly I shall," I answered, coughing, "and I beg that you will not play such a joke upon me again."

As a matter of fact, whatever may have been the reason, I never forgot any detail of that extremely intricate map.

"That big river must be the Zambezi," I stuttered, "and even then the mountain of your Queen, if it be her mountain, is far away, and how can I come there alone?"

"I don't know, Macumazahn, though perhaps you might do so in company. At least I believe that in the old days people used to travel to the place, since I have heard a great city stood there once which was the heart of a mighty empire."

Now I pricked up my ears, for though I believed nothing of Zikali's story of a wonderful Queen, I was always intensely interested in past civilisations and their relics. Also I knew that the old wizard's knowledge was extensive and peculiar, however he came by it, and I did not think that he would lie to me in this matter. Indeed to tell the truth, then and there I made up my mind that if it were in any way possible, I would attempt this journey.

"How did people travel to the city, Zikali?"

"By sea, I suppose, Macumazahn, but I think that you will be wise not to try that road, since I believe that on the sea side the marshes are now impassable and you will be safer on your feet."

"You want me to go on this adventure, Zikali. Why? I know you never do anything without motive."

"Oho! Macumazahn, you are clever and see deeper into the trunk of a tree than most. Yes, I want you to go for three reasons. First, that you may satisfy your soul on certain matters and I would help you to do so. Secondly, because I want to satisfy mine, and thirdly, because I know that you will come back safe to be a prop to me in things that will happen in days unborn. Otherwise I would have told you nothing of this story, since it is necessary to me that you should remain living beneath the sun."

"Have done, Zikali. What is it that you desire?"

"Oh! a great deal that I shall get, but chiefly two things, so with the rest I will not trouble you. First I desire to know to know whether these dreams of mine of a wonderful white witch-doctoress, or witch, and of my converse with her are indeed more than dreams. Next I would learn whether certain plots of mine at which I have worked for years, will succeed."

"What plots, Zikali, and how can my taking a distant journey tell you anything about them?"

"You know them well enough, Macumazahn; they have to do with the overthrow of a Royal House that has worked me bitter wrong. As to how your journey can help me, why, thus. You shall promise to me to ask of this Queen whether Zikali, Opener-of-Roads, shall triumph or be overthrown in that on which he has set his heart."

"As you seem to know this witch so well, why do you not ask her yourself, Zikali?"

"To ask is one thing, Macumazahn. To get an answer is another. I have asked in the watches of the night, and the reply was, 'Come hither and perchance I will tell you.' 'Queen,' I said, 'how can I come save in the spirit, who am an ancient and a crippled dwarf scarcely able to stand upon my feet?'

"'Then send a messenger, Wizard, and be sure that he is white, for of black savages I have seen more than enough. Let him bear a token also that he comes from you and tell me of it in your sleep. Moreover let that token be something of power which will protect him on the journey.'

21

"Such is the answer that comes to me in my dreams, Macumazahn."

"Well, what token will you give me, Zikali?"

He groped about in his robe and produced a piece of ivory of the size of a large chessman, that had a hole in it, through which ran a plaited cord of the stiff hairs from an elephant's tail. On this article, which was of a rusty brown colour, he breathed, then having whispered to it for a while, handed it to me.

I took the talisman, for such I guessed it to be, idly enough, held it to the light to examine it, and started back so violently that almost I let it fall. I do not quite know why I started, but I think it was because some influence seemed to leap from it to me. Zikali started also and cried out, "Have a care, Macumazahn. Am I young that I can bear bring dashed to the ground?"

"What do you mean?" I asked, still staring at the thing which I perceived to be a most wonderfully fashioned likeness of the old dwarf himself as he appeared before me crouched upon the ground. There were the deep-set eyes, the great head, the toad-like shape, the long hair, all.

"It is a clever carving, is it not, Macumazahn? I am skilled in that art, you know, and therefore can judge of carving."

"Yes, I know," I answered, bethinking me of another statuette of his which he had given to me on the morrow of the death of her from whom it was modelled. "But what of the thing?"

"Macumazahn, it has come down to me through the ages. As you may have heard, all great doctors when they die pass on their wisdom and something of their knowledge to another doctor of spirits who is still living on the earth, that nothing may be lost, or as little as possible. Also I have learned that to such likenesses as these may be given the strength of him or her from whom they were shaped."

Now I bethought me of the old Egyptians and their *Ka* statues of which I had read, and that these statues, magically charmed and set in the tombs of the departed, were supposed to be inhabited everlastingly by the Doubles of the dead endued with more power even than ever these possessed in life. But of this I said nothing to Zikali, thinking that it would take too much explanation, though I wondered very much how he had come by the same idea.

"When that ivory is hung over your heart, Macumazahn, where you must always wear it, learn that with it goes the strength of Zikali; the thought that would have been his thought and the wisdom that is his wisdom, will be your companions, as much as though he walked at your side and could instruct you in every peril. Moreover north and south and east and west this image is known to men who, when they see it, will bow down and obey, opening a road to him who wears the medicine of the Opener-of-Roads."

"Indeed," I said, smiling, "and what is this colour on the ivory?"

"I forget, Macumazahn, who have had it a great number of years, ever since it descended to me from a forefather of mine, who was fashioned in the same mould as I am. It looks like blood, does it not? It is a pity that Mameena is not still alive, since she whose memory was so excellent might have been able to tell you," and as he spoke, with a motion that was at once sure and swift, he threw the loop of elephant hair over my head.

Hastily I changed the subject, feeling that after his wont this old wizard, the most terrible man whom ever I knew, who had been so much concerned with the tragic death of Mameena, was stabbing at me in some hidden fashion.

"You tell me to go on this journey," I said, "and not alone. Yet for companion you give me only an ugly piece of ivory shaped as no man ever was," here I got one back at Zikali, "and from the look of it, steeped in blood, which ivory, if I had my way, I would throw into the camp fire. Who, then, am I to take with me?"

"Don't do that, Macumazahn—I mean throw the ivory into the fire—since I have no wish to burn before my time, and if you do, you who have worn it might burn with me. At least certainly you would die with the magic thing and go to acquire knowledge more quickly than you desire. No, no, and do not try to take it off your neck, or rather try if you will."

I did try, but something seemed to prevent me from accomplishing my purpose of giving the carving back to Zikali as I wished to do. First my pipe got in the way of my hand, then the elephant hairs caught in the collar of my coat; then a pang of rheumatism to which I was accustomed from an old lion-bite, developed of a sudden in my arm, and lastly I grew tired of bothering about the thing.

Zikali, who had been watching my movements, burst out into one of his terrible laughs that seemed to fill the whole kloof and to re-echo from its rocky walls. It died away and he went on, without further reference to the talisman or image.

"You asked whom you were to take with you, Macumazahn. Well, as to this I must make inquiry of those who know. Man, my medicines!"

From the shadows in the hut behind darted out a tall figure carrying a great spear in one hand and in the other a cat-skin bag which with a salute he laid down at the feet of his master. This salute, by the way, was that of a Zulu word which means "Lord" or "Home" of Ghosts.

Zikali groped in the bag and produced from it certain knuckle-bones.

"A common method," he muttered, "such as every vulgar wizard uses, but one that is quick and, as the matter concerned is small, will serve my turn. Let us see now, whom you shall take with you, Macumazahn."

Then he breathed upon the bones, shook them up in his thin hands and with a quick turn of the wrist, threw them into the air. After this he studied them carefully, where they lay among the ashes which he had raked out of the fire, those that he had used for the making of his map.

"Do you know a man named Umslopogaas, Macumazahn, the chief of a tribe that is called The People of the Axe, whose titles of praise are Bulalio or the Slaughterer, and Woodpecker, the latter from the way he handles his ancient axe? He is a savage fellow, but one of high blood and higher courage, a great captain in his way, though he will never come to anything, save a glorious death—in your company, I think, Macumazahn." (Here he studied the bones again for a while.) "Yes, I am sure, in your company, though not upon this journey."

"I have heard of him," I answered cautiously. "It is said in the land that he is a son of Chaka, the great king of the Zulus."

"Is it, Macumazahn? And is it said also that he was the slayer of Chaka's brother, Dingaan, also the lover of the fairest woman that the Zulus have ever seen, who was called Nada the Lily? Unless indeed a certain Mameena, who, I seem to remember, was a friend of yours, may have been even more beautiful?"

"I know nothing of Nada the Lily," I answered.

"No, no, Mameena, 'the Waiting Wind,' has blown over her fame, so why should you know of one who has been dead a long while? Why also, Macumazahn, do you always bring women into every business? I begin to believe that although you are so strict in a white man's fashion, you must be too fond of them, a weakness which makes for ruin to any man. Well, now, I think that this wolf-man, this axe-man, this warrior, Umslopogaas should be a good fellow to you on your journey to visit the white witch, Queen—another woman by the way, Macumazahn, and therefore one of whom you should be careful. Oh! yes, he will come with you—because of a man called Lousta and a woman named Monazi, a wife of his who hates him and does—not hate Lousta. I am almost sure that he will come with you, so do not stop to ask questions about him."

"Is there anyone else?" I inquired.

Zikali glanced at the bones again, poking them about in the ashes with his toe, then replied with a yawn, "You seem to have a little yellow man in your service, a clever snake who knows how to creep through grass, and when to strike and when to lie hidden. I should take him too, if I were you."

"You know well that I have such a man, Zikali, a Hottentot named Hans, clever in his way but drunken, very faithful too, since he loved my father before me. He is cooking my supper in the wagon now. Are there to be any others?"

"No, I think you three will be enough, with a guard of soldiers from the People of the Axe, for you will meet with fighting and a ghost or two. Umslopogaas has always one at his elbow named Nada, and perhaps you have several. For instance, there was a certain Mameena whom I always seem to feel about me when you are near, Macumazahn.

"Why, the wind is rising again, which is odd on so still an evening. Listen to how it wails, yes, and stirs your hair, though mine hangs straight enough. But why do I talk of ghosts, seeing that you travel to seek other ghosts, white ghosts, beyond my ken, who can only deal with those who were black?

"Good-night, Macumazahn, good-night. When you return from visiting the white Queen, that Great One beneath those feet I, Zikali, who am also great in my way, am but a grain of dust, come and tell me her answer to my question.

"Meanwhile, be careful always to wear that pretty little image which I have given you, as a young lover sometimes wears a lock of hair cut from the head of some fool-girl that he thinks is fond of him. It will bring you safety and luck, Macumazahn, which, for the most part, is more than the lock of hair does to the lover. Oh! it is a strange world, full of jest to those who can see the strings that work it. I am one of them, and perhaps, Macumazahn, you are another, or will be before all is done—or begun.

"Good-night, and good fortune to you on your journeyings, and, Macumazahn, although you are so fond of women, be careful not to fall in love with that white Queen, because it would make others jealous; I mean some who you have lost sight of for a while, also I think that being under a curse of her own, she is not one whom you can put into your sack. *Oho! Oho-ho!* Slave, bring me my blanket, it grows cold, and my medicine also, that which protects me from the ghosts, who are thick tonight. Macumazahn brings them, I think. *Oho-ho!*"

I turned to depart but when I had gone a little way Zikali called me back again and said, speaking very low, "When you meet this Umslopogaas, as you will meet him, he who is called the Woodpecker and the Slaughterer, say these words to him, "'A bat has been twittering round the hut of the Opener-of-Roads, and to his ears it squeaked the name of a certain Lousta and the name of a woman called Monazi. Also it twittered another greater name that may not be uttered, that of an elephant who shakes the earth, and said that this elephant sniffs the air with his trunk and grows angry, and sharpens his tusks to dig a certain Woodpecker out of his hole in a tree that grows near the Witch Mountain. Say, too, that the Opener-of-Roads thinks that this Woodpecker would be wise to fly north for a while in the company of one who watches by night, lest harm should come to a bird that pecks at the feet of the great and chatters of it in his nest.'"

Then Zikali waved his hand and I went, wondering into what plot I had stumbled.

## CHAPTER 2

# The Messengers

I did not rest as I should that night who somehow was never able to sleep well in the neighbourhood of the Black Kloof. I suppose that Zikali's constant talk about ghosts, with his hints and innuendoes concerning those who were dead, always affected my nerves till, in a subconscious way, I began to believe that such things existed and were hanging about me. Many people are open to the power of suggestion, and I am afraid that I am one of them.

However, the sun which has such strength to kill noxious things, puts an end to ghosts more quickly even than it does to other evil vapours and emanations, and when I woke up to find it shining brilliantly in a pure heaven, I laughed with much heartiness over the whole affair.

Going to the spring near which we were outspanned, I took off my shirt to have a good wash, still chuckling at the memory of all the hocus-pocus of my old friend, the Opener-of-Roads.

While engaged in this matutinal operation I struck my hand against something and looking, observed that it was the hideous little ivory image of Zikali, which he had set about my neck. The sight of the thing and the memory of his ridiculous talk about it, especially of its assertion that it had come down to him through the ages, which it could not have done, seeing that it was a likeness of himself, irritated me so much that I proceeded to take it off with the full intention of throwing it into the spring.

As I was in the act of doing this, from a clump of reeds mixed with bushes, quite close to me, there came a sound of hissing, and suddenly above them appeared the head of a great black *immamba*, perhaps the deadliest of all our African snakes, and the only one I know which will attack man without provocation.

Leaving go of the image, I sprang back in a great hurry towards where my gun lay. Then the snake vanished and making sure that it had departed to its hole, which was probably at a distance, I returned to the pool, and once more began to take off the talisman in order to consign it to the bottom of the pool.

After all, I reflected, it was a hideous and probably a blood-stained thing which I did not in the least wish to wear about my neck like a lady's love-token.

Just as it was coming over my head, suddenly from the other side of the bush that infernal snake popped up again, this time, it was clear, really intent on business. It began to move towards me in the lightning-like way *immamba*s have, hissing and flicking its tongue.

I was too quick for my friend, however, for snatching up the gun that I had lain down beside me, I let it have a charge of buckshot in the neck which nearly cut it in two, so that it fell down and expired with hideous convulsive writhings.

Hearing the shot Hans came running from the wagon to see what was the matter. Hans, I should say, was that same Hottentot who had been the companion of most of my journeyings since my father's day. He was with me when as a young fellow I accompanied Retief to Dingaan's kraal, and like myself, escaped the massacre.[1] Also we shared many other adventures, including the great one in the Land of the Ivory Child where he slew the huge elephant-god, Jana, and himself was slain. But of this journey we did not dream in those days.

For the rest Hans was a most entirely unprincipled person, but as the Boers say, "as clever as a wagonload of monkeys." Also he drank when he got the chance. One good quality he had, however; no man was ever more faithful, and perhaps it would be true to say that neither man nor woman ever loved me, unworthy, quite so well.

In appearance he rather resembled an antique and dilapidated baboon; his face was wrinkled like a dried nut and his quick little eyes were bloodshot. I never knew what his age was, any more than he did himself, but the years had left him tough as whipcord and absolutely untiring. Lastly he was perhaps the best hand at following a spoor that ever I knew and up to a hundred and fifty yards or so, a very deadly shot with a rifle especially when he used a little single-barrelled, muzzle-loading gun of mine made by Purdey which he named *Intombi* or Maiden. Of that gun, however, I have written in *The Holy Flower* and elsewhere.

"What is it, Baas?" he asked. "Here there are no lions, nor any game."

"Look the other side of the bush, Hans."

He slipped round it, making a wide circle with his usual caution, then, seeing the snake which was, by the way, I think, the biggest *im-*

1. See the book called *Marie.*—Editor.

*mamba* I ever killed, suddenly froze, as it were, in a stiff attitude that reminded me of a pointer when it scents game. Having made sure that it was dead, he nodded and said, "Black '*mamba*, or so you would call it, though I know it for something else."

"What else, Hans?"

"One of the old witch-doctor Zikali's spirits which he sets at the mouth of this kloof to warn him of who comes or goes. I know it well, and so do others. I saw it listening behind a stone when you were up the kloof last evening talking with the Opener-of-Roads."

"Then Zikali will lack a spirit," I answered, laughing, "which perhaps he will not miss amongst so many. It serves him right for setting the brute on me."

"Quite so, Baas. He will be angry. I wonder why he did it?" he added suspiciously, "seeing that he is such a friend of yours."

"He didn't do it, Hans. These snakes are very fierce and give battle, that is all."

Hans paid no attention to my remark, which probably he thought only worthy of a white man who does not understand, but rolled his yellow, bloodshot eyes about, as though in search of explanations. Presently they fell upon the ivory that hung about my neck, and he started.

"Why do you wear that pretty likeness of the Great One yonder over your heart, as I have known you do with things that belonged to women in past days, Baas? Do you know that it is Zikali's Great Medicine, nothing less, as everyone does throughout the land? When Zikali sends an order far away, he always sends that image with it, for then he who receives the order knows that he must obey or die. Also the messenger knows that he will come to no harm if he does not take it off, because, Baas, the image is Zikali himself, and Zikali is the image. They are one and the same. Also it is the image of his father's father's father—or so he says."

"That is an odd story," I said.

Then I told Hans as much as I thought advisable of how this horrid little talisman came into my possession.

Hans nodded without showing any surprise.

"So we are going on a long journey," he said. "Well, I thought it was time that we did something more than wander about these tame countries selling blankets to stinking old women and so forth, Baas. Moreover, Zikali does not wish that you should come to harm, doubtless because he does wish to make use of you afterwards—oh! it's safe to talk now when that spirit is away looking for another snake. What were you doing with the Great Medicine, Baas, when the '*mamba* attacked you?"

29

"Taking it off to throw it into the pool, Hans, as I do not like the thing. I tried twice and each time the *immamba* appeared."

"Of course it appeared, Baas, and what is more, if you had taken that Medicine off and thrown it away *you* would have disappeared, since the *'mamba* would have killed you. Zikali wanted to show you that, Baas, and that is why he set the snake at you."

"You are a superstitious old fool, Hans."

"Yes, Baas, but my father knew all about that Great Medicine before me, for he was a bit of a doctor, and so does every wizard and witch for a thousand miles or more. I tell you, Baas, it is known by all though no one ever talks about it, no, not even the king himself. Baas, speaking to you, not with the voice of Hans the old drunkard, but with that of the Predikant, your reverend father, who made so good a Christian of me and who tells me to do so from up in Heaven where the hot fires are which the wood feeds of itself, I beg you not to try to throw away the Medicine again, or if you wish to do so, to leave me behind on this journey. For you see, Baas, although I am now so good, almost like one of those angels with the pretty goose's wings in the pictures, I feel that I should like to grow a little better before I go to the Place of Fires to make report to your reverend father, the Predikant."

Thinking of how horrified my dear father would be if he could hear all this string of ridiculous nonsense and learn the result of his moral and religious lessons on raw Hottentot material, I burst out laughing. But Hans went on as gravely as a judge, "Wear the Great Medicine, Baas, wear it; part with the liver inside you before you part with that, Baas. It may not be as pretty or smell as sweet as a woman's hair in a little gold bottle, but it is much more useful. The sight of the woman's hair will only make you sick in your stomach and cause you to remember a lot of things which you had much better forget, but the Great Medicine, or rather Zikali who is in it, will keep the assegais and sickness out of you and turn back bad magic on to the heads of those who sent it, and always bring us plenty to eat and perhaps, if we are lucky, a little to drink too sometimes."

"Go away," I said, "I want to wash."

"Yes, Baas, but with the Baas's leave I will sit on the other side of that bush with the gun—not to look at the Baas without his clothes, because white people are always so ugly that it makes me feel ill to see them undressed, also because—the Baas will forgive me—but because they smell. No, not for that, but just to see that no other snake comes."

"Get out of the road, you dirty little scoundrel, and stop your impudence," I said, lifting my foot suggestively.

Thereon he scooted with a subdued grin round the other side of the bush, whence as I knew well he kept his eye fixed on me to be sure that I made no further attempt to take off the Great Medicine.

\* \* \* \* \* \* \* \*

Now of this talisman I may as well say at once that I am no believer in it or its precious influences. Therefore, although it was useful sometimes, notably twice when Umslopogaas was concerned, I do not know whether personally I should have done better or worse upon that journey if I had thrown it into the pool.

It is true, however, that until quite the end of this history when it became needful to do so to save another, I never made any further attempt to remove it from my neck, not even when it rubbed a sore in my skin, because I did not wish to offend the prejudices of Hans.

It is true, moreover, that this hideous ivory had a reputation which stretched very far from the place where it was made and was regarded with great reverence by all kinds of queer people, even by the Amahagger themselves, of whom presently, as they say in pedigrees, a fact of which I found sundry proofs. Indeed, I saw a first example of it when a little while later I met that great warrior, Umslopogaas, Chief of the People of the Axe.

For, after determining firmly, for reasons which I will set out, that I would not visit this man, in the end I did so, although by then I had given up any idea of journeying across the Zambezi to look for a mysterious and non-existent witch-woman, as Zikali had suggested that I should do. To begin with I knew that his talk was all rubbish and, even if it were not, that at the bottom of it was some desire of the Opener-of-Roads that I should make a path for him to travel towards an indefinite but doubtless evil object of his own. Further, by this time I had worn through that mood of mine which had caused me to yearn for correspondence with the departed and a certain knowledge of their existence.

I wonder whether many people understand, as I do, how entirely distinct and how variable are these moods which sway us, or at any rate some of us, at sundry periods of our lives. As I think I have already suggested, at one time we are all spiritual; at another all physical; at one time we are sure that our lives here are as a dream and a shadow and that the real existence lies elsewhere; at another that these brief days of ours are the only business with which we have to do and that of it we must make the best. At one time we think our loves much more immortal than the stars; at another that they are mere shadows cast by the baleful sun of desire upon the shallow and fleeting water we call Life which seems to flow out of nowhere into nowhere. At one time we are full of faith, at another all such hopes are blotted out by a black wall of Nothingness, and so on *ad infinitum*. Only very stupid people, or humbugs, are or pretend to be, always consistent and unchanging.

To return, I determined not only that I would not travel north to seek that which no living man will ever find, certainty as to the future, but also, to show my independence of Zikali, that I would not visit this chief, Umslopogaas. So, having traded all my goods and made a fair profit (on paper), I set myself to return to Natal, proposing to rest awhile in my little house at Durban, and told Hans my mind.

"Very good, Baas," he said. "I, too, should like to go to Durban. There are lots of things there that we cannot get here," and he fixed his roving eye upon a square-faced gin bottle, which as it happened was filled with nothing stronger than water, because all the gin was drunk. "Yet, Baas, we shall not see the Berea for a long while."

"Why do you say that?" I asked sharply.

"Oh! Baas, I don't know, but you went to visit the Opener-of-Roads, did you not, and he told you to go north and lent you a certain Great Medicine, did he not?"

Here Hands proceeded to light his corncob pipe with an ash from the fire, all the time keeping his beady eyes fixed upon that part of me where he knew the talisman was hung.

"Quite true, Hans, but now I mean to show Zikali that I am not his messenger, for south or north or east or west. So tomorrow morning we cross the river and trek for Natal."

"Yes, Baas, but then why not cross it this evening? There is still light."

"I have said that we will cross it tomorrow morning," I answered with that firmness which I have read always indicates a man of character, "and I do not change my word."

"No, Baas, but sometimes other things change besides words. Will the Baas have that buck's leg for supper, or the stuff out of a tin with a dint in it, which we bought at a store two years ago? The flies have got at the buck's leg, but I cut out the bits with the maggots on it and ate them myself."

\*\*\*\*\*\*\*\*

Hans was right, things do change, especially the weather. That night, unexpectedly, for when I turned in the sky seemed quite serene, there came a terrible rain long before it was due, which lasted off and on for three whole days and continued intermittently for an indefinite period. Needless to say the river, which it would have been so easy to cross on this particular evening, by the morning was a raging torrent, and so remained for several weeks.

In despair at length I trekked south to where a ford was reported, which, when reached, proved impracticable.

I tried another, a dozen miles further on, which was very hard to come to over boggy land. It looked all right and we were getting across finely, when suddenly one of the wheels sank in an unsuspected hole and there we stuck. Indeed, I believe the wagon, or bits of it, would have remained in the neighbourhood of that ford to this day, had I not managed to borrow some extra oxen belonging to a Christian *Kaffir*, and with their help to drag it back to the bank whence we had started.

As it happened I was only just in time, since a new storm which had burst further up the river, brought it down in flood again, a very heavy flood.

In this country, England, where I write, there are bridges everywhere and no one seems to appreciate them. If they think of them at all it is to grumble about the cost of their upkeep. I wish they could have experienced what a lack of them means in a wild country during times of excessive rain, and the same remark applied to roads. You should think more of your blessings, my friends, as the old woman said to her complaining daughter who had twins two years running, adding that they might have been triplets.

To return—after this I confessed myself beaten and gave up until such time as it should please Providence to turn off the water-tap. Trekking out of sight of that infernal river which annoyed me with its constant gurgling, I camped on a comparatively dry spot that overlooked a beautiful stretch of rolling *veld*. Towards sunset the clouds lifted and I saw a mile or two away a most extraordinary mountain on the lower slopes of which grew a dense forest. Its upper part, which was of bare rock, looked exactly like the seated figure of a grotesque person with the chin resting on the breast. There was the head, there were the arms, there were the knees. Indeed, the whole mass of it reminded me strongly of the effigy of Zikali which was tied about my neck, or rather of Zikali himself.

"What is that called?" I said to Hans, pointing to this strange hill, now blazing in the angry fire of the setting sun that had burst out between the storm clouds, which made it appear more ominous even than before.

"That is the Witch Mountain, Baas, where the Chief Umslopogaas and a blood brother of his who carried a great club used to hunt with the wolves. It is haunted and in a cave at the top of it lie the bones of Nada the Lily, the fair woman whose name is a song, she who was the love of Umslopogaas."[2]

"Rubbish," I said, though I had heard something of all that story and remembered that Zikali had mentioned this Nada, comparing her beauty to that of another whom once I knew.

"Where then lives the Chief Umslopogaas?"

"They say that his town is yonder on the plain, Baas. It is called the Place of the Axe and is strongly fortified with a river round most of it, and his people are the People of the Axe. They are a fierce people, and all the country round here is uninhabited because Umslopogaas has cleaned out the tribes who used to live in it, first with his wolves and afterwards in war. He is so strong a chief and so terrible in battle that even Chaka himself was afraid of him, and they say that he brought Dingaan the King to his end because of a quarrel about this Nada. Cetywayo, the present king, too leaves him alone and to him he pays no tribute."

Whilst I was about to ask Hans from whom he had collected all this information, suddenly I heard sounds, and looking up, saw three tall men clad in full herald's dress rushing towards us at great speed.

"Here come some chips from the Axe," said Hans, and promptly bolted into the wagon.

I did not bolt because there was no time to do so without loss of dignity, but, although I wished I had my rifle with me, just sat still upon my stool and with great deliberation lighted my pipe, taking not the slightest notice of the three savage-looking fellows.

These, who I noted carried axes instead of assegais, rushed straight at me with the axes raised in such a fashion that anyone unacquainted with the habits of Zulu warriors of the old school, might have thought that they intended nothing short of murder.

As I expected, however, within about six feet of me they halted suddenly and stood there still as statues. For my part I went on lighting my pipe as though I did not see them and when at length I was obliged to lift my head, surveyed them with an air of mild interest.

Then I took a little book out of my pocket, it was my favourite copy of the *Ingoldsby Legends*—and began to read.

The passage which caught my eye, if "axe" be substituted for "knife" was not inappropriate. It was from *The Nurse's Story*, and runs:

2. For the story of Umslopogaas and Nada see the book called *Nada the Lily*.—Editor.

*But, oh! what a thing 'tis to see and to know*
*That the bare knife is raised in the hand of the foe,*
*Without hope to repel or to ward off the blow!*

This proceeding of mine astonished them a good deal who felt that they had, so to speak, missed fire. At last the soldier in the middle said, "Are you blind, White Man?"

"No, Black Fellow," I answered, "but I am short-sighted. Would you be so good as to stand out of my light?" a remark which puzzled them so much that all three drew back a few paces.

When I had read a little further I came to the following lines, "'Tis plain, As anatomists tell us, that never again, Shall life revisit the foully slain When once they've been cut through the jugular vein."

In my circumstances at that moment this statement seemed altogether too suggestive, so I shut up the book and remarked, "If you are wanderers who want food, as I judge by your being so thin, I am sorry that I have little meat, but my servants will give you what they can."

"*Ow!*" said the spokesman, "he calls us wanderers! Either he must be a very great man or he is mad."

"You are right. I *am* a great man," I answered, yawning, "and if you trouble me too much you will see that I can be mad also. Now what do you want?"

"We are messengers from the great Chief Umslopogaas, Captain of the People of the Axe, and we want tribute," answered the man in a somewhat changed tone.

"Do you? Then you won't get it. I thought that only the King of Zululand had a right to tribute, and your Captain's name is not Cetywayo, is it?"

"Our Captain is King here," said the man still more uncertainly.

"Is he indeed? Then away with you back to him and tell this King of whom I have never heard, though I have a message for a certain Umslopogaas, that Macumazahn, Watcher-by-Night, intends to visit him tomorrow, if he will send a guide at the first light to show the best path for the wagon."

"Hearken," said the man to his companions, "this is Macumazahn himself and no other. Well, we thought it, for who else would have dared——"

Then they saluted with their axes, calling me "Chief" and other fine names, and departed as they had come, at a run, calling out that my message should be delivered and that doubtless Umslopogaas would send the guide.

\* \* \* \* \* \* \* \*

So it came about that, quite contrary to my intention, after all circumstances brought me to the Town of the Axe. Even to the last moment I had not meant to go there, but when the tribute was demanded I saw that it was best to do so, and having once passed my word it could not be altered. Indeed, I felt sure that in this event there would be trouble and that my oxen would be stolen, or worse.

So Fate having issued its decree, of which Hans's version was that Zikali, or his Great Medicine, had so arranged things, I shrugged my shoulders and waited.

## CHAPTER 3

# Umslopogaas of the Axe

Next morning at the dawn guides arrived from the Town of the Axe, bringing with them a yoke of spare oxen, which showed that its Chief was really anxious to see me. So, in due course we inspanned and started, the guides leading us by a rough but practicable road down the steep hillside to the saucer-like plain beneath, where I saw many cattle grazing. Travelling some miles across this plain, we came at last to a river of no great breadth that encircled a considerable *Kaffir* town on three sides, the fourth being protected by a little line of *koppies* which were joined together with walls. Also the place was strongly fortified with fences and in every other way known to the native mind.

With the help of the spare oxen we crossed the river safely at the ford, although it was very full, and on the further side were received by a guard of men, tall, soldierlike fellows, all of them armed with axes as the messengers had been. They led us up to the cattle enclosure in the centre of the town, which although it could be used to protect beasts in case of emergency, also served the practical purpose of a public square.

Here some ceremony was in progress, for soldiers stood round the kraal while heralds pranced and shouted. At the head of the place in front of the chief's big hut was a little group of people, among whom a big, gaunt man sat upon a stool clad in a warrior's dress with a great and very long axe hafted with wire-lashed rhinoceros horn, laid across his knees.

Our guides led me, with Hans sneaking after me like a dejected and low-bred dog (for the wagon had stopped outside the gate), across the kraal to where the heralds shouted and the big man sat yawning. At once I noted that he was a very remarkable person, broad and tall and spare of frame, with long, tough-looking arms and a fierce face which reminded me of that of the late King Dingaan. Also he had a great hole in his head above the temple where the skull had been driven in by some blow, and keen, royal-looking eyes.

He looked up and seeing me, cried out, "What! Has a white man come to fight me for the chieftainship of the People of the Axe? Well, he is a small one."

"No," I answered quietly, "but Macumazahn, Watcher-by-Night, has come to visit you in answer to your request, O Umslopogaas; Macumazahn whose name was known in this land before yours was told of, O Umslopogaas."

The Chief heard and rising from his seat, lifted the big axe in salute.

"I greet you, O Macumazahn," he said, "who although you are small in stature, are very great indeed in fame. Have I not heard how you conquered Bangu, although Saduko slew him, and of how you gave up the six hundred head of cattle to Tshoza and the men of the Amangwane who fought with you, the cattle that were your own? Have I not heard how you led the Tulwana against the Usutu and stamped flat three of Cetywayo's regiments in the days of Panda, although, alas! because of an oath of mine I lifted no steel in that battle, I who will have nothing to do with those that spring from the blood of Senzangacona—perhaps because I smell too strongly of it, Macumazahn. Oh! yes, I have heard these and many other things concerning you, though until now it has never been my fortune to look upon your face, O Watcher-by-Night, and therefore I greet you well, Bold one, Cunning one, Upright one, Friend of us Black People."

"Thank you," I answered, "but you said something about fighting. If there is to be anything of the sort, let us get it over. If you want to fight, I am quite ready," and I tapped the rifle which I carried.

The grim Chief broke into a laugh and said, "Listen. By an ancient law any man on this day in each year may fight me for this Chieftainship, as I fought and conquered him who held it before me, and take it from me with my life and the axe, though of late none seems to like the business. But that law was made before there were guns, or men like Macumazahn who, it is said, can hit a lizard on a wall at fifty paces. Therefore I tell you that if you wish to fight me with a rifle, O Macumazahn, I give in and you may have the chieftainship," and he laughed again in his fierce fashion.

"I think it is too hot for fighting either with guns or axes, and Chieftainships are honey that is full of stinging bees," I answered.

Then I took my seat on a stool that had been brought for me and placed by the side of Umslopogaas, after which the ceremony went on.

The heralds cried out the challenge to all and sundry to come and fight the Holder of the Axe for the chieftainship of the Axe without the slightest result, since nobody seemed to desire to do anything of the sort. Then, after a pause, Umslopogaas rose, swinging his formidable weapon round his head and declared that by right of conquest he was Chief of the Tribe for the ensuing year, an announcement that everybody accepted without surprise.

Again the heralds summoned all and sundry who had grievances, to come forward and to state them and receive redress.

After a little pause there appeared a very handsome woman with large eyes, particularly brilliant eyes that rolled as though they were in search of someone. She was finely dressed and I saw by the ornaments she wore that she held the rank of a chief's wife.

"I, Monazi, have a complaint to make," she said, "as it is the right of the humblest to do on this day. In succession to Zinita whom Dingaan slew with her children, I am your *Inkosikaas*, your head-wife, O Umslopogaas."

"That I know well enough," said Umslopogaas, "what of it?"

"This, that you neglect me for other women, as you neglected Zinita for Nada the Beautiful, Nada the witch. I am childless, as are all your wives because of the curse that this Nada left behind her. I demand that this curse should be lifted from me. For your sake I abandoned Lousta the Chief, to whom I was betrothed, and this is the end of it, that I am neglected and childless."

"Am I the Heavens Above that I can cause you to bear children, woman?" asked Umslopogaas angrily. "Would that you had clung to Lousta, my blood-brother and my friend, whom you lament, and left me alone."

"That still may chance, if I am not better treated," answered Monazi with a flash of her eyes. "Will you dismiss yonder new wife of yours and give me back my place, and will you lift the curse of Nada off me, or will you not?"

"As to the first," answered Umslopogaas, "learn, Monazi, that I will not dismiss my new wife, who at least is gentler-tongued and truer-hearted than you are. As to the second, you ask that which it is not in my power to give, since children are the gift of Heaven, and barrenness is its bane. Moreover, you have done ill to bring into this matter the name of one who is dead, who of all women was the sweetest and most innocent. Lastly, I warn you before the people to cease from your plottings or traffic with Lousta, lest ill come of them to you, or him, even though he be my blood-brother, or to both."

"Plottings!" cried Monazi in a shrill and furious voice. "Does Umslopogaas talk of plottings? Well, I have heard that Chaka the Lion left a son, and that this son has set a trap for the feet of him who sits on Chaka's throne. Perchance that king has heard it also; perchance the People of the Axe will soon have another Chief."

"Is it thus?" said Umslopogaas quietly. "And if so, will he be named Lousta?"

Then his smouldering wrath broke out and in a kind of roaring voice he went on, "What have I done that the wives of my bosom should be my betrayers, those who would give me to death? Zinita betrayed me to Dingaan and in reward was slain, and my children with her. Now would you, Monazi, betray me to Cetywayo—though in truth there is naught to betray? Well, if so, bethink you and let Lousta bethink him of what chanced to Zinita, and of what chances to those who stand before the axe of Umslopogaas. What have I done, I say, that women should thus strive to work me ill?"

"This," answered Monazi with a mocking laugh, "that you have loved one of them too well. If he would live in peace, he who has wives should favour all alike. Least of anything should he moan continually over one who is dead, a witch who has left a curse behind her and thus insulted and do wrong to the living. Also he would be wise to attend to the matters of his own tribe and household and to cease from ambitions that may bring him to the assegai, and them with him."

"I have heard your counsel, Wife, so now begone!" said Umslopogaas, looking at her very strangely, and it seemed to me not without fear.

"Have you wives, Macumazahn?" he asked of me in a low voice when she was out of hearing.

"Only among the spirits," I answered.

"Well for you then; moreover, it is a bond between us, for I too have but one true wife and she also is among the spirits. But go rest a while, and later we will talk."

So I went, leaving the Chief to his business, thinking as I walked away of a certain message with which I was charged for him and of how into that message came names that I had just heard, namely that of a man called Lousta and of a woman called Monazi. Also I thought of the hints which in her jealous anger and disappointment at her lack of children, this woman had dropped about a plot against him who sat on the throne of Chaka, which of course must mean King Cetywayo himself.

I came to the guest-hut, which proved to be a very good place and clean; also in it I found plenty of food made ready for me and for my servants. After eating I slept for a time as it is always my fashion to do when I have nothing else on hand, since who knows for how long he may be kept awake at night? Indeed, it was not until the sun had begun to sink that a messenger came, saying that the Chief desired to see me if I had rested. So I went to his big hut which stood alone with a strong fence set round it at a distance, so that none could come within hearing of what was said, even at the door of the hut. I observed also that a man armed with an axe kept guard at the gateway in this fence round which he walked from time to time.

The Chief Umslopogaas was seated on a stool by the door of his hut with his rhinoceros-horn-handled axe which was fastened to his right wrist by a thong, leaning against his thigh, and a wolf-skin hanging from his broad shoulders. Very grim and fierce he looked thus, with the red light of the sunset playing on him. He greeted me and pointed to another stool on which I sat myself down. Apparently he had been watching my eyes, for he said, "I see that like other creatures which move at night, such as leopards and hyenas, you take note of all, O Watcher-by-Night, even of the soldier who guards this place and of where the fence is set and of how its gate is fashioned."

"Had I not done so I should have been dead long ago, O Chief."

"Yes, and because it is not my nature to do so as I should, perchance I shall soon be dead. It is not enough to be fierce and foremost in the battle, Macumazahn. He who would sleep safe and of whom, when he dies, folk will say 'He has eaten' (i.e., he has lived out his life), must do more than this. He must guard his tongue and even his thoughts! he must listen to the stirring of rats in the thatch and look for snakes in the grass; he must trust few, and least of all those who sleep upon his bosom. But those who have the Lion's blood in them or who are prone to charge like a buffalo, often neglect these matters and therefore in the end they fall into a pit."

"Yes," I answered, "especially those who have the lion's blood in them, whether that lion be man or beast."

This I said because of the rumours I had heard that this Slaughterer was in truth the son of Chaka. Therefore not knowing whether or no he were playing on the word "lion," which was Chaka's title, I wished to draw him, especially as I saw in his face a great likeness to Chaka's brother Dingaan, whom, it was whispered, this same Umslopogaas had slain. As it happened I failed, for after a pause he said, "Why do you come to visit me, Macumazahn, who have never done so before?"

"I do not come to visit you, Umslopogaas. That was not my intention. You brought me, or rather the flooded rivers and you together brought me, for I was on my way to Natal and could not cross the drifts."

"Yet I think you have a message for me, White Man, for not long ago a certain wandering witch-doctor who came here told me to expect you and that you had words to say to me."

41

"Did he, Umslopogaas? Well, it is true that I have a message, though it is one that I did not mean to deliver."

"Yet being here, perchance you will deliver it, Macumazahn, for those who have messages and will not speak them, sometimes come to trouble."

"Yes, being here, I will deliver it, seeing that so it seems to be fated. Tell me, do you chance to know a certain Small One who is great, a certain Old One whose brain is young, a doctor who is called Opener-of-Roads?"

"I have heard of him, as have my forefathers for generations."

"Indeed, and if it pleases you to tell me, Umslopogaas, what might be the names of those forefathers of yours, who have heard of this doctor for generations? They must have been short-lived men and as such I should like to know of them."

"That you cannot," replied Umslopogaas shortly, "since they are *hlonipa* (i.e. not to be spoken) in this land."

"Indeed," I said again. "I thought that rule applied only to the names of kings, but of course I am but an ignorant white man who may well be mistaken on such matters of your Zulu customs."

"Yes, O Macumazahn, you may be mistaken or—you may not. It matters nothing. But what of this message of yours?"

"It came at the end of a long story, O Bulalio. But since you seek to know, these were the words of it, so nearly as I can remember them."

Then sentence by sentence I repeated to him all that Zikali had said to me when he called me back after bidding me farewell, which doubtless he did because he wished to cut his message more deeply into the tablets of my mind. Umslopogaas listened to every syllable with a curious intentness, and then asked me to repeat it all again, which I did.

"Lousta! Monazi!" he said slowly. "Well, you heard those names today, did you not, White Man? And you heard certain things from the lips of this Monazi who was angry, that give colour to that talk of the Opener-of-Roads. It seems to me," he added, glancing about him and speaking in a low voice, "that what I suspected is true and that without doubt I am betrayed."

"I do not understand," I replied indifferently. "All this talk is dark to me, as is the message of the Opener-of-Roads, or rather its meaning. By whom and about what are you betrayed?"

"Let that snake sleep. Do not kick it with your foot. Suffice it you to know that my head hangs upon this matter; that I am a rat in a forked stick, and if the stick is pressed on by a heavy hand, then where is the rat?"

"Where all rats go, I suppose, that is, unless they are wise rats that bite the hand which holds the stick before it is pressed down."

"What is the rest of this story of yours, Macumazahn, which was told before the Opener-of-Roads gave you that message? Does it please you to repeat it to me that I may judge of it with my ears?"

"Certainly," I answered, "on one condition, that what the ears hear, the heart shall keep to itself alone."

Umslopogaas stooped and laid his hand upon the broad blade of the weapon beside him, saying, "By the Axe I swear it. If I break the oath be the Axe my doom."

Then I told him the tale, as I have set it down already, thinking to myself that of it he would understand little, being but a wild warrior-man. As it chanced, however, I was mistaken, for he seemed to understand a great deal, perchance because such primitive natures are in closer touch with high and secret things than we imagine; perchance for other reasons with which I became acquainted later.

"It stands thus," he said when I had finished, "or so I think. You, Macumazahn, seek certain women who are dead to learn whether they still live, or are really dead, but so far have failed to find them. Still seeking, you asked the counsel of Zikali, Opener-of-Roads, he who among other titles is also called 'Home of Spirits.' He answered that he could not satisfy your heart because this tree was too tall for him to climb, but that far to the north there lives a certain white witch who has powers greater than his, being able to fly to the top of any tree, and to this white witch he bade you go. Have I the story right thus far?"

I answered that he had.

"Good! Then Zikali went on to choose you companions for your journey, but two, leaving out the guards or servants. I, Umhlopekazi, called Bulalio the Slaughterer, called the Woodpecker also, was one of these, and that little yellow monkey of a man whom I saw with you today, called Hansi, was the other. Then you made a mock of Zikali by determining not to visit me, Umhlopekazi, and not to go north to find the great white Queen of whom he had told you, but to return to Natal. Is that so?"

I said it was.

"Then the rain fell and the winds blew and the rivers rose in wrath so that you could not return to Natal, and after all by chance, or by fate, or by the will of Zikali, the wizard of wizards, you drifted here to the kraal of me, Umhlopekazi, and told me this story."

"Just so," I answered.

"Well, White Man, how am I to know that all this is not but a trap

43

for my feet which already seem to feel cords between the toes of both of them? What token do you bring, O Watcher-by-Night? How am I to know that the Opener-of-Roads really sent me this message which has been delivered so strangely by one who wished to travel on another path? The wandering witch-doctor told me that he who came would bear some sign."

"I can't say," I answered, "at least in words. But," I added after reflection, "as you ask for a token, perhaps I might be able to show you something that would bring proof to your heart, if there were any secret place——"

Umslopogaas walked to the gateway of the fence and saw that the sentry was at his post. Then he walked round the hut casting an eye upon its roof, and muttered to me as he returned.

"Once I was caught thus. There lived a certain wife of mine who set her ear to the smoke-hole and so brought about the death of many, and among them of herself and of our children. Enter. All is safe. Yet if you talk, speak low."

So we went into the hut taking the stools with us, and seated ourselves by the fire that burned there on to which Umslopogaas threw chips of resinous wood.

"Now," he said.

I opened my shirt and by the clear light of the flame showed him the image of Zikali which hung about my neck. He stared at it, though touch it he would not. Then he stood up and lifting his great axe, he saluted the image with the word "*Makosi!*" the salute that is given to great wizards because they are supposed to be the home of many spirits.

"It is the big Medicine, the Medicine itself," he said, "that which has been known in the land since the time of Senzangacona, the father of the Zulu Royal House, and as it is said, before him."

"How can that be?" I asked, "seeing that this image represents Zikali, Opener-of-Roads, as an old man, and Senzangacona died many years ago?"

"I do not know," he answered, "but it is so. Listen. There was a certain Mopo, or as some called him, Umbopo, who was Chaka's body-servant and my foster-father, and he told me that twice this Medicine," and he pointed to the image, "was sent to Chaka, and that each time the Lion obeyed the message that came with it. A third time it was sent, but he did not obey the message and then—where was Chaka?"

Here Umslopogaas passed his hand across his mouth, a significant gesture amongst the Zulus.

"Mopo," I said, "yes, I have heard the story of Mopo, also that

Chaka's body became *his* servant in the end, since Mopo killed him with the help of the princes Dingaan and Umhlangana. Also I have heard that this Mopo still lives, though not in Zululand."

"Does he, Macumazahn?" said Umslopogaas, taking snuff from a spoon and looking at me keenly over the spoon. "You seem to know a great deal, Macumazahn; too much as some might think."

"Yes," I answered, "perhaps I do know too much, or at any rate more than I want to know. For instance, O fosterling of Mopo and son of—was the lady named Baleka?—I know a good deal about *you*."

Umslopogaas stared at me and laying his hand upon the great axe, half rose. Then he sat down again.

"I think that this," and I touched the image of Zikali upon my breast, "would turn even the blade of the axe named Groan-maker," I said and paused. As nothing happened, I went on, "For instance, again I think I know—or have I dreamed it?—that a certain chief, whose mother's name I believe was Baleka—by the way, was she not one of Chaka's 'sisters'?—has been plotting against that son of Panda who sits upon the throne, and that his plots have been betrayed, so that he is in some danger of his life."

"Macumazahn," said Umslopogaas hoarsely, "I tell you that did you not wear the Great Medicine on your breast, I would kill you where you sit and bury you beneath the floor of the hut, as one who knows—too much."

"It would be a mistake, Umslopogaas, one of the many that you have made. But as I *do* wear the Medicine, the question does not arise, does it?"

Again he made no answer and I went on, "And now, what about this journey to the north? If indeed I must make it, would you wish to accompany me?"

Umslopogaas rose from the stool and crawled out of the hut, apparently to make some inspection. Presently he returned and remarked that the night was clear although there were heavy storm clouds on the horizon, by which I understood him to convey in Zulu metaphor that it was safe for us to talk, but that danger threatened from afar.

"Macumazahn," he said, "we speak under the blanket of the Opener-of-Roads who sits upon your heart, and whose sign you bring to me, as he sent me word that you would, do we not?"

"I suppose so," I answered. "At any rate we speak as man to man, and hitherto the honour of Macumazahn has not been doubted in Zululand. So if you have anything to say, Chief Bulalio, say it at once, for I am tired and should like to eat and rest."

"Good, Macumazahn. I have this to say. I who am the son of one who was greater than he, have plotted to seize the throne of Zululand from him who sits upon that throne. It is true, for I grew weary of my idleness as a petty chief. Moreover, I should have succeeded with the help of Zikali, who hates the House of Senzangacona, though me, who am of its blood, he does not hate, because ever I have striven against that House. But it seems from his message and those words spoken by an angry woman, that I have been betrayed, and that to-night or tomorrow night, or by the next moon, the slayers will be upon me, smiting me before I can smite, at which I cannot grumble."

"By whom have you been betrayed, Umslopogaas?"

"By that wife of mine, as I think, Macumazahn. Also by Lousta, my blood-brother, over whom she has cast her net and made false to me, so that he hopes to win her whom he has always loved and with her the Chieftainship of the Axe. Now what shall I do?—Tell me, you whose eyes can see in the dark."

I thought a moment and answered, "I think that if I were you, I would leave this Lousta to sit in my place for a while as Chief of the People of the Axe, and take a journey north, Umslopogaas. Then if trouble comes from the Great House where a king sits, it will come to Lousta who can show that the People of the Axe are innocent and that you are far away."

"That is cunning, Macumazahn. There speaks the Great Medicine. If I go north, who can say that I have plotted, and if I leave my betrayer in my place, who can say that I was a traitor, who have set him where I used to sit and left the land upon a private matter? And now tell me of this journey of yours."

So I told him everything, although until that moment I had not made up my mind to go upon this journey, I who had come here to his kraal by accident, or so it seemed, and by accident had delivered to him a certain message.

"You wish to consult a white witch-doctoress, Macumazahn, who according to Zikali lives far to the north, as to the dead. Now I too, though perchance you will not think it of a black man, desire to learn of the dead; yes, of a certain wife of my youth who was sister and friend as well as wife, whom too I loved better than all the world. Also I desire to learn of a brother of mine whose name I never speak, who ruled the wolves with me and who died at my side on yonder Witch-Mountain, having made him a mat of men to lie on in a great and glorious fight. For of him as of the woman I think all day and dream all night, and I would know if they still live anywhere and I may look to see them again when I have died as a warrior should and as I hope to do. Do you understand, Watcher-by-Night?"

I answered that I understood very well, as his case seemed to be like my own.

"It may happen," went on Umslopogaas, "that all this talk of the dead who are supposed to live after they are dead, is but as the sound of wind whispering in the reeds at night, that comes from nowhere and goes nowhere and means nothing. But at least ours will be a great journey in which we shall find adventure and fighting, since it is well known in the land that wherever Macumazahn goes there is plenty of both. Also it seems well for reasons that have been spoken of between us, as Zikali says, that I should leave the country of the Zulus for a while, who desire to die a man's death at the last and not to be trapped like a jackal in a pit. Lastly I think that we shall agree well together though my temper is rough at times, and that neither of us will desert the other in trouble, though of that little yellow dog of yours I am not so sure."

"I answer for him," I replied. "Hans is a true man, cunning also when once he is away from drink."

Then we spoke of plans for our journey, and of when and where we should meet to make it, talking till it was late, after which I went to sleep in the guest-hut.

## CHAPTER 4

# The Lion and the Axe

Next day early I left the town of the People of the Axe, having bid a formal farewell to Umslopogaas, saying in a voice that all could hear that as the rivers were still flooded, I proposed to trek to the northern parts of Zululand and trade there until the weather was better. Our private arrangement, however, was that on the night of the next full moon, which happened about four weeks later, we should meet at the eastern foot of a certain great, flat-topped mountain known to both of us, which stands to the north of Zululand but well beyond its borders.

So northward I trekked, slowly to spare my oxen, trading as I went. The details do not matter, but as it happened I met with more luck upon that journey than had come my way for many a long year. Although I worked on credit since nearly all my goods were sold, as owing to my repute I could always do in Zululand, I made some excellent bargains in cattle, and to top up with, bought a large lot of ivory so cheap that really I think it must have been stolen.

All of this, cattle, and ivory together, I sent to Natal in charge of a white friend of mine whom I could trust, where the stuff was sold very well indeed, and the proceeds paid to my account, the "trade" equivalents being duly remitted to the native vendors.

In fact, my good fortune was such that if I had been superstitious like Hans, I should have been inclined to attribute it to the influence of Zikali's "Great Medicine." As it was I knew it to be one of the chances of a trader's life and accepted it with a shrug as often as I had been accustomed to do in the alternative of losses.

Only one untoward incident happened to me. Of a sudden a party of the King's soldiers under the command of a well-known *Induna* or Councillor, arrived and insisted upon searching my wagon, as I thought at first in connection with that cheap lot of ivory which had already departed to Natal. However, never a word did they say of ivory, nor indeed was a single thing belonging to me taken by them.

I was very indignant and expressed my feelings to the *Induna* in no measured terms. He on his part was most apologetic, and explained that what he did he was obliged to do "by the King's orders." Also he let it slip that he was seeking for a certain "evil-doer" who, it was thought, might be with me without my knowing his real character, and as this "evil-doer," whose name he would not mention, was a very fierce man, it had been necessary to bring a strong guard with him.

Now I bethought me of Umslopogaas, but merely looked blank and shrugged my shoulders, saying that I was not in the habit of consorting with evil-doers.

Still unsatisfied, the *Induna* questioned me as to the places where I had been during this journey of mine in the Zulu country. I told him with the utmost frankness, mentioning among others—because I was sure that already he knew all my movements well—the town of the People of the Axe.

Then he asked me if I had seen its Chief, a certain Umslopogaas or Bulalio. I answered, Yes, that I had met him there for the first time and thought him a very remarkable man.

With this the *Induna* agreed emphatically, saying that perhaps I did not know *how* remarkable. Next he asked me where he was now, to which I replied that I had not the faintest idea, but I presumed in his kraal where I had left him. The *Induna* explained that he was *not* in his kraal; that he had gone away leaving one Lousta and his own head wife Monazi to administer the chieftainship for a while, because, as he stated, he wished to make a journey.

I yawned as if weary of the subject of this chief, and indeed of the whole business. Then the *Induna* said that I must come to the King and repeat to him all the words that I had spoken. I replied that I could not possibly do so as, having finished my trading, I had arranged to go north to shoot elephants. He answered that elephants lived a long while and would not die while I was visiting the King.

Then followed an argument which grew heated and ended in his declaring that to the King I must come, even if he had to take me there by force.

I sat silent, wondering what to say or do and leant forward to pick a piece of wood out of the fire wherewith to light my pipe. Now my shirt was not buttoned and as it chanced this action caused the ivory image of Zikali that hung about my neck to appear between its edges. The *Induna* saw it and his eyes grew big with fear.

"Hide that!" he whispered, "hide that, lest it should bewitch me. Indeed, already I feel as though I were being bewitched. It is the Great Medicine itself."

"That will certainly happen to you," I said, yawning again, "if you insist upon my taking a week's trek to visit the Black One, or interfere with me in any way now or afterwards," and I lifted my hand towards the talisman, looking him steadily in the face.

"Perhaps after all, Macumazahn, it is not necessary for you to visit the King," he said in an uncertain voice. "I will go and make report to him that you know nothing of this evil-doer."

And he went in such a hurry that he never waited to say good-bye. Next morning before the dawn I went also and trekked steadily until I was clear of Zululand.

* * * * * * * *

In due course and without accident, for the weather, which had been so wet, had now turned beautifully fine and dry, we came to the great, flat-topped hill that I have mentioned, trekking thither over high, sparsely-timbered *veld* that offered few difficulties to the wagon. This peculiar hill, known to such natives as lived in those parts by a long word that means Hut-with-a-flat-roof, is surrounded by forest, for here trees grow wonderfully well, perhaps because of the water that flows from its slopes. Forcing our way through this forest, which was full of game, I reached its eastern foot and there camped, five days before that night of full moon on which I had arranged to meet Umslopogaas.

That I should meet him I did not in the least believe, firstly because I thought it very probable that he would have changed his mind about coming, and secondly for the excellent reason that I expected he had gone to call upon the King against his will, as I had been asked to do. It was evident to me that he was up to his eyes in some serious plot against Cetywayo, in which he was the old dwarf Zikali's partner, or rather, tool; also that his plot had been betrayed, with the result that he was "wanted" and would have little chance of passing safely through Zululand. So taking one thing with another I imagined that I had seen his grim face and his peculiar, ancient-looking axe for the last time.

To tell the truth I was glad. Although at first the idea had appealed to me a little, I did not want to make this wild-goose, or wild-witch chase through unknown lands to seek for a totally fabulous person who dwelt far across the Zambezi. I had, as it were, been forced into the thing, but if Umslopogaas did not appear, my obligations would be at an end and I should return to Natal at my leisure. First, however, I would do a little shooting since I found that a large herd of elephants haunted this forest. Indeed I was tempted to attack them at once, but did not do so since, as Hans pointed out, if we were going north it would be difficult to carry the ivory, especially if we had to leave the wagon, and I was too old a hunter to desire to kill the great beasts for the fun of the thing.

So I just sat down and rested, letting the oxen feed throughout the hours of light on the rich grasses which grew upon the bottom-most slopes of the big mountain where we were camped by a stream, not more than a hundred yards above the timber line.

At some time or other there had been a native village at this spot; probably the Zulus had cleaned it out in long past years, for I found human bones black with age lying in the long grass. Indeed, the cattle-kraal still remained and in such good condition that by piling up a few stones here and there on the walls and closing the narrow entrances with thorn bushes, we could still use it to enclose our oxen at night. This I did for fear lest there should be lions about, though I had neither seen nor heard them.

So the days went by pleasantly enough with lots to eat, since whenever we wanted meat I had only to go a few yards to shoot a fat buck at a spot whither they trekked to drink in the evening, till at last came the time of full moon. Of this I was also glad, since, to tell the truth, I had begun to be bored. Rest is good, but for a man who has always led an active life too much of it is very bad, for then he begins to think and thought in large doses is depressing.

Of the fire-eating Umslopogaas there was no sign, so I made up my mind that on the morrow I would start after those elephants and when I had shot—or failed to shoot—some of them, return to Natal. I felt unable to remain idle any more; it never was my gift to do so, which is perhaps why I employ my ample leisure here in England in jotting down such reminiscences as these.

Well, the full moon came up in silver glory and after I had taken a good look at her for luck, also at all the *veld* within sight, I turned in. An hour or two later some noise from the direction of the cattle-kraal woke me up. As it did not recur, I thought that I would go to sleep again. Then an uneasy thought came to me that I could not remember having looked to see whether the entrance was properly closed, as it was my habit to do. It was the same sort of troublesome doubt which in a civilised house makes a man get out of bed and go along the cold passages to the sitting-room to see whether he has put out the lamp. It always proves that he *has* put it out, but that does not prevent a repetition of the performance next time the perplexity arises.

I reflected that perhaps the noise was caused by the oxen pushing their way through the carelessly-closed entrance, and at any rate that I had better go to see. So I slipped on my boots and a coat and went without waking Hans or the boys, only taking with me a loaded, single-barrelled rifle which I used for shooting small buck, but no spare cartridges.

Now in front of the gateway of the cattle-kraal, shading it, grew a single big tree of the wild fig order. Passing under this tree I looked and saw that the gateway was quite securely closed, as now I remembered I had noted at sunset. Then I started to go back but had not stepped more than two or three paces when, in the bright moonlight, I saw the head of my smallest ox, a beast of the Zulu breed, suddenly appear over the top of the wall. About this there would have been nothing particularly astonishing, had it not been for the fact that this head belonged to a dead animal, as I could tell from the closed eyes and the hanging tongue.

"What in the name of goodness——" I began to myself, when my reflections were cut short by the appearance of another head, that of one of the biggest lions I ever saw, which had the ox by the throat, and with the enormous strength that is given to these creatures, by getting its back beneath the body, was deliberately hoisting it over the wall, to drag it away to devour at its leisure.

There was the brute within twelve feet of me, and what is more, it saw me as I saw it, and stopped, still holding the ox by the throat.

"What a chance for Allan Quatermain! Of course he shot it dead," one can fancy anyone saying who knows me by repute, also that by the gift of God I am handy with a rifle. Well, indeed, it should have been, for even with the small-bore piece that I carried, a bullet ought to have pierced through the soft parts of its throat to the brain and to have killed that lion as dead as Julius Caesar. Theoretically the thing was easy enough; indeed, although I was startled for a moment, by the time that I had the rifle to my shoulder I had little fear of the issue, unless there was a miss-fire, especially as the beast seemed so astonished that it remained quite still.

Then the unexpected happened as generally it does in life, particularly in hunting, which, in my case, is a part of life. I fired, but by misfortune the bullet struck the tip of the horn of that confounded ox, which tip either was or at that moment fell in front of the spot on the lion's throat whereat half-unconsciously I had aimed. Result: the ball was turned and, departing at an angle, just cut the skin of the lion's neck deeply enough to hurt it very much and to make it madder than all the hatters in the world.

Dropping the ox, with a most terrific roar it came over the wall at me—I remember that there seemed to be yards of it—I mean of the lion—in front of which appeared a cavernous mouth full of gleaming teeth.

I skipped back with much agility, also a little to one side, because there was nothing else to do, reflecting in a kind of inconsequent way, that after all Zikali's Great Medicine was not worth a curse. The lion landed on my side of the wall and reared itself upon its hind legs before getting to business, towering high above me but slightly to my left.

Then I saw a strange thing. A shadow thrown by the moon flitted past me—all I noted of it was the distorted shape of a great, lifted axe, probably because the axe came first. The shadow fell and with it another shadow, that of a lion's paw dropping to the ground. Next there was a most awful noise of roaring, and wheeling round I saw such a fray as never I shall see again. A tall, grim, black man was fighting the great lion, that now lacked one paw, but still stood upon its hind legs, striking at him with the other.

The man, who was absolutely silent, dodged the blow and hit back with the axe, catching the beast upon the breast with such weight that it came to the ground in a lopsided fashion, since now it had only one fore-foot on which to light.

The axe flashed up again and before the lion could recover itself, or do anything else, fell with a crash upon its skull, sinking deep into the head. After this all was over, for the beast's brain was cut in two.

"I am here at the appointed time, Macumazahn," said Umslopogaas, for it was he, as with difficulty he dragged his axe from the lion's severed skull, "to find you watching by night as it is reported that you always do."

"No," I retorted, for his tone irritated me, "you are late, Bulalio, the moon has been up some hours."

"I said, O Macumazahn, that I would meet you on the *night* of the full moon, not at the rising of the moon."

"That is true," I replied, mollified, "and at any rate you came at a good moment."

"Yes," he answered, "though as it happens in this clear light the thing was easy to anyone who can handle an axe. Had it been darker the end might have been different. But, Macumazahn, you are not so clever as I thought, since otherwise you would not have come out against a lion with a toy like that," and he pointed to the little rifle in my hand.

"I did not know that there was a lion, Umslopogaas."

"That is why you are not so clever as I thought, since of one sort or another there is always a lion which wise men should be prepared to meet, Macumazahn."

"You are right again," I replied.

At that moment Hans arrived upon the scene, followed at a discreet distance by the wagon boys, and took in the situation at a glance.

"The Great Medicine of the Opener-of-Roads has worked well," was all he said.

"The great medicine of the Opener-of-Heads has worked better," remarked Umslopogaas with a little laugh and pointing to his red axe. "Never before since she came into my keeping has *Inkosikaas* (i.e. 'Chieftainess,' for so was this famous weapon named) sunk so low as to drink the blood of beasts. Still, the stroke was a good one so she need not be ashamed. But, Yellow Man, how comes it that you who, I have been told, are cunning, watch your master so ill?"

"I was asleep," stuttered Hans indignantly.

"Those who serve should never sleep," replied Umslopogaas sternly. Then he turned and whistled, and behold! out of the long grass that grew at a little distance, emerged twelve great men, all of them bearing axes and wearing cloaks of hyena skins, who saluted me by raising their axes.

"Set a watch and skin me this beast by dawn. It will make us a mat," said Umslopogaas, whereon again they saluted silently and melted away.

"Who are these?" I asked.

"A few picked warriors whom I brought with me, Macumazahn. There were one or two more, but they got lost on the way."

Then we went to the wagon and spoke no more that night.

\* \* \* \* \* \* \* \*

Next morning I told Umslopogaas of the visit I had received from the *Induna* of the King who wished me to come to the royal kraal. He nodded and said, "As it chances certain thieves attacked me on my journey, which is why one or two of my people remain behind who will never travel again. We made good play with those thieves; not one of them escaped," he added grimly, "and their bodies we threw into a river where are many crocodiles. But their spears I brought away

54

and I think that they are such as the King's guard use. If so, his search for them will be long, since the fight took place where no man lives and we burned the shields and trappings. Oho! he will think that the ghosts have taken them."

That morning we trekked on fast, fearing lest a regiment searching for these "thieves" should strike and follow our spoor. Luckily the ox that the lion had killed was one of some spare cattle which I was driving with me, so its loss did not inconvenience us. As we went Umslopogaas told me that he had duly appointed Lousta and his wife Monazi to rule the tribe during his absence, an office which they accepted doubtfully, Monazi acting as Chieftainess and Lousta as her head *Induna* or Councillor.

I asked him whether he thought this wise under all the circumstances, seeing that it had occurred to me since I made the suggestion, that they might be unwilling to surrender power on his return, also that other domestic complications might ensue.

"It matters little, Macumazahn," he said with a shrug of his great shoulders, "for of this I am sure, that I have played my part with the People of the Axe and to stop among them would have meant my death, who am a man betrayed. What do I care who love none and now have no children? Still, it is true that I might have fled to Natal with the cattle and there have led a fat and easy life. But ease and plenty I do not desire who would live and fall as a warrior should.

"Never again, mayhap, shall I see the Ghost-Mountain where the wolves ravened and the old Witch sits in stone waiting for the world to die, or sleep in the town of the People of the Axe. What do I want with wives and oxen while I have *Inkosikaas* the Groan-maker and she is true to me?" he added, shaking the ancient axe above his head so that the sun gleamed upon the curved blade and the hollow gouge or point at the back beyond the shaft socket. "Where the Axe goes, there go the strength and virtue of the Axe, O Macumazahn."

"It is a strange weapon," I said.

"Aye, a strange and an old, forged far away, says Zikali, by a warrior-wizard hundreds of years ago, a great fighter who was also the first of smiths and who sits in the Under-world waiting for it to return to his hand when its work is finished beneath the sun. That will be soon, Macumazahn, since Zikali told me that I am the last Holder of the Axe."

"Did you then see the Opener-of-Roads?" I asked.

"Aye, I saw him. He it was who told me which way to go to escape from Zululand. Also he laughed when he heard how the flooded rivers brought you to my kraal, and sent you a message in which he said that the spirit of a snake had told him that you tried to throw the Great Medicine into a pool, but were stopped by that snake, whilst it was still alive. This, he said, you must do no more, lest he should send another snake to stop *you*."

"Did he?" I replied indignantly, for Zikali's power of seeing or learning about things that happened at a distance puzzled and annoyed me.

Only Hans grinned and said, "I told you so, Baas."

\* \* \* \* \* \* \* \*

On we travelled from day to day, meeting with such difficulties and dangers as are common on roadless *veld* in Africa, but no more, for the grass was good and there was plenty of game, of which we shot what we wanted for meat. Indeed, here in the back regions of what is known as Portuguese South East Africa, every sort of wild animal was so numerous that personally I wished we could turn our journey into a shooting expedition.

But of this Umslopogaas, whom hunting bored, would not hear. In fact, he was much more anxious than myself to carry out our original purpose. When I asked him why, he answered because of something Zikali had told him. What this was he would not say, except that in the country whither we wandered he would fight a great fight and win much honour.

Now Umslopogaas was by nature a fighting man, one who took a positive joy in battle, and like an old Norseman, seemed to think that thus only could a man decorously die. This amazed me, a peaceful person who loves quiet and a home. Still, I gave way, partly to please him, partly because I hoped that we might discover something of interest, and still more because, having once undertaken an enterprise, my pride prompted me to see it through.

Now while he was preparing to draw his map in the ashes, or afterwards, I forget which, Zikali had told me that when we drew near to the great river we should come to a place on the edge of bush-*veld* that ran down to the river, where a white man lived, adding, after casting his bones and reading from them, that he thought this white man was a "trek-Boer." This, I should explain, means a Dutchman who has travelled away from wherever he lived and made a home for himself in the wilderness, as some wandering spirit and the desire to be free of authority often prompt these people to do. Also, after another inspection of his enchanted knuckle-bones, he had declared that something remarkable would happen to this man or his family, while I was visiting him. Lastly in that map he drew in the ashes, the details of which were impressed so indelibly upon my memory, he had shown me where I should find the dwelling of this white man, of whom and of whose habitation doubtless he knew through the many spies who seemed to be at the service of all witch-doctors, and more especially of Zikali, the greatest among them.

Travelling by the sun and the compress I had trekked steadily in the exact direction which he indicated, to find that in this useful particular he was well named the "Opener-of-Roads," since always before me I found a practicable path, although to the right or to the left there would have been none. Thus when we came to mountains, it was at a spot where we discovered a pass; when we came to swamps it was where a ridge of high ground ran between, and so forth. Also such tribes as we met upon our journey always proved of a friendly character, although perhaps the aspect of Umslopogaas and his fierce band whom, rather irreverently, I named his twelve Apostles, had a share in inducing this peaceful attitude.

So smooth was our progress and so well marked by water at certain intervals, that at last I came to the conclusion that we must be following some ancient road which at a forgotten period of history, had run from south to north, or *vice versa*. Or rather, to be honest, it was the observant Hans who made this discovery from various indications which had escaped my notice. I need not stop to detail them, but one of these was that at certain places the water-holes on a high, rather barren land had been dug out, and in one or more instances, lined with stones after the fashion of an ancient well. Evidently we were following an old trade route made, perhaps, in forgotten ages when Africa was more civilised than it is now.

Passing over certain high, misty lands during the third week of our trek, where frequently at this season of the year the sun never showed itself before ten o'clock and disappeared at three or four in the afternoon, and where twice we were held up for two whole days by dense fog, we came across a queer nomadic people who seemed to live in movable grass huts and to keep great herds of goats and long-tailed sheep.

These folk ran away from us at first, but when they found that we did them no harm, became friendly and brought us offerings of milk, also of a kind of slug or caterpillar which they seemed to eat. Hans, who was a great master of different native dialects, discovered a tongue, or a mixture of tongues, in which he could make himself understood to some of them.

They told him that in their day they had never seen a white man, although their fathers' fathers (an expression by which they meant their remote ancestors) had known many of them. They added, however, that if we went on steadily towards the north for another seven days' journey, we should come to a place where a white man lived, one, they had heard, who had a long beard and killed animals with guns, as we did.

Encouraged by this intelligence we pushed forward, now travelling down hill out of the mists into a more genial country. Indeed, the *veld* here was beautiful, high, rolling plains like those of the East African plateau, covered with a deep and fertile chocolate-coloured soil, as we could see where the rains had washed out dongas. The climate, too, seemed to be cool and very healthful. Altogether it was a pity to see such lands lying idle and tenanted only by countless herds of game, for there were not any native inhabitants, or at least we met none.

On we trekked, our road still sloping slightly down hill, till at length we saw far away a vast sea of bush-*veld* which, as I guessed correctly, must fringe the great Zambezi River. Moreover we, or rather Hans, whose eyes were those of a hawk, saw something else, namely buildings of a more or less civilised kind, which stood among trees by the side of a stream several miles on this side of the great belt of bush.

"Look, Baas," said Hans, "those wanderers did not lie; there is the house of the white man. I wonder if he drinks anything stronger than water," he added with a sigh and a kind of reminiscent contraction of his yellow throat.

As it happened, he did.

## CHAPTER 5

# Inez

We had sighted the house from far away shortly after sunrise and by midday we were there. As we approached I saw that it stood almost immediately beneath two great baobab trees, babyan trees we call them in South Africa, perhaps because monkeys eat their fruit. It was a thatched house with whitewashed walls and a *stoep* or veranda round it, apparently of the ordinary Dutch type. Moreover, beyond it, at a little distance were other houses or rather shanties with wagon sheds, etc., and beyond and mixed up with these a number of native huts. Further on were considerable fields green with springing corn; also we saw herds of cattle grazing on the slopes. Evidently our white man was rich.

Umslopogaas surveyed the place with a soldier's eye and said to me, "This must be a peaceful country, Macumazahn, where no attack is feared, since of defences I see none."

"Yes," I answered, "why not, with a wilderness behind it and bush-*veld* and a great river in front?"

"Men can cross rivers and travel through bush-*veld*," he answered, and was silent.

Up to this time we had seen no one, although it might have been presumed that a wagon trekking towards the house was a sufficiently unusual sight to have attracted attention.

"Where can they be?" I asked.

"Asleep, Baas, I think," said Hans, and as a matter of fact he was right. The whole population of the place was indulging in a noonday siesta.

At last we came so near to the house that I halted the wagon and descended from the driving-box in order to investigate. At this moment someone did appear, the sight of whom astonished me not a little, namely, a very striking-looking young woman. She was tall, handsome, with large dark eyes, good features, a rather pale complexion, and I think the saddest face that I ever saw. Evidently she had heard the noise of the wagon and had come out to see what caused it, for she had nothing on her head, which was covered with thick hair of a raven blackness. Catching sight of the great Umslopogaas with his gleaming axe and of his savage-looking bodyguard, she uttered an exclamation and not unnaturally turned to fly.

"It's all right," I sang out, emerging from behind the oxen, and in English, though before the words had left my lips I reflected that there was not the slightest reason to suppose that she would understand them. Probably she was Dutch, or Portuguese, although by some instinct I had addressed her in English.

To my surprise she answered me in the same tongue, spoken, it is true, with a peculiar accent which I could not place, as it was neither Scotch nor Irish.

"Thank you," she said. "I, sir, was frightened. Your friends look——" Here she stumbled for a word, then added, "terrocious."

I laughed at this composite adjective and answered, "Well, so they are in a way, though they will not harm you or me. But, young lady, tell me, can we outspan here? Perhaps your husband——"

"I have no husband, I have only a father, sir," and she sighed.

"Well, then, could I speak to your father? My name is Allan Quatermain and I am making a journey of exploration, to find out about the country beyond, you know."

"Yes, I will go to wake him. He is asleep. Everyone sleeps here at midday—except me," she said with another sigh.

"Why do you not follow their example?" I asked jocosely, for this young woman puzzled me and I wanted to find out about her.

"Because I sleep little, sir, who think too much. There will be plenty of time to sleep soon for all of us, will there not?"

I stared at her and inquired her name, because I did not know what else to say.

"My name is Inez Robertson," she answered. "I will go to wake my father. Meanwhile please unyoke your oxen. They can feed with the others; they look as though they wanted rest, poor things." Then she turned and went into the house.

"Inez Robertson," I said to myself, "that's a queer combination. English father and Portuguese mother, I suppose. But what can an Englishman be doing in a place like this? If it had been a trek-Boer I should not have been surprised." Then I began to give directions about out-spanning.

We had just got the oxen out of the yokes, when a big, raw-boned, red-bearded, blue-eyed, roughly-clad man of about fifty years of age appeared from the house, yawning. I threw my eye over him as he advanced with a peculiar rolling gait, and formed certain conclusions. A drunkard who has once been a gentleman, I reflected to myself, for there was something peculiarly dissolute in his appearance, also one who has had to do with the sea, a diagnosis which proved very accurate.

"How do you do, Mr. Allan Quatermain, which I think my daughter said is your name, unless I dreamed it, for it is one that I seem to have heard before," he exclaimed with a broad Scotch accent which I do not attempt to reproduce. "What in the name of blazes brings you here where no real white man has been for years? Well, I am glad enough to see you any way, for I am sick of half-breed Portuguese and niggers, and snuff-and-butter girls, and gin and bad whisky. Leave your people to attend to those oxen and come in and have a drink."

"Thank you, Mr. Robertson——"

"Captain Robertson," he interrupted. "Man, don't look astonished. You mightn't guess it, but I commanded a mail-steamer once and should like to hear myself called rightly again before I die."

"I beg your pardon—Captain Robertson, but myself, I don't drink anything before sundown. However, if you have something to eat——?"

"Oh yes, Inez—she's my daughter—will find you a bite. Those men of yours," and he also looked doubtfully at Umslopogaas and his savage company, "will want food as well. I'll have a beast killed for them; they look as if they could eat it, horns and all. Where are my people? All asleep, I suppose, the lazy lubbers. Wait a bit, I'll wake them up."

Going to the house he snatched a great *sjambok* cut from hippopotamus hide, from where it hung on a nail in the wall, and ran towards the group of huts which I have mentioned, roaring out the name Thomaso, also a string of oaths such as seamen use, mixed with others of a Portuguese variety. What happened there I could not see because boughs were in the way, but presently I heard blows and screams, and caught sight of people, all dark-skinned, flying from the huts.

A little later a fat, half-breed man—I should say from his curling hair that his mother was a negress and his father a Portuguese—appeared with some other nondescript fellows and began to give directions in a competent fashion about our oxen, also as to the killing of a calf. He spoke in bastard Portuguese, which I could understand, and I heard him talk of Umslopogaas to whom he pointed, as "that nig-

61

ger," after the fashion of such cross-bred people who choose to consider themselves white men. Also he made uncomplimentary remarks about Hans, who of course understood every word he said. Evidently Thomaso's temper had been ruffled by this sudden and violent disturbance of his nap.

Just then our host appeared puffing with his exertions and declaring that he had stirred up the swine with a vengeance, in proof of which he pointed to the *sjambok* that was reddened with blood.

"Captain Robertson," I said, "I wish to give you a hint to be passed on to Mr. Thomaso, if that is he. He spoke of the Zulu soldier there as a nigger, etc. Well, he is a chief of a high rank and rather a terrible fellow if roused. Therefore I recommend Mr. Thomaso not to let him understand that he is insulting him."

"Oh! that's the way of these 'snuff-and-butters' one of whose grandmothers once met a white man," replied the Captain, laughing, "but I'll tell him," and he did in Portuguese.

His retainer listened in silence, looking at Umslopogaas rather sulkily. Then we walked into the house. As we went the Captain said, "*Señor* Thomaso—he calls himself *Señor*—is my manager here and a clever man, honest too in his way and attached to me, perhaps because I saved his life once. But he has a nasty temper, as have all these cross-breeds, so I hope he won't get wrong with that native who carries a big axe."

"I hope so too, for his own sake," I replied emphatically.

The Captain led the way into the sitting-room; there was but one in the house. It proved a queer kind of place with rude furniture seated with strips of hide after the Boer fashion, and yet bearing a certain air of refinement which was doubtless due to Inez, who, with the assistance of a stout native girl, was already engaged in setting the table. Thus there was a shelf with books, Shakespeare was one of these, I noticed—over which hung an ivory crucifix, which suggested that Inez was a Catholic. On the walls, too, were some good portraits, and on the window-ledge a jar full of flowers. Also the forks and spoons were of silver, as were the mugs, and engraved with a tremendous coat-of-arms and a Portuguese motto.

Presently the food appeared, which was excellent and plentiful, and the Captain, his daughter and I sat down and ate. I noted that he drank gin and water, an innocent-looking beverage but strong as he took it. It was offered to me, but like Miss Inez, I preferred coffee.

During the meal and afterwards while we smoked upon the veranda, I told them as much as I thought desirable of my plans. I said that I was engaged upon a journey of exploration of the country beyond the Zambezi, and that having heard of this settlement, which, by the way, was called Strathmuir, as I gathered after a place in far away Scotland where the Captain had been born and passed his childhood, I had come here to inquire as to how to cross the great river, and about other things.

The Captain was interested, especially when I informed him that I was that same Hunter Quatermain of whom he had heard in past years, but he told me that it would be impossible to take the wagon down into the low bush-*veld* which we could see beneath us, as there all the oxen would die of the bite of the tsetse fly. I answered that I was aware of this and proposed to try to make an arrangement to leave it in his charge till I returned.

"That might be managed, Mr. Quatermain," he answered. "But, man, will you ever return? They say there are queer folk living on the other side of the Zambezi, savage men who are cannibals, Amahagger I think they call them. It was they who in past years cleaned out all this country, except a few river tribes who live in floating huts or on islands among the reeds, and that's why it is so empty. But this happened long ago, much before my time, and I don't suppose they will ever cross the river again."

"If I might ask, what brought you here, Captain?" I said, for the point was one on which I felt curious.

"That which brings most men to wild places, Mr. Quatermain— trouble. If you want to know, I had a misfortune and piled up my ship. There were some lives lost and, rightly or wrongly, I got the sack. Then I started as a trader in a God-forsaken hole named Chinde, one of the Zambezi mouths, you know, and did very well, as we Scotchmen have a way of doing.

"There I married a Portuguese lady, a real lady of high blood, one of the old sort. When my girl, Inez, was about twelve years old I got into more trouble, for my wife died and it pleased a certain relative of hers to say that it was because I had neglected her. This ended in a row and the truth is that I killed him—in fair fight, mind you. Still, kill him I did though I scarcely knew that I had done it at the time, after which the place grew too hot to hold me. So I sold up and swore that I would have no more to do with what they are pleased to call civilisation on the East Coast.

"During my trading I had heard that there was fine country up this way, and here I came and settled years ago, bringing my girl and Thomaso, who was one of my managers, also a few other people with me. And here I have been ever since, doing very well as before, for I trade a lot of ivory and other things and grow stuff and cattle, which I sell to the River natives. Yes, I am a rich man now and could go to live on my means in Scotland, or anywhere."

"Why don't you?" I asked.

"Oh! for many reasons. I have lost touch with all that and become half wild and I like this life and the sunshine and being my own master. Also, if I did, things might be raked up against me, about that man's death. Also, though I daresay it will make you think badly of me for it, Mr. Quatermain, I have ties down there," and he waved is hand towards the village, if so it could be called, "which it wouldn't be easy for me to break. A man may be fond of his children, Mr. Quatermain, even if their skins ain't so white as they ought to be. Lastly I have habits—you see, I am speaking out to you as man to man—which might get me into trouble again if I went back to the world," and he nodded his fine, capable-looking head in the direction of the bottle on the table.

"I see," I said hastily, for this kind of confession bursting out of the man's lonely heart when what he had drunk took a hold of him, was painful to hear. "But how about your daughter, Miss Inez?"

"Ah!" he said, with a quiver in his voice, "there you touch it. She ought to go away. There is no one for her to marry here, where we haven't seen a white man for years, and she's a lady right enough, like her mother. But who is she to go to, being a Roman Catholic whom my own dour Presbyterian folk in Scotland, if any of them are left, would turn their backs on? Moreover, she loves me in her own fashion, as I love her, and she wouldn't leave me because she thinks it her duty to stay and knows that if she did, I should go to the devil altogether. Still—perhaps you might help me about her, Mr. Quatermain, that is if you live to come back from your journey," he added doubtfully.

I felt inclined to ask how I could possibly help in such a matter, but thought it wisest to say nothing. This, however, he did not notice, for he went on, "Now I think I will have a nap, as I do my work in the early morning, and sometimes late at night when my brain seems to clear up again, for you see I was a sailor for many years and accustomed to keeping watches. You'll look after yourself, won't you, and treat the place as your own?" Then he vanished into the house to lie down.

When I had finished my pipe I went for a walk. First I visited the wagon where I found Umslopogaas and his company engaged in cooking the beast that had been given them, Zulu fashion; Hans with his usual cunning had already secured a meal, probably from the servants, or from Inez herself; at least he left them and followed me. First we went down to the huts, where we saw a number of good-looking young women of mixed blood, all decently dressed and engaged about their household duties. Also we saw four or five boys and girls, to say nothing of a baby in arms, fine young people, one or two of whom were more white than coloured.

"Those children are very like the Baas with the red beard," remarked Hans reflectively.

"Yes," I said, and shivered, for now I understood the awfulness of this poor man's case. He was the father of a number of half-breeds who tied him to this spot as anchors tie a ship. I went on rather hastily past some sheds to a long, low building which proved to be a store. Here the quarter-blood called Thomaso, and some assistants were engaged in trading with natives from the Zambezi swamps, men of a kind that I had never seen, but in a way more civilised than many further south. What they were selling or buying, I did not stop to see, but I noticed that the store was full of goods of one sort or another, including a great deal of ivory, which, as I supposed, had come down the river from inland.

Then we walked on to the cultivated fields where we saw corn growing very well, also tobacco and other crops. Beyond this were cattle kraals and in the distance we perceived a great number of cattle and goats feeding on the slopes.

"This red-bearded Baas must be very rich in all things," remarked the observant Hans when we had completed our investigations.

"Yes," I answered, "rich and yet poor."

"How can a man be both rich and yet poor, Baas?" asked Hans.

Just at that moment some of the half-breed children whom I have mentioned, ran past us more naked than dressed and whooping like little savages. Hans contemplated them gravely, then said, "I think I understand now, Baas. A man may be rich in things he loves and yet does not want, which makes him poor in other ways."

"Yes," I answered, "as you *are*, Hans, when you take too much to drink."

Just then we met the stately Miss Inez returning from the store, carrying some articles in a basket, soap, I think, and tea in a packet, amongst them. I told Hans to take the basket and bear it to the house for her. He went off with it and, walking slowly, we fell into conversation.

"Your father must do very well here," I said, nodding at the store with the crowd of natives round it.

"Yes," she answered, "he makes much money which he puts in a bank at the coast, for living costs us nothing and there is great profit in what he buys and sells, also in the crops he grows and in the cattle. But," she added pathetically, "what is the use of money in a place like this?"

"You can get things with it," I answered vaguely.

"That is what my father says, but what does he get? Strong stuff to drink; dresses for those women down there, and sometimes pearls, jewels and other things for me which I do not want. I have a box full of them set in ugly gold, or loose which I cannot use, and if I put them on, who is there to see them? That clever half-breed, Thomaso—for he is clever in his way, faithful too—or the women down there—no one else."

"You do not seem to be happy, Miss Inez."

"No. I cannot tell how unhappy others are, who have met none, but sometimes I think that I must be the most miserable woman in the world."

"Oh! no," I replied cheerfully, "plenty are worse off."

"Then, Mr. Quatermain, it must be because they cannot feel. Did you ever have a father whom you loved?"

"Yes, Miss Inez. He is dead, but he was a very good man, a kind of saint. Ask my servant, the little Hottentot Hans; he will tell you about him."

"Ah! a very good man. Well, as you may have guessed, mine is not, though there is much good in him, for he has a kind heart, and a big brain. But the drink and those women down there, they ruin him," and she wrung her hands.

"Why don't you go away?" I blurted out.

"Because it is my duty to stop. That is what my religion teaches me, although of it I know little except through books, who have seen no priest for years except one who was a missionary, a Baptist, I think, who told me that my faith was false and would lead me to hell. Yes, not understanding how I lived, he said that, who did not know that hell is here. No, I cannot go, who hopes always that still God and the Saints will show me how to save my father, even though it be with my blood. And now I have said too much to you who are quite a stranger. Yet, I do not know why, I feel that you will not betray me, and what is more, that you will help me if you can, since you are not one of those who drink, or——" and she waved her hand towards the huts.

"I have my faults, Miss Inez," I answered.

"Yes, no doubt, else you would be a saint, not a man, and even the saints had their faults, or so I seem to remember, and became saints by repentance and conquering them. Still, I am sure that you will help me if you can."

Then with a sudden flash of her dark eyes that said more than all her words, she turned and left me.

Here's a pretty kettle of fish, thought I to myself as I strolled back to the wagon to see how things were going on there, and how to get the live fish out of the kettle before they boil or spoil is more than I know. I wonder why fate is always finding me such jobs to do.

Even as I thought thus a voice in my heart seemed to echo that poor girl's words—because it is your duty—and to add others to them—woe betide him who neglects his duty. I was appointed to try to hook a few fish out of the vast kettle of human woe, and therefore I must go on hooking. Meanwhile this particular problem seemed beyond me. Perhaps Fate would help, I reflected. As a matter of fact, in the end Fate did, if Fate is the right word to use in this connection.

## CHAPTER 6

# The Sea-Cow Hunt

Now it had been my intention to push forward across the river at once, but here luck, or our old friend, Fate, was against me. To begin with several of Umslopogaas' men fell sick with a kind of stomach trouble, arising no doubt from something they had eaten. This, however, was not their view, or that of Umslopogaas himself. It happened that one of these men, Goroko by name, who practised as a witch-doctor in his lighter moments, naturally suspected that a spell had been cast upon them, for such people see magic in everything.

Therefore he organised a "smelling-out" at which Umslopogaas, who was as superstitious as the rest, assisted. So did Hans, although he called himself a Christian, partly out of curiosity, for he was as curious as a magpie, and partly from fear lest some implication should be brought against him in his absence. I saw the business going on from a little distance, and, unseen myself, thought it well to keep an eye upon the proceedings in case anything untoward should occur. This I did with Miss Inez, who had never witnessed anything of the sort, as a companion.

The circle, a small one, was formed in the usual fashion; Goroko rigged up in the best witch-doctor's costume that he could improvise, duly came under the influence of his *Spirit* and skipped about, waving a wildebeeste's tail, and so forth.

Finally to my horror he broke out of the ring, and running to a group of spectators from the village, switched Thomaso, who was standing among them with a lordly and contemptuous air, across the face with the gnu's tail, shouting out that he was the wizard who had poisoned the bowels of the sick men. Thereon Thomaso, who although he could be insolent, like most crossbreeds was not remarkable for courage, seeing the stir that this announcement created amongst the fierce-faced Zulus and fearing developments, promptly bolted, none attempting to follow him.

After this, just as I thought that everything was over and that the time had come for me to speak a few earnest words to Umslopogaas, pointing out that matters must go no further as regards Thomaso, whom I knew that he and his people hated, Goroko went back to the circle and was seized with a new burst of inspiration.

Throwing down his whisk, he lifted his arms above his head and stared at the heavens. Then he began to shout out something in a loud voice which I was too far off to catch. Whatever it may have been, evidently it frightened his hearers, as I could see from the expressions on their faces. Even Umslopogaas was alarmed, for he let his axe fall for a moment, rose as though to speak, then sat down again and covered his eyes with his hands.

In a minute it was over; Goroko seemed to become normal, took some snuff and as I guessed, after the usual fashion of these doctors, began to ask what he had been saying while the Spirit possessed him, which he either had, or affected to have, forgotten. The circle, too, broke up and its members began to talk to each other in a subdued way, while Umslopogaas remained seated on the ground, brooding, and Hans slipped away in his snake-like fashion, doubtless in search of me.

"What was it all about, Mr. Quatermain?" asked Inez.

"Oh! a lot of nonsense," I said. "I fancy that witch-doctor declared that your friend Thomaso put something into those men's food to make them sick."

"I daresay that he did; it would be just like him, Mr. Quatermain, as I know that he hates them, especially Umslopogaas, of whom I am very fond. He brought me some beautiful flowers this morning which he had found somewhere, and made a long speech which I could not understand."

The idea of Umslopogaas, that man of blood and iron, bringing flowers to a young lady, was so absurd that I broke out laughing and even the sad-faced Inez smiled. Then she left me to see about something and I went to speak to Hans and asked him what had happened.

"Something rather queer, I think, Baas," he answered vacuously, "though I did not quite understand the last part. The doctor, Goroko, smelt out Thomaso as the man who had made them sick, and though they will not kill him because we are guests here, those Zulus are very angry with Thomaso and I think will beat him if they get a chance. But that is only the small half of the stick," and he paused.

"What is the big half, then?" I asked with irritation.

"Baas, the Spirit in Goroko———"

"The jackass in Goroko, you mean," I interrupted. "How can you, who are a Christian, talk such rubbish about spirits? I only wish that my father could hear you."

"Oh! Baas, your reverend father, the Predikant, is now wise enough to know all about Spirits and that there are some who come into black witch-doctors though they turn up their noses at white men and leave them alone. However, whatever it is that makes Goroko speak, got hold of him so that his lips said, though he remembered nothing of it afterwards, that soon this place would be red with blood—that there would be a great killing here, Baas. That is all."

"Red with blood! Whose blood? What did the fool mean?"

"I don't know, Baas, but what you call the jackass in Goroko, declared that those who are 'with the Great Medicine'—meaning what you wear, Baas—will be quite safe. So I hope that it will not be our blood; also that you will get out of this place as soon as you can."

Well, I scolded Hans because he believed in what this doctor said, for I could see that he did believe it, then went to question Umslopogaas, whom I found looking quite pleased, which annoyed me still more.

"What is it that Goroko has been saying and why do you smile, Bulalio?" I asked.

"Nothing much, Macumazahn, except that the man who looks like tallow that has gone bad, put something in our food which made us sick, for which I would kill him were he not Red-beard's servant and that it would frighten the lady his daughter. Also he said that soon there will be fighting, which is why I smiled, who grow weary of peace. We came out to fight, did we not?"

"Certainly not," I answered. "We came out to make a quiet journey in strange lands, which is what I mean to do."

"Ah! well, Macumazahn, in strange lands one meets strange men with whom one does not always agree, and then *Inkosikaas* begins to talk," and he whirled the great axe round his head, making the air whistle as it was forced through the gouge at its back.

I could get no more out of him, so having extracted a promise from him that nothing should happen to Thomaso who, I pointed out, was probably quite unjustly accused, I went away.

Still, the whole incident left a disagreeable impression on my mind, and I began to wish that we were safe across the Zambezi without more trouble. But we could not start at once because two of the Zulus were still not well enough to travel and there were many preparations to be made about the loads, and so forth, since the wagon must be left behind. Also, and this was another complication—Hans had a sore upon his foot, resulting from the prick of a poisonous thorn, and it was desirable that this should be quite healed before we marched.

So it came about that I was really glad when Captain Robertson suggested that we should go down to a certain swamp formed, I gathered, by some small tributary of the Zambezi to take part in a kind of hippopotamus battue. It seemed that at this season of the year these great animals always frequented the place in numbers, also that by barring a neck of deep water through which they gained it, they, or a proportion of them, could be cut off and killed.

This had been done once or twice in the past, though not of late, perhaps because Captain Robertson had lacked the energy to organise such a hunt. Now he wished to do so again, taking advantage of my presence, both because of the value of the hides of the sea-cows which were cut up to be sent to the coast and sold as *sjamboks* or whips, and because of the sport of the thing. Also I think he desired to show me that he was not altogether sunk in sloth and drink.

I fell in with the idea readily enough, since in all my hunting life I had never seen anything of the sort, especially as I was told that the expedition would not take more than a week and I reckoned that the sick men and Hans would not be fit to travel sooner. So great preparations were made. The riverside natives, whose share of the spoil was to be the carcases of the slain sea-cows, were summoned by hundreds and sent off to their appointed stations to beat the swamps at a signal given by the firing of a great pile of reeds. Also many other things were done upon which I need not enter.

Then came the time for us to depart to the appointed spot over twenty miles away, most of which distance it seemed we could trek in the wagon. Captain Robertson, who for the time had cut off his gin, was as active about the affair as though he were once more in command of a mail-steamer. Nothing escaped his attention; indeed, in the care which he gave to details he reminded me of the captain of a great ship that is leaving port, and from it I learned how able a man he must once have been.

"Does your daughter accompany us?" I asked on the night before we started.

"Oh! no," he answered, "she would only be in the way. She will be quite safe here, especially as Thomaso, who is no hunter, remains in charge of the place with some of the older natives to look after the women and children."

Later I saw Inez herself, who said that she would have liked to

71

come, although she hated to see great beasts killed, but that her father was against it because he thought she might catch fever. So she supposed that she had better remain where she was.

I agreed, though in my heart I was doubtful, and said that I would leave Hans, whose foot was not as yet quite well, and with whom she had made friends as she had done with Umslopogaas, to look after her. Also there would be with him the two great Zulus who were now recovering from their attack of stomach sickness, so that she would have nothing to fear. She answered with her slow smile that she feared nothing, still, she would have liked to come with us. Then we parted, as it proved for a long time.

It was quite a ceremony. Umslopogaas, "in the name of the Axe" solemnly gave over Inez to the charge of his two followers, bidding them guard her with so much earnestness that I began to suspect he feared something which he did not choose to mention. My mind went back indeed to the prophecy of the witch-doctor Goroko, of which it was possible that he might be thinking, but as while he spoke he kept his fierce eyes fixed upon the fat and pompous quarter-breed, Thomaso, I concluded that here was the object of his doubts.

It might have occurred to him that this Thomaso would take the opportunity of her father's absence to annoy Inez. If so I was sure that he was mistaken for various reasons, of which I need only quote one, namely, that even if such an idea had ever entered his head, Thomaso was far too great a coward to translate it into action. Still, suspecting something, I also gave Hans instructions to keep a sharp eye on Inez and generally to watch the place, and if he saw anything suspicious, to communicate with us at once.

"Yes, Baas," said Hans, "I will look after Sad-Eyes"—for so with their usual quickness of observation our Zulus had named Inez—"as though she were my grandmother, though what there is to fear for her, I do not know. But, Baas, I would much rather come and look after you, as your reverend father, the Predikant, told me to do always, which is my duty, not girl-herding, Baas. Also my foot is now quite well and—I want to shoot sea-cows, and——" Here he paused.

"And what, Hans?"

"And Goroko said that there was going to be much fighting and if there should be fighting and you should come to harm because I was not there to protect you, what would your reverend father think of me then?"

All of which meant two things: that Hans never liked being separated from me if he could help it, and that he much preferred a shooting trip to stopping alone in this strange place with nothing to do except eat and sleep. So I concluded, though indeed I did not get quite to the bottom of the business. In reality Hans was putting up a most gallant struggle against temptation.

As I found out afterwards, Captain Robertson had been giving him strong drink on the sly, moved thereto by sympathy with a fellow toper. Also he had shown him where, if he wanted it, he could get more, and Hans always wanted gin very badly indeed. To leave it within his reach was like leaving a handful of diamonds lying about in the room of a thief. This he knew, but was ashamed to tell me the truth, and thence came much trouble.

"You will stop here, Hans, look after the young lady and nurse your foot," I said sternly, whereon he collapsed with a sigh and asked for some tobacco.

Meanwhile Captain Robertson, who I think had been taking a stirrup cup to cheer him on the road, was making his farewells down in what was known as "the village," for I saw him there kissing a collection of half-breed children, and giving Thomaso instructions to look after them and their mothers. Returning at length, he called to Inez, who remained upon the veranda, for she always seemed to shrink from her father after his visits to the village, to "keep a stiff upper lip" and not feel lonely, and commanded the cavalcade to start.

So off we went, about twenty of the village natives, a motley crew armed with every kind of gun, marching ahead and singing songs. Then came the wagon with Captain Robertson and myself seated on the driving-box, and lastly Umslopogaas and his Zulus, except the two who had been left behind.

We trekked along a kind of native road over fine *veld* of the same character as that on which Strathmuir stood, having the lower-lying bush-*veld* which ran down to the Zambezi on our right. Before nightfall we came to a ridge whereon this bush-*veld* turned south, fringing that tributary of the great river in the swamps of which we were to hunt for sea-cows. Here we camped and next morning, leaving the wagon in charge of my *voorlooper* and a couple of the Strathmuir natives, for the driver was to act as my gun-bearer—we marched down into the sea of bush-*veld*. It proved to be full of game, but at this we dared not fire for fearing of disturbing the hippopotami in the swamps beneath, whence in that event they might escape us back to the river.

About midday we passed out of the bush-*veld* and reached the place where the drive was to be. Here, bordered by steep banks covered with bush, was swampy ground not more than two hundred yards wide, down the centre of which ran a narrow channel of rather deep water, draining a vast expanse of morass above. It was up this channel that the sea-cows travelled to the feeding ground where they loved to collect at that season of the year.

There with the assistance of some of the riverside natives we made our preparations under the direction of Captain Robertson. The rest of these men, to the number of several hundreds, had made a wide detour to the head of the swamps, miles away, whence they were to advance at a certain signal. These preparations were simple. A quantity of thorn trees were cut down and by means of heavy stones fastened to their trunks, anchored in the narrow channel of deep water. To their tops, which floated on the placid surface, were tied a variety of rags which we had brought with us, such as old red flannel shirts, gay-coloured but worn-out blankets, and I know not what besides. Some of these fragments also were attached to the anchored ropes under water.

Also we selected places for the guns upon the steep banks that I have mentioned, between which this channel ran. Foreseeing what would happen, I chose one for myself behind a particularly stout rock and what is more, built a stone wall to the height of several feet on the landward side of it, as I guessed that the natives posted near to me would prove wild in their shooting.

These labours occupied the rest of that day, and at night we retired to higher ground to sleep. Before dawn on the following morning we returned and took up our stations, some on one side of the channel and some on the other which we had to reach in a canoe brought for the purpose by the river natives.

Then, before the sun rose, Captain Robertson fired a huge pile of dried reeds and bushes, which was to give the signal to the river natives far away to begin their beat. This done, we sat down and waited, after making sure that every gun had plenty of ammunition ready.

As the dawn broke, by climbing a tree near my *schanze* or shelter, I saw a good many miles away to the south a wide circle of little fires, and guessed that the natives were beginning to burn the dry reeds of the swamp. Presently these fires drew together into a thin wall of flame. Then I knew that it was time to return to the *schanze* and prepare. It was full daylight, however, before anything happened.

Watching the still channel of water, I saw ripples on it and bubbles of air rising. Suddenly there appeared the head of a great bull-hippopotamus which, having caught sight of our rag barricade, either above or below water, had risen to the surface to see what it might be. I put a bullet from an eight-bore rifle through its brain, whereon it sank, as I guessed, stone dead to the bottom of the channel, thus helping to increase the barricade by the bulk of its great body. Also it had another effect. I have observed that sea-cows cannot bear the smell and taint of blood, which frightens them horribly, so that they will expose themselves to almost any risk, rather than get it into their nostrils.

Now, in this still water where there was no perceptible current, the blood from the dead bull soon spread all about so that when the herd, following their leader, began to arrive they were much alarmed. Indeed, the first of them on winding or tasting it, turned and tried to get back up the channel where, however, they met others following, and there ensued a tremendous confusion. They rose to the surface, blowing, snorting, bellowing and scrambling over each other in the water, while continually more and more arrived behind them, till there was a perfect pandemonium in that narrow place.

All our guns opened fire wildly upon the mass; it was like a battle and through the smoke I caught sight of the riverside natives who were acting as beaters, advancing far away, fantastically dressed, screaming with excitement and waving spears, or sometimes torches of flaming reeds. Most of these were scrambling along the banks, but some of the bolder spirits advanced over the lagoon in canoes, driving the hippopotami towards the mouth of the channel by which alone they could escape into the great swamps below and so on to the river. In all my hunting experience I do not think I ever saw a more remarkable scene. Still, in a way, to me it was unpleasant, for I flatter myself that I am a sportsman and a battle of this sort is not sport as I understand the term.

At length it came to this; the channel for quite a long way was literally full of hippopotami—I should think there must have been a hundred of them or more of all sorts and sizes, from great bulls down to little calves. Some of these were killed, not many, for the shooting of our gallant company was execrable and almost at hazard. Also for every sea-cow that died, of which number I think that Captain Robertson and myself accounted for most—many were only wounded.

Still, the unhappy beasts, crazed with noise and fire and blood, did not seem to dare to face our frail barricade, probably for the reason that I have given. For a while they remained massed together in the water, or under it, making a most horrible noise. Then of a sudden they seemed to take a resolution. A few of them broke back towards the burning reeds, the screaming beaters and the advancing canoes. One of these, indeed, a wounded bull, charged a canoe, crushed it in its huge jaws and killed the rower, how exactly I do not know, for his body was never found. The majority of them, however, took another counsel, for emerging from the water on either side, they began to scramble towards us along the steep banks, or even to climb up them with surprising agility. It was at this point in the proceedings that I congratulated myself earnestly upon the solid character of the water-worn rock which I had selected as a shelter.

Behind this rock together with my gun-bearer and Umslopogaas, who, as he did not shoot, had elected to be my companion, I crouched and banged away at the unwieldy creatures as they advanced. But fire fast as I might with two rifles, I could not stop the half of them—they were drawing unpleasantly near. I glanced at Umslopogaas and even then was amused to see that probably for the first time in his life that redoubtable warrior was in a genuine fright.

"This is madness, Macumazahn," he shouted above the din. "Are we to stop here and be stamped flat by a horde of water-pigs?"

"It seems so," I answered, "unless you prefer to be stamped flat outside—or eaten," I added, pointing to a great crocodile that had also emerged from the channel and was coming along towards us with open jaws.

"By the Axe!" shouted Umslopogaas again, "I—a warrior—will not die thus, trodden on like a slug by an ox."

Now I have mentioned a tree which I climbed. In his extremity Umslopogaas rushed for that tree and went up it like a lamplighter, just as the crocodile wriggled past its trunk, snapping at his retreating legs.

After this I took no more note of him, partly because of the advancing sea-cows, and more for the reason that one of the village natives posted above me, firing wildly, put a large round bullet through the sleeve of my coat. Indeed, had it not been for the wall which I built that protected us, I am certain that both my bearer and I would have been killed, for afterwards I found it splashed over with lead from bullets which had struck the stones.

Well, thanks to the strength of my rock and to the wall, or as Hans said afterwards, to Zikali's Great Medicine, we escaped unhurt. The rush went by me; indeed, I killed one sea-cow so close that the powder from the rifle actually burned its hide. But it did go by, leaving us untouched. All, however, were not so fortunate, since of the village natives two were trampled to death, while a third had his leg broken.

Also, and this was really amusing—a bewildered bull charging at full speed, crashed into the trunk of Umslopogaas' tree, and as it was not very thick, snapped it in two. Down came the top in which the dignified chief was ensconced like a bird in a nest, though at that moment there was precious little dignity about him. However, except for scratches he was not hurt, as the hippopotamus had other business in urgent need of attention and did not stop to settle with him.

"Such are the things which happen to a man who mixes himself up with matters of which he knows nothing," said Umslopogaas sententiously to me afterwards. But all the same he could never bear any allusion to this tree-climbing episode in his martial career, which, as it happened, had taken place in full view of his retainers, among whom it remained the greatest of jokes. Indeed, he wanted to kill a man, the wag of the party, who gave him a slang name which, being translated, means "*He-who-is-so-brave-that-he-dares-to-ride-a-water-horse-up-a-tree.*"

It was all over at last, for which I thanked Providence devoutly. A good many of the sea-cows were dead, I think twenty-one was out exact bag, but the majority of them had escaped in one way or another, many as I fear, wounded. I imagine that at the last the bulk of the herd overcame its fears and swimming through our screen, passed away down the channel. At any rate they were gone, and having ascertained that there was nothing to be done for the man who had been trampled on my side of the channel, I crossed it in the canoe with the object of returning quietly to our camp to rest.

But as yet there was to be no quiet for me, for there I found Captain Robertson, who I think had been refreshing himself out of a bottle and was in a great state of excitement about a native who had been killed near him who was a favourite of his, and another whose leg was broken. He declared vehemently that the hippopotamus which had done this had been wounded and rushed into some bushes a few hundred yards away, and that he meant to take vengeance upon it. Indeed, he was just setting off to do so.

Seeing his agitated state I thought it wisest to follow him. What happened need not be set out in detail. It is sufficient to say that he found that hippopotamus and blazed both barrels at it in the bushes, hitting it, but not seriously. Out lumbered the creature with its mouth open, wishing to escape. Robertson turned to fly as he was in its path, but from one cause or another, tripped and fell down. Certainly he would have been crushed beneath its huge feet had I not stepped in front of him and sent two solid eight-bore bullets down that yawning throat, killing it dead within three feet of where Robertson was trying to rise, and I may add, of myself.

This narrow escape sobered him, and I am bound to say that his gratitude was profuse.

"You are a brave man," he said, "and had it not been for you by now I should be wherever bad people go. I'll not forget it, Mr. Quatermain, and if ever you want anything that John Robertson can give, why, it's yours."

"Very well," I answered, being seized by an inspiration, "I do want something that you can give easily enough."

"Give it a name and it's yours, half my place, if you like."

"I want," I went on as I slipped new cartridges into the rifle, "I want you to promise to give up drink for your daughter's sake. That's what nearly did for you just now, you know."

"Man, you ask a hard thing," he said slowly. "But by God I'll try for her sake and for yours too."

Then I went to help to set the leg of the injured man, which was all the rest I got that morning.

CHAPTER 7

# The Oath

We spent three more days at that place. First it was necessary to allow time to elapse before the gases which generated in their great bodies caused those of the sea-cows which had been killed in the water, to float. Then they must be skinned and their thick hides cut into strips and pieces to be traded for *sjamboks* or to make small native shields for which some of the East Coast tribes will pay heavily.

All this took a long while, during which I amused, or disgusted myself in watching those river natives devouring the flesh of the beasts. The lean, what there was of it, they dried and smoked into a kind of *biltong*, but a great deal of the fat they ate at once. I had the curiosity to weigh a lump which was given to one thin, hungry-looking fellow. It scaled quite twenty pounds. Within four hours he had eaten it to the last ounce and lay there, a distended and torpid log. What would not we white people give for such a digestion!

At last all was over and we started homewards, the man with a broken leg being carried in a kind of litter. On the edge of the bush-*veld* we found the wagon quite safe, also one of Captain Robertson's that had followed us from Strathmuir in order to carry the expected load of hippopotamus' hides and ivory. I asked my *voorlooper* if anything had happened during our absence. He answered nothing, but on the previous evening after dark, he had seen a glow in the direction of Strathmuir which lay on somewhat lower ground about twenty miles away, as though numerous fires had been lighted there. It struck him so much, he added, that he climbed a tree to observe it better. He did not think, however, that any building had been burned there, as the glow was not strong enough for that.

I suggested that it was caused by some grass fire or reed-burning, to which he replied indifferently that he did not think so as the line of the glow was not sufficiently continuous.

There the matter ended, though I confess that the story made me anxious, for what exact reason I could not say. Umslopogaas also, who had listened to it, for our talk was in Zulu, looked grave, but made no remark. But as since his tree-climbing experience he had been singularly silent, of this I thought little.

We had trekked at a time which we calculated would bring us to Strathmuir about an hour before sundown, allowing for a short halt half way. As my oxen were got in more quickly than those of the other wagon after this outspan, I was the first away, followed at a little distance by Umslopogaas, who preferred to walk with his Zulus. The truth was that I could not get that story about the glow of fires out of my mind and was anxious to push on, which had caused me to hurry up the *inspanning*.

Perhaps we had covered a couple of miles of the ten or twelve which still lay between us and Strathmuir, when far off on the crest of one of the waves of the *veld* which much resembled those of the swelling sea frozen while in motion, I saw a small figure approaching us at a rapid trot. Somehow that figure suggested Hans to my mind, so much so that I fetched my glasses to examine it more closely. A short scrutiny through them convinced me that Hans it was, Hans and no other, advancing at a great pace.

Filled with uneasiness, I ordered the driver to flog up the oxen, with the result that in a little over five minutes we met. Halting the wagon, I leapt from the wagon-box and calling to Umslopogaas who had kept up with us at a slow, swinging trot, went to Hans, who, when he saw me, stood still at a little distance, swinging his apology for a hat in his hand, as was his fashion when ashamed or perplexed.

"What is the matter, Hans?" I asked when we were within speaking distance.

"Oh! Baas, everything," he answered, and I noticed that he kept his eyes fixed upon the ground and that his lips twitched.

"Speak, you fool, and in Zulu," I said, for by now Umslopogaas had joined me.

"Baas," he answered in that tongue, "a terrible thing has come about at the farm of Red-Beard yonder. Yesterday afternoon at the time when people are in the habit of sleeping there till the sun grows less hot, a body of great men with fierce faces who carried big spears—perhaps there were fifty of them, Baas—crept up to the place through the long grass and growing crops, and attacked it."

"Did you see them come?" I asked.

"No, Baas. I was watching at a little distance as you bade me do and the sun being hot, I shut my eyes to keep out the glare of it, so that I did not see them until they had passed me and heard the noise."

"You mean that you were asleep or drunk, Hans, but go on."

"Baas, I do not know," he answered shamefacedly, "but after that I climbed a tall tree with a kind of bush at the top of it" (I ascertained afterwards that this was a sort of leafy-crowned palm), "and from it I saw everything without being seen."

"What did you see, Hans?" I asked him.

"I saw the big men run up and make a kind of circle round the village. Then they shouted, and the people in the village came out to see what was the matter. Thomaso and some of the men caught sight of them first and ran away fast into the hillside at the back where the trees grow, before the circle was complete. Then the women and the children came out and the big men killed them with their spears—all, all!"

"Good God!" I exclaimed. "And what happened at the house and to the lady?"

"Baas, some of the men had surrounded that also and when she heard the noise the lady Sad-Eyes came out on to the *stoep* and with her came the two Zulus of the Axe who had been left sick but were now quite recovered. A number of the big men ran as though to take her, but the two Zulus made a great fight in front of the little steps to the *stoep*, having their backs protected by the *stoep*, and killed six of them before they themselves were killed. Also Sad-Eyes shot one with a pistol she carried, and wounded another so that the spear fell out of his hand.

"Then the rest fell on her and tied her up, setting her in a chair on the *stoep* where two remained to watch her. They did her no hurt, Baas; indeed, they seemed to treat her as gently as they could. Also they went into the house and there they caught that tall fat yellow girl who always smiles and is called Janee, she who waits upon the Lady Sad-Eyes, and brought her out to her. I think they told her, Baas, that she must look after her mistress and that if she tried to run away she would be killed, for afterwards I saw Janee bring her food and other things."

"And then, Hans?"

"Then, Baas, most of the great men rested a while, though some of them went through the store gathering such things as they liked, blankets, knives and iron cooking-pots, but they set fire to nothing, nor did they try to catch the cattle. Also they took dry wood from the pile and lit big fires, eight or nine of them, and when the sun set they began to feast."

"What did they feast on, Hans, if they took no cattle?" I asked with a shiver, for I was afraid of I knew not what.

"Baas," answered Hans, turning his head away and looking at the ground, "they feasted on the children whom they had killed, also on some of the young women. These tall soldiers are men-eaters, Baas."

At this horrible intelligence I turned faint and felt as though I was going to fall, but recovering myself, signed to him to go on with his story.

"They feasted quite nicely, Baas," he continued, "making no noise. Then some of them slept while others watched, and that went on all night. As soon as it was dark, but before the moon rose, I slid down the tree and crept round to the back of the house without being seen or heard, as I can, Baas. I got into the house by the back door and crawled to the window of the sitting-room. It was open and peeping through I saw Sad-Eyes still tied to the seat on the *stoep* not more than a pace away, while the girl Janee crouched on the floor at her feet—I think she was asleep or fainting.

"I made a little noise, like a night-adder hissing, and kept on making it, till at last Sad-Eyes turned her head. Then I spoke in a very low whisper, for fear lest I should wake the two guards who were dozing on either side of her wrapped in their blankets, saying, 'It is I, Hans, come to help you.' 'You cannot,' she answered, also speaking very low. 'Get to your master and tell him and my father to follow. These men are called Amahagger and live far away across the river. They are going to take me to their home, as I understand, to rule them, because they want a white woman to be a queen over them who have always been ruled by a certain white queen, against whom they have rebelled. I do not think they mean to do me any harm, unless perhaps they want to marry me to their chief, but of this I am not sure from their talk which I understand badly. Now go, before they catch you.'

"'I think you might get away,' I whispered back. 'I will cut your bonds. When you are free, slip through the window and I will guide you.'

"'Very well, try it,' she said.

"So I drew my knife and stretched out my arm. But then, Baas, I showed myself a fool—if the Great Medicine had still been there I might have known better. I forgot the starlight which shone upon the blade of the knife. That girl Janee came out of her sleep or swoon, lifted her head and saw the knife. She screamed once, then at a word from her mistress was silent. But it was enough, for it woke up the guards who glared about them and threatened Janee with their great spears, also they went to sleep no more, but began to talk together, though what they said I could not hear, for I was hiding on the floor of the room. After this, knowing that I could do no good and might do harm and get myself killed, I crept out of the house as I had crept in, and crawled back to my tree."

"Why did you not come to me?" I asked.

"Because I still hoped I might be able to help Sad-Eyes, Baas. Also I wanted to see what happened, and I knew that I could not bring you here in time to be any good. Yet it is true I thought of coming though I did not know the road."

"Perhaps you were right."

"At the first dawn," continued Hans, "the great men who are called Amahagger rose and ate what was left over from the night before. Then they gathered themselves together and went to the house. Here they found a large chair, that seated with *rimpis* in which the Baas Red-Beard sits, and lashed two poles to the chair. Beneath the chair they tied the garments and other things of the Lady Sad-Eyes which they made Janee gather as Sad-Eyes directed her. This done, very gently they sat Sad-Eyes herself in the chair, bowing while they made her fast. After this eight of them set the poles upon their shoulders, and they all went away at a trot, heading for the bush-*veld*, driving with them a herd of goats which they had stolen from the farm, and making Janee run by the chair. I saw everything, Baas, for they passed just beneath my tree. Then I came to seek you, following the outward spoor of the wagons which I could not have done well at night. That is all, Baas."

"Hans," I said, "you have been drinking and because of it the lady Sad-Eyes is taken a prisoner by cannibals; for had you been awake and watching, you might have seen them coming and saved her and the rest. Still, afterwards you did well, and for the rest you must answer to Heaven."

"I must tell your reverend father, the Predikant, Baas, that the white master, Red-Beard, gave me the liquor and it is rude not to do as a great white master does, and drink it up. I am sure he will understand, Baas," said Hans abjectly.

I thought to myself that it was true and that the spear which Robertson cast had fallen upon his own head, as the Zulus say, but I made no answer, lacking time for argument.

"Did you say," asked Umslopogaas, speaking for the first time, "that my servants killed only six of these men-eaters?"

Hans nodded and answered, "Yes, six. I counted the bodies."

"It was ill done, they should have killed six each," said Umslopogaas moodily. "Well, they have left the more for us to finish," and he fingered the great axe.

Just then Captain Robertson arrived in his wagon, calling out anxiously to know what was the matter, for some premonition of evil seemed to have struck him. My heart sank at the sight of him, for how was I to tell such a story to the father of the murdered children and of the abducted girl?

In the end I felt that I could not. Yes, I turned coward and saying that I must fetch something out of the wagon, bolted into it, bidding Hans go forward and repeat his tale. He obeyed unwillingly enough and looking out between the curtains of the wagon tent I saw all that happened, though I could not hear the words that passed.

Robertson had halted the oxen and jumping from the wagon-box strode forward and met Hans, who began to speak with him, twitching his hat in his hands. Gradually as the tale progressed, I saw the Captain's face freeze into a mask of horror. Then he began to argue and deny, then to weep—oh! it was a terrible sight to see that great man weeping over those whom he had lost, and in such a fashion.

After this a kind of blind rage seized him and I thought he was going to kill Hans, who was of the same opinion, for he ran away. Next he staggered about, shaking his fists, cursing and shouting, till presently he fell of a heap and lay face downwards, beating his head against the ground and groaning.

Now I went to him and sat up.

"That's a pretty story, Quatermain, which this little yellow monkey has been gibbering at me. Man, do you understand what he says? He says that all those half-blood children of mine are dead, murdered by savages from over the Zambezi, yes, and eaten, too, with their mothers. Do you take the point? Eaten like lambs. Those fires your man saw last night were the fires on which they were cooked, my little *so-and-so* and *so-and-so*," and he mentioned half a dozen different names. "Yes, cooked, Quatermain. And that isn't all of it, they have taken Inez too. They didn't eat her, but they have dragged her off a captive for God knows what reason. I couldn't understand. The whole ship's crew is gone, except the captain absent on leave and the first officer, Thomaso, who deserted with some Lascar stokers, and left the women and children to their fate. My God, I'm going mad. I'm going mad! If you have any mercy in you, give me something to drink."

"All right," I said, "I will. Sit here and wait a minute."

Then I went to the wagon and poured out a stiff tot of spirits into which I put an amazing doze of bromide from a little medicine chest I always carry with me, and thirty drops of *chlorodyne* on the top of it. All this compound I mixed up with a little water and took it to him in a tin cup so that he could not see the colour.

He drank it at a gulp and throwing the pannikin aside, sat down on the *veld*, groaning while the company watched him at a respectful distance, for Hans had joined the others and his tale had spread like fire in drought-parched grass.

In a few minutes the drugs began to take effect upon Robertson's tortured nerves, for he rose and said quietly, "What now?"

"Vengeance, or rather justice," I answered.

"Yes," he exclaimed, "vengeance. I swear that I will be avenged, or die—or both."

Again I saw my opportunity and said, "You must swear more than that, Robertson. Only sober men can accomplish great things, for drink destroys the judgment. If you wish to be avenged for the dead and to rescue the living, you must be sober, or I for one will not help you."

"Will you help me if I do, to the end, good or ill, Quatermain?" he added.

I nodded.

"That's as much as another's oath," he muttered. "Still, I will put my thought in words. I swear by God, by my mother—like these natives—and by my daughter born in honest marriage, that I will never touch another drop of strong drink, until I have avenged those poor women and their little children, and rescued Inez from their murderers. If I do you may put a bullet through me."

"That's all right," I said in an offhand fashion, though inwardly I glowed with pride at the success of my great idea, for at the time I thought it great, and went on, "Now let us get to business. The first thing to do is to trek to Strathmuir and make preparations; the next to start upon the trail. Come to sit on the wagon with me and tell me what guns and ammunition you have got, for according to Hans those savages don't seem to have touched anything, except a few blankets and a herd of goats."

He did as I asked, telling me all he could remember. Then he said, "It is a strange thing, but now I recall that about two years ago a great savage with a high nose, who talked a sort of Arabic which, like Inez, I understand, having lived on the coast, turned up one day and said he wanted to trade. I asked him what in, and he answered that he would like to buy some children. I told him that I was not a slave-dealer. Then he looked at Inez, who was moving about, and said that he would like to buy her to be a wife for his Chief, and offered some fabulous sum in ivory and in gold, which he said should be paid before she was taken away. I snatched his big spear from his hand, broke it over his head and gave him the best hiding with its shaft that he had ever heard of. Then I kicked him off the place. He limped away but when he was out of reach, turned and called out that one day he would come again with others and take her, meaning Inez, without leaving the price in ivory and gold. I ran for my gun, but when I got back he had gone and I never thought of the matter again from that day to this."

"Well, he kept his promise," I said, but Robertson made no answer, for by this time that thundering dose of bromide and laudanum had taken effect on him and he had fallen asleep, of which I was glad, for I thought that this sleep would save his sanity, as I believe it did for a while.

We reached Strathmuir towards sunset, too late to think of attempting the pursuit that day. Indeed, during our trek, I had thought the matter out carefully and come to the conclusion that to try to do so would be useless. We must rest and make preparations; also there was no hope of our overtaking these brutes who already had a clear twelve hours' start, by a sudden spurt. They must be run down patiently by following their spoor, if indeed they could be run down at all before they vanished into the vast recesses of unknown Africa. The most we could do this night was to get ready.

Captain Robertson was still sleeping when we passed the village and of this I was heartily glad, since the remains of a cannibal feast are not pleasant to behold, especially when they are——! Indeed, of these I determined to be rid at once, so slipping off the wagon with Hans and some of the farm boys, for none of the Zulus would defile themselves by touching such human remnants—I made up two of the smouldering fires, the light of which the *voorlooper* had seen upon the sky, and on to them cast, or caused to be cast, those poor fragments. Also I told the farm natives to dig a big grave and in it to place the other bodies and generally to remove the traces of murder.

Then I went on to the house, and not too soon. Seeing the wagons arrive and having made sure that the Amahagger were gone, Thomaso and the other cowards emerged from their hiding-places and returned. Unfortunately for the former the first person he met was Umslopogaas, who began to revile the fat half-breed in no measured terms, calling him dog, coward, and other opprobrious names, such as deserter of women and children, and so forth—all of which someone translated.

Thomaso, an insolent person, tried to swagger the matter out, saying that he had gone to get assistance. Infuriated at this lie, Umslopogaas leapt upon him with a roar and though he was a strong man, dealt with him as a lion does with a buck. Lifting him from his feet, he hurled him to the ground, then as he strove to rise and run, caught him again and as it seemed to me, was about to break his back across his knee. Just at this juncture I arrived.

"Let the man go," I shouted to him. "Is there not enough death here already?"

"Yes," answered Umslopogaas, "I think there is. Best that this jackal should live to eat his own shame," and he cast Thomaso to the ground, where he lay groaning.

Robertson, who was still asleep in the wagon, woke up at the noise, and descended from it, looking dazed. I got him to the house and in doing so made my way past, or rather between the bodies of the two Zulus and of the six men whom they had killed, also of him whom Inez had shot. Those Zulus had made a splendid fight for they were covered with wounds, all of them in front, as I found upon examination.

Having made Robertson lie down upon his bed, I took a good look at the slain Amahagger. They were magnificent men, all of them; tall, spare and shapely with very clear-cut features and rather frizzled hair. From these characteristics, as well as the lightness of their colour, I concluded that they were of a Semitic or Arab type, and that the admixture of their blood with that of the Bantus was but slight, if indeed there were any at all. Their spears, of which one had been cut through by a blow of a Zulu's axe, were long and broad, not unlike to those used by the Masai, but of finer workmanship.

By this time the sun was setting and thoroughly tired by all that I had gone through, I went into the house to get something to eat, having told Hans to find food and prepare a meal. As I sat down Robertson joined me and I made him also eat. His first impulse was to go to the cupboard and fetch the spirit bottle; indeed, he rose to do so.

"Hans is making coffee," I said warningly.

"Thank you," he answered, "I forgot. Force of habit, you know."

Here I may state that never from that moment did I see him touch another drop of liquor, not even when I drank my modest tot in front of him. His triumph over temptation was splendid and complete, especially as the absence of his accustomed potations made him ill for some time and of course depressed his spirits, with painful results that were apparent in due course.

In fact, the man became totally changed. He grew gloomy but resourceful, also full of patience. Only one idea obsessed him—to rescue his daughter and avenge the murder of his people; indeed, except his sins, he thought of and found interest in nothing else. Moreover, his iron constitution cast off all the effects of his past debauchery and he grew so strong that although I was pretty tough in those days, he could out-tire me.

To return; I engaged him in conversation and with his help made a list of what we should require on our vendetta journey, all of which served to occupy his mind. Then I sent him to bed, saying that I would call him before dawn, having first put a little more bromide into his third cup of coffee. After this I turned in and notwithstanding the sight of those remains of the cannibal feast and the knowledge of the dead men who lay outside my window, I slept like a top.

Indeed, it was the Captain who awakened me, not I the Captain, saying that daylight was on the break and we had better be stirring. So we went down to the Store, where I was thankful to find that everything had been tidied up in accordance with my directions.

On our way Robertson asked me what had become of the remains, whereon I pointed to the smouldering ashes of one of the great fires. He went to it and kneeling down, said a prayer in broad Scotch, doubtless one that he had learned at his mother's knee. Then he took some of the ashes from the edge of the pyre—for such it was—and threw them into the glowing embers where, as he knew, lay all that was left of those who had sprung from him. Also he tossed others of them into the air, though what he meant by this I did not understand and never asked. Probably it was some rite indicative of expiation or of revenge, or both, which he had learned from the savages among whom he had lived so long.

After this we went into the Store and with the help of some of the natives, or half-breeds, who had accompanied us on the sea-cow expedition, selected all the goods we wanted, which we sent to the house.

As we returned thither I saw Umslopogaas and his men engaged, with the usual Zulu ceremonies, in burying their two companions in a hole they had made in the hillside. I noted, however, that they did not inter their war-axes or their throwing-spears with them as usual, probably because they thought that these might be needed. In place of them they put with the dead little models roughly shaped of bits of wood, which models they "killed" by first breaking them across.

I lingered to watch the funeral and heard Goroko, the witch-doctor, make a little speech.

"O Father and Chief of the Axe," he said, addressing Umslopogaas, who stood silent leaning on his weapon and watching all, a portentous figure in the morning mist, "O Father, O Son of the Heavens" (this was an allusion to the royal blood of Umslopogaas of which the secret was well known, although it would never have been spoken aloud in Zululand), "O Slaughterer (Bulalio), O Woodpecker who picks at the hearts of men; O King-Slayer; O Conqueror of the Halakazi; O Victor in a hundred fights; O Gatherer of the Lily-bloom that faded in the hand; O Wolf-man, Captain of the Wolves that ravened; O Slayer of Faku; O Great One whom it pleases to seem small, because he must follow his blood to the end appointed——"

This was the opening of the speech, the "*bonga*-ing" or giving of Titles of Praise to the person addressed, of which I have quoted but a sample, for there were many more of them that I have forgotten. Then the speaker went on, "It was told to me, though of it I remember nothing, that when my Spirit was in me a while ago I prophesied that this place would flow with blood, and lo! the blood has flowed, and with it that of these our brothers," and he gave the names of the two dead Zulus, also those of their forefathers for several generations.

"It seems, Father, that they died well, as you would have wished them to die, and as doubtless they desired to die themselves, leaving a tale behind them, though it is true that they might have died better, killing more of the men-eaters, as it is certain they would have done, had they not been sick inside. They are finished; they have gone beyond to await us in the Under-world among the ghosts. Their story is told and soon to their children they will be but names whispered in honour after the sun has set. Enough of them who have showed us how to die as our fathers did before them."

Goroko paused a while, then added with a waving of his hands, "My Spirit comes to me again and I know that these our brothers shall not pass unavenged. Chief of the Axe, great glory awaits the Axe, for it shall feed full. I have spoken."

"Good words!" grunted Umslopogaas. Then he saluted the dead by raising *Inkosikaas* and came to me to consult about our journey.

## CHAPTER 8

# Pursuit

After all we did not get away much before noon, because first there was a great deal to be done. To begin with the loads had to be arranged. These consisted largely of ammunition, everything else being cut down to an irreducible minimum. To carry them we took two donkeys there were on the place, also half a dozen pack oxen, all of which animals were supposed to be "salted"—that is, to have suffered and recovered from every kind of sickness, including the bite of the deadly tsetse fly. I suspected, it is true, that they would not be proof against further attacks, still, I hoped that they would last for some time, as indeed proved to be the case.

In the event of the beasts failing us, we took also ten of the best of those Strathmuir men who had accompanied us on the sea-cow trip, to serve as bearers when it became necessary. It cannot be said that these snuff-and-butter fellows—for most, if not all of them had some dash of white blood in their veins—were exactly willing volunteers. Indeed, if a choice had been left to them, they would, I think, have declined this adventure.

But there was no choice. Their master, Robertson, ordered them to come and after a glance at the Zulus they concluded that the command was one which would be enforced and that if they stopped behind, it would not be as living men. Also some of them had lost wives or children in the slaughter, which, if they were not very brave, filled them with a desire for revenge. Lastly, they could all shoot after a fashion and had good rifles; moreover if I may say so, I think that they put confidence in my leadership. So they made the best of a bad business and got themselves ready.

Then arrangements must be made about the carrying on of the farm and store during our absence. These, together with my wagon and oxen, were put in the charge of Thomaso, since there was no one else who could be trusted at all—a very battered and crestfallen Thomaso, by the way. When he heard of it he was much relieved, since I think he feared lest he also should be expected to take part in the hunt of the Amahagger man-eaters. Also it may have occurred to him that in all probability none of us would ever come back at all, in which case by a process of natural devolution, he might find himself the owner of the business and much valuable property. However, he swore by sundry saints—for Thomaso was nominally a Catholic—that he would look after everything as though it were his own, as no doubt he hoped it might become.

"Hearken, fat pig," said Umslopogaas, Hans obligingly translating so that there might be no mistake, "if I come back, and come back I shall who travel with the Great Medicine—and find even one of the cattle of the white lord, Macumazahn, Watcher-by-Night, missing, or one article stolen from his wagon, or the fields of your master not cultivated or his goods wasted, I swear by the Axe that I will hew you into pieces with the axe; yes, if to do it I have to hunt you from where the sun rises to where it sets and down the length of the night between. Do you understand, fat pig, deserter of women and children, who to save yourself could run faster than a buck?"

Thomaso replied that he understood very clearly indeed, and that, Heaven helping him, all should be kept safe and sound. Still, I was sure that in his manly heart he was promising great gifts to the saints if they would so arrange matters that Umslopogaas and his axe were never seen at Strathmuir again, and reflecting that after all the Amahagger had their uses. However, as I did not trust him in the least, much against their will, I left my driver and *voorlooper* to guard my belongings.

At last we did get off, pursued by the fervent blessings of Thomaso and the prayers of the others that we would avenge their murdered relatives. We were a curious and motley procession. First went Hans, because at following a spoor he was, I believe, almost unequalled in Africa, and with him, Umslopogaas, and three of his Zulus to guard against surprise. These were followed by Captain Robertson, who seemed to prefer to walk alone and whom I thought it best to leave undisturbed. Then I came and after me straggled the Strathmuir boys with the pack animals, the cavalcade being closed by the remaining Zulus under the command of Goroko. These walked last in case any of the mixed-bloods should attempt to desert, as we thought it quite probable that they would.

Less than an hour's tramp brought us to the bush-*veld* where I feared that our troubles might begin, since if the Amahagger were cunning, they would take advantage of it to confuse or hide their spoor. As it chanced, however, they had done nothing of the sort and a child could have followed their march. Just before nightfall we came to their first halting-place where they had made a fire and eaten one of the herd of farm goats which they had driven away with them, although they left the cattle, I suppose, because goats are docile and travel well.

Hans showed us everything that had happened; where the chair in which Inez was carried was set down, where she and Janee had been allowed to walk that she might stretch her stiff limbs, the dregs of some coffee that evidently Janee had made in a saucepan, and so forth.

He even told us the exact number of the Amahagger, which he said totalled forty-one, including the man whom Inez had wounded. His spoor he distinguished from that of the others both by an occasional drop of blood and because he walked lightly on his right foot, doubt-less for the reason that he wished to avoid jarring his wound, which was on that side.

At this spot we were obliged to stay till daybreak, since it was impossible to follow the spoor by night, a circumstance that gave the cannibals a great advantage over us.

The next two days were repetitions of the first, but on the fourth we passed out of the bush-*veld* into the swamp country that bordered the great river. Here our task was still easy since the Amahagger had followed one of the paths made by the river-dwellers who had their habitations on mounds, though whether these were natural or artifi-cial I am not sure, and sometimes on floating islands.

On our second day in the reeds we came upon a sad sight. To our left stood one of these mound villages, if a village it could be called, since it consisted only of four or five huts inhabited perhaps by twenty people. We went up to it to obtain information and stumbled across the body of an old man lying in the pathway. A few yards further on we found the ashes of a big fire and by it such remains as we had seen at Strathmuir. Here there had been another cannibal feast. The miser-able huts were empty, but as at Strathmuir, had not been burnt.

We were going away when the acute ears of Hans caught the sound of groans. We searched about and in a clump of reeds near the foot of the mound, found an old woman with a great spear wound just above her skinny thigh piercing deep into the vitals, but of a nature which is not immediately mortal. One of Robertson's people who understood the language of these swamp-dwellers well, spoke to her. She told him that she wanted water. It was brought and she drank copiously. Then in answer to his questions she began to talk.

She said that the Amahagger had attacked the village and killed all who could not escape. They had eaten a young woman and three children. She had been wounded by a spear and fled away into the place where we found her, where none of them took the trouble to follow her as she "was not worth eating."

By my direction the man asked her whether she knew anything of these Amahagger. She replied that her grandfathers had, though she had heard nothing of them since she was a child, which must have been seventy years before. They were a fierce people who lived far up north across the Great River, the remnants of a race that had once "ruled the world."

Her grandfathers used to say that they were not always cannibals, but had become so long before because of a lack of food and now had acquired the taste. It was for this purpose that they still raided to get other people to eat, since their ruler would not allow them to eat one another. The flesh of cattle they did not care for, although they had plenty of them, but sometimes they ate goats and pigs because they said they tasted like man. According to her grandfathers they were a very evil people and full of magic.

All of this the old woman told us quite briskly after she had drunk the water, I think because her wound had mortified and she felt no pain. Her information, however, as is common with the aged, dealt entirely with the far past; of the history of the Amahagger since the days of her forebears she knew nothing, nor had she seen anything of Inez. All she could tell us was that some of them had attacked her village at dawn and that when she ran out of the hut she was speared.

While Robertson and I were wondering what we should do with the poor old creature whom it seemed cruel to leave here to perish, she cleared up the question by suddenly expiring before our eyes. Uttering the name of someone with whom, doubtless, she had been familiar in her youth, three or four times over, she just sank down and seemed to go to sleep and on examination we found that she was dead. So we left her and went on.

Next day we came to the edge of the Great River, here a sheet of placid running water about a mile across, for at this time of the year it was low. Perceiving quite a big village on our left, we went to it and made enquiries, to find that it had not been attacked by the cannibals, probably because it was too powerful, but that three nights before some of their canoes had been stolen, in which no doubt these had crossed the river.

As the people of this village had traded with Robertson at Strathmuir, we had no difficulty in obtaining other canoes from them in which to cross the Zambezi in return for one of our oxen that I could see was already sickening from tsetse bite. These canoes were large enough to take the donkeys that were patient creatures and stood still, but the cattle we could not get into them for fear of an upset. So we killed the two driven beasts that were left to us and took them with us as dead meat for food, while the three remaining pack oxen we tried to swim across, dragging them after the canoes with hide *reims* round their horns. As a result two were drowned, but one, a bold-hearted and enterprising animal, gained the other bank.

Here again we struck a sea of reeds in which, after casting about, Hans once more found the spoor of the Amahagger. That it was theirs beyond doubt was proved by the circumstance that on a thorny kind of weed we found a fragment of a cotton dress which, because of the pattern stamped on it, we all recognised as one that Inez had been wearing. At first I thought that this had been torn off by the thorns, but on examination we became certain that it had been placed there purposely, probably by Janee, to give us a clue. This conclusion was confirmed when at subsequent periods of the hunt we found other fragments of the same garment.

Now it would be useless for me to set out the details of this pro-longed and arduous chase which in all endured for something over three weeks. Again and again we lost the trail and were only able to recover it by long and elaborate search, which occupied much time. Then, after we escaped from the reeds and swamps, we found our-selves upon stony uplands where the spoor was almost impossible to follow, indeed, we only rediscovered it by stumbling across the dead body of that cannibal whom Inez had wounded. Evidently he had perished from his hurt, which I could see had mortified. From the state of his remains we gathered that the raiders must be about two days' march ahead of us.

Striking their spoor again on softer ground where the impress of their feet remained—at any rate to the cunning sight of Hans—we followed them down across great valleys wherein trees grew sparsely, which valleys were separated from each other by ridges of high and barren land. On these belts of rocky soil our difficulties were great, but here twice we were put on the right track by more fragments torn from the dress of Inez.

At length we lost the spoor altogether; not a sign of it was to be found. We had no idea which way to go. All about us appeared these valleys covered with scattered bush running this way and that, so that we could not tell which of them to follow or to cross. The thing seemed hopeless, for how could we expect to find a little body of men in that immensity? Hans shook his head and even the fierce and steadfast Robertson was discouraged.

"I fear my poor lassie is gone," he said, and relapsed into brooding as had become his wont.

"Never say die! It's dogged as does it!" I replied cheerfully in the words of Nelson, who also had learned what it meant to hunt an enemy over trackless wastes, although his were of water.

I walked to the top of the rise where we were encamped, and sat down alone to think matters over. Our condition was somewhat parlous; all our beasts were now dead, even the second donkey, which was the last of them, having perished that morning, and been eaten, for food was scanty since of late we had met with little game. The Strathmuir men, who now must carry the loads, were almost worn out and doubtless would have deserted, except for the fact that there was no place to which they could go. Even the Zulus were discouraged, and said they had come away from home across the Great River to fight, not to run about in wildernesses and starve, though Umslopogaas made no complaint, being buoyed up by the promise of his soothsayer, Goroko, that battle was ahead of him in which he would win great glory.

Hans, however, remained cheerful, for the reason, as he remarked vacuously, that the Great Medicine was with us and that therefore, however bad things seemed to be, all in fact was well; an argument that carried no conviction to my soul.

It was on a certain evening towards sunset that I went away thus alone. I looked about me, east and west and north. Everywhere appeared the same bush-clad valleys and barren rises, miles upon miles of them. I bethought me of the map that old Zikali had drawn in the ashes, and remembered that it showed these valleys and rises and that beyond them there should be a great swamp, and beyond the swamp a mountain. So it seemed that we were on the right road to the home of his white Queen, if such a person existed, or at any rate we were passing over country similar to that which he had pictured or imagined.

But at this time I was not troubling my head about white queens. I was thinking of poor Inez. That she was alive a few days before we knew from the fragments of her dress. But where was she now? The spoor was utterly lost on that stony ground, or if any traces of it remained a heavy deluge of rain had washed them away. Even Hans had confessed himself beaten.

I stared about me helplessly, and as I did so a flying ray of light from the setting sun reflected downwards from a storm-cloud, fell upon a white patch on the crest of one of the distant land-waves. It struck me that probably limestone outcropped at this spot, as indeed proved to be the case; also that such a patch of white would be a convenient guide for any who were travelling across that sea of bush. Further, some instinct within seemed to impel me to steer for it, although I had all but made up my mind to go in a totally different direction many more points to the east. It was almost as though a voice were calling to me to take this path and no other. Doubtless this was an effect produced by weariness and mental overstrain. Still, there it was, very real and tangible, one that I did not attempt to combat.

So next morning at the dawn I headed north by west, laying my course for that white patch and for the first time breaking the straight line of our advance. Captain Robertson, whose temper had not been bettered by prolonged and frightful anxiety, or I may add, by his unaccustomed abstinence, asked me rather roughly why I was altering the course.

"Look here, Captain," I answered, "if we were at sea and you did something of the sort, I should not put such a question to you, and if by any chance I did, I should not expect you to answer. Well, by your own wish I am in command here and I think that the same argument holds."

"Yes," he replied. "I suppose you have studied your chart, if there is any of this God-forsaken country, and at any rate discipline is discipline. So steam ahead and don't mind me."

The others accepted my decision without comment; most of them were so miserable that they did not care which way we went, also they were good enough to repose confidence in my judgment.

"Doubtless the Baas has reasons," said Hans dubiously, "although the spoor, when last we saw it, headed towards the rising sun and as the country is all the same, I do not see why those man-eaters should have returned."

"Yes," I said, "I have reasons," although in fact I had none at all.

Hans surveyed me with a watery eye as though waiting for me to explain them, but I looked haughty and declined to oblige.

"The Baas has reasons," continued Hans, "for taking us on what I think to be the wrong side of that great ridge, there to hunt for the spoor of the men-eaters, and they are so deep down in his mind that he cannot dig them up for poor old Hans to look at. Well, the Baas wears the Great Medicine and perhaps it is there that the reasons sit. Those Strathmuir fellows say that they can go no further and wish to die. Umslopogaas has just gone to them with his axe to tell them that he is ready to help them to their wish. Look, he has got there, for they are coming quickly, who after all prefer to live."

Well, we started for my white patch of stones which no one else had noticed and of which I said nothing to anyone, and reached it by the following evening, to find, as I expected, that it was a lime outcrop.

By now we were in a poor way, for we had practically nothing left to eat, which did not tend to raise the spirits of the party. Also that lime outcrop proved to be an uninteresting spot overlooking a wide valley which seemed to suggest that there were other valleys of a similar sort beyond it, and nothing more.

Captain Robertson sat stern-faced and despondent at a distance muttering into his beard, as had become a habit with him. Umslopogaas leaned upon his axe and contemplated the heavens, also occasionally the Strathmuir men who cowered beneath his eye. The Zulus squatted about sharing such snuff as remained to them in economic pinches. Goroko, the witch-doctor, engaged himself in consulting his "Spirit," by means of bone-throwing, upon the humble subject of whether or no we should succeed in killing any game for food tomorrow, a point on which I gathered that his "Spirit" was quite uncertain. In short, the gloom was deep and universal and the sky looked as though it were going to rain.

Hans became sarcastic. Sneaking up to me in his most aggravating way, like a dog that means to steal something and cover up the theft with simulated affection, he pointed out one by one all the disadvantages of our present position. He indicated *per contra*, that if *his* advice had been followed, his conviction was that even if we had not found the man-eaters and rescued the lady called Sad-Eyes, our state would have been quite different. He was sure, he added, that the valley which he had suggested we should follow, was one full of game, inasmuch as he had seen their spoor at its entrance.

"Then why did you not say so?" I asked.

Hans sucked at his empty corn-cob pipe, which was his way of indicating that he would like me to give him some tobacco, much as a dog groans heavily under the table when he wants a bit to eat, and answered that it was not for him to point out things to one who knew everything, like the great Macumazahn, Watcher-by-Night, his honoured master. Still, the luck did seem to have gone a bit wrong. The privations could have been put up with (here he sucked very loudly at the empty pipe and looked at mine, which was alight), everything could have been put up with, if only there had been a chance of coming even with those men-eaters and rescuing the Lady Sad-Eyes, whose face haunted his sleep. As it was, however, he was convinced that by following the course I had mapped out we had lost their spoor finally and that probably they were now three days' march away in another direction. Still, the Baas had said that he had his reasons, and that of course was enough for him, Hans, only if the Baas would condescend to tell him, he would as a matter of curiosity like to know what the reasons were.

At that moment I confess that, much as I was attached to him, I should have liked to murder Hans, who, I felt, believing that he had me "on toast," to use a vulgar phrase, was taking advantage of my position to make a mock of me in his sly, Hottentot way.

I tried to continue to look grand, but felt that the attitude did not impress. Then I stared about me as though taking counsel with the Heavens, devoutly hoping that the Heavens would respond to my mute appeal. As a matter of fact they did.

"There is my reason, Hans," I said in my most icy voice, and I pointed to a faint line of smoke rising against the twilight sky on the further side of the intervening valley.

"You will perceive, Hans," I added, "that those Amahagger cannibals have forgotten their caution and lit a fire yonder, which they have not done for a long time. Perhaps you would like to know why this has happened. If so I will tell you. It is because for some days past I have purposely lost their spoor, which they knew we were following, and lit fires to puzzle them. Now, thinking that they have done with us, they have become incautious and shown us where they are. That is my reason, Hans."

He heard and, although of course he did not believe that I had lost the spoor on purpose, stared at me till I thought his little eyes were going to drop out of his head. But even in his admiration he contrived to convey an insult as only a native can.

"How wonderful is the Great Medicine of the Opener-of-Roads, that it should have been able thus to instruct the Baas," he said. "Without doubt the Great Medicine is right and yonder those men-eaters are encamped, who might just as well as have been anywhere else within a hundred miles."

"Drat the Great Medicine," I replied, but beneath my breath, then added aloud, "Be so good, Hans, as to go to Umslopogaas and to tell him that Macumazahn, or the Great Medicine, proposes to march at once to attack the camp of the Amahagger, and—here is some tobacco."

"Yes, Baas," answered Hans humbly, as he snatched the tobacco and wriggled away like a worm.

Then I went to talk with Robertson.

The end of it was that within an hour we were creeping across that valley towards the spot where I had seen the line of smoke rising against the twilight sky.

Somewhere about midnight we reached the neighbourhood of this place. How near or how far we were from it, we could not tell since the moon was invisible, as of course the smoke was in the dark. Now the question was, what should we do?

Obviously there would be enormous advantages in a night attack, or at least in locating the enemy, so that it might be carried out at dawn before he marched. Especially was this so, since we were scarcely in a condition even if we could come face to face with them, to fight these savages when they were prepared and in the light of day. Only we two white men, with Hans, Umslopogaas and his Zulus, could be relied upon in such a case, since the Strathmuir mixed-bloods had become entirely demoralised and were not to be trusted at a pinch. Indeed, tired and half starving as we were, none of us was at his best. Therefore a surprise seemed our only chance. But first we must find those whom we wished to surprise.

Ultimately, after a hurried consultation, it was agreed that Hans and I should go forward and see if we could locate the Amahagger. Robertson wished to come too, but I pointed out that he must remain to look after his people, who, if he left them, might take the opportunity to melt away in the darkness, especially as they knew that heavy fighting was at hand. Also if anything happened to me it was desirable that one white man should remain to lead the party. Umslopogaas, too, volunteered, but knowing his character, I declined his help. To tell the truth, I was almost certain that if we came upon the men-eaters, he would charge the whole lot of them and accomplish a fine but futile end after hacking down a number of cannibal barbarians, whose extinction or escape remained absolutely immaterial to our purpose, namely, the rescue of Inez.

So it came about that Hans and I started alone, I not at all enjoying the job. I suppose that there lurks in my nature some of that primeval terror of the dark, which must continually have haunted our remote forefathers of a hundred or a thousand generations gone and still lingers in the blood of most of us. At any rate even if I am named the Watcher-by-Night, greatly do I prefer to fight or to face peril in the sunlight, though it is true that I would rather avoid both at any time.

In fact, I wished heartily that the Amahagger were at the other side of Africa, or in heaven, and that I, completely ignorant of the person

99

called Inez Robertson, were seated smoking the pipe of peace on my own *stoep* in Durban. I think that Hans guessed my state of mind, since he suggested that he should go alone, adding with his usual unveiled rudeness, that he was quite certain that he would do much better without me, since white men always made a noise.

"Yes," I replied, determined to give him a Roland for his Oliver, "I have no doubt you would—under the first bush you came across, where you would sleep till dawn, and then return and say that you could not find the Amahagger."

Hans chuckled, quite appreciating the joke, and having thus mutually affronted each other, we started on our quest.

## CHAPTER 9

# The Swamp

Neither Hans nor I carried rifles that we knew would be in the way on our business, which was just to scout. Moreover, one is always tempted to shoot if a gun is at hand, and this I did not want to do at present. So, although I had my revolver in case of urgent necessity, my only other weapon was a Zulu axe, that formerly had belonged to one of those two men who died defending Inez on the veranda at Strathmuir, while Hans had nothing but his long knife. Thus armed, or unarmed, we crept forward towards that spot whence, as we conjectured, we had seen the line of smoke rising some hours before.

For about a quarter of a mile we went on thus without seeing or hearing anything, and a difficult job it was in that gloom among the scattered trees with no light save such as the stars gave us. Indeed, I was about to suggest that we had better abandon the enterprise until daybreak when Hans nudged me, whispering, "Look to the right between those twin thorns."

I obeyed and following the line of sight which he had indicated, perceived, at a distance of about two hundred yards a faint glow, so faint indeed that I think only Hans would have noticed it. Really it might have been nothing more than the phosphorescence rising from a heap of fungus, or even from a decaying animal.

"The fire of which we saw the smoke that has burnt to ashes," whispered Hans again. "I think that they have gone, but let us look."

So we crawled forward very cautiously to avoid making the slightest noise; so cautiously, indeed, that it must have taken us nearly half an hour to cover those two hundred yards. At length we were within about forty yards of that dying fire and, afraid to go further, came to a stand—or rather, a lie-still—behind some bushes until we knew more. Hans lifted his head and sniffed with his broad nostrils; then he whispered into my ear, but so low that I could scarcely hear him.

"Amahagger there all right, Baas, I smell them."

This of course was possible, since what wind there was blew from the direction of the fire, although I whose nose is fairly keen could smell nothing at all. So I determined to wait and watch a while, and indicated my decision to Hans, who, considering our purpose accomplished, showed signs of wishing to retreat.

Some minutes we lay thus, till of a sudden this happened. A branch of resinous wood of which the stem had been eaten through by the flames, fell upon the ashes of the fire and burnt up with a brilliant light. In it we saw that the Amahagger were sleeping in a circle round the fire wrapped in their blankets.

Also we saw another thing, namely that nearer to us, not more than a dozen yards away, indeed, was a kind of little tent, also made of fur rugs or blankets, which doubtless sheltered Inez. Indeed, this was evident from the fact that at the mouth of it, wrapped up in something, lay none other than her maid, Janee, for her face being towards us, was recognised by us both in the flare of the flaming branch. One more thing we noted, namely, that two of the cannibals, evidently a guard, were sleeping between us and the little tent. Of course they ought to have been awake, but fatigue had overcome them and there they slumbered, seated on the ground, their heads hanging forward almost upon their knees.

An idea came to me. If we could kill those men without waking the others in that gloom, it might be possible to rescue Inez at once. Rapidly I weighed the *pros* and *cons* of such an attempt. Its advantages, if successful, were that the object of our pursuit would be carried through without further trouble and that it was most doubtful whether we should ever get such a chance again. If we returned to fetch the others and attacked in force, the probability was that those Amahagger, or one of them, would hear some sound made by the advance of a number of men, and fly into the darkness; or, rather than lose Inez, they might kill her. Or if they stood and fought, she might be slain in the scrimmage. Or, as after all we had only about a dozen effectives, for the Strathmuir bearers could not be relied upon, they might defeat and kill us whom they outnumbered by two or three to one.

These were the arguments for the attempt. Those for not making it were equally obvious. To begin with it was one of extraordinary risk; the two guards or someone else behind them might wake up—for such people, like dogs, mostly sleep with one eye open, especially when they knew that they are being pursued. Or if they did not we might bungle the business so that they raised an outcry before they grew silent for ever, in which case both of us and perhaps Inez also would probably pay the penalty before we could get away.

Such was the horned dilemma upon one point or other of which we ran the risk of being impaled. For a full minute or more I considered the matter with an earnestness almost amounting to mental agony, and at last all but came to the conclusion that the danger was too enormous. It would be better, notwithstanding the many disadvantages of that plan, to go back and fetch the others.

But then it was that I made one of my many mistakes in life. Most of us do more foolish things than wise ones and sometimes I think that in spite of a certain reputation for caution and far-sightedness, I am exceptionally cursed in this respect. Indeed, when I look back upon my past, I can scarcely see the scanty flowers of wisdom that decorate its path because of the fat, ugly trees of error by which it is overshadowed.

On that occasion, forgetting past experiences where Hans was concerned, my natural tendency to blunder took the form of relying upon another's judgment instead of on my own. Although I had formed a certain view as to what should be done, the *pros* and *cons* seemed so evenly balanced that I determined to consult the little Hottentot and accept his verdict. This, after all, was but a form of gambling like pitch and toss, since, although it is true Hans was a clever, or at any rate a cunning man according to his lights, and experienced, it meant that I was placing my own judgment in abeyance, which no one considering a life-and-death enterprise should do, taking the chance of that of another, whatever it might be. However, not for the first time, I did so—to my grief.

In the tiniest of whispers with my lips right against his smelly head, I submitted the problem to Hans, asking him what we should do, go on or go back. He considered a while, then answered in a voice which he contrived to make like the drone of a night beetle.

"Those men are fast asleep, I know it by their breathing. Also the Baas has the Great Medicine. Therefore I say go on, kill them and rescue Sad-Eyes."

Now I saw that the Fates to which I had appealed had decided against me and that I must accept their decree. With a sick and sinking heart—for I did not at all like the business—I wondered for a moment what had led Hans to take this view, which was directly opposite to any I had expected from him. Of course his superstition about the Great Medicine had something to do with it, but I felt convinced that this was not all.

Even then I guessed that two arguments appealed to him, of which the first was that he desired, if possible, to put an end to this intolerable and unceasing hunt which had worn us all out, no matter what that end might be. The second and more powerful, however, was, I believed, and rightly, that the idea of this stealthy, midnight blow appealed irresistibly to the craft of his half-wild nature in which the strains of the leopard and the snake seemed to mingle with that of the human being. For be it remembered that notwithstanding his veneer of civilisation, Hans was a savage whose forefathers for countless ages had preserved themselves alive by means of such attacks and stratagems.

The die having been cast, in the same infinitesimal whispers we made our arrangements, which were few and simple. They amounted to this—that we were to creep on to the men and each of us to kill that one who was opposite to him, I with the axe and Hans with his knife, remembering that it must be done with a single stroke—that is, if they did not wake up and kill us—after which we were to get Inez out of her shelter, dressed or undressed, and make off with her into the darkness where we were pretty sure of being able to baffle pursuit until we reached our own camp.

Provided that we could kill the two guards in the proper fashion—rather a large proviso, I admit—the thing was simple as shelling peas which, notwithstanding the proverb, in my experience is not simple at all, since generally the shells crack the wrong way and at least one of the peas remained in the pod. So it happened in this case, for Janee, whom we had both forgotten, remained in the pod.

I am sure I don't know why we overlooked her; indeed, the error was inexcusable, especially as Hans had already experienced her foolishness and she was lying there before our eyes. I suppose that our minds were so concentrated upon the guard-killing and the tragic and impressive Inez that there was no room in them for the stolid and matter-of-fact Janee. At any rate she proved to be the pea that would not come out of the pod.

Often in my life I have felt terrified, not being by nature one of those who rejoices in dangers and wild adventures for their own sake, which only the stupid do, but who has, on the contrary, been forced to undertake them by the pressure of circumstances, a kind of hydraulic force that no one can resist, and who, having undertaken, has been carried through them, triumphing over the shrinkings of his flesh by some secret reserve of nerve power. Almost am I tempted to call it spirit-power, something that lives beyond and yet inspires our frail and fallible bodies.

Well, rarely have I been more frightened than I was at this moment. Actually I hung back until I saw that Hans slithering through the grass like a thick yellow snake with the great knife in his right hand, was quite a foot ahead of me. Then my pride came to the rescue and I spurted, if one can spurt upon one's stomach, and drew level with him. After this we went at a pace so slow that any able-bodied snail would have left us standing still. Inch by inch we crept forward, lying motionless a while after each convulsive movement, once for quite a long time, since the left-hand cannibal seemed about to wake up, for he opened his mouth and yawned. If so, he changed his mind and rolling from a sitting posture on to his side, went to sleep much more soundly than before.

A minute or so later the right-hand ruffian, my man, also stirred, so sharply that I thought he had heard something. Apparently, however, he was only haunted by dreams resulting from an evil life, or perhaps by the prescience of its end, for after waving his arm and muttering something in a frightened voice, he too, wearied out, poor devil, sank back into sleep.

At last we were on them, but paused because we could not see exactly where to strike and knew, each of us, that our first blow must be the last and fatal. A cloud had come up and dimmed what light there was, and we must wait for it to pass. It was a long wait, or so it seemed.

At length that cloud did pass and in faint outline I saw the classical head of my Amahagger bowed in deep sleep. With a heart beating as it does only in the fierce extremities of love or war, I hissed like a snake, which was our agreed signal. Then rising to my knees, I lifted the Zulu axe and struck with all my strength.

The blow was straight and true; Umslopogaas himself could not have dealt a better. The victim in front of me uttered no sound and made no movement; only sank gently on to his side, and there lay as dead as though he had never been born.

It appeared that Hans had done equally well, since the other man kicked out his long legs, which struck me on the knees. Then he also became strangely still. In short, both of them were stone dead and would tell no stories this side of Judgment Day.

Recovering my axe, which had been wrenched from my hand, I crept forward and opened the curtain-like rugs or blankets, I do not know which they were, that covered Inez. I heard her stir at once. The movement had wakened her, since captives sleep lightly.

"Make no noise, Inez," I whispered. "It is I, Allan Quatermain, come to rescue you. Slip out and follow me; do you understand?"

"Yes, quite," she whispered back and began to rise.

At this moment a blood-curdling yell seemed to fill earth and heaven, a yell at the memory of which even now I feel faint, although I am writing years after its echoes died away.

I may as well say at once that it came from Janee who, awaking suddenly, had perceived against the background of the sky, Hans standing over her, looking like a yellow devil with a long knife in his hand, which she thought was about to be used to murder her.

So, lacking self-restraint, she screamed in the most lusty fashion, for her lungs were excellent, and—the game was up.

Instantly every man sleeping round the fire leapt to his feet and rushed in the direction of the echoes of Janee's yell. It was impossible to get Inez free of her tent arrangement or to do anything, except whisper to her, "Feign sleep and know nothing. We will follow you. Your father is with us."

Then I bolted back into the bushes, which Hans had reached already.

A minute or two later when we were clear of the hubbub and nearing our own camp, Hans remarked to me sententiously, "The Great Medicine worked well, Baas, but not quite well enough, for what medicine can avail against a woman's folly?"

"It was our own folly we should blame," I answered. "We ought to have known that fool-girl would shriek, and taken precautions."

"Yes, Baas, we ought to have killed her too, for nothing else would have kept her quiet," replied Hans in cheerful assent. "Now we shall have to pay for our mistake, for the hunt must go on."

At this moment we stumbled across Robertson and Umslopogaas who, with the others, and every living thing within a mile or two had also heard Janee's yell, and briefly told our story. When he learned how near we had been to rescuing his daughter, Robertson groaned, but Umslopogaas only said, "Well, there are two less of the men-eaters left to deal with. Still, for once your wisdom failed you, Macumazahn. When you had found the camp you should have returned, so that we might all attack it together. Had we done so, before the dawn there would not have been one of them left."

"Yes," I answered, "I think that my wisdom did fail me, if I have any to fail. But come; perhaps we may catch them yet."

So we advanced, Hans and I showing the road. But when we reached the place it was too late, for all that remained of the Amahagger, or of Inez and Janee, were the two dead men whom we had killed, and in that darkness pursuit was impossible. So we went back to our own camp to rest and await the dawn before taking up the trail, only to find ourselves confronted with a new trouble. All the Strathmuir half-breeds whom we had left behind as useless, had taken advantage of our absence and that of the Zulus, to desert. They had just bolted back upon our tracks and vanished into the sea of bush. What became of them I do not know, as we never saw them again, but my belief is that these cowardly fellows all perished, for certainly not one of them reached Strathmuir.

Fortunately for us, however, they departed in such a hurry that they left all their loads behind them, and even some of the guns they carried. Evidently Janee's yell was the last straw which broke the back of such nerve as remained to them. Doubtless they believed it to be the signal of attack by hordes of cannibals.

As there was nothing to said or done, since any pursuit of these curs was out of the question, we made the best of things as they were. It proved a simple business. From the loads we selected such articles as were essential, ammunition for the most part, to carry ourselves—and the rest we abandoned, hiding it under a pile of stones in case we should ever come that way again.

The guns they had thrown aside we distributed among the Zulus who had none, though the thought that they possessed them, so far as I was concerned, added another terror to life. The prospect of going into battle with those wild axemen letting off bullets in every direction was not pleasant, but fortunately when that crisis came, they cast them away and reverted to the weapons to which they were accustomed.

Now all this sounds much like a tale of disaster, or at any rate of failure. It is, however, wonderful by what strange ways good results are brought about, so much so that at times I think that these seeming accidents must be arranged by an Intelligence superior to our own, to fulfil through us purposes of which we know nothing, and frequently, be it admitted, of a nature sufficiently obscure. Of course this is a fatalistic doctrine, but then, as I have said before, within certain limits I am a fatalist.

To take the present case, for instance, the whole Inez episode at first sight might appear to be an excrescence on my narrative, of which the object is to describe how I met a certain very wonderful woman and what I heard and experienced in her company. Yet it is not really so, since had it not been for the Inez adventure, it is quite clear that I should never have reached the home of this woman, if woman she were, or have seen her at all. Before long this became very obvious to me, as shall be told.

From the night upon which Hans and I failed to rescue Inez we had no more difficulty in following the trail of the cannibals, who thenceforward were never more than a few hours ahead of us and had no time to be careful or to attempt to hide their spoor. Yet so fast did they travel that do what we would, burdened and wearied as we were, it proved impossible to overtake them.

For the first three days the track ran on through scattered, rolling bush-*veld* of the character that I have described, but tending continually down hill. When we broke camp on the morning of the fourth day, eating a hasty meal at dawn (for now game had become astonishingly plentiful, so that we did not lack food) the rising sun showed beneath us an endless sea of billowy mist stretching in every direction far as the sight could carry.

To the north, however, it did come to an end, for there, as I judged fifty or sixty miles away, rose the grim outline of what looked like a huge fortress, which I knew must be one of those extraordinary mountain formations, probably owing their origin to volcanic action, that are to be met with here and there in the vast expanses of Central and Eastern Africa. Being so distant it was impossible to estimate its size, which I guessed must be enormous, but in looking at it I bethought me of that great mountain in which Zikali said the marvellous white Queen lived, and wondered whether it could be the same, as from my memory of his map upon the ashes, it well might be, that is, if such a place existed at all. If so the map had shown it as surrounded by swamps and—well, surely that mist hid the face of a mighty swamp?

It did indeed, since before nightfall, following the spoor of those Amahagger, we had plunged into a morass so vast that in all my experience I have never seen or heard of its like. It was a veritable ocean of papyrus and other reeds, some of them a dozen or more feet high, so that it was impossible to see a yard in any direction.

Here it was that the Amahagger ahead of us proved our salvation, since without them to guide us we must soon have perished. For through that gigantic swamp there ran a road, as I think an ancient road, since in one or two places I saw stone work which must have been laid by man. Yet it was not a road which it would have been possible to follow without a guide, seeing that it also was overgrown with reeds. Indeed, the only difference between it and the surrounding swamp was that on the road the soil was comparatively firm, that is to say, one seldom sank into it above the knee, whereas on either side of it quagmires were often apparently bottomless, and what is more, partook of the nature of quicksand.

This we found out soon after we entered the swamp, since Robertson, pushing forward with the fierce eagerness which seemed to consume him, neglected to keep his eye upon the spoor and stepped off the edge on to land that appeared to be exactly similar to its surface. Instantly he began to sink in greasy and tenacious mud. Umslopogaas and I were only twenty yards behind, yet by the time we reached him in answer to his shouts, already he was engulfed up to his middle and going down so rapidly that in another minute he would have vanished altogether. Well, we got him out but not with ease, for that mud clung to him like the tentacles of an octopus. After this we were more careful.

Nor did this road run straight; on the contrary, it curved about and sometimes turned at right angles, doubtless to avoid a piece of swamp over which it had proved impossible for the ancients to construct a causeway, or to follow some out-crop of harder soil beneath.

The difficulties of that horrible place are beyond description, and indeed can scarcely be imagined. First there was that of a kind of grass which grew among the roots of the reeds and had edges like to those of knives. As Robertson and I wore gaiters we did not suffer so much from it, but the poor Zulus with their bare legs were terribly cut about and in some cases lame.

Then there were the mosquitoes which lived here by the million and all seemed anxious for a bite; also snakes of a peculiarly deadly kind were numerous. A Zulu was bitten by one of them of so poisonous a nature that he died within three minutes, for the venom seemed to go straight to his heart. We threw his body into the swamp, where it vanished at once.

Lastly there was the all-pervading stench and the intolerable heat of the place, since no breath of air could penetrate that forest of reeds, while a minor trouble was that of the multitude of leeches which fastened on to our bodies. By looking one could see the creatures sitting on the under side of leaves with their heads stretched out waiting to attack anything that went by. As wayfarers there could not have been numerous, I wondered what they had lived on for the last few thousand years. By the way, I found that paraffin, of which we had a small supply for our hand-lamps, rubbed over all exposed surfaces, was to some extent a protection against these blood-sucking worms and the gnats, although it did make one go about smelling like a dirty oil tin.

During the day, except for the occasional rush of some great iguana or other reptile, and the sound of the wings of the flocks of wildfowl passing over us from time to time, the march was deathly silent. But at night it was different, for then the bull-frogs boomed incessantly, as did the bitterns, while great swamp owls and other night-flying birds uttered their weird cries. Also there were mysterious sucking noises caused, no doubt, by the sinking of areas of swamp, with those of bursting bubbles of foul, up-rushing gas.

Strange lights, too, played about, will-o'-the-wisps or St. Elmo fires, as I believe they are called, that frightened the Zulus very much, since they believed them to be spirits of the dead. Perhaps this super-stition had something to do with their native legend that mankind was "torn out of the reeds." If so, they may have imagined that the ghosts of men went back to the reeds, of which there were enough here to accommodate those of the entire Zulu nation. Any way they were much scared; even the bold witch-doctor, Goroko, was scared and went through incantations with the little bag of medicines he carried to secure protection for himself and his companions. Indeed, I think even the iron Umslopogaas himself was not as comfortable as he might have been, although he did inform me that he had come out to fight and did not care whether it were with man, or wizard, or spirit.

In short, of all the journeys that I have made, with the exception of the passage of the desert on our way to King Solomon's Mines, I think that through this enormous swamp was the most miserable. Heartily did I curse myself for ever having undertaken such a quest in a wild attempt to allay that sickness, or rather to quench that thirst of the soul which, I imagine, at times assails most of those who have hearts and think or dream.

For this was at the bottom of the business: this it was which had delivered me into the hands of Zikali, Opener-of-Roads, who, as now I am sure, was merely making use of me for his private occult purpos-es. He desired to consult the distant Oracle, if such a person existed, as to great schemes of his own, and therefore, to attain his end, made use of my secret longings which I had been so foolish as to reveal to him, quite careless of what happened to me in the process.

Well, I was in for the business and must follow it to the finish whatever that might be. After all it was very interesting and if there were anything in what Zikali said (if there were not I could not con-ceive what object he had in sending me on such a wild-goose chase through this home of geese and ducks), it might become more inter-esting still. For being pretty well fever-proof I did not think I should die in that morass, as of course nine white men out of ten would have done, and, beyond it lay the huge mountain which day by day grew larger and clearer.

Nor did Hans, who, with a childlike trust, pinned his faith to the Great Medicine. This, he remarked, was the worst *veld* through which he had ever travelled, but as the Great Medicine would never consent to be buried in that stinking mud, he had no doubt that we should come safely through it some time. I replied that this wonderful medicine of his had not saved one of our companions who had now made a grave in the same mud.

"No, Baas," he said, "but those Zulus have nothing to do with the Medicine which was given to you, and to me who accompanied you when we saw the Opener-of-Roads. Therefore perhaps they will all die, except Umslopogaas, whom you were told to take with you. If so, what does it matter, since there are plenty of Zulus, although there be but one Macumazahn or one Hans? Also the Baas may remember that he began by offending a snake and therefore it is quite natural that this snake's brother should have bitten the Zulu."

"If you are right, he should have bitten me, Hans."

"Yes, Baas, and so no doubt he would have done had you not been protected by the Great Medicine, and me too had not my grandfather been a snake-charmer, to say nothing of the smell of the Medicine being on me as well. The snakes know those that they should bite, Baas."

"So do the mosquitoes," I answered, grabbing a handful of them. "The Great Medicine has no effect upon them."

"Oh! yes, Baas, it has, since though it pleases them to bite, the bites do us no harm, or at least not much, and all are made happy. Still, I wish we could get out of these reeds of which I never want to see another, and Baas, please keep your rifle ready for I think I hear a crocodile stirring there."

"No need, Hans," I remarked sarcastically. "Go and tell him that I have the Great Medicine."

"Yes, Baas, I will; also that if he is very hungry, there are some Zulus camped a few yards further down the road," and he went solemnly to the reeds a little way off and began to talk to them.

"You infernal donkey!" I murmured, and drew my blanket over my head in a vain attempt to keep out the mosquitoes and smoking furiously with the same object, tried to get to sleep.

\* \* \* \* \* \* \*

At last the swamp bottom began to slope upwards a little, with the result that as the land dried through natural drainage, the reeds grew thinner by degrees, until finally they ceased and we found ourselves on firmer ground; indeed, upon the lowest slopes of the great mountain that I have mentioned, that now towered above us, forbidden and majestic.

I had made a little map in my pocket-book of the various twists and turns of the road through that vast Slough of Despond, marking them from hour to hour as we followed its devious wanderings. On studying this at the end of that part of our journey I realised afresh how utterly impossible it would have been for us to thread that misty maze where a few false steps would always have meant death by suffocation, had it not been for the spoor of those Amahagger travelling immediately ahead of us who were acquainted with its secrets. Had they been friendly guides they could not have done us a better turn.

What I wondered was why they had not tried to ambush us in the reeds, since our fires must have shown them that we were close upon their heels. That they did try to burn us out was clear from certain evidences that I found, but fortunately at this season of the year in the absence of a strong wind the rank reeds were too green to catch fire. For the rest I was soon to learn the reason of their neglect to attack us in that dense cover.

They were waiting for a better opportunity!

## CHAPTER 10

# The Attack

We won out of the reeds at last, for which I fervently thanked God, since to have crossed that endless marsh unguided, with the loss of only one man, seemed little less than miraculous. We emerged from them late in the afternoon and being wearied out, stopped for a while to rest and eat of the flesh of a buck that I had been fortunate enough to shoot upon their fringe. Then we pushed forward up the slope, proposing to camp for the night on the crest of it a mile or so away where I thought we should escape from the deadly mist in which we had been enveloped for so long, and obtain a clear view of the country ahead.

Following the bank of a stream which here ran down into the marsh, we came at length to this crest just as the sun was sinking. Below us lay a deep valley, a fold, as it were, in the skin of the mountain, well but not densely bushed. The woods of this valley climbed up the mountain flank for some distance above it and then gave way to grassy slopes that ended in steep sides of rock, which were crowned by a black and frowning precipice of unknown height.

There was, I remember, something very impressive about this towering natural wall, which seemed to shut off whatever lay beyond the gaze of man, as though it veiled an ancient mystery. Indeed, the aspect of it thrilled me, I knew not why. I observed, however, that at one point in the mighty cliff there seemed to be a narrow cleft down which, no doubt, lava had flowed in a remote age, and it occurred to me that up this cleft ran a roadway, probably a continuation of that by which we had threaded the swamp. The fact that through my glasses I could see herds of cattle grazing on the slopes of the mountain went to confirm this view, since cattle imply owners and herdsmen, and search as I would, I could find no native villages on the slopes. The inference seemed to be that those owners dwelt beyond or within the mountain.

All of these things I saw and pointed out to Robertson in the light of the setting sun.

Meanwhile Umslopogaas had been engaged in selecting the spot where we were to camp for the night. Some soldierlike instinct, or perchance some prescience of danger, caused him to choose a place particularly suitable to defence. It was on a steep-sided mound that more or less resembled a gigantic ant-heap. Upon one side this mound was protected by the stream which because of a pool was here rather deep, while at the back of it stood a collection of those curious and piled-up water-worn rocks that are often to be found in Africa. These rocks, lying one upon another like the stones of a Cyclopean wall, curved round the western side of the mound, so that practically it was only open for a narrow space, say thirty or forty feet, upon that face of it which looked on to the mountain.

"Umslopogaas expects battle," remarked Hans to me with a grin, "otherwise with all this nice plain round us he would not have chosen to camp in a place which a few men could hold against many. Yes, Baas, he thinks that those cannibals are going to attack us."

"Stranger things have happened," I answered indifferently, and having seen to the rifles, went to lie down, observing as I did so that the tired Zulus seemed already to be asleep. Only Umslopogaas did not sleep. On the contrary, he stood leaning on his axe staring at the dim outlines of the opposing precipice.

"A strange mountain, Macumazahn," he said, "compared to it that of the Witch, beneath which my kraal lies, is but a little baby. I wonder what we shall find within it. I have always loved mountains, Macumazahn, ever since a dead brother of mine and I lived with the wolves in the Witch's lap, for on them I have had the best of my fighting."

"Perhaps it is not done with yet," I answered wearily.

"I hope not, Macumazahn, since some is due for us, after all these days of mud and stench. Sleep a while now, Macumazahn, for that head of yours which you use so much, must need rest. Fear not, I and the little yellow man who do not think as much as you do, will keep watch and wake you if there is need, as mayhap there will be before the dawn. Here none can come at us except in front, and the place is narrow."

So I lay down and slept as soundly as ever I had done in my life, for a space of four or five hours I suppose. Then, by some instinct perhaps, I awoke suddenly, feeling much refreshed in that sweet mountain air, a new man indeed, and in the moonlight saw Umslopogaas striding towards me.

"Arise, Macumazahn," he said, "I hear men stirring below us."

At this moment Hans slipped past him, whispering, "The cannibals are coming, Baas, a good number of them. I think they mean to attack before dawn."

Then he passed behind me to warn the Zulus. As he went by, I said to him, "If so, Hans, now is the time for your Great Medicine to show what it can do."

"The Great Medicine will look after you and me all right, Baas," he replied, pausing and speaking in Dutch, which Umslopogaas did not understand, "but I expect there will be fewer of those Zulus to cook for before the sun grows hot. Their spirits will be turned into snakes and go back into the reeds from which they say they were 'torn out,'" he added over his shoulder.

I should explain that Hans acted as cook to our party and it was a grievance with him that the Zulus ate so much of the meat which he was called upon to prepare. Indeed, there is never much sympathy between Hottentots and Zulus.

"What is the little yellow man saying about us?" asked Umslopogaas suspiciously.

"He is saying that if it comes to battle, you and your men will make a great fight," I replied diplomatically.

"Yes, we will do that, Macumazahn, but I thought he said that we should be killed and that this pleased him."

"Oh dear no!" I answered hastily. "How could he be pleased if that happened, since then he would be left defenceless, if he were not killed too. Now, Umslopogaas, let us make a plan for this fight."

So, together with Robertson, rapidly we discussed the thing. As a result, with the help of the Zulus, we dragged together some loose stones and the tops of three small thorn trees which we had cut down, and with them made a low breastwork, sufficient to give us some protection if we lay down to shoot. It was the work of a few minutes since we had prepared the material when we camped in case an emergency should arise.

Behind this breastwork we gathered and waited, Robertson and I being careful to get a little to the rear of the Zulus, who it will be remembered had the rifles which the Strathmuir bastards had left behind them when they bolted, in addition to their axes and throwing assegais. The question was how these cannibals would fight. I knew that they were armed with long spears and knives but I did not know if they used those spears for thrusting or for throwing. In the former case it would be difficult to get at them with the axes because they must have the longer reach. Fortunately as it turned out, they did both.

At length all was ready and there came that long and trying wait, the most disagreeable part of a fight in which one grows nervous and begins to reflect earnestly upon one's sins. Clearly the Amahagger, if they really intended business, did not mean to attack till just before dawn, after the common native fashion, thinking to rush us in the low and puzzling light. What perplexed me was that they should wish to attack us at all after having let so many opportunities of doing so go by. Apparently these men were now in sight of their own home, where no doubt they had many friends, and by pushing on could reach its shelter before us, especially as they knew the roads and we did not.

They had come out for a secret purpose that seemed to have to do with the abduction of a certain young white woman for reasons connected with their tribal statecraft or ritual, which is the kind of thing that happens not infrequently among obscure and ancient African tribes. Well, they had abducted their young woman and were in sight of safety and success in their objects, whatever these might be. For what possible reason, then, could they desire to risk a fight with the outraged friends and relatives of that young woman?

It was true that they outnumbered us and therefore had a good chance of victory, but on the other hand, they must know that it would be very dearly won, and if it were not won, that we should retake their captive, so that all their trouble would have been for nothing. Further they must be as exhausted and travel-worn as we were ourselves and in no condition to face a desperate battle.

The problem was beyond me and I gave it up with the reflection that either this threatened attack was a mere feint to delay us, or that behind it was something mysterious, such as a determination to prevent us at all hazards from discovering the secrets of that mountain stronghold.

When I put the riddle to Hans, who was lying next to me, he was ready with another solution.

"They are men-eaters, Baas," he said, "and being hungry, wish to eat us before they get to their own land where doubtless they are not allowed to eat each other."

"Do you think so," I answered, "when we are so thin?" and I surveyed Hans' scraggy form in the moonlight.

"Oh! yes, Baas, we should be quite good boiled—like old hens, Baas. Also it is the nature of cannibals to prefer thin man to fat beef. The devil that is in them gives them that taste, Baas, just as he makes me like gin, or you turn your head to look at pretty women, as those Zulus say you always did in their country, especially at a certain witch who was named Mameena and whom you kissed before everybody——"

Here I turned my head to look at Hans, proposing to smite him with words, or physically, since to have this Mameena myth, of which I have detailed the origin in the book called *Child of Storm*, re-arise out of his hideous little mouth was too much. But before I could get out a syllable he held up his finger and whispered, "Hush! the dawn breaks and they come. I hear them."

I listened intently but could distinguish nothing. Only straining my eyes, presently I thought that about a hundred yards down the slope beneath us in the dim light I caught sight of ghostlike figures flitting from tree to tree; also that these figures were drawing nearer.

"Look out!" I said to Robertson, "I believe they are coming."

"Man," he answered sternly, "I hope so, for whom else have I wanted to meet all these days?"

Now the figures vanished into a little fold of the ground. A minute or so later they re-appeared upon its hither side where such light as there was from the fading stars and the gathering dawn fell full upon them, for here were no trees. I looked and a thrill of horror went through me, for with one glance I recognised that these were *not the men whom we had been following.* To begin with, there were many more of them, quite a hundred, I should think, also they had painted shields, wore feathers in their hair, and generally so far as I could judge, seemed to be fat and fresh.

"We have been led into an ambush," I said first in Zulu to Umslopogaas immediately in front, and then in English to Robertson.

"If so, man, we must just do the best we can," answered the latter, "but God help my poor daughter, for those other devils will have taken her away, leaving their brethren to make an end of us."

"It is so, Macumazahn," broke in Umslopogaas. "Well, whatever the end of it, we shall have a better fight. Now do you give the word and we will obey."

The savages, for so I call them, although I admit that cannibals or not, they looked more like high-class Arabs than savages, came on in perfect silence, hoping, I suppose, to catch us asleep. When they were about fifty yards away, running in a treble line with spears advanced, I called out "Fire!" in Zulu, and set the example by loosing off both barrels of my express rifle at men whom I had picked out as leaders, with results that must have been more satisfactory to me than to the two Amahagger whose troubles in this world came to an end.

There followed a tremendous fusillade, the Zulus banging off their guns wildly, but even at that distance managing for the most part to shoot over the enemy's heads. Captain Robertson and Hans, however, did better and the general result was that the Amahagger, who appeared to be unaccustomed to firearms, retreated in a hurry to a fold of the ground whence they had emerged. Before the last of them got there I loaded again, so that two more stopped behind. Altogether we had put nine or ten of them out of action.

Now I hoped that they would give the business up. But this was not so, for being brave fellows, after a pause of perhaps five minutes, once more they charged in a body, hoping to overwhelm us. Again we greeted them with bullets and knocked out several, whereon the rest threw a volley of their long spears at us. I was glad to see them do this although one of the Zulus got his death from it, while two more were wounded. I myself had a very narrow escape, for a spear passed between my neck and shoulder. Each of them carried but one of these weapons and I knew that if they used them up in throwing, only their big knives would remain to them with which to attack us.

After this discharge of spears which was kept up for some time, they rushed at us and there followed a great fight. The Zulus, throwing down their guns, rose to their feet and holding their little fighting shields which had been carried in their mats, in the left hand, wielded their axes with the right. Umslopogaas, who stood in the centre of them, however, had no shield and swung his great axe with both arms. This was the first time that I had seen him fight and the spectacle was in a way magnificent. Again and again the axe crashed down and every time it fell it left one dead beneath the stroke, till at length those Amahagger shrank back out of his reach.

Meanwhile Robertson, Hans and I, standing on some stones at the back, kept up a continual fire upon them, shooting over the heads of the Zulus, who were playing their part like men. Yes, they shrank back, leaving many dead behind them. Then a captain tried to gather them for another rush, and once more they moved forward. I killed that captain with a revolver shot, for my rifle had become too hot to hold, and at the sight of his fall, they broke and ran back into the little hollow where our bullets could not reach them.

So far we had held our own, but at a price, for three of the Zulus were now dead and three more wounded, one of them severely, the other two but enough to cripple them. In fact, now there were left of them but three untouched men, and Umslopogaas, so that in all for fighting purposes we were but seven. What availed it that we had killed a great number of these Amahagger, when we were but seven? How could seven men withstand such another onslaught? There in the pale light of the dawn we looked at each other dismayed.

"Now," said Umslopogaas, leaning on his red axe, "there remains but one thing to do, make a good end, though I would that it were in a greater cause. At least we must either fight or fly," and he looked down at the wounded.

"Think not of us, Father," murmured one of them, the man who had a mortal hurt. "If it is best, kill us and begone that you may live to bear the Axe in years to come."

"Well spoken!" said Umslopogaas, and again stood still a while, then added, "The word is with you, Macumazahn, who are our captain."

I set out the situation to Robertson and Hans as briefly as I could, showing that there was a chance of life if we ran, but so far as I could see, none if we stayed.

"Go if you like, Quatermain," answered the Captain, "but I shall stop and die here, for since my girl is gone I think I'm better dead."

I motioned to Hans to speak.

"Baas," he answered, "the Great Medicine is here with us upon the earth and your reverend father, the Predikant, is with us in the sky, so I think we had better stop here and do what we can, especially as I do not want to see those reeds any more at present."

"So do I," I said briefly, giving no reasons.

So we made ready for the next attack which we knew would be the last, strengthening our little wall and dragging the dead Amahagger up against it as an added protection. As we were thus engaged the sun rose and in its first beams, some miles away on the opposing slopes of the mountain looking tiny against the black background of the precipice, we saw a party of men creeping forward. Lifting my glasses I studied it and perceived that in its midst was a litter.

"There goes your daughter," I said, and handed the glasses to Robertson.

"Oh! my God," he answered, "those villains have outwitted us after all."

Another minute and the litter, or rather the chair with its escort, had vanished into the shadow of the great cliffs, probably up some pass which we could not see.

Next moment our thoughts were otherwise engaged, since from various symptoms we gathered that the attack was about to be renewed. Spears upon which shone the light of the rising sun, appeared above the edge of the ground-fold that I have mentioned, which to the east increased to a deep, bush-clad ravine. Also there were voices as of leaders encouraging their men to a desperate effort.

"They are coming," I said to Robertson.

"Yes," he answered, "they are coming and we are going. It's a queer end to the thing we call life, isn't it, Quatermain, and hang it all! I wonder what's beyond? Not much for me, I expect, but whatever it is could scarcely be worse than what I've gone through here below in one way and another."

"There's hope for all of us," I replied as cheerfully as I could, for the man's deep depression disturbed me.

"Mayhap, Quatermain, for who knows the infinite mercy of whatever made us as we are? My old mother used to preach of it and I remember her words now. But in my case I expect it will stop at hope, or sleep, and if it wasn't for Inez, I'd not mind so much, for I tell you I've had enough of the world and life. Look, there's one of them. Take that, you black devil!" and lifting his rifle he aimed and fired at an Amahagger who appeared upon the edge of the fold of ground. What is more he hit him, for I saw the man double up and fall backwards.

Then the game began afresh, for the cannibals (I suppose they were cannibals like their brethren) crept out of shelter, advancing on their stomachs or their hands and knees, so as to offer a smaller mark, and dragging between them a long and slender tree-trunk with which clearly they intended to batter down our wall.

Of course I blazed away at them, pretty carefully too, for I was determined that what I believed to be the last exercise of the gift of shooting that has been given to me, should prove a record. Therefore I selected my men and even where I would hit them, and as subsequent examination showed, I made no mistakes in the seven or eight shots that I fired. But all the while, like poor Captain Robertson, I was thinking of other things; namely, where I was bound for presently and if I should meet certain folk there and what was the meaning of this show called Life, which unless it leads somewhere, according to my judgment has none at all. Until these questions were solved, however, my duty was to kill as many of those ruffians as I could, and this I did with finish and despatch.

Robertson and Hans were firing also, with more or less success, but there were too many to be stopped by our three rifles. Still they came on till at length their fierce faces were within a few yards of our little parapet and Umslopogaas had lifted his great axe to give them greeting. They paused a moment before making their final rush, and so did we to slip in fresh cartridges.

"Die well, Hans," I said, "and if you get there first, wait for me on the other side."

"Yes, Baas, I always meant to do that, though not yet. We are not going to die this time, Baas. Those who have the Great Medicine don't die; it is the others who die, like that fellow," and he pointed to an Amahagger who went reeling round and round with a bullet from his Winchester through the middle, for he had fired in the midst of his remarks.

"Curse—I mean bless—the Great Medicine," I said as I lifted my rifle to my shoulder.

At that moment all those Amahagger—there were about sixty of them left—became seized with a certain perturbation. They stood still, they stared towards the fold of ground out of which they had emerged; they called to each other words which I did not catch, and then—they turned to run.

Umslopogaas saw, and with a leader's instinct, acted. Springing over the parapet, followed by his remaining Zulus of the Axe, he leapt upon them with a roar. Down they went before *Inkosikaas*, like corn before a sickle. The thing was marvellous to see, it was like the charge of a leopard, so swift was the rush and so lightning-like were the strokes or rather the pecks of that flashing axe, for now he was tapping at their heads or spines with the gouge-like point upon its back. Nor were these the only victims, for those brave followers of his also did their part. In a minute all who remained upon their feet of the Amahagger were in full flight, vanishing this way and that among the trees. Hans fired a parting shot after the last of them, then sat down upon a stone and finding his corn-cob pipe, proceeded to fill it.

"The Great Medicine, Baas," he began sententiously, "or perhaps your reverend father, the Predikant——" Here he paused and pointed doubtfully with the bowl of the pipe towards the fold in the ground, adding, "Here it is, but I think it must be your reverend father, not the Great Medicine, yes, the Predikant himself, returned from Heaven, the Place of Fires!"

Looking vaguely in the direction indicated, for I could not conceive what he meant and thought that the excitement must have made him mad, I perceived a venerable old man with a long white beard and clothed in a flowing garment, also white, who reminded me of Father Christmas at a child's party, walking towards us and radiating benignancy. Also behind him I perceived a whole forest of spear points emerging from the gully. He seemed to take it for granted that we should not shoot at him, for he came on quite unconcerned, carefully picking his way among the corpses. When he was near enough he stopped and said in a kind of Arabic which I could understand, "I greet you, Strangers, in the name of her I serve. I see that I am just in time, but this does not surprise me, since she said that it would be so. You seem to have done very well with these dogs," and he prodded a dead Amahagger with his sandaled foot. "Yes, very well indeed. You must be great warriors."

Then he paused and we stared at each other.

# Through the Mountain Wall

"These do not seem to be friends of yours," I said, pointing to the fallen. "And yet," I added, nodding towards the spearmen who were now emerging from the gully, "they are very like your friends."

"Puppies from the same litter are often alike, yet when they grow up sometimes they fight each other," replied Father Christmas blandly. "At least these come to save and not to kill you. Look! they kill the others!" and he pointed to them making an end of some of the wounded men. "But who are these?" and he glanced with evident astonishment, first at the fearsome-looking Umslopogaas and then at the grotesque Hans. "Nay, answer not, you must be weary and need rest. Afterwards we can talk."

"Well, as a matter of fact we have not yet breakfasted," I replied. "Also I have business to attend to here," and I glanced at our wounded.

The old fellow nodded and went to speak to the captains of his force, doubtless as to the pursuit of the enemy, for presently I saw a company spring forward on their tracks. Then, assisted by Hans and the remaining Zulus, of whom one was Goroko, I turned to attend to our own people. The task proved lighter than I expected, since the badly injured man was dead or dying and the hurts of the two others were in their legs and comparatively slight, such as Goroko could doctor in his own native fashion.

After this, taking Hans to guard my back, I went down to the stream and washed myself. Then I returned and ate, wondering the while that I could do so with appetite after the terrible dangers which we had passed. Still, we had passed them, and Robertson, Umslopogaas with three of his men, I and Hans were quite unharmed, a fact for which I returned thanks in silence but sincerely enough to Providence.

Hans also returned thanks in his own fashion, after he had filled himself, not before, and lit his corn-cob pipe. But Robertson made no remark; indeed, when he had satisfied his natural cravings, he rose and walking a few paces forward, stood staring at the cleft in the mountain cliff into which he had seen the litter vanish that bore his daughter to some fate unknown.

Even the great fight that we had fought and the victory we had won against overpowering odds did not appear to impress him. He only glared at the mountain into the heart of which Inez had been raped away, and shook his fist. Since she was gone all else went for nothing, so much so that he did not offer to assist with the wounded Zulus or show curiosity about the strange old man by whom we had been rescued.

"The Great Medicine, Baas," said Hans in a bewildered way, "is even more powerful than I thought. Not only has it brought us safely through the fighting and without a scratch, for those Zulus there do not matter and there will be less cooking for me to do now that they are gone; it has also brought down your reverend father the Predikant from the Place of Fires in Heaven, somewhat changed from what I remember him, it is true, but still without doubt the same. When I make my report to me presently, if he can understand my talk, I shall——"

"Stop your infernal nonsense, you son of a donkey," I broke in, for at this moment old Father Christmas, smiling more benignly than before, re-appeared from the kloof into which he had vanished and advanced towards us bowing with much politeness.

Having seated himself upon the little wall that we had built up, he contemplated us, stroking his beautiful white beard, then said, addressing me, "Of a certainty you should be proud who with a few have defeated so many. Still, had I not been ordered to come at speed, I think that by now you would have been as those are," and he looked towards the dead Zulus who were laid out at a distance like men asleep, while their companions sought for a place to bury them.

"Ordered by whom?" I asked.

"There is only one who can order," he answered with mild astonishment. "'She-who-commands, She-who-is-everlasting'!"

It occurred to me that this must be some Arabic idiom for the Eternal Feminine, but I only looked vague and said, "It would appear that there are some whom this exalted everlasting She cannot command; those who attacked us; also those who have fled away yonder," and I waved my hand towards the mountain.

"No command is absolute; in every country there are rebels, even, as I have heard, in Heaven above us. But, Wanderer, what is your name?"

"Watcher-by-Night," I answered.

"Ah! a good name for one who must have watched well by night, and by day too, to reach this country living where She-who-commands says that no man of your colour has set foot for many generations. Indeed, I think she told me once that two thousand years had gone by since she spoke to a white man in the City of Kôr."

"Did she indeed?" I exclaimed, stifling a cough.

"You do not believe me," he went on, smiling. "Well, She-who-commands can explain matters for herself better than I who was not alive two thousand years ago, so far as I remember. But what must I call him with the Axe?"

"Warrior is his name."

"Again a good name, as to judge by the wounds on them, certain of those rebels I think are now telling each other in Hell. And this man, if indeed he be a man——" he added, looking doubtfully at Hans.

"Light-in-Darkness is his name."

"I see, doubtless because his colour is that of the winter sun in thick fog, or a bad egg broken into milk. And the other white man who mutters and whose brow is like a storm?"

"He is called Avenger; you will learn why later on," I answered impatiently, for I grew tired of this catechism, adding, "And what are you called and, if you are pleased to tell it to us, upon what errand do you visit us in so fortunate an hour?"

"I am named Billali," he answered, "the servant and messenger of She-who-commands, and I was sent to save you and to bring you safely to her."

"How can this be, Billali, seeing that none knew of our coming?"

"Yet She-who-commands knew," he said with his benignant smile. "Indeed, I think that she learned of it some moons ago through a message that was sent to her and so arranged all things that you should be guided safely to her secret home; since otherwise how would you have passed a great pathless swamp with the loss, I think she said, of but one man whom a snake bit?"

Now I stared at the old fellow, for how could he know of the death of this man, but thought it useless to pursue the conversation further.

"When you are rested and ready," he went on, "we will start. Meanwhile I leave you that I may prepare litters to carry those wounded men, and you also, Watcher-by-Night, if you wish." Then with a dignified bow, for everything about this old fellow was stately, he turned and vanished into the kloof.

The next hour or so was occupied in the burial of the dead Zulus, a ceremony in which I took no part beyond standing up and raising my hat as they were borne away, for as I have said somewhere, it is best to leave natives alone on these occasions. Indeed, I lay down, reflecting that strangely enough there seemed to be something in old Zikali's tale of a wonderful white Queen who lived in a mountain fastness, since there was the mountain as he had drawn it on the ashes, and the servants of that Queen who, apparently, had knowledge of our coming, appeared in the nick of time to rescue us from one of the tightest fixes in which ever I found myself.

Moreover, the antique and courteous individual called Billali, spoke of her as "She-who-is-everlasting." What the deuce could he mean by that, I wondered? Probably that she was very old and therefore disagreeable to look on, which I confessed to myself would be a disappointment.

And how did she know that we were coming? I could not guess and when I asked Robertson, he merely shrugged his shoulders and intimated that he took no interest in the matter. The truth is that nothing moved the man, whose whole soul was wrapped in one desire, namely to rescue, or avenge, the daughter against whom he knew he had so sorely sinned.

In fact, this loose-living but reformed seaman was becoming a monomaniac, and what is more, one of the religious type. He had a Bible with him that had been given to him by his mother when he was a boy, and in this he read constantly; also he was always on his knees and at night I could hear him groaning and praying aloud. Doubtless now that the chains of drink had fallen off him, the instincts and the blood of the dour old Covenanters from whom he was descended, were asserting themselves. In a way this was a good thing though for some time past I had feared lest it should end in his going mad, and certainly as a companion he was more cheerful in his unregenerate days.

Abandoning speculation as useless and taking my chance of being murdered where I lay, for after all Billali's followers were singularly like the men with whom we had been fighting and for aught I knew might be animated by identical objects—I just went to sleep, as I can do at any time, to wake up an hour or so later feeling wonderfully refreshed. Hans, who when I closed my eyes was already asleep slumbering at my feet curled up like a dog on a spot where the sun struck hotly, roused me by saying:

"Awake, Baas, they are here!"

I sprang up, snatching at my rifle, for I thought that he meant that we were being attacked again, to see Billali advancing at the head of a train of four litters made of bamboo with grass mats for curtains and coverings, each of which was carried by stalwart Amahagger, as I supposed that they must be. Two of these, the finest, Billali indicated were for Robertson and myself, and the two others for the wounded. Umslopogaas and the remaining Zulus evidently were expected to walk, as was Hans.

"How did you make these so quickly," I asked, surveying their elegant and indeed artistic workmanship.

"We did not make them, Watcher-by-Night, we brought them with us folded up. She-who-commands looked in her glass and said that four would be needed, besides my own which is yonder, two for white lords and two for wounded black men, which you see is the number required."

"Yes," I answered vaguely, marvelling what kind of a glass it was that gave the lady this information.

Before I could inquire upon the point Billali added, "You will be glad to learn that my men caught some of those rebels who dared to attack you, eight or ten of them who had been hurt by your missiles or axe-cuts, and put them to death in the proper fashion—yes, quite the proper fashion," and he smiled a little. "The rest had gone too far where it would have been dangerous to follow them among the rocks. Enter now, my lord Watcher-by-Night, for the road is steep and we must travel fast if we would reach the place where She-who-commands is camped in the ancient holy city, before the moon sinks behind the cliffs tonight."

So having explained matters to Robertson and Umslopogaas, who announced that nothing would induce *him* to be carried like an old woman, or a corpse upon a shield, and seen that the hurt Zulus were comfortably accommodated, Robertson and I got into our litters, which proved to be delightfully easy and restful.

Then when our gear was collected by the hook-nosed bearers to whom we were obliged to trust, though we kept with us our rifles and a certain amount of ammunition, we started. First went a number of Billali's spearmen, then came the litters with the wounded alongside of which Umslopogaas and his three uninjured Zulus talked or trotted, then another litter containing Billali, then my own by which ran Hans, and Robertson's, and lastly the rest of the Amahagger and the relief bearers.

"I see now, Baas," said Hans, thrusting his head between my curtains, "that yonder Whitebeard cannot be your reverend father, the Predikant, after all."

"Why not?" I asked, though the fact was fairly obvious.

"Because, Baas, if he were, he would not have left Hans, of whom he always thought so well, to run in the sun like a dog, while he and others travel in carriages like great white ladies."

"You had better save your breath instead of talking nonsense, Hans," I said, "since I believe that you have a long way to go."

In fact, it proved to be a very long way indeed, especially as after we began to breast the mountain, we must travel slowly. We started about ten o'clock in the morning, for the fight which after all did not take long—had, it will be remembered, begun shortly after dawn, and it was three in the afternoon before we reached the base of the towering cliff which I have mentioned.

Here, at the foot of a remarkable, isolated column of rock, on which I was destined to see a strange sight in the after days, we halted and ate of the remaining food which we had brought with us, while the Amahagger consumed their own, that seemed to consist largely of curdled milk, such as the Zulus call *maas*, and lumps of a kind of bread.

I noted that they were a very curious people who fed in silence and on whose handsome, solemn faces one never saw a smile. Somehow it gave me the creeps to look at them. Robertson was affected in the same way, for in one of the rare intervals of his abstraction he remarked that they were "no canny." Then he added, "Ask yon old wizard who might be one of the Bible prophets come to life—what those man-eating devils have done with my daughter."

I did so, and Billali answered, "Say that they have taken her away to make a queen of her, since having rebelled against their own queen, they must have another who is white. Say too that She-who-commands will wage war on them and perhaps win her back, unless they kill her first."

"Ah!" Robertson repeated when I had translated, "unless they kill her first—or worse." Then he relapsed into his usual silence.

Presently we started on again, heading straight for what looked like a sheer wall of black rock a thousand feet or more in height, up a path so steep that Robertson and I got out and walked, or rather scrambled, in order to ease the bearers. Billali, I noticed, remained in his litter. The convenience of the bearers did not trouble him; he only ordered an extra gang to the poles. I could not imagine how we were to negotiate this precipice. Nor could Umslopogaas, who looked at it and said, "If we are to climb that, Macumazahn, I think that the only one who will live to get to the top will be that little yellow monkey of yours," and he pointed with his axe at Hans.

"If I do," replied that worthy, much nettled, for he hated to be called a "yellow monkey" by the Zulus, "be sure that I will roll down stones upon any black butcher whom I see sprawling upon the cliff below."

Umslopogaas smiled grimly, for he had a sense of humour and could appreciate a repartee even when it hit him hard. Then we stopped talking for the climb took all our breath.

At length we came to the cliff face where, to all appearance, our journey must end. Suddenly, however, out of the blind black wall in front of us started the apparition of a tall man armed with a great spear and wearing a white robe, who challenged us hoarsely.

Suddenly he stood before us, as a ghost might do, though whence he came we could not see. Presently the mystery was explained. Here in the cliff face there was a cleft, though one invisible even from a few paces away, since its outer edge projected over the inner wall of rock. Moreover, this opening was not above four feet in width, a mere split in the huge mountain mass caused by some titanic convulsion in past ages. For it was a definite split since, once entered, far, far above could be traced a faint line of light coming from the sky, although the gloom of the passage was such that torches, which were stored at hand, must be used by those who threaded it. One man could have held the place against a hundred—until he was killed. Still, it was guarded, not only at the mouth where the warrior had appeared, but further along at every turn in the jagged chasm, and these were many.

Into this grim place we went. The Zulus did not like it at all, for they are a light-loving people and I noted that even Umslopogaas seemed scared and hung back a little. Nor did Hans, who with his usual suspicion, feared some trap; nor, for the matter of that, did I, though I thought it well to appear much interested. Only Robertson seemed quite indifferent and trudged along stolidly after a man carrying a torch.

Old Billali put his head out of the litter and shouted back to me to fear nothing, since there were no pitfalls in the path, his voice echoing strangely between those narrow walls of measureless height.

For half an hour or more we pursued this dreary, winding path round the corners of which the draught tore in gusts so fierce that more than once the litters with the wounded men and those who bore them were nearly blown over. It was safe enough, however, since on either side of us, smooth and without break, rose the sheer walls of rock over which lay the tiny ribbon of blue sky. At length the cleft widened somewhat and the light grew stronger, making the torches unnecessary.

Then of a sudden we came to its end and found ourselves upon a little plateau in the mountainside. Behind us for a thousand feet or so rose the sheer rock wall as it did upon the outer face, while in front and beneath, far beneath, was a beautiful plain circular in shape and of great extent, which plain was everywhere surrounded, so far as I could see, by the same wall of rock. In short, notwithstanding its enormous size, without doubt it was neither more nor less than the crater of a vast extinct volcano. Lastly, not far from the centre of this plain was what appeared to be a city, since through my glasses I could see great walls built of stone, and what I thought were houses, all of them of a character more substantial than any that I had discovered in the wilds of Africa.

I went to Billali's litter and asked him who lived in the city.

"No one," he answered, "it has been dead for thousands of years, but She-who-commands is camped there at present with an army, and thither we go at once. Forward, bearers."

So, Robertson and I having re-entered our litters, we started on down hill at a rapid pace, for the road, though steep, was safe and kept in good order. All the rest of that afternoon we travelled and by sunset reached the edge of the plain, where we halted a while to rest and eat, till the light of the growing moon grew strong enough to enable us to proceed. Umslopogaas came up and spoke to me.

"Here is a fortress indeed, Macumazahn," he said, "since none can climb that fence of rock in which the holes seem to be few and small."

"Yes," I answered, "but it is one out of which those who are in, would find it difficult to get out. We are buffaloes in a pit, Umslopogaas."

"That is so," he answered, "I have thought it already. But if any would meddle with us we still have our horns and can toss for a while."

Then he went back to his men.

The sunset in that great solemn place was a wonderful thing to see. First of all the measureless crater was filled with light like a bowl with fire. Then as the great orb sank behind the western cliff, half of the plain became quite dark while shadows seemed to rush forward over the eastern part of its surface, till that too was swallowed up in gloom and for a little while there remained only a glow reflected from the cliff face and from the sky above, while on the crest of the parapet of rock played strange and glorious fires. Presently these too vanished and the world was dark.

Then the half moon broke from behind a bank of clouds and by its silver, uncertain light we struggled forward across the flat plain, rather slowly now, for even the iron muscles of those bearers grew tired. I could not see much of it, but I gathered that we were passing through crops, very fine crops to judge by their height, as doubtless they would be upon this lava soil; also once or twice we splashed through streams.

At length, being tired and lulled by the swaying of the litter and by the sound of a weird, low chant that the bearers had set up now that they neared home and were afraid of no attack, I sank into a doze. When I awoke again it was to find that the litter had halted and to hear the voice of Billali say, "Descend, White Lords, and come with your companions, the black Warrior and the yellow man who is named Light-in-Darkness. She-who-commands desires to see you at once before you eat and sleep, and must not be kept waiting. Fear not for the others, they will be cared for till you return."

## CHAPTER 12

# The White Witch

I descended from the litter and told the others what the old fellow had said. Robertson did not want to come, and indeed refused to do so until I suggested to him that such conduct might prejudice a powerful person against us. Umslopogaas was indifferent, putting, as he remarked, no faith in a ruler who was a woman.

Only Hans, although he was so tired, acquiesced with some eagerness, the fact being that his brain was more alert and that he had all the curiosity of the monkey tribe which he so much resembled in appearance, and wanted to see this queen whom Zikali revered.

In the end we started, conducted by Billali and by men who carried torches whereof the light showed me that we were passing between houses, or at any rate walls that had been those of houses, and along what seemed to be a paved street.

Walking under what I took to be a great arch or portico, we came into a court that was full of towering pillars but unroofed, for I could see the stars above. At its end we entered a building of which the doorway was hung with mats, to find that it was lighted with lamps and that all down its length on either side guards with long spears stood at intervals.

"Oh, Baas," said Hans hesitatingly, "this is the mouth of a trap," while Umslopogaas glared about him suspiciously, fingering the handle of his great axe.

"Be silent," I answered. "All this mountain is a trap, therefore another does not matter, and we have our pistols."

Walking forward between the double line of guards who stood immovable as statues, we came to some curtains hung at the end of a long, narrow hall which, although I know little of such things, were, I noted, made of rich stuff embroidered in colours and with golden threads. Before these curtains Billali motioned us to halt.

After a whispered colloquy with someone beyond carried on through the join of the curtains, he vanished between them, leaving us alone for five minutes or more. At length they opened and a tall and elegant woman with an Arab cast of countenance and clad in white robes, appeared and beckoned to us to enter. She did not speak or answer when I spoke to her, which was not wonderful as afterwards I discovered that she was a mute. We went in, I wondering very much what we were going to see.

On the further side of the curtains was a room of no great size illumined with lamps of which the light fell upon sculptured walls. It looked to me as though it might once have been the inmost court or a sanctuary of some temple, for at its head was a dais upon which once perhaps had stood the shrine or statue of a god. On this dais there was now a couch and on the couch—a goddess!

There she sat, straight and still, clothed in shining white and veiled, but with her draperies so arranged that they emphasised rather than concealed the wonderful elegance of her tall form. From beneath the veil, which was such as a bride wears, appeared two plaits of glossy, raven hair of great length, to the end of each of which was suspended a single large pearl. On either side of her stood a tall woman like to her who had led us through the curtains, and on his knees in front, but to the right, knelt Billali.

About this seated personage there was an air of singular majesty, such as might pervade a queen as fancy paints her, though she had a nobler figure than any queen I ever saw depicted. Mystery seemed to flow from her; it clothed her like the veil she wore, which of course heightened the effect. Beauty flowed from her also; although it was shrouded I knew that it was there, no veil or coverings could obscure it—at least, to my imagination. Moreover she breathed out power also; one felt it in the air as one feels a thunderstorm before it breaks, and it seemed to me that this power was not quite human, that it drew its strength from afar and dwelt a stranger to the earth.

To tell the truth, although my curiosity, always strong, was enormously excited and though now I felt glad that I had attempted this journey with all its perils, I was horribly afraid, so much afraid that I should have liked to turn and run away. From the beginning I knew myself to be in the presence of an unearthly being clothed in soft and perfect woman's flesh, something alien, too, and different from our human race.

What a picture it all made! There she sat, quiet and stately as a perfect marble statue; only her breast, rising and falling beneath the white robe, showed that she was alive and breathed as others do. Another thing showed it also—her eyes. At first I could not see them through the veil, but presently either because I grew accustomed to the light, or because they brightened as those of certain animals have power to do when they watch intently, it ceased to be a covering to them. Distinctly I saw them now, large and dark and splendid with a tinge of deep blue in the iris; alluring and yet awful in their majestic aloofness which seemed to look through and beyond, to embrace all without seeking and without effort. Those eyes were like windows through which light flows from within, a light of the spirit.

I glanced round to see the effect of this vision upon my companions. It was most peculiar. Hans had sunk to his knees; his hands were joined in the attitude of prayer and his ugly little face reminded me of that of a big fish out of water and dying from excess of air. Robertson, startled out of his abstraction, stared at the royal-looking woman on the couch with his mouth open.

"Man," he whispered, "I've got them back although I have touched nothing for weeks, only this time they are lovely. For yon's no human lady, I feel it in my bones."

Umslopogaas stood great and grim, his hands resting on the handle of his tall axe; and he stared also, the blood pulsing against the skin that covered the hole in his head.

"Watcher-by-Night," he said to me in his deep voice, but also speaking in a whisper, "this chieftainess is not one woman, but all women. Beneath those robes of hers I seem to see the beauty of one who has 'gone Beyond,' of the Lily who is lost to me. Do you not feel it thus, Macumazahn?"

Now that he mentioned it, certainly I did; indeed, I had felt it all along although amid the rush of sensations this one had scarcely disentangled itself in my mind. I looked at the draped shape and saw—well, never mind whom I saw; it was not one only but several in sequence; also a woman who at that time I did not know although I came to know her afterwards, too well, perhaps, or at any rate quite enough to puzzle me. The odd thing was that in this hallucination the personalities of these individuals seemed to overlap and merge, till at last I began to wonder whether they were not parts of the same entity or being, manifesting itself in sundry shapes, yet springing from one centre, as different coloured rays flow from the same crystal, while the beams from their source of light shift and change. But the fancy is too metaphysical for my poor powers to express as clearly as I would. Also no doubt it was but a hallucination that had its origin, perhaps, in the mischievous brain of her who sat before us.

At length she spoke and her voice sounded like silver bells heard over water in a great calm. It was low and sweet, oh! so sweet that at its first notes for a moment my senses seemed to swoon and my pulse to stop. It was to me that she addressed herself.

"My servant here," and ever so slightly she turned her head towards the kneeling Billali, "tells me that you who are named Watcher-in-the-Night, understand the tongue in which I speak to you. Is it so?"

"I understand Arabic of a kind well enough, having learned it on the East Coast and from Arabs in past years, but not such Arabic as you use, O——" and I paused.

"Call me Hiya," she broke in, "which is my title here, meaning, as you know, She, or Woman. Or if that does not please you, call me Ayesha. It would rejoice me after so long to hear the name I bore spoken by the lips of one of my colour and of gentle blood."

I blushed at the compliment so artfully conveyed, and repeated stupidly enough, "—Not such Arabic as you use, O—Ayesha."

"I thought that you would like the sound of the word better than that of Hiya, though afterwards I will teach you to pronounce it as you should, O—have you any other name save Watcher-by-Night, which seems also to be a title?"

"Yes," I answered. "Allan."

"—O—Allan. Tell me of these," she went on quickly, indicating my companions with a sweep of her slender hand, "for they do not speak Arabic, I think. Or stay, I will tell you of them and you shall say if I do so rightly. This one," and she nodded towards Robertson, "is a man bemused. There comes from him a colour which I see if you cannot, and that colour betokens a desire for revenge, though I think that in his time he has desired other things also, as I remember men always did from the beginning, to their ruin. Human nature does not change, Allan, and wine and women are ancient snares. Enough of him for this time. The little yellow one there is afraid of me, as are all of you. That is woman's greatest power, although she is so weak and gentle, men are still afraid of her just because they are so foolish that they cannot understand her. To them after a million years she still remains the Unknown and to us all the Unknown is also the awful. Do you remember the proverb of the Romans that says it well and briefly?"

I nodded, for it was one of the Latin tags that my father had taught me.

"Good. Well, he is a little wild man, is he not, nearer to the apes from whose race our bodies come? But do you know that, Allan?"

I nodded again, and said, "There are disputes upon the point, Ayesha."

"Yes, they had begun in my day and we will discuss them later. Still, I say—nearer to the ape than you or I, and therefore of interest, as the germ of things is always. Yet he has qualities, I think; cunning, and fidelity and love which in its round is all in all. Do you understand, Allan, that love is all in all?"

I answered warily that it depended upon what she meant by love, to which she replied that she would explain afterwards when we had leisure to talk, adding, "What this little yellow monkey understands by it at least has served you well, or so I believe. You shall tell me the tale of it some day. Now of the last, this Black One. Here I think is a man indeed, a warrior of warriors such as there used to be in the early world, if a savage. Well, believe me, Allan, savages are often the best. Moreover, all are still savage at heart, even you and I. For what is termed culture is but coat upon coat of paint laid on to hide our native colour, and often there is poison in the paint. That axe of his has drunk deep, I think, though always in fair fight, and I say that it shall drink deeper yet. Have I read these men aright, Allan?"

"Not so ill," I answered.

"I thought it," she said with a musical laugh, "although at this place I rust and grow dull like an unused sword. Now you would rest. Go— all of you. Tomorrow you and I will talk alone. Fear nothing for your safety; you are watched by my slaves and I watch my slaves. Until tomorrow, then, farewell. Go now, eat and sleep, as alas we all must do who linger on this ball of earth and cling to a life we should do well to lose. Billali, lead them hence," and she waved her hand to signify that the audience was ended.

At this sign Hans, who apparently was still much afraid, rose from his knees and literally bolted through the curtains. Robertson followed him. Umslopogaas stood a moment, drew himself up and lifting the great axe, cried *Bayéte*, after which he too turned and went.

"What does that word mean, Allan?" she asked.

I explained that it was the salutation which the Zulu people only give to kings.

"Did I not say that savages are often the best?" she exclaimed in a gratified voice. "The white man, your companion, gave me no salute, but the Black One knows when he stands before a woman who is royal."

"He too is of royal blood in his own land," I said.

"If so, we are akin, Allan."

Then I bowed deeply to her in my best manner and rising from her couch for the first time she stood up, looking very tall and commanding, and bowed back.

After this I went to find the others on the further side of the curtains, except Hans, who had run down the long narrow hall and through the mats at its end. We followed, marching with dignity behind Billali and between the double line of guards, who raised their spears as we passed them, and on the further side of the mats discovered Hans, still looking terrified.

"Baas," he said to me as we threaded our way through the court of columns, "in my life I have seen all kinds of dreadful things and faced them, but never have I been so much afraid as I am of that white witch. Baas, I think that she is the devil of whom your reverend father, the Predikant, used to talk so much, or perhaps his wife."

"If so, Hans," I answered, "the devil is not so black as he is painted. But I advise you to be careful of what you say as she may have long ears."

"It doesn't matter at all what one says, Baas, because she reads thoughts before they pass the lips. I felt her doing it there in that room. And do you be careful, Baas, or she will eat up your spirit and make you fall in love with her, who, I expect, is very ugly indeed, since otherwise she would not wear a veil. Whoever saw a pretty woman tie up her head in a sack, Baas?"

"Perhaps she does this because she is so beautiful, Hans, that she fears the hearts of men who look upon her would melt."

"Oh, no, Baas, all women want to melt men's hearts; the more the better. They seem to have other things in their minds, but really they think of nothing else until they are too old and ugly, and it takes them a long while to be sure of that."

So Hans went on talking his shrewd nonsense till, following so far as I could see, the same road as that by which we had come, we reached our quarters, where we found food prepared for us, broiled goat's flesh with corn cakes and milk, I think it was; also beds for us two white men covered with skin rugs and blankets woven of wool.

These quarters, I should explain, consisted of rooms in a house built of stone of which the walls had once been painted. The roof of the house was gone now, for we could see the stars shining above us, but as the air was very soft in this sheltered plain, this was an advantage rather than otherwise. The largest room was reserved for Robertson and myself, while another at the back was given to Umslopogaas and his Zulus, and a third to the two wounded men.

Billali showed us these arrangements by the light of lamps and apologised that they were not better because, as he explained, the place was a ruin and there had been no time to build us a house. He added that we might sleep without fear as we were guarded and none would dare to harm the guests of She-who-commands, on whom he was sure we, or at any rate I and the black Warrior, had produced an excellent impression. Then he bowed himself out, saying that he would return in the morning, and left us to our own devices.

Robertson and I sat down on stools that had been set for us, and ate, but he seemed so overcome by his experiences, or by his sombre thoughts, that I could not draw him into conversation. All he remarked was that we had fallen into queer company and that those who supped with Satan needed a long spoon. Having delivered himself of this sentiment he threw himself upon the bed, prayed aloud for a while as had become his fashion, to be "protected from warlocks and witches," amongst other things, and went to sleep.

Before I turned in I visited Umslopogaas's room to see that all was well with him and his people, and found him standing in the doorway staring at the star-spangled sky.

"Greeting, Macumazahn," he said, "you who are white and wise and I am black and a fighter have seen many strange things beneath the sun, but never such a one as we have looked upon tonight. Who and what is that chieftainess, Macumazahn?"

"I do not know," I said, "but it is worth while to have lived to see her, even though she be veiled."

"Nor do I, Macumazahn. Nay, I do know, for my heart tells me that she is the greatest of all witches and that you will do well to guard your spirit lest she should steal it away. If she were not a witch, should I have seemed to behold the shape of Nada the Lily who was the wife of my youth, beneath those white robes of hers, and though the tongue in which she spoke was strange to me, to hear the murmur of Nada's voice between her lips, of Nada who has gone further from me than those stars. It is good that you wear the Great Medicine of Zikali upon your breast, Macumazahn, for perhaps it will shield you from harm at those hands that are shaped of ivory."

"Zikali is another of the tribe," I answered, laughing, "although less beautiful to see. Also I am not afraid of any of them, and from this one, if she be more than some white woman whom it pleases to veil herself, I shall hope to gather wisdom."

"Yes, Macumazahn, such wisdom as Spirits and the dead have to give."

"Mayhap, Umslopogaas, but we came here to seek Spirits and the dead, did we not?"

"Aye," answered Umslopogaas, "these and war, and I think that we shall find enough of all three. Only I hope that war will come the first, lest the Spirits and the dead should bewitch me and take away my skill and courage."

Then we parted, and too tired even to wonder any more, I threw myself down on my bed and slept.

* * * * * * * *

I was awakened when the sun was already high, by the sound of Robertson, who was on his knees, praying aloud as usual, a habit of his which I confess got on my nerves. Prayer, in my opinion, is a private matter between man and his Creator, that is, except in church; further, I did not in the least wish to hear all about Robertson's sins, which seemed to have been many and peculiar. It is bad enough to have to bear the burden of one's own transgressions without learning of those of other people, that is, unless one is a priest and must do so professionally. So I jumped up to escape and make arrangements for a wash, only to butt into old Billali, who was standing in the doorway contemplating Robertson with much interest and stroking his white beard.

He greeted me with his courteous bow and said, "Tell your companion, O Watcher, that it is not necessary for him to go upon his knees to She-who-commands—and must be obeyed," he added with emphasis, "when he is not in her presence, and that even then he would do well to keep silent, since so much talking in a strange tongue might trouble her."

I burst out laughing and answered, "He does not go upon his knees and pray to She-who-commands, but to the Great One who is in the sky."

"Indeed, Watcher. Well, here we only know a Great One who is upon the earth, though it is true that perhaps she visits the skies sometimes."

"Is it so, Billali?" I answered incredulously. "And now, I would ask you to take me to some place where I can bathe."

"It is ready," he replied. "Come."

So I called to Hans, who was hanging about with a rifle on his arm, to follow with a cloth and soap, of which fortunately we had a couple of pieces left, and we started along what had once been a paved roadway running between stone houses, whereof the time-eaten ruins still remained on either side.

"Who and what is this Queen of yours, Billali?" I asked as we went. "Surely she is not of the Amahagger blood."

139

"Ask it of herself, O Watcher, for I cannot tell you. All I know is that I can trace my own family for ten generations and that my tenth forefather told his son on his deathbed, for the saying has come down through his descendants—that when he was young She-who-commands had ruled the land for more scores of years than he could count months of life."

I stopped and stared at him, since the lie was so amazing that it seemed to deprive me of the power of motion. Noting my very obvious disbelief he continued blandly, "If you doubt, ask. And now here is where you may bathe."

Then he led me through an arched doorway and down a wrecked passage to what very obviously once had been a splendid bath-house such as some I have seen pictures of that were built by the Romans. Its size was that of a large room; it was constructed of a kind of marble with a sloping bottom that varied from three to seven feet in depth, and water still ran in and out of it through large glazed pipes. Moreover round it was a footway about five feet across, from which opened chambers, unroofed now, that the bathers used as dressing-rooms, while between these chambers stood the remains of statues. One at the end indeed, where an alcove had protected it from sun and weather, was still quite perfect, except for the outstretched arms which were gone (the right hand I noticed lying at the bottom of the bath). It was that of a nude young woman in the attitude of diving, a very beautiful bit of work, I thought, though of course I am no judge of sculpture. Even the smile mingled with trepidation upon the girl's face was most naturally portrayed.

This statue showed two things, that the bath was used by females and that the people who built it were highly civilised, also that they belonged to an advanced if somewhat Eastern race, since the girl's nose was, if anything, Semitic in character, and her lips, though prettily shaped, were full. For the rest, the basin was so clean that I presume it must have been made ready for me or other recent bathers, and at its bottom I discovered gratings and broken pipes of earthenware which suggested that in the old days the water could be warmed by means of a furnace.

This relic of a long-past civilisation excited Hans even more than it did myself, since having never seen anything of the sort, he thought it so strange that, as he informed me, he imagined that it must have been built by witchcraft. In it I had a most delightful and much-needed bath. Even Hans was persuaded to follow my example—a thing I had rarely known him to do before—and seated in its shallowest part, splashed some water over his yellow, wrinkled anatomy. Then we returned to our house, where I found an excellent breakfast had been provided which was brought to us by tall, silent, handsome women who surveyed us out of the corners of their eyes, but said nothing.

Shortly after I had finished my meal, Billali, who had disappeared, came back again and said that She-who-commands desired my presence as she would speak with me; also that I must come alone. So, after attending to the wounded, who both seemed to be getting on well, I went, followed by Hans armed with his rifle, though I only carried my revolver. Robertson wished to accompany me, as he did not seem to care about being left alone with the Zulus in that strange place, but this Billali would not allow. Indeed, when he persisted, two great men stepped forward and crossed their spears before him in a somewhat threatening fashion. Then at my entreaty, for I feared lest trouble should arise, he gave in and returned to the house.

Following our path of the night before, we walked up a ruined street which I could see was only one of scores in what had once been a very great city, until we came to the archway that I have mentioned, a large one now overgrown with plants that from their yellow, sweet-scented bloom I judged to be a species of wallflower, also with a kind of houseleek or saxifrage.

Here Hans was stopped by guards, Billali explaining to me that he must await my return, an order which he obeyed unwillingly enough. Then I went on down the narrow passage, lined as before by guards who stood silent as statues, and came to the curtains at the end. Before these at a motion from Billali, who did not seem to dare to speak in this place, I stood still and waited.

## Chapter 13

# Allan Hears a Strange Tale

For some minutes I remained before those curtains until, had it not been for something electric in the air which got into my bones, a kind of force that, perhaps in my fancy only, seemed to pervade the place, I should certainly have grown bored. Indeed I was about to ask my companion why he did not announce our arrival instead of standing there like a stuck pig with his eyes shut as though in prayer or meditation, when the curtains parted and from between them appeared one of those tall waiting women whom we had seen on the previous night. She contemplated us gravely for a few moments, then moved her hand twice, once forward, towards Billali as a signal to him to retire, which he did with great rapidity, and next in a beckoning fashion towards myself to invite me to follow her.

I obeyed, passing between the thick curtains which she fastened in some way behind me, and found myself in the same roofed and sculptured room that I have already described. Only now there were no lamps, such light as penetrated it coming from an opening above that I could not see, and falling upon the dais at its head, also on her who sat upon the dais.

Yes, there she was in her white robes and veil, the point and centre of a little lake of light, a wondrous and in a sense a spiritual vision, for in truth there was something about her which was not of the world, something that drew and yet frightened me. Still as a statue she sat, like one to whom time is of no account and who has grown weary of motion, and on either side of her yet more still, like caryatides supporting a shrine, stood two of the stately women who were her attendants.

For the rest a sweet and subtle odour pervaded the chamber which took hold of my senses as *hasheesh* might do, which I was sure proceeded from her, or from her garments, for I could see no perfumes burning. She spoke no word, yet I knew she was inviting me to come nearer and moved forward till I reached a curious carved chair that was placed just beneath the dais, and there halted, not liking to sit down without permission.

For a long while she contemplated me, for as before I could feel her eyes searching me from head to foot and as it were looking through me as though she would discover my very soul. Then at length she moved, waving those two ivory arms of hers outwards with a kind of swimming stroke, whereon the women to right and left of her turned and glided away, I know not whither.

"Sit, Allan," she said, "and let us talk, for I think we have much to say to each other. Have you slept well? And eaten?—though I fear that the food is but rough. Also was the bath made ready for you?"

"Yes, Ayesha," I answered to all three questions, adding, for I knew not what to say, "It seems to be a very ancient bath."

"When I last saw it," she replied, "it was well enough with statues standing round it worked by a sculptor who had seen beauty in his dreams. But in two thousand years—or is it more?—the tooth of Time bites deep, and doubtless like all else in this dead place it is now a ruin."

I coughed to cover up the exclamation of disbelief that rose to my lips and remarked blandly that two thousand years was certainly a long time.

"When you say one thing, Allan, and mean another, your Arabic is even more vile than usual and does not serve to cloak your thought."

"It may be so, Ayesha, for I only know that tongue as I do many other of the dialects of Africa by learning it from common men. My own speech is English, in which, if you are acquainted with it, I should prefer to talk."

"I know not English, which doubtless is some language that has arisen since I left the world. Perhaps later you shall teach it to me. I tell you, you anger me whom it is not well to anger, because you believe nothing that passes my lips and yet do not dare to say so."

"How can I believe one, Ayesha, who if I understand aright, speaks of having seen a certain bath two thousand years ago, whereas one hundred years are the full days of man? Forgive me therefore if I cannot believe what I know to be untrue."

Now I thought that she would be very angry and was sorry that I had spoken. But as it happened she was not.

"You must have courage to give me the lie so boldly—and I like courage," she said, "who have been cringed to for so long. Indeed, I know that you are brave, who have heard how you bore yourself in the fight yesterday, and much else about you. I think that we shall be friends, but—seek no more."

"What else should I seek, Ayesha?" I asked innocently.

"Now you are lying again," she said, "who know well that no man who is a man sees a woman who is beautiful and pleases him, without wondering whether, should he desire it, she could come to love him, that is, if she be young."

"Which at least is not possible if she has lived two thousand years. Then naturally she would prefer to wear a veil," I said boldly, seeking to avoid the argument into which I saw she wished to drag me.

"Ah!" she answered, "the little yellow man who is named Light-in-Darkness put that thought into your heart, I think. Oh, do not trouble as to how I know it, who have many spies here, as he guessed well enough. So a woman who has lived two thousand years must be hideous and wrinkled, must she? The stamp of youth and loveliness must long have fled from her; of that you, the wise man, are sure. Very well. Now you tempt me to do what I had determined I would not do and you shall pluck the fruit of that tree of curiosity which grows so fast within you. Look, Allan, and say whether I am old and hideous, even though I have lived two thousand years upon the earth and mayhap many more."

Then she lifted her hands and did something to her veil, so that for a moment—only one moment—her face was revealed, after which the veil fell into its place.

I looked, I saw, and if that chair had lacked a back I believe that I should have fallen out of it to the ground. As for what I saw—well, it cannot be described, at any rate by me, except perhaps as a flash of glory.

Every man has dreamed of perfect beauty, basing his ideas of it perhaps on that of some woman he has met who chanced to take his fancy, with a few accessories from splendid pictures or Greek statues thrown in, *plus* a garnishment of the imagination. At any rate I have, and here was that perfect beauty multiplied by ten, such beauty, that at the sight of it the senses reeled. And yet I repeat that it is not to be described.

I do not know what the nose or the lips were like; in fact, all that I can remember with distinctness is the splendour of the eyes, of which I had caught some hint through her veil on the previous night. Oh, they were wondrous, those eyes, but I cannot tell their colour save that the groundwork of them was black. Moreover they seemed to be more than eyes as we understand them. They were indeed windows of the soul, out of which looked thought and majesty and infinite wisdom, mixed with all the allurements and the mystery that we are accustomed to see or to imagine in woman.

Here let me say something at once. If this marvellous creature expected that the revelation of her splendour was going to make me her slave; to cause me to fall in love with her, as it is called, well, she must have been disappointed, for it had no such effect. It frightened and in a sense humbled me, that is all, for I felt myself to be in the presence of something that was not human, something alien to me as a man, which I could fear and even adore as humanity would adore that which is Divine, but with which I had no desire to mix. Moreover, was it divine, or was it something very different? I did not know, I only knew that it was not for me; as soon should I have thought of asking for a star to set within my lantern.

I think that she felt this, felt that her stroke had missed, as the French say, that is if she meant to strike at all at this moment. Of this I am not certain, for it was in a changed voice, one with a suspicion of chill in it that she said with a little laugh, "Do you admit now, Allan, that a woman may be old and still remain fair and unwrinkled?"

"I admit," I answered, although I was trembling so much that I could hardly speak with steadiness, "that a woman may be splendid and lovely beyond anything that the mind of man can conceive, whatever her age, of which I know nothing. I would add this, Ayesha, that I thank you very much for having revealed to me the glory that is hid beneath your veil."

"Why?" she asked, and I thought that I detected curiosity in her question.

"For this reason, Ayesha. Now there is no fear of my troubling you in such a fashion as you seemed to dread a little while ago. As soon would a man desire to court the moon sailing in her silver loveliness through heaven."

"The moon! It is strange that you should compare me to the moon," she said musingly. "Do you know that the moon was a great goddess in Old Egypt and that her name was Isis and—well, once I had to do with Isis? Perhaps you were there and knew it, since more lives than one are given to most of us. I must search and learn. For the rest, all have not thought as you do, Allan. Many, on the contrary, love and seek to win the Divine."

"So do I at a distance, Ayesha, but to come too near to it I do not aspire. If I did perhaps I might be consumed."

"You have wisdom," she replied, not without a note of admiration in her voice. "The moths are few that fear the flame, but those are the moths which live. Also I think that you have scorched your wings before and learned that fire hurts. Indeed, now I remember that I have heard of three such fires of love through which you have flown, Allan, though all of them are dead ashes now, or shine elsewhere. Two burned in your youth when a certain lady died to save you, a great woman that, is it not so? And the third, ah! she was fire indeed, though of a copper hue. What was her name? I cannot remember, but I think it had something to do with the wind, yes, with the wind when it wails."

I stared at her. Was this Mameena myth to be dug up again in a secret place in the heart of Africa? And how the deuce did she know anything about Mameena? Could she have been questioning Hans or Umslopogaas? No, it was not possible, for she had never seen them out of my presence.

"Perhaps," she went on in a mocking voice, "perhaps once again you disbelieve, Allan, whose cynic mind is so hard to open to new truths. Well, shall I show you the faces of these three? I can," and she waved her hand towards some object that stood on a tripod to the right of her in the shadow—it looked like a crystal basin. "But what would it serve when you who know them so well, believed that I drew their pictures out of your own soul? Also perchance but one face would appear and that one strange to you.

"Have you heard, Allan, that among the wise some hold that not all of us is visible at once here on earth within the same house of flesh; that the whole self in its home above, separates itself into sundry parts, each of which walks the earth in different form, a segment of life's circle that can never be dissolved and must unite again at last?"

I shook my head blankly, for I had never heard anything of the sort.

"You have still much to learn, Allan, although doubtless there are some who think you wise," she went on in the same mocking voice. "Well, I hold that this doctrine is built upon a rock of truth; also," she added after studying me for a minute, "that in your case these three women do not complete that circle. I think there is a fourth who as yet is strange to you in this life, though you have known her well enough in others."

I groaned, imagining that she alluded to herself, which was foolish of me, for at once she read my mind and went on with a rather acid little laugh, "No, no, not the humble slave who sits before you, whom, as you have told me, it would please you to reject as unworthy were she brought to you in offering, as in the old days was done at the courts of the great kings of the East. O fool, fool! who hold yourself so

146

strong and do not know that if I chose, before yon shadow had moved a finger's breadth, I could bring you to my feet, praying that you might be suffered to kiss my robe, yes, just the border of my robe."

"Then I beg of you not to choose, Ayesha, since I think that when there is work to be done by both of us, we shall find more comfort side by side than if I were on the ground seeking to kiss a garment that doubtless then it would delight you to snatch away."

At these words her whole attitude seemed to change. I could see her lovely shape brace itself up, as it were, beneath her robes and felt in some way that her mind had also changed; that it had rid itself of mockery and woman's pique and like a shifting searchlight, was directed upon some new objective.

"Work to be done," she repeated after me in a new voice. "Yes, I thank you who bring it to my mind, since the hours pass and that work presses. Also I think there is a bargain to be made between us who are both of the blood that keeps bargains, even if they be not written on a roll and signed and sealed. Why do you come to me and what do you seek of me, Allan, Watcher-in-the-Night? Say it and truthfully, for though I may laugh at lies and pass them by when they have to do with the eternal sword-play which Nature decrees between man and woman, until these break apart or, casting down the swords, seek arms in which they agree too well, when they have to do with policy and high purpose and ambition's ends, why then I avenge them upon the liar."

Now I hesitated, as what I had to tell her seemed so foolish, indeed so insane, while she waited patiently as though to give me time to shape my thoughts. Speaking at last because I must, I said, "I come to ask you, Ayesha, to show me the dead, if the dead still live elsewhere."

"And who told you, Allan, that I could show you the dead, if they are not truly dead? There is but one, I think, and if you are his messenger, show me his token. Without it we do not speak together of this business."

"What token?" I asked innocently, though I guessed her meaning well enough.

She searched me with her great eyes, for I felt, and indeed saw them on me through the veil, then answered, "I think—nay, let me be sure," and half rising from the couch, she bent her heard over the tripod that I have described, and stared into what seemed to be a crystal bowl. "If I read aright," she said, straightening herself presently, "it is a hideous thing enough, the carving of an abortion of a man such as no woman would care to look on lest her babe should bear its stamp. It is a charmed thing also that has virtues for him who wears it, especially for you, Allan, since something tells me that it is dyed with the blood of one who loved you. If you have it, let it be revealed, since without it I do not talk with you of these dead you seek."

Now I drew Zikali's talisman from its hiding-place and held it towards her.

"Give it to me," she said.

I was about to obey when something seemed to warn me not to do so.

"Nay," I answered, "he who lent me this carving for a while, charged me that except in emergency and to save others, I must wear it night and day till I returned it to his hand, saying that if I parted from it fortune would desert me. I believe none of this talk and tried to be rid of it, whereon death drew near to me from a snake, such a snake as I see you wear about you, which doubtless also has poison in its fangs, if of another sort, Ayesha."

"Draw near," she said, "and let me look. Man, be not afraid."

So I rose from my chair and knelt before her, hoping secretly that no one would see me in that ridiculous position, which the most un-suspicious might misinterpret. I admit, however, that it proved to have compensations, since even through the veil I saw her marvellous eyes better than I had done before, and something of the pure outline of her classic face; also the fragrance of her hair was wonderful.

She took the talisman in her hand and examined it closely.

"I have heard of this charm and it is true that the thing has power," she said, "for I can feel it running through my veins, also that it is a shield of defence to him who wears it. Yes, and now I understand what perplexed me somewhat, namely, how it came about that when you vexed me into unveiling—but let that matter be. The wisdom was not your own, but another's, that is all. Yes, the wisdom of one whose years have borne him beyond the shafts that fly from woman's eyes, the ruinous shafts which bring men down to doom and nothingness. Tell me, Allan, is this the likeness of him who gave it to you?"

"Yes, Ayesha, the very picture, as I think, carved by himself, though he said that it is ancient, and others tell that it has been known in the land for centuries."

"So perchance has he," she answered drily, "since some of our company live long. Now tell me this wizard's names. Nay, wait awhile for I would prove that indeed you are his messenger with whom I may talk about the dead, and other things, Allan. You can read Arabic, can you not?"

"A little," I answered.

Then from a stool at her side she took paper, or rather papyrus and a reed pen, and on her knee wrote something on the sheet which she gave to me folded up.

"Now tell me the names," she said, "and then let us see if they tally with what I have written, for if so you are a true man, not a mere wanderer or a spy."

"The principal names of this doctor are Zikali, the Opener-of-Roads, the *Thing-that-should-never-have-been-born*," I answered.

"Read the writing, Allan," she said.

I unfolded the sheet and read Arabic words which meant, "Weapons, Cleaver-of-Rocks, One-at-whom-dogs-bark-and-children-wail."

"The last two are near enough," she said, "but the first is wrong."

"Nay, Ayesha, since in this man's tongue the word *Zikali* means 'Weapons'"; intelligence at which she clapped her hands as a merry girl might do. "The man," I went on, "is without doubt a great doctor, one who sees and knows things that others do not, but I do not understand why this token carved in his likeness should have power, as you say it has."

"Because with it goes his spirit, Allan. Have you never heard of the Egyptians, a very wise people who, as I remember, declared that man has a *Ka* or Double, a second self, that can either dwell in his statue or be sent afar?"

I answered that I had heard this.

"Well the *Ka* of this Zikali goes with that hideous image of him, which is perhaps why you have come safe through many dangers and why also I seemed to dream so much of him last night. Tell me now, what does Zikali want of me whose power he knows very well?"

"An oracle, the answer to a riddle, Ayesha."

"Then set it out another time. So you decide to see the dead, and this old dwarf, who is a home of wisdom, desires an oracle from one who is greater than he. Good. And what are you, or both of you, prepared to pay for these boons? Know, Allan, that I am a merchant who sells my favours dear. Tell me then, will you pay?"

"I think that it depends upon the price," I answered cautiously. "Set out the price, Ayesha."

"Be not afraid, O cunning dealer," she mocked. "I do not ask your soul or even that love of yours which you guard so jealously, since these things I could take without the asking. Nay, I ask only what a brave and honest man may give without shame: your help in war, and perhaps," she added with a softer tone, "your friendship. I think, Allan, that I like you well, perhaps because you remind me of another whom I knew long ago."

I bowed at the compliment, feeling proud and pleased at the prospect of a friendship with this wonderful and splendid creature, although I was aware that it had many dangers. Then I sat still and waited. She also waited, brooding.

"Listen," she said after a while, "I will tell you a story and when you have heard it you shall answer, even if you do not believe it, but not before. Does it please you to listen to something of the tale of my life which I am moved to tell you, that you may know with whom you have to deal?"

Again I bowed, thinking to myself that I knew nothing that would please me more, who was eaten up with a devouring curiosity about this woman.

Now she rose from her couch and descending off the dais, began to walk up and down the chamber. I say, to walk, but her movements were more like the gliding of an eagle through the air or the motion of a swan upon still water, so smooth were they and gracious. As she walked she spoke in a low and thrilling voice.

"Listen," she said again, "and even if my story seems marvellous to you, interrupt, and above all, mock me not, lest I should grow angry, which might be ill for you. I am not as other women are, O Allan, who having conquered the secrets of Nature," here I felt an intense desire to ask what secrets, but remembered and held my tongue, "to my sorrow have preserved my youth and beauty through many ages. Moreover in the past, perhaps in payment for my sins, I have lived other lives of which some memory remains with me.

"By my last birth I am an Arab lady of royal blood, a descendant of the Kings of the East. There I dwelt in the wilderness and ruled a people, and at night I gathered wisdom from the stars and the spirits of the earth and air. At length I wearied of it all and my people too wearied of me and besought me to depart, for, Allan, I would have naught to do with men, yet men went mad because of my beauty and slew each other out of jealousy. Moreover other peoples made war upon my people, hoping to take me captive that I might be a wife to their kings. So I left them, and being furnished with great wealth in hoarded gold and jewels, together with a certain holy man, my master, I wandered through the world, studying the nations and their worships. At Jerusalem I tarried and learned of Jehovah who is, or was, its God.

"At Paphos in the Isle of Chitim I dwelt a while till the folk of that city thought that I was Aphrodite returned to earth and sought to worship me. For this reason and because I made a mock of Aphrodite, I, who, as I have said, would have naught to do with men, she through

150

her priests cursed me, saying that her yoke should lie more heavily upon my neck from age to age than on that of any woman who had breathed beneath the sun.

"It was a wondrous scene," she added reflectively, "that of the cursing, since for every word I gave back two. Moreover I told the hoary villain of a high-priest to make report to his goddess that long after she was dead in the world, I would live on, for the spirit of prophecy was on me in that hour. Yet the curse fell in its season, since in her day, doubt it or not, Aphrodite had strength, as indeed under other names she has and will have while the world endures, and for aught I know, beyond it. Do they worship her now in any land, Allan?"

"No, only her statues because of their beauty, though Love is always worshipped."

"Yes, who can testify to that better than you yourself, Allan, if he who is called Zikali tells me the truth concerning you in the dreams he sends? As for the statues, I saw some of them as they left the master's hand in Greece, and when I told him that he might have found a better model, once I was that model. If this marble still endures, it must be the most famous of them all, though perchance Aphrodite has shattered it in her jealous rage. You shall tell me of these statues afterwards; mine had a mark on the left shoulder like to a mole, but the stone was imperfect, not my flesh, as I can prove if you should wish."

Thinking it better not to enter on a discussion as to Ayesha's shoulder, I remained silent and she went on.

"I dwelt in Egypt also, and there, to be rid of men who wearied me with their sighs and importunities, also to acquire more wisdom of which she was the mistress, I entered the service of the goddess Isis, Queen of Heaven, vowing to remain virgin for ever. Soon I became her high-priestess and in her most sacred shrines upon the Nile, I communed with the goddess and shared her power, since from me her daughter, she withheld none of her secrets. So it came about that though Pharaohs held the sceptre, it was I who ruled Egypt and brought it and Sidon to their fall, it matters not how or why, as it was fated that I must do. Yes, kings would come to seek counsel from me where I sat throned, dressed in the garb of Isis and breathing out her power. Yet, my task accomplished, of it all I grew weary, as men will surely do of the heavens that they preach, should they chance to find them."

I wondered what this "task" might be, but only asked, "Why?"

"Because in their pictured heaven all things lie to their hands and man, being man, cannot be happy without struggle, and woman, being woman, without victory over others. What is cheaply bought, or given, has no value, Allan; to be enjoyed, it must first be won. But I bade you not to break my thought."

I asked pardon and she went on, "Then it was that the shadow of the curse of Aphrodite fell upon me, yes, and of the curse of Isis also, so that these twin maledictions have made me what I am, a lost soul dwelling in the wilderness waiting the fulfilment of a fate whereof I know not the end. For though I have all wisdom, all knowledge of the Past and much power together with the gift of life and beauty, the future is as dark to me as night without its moon and stars.

"Hearken, this chanced to me. Though it be to my shame I tell it you that all may be clear. At a temple of Isis on the Nile where I ruled, there was a certain priest, a Greek by birth, vowed like myself to the service of the goddess and therefore to wed none but her, the goddess herself—that is, in the spirit. He was named Kallikrates, a man of courage and of beauty, such an one as those Greeks carved in the statues of their god Apollo. Never, I think, was a man more beautiful in face and form, though in soul he was not great, as often happens to men who have all else, and well-nigh always happens to women, save myself and perhaps one or two others that history tells of, doubtless magnifying their fabled charms.

"The Pharaoh of that day, the last of the native blood, him whom the Persians drove to doom, had a daughter, the Princess of Egypt, Amenartas by name, a fair woman in her fashion, though somewhat swarthy. In her youth this Amenartas became enamoured of Kallikrates and he of her, when he was a captain of the Grecian Mercenaries at Pharaoh's Court. Indeed, she brought blood upon his hands because of her, wherefore he fled to Isis for forgiveness and for peace. Thither in after time she followed him and again urged her love.

"Learning of the thing and knowing it for sacrilege, I summoned this priest and warned him of his danger and of the doom which awaited him should he continue in that path. He grew affrighted. He flung himself upon the ground before me with groans and supplications, and kissing my feet, vowed most falsely to me that his dealings with the royal Amenartas were but a veil and that it was I whom he worshipped. His unhallowed words filled me with horror and sternly I bade him begone and do penance for his crime, saying that I would pray the goddess on behalf of him.

"He went, leaving me alone lost in thought in the darkening shrine. Then sleep fell on me and in my sleep I dreamed a dream, or saw a vision. For suddenly there stood before me a woman beauteous as myself clad in nothing save a golden girdle and a veil of gossamer.

"'O Ayesha,' she said in a honeyed voice, 'priestess of Isis of the Egyptians, sworn to the barren worship of Isis and fed on the ashes of her unprofitable wisdom, know that I am Aphrodite of the Greeks whom many times thou hast mocked and defied, and Queen of the breathing world, as Isis is Queen of the world that is dead. Now because thou didst despise me and pour contempt upon my name, I smite thee with my strength and lay a curse upon thee. It is that thou shalt love and desire this man who but now hath kissed thy feet, ever longing till the world's end to kiss his lips in payment, although thou art as far above him as the moon thou servest is above the Nile. Think not that thou shalt escape my doom, for know that however strong the spirit, here upon the earth the flesh is stronger still and of all flesh I am the queen.'

"Then she laughed softly and smiting me across the eyes with a lock of her scented hair, was gone.

"Allan, I awoke from my sleep and a great trouble fell upon me, for I who had never loved before now was rent with a rage of love and for this man who till that moment had been naught to me but as some beauteous image of gold and ivory. I longed for him, my heart was racked with jealousy because of the Egyptian who favoured him, an eating flame possessed my breast. I grew mad. There in the shrine of Isis the divine I cast myself upon my knees and cried to Aphrodite to return and give me him I sought, for whose sake I would renounce all else, even if I must pour my wisdom into a beauteous, empty cup. Yes, thus I prayed and lay upon the ground and wept until, outworn, once more sleep fell upon me.

"Now in the darkness of the holy place once more there came a dream or vision, since before me in her glory stood the goddess Isis crowned with the crescent of the young moon and holding in her hand the jewelled *sistrum* that is her symbol, from which came music like to the melody of distant bells. She gazed at me and in her great eyes were scorn and anger.

"'O Ayesha, Daughter of Wisdom,' she said in a solemn voice, 'whom I, Isis, had come to look upon rather as a child than a servant, since in none other of my priestesses was such greatness to be found, and whom in a day to be I had purposed to raise to the very steps of my heavenly throne, thou hast broken thine oath and, forsaking me, hast worshipped false Aphrodite of the Greeks who is mine enemy. Yea, in the eternal war between the spirit and the flesh, thou hast chosen the part of flesh. Therefore I hate thee and add my doom to that which Aphrodite laid upon thee, which, hadst thou prayed to me and not to her, I would have lifted from thy heart.

"'Hearken! The Grecian whom thou hast chosen, by Aphrodite's will, thou shalt love as the Pathian said. More, thy love shall bring his blood upon thy hands, nor mayest thou follow him to the grave. For I will show thee the Source of Life and thou shalt drink of it to make thyself more fair even than thou art and thus outpace thy rival, and when thy lover is dead, in a desolate place thou shalt wait in grief and solitude till he is born again and find thee there.

"'Yet shall this be but the beginning of thy sorrows, since through all time thou shalt pursue thy fate till at length thou canst draw up this man to the height on which thine own soul stands by the ropes of love and loss and suffering. Moreover through it all thou shalt despise thyself, which is man's and woman's hardest lot, thou who having the rare feast of spirit spread out before thee, hast chosen to fill thyself from the troughs of flesh.'

"Then, Allan, in my dream I made a proud answer to the goddess, saying, 'Hear me, mighty mistress of many Forms who dost appear in all that lives! An evil fate has fallen upon me, but was it I who chose that fate? Can the leaf contend against the driving gale? Can the falling stone turn upwards to the sky, or when Nature draws it, can the tide cease to flow? A goddess whom I have offended, that goddess whose strength causes the whole world to be, has laid her curse upon me and because I have bent before the storm, as bend I must, or break, another goddess whom I serve, thou thyself, Mother Isis, hast added to the curse. Where then is Justice, O Lady of the Moon?'

"'Not here, Woman,' she answered. 'Yet far away Justice lives and shall be won at last and mayhap because thou art so proud and high-stomached, it is laid upon thee to seek her blinded eyes through many an age. Yet at last I think thou shalt set thy sins against her weights and find the balance even. Therefore cease from questioning the high decrees of destiny which thou canst not understand and be content to suffer, remembering that all joy grows from the root of pain. Moreover, know this for thy comfort, that the wisdom which thou hast shall grow and gather on thee and with it thy beauty and thy power; also that at the last thou shalt look upon my face again, in token whereof I leave to thee my symbol, the *sistrum* that I bear, and with it this command. Follow that false priest of mine wherever he may go and avenge me upon him, and if thou lose him there, wait while the generations pass till he return again. Such and no other is thy destiny.'

"Allan, the vision faded and when I awoke the lights of dawn played upon the image of the goddess in the sanctuary. They played, moreover, upon the holy jewelled thing that in my dream her hand had held, the *sistrum* of her worship, shaped like the loop of life, the magic symbol that she had vowed to me, wherewith goes her power, which henceforth was mine.

"I took it and followed after the priest Kallikrates, to whom thenceforward I was bound by passion's ties that are stronger than all the goddesses in this wide universe."

Here I, Allan, could contain myself no longer and asked, "What for?" then, fearing her wrath, wished that I had been silent.

But she was not angry, perhaps because this tale of her interviews with goddesses, doubtless fabled, had made her humble, for she answered quietly, "By Aphrodite, or by Isis, or both of them I did not know. All I knew was that I *must* seek him, then and evermore, as seek I do today and shall perchance through aeons yet unborn. So I followed, as I was taught and commanded, the *sistrum* being my guide, how it matters not, and giving me the means, and so at last I came to this ancient land whereof the ruin in which you sit was once known as Kôr."

## CHAPTER 14

# Allan Misses Opportunity

All the while that she was talking thus the Lady or the Queen or the Witch-woman, Ayesha, had been walking up and down the place from the curtains to the foot of the dais, sweeping me with her scented robes as she passed to and fro, and as she walked she waved her arms as an orator might do to emphasise the more moving passages of her tale. Now at the end of it, or what I took to be the end, she stepped on to the dais and sank upon the couch as if exhausted, though I think her spirit was weary rather than her body.

Here she sat awhile, brooding, her chin resting on her hand, then suddenly looked up and fixing her glance upon me—for I could see the flash of it through her thin veil—said, "What think you of this story, Allan? Do you believe it and have you ever heard its like?"

"*Never*," I answered with emphasis, "and of course I believe every word. Only there are one or two questions that with your leave I would wish to ask, Ayesha."

"By which you mean, Allan, that you believe nothing, being by nature without faith and doubtful of all that you cannot see and touch and handle. Well, perhaps you are wise, since what I have told you is not all the truth. For example, it comes back to me now that it was not in the temple on the Nile, or indeed upon the Earth, that I saw the vision of Aphrodite and of Isis, but elsewhere; also that it was here in Kôr that I was first consumed by passion for Kallikrates whom hitherto I had scorned. In two thousand years one forgets much, Allan. Out with your questions and I will answer them, unless they be too long."

"Ayesha," I said humbly, reflecting to myself that my questions would, at any rate, be shorter than her varying tale, "even I who am not learned have heard of these goddesses of whom you speak, of the Grecian Aphrodite who rose from the sea upon the shores of Cyprus and dwelt at Paphos and elsewhere——"

"Yes, doubtless like most men you have heard of her and perchance also have been struck across the eyes with her hair, like your betters before you," she interrupted with sarcasm.

"——Also," I went on, avoiding argument, "I have heard of Isis of the Egyptians, Lady of the Moon, Mother of Mysteries, Spouse of Osiris whose child was Horus the Avenger."

"Aye, and I think will hear more of her before you have done, Allan, for now something comes back to me concerning you and her and another. I am not the only one who has broken the oaths of Isis and received her curse, Allan, as *you* may find out in the days to come. But what of these heavenly queens?"

"Only this, Ayesha; I have been taught that they were but phantasms fabled by men with many another false divinity, and could have sworn that this was true. And yet you talk of them as real and living, which perplexes me."

"Being dull of understanding doubtless it perplexes you, Allan. Yet if you had imagination you might understand that these goddesses are great *principles of nature*; Isis, of throned Wisdom and strait virtue, and Aphrodite, of Love, as it is known to men and women who, being human, have it laid upon them that they must hand on the torch of Life in their little hour. Also you would know that such *principles* can seem to take shape and form and at certain ages of the world appear to their servants visible in majesty, though perchance today others with changed names wield their sceptres and work their will. Now you are answered on this matter. So to the next."

Privately I did not feel as though I were answered at all and I was sure that I know nothing of the kind she indicated, but thinking it best to leave the subject, I went on, "If I understood rightly, Ayesha, the events which you have been pleased first to describe to me, and then to qualify or contradict, took place when the Pharaohs reigned. Now no Pharaoh has sat upon the throne of Egypt for near two thousand years, for the last was a Grecian woman whom the Romans conquered and drove to death. And yet, Ayesha, you speak as though you have lived all through that gulf of time, and in this there must be error, because it is impossible. Therefore I suppose you to mean that this history has come down to you in writing, or perhaps in dreams. I believe that even in such far-off times there were writers of romance, and we all know of what stuff dreams are made. At least this thought comes to me," I added hurriedly, fearing lest I had said too much, "and one so wise as you are, I repeat, knows well that a woman who says she has lived two thousand years must be mad or—suffer from delusions, because I repeat, it is impossible."

At these quite innocent remarks she sprang to her feet in a rage that might truly be called royal in every sense.

"Impossible! Romance! Dreams! Delusions! Mad!" she cried in a ringing voice. "Oh! of a truth you weary me, and I have a mind to send you whither you will learn what is impossible and what is not. Indeed, I would do it, and now, only I need your services, and if I did there would be none left for me to talk with, since your companion is moonstruck and the others are but savages of whom I have seen enough.

"Hearken, fool! *Nothing* is impossible. Why do you seek, you who talk of the impossible, to girdle the great world in the span of your two hands and to weigh the secrets of the Universe in the balance of your petty mind and, of that which you cannot understand, to say that it is not? Life you admit because you see it all about you. But that it should endure for two thousand years, which after all is but a second's beat in the story of the earth, that to you is 'impossible,' although in truth the buried seed or the sealed-up toad can live as long. Doubtless, also, you have some faith which promises you this same boon to all eternity, after the little change called Death.

"Nay, Allan, it is possible enough, like to many other things of which you do not dream today that will be common to the eyes of those who follow after you. Mayhap you think it impossible that I should speak with and learn of you from yonder old black wizard who dwells in the country whence you came. And yet whenever I will I do so in the night because he is in tune with me, and what I do shall be done by all men in the years unborn. Yes, they shall talk together across the wide spaces of the earth, and the lover shall hear her lover's voice although great seas roll between them. Nor perchance will it stop at this; perchance in future time men shall hold converse with the denizens of the stars, and even with the dead who have passed into silence and the darkness. Do you hear and understand me?"

"Yes, yes," I answered feebly.

"You lie, as you are too prone to do. You hear but you do not understand nor believe, and oh! you vex me sorely. Now I had it in my mind to tell you the secret of this long life of mine; long, mark you, but not endless, for doubtless I must die and change and return again, like others, and even to show you how it may be won. But you are not worthy in your faithlessness."

"No, no, I am not worthy," I answered, who at that moment did not feel the least desire to live two thousand years, perhaps with this woman as a neighbour, rating me from generation to generation. Yet it is true, that now when I am older and a certain event cannot be postponed much longer, I do often regret that I neglected to take this unique chance, if in truth there was one, of prolonging an existence which after all has its consolations—especially when one has made one's pile. Certainly it is a case, a flagrant case, of neglected opportunities, and my only consolation for having lost them is that this was due to the uprightness of my nature which made it so hard for me to acquiesce in alternative statements that I had every cause to disbelieve and thus to give offence to a very powerful and petulant if attractive lady.

"So that is done with," she went on with a little stamp of indignation, "as soon you will be also, who, had you not crossed and doubted me, might have lived on for untold time and become one of the masters of the world, as I am."

Here she paused, choked, I think, with her almost childish anger, and because I could not help it, I said, "Such place and power, if they be yours, Ayesha, do not seem to bring you much reward. If I were a master of the world I do not think that I should choose to dwell unchangingly among savages who eat men and in a pile of ruins. But perhaps the curses of Aphrodite and of Isis are stronger masters still?" and I paused inquiringly.

This bold argument—for now I see that it was bold—seemed to astonish and even bewilder my wonderful companion.

"You have more wisdom than I thought," she said reflectively, "who have come to understand that no one is really lord of anything, since above there is always a more powerful lord who withers all his pomp and pride to nothingness, even as the great kings learned in olden days, and I, who am higher than they are, am learning now. Hearken. Troubles beset me wherein I would have your help and that of your companions, for which I will pay each of you the fee that he desires. The brooding white man who is with you shall free his daughter and unharmed; though that *he* will be unharmed I do not promise. The black savage captain shall fight his fill and gain the glory that he seeks, also something that he seeks still more. The little yellow man asks nothing save to be with his master like a dog and to satisfy at once his stomach and his apish curiosity. You, Allan, shall see those dead over whom you brood at night, though the other guerdon that you might have won is now passed from your reach because you mock me in your heart."

"What must we do to gain these things?" I asked. "How can we humble creatures help one who is all powerful and who has gathered in her breast the infinite knowledge of two thousand years?"

"You must make war under my banner and rid me of my foes. As for the reason, listen to the end of my tale and you shall learn."

I reflected that it was a marvellous thing that this queen who claimed supernatural powers should need our help in a war, but thinking it wiser to keep my meditations to myself, said nothing. As a matter of fact I might just as well have spoken, since as usual she read my thoughts.

"You are thinking that it is strange, Allan, that I, the Mighty and Undying, should seek your aid in some petty tribal battle, and so it would be were my foes but common savages. But they are more; they are men protected by the ancient god of this immemorial city of Kôr, a great god in his day whose spirit still haunts these ruins and whose strength still protects the worshippers who cling to him and practise his unholy rites of human sacrifice."

"How was this god named?" I asked.

"*Rezu* was his name, and from him came the Egyptian Re or Ra, since in the beginning Kôr was the mother of Egypt and the conquering people of Kôr took their god with them when they burst into the valley of the Nile and subdued its peoples long before the first Pharaoh, Menes, wore Egypt's crown."

"Ra was the sun, was he not?" I asked.

"Aye, and Rezu also was a sun-god whom from his throne in the fires of the Lord of Day, gave life to men, or slew them if he willed with his thunderbolts of drought and pestilence and storm. He was no gentle king of heaven, but one who demanded blood-sacrifice from his worshippers, yes, even that of maids and children. So it came about that the people of Kôr, who saw their virgins slain and eaten by the priests of Rezu, and their infants burned to ashes in the fires that his rays lit, turned themselves to the worship of the gentle moon, the goddess whom they named *Lulala*, while some of them chose Truth for their queen, since Truth, they said, was greater and more to be desired than the fierce Sun-King or even the sweet Moon-Lady, Truth, who sat above them both throned in the furthest stars of Heaven. Then the demon, Rezu, grew wroth and sent a pestilence upon Kôr and its subject lands and slew their people, save those who clung to him in the great apostasy, and with them some others who served Lulala and Truth the Divine, that escaped I know not how."

"Did you see this great pestilence?" I asked, much interested.

"Nay, it befell generations before I came to Kôr. One Junis, a priest, wrote a record of it in the caves yonder where I have my home and where is the burying-place of the countless thousands that it slew. In my day Kôr, of which, should you desire to hear it, I will tell you the history, was a ruin as it is now, though scattered in the lands amidst

160

the tumbled stones which once built up her subject cities, a people named the Amahagger dwelt in Households, or Tribes and there sacrificed men by fire and devoured them, following the rites of the demon Rezu. For these were the descendants of those who escaped the pestilence. Also there were certain others, children of the worshippers of Lulala whose kingdom is the moon, and of Truth the Queen, who clung to the gentle worship of their forefathers and were ever at war with the followers of Rezu."

"What brought *you* to Kôr, Ayesha?" I asked irrelevantly.

"Have I not said that I was led hither by the command and the symbol of great Isis whom I serve? Also," she added after a pause, "that I might find a certain pair, one of whom had broken his oaths to her, tempted thereto by the other."

"And did you find them, Ayesha?" I asked.

"Aye, I found them, or rather they found me, and in my presence the goddess executed her decree upon her false priest and drove his temptress back to the world."

"That must have been dreadful for you, Ayesha, since I understood that you also—liked this priest."

She sprang from her couch and in a low, hissing voice which resembled the sound made by an angry snake and turned my blood cold to hear, exclaimed, "Man, do you dare to mock me? Nay, you are but a blundering, curious fool, and it is well for you that this is so, since otherwise like Kallikrates, never should you leave Kôr living. Cease from seeking that which you may not learn. Suffice it for you to know that the doom of Isis fell upon the lost Kallikrates, her priest forsworn, and that on me also fell her doom, who must dwell here, dead yet living, till he return again and the play begins afresh.

"Stranger," she went on in a softer voice, "perchance your faith, whate'er it be, parades a hell to terrify its worshippers and give strength to the arms of its prophesying priests, who swear they hold the keys of doom or of the eternal joys. I see you sign assent" (I had nodded at her extremely accurate guess) "and therefore can understand that in such a hell as this, here upon the earth I have dwelt for some two thousand years, expiating the crime of Powers above me whereof I am but the hand and instrument, since those Powers which decreed that I should love, decree also that I must avenge that love."

She sank down upon the couch as though exhausted by emotion, of which I could only guess the reasons, hiding her face in her hands. Presently she let them fall again and continued, "Of these woes ask me no more. They sleep till the hour of their resurrection, which I think draws nigh; indeed, I thought that you perchance——But let that be. 'Twas near the mark; nearer, Allan, than you know, not in it! Therefore leave them to their sleep as I would if I might—ah! if I might, whose companions they are throughout the weary ages. Alas! that through the secret which was revealed to me I remain undying on the earth who in death might perhaps have found a rest, and being human although half divine, must still busy myself with the affairs of earth.

"Look you, Wanderer, after that which was fated had happened and I remained in my agony of solitude and sorrow, after, too, I had drunk of the cup of enduring life and like the Prometheus of old fable, found myself bound to this changeless rock, whereon day by day the vultures of remorse tear out my living heart which in the watches of the night is ever doomed to grow again within my woman's breast, I was plunged into petty troubles of the flesh, aye and welcomed them because their irk at times gave me forgetfulness. When the savage dwellers in this land came to know that a mighty one had arisen among them who was the servant of the Lady of the Moon, those of them who still worshipped their goddess Lulala, gathered themselves about me, while those of them who worshipped Rezu sought to overthrow me.

"'Here,' they said, 'is the goddess Lulala come to earth. In the name of Rezu let us slay her and make an end,' for these fools thought that I could be killed. Allan, I conquered them, but their captain, who also is named Rezu and whom they held and hold to be an emanation of the god himself walking the earth, I could not conquer."

"Why not?" I asked.

"For this reason, Allan. In some past age his god showed him the same secret that was shown to me. He too had drunk of the Cup of Life and lives on unharmed by Time, so that being in strength my equal, no spear of mine can reach his heart clad in the armour of his evil god."

"Then what spear can?" I inquired helplessly, who was bewildered.

"None at all, Allan, yet an *axe* may, as you shall hear, or so I think. For many generations there has been peace of a sort between the worshippers of Lulala who dwell with me in the Plain of Kôr, or rather of myself, since to these people *I* am Lulala, and the worshippers of Rezu, who dwell in the strongholds beyond the mountain crest. But of late years their chief Rezu, having devastated the lands about, has grown restless and threatened to attack on Kôr, which is not strong enough to stand against him. Moreover he has sought for a white queen to rule under him, purposing to set her up to mock my majesty."

"Is that why those cannibals carried away the daughter of my companion, the Sea-Captain who is named Avenger?" I asked.

"It is, Allan, since presently he will give it out that I am dead or fled, if he has not done so already, and that this new queen has arisen in my place. Thereby he hopes to draw away many who cling to me ere he advances upon Kôr, carrying with him this girl veiled as I am, so that none may know the difference between us, since not a man of them has ever looked upon my face, Allan. Therefore this Rezu must die, if die he can; otherwise, although it is impossible that he should harm me, he may slay or draw away my people and leave me with none to rule in this place where by the decree of Fate I must dwell on until he whom I seek returns. You are thinking in your heart that such savages would be little loss and this is so, but still they serve as slaves to me in my loneliness. Moreover I have sworn to protect them from the demon Rezu and they have trusted in me and therefore my honour is at stake, for never shall it be said that those who trusted in She-who-commands, were overthrown because they put faith in one who was powerless."

"What do you mean about an axe, Ayesha?" I asked. "Why can an axe alone kill Rezu?"

"The thing is a mystery, O Allan, of which I may not tell you all, since to do so I must reveal secrets which I have determined you shall not learn. Suffice it to you to know that when this Rezu drank of the Cup of Life he took with him his axe. Now this axe was an ancient weapon rumoured to have been fashioned by the gods and, as it chanced, that axe drew to itself more and stronger life than did Rezu, how, it does not matter, if indeed the tale be more than a fable. At least this I know is true, for he who guarded the Gate of Life, a certain Noot, a master of mysteries, and mine also in my day of youth, who being a philosopher and very wise, chose never to pass that portal which was open to him, said it to me himself ere he went the way of flesh. He told this Rezu also that now he had naught to fear save his own axe and therefore he counselled him to guard it well, since if it was lifted against him in another's hands it would bring him down to death, which nothing else could do. Like to the heel of Achilles whereof the great Homer sings—have you read Homer, Allan?"

"In a translation," I answered.

"Good, then you will remember the story. Like to the heel of Achilles, I say, that axe would be the only gate by which death could enter his invulnerable flesh, or rather it alone could make the gate."

"How did Noot know that?" I asked.

"I cannot say," she answered with irritation. "Perchance he did not know it. Perchance it is all an idle tale, but at least it is true that Rezu

163

believed and believes it, and what a man believes is true for him and will certainly befall. If it were otherwise, what is the use of faith which in a thousand forms supports our race and holds it from the horrors of the Pit? Only those who believe nothing inherit what they believe— nothing, Allan."

"It may be so," I replied prosaically, "but what happened about the axe?"

"In the end it was lost, or as some say stolen by a woman whom Rezu had deserted, and therefore he walks the world in fear from day to day. Nay, ask no more empty questions" (I had opened my mouth to speak) "but hear the end of the tale. In my trouble concerning Rezu I remembered this wild legend of the axe and since, when lost in a forest every path that may lead to safety should be explored, I sent my wisdom forth to make inquiry concerning it, as I who am great, have the power to do, of certain who are in tune with me through-out this wide land of Africa. Amongst others, I inquired of that old wizard whom you named Zikali, Opener of Roads, and he gave me an answer that there lived in his land a certain warrior who ruled a tribe called the People of the Axe by right of the Axe, of which axe none, not even he, knew the beginning or the legend. On the chance, though it was a small one, I bade the wizard send that warrior here with his axe. Last night he stood before me and I looked upon him and the axe, which at least is ancient and has a story. Whether it be the same that Rezu bore I do not know who never saw it, yet perchance he who bears it now is prepared to hold it aloft in battle even against Rezu, though he be terrible to see, and then we shall learn."

"Oh! yes," I answered, "he is quite prepared, for that is his nature. Also among this man's people, the holder of the Axe is thought to be unconquerable."

"Yet some must have been conquered who held it," she replied musingly. "Well, you shall tell me that tale later. Now we have talked long and you are weary and astonished. Go, eat and rest yourself. To-night when the moon rises I will come to where you are, not before, for I have much that must be done, and show you those with whom you must fight against Rezu, and make a plan of battle."

"But I do not want to fight," I answered, "who have fought enough and came here to seek wisdom, not bloodshed."

"First the sacrifice, then the reward," she answered, "that is if any are left to be rewarded. Farewell."

## CHAPTER 15

# Robertson is Lost

So I went and was conducted by Billali, the old chamberlain, for such seemed to be his office, who had been waiting patiently without all this while, back to our rest-house. On my way I picked up Hans, whom I found sitting outside the arch, and found that as usual that worthy had been keeping his eyes and ears open.

"Baas," he said, "did the White Witch tell you that there is a big *impi* encamped over yonder outside the houses, in what looks like a great dry ditch, and on the edge of the plain beyond?"

"No, Hans, but she said that this evening she would show us those in whose company we must fight."

"Well, Baas, they are there, some thousands of them, for I crept through the broken walls like a snake and saw them. And, Baas, I do not think they are men, I think that they are evil spirits who walk at night only."

"Why, Hans?"

"Because when the sun is high, Baas, as it is now, they are all sleeping. Yes, there they lie abed, fast asleep, as other people do at night, with only a few sentries out on guard, and these are yawning and rubbing their eyes."

"I have heard that there are folk like that in the middle of Africa where the sun is very hot, Hans," I answered, "which perhaps is why She-who-commands is going to take us to see them at night. Also these people, it seems, are worshippers of the moon."

"No, Baas, they are worshippers of the devil and that White Witch is his wife."

"You had better keep your thoughts to yourself, Hans, for whatever she is I think that she can read thoughts from far away, as you guessed last night. Therefore I would not have any if I were you."

"No, Baas, or if I must think, henceforth, it shall be only of gin which in this place is also far away," he replied, grinning.

Then we came to the rest-house where I found that Robertson had already eaten his midday meal and like the Amahagger gone to sleep, while apparently Umslopogaas had done the same; at least I saw nothing of him. Of this I was glad, since that wondrous Ayesha seemed to draw vitality out of me and after my long talk with her I felt very tired. So I too ate and then went to lie down under an old wall in the shade at a little distance, and to reflect upon the marvellous things that I had heard.

Here be it said at once that I believed nothing of them, or at least very little indeed. All the involved tale of Ayesha's long life I dismissed at once as incredible. Clearly she was some beautiful woman who was more or less mad and suffered from megalomania; probably an Arab, who had wandered to this place for reasons of her own, and become the chieftainess of a savage tribe whose traditions she had absorbed and reproduced as personal experiences, again for reasons of her own.

For the rest, she was now threatened by another tribe and knowing that we had guns and could fight from what happened on the yesterday, wished naturally enough for our assistance in the coming battle. As for the marvellous chief Rezu, or rather for his supernatural attributes and all the cock-and-bull story about an axe—well, it was humbug like the rest, and if she believed in it she must be more foolish than I took her to be—even if she were unhinged on certain points. For the rest, her information about myself and Umslopogaas doubtless had reached her from Zikali in some obscure fashion, as she herself acknowledged.

But heavens! how beautiful she was! That flash of loveliness when out of pique or coquetry she lifted her veil, blinded like the lightning. But thank goodness, also like the lightning it frightened; instinctively one felt that it was very dangerous, even to death, and with it I for one wished no closer acquaintance. Fire may be lovely and attractive, also comforting at a proper distance, but he who sits on the top of it is cremated, as many a moth has found.

So I argued, knowing well enough all the while that if this particular human—or inhuman—fire desired to make an holocaust of me, it could do so easily enough, and that in reality I owed my safety so far to a lack of that desire on its part. The glorious Ayesha saw nothing to attract her in an insignificant and withered hunter, or at any rate in his exterior, though with his mind she might find some small affinity. Moreover to make a fool of him just for the fun of it would not serve her purpose, since she needed his assistance in a business that necessitated clear wits and unprejudiced judgment.

Lastly she had declared herself to be absorbed in some tiresome complication with another man, of which it was rather difficult to follow the details. It is true that she described him as a handsome but somewhat empty-headed person whom she had last seen two thousand years ago, but probably this only meant that she thought poorly of him because he had preferred some other woman to herself, while the two thousand years were added to the tale to give it atmosphere.

The worst of scandals becomes romantic and even respectable in two thousand years; witness that of Cleopatra with Caesar, Mark Antony and other gentlemen. The most virtuous read of Cleopatra with sympathy, even in boarding-schools, and it is felt that were she by some miracle to be blotted out of the book of history, the loss would be enormous. The same applied to Helen, Phryne, and other bad lots. In fact now that one comes to think of it, most of the attractive personages in history, male or female, especially the latter, were bad lots. When we find someone to whose name is added "the good" we skip. No doubt Ayesha, being very clever, appreciated this regrettable truth, and therefore moved her murky entanglements of the past decade or so back for a couple of thousand years, as many of us would like to do.

There remained the very curious circumstance of her apparent correspondence with old Zikali who lived far away. This, however, after all was not inexplicable. In the course of a great deal of experience I have observed that all the witch-doctor family, to which doubtless she belonged, have strange means of communication.

In most instances these are no doubt physical, carried on by help of messengers, or messages passed from one to the other. But sometimes it is reasonable to assume what is known as telepathy, as their link of intercourse. Between two such highly developed experts as Ayesha and Zikali, it might for the sake of argument safely be supposed that it was thus they learned each other's mind and co-operated in each other's projects, though perhaps this end was effected by commoner methods.

Whatever its interpretations, the issue of the business seemed to be that I was to be let in for more fighting. Well, in any case this could not be avoided, since Robertson's daughter, Inez, had to be saved at all costs, if it could possibly be done, even if we lost our lives in the attempt. Therefore fight we must, so there was nothing more to be said. Also without doubt this adventure was particularly interesting and I could only hope that good luck, or Zikali's Great Medicine, or rather Providence, would see me through it safely.

For the rest the fact that our help was necessary to her in this war-like venture showed me clearly enough that all this wonderful woman's pretensions to supernatural powers were the sheerest nonsense. Had they been otherwise she would not have needed our help in her tribal fights, notwithstanding the rubbish she talked about the chief, Rezu, who according to her account of him, must resemble one of the fabulous "trolls," half-human and half-ghostly evil creatures, of whom I have read in the Norse Sagas, who could only be slain by some particular hero armed with a particular weapon.

********

Reflecting thus I went to sleep and did not wake until the sun was setting. Finding that Hans was also sleeping at my feet just like a faithful dog, I woke him up and we went back together to the rest-house, which we reached as the darkness fell with extraordinary swiftness, as it does in those latitudes, especially in a place surrounded by cliffs.

Not finding Robertson in the house, I concluded that he was somewhere outside, possibly making a reconnaissance on his own account, and told Hans to get supper ready for both of us. While he was doing so, by aid of the Amahagger lamps, Umslopogaas suddenly appeared in the circle of light, and looking about him, said, "Where is Red-Beard, Macumazahn?"

I answered that I did not know and waited, for I felt sure that he had something to say.

"I think that you had better keep Red-Beard close to you, Macumazahn," he went on. "This afternoon, when you had returned from visiting the white doctoress and having eaten, had gone to sleep under the wall yonder, I saw Red-Beard come out of the house carrying a gun and a bag of cartridges. His eyes rolled wildly and he turned first this way and then that, sniffing at the air, like a buck that scents danger. Then he began to talk aloud in his own tongue and as I saw that he was speaking with his Spirit, as those do who are mad, I went away and left him."

"Why?" I asked.

"Because, as you know, Macumazahn, it is a law among us Zulus never to disturb one who is mad and engaged in talking with his Spirit. Moreover, had I done so, probably he would have shot me, nor should I have complained who would have thrust myself in where I had no right to be."

"Then why did you not come to call me, Umslopogaas?"

"Because then he might have shot you, for, as I have seen for some time he is inspired of heaven and knows not what he does upon the earth, thinking only of the Lady Sad-Eyes who has been stolen away from him, as is but natural. So I left him walking up and down, and when I returned later to look, saw that he was gone, as I thought into this walled hut. Now when Hansi tells me that he is not here, I have come to speak to you about him."

"No, certainly he is not here," I said, and I went to look at the bed where Robertson slept to see if it had been used that evening.

Then for the first time I saw lying on it a piece of paper torn from a pocketbook and addressed to myself. I seized and read it. It ran thus:

> The merciful Lord has sent me a vision of Inez and shown me where she is over the cliff-edge away to the west, also the road to her. In my sleep I heard her talking to me. She told me that she is in great danger—that they are going to marry her to some brute—and called to me to come at once and save her; yes, and to come alone without saying anything to anyone. So I am going at once. Don't be frightened or trouble about me. All will be well, all will be quite well. I will tell you the rest when we meet.

Horror-struck I translated this insane screed to Umslopogaas and Hans. The former nodded gravely.

"Did I not tell you that he was talking with his Spirit, Macumazahn?" (I had rendered "the merciful Lord" as the Good Spirit.) "Well, he has gone and doubtless his Spirit will take care of him. It is finished."

"At any rate we cannot, Baas," broke in Hans, who I think feared that I might send him out to look for Robertson. "I can follow most spoors, but not on such a night as this when one could cut the blackness into lumps and build a wall of it."

"Yes," I answered, "he has gone and nothing can be done at present," though to myself I reflected that probably he had not gone far and would be found when the moon rose, or at any rate on the following morning.

Still I was most uneasy about the man who, as I had noted for a long while, was losing his balance more and more. The shock of the barbarous and dreadful slaughter of his half-breed children and of the abduction of Inez by these grim, man-eating savages began the business, and I think that it was increased and accentuated by his sudden conversion to complete temperance after years of heavy drinking.

When I persuaded him to this course I was very proud of myself, thinking that I had done a clever thing, but now I was not so sure. Perhaps it would have been better if he had continued to drink something, at any rate for a while, but the trouble is that in such cases there is generally no half-way house. A man, or still more a woman, given to this frailty either turns aggressively sober or remains very drunken. At any rate, even if I had made a mess of it, I had acted for the best and could not blame myself.

For the rest it was clear that in his new phase the religious associations of his youth had re-asserted themselves with remarkable vigour, for I gathered that he had been brought up almost as a Calvinist, and in the rush of their return, had overset his equilibrium. As I have said, he prayed night and day without any of those reserves which most people prefer in their religious exercises, and when he talked of matters outside our quest, his conversation generally revolved round the devil, or hell and its torments, which, to say the truth, did not make him a cheerful companion. Indeed in this respect I liked him much better in his old, unregenerate days, being, I fear, myself a somewhat worldly soul.

Well, the sum of it was that the poor fellow had gone mad and given us the slip, and as Hans said, to search for him at once in that darkness was impossible. Indeed, even if it had been lighter, I do not think that it would have been safe among these Amahagger night birds whom I did not trust. Certainly I could not have asked Hans to undertake the task, and if I had, I do not think he would have gone since he was afraid of the Amahagger. Therefore there was nothing to be done except wait and hope for the best.

So I waited till at last the moon came and with it Ayesha, as she had promised. Clad in a rich, dark cloak she arrived in some pomp, heralded by Billali, followed by women, also cloaked, and surrounded by a guard of tall spearmen. I was seated outside the house, smoking, when suddenly she arrived from the shadows and stood before me.

I rose respectfully and bowed, while Umslopogaas, Goroko and the other Zulus who were with me, gave her the royal salute, and Hans cringed like a dog that is afraid of being kicked.

After a swift glance at them, as I guessed by the motion of her veiled head, she seemed to fix her gaze upon my pipe that evidently excited her curiosity, and asked me what it was. I explained as well as I could, expatiating on the charms of smoking.

"So men have learned another useless vice since I left the world, and one that is filthy also," she said, sniffing at the smoke and waving her hand before her face, whereon I dropped the pipe into my pocket, where, being alight, it burnt a hole in my best remaining coat.

I remember the remark because it showed me what a clever actress she was who, to keep up her character of antiquity, pretended to be astonished at a habit with which she must have been well acquainted, although I believe that it was unknown in the ancient world.

"You are troubled," she went on, swiftly changing the subject, "I read it in your face. One of your company is missing. Who is it? Ah! I see, the white man you name Avenger. Where is he gone?"

"That is what I wish to ask you, Ayesha," I said.

"How can I tell you, Allan, who in this place lack any glass into which to look for things that pass afar. Still, let me try," and pressing her hands to her forehead, she remained silent for perhaps a minute, then spoke slowly.

"I think that he has gone over the mountain lip towards the worshippers of Rezu. I think that he is mad; sorrow and something else which I do not understand have turned his brain; something that has to do with the Heavens. I think also that we shall recover him living, if only for a little while, though of this I cannot be sure since it is not given to me to read the future, but only the past, and sometimes the things that happen in the present though they be far away."

"Will you send to search for him, O Ayesha?" I asked anxiously.

"Nay, it is useless, for he is already distant. Moreover those who went might be taken by the outposts of Rezu, as perchance has happened to your companion wandering in his madness. Do you know what he went to seek?"

"More or less," I answered and translated to her the letter that Robertson had left for me.

"It may be as the man writes," she commented, "since the mad often see well in their dreams, though these are not sent by a god as he imagines. The mind in its secret places knows all things, O Allan, although it seems to know little or nothing, and when the breath of vision or the fury of a soul distraught blows away the veils or burns through the gates of distance, then for a while it sees and learns, since, whatever fools may think, often madness is true wisdom. Now follow me with the little yellow man and the Warrior of the Axe. Stay, let me look upon that axe."

I interpreted her wish to Umslopogaas who held it out to her but refused to loose it from his wrist to which it was attached by the leathern thong.

"Does the Black One think that I shall cut him down with his own weapon, I who am so weak and gentle?" she asked, laughing.

"Nay, Ayesha, but it is his law not to part with this Drinker of Lives, which he names 'Chieftainess and Groan-maker,' and clings to closer by day and night than a man does to his wife."

"There he is wise, Allan, since a savage captain may get more wives but never such another axe. The thing is ancient," she added musingly after examining its every detail, "and who knows? It may be that whereof the legend tells which is fated to bring Rezu to the dust. Now ask this fierce-eyed Slayer whether, armed with his axe he can find courage to face the most terrible of all men and the strongest, one who is a wizard also, of whom it is prophesied that only by such an axe as this can he be made to bite the dust."

I obeyed. Umslopogaas laughed grimly and answered, "Say to the White Witch that there is no man living upon the earth whom I would not face in war, I who have never been conquered in fair fight, though once a chance blow brought me to the doors of death," and he touched the great hole in his forehead. "Say to her also that I have no fear of defeat, I from whom doom is, as I think, still far away, though the Opener-of-Roads has told me that among a strange people I shall die in war at last, as I desire to do, who from my boyhood have lived in war."

"He speaks well," she answered with a note of admiration in her voice. "By Isis, were he but white I would set him to rule these Amahagger under me. Tell him, Allan, that if he lays Rezu low he shall have a great reward."

"And tell the White Witch, Macumazahn," Umslopogaas replied when I had translated, "that I seek no reward, save glory only, and with it the sight of one who is lost to me but with whom my heart still dwells, if indeed this Witch has strength to break the wall of blackness that is built between me and her who is 'gone down.'"

"Strange," reflected Ayesha when she understood, "that this grim Destroyer should yet be bound by the silken bonds of love and yearn for one whom the grave has taken. Learn from it, Allan, that all humanity is cast in the same mould, since my longings and your longings are his also, though the three of us be far apart as are the sun and the moon and the earth, and as different in every other quality. Yet it is true that sun and moon and earth are born of the same black womb of chaos. Therefore in the beginning they were identical, as doubtless they will be in the end when, their journeyings done, they rush together to light space with a flame at which the mocking gods that made them may warm their hands. Well, so it is with men, Allan, whose soul-stuff is drawn from the gulf of Spirit by Nature's hand, and, cast upon the cold air of this death-driven world, freezes into a million shapes each different to the other and yet, be sure, the same. Now talk no more, but follow me. Slave" (this was addressed to Billali), "bid the guards lead on to the camp of the servants of Lulala."

So we went through the silent ruins. Ayesha walked, or rather glided a pace or two ahead, then came Umslopogaas and I side by side, while at our heels followed Hans, very close at our heels since he did not wish to be out of reach of the virtue of the Great Medicine and incidentally of the protection of axe and rifle.

Thus we marched surrounded by the solemn guard for something between a quarter and half a mile, till at length we climbed the debris of a mighty wall that once had encompassed the city, and by the moonlight saw beneath us a vast hollow which clearly at some unknown time had been the bed of an enormous moat and filled with water.

Now, however, it was dry and all about its surface were dotted numerous camp-fires round which men were moving, also some women who appeared to be engaged in cooking food. At a little distance too, upon the further edge of the moat-like depression were a number of white-robed individuals gathered in a circle about a large stone upon which something was stretched that resembled the carcase of a sheep or goat, and round these a great number of spectators.

"The priests of Lulala who make sacrifice to the moon, as they do night by night, save when she is dead," said Ayesha, turning back towards me as though in answer to the query which I had conceived but left unuttered.

What struck me about the whole scene was its extraordinary animation and briskness. All the folk round the fires and outside of them moved about quickly and with the same kind of liveliness which might animate a camp of more natural people at the rising of the sun. It was as though they had just got up full of vigour to commence their daily, or rather their nightly round, which in truth was the case, since as Hans discovered, by habitude these Amahagger preferred to sleep during the day unless something prevented them, and to carry on the activities of life at night. It only remains to add that there seemed to be a great number of them, for their fires following the round of the dry moat, stretched further than I could see.

Scrambling down the crumpled wall by a zigzag pathway, we came upon the outposts of the army beneath us who challenged, then seeing with whom they had to do, fell flat upon their faces, leaving their great spears, which had iron spikes on their shafts like to those of the Masai, sticking in the ground beside them.

We passed on between some of the fires and I noted how solemn and gloomy, although handsome, were the countenances of the folk by whom these were surrounded. Indeed, they looked like denizens of a different world to ours, one alien to the kindly race of men. There was nothing social about these Amahagger, who seemed to be a people labouring under some ancient ancestral curse of which they could never shake off the memory. Even the women rarely smiled; their clear-cut, stately countenances remained stern and set, except when they glowered at us incuriously. Only when Ayesha passed they prostrated themselves like the rest.

We went on through them and across the moat, climbing its further slope and here suddenly came upon a host of men gathered in a hollow square, apparently in order to receive us. They stood in ranks of five or six deep and their spear-points glimmering in the moonlight looked like long bands of level steel. As we entered the open side of the square all these spears were lifted. Thrice they were lifted and at each uplifting there rose a deep-throated cry of *Hiya*, which is the Arabic for She, and I suppose was a salutation to Ayesha.

She swept on taking no heed, till we came to the centre of the square where a number of men were gathered who prostrated themselves in the usual fashion. Motioning to them to rise she said, "Captains, this very night within two hours we march against Rezu and the sun-worshippers, since otherwise as my arts tell me, they march against us. She-who-commands is immortal, as your fathers have known from generation to generation, and cannot be destroyed; but you, her servants, can be destroyed, and Rezu, who also has drunk of the Cup of Life, out-numbers you by three to one and prepares a queen to set up in my place over his own people and such of you as remain. As though," she added with a contemptuous laugh, "any woman of a day could take my place."

She paused and the spokesman of the captains said, "We hear, O Hiya, and we understand. What wouldst thou have us do, O Lulala-come-to-earth? The armies of Rezu are great and from the beginning he has hated thee and us, also his magic is as thy magic and his length of days as thy length of days. How then can we who are few, three thousand men at the most, match ourselves against Rezu, Son of the Sun? Would it not be better that we should accept the terms of Rezu, which are light, and acknowledge him as our king?"

As she heard these words I saw the tall shape of Ayesha quiver beneath her robes, as I think, not with fear but with rage, because the meaning of them was clear enough, namely that rather than risk a battle with Rezu, these people were contemplating surrender and her own deposition, if indeed she could be deposed. Still she answered in a quiet voice, "It seems that I have dealt too gently with you and with your fathers, Children of Lulala, whose shadow I am here upon the earth, so that because you only see the scabbard, you have forgotten the sword within and that it can shine forth and smite. Well, why should I be wrath because the brutish will follow the law of brutes, though it be true that I am minded to slay you where you stand? Hearken! Were I less merciful I would leave you to the clutching hands of Rezu, who would drag you one by one to the stone of sacrifice and there offer up your hearts to his god of fire and devour your bodies with his heat. But I bethink me of your wives and children and of your forefathers whom I knew in the dead days, and therefore, if I may, I still would save you from yourselves and your heads from the glowing pot.

"Take counsel together now and say—Will you fight against Rezu, or will you yield? If that is your desire, speak it, and by tomorrow's sun I will begone, taking these with me," and she pointed to us, "whom I have summoned to help us in the war. Aye, I will begone, and when you are stretched upon the stone of sacrifice, and your women and children are the slaves of the men of Rezu, then shall you cry, "'Oh, where is Hiya whom our fathers knew? Oh, will she not return and save us from this hell?'

"Yes, so shall you cry but there shall come no answer, since then she will have departed to her own habitations in the moon and thence appear no more. Now consult together and answer swiftly, since I weary of you and your ways."

The captains drew apart and began to talk in low voices, while Ayesha stood still, apparently quite unconcerned, and I considered the situation.

It was obvious to me that these people were almost in rebellion against their strange ruler, whose power over them was of a purely moral nature, one that emanated from her personality alone. What I wondered was, being what she seemed to be, why she thought it worth while to exercise it at all. Then I remembered her statement that here and nowhere else she must abide for some secret reason, until a certain mystical gentleman with a Greek name came to fetch her away from this appointed *rendezvous*. Therefore I supposed she had no choice, or rather, suffering as she did from hallucinations, believed herself to have no choice and was obliged to put up with a crowd of disagreeable savages in quarters which were sadly out of repair.

Presently the spokesman returned, saluted with his spear, and asked, "If we go up to fight against Rezu, who will lead us in the battle, O Hiya?"

"My wisdom shall be your guide," she answered, "this white man shall be your General and there stands the warrior who shall meet Rezu face to face and bring him to the dust," and she pointed to Umslopogaas leaning upon his axe and watching them with a contemptuous smile.

This reply did not seem to please the man for he withdrew to consult again with his companions. After a debate which I suppose was animated for the Amahagger, men of few words who did not indulge in oratory, all of them advanced on us and the spokesman said, "The choice of a General does not please us, Hiya. We know that the white man is brave because of the fight he made against the men of Rezu over the mountain yonder; also that he and his followers have weapons that deal death from afar. But there is a prophecy among us of which none know the beginning, that he who commands in the last great battle between Lulala and Rezu must produce before the eyes of the People of Lulala a certain holy thing, a charm of power, without which defeat will be the portion of Lulala. Of this holy thing, this spirit-haunted shape of power, we know the likeness and the fashion, for these have come down among our priests, though who told it to them we cannot tell, but of it I will say this only, that it speaks both of the spirit and the body, of man and yet of more than man."

"And if this wondrous charm, this talisman of might, cannot be shown by the white lord here, what then?" asked Ayesha coldly.

"Then, Hiya, this is the word of the People of Lulala, that we will not serve under him in the battle, and this also is their word that we will not go up against Rezu. That thou art mighty we know well, Hiya, also that thou canst slay if thou wilt, but we know also that Rezu is mightier and that against him thou hast no power. Therefore kill us if thou dost so desire, until thy heart is satisfied with death. For it is better that we should perish thus than upon the altar of sacrifice wearing the red-hot crowns of Rezu."

"So say we all," exclaimed the rest of the company when he had finished.

"The thought comes to me to begin to satisfy my heart with thy coward blood and that of thy companions," said Ayesha contemptuously. Then she paused and turning to me, added, "O Watcher-by-Night, what counsel? Is there aught that will convince these chicken-hearted ones over whom I have spread my feathers for so long?"

I shook my head blankly, whereat they murmured together and made as though they would go.

Then it was that Hans, who understood something of Arabic as he did of most African tongues, pulled my sleeve and whispered in my ear.

"The Great Medicine, Baas! Show them Zikali's Great Medicine."

Here was an idea. The description of the article required, a "spirit-haunted shape of power" that spoke "both of the spirit and the body of man and yet of more than man," was so vague that it might mean anything or nothing. And yet——

I turned to Ayesha and prayed her to ask them if what they wanted should be produced, whether they would follow me bravely and fight Rezu to the death. She did so and with one voice they replied, "Aye, bravely and to the death, him and the Bearer of the Axe of whom also our legend tells."

Then with deliberation I opened my shirt and holding out the image of Zikali as far as the chain of elephant hair would allow, I asked, "Is this the holy thing, the charm of power, of which your legend tells, O People of the Amahagger and worshippers of Lulala?"

The spokesman glanced at it, then snatching a brand from a watch-fire that burnt near by held it over the carving and stared, and stared again; and as he did, so did the others bending over him.

"Dog! would you singe my beard?" I cried in affected rage, and seizing the brand from his hand I smote him with it over the head.

But he took no heed of the affront which I had offered to him merely to assert my authority. Still for a few moments he stared although the sparks from the wood were frizzling in his greasy hair, then of a sudden went down on his face before me, as did all the others and cried out, "It is the Holy Thing! It is the spirit-haunted Shape of Power itself, and we the Worshippers of Lulala will follow thee to the death, O white lord, Watcher-by-Night. Yes, where thou goest and he goes who bears the Axe, thither will we follow till not one of us is left upon his feet."

"Then that's settled," I said, yawning, since it is never wise to show concern about anything before savages. Indeed personally I had no wish to be the leader of this very peculiar tribe in an adventure of which I knew nothing, and therefore had hoped that they would leave that honour to someone else. Then I turned and told Umslopogaas what had passed, a tale at which he only shrugged his great shoulders, handling his axe as though he were minded to try its edge upon some of these "Dark-lovers," as he named the Amahagger people because of their nocturnal habits.

Meanwhile Ayesha gave certain orders. Then she came to me and said, "These men march at once, three thousand strong, and by dawn will camp on the northern mountain crest. At sunrise litters will come to bear you and those with you if they will, to join them, which you should do by midday. In the afternoon marshal them as you think wise, for the battle will take place in the small hours of the following morning, since the People of Lulala only fight at night. I have said."

"Do you not come with us?" I asked, dismayed.

"Nay, not in a war against Rezu, why it matters not. Yet my Spirit will go with you, for I shall watch all that passes, how it matters not and perchance you may see it there—I know not. On the third day from tomorrow we shall meet again in the flesh or beyond it, but as I think in the flesh, and you can claim the reward which you journeyed here to seek. A place shall be prepared for the white lady whom Rezu would have set up as a rival queen to me. Farewell, and farewell also to yonder Bearer of the Axe that shall drink the blood of Rezu, also to the little yellow man who is rightly named Light-in-Darkness, as you shall learn ere all is done."

Then before I could speak she turned and glided away, swiftly surrounded by her guards, leaving me astonished and very uncomfortable.

# Allan's Vision

The old chamberlain, Billali, conducted us back to our camp. As we went he discoursed to me of these Amahagger, of whom it seemed he was himself a developed specimen, one who threw back, perhaps tens of generations, to some superior ancestor who lived before they became debased. In substance he told me that they were a wild and lawless lot who lived amongst ruins or in caves, or some of them in swamp dwellings, in small separate communities, each governed by its petty headman who was generally a priest of their goddess Lulala.

Originally they and the people of Rezu were the same, in times when they worshipped the sun and the moon jointly, but "thousands of years" ago, as he expressed it, they had separated, the Rezuites having gone to dwell to the north of the Great Mountain, whence they continually threatened the Lulalaites whom, had it not been for She-who-commands, they would have destroyed long before. The Rezuites, it seemed, were habitual cannibals, whereas the Lulalaite branch of the Amahagger only practised cannibalism occasionally when by a lucky chance they got hold of strangers. "Such as yourself, Watcher-by-Night, and your companions," he added with meaning. If their crime were discovered, however, Hiya, She-who-commands, punished it by death.

I asked if she exercised an active rule over these people. He answered that she did not, as she lacked sufficient interest in them; only when she was angry with individuals she would destroy some of them by "her arts," as she had power to do if she chose. Most of them indeed had never seen her and only knew of her existence by rumour. To them she was a spirit or a goddess who inhabited the ancient tombs that lay to the south of the old city whither she had come because of the threatened war with Rezu, whom alone she feared, he did not know why. He told me again, moreover, that she was the greatest magician who had ever been, and that it was certain she did not die, since their forefathers knew her generations ago. Still she seemed to be under some curse, like the Amahagger themselves, who were the descendants of those who had once inhabited Kôr and the country round it, as far as the sea-coast and for hundreds of miles inland, having been a mighty people in their day before a great plague destroyed them.

For the rest he thought that she was a very unhappy woman who "lived with her own soul mourning the dead" and consorting with none upon the earth.

I asked him why she stayed here, whereat he shook his head and replied, he supposed because of the "curse," since he could conceive of no other reason. He informed me also that her moods varied very much. Sometimes she was fierce and active and at others by comparison mild and low-spirited. Just now she was passing through one of the latter stages, perhaps because of the Rezu trouble, for she did not wish her people to be destroyed by this terrible person; or perhaps for some other reason with which he was not acquainted.

When she chose, she knew all things, except the distant future. Thus she knew that we were coming, also the details of our march and that we should be attacked by the Rezuites who were going out to meet their returning company that had been sent afar to find a white queen. Therefore she had ordered him to go with soldiers to our assistance. I asked why she went veiled, and he replied, because of her beauty which drove even savage men mad, so that in old days she had been obliged to kill a number of them.

That was all he seemed to know about her, except that she was kind to those who served her well, like himself, and protected them from evil of every sort.

Then I asked him about Rezu. He answered that he was a dreadful person, undying, it was said, like She-who-commands, though he had never seen the man himself and never wanted to do so. His followers being cannibals and having literally eaten up all those that they could reach, were now desirous of conquering the people of Lulala that they might eat them also at their leisure. Each other they did not eat, because dog does not eat dog, and therefore they were beginning to grow hungry, although they had plenty of grain and cattle of which they used the milk and hides.

As for the coming battle, he knew nothing about it or what would happen, save that She-who-commands said that it would go well for the Lulalaites under my direction. She was so sure that it would go well, that she did not think it worth while to accompany the army, for she hated noise and bloodshed.

It occurred to me that perhaps she was afraid that she too would be taken captive and eaten, but I kept my reflection to myself.

Just then we arrived at our camp-house, where Billali bade me farewell, saying that he wished to rest as he must be back at dawn with litters, when he hoped to find us ready to start. Then he departed. Umslopogaas and Hans also went away to sleep, leaving me alone who, having taken my repose in the afternoon, did not feel drowsy at the moment. So lovely was the night indeed that I made up my mind to take a little walk during the midnight hours, after the manner of the Amahagger themselves, for having now been recognised as Generalissimo of their forces, I had little fear of being attacked, especially as I carried a pistol in my pocket. So off I set strolling slowly down what seemed to have been a main street of the ancient city, which in its general appearance resembled excavated Pompeii, only on an infinitely larger scale.

As I went I meditated on the strange circumstances in which I found myself. Really they tempted me to believe that I was suffering from delusions and perhaps all the while in fact lay stretched upon a bed in the delirium of fever. That marvellous woman, for instance— even rejecting her tale of miraculously extended life, which I did— what was I to make of her? I did not know, except that wondrous as she was, it remained clear that she claimed a great deal more power than she possessed. This was evident from her tone in the interview with the captains, and from the fact that she had shuffled off the command of her tribe on to my shoulders. If she were so mighty, why did she not command it herself and bring her celestial, or infernal, powers to bear upon the enemy? Again, I could not say, but one fact emerged, namely that she was as interesting as she was beautiful, and uncommonly clever into the bargain.

But what a task was this that she had laid upon me, to lead into battle, with a foe of unascertained strength, a mob of savages probably quite undisciplined, of whose fighting qualities I knew nothing and whom I had no opportunity of organising. The affair seemed madness and I could only hope that luck or destiny would take me through somehow.

To tell the truth, I believed it would, for I had grown almost as superstitious about Zikali and his Great Medicine as was Hans himself. Certainly the effect of it upon those captains was very odd, or would have been had not the explanation come to me in a flash. On the first night of our meeting, as I have described, I showed this talisman to Ayesha, as a kind of letter of credentials, and now I could see that it was she who had arranged all the scene with the captains, or their tribal magician, in order to get her way about my appointment to the command.

Everything about her conduct bore this out, even her feigning ignorance of the existence of the charm and the leaving of it to Hans to suggest its production, which perhaps she did by influencing his mind subconsciously. No doubt more or less it fitted in with one of those nebulous traditions which are so common amongst ancient savage races, and therefore once shown to her confederate, or confederates, would be accepted by the common people as a holy sign, after which the rest was easy.

Such an obvious explanation involved the death of any illusions I might still cherish about this Arab lady, Ayesha, and it is true that I parted with them with regret, as we all do when we think we have discovered something wonderful in the female line. But there it was, and to bother any more about her, her history and aims, seemed useless.

So dismissing her and all present anxieties from my mind, I began to look about me and to wonder at the marvellous scene which unfolded itself before me in the moonlight. That I might see it better, although I was rather afraid of snakes which might hide among the stones, by an easy ascent I climbed a mount of ruins and up the broad slope of a tumbled massive wall, which from its thickness I judged must have been that of some fort or temple. On the crest of this wall, some seventy or eighty feet above the level of the streets, I sat down and looked about me.

Everywhere around me stretched the ruins of the great city, now as fallen and as deserted as Babylon herself. The majestic loneliness of the place was something awful. Even the vision of companies and battalions of men crossing the plain towards the north with the moonlight glistening on their spear-points, did little to lessen this sense of loneliness. I knew that these were the regiments which I was destined to command, travelling to the camp where I must meet them. But in such silence did they move that no sound came from them even in the deathly stillness of the perfect night, so that almost I was tempted to believe them to be the shadow-ghosts of some army of old Kôr.

They vanished, and musing thus I think I must have dozed. At any rate it seemed to me that of a sudden the city was as it had been in the days of its glory. I saw it brilliant with a hundred colours; everywhere was colour, on the painted walls and roofs, the flowering trees that lined the streets and the bright dresses of the men and women who by thousands crowded them and the marts and squares. Even the chariots that moved to and fro were coloured as were the countless banners which floated from palace walls and temple tops.

The enormous place teemed with every activity of life; brides being borne to marriage and dead men to burial; squadrons marching, clad in glittering armour; merchants chaffering; white-robed priests and priestesses passing in procession (who or what did they worship? I wondered); children breaking out of school; grave philosophers debating in the shadow of a cool arcade; a royal person making a progress preceded by runners and surrounded by slaves, and lastly the multitudes of citizens going about the daily business of life.

Even details were visible, such as those of officers of the law chasing an escaped prisoner who had a broken rope tied to his arm, and a collision between two chariots in a narrow street, about the wrecks of which an idle mob gathered as it does today if two vehicles collide, while the owners argued, gesticulating angrily, and the police and grooms tried to lift a fallen horse on to its feet. Only no sound of the argument or of anything else reached me. I saw, and that was all. The silence remained intense, as well it might do, since those chariots must have come to grief thousands upon thousands of years ago.

A cloud seemed to pass before my eyes, a thin, gauzy cloud which somehow reminded me of the veil that Ayesha wore. Indeed at the moment, although I could not see her, I would have sworn that she was present at my side, and what is more, that she was mocking me who had set her down as so impotent a trickstress, which doubtless was part of the dream.

At any rate I returned to my normal state, and there about me were the miles of desolate streets and the thousands of broken walls, and the black blots of roofless houses and the wide, untenanted plain bounded by the battlemented line of encircling mountain crests, and above all, the great moon shining softly in a tender sky.

I looked and thrilled, though oppressed by the drear and desolate beauty of the scene around me, descended the wall and the ruined slope and made my way homewards, afraid even of my own shadow. For I seemed to be the only living thing among the dead habitations of immemorial Kôr.

********

Reaching our camp I found Hans awake and watching for me.

"I was just coming to look for you, Baas," he said. "Indeed I should have done so before, only I knew that you had gone to pay a visit to that tall white 'Missis' who ties up her head in a blanket, and thought that neither of you would like to be disturbed."

"Then you thought wrong," I answered, "and what is more, if you had made that visit I think it might have been one from which you would never have come back."

183

"Oh yes, Baas," sniggered Hans. "The tall white lady would not have minded. It is you who are so particular, after the fashion of men whom Heaven made very shy."

Without deigning to reply to the gibes of Hans I went to lie down, wondering what kind of a bed poor Robertson occupied that night, and soon fell asleep, as fortunately for myself I have the power to do, whatever my circumstances at the moment. Men who can sleep are those who do the work of the world and succeed, though personally I have had more of the work than of the success.

\* \* \* \* \* \* \* \*

I was awakened at the first grey dawn by Hans, who informed me that Billali was waiting outside with litters, also that Goroko had already made his incantations and doctored Umslopogaas and his two men for war after the Zulu fashion when battle was expected. He added that these Zulus had refused to be left behind to guard and nurse their wounded companions, and said that rather than do so, they would kill them.

Somehow, he informed me, in what way he could not guess, this had come to the ears of the White Lady who "hid her face from men because it was so ugly," and she had sent women to attend to the sick ones, with word that they should be well cared for. All of this proved to be true enough, but I need not enter into the details.

In the end off we went, I in my litter following Billali's, with an express and a repeating rifle and plenty of ammunition for both, and Hans, also well armed, in that which had been sent for Umslopogaas, who preferred to walk with Goroko and the two other Zulus.

For a little while Hans enjoyed the sensation of being carried by somebody else, and lay upon the cushions smoking with a seraphic smile and addressing sarcastic remarks to the bearers, who fortunately did not understand them. Soon, however, he wearied of these novel delights and as he was still determined not to walk until he was obliged, climbed on to the roof of the litter, astride of which he sat as though it were a horse, looking for all the world like a toy monkey on a horizontal stick.

Our road ran across the level, fertile plain but a small portion of which was cultivated, though I could see that at some time or other, when its population was greater, every inch of it had been under crop. Now it was largely covered by trees, many of them fruit-bearing, between which meandered streams of water which once, I think, had been irrigation channels.

About ten o'clock we reached the foot of the encircling cliffs and began the climb of the escarpment, which was steep, tortuous and difficult. By noon we reached its crest and here found all our little army encamped and, except for the sentries, sleeping, as seemed to be the invariable custom of these people in the daytime.

I caused the chief captains to be awakened and with them made a circuit of the camp, reckoning the numbers of the men which came to about 3,250 and learning what I could concerning them and their way of fighting. Then, accompanied by Umslopogaas and Hans with the Zulus as a guard, also by three of the head-captains of the Amahagger, I walked forward to study the lie of the land.

Coming to the further edge of the escarpment, I found that at this place two broad-based ridges, shaped like those that spring from the boles of certain tropical forest trees, ran from its crest to the plain beneath at a gentle slope. Moreover I saw that on this plain between the ends of the ridges an army was encamped which, by the aid of my glasses, I examined and estimated to number at least ten thousand men.

This army, the Amahagger captains informed me, was that of Rezu, who, they said, intended to commence his attack at dawn on the following morning, since the People of Rezu, being sun-worshippers, would never fight until their god appeared above the horizon. Having studied all there was to see I asked the captains to set out their plan of battle, if they had a plan.

The chief of them answered that it was to advance halfway down the right-hand ridge to a spot where there was a narrow flat piece of ground, and there await attack, since at this place their smaller numbers would not so much matter, whereas these made it impossible for them to assail the enemy.

"But suppose that Rezu should choose to come up to the other ridge and get behind you. What would happen then?" I inquired.

He replied that he did not know, his ideas of strategy being, it was clear, of a primitive order.

"Do your people fight best at night or in the day?" I went on.

He said undoubtedly at night, indeed in all their history there was no record of their having done so in the daytime.

"And yet you propose to let Rezu join battle with you when the sun is high, or in other words to court defeat," I remarked.

Then I went aside and discussed things for a while with Umslopogaas and Hans, after which I returned and gave my orders, declining all argument. Briefly these were that in the dusk before the rising of the moon, our Amahagger must advance down the right-hand ridge in complete silence, and hide themselves among the scrub which I saw grew thickly near its root. A small party, however, under the leadership of Goroko, whom I knew to be a brave and clever captain, was to pass halfway down the left-hand ridge and there light fires over a wide area, so as to make the enemy think that our whole force had encamped there. Then at the proper moment which I had not yet decided upon, we would attack the army of Rezu.

The Amahagger captains did not seem pleased with this plan which I think was too bold for their fancy, and began to murmur together. Seeing that I must assert my authority at once, I walked up to them and said to their chief man, "Hearken, my friend. By your own wish, not mine, I have been appointed your general and I expect to be obeyed without question. From the moment that the advance begins you will keep close to me and to the Black One, and if so much as one of your men hesitates or turns back, you will die," and I nodded towards the axe of Umslopogaas. "Moreover, afterwards She-who-commands will see that others of you die, should you escape in the fight."

Still they hesitated. Thereon without another word, I produced Zikali's Great Medicine and held it before their eyes, with the result that the sight of this ugly thing did what even the threat of death could not do. They went flat on the ground, every one of them, and swore by Lulala and by She-who-commands, her priestess, that they would do all I said, however mad it seemed to them.

"Good," I answered. "Now go back and make ready, and for the rest, by this time tomorrow we shall know who is or is not mad."

From that moment till the end I had no more trouble with these Amahagger.

********

I will get on quickly with the story of this fight whereof the preliminary details do not matter. At the proper time Goroko went off with two hundred and fifty men and one of the two Zulus to light the fires and, at an agreed signal, namely the firing of two shots in rapid succession by myself, to begin shouting and generally make as much noise as they could.

We also went off with the remaining three thousand, and before the moon rose, crept as quietly as ghosts down the right-hand ridge. Being such a silent folk who were accustomed to move at night and could see in the dark almost as well as cats, the Amahagger executed this manoeuvre splendidly, wrapping their spear-blades in bands of dry grass lest light should glint on them and betray our movements. So in due course we came to the patch of bush where the ridge widened out about five hundred yards from the plain beneath, and there lay down in four companies or regiments, each of them about seven hundred and fifty strong.

Now the moon had risen, but because of the mist which covered the surface of the plain, we could see nothing of the camp of Rezu which we knew must be within a thousand yards of us, unless indeed it had been moved, as the silence seemed to suggest.

This circumstance gave me much anxiety, since I feared lest abandoning their reputed habits, these Rezuites were also contemplating a night attack. Umslopogaas, too, was disturbed on the subject, though because of Goroko and his men whose fires began to twinkle on the opposing ridge something over a mile away, they could not pass up there without our knowledge.

Still, for aught I knew there might be other ways of scaling this mountain. I did not trust the Amahagger, who declared that none existed, since their local knowledge was slight as they never visited these northern slopes because of their fear of Rezu. Supposing that the enemy gained the crest and suddenly assaulted us in the rear! The thought of it made me feel cold down the back.

While I was wondering how I could find out the truth, Hans, who was squatted behind a bush, suddenly rose and gave the rifle he was carrying to the remaining Zulu.

"Baas," he said, "I am going to look and find out what those people are doing, if they are still there, and then you will know how and when to attack them. Don't be afraid for me, Baas, it will be easy in that mist and you know I can move like a snake. Also if I should not come back, it does not matter and it will tell you that they *are* there."

I hesitated who did not wish to expose the brave little Hottentot to such risks. But when he understood, Umslopogaas said, "Let the man go. It is his gift and duty to spy, as it is mine to smite with the axe, and yours to lead, Macumazahn. Let him go, I say."

I nodded my head, and having kissed my hand in his silly fashion in token of much that he did not wish to say, Hans slipped out of sight, saying that he hoped to be back within an hour. Except for his great knife, he went unarmed, who feared that if he took a pistol he might be tempted to fire it and make a noise.

## CHAPTER 17

# The Midnight Battle

That hour went by very slowly. Again and again I consulted my watch by the light of the moon, which was now rising high in the heavens, and thought that it would never come to an end. Listen as I would, there was nothing to be heard, and as the mist still prevailed the only thing I could see except the heavens, was the twinkling of the fires lit by Goroko and his party.

At length it was done and there was no sign of Hans. Another half hour passed and still no sign of Hans.

"I think that Light-in-Darkness is dead or taken prisoner," said Umslopogaas.

I answered that I feared so, but that I would give him another fifteen minutes and then, if he did not appear, I proposed to order an advance, hoping to find the enemy where we had last seen them from the top of the mountain.

The fifteen minutes went by also, and as I could see that the Amahagger captains who sat at a little distance were getting very nervous, I picked up my double-barrelled rifle and turned round so that I faced up hill with a view of firing it as had been agreed with Goroko, but in such a fashion that the flashes perhaps would not be seen from the plain below. For this purpose I moved a few yards to the left to get behind the trunk of a tree that grew there, and was already lifting the rifle to my shoulder, when a yellow hand clasped the barrel and a husky voice said, "Don't fire yet, Baas, as I want to tell you my story first."

I looked down and there was the ugly face of Hans wearing a grin that might have frightened the man in the moon.

"Well," I said with cold indifference, assumed I admit to hide my excessive joy at his safe return, "tell on, and be quick about it. I suppose you lost your way and never found them."

"Yes, Baas, I lost my way for the fog was very thick down there. But in the end I found them all right, by my nose, Baas, for those man-eating people smell strong and I got the wind of one of their sentries. It was easy to pass him in the mist, Baas, so easy that I was tempted to cut his throat as I went, but I didn't for fear lest he should make a noise. No, I walked on right into the middle of them, which was easy too, for they were all asleep, wrapped up in blankets. They hadn't any fires perhaps because they didn't want them to be seen, or perhaps because it is so hot down in that low land, I don't know which.

"So I crept on taking note of all I saw, till at last I came to a little hill of which the top rose above the level of the mist, so that I could see on it a long hut built of green boughs with the leaves still fresh upon them. Now I thought that I would crawl up to the hut since it came into my mind that Rezu himself must be sleeping there and that I might kill him. But while I stood hesitating I heard a noise like to that made by an old woman whose husband had thrown a blanket over her head to keep her quiet, or to that of a bee in a bottle, a sort of droning noise that reminded me of something.

"I thought a while and remembered that when Red Beard was on his knees praying to Heaven, as is his habit when he has nothing else to do, Baas, he makes a noise just like that. I crept towards the sound and presently there I found Red Beard himself tied upon a stone and looking as mad as a buffalo bull stuck in a swamp, for he shook his head and rolled his eyes about, just as though he had had two bottles of bad gin, Baas, and all the while he kept saying prayers. Now I thought that I would cut him loose, and bent over him to do so, when by ill-luck he saw my face and began to shout, saying, "'Go away, you yellow devil. I know you have come to take me to hell, but you are too soon, and if my hands were loose I would twist your head off your shoulders.'

"He said this in English, Baas, which as you know I can understand quite well, after which I was sure that I had better leave him alone. Whilst I was thinking, there came out of the hut above two old men dressed in night-shirts, such as you white people wear, with yellow things upon their heads that had a metal picture of the sun in front of them."

"Medicine-men," I suggested.

"Yes, Baas, or Predikants of some sort, for they were rather like your reverend father when he dressed himself up and went into a box to preach. Seeing them I slipped back a little way to where the mist began, lay down and listened. They looked at Red Beard, for his shouts at me had brought them out, but he took no notice of them, only went on making a noise like a beetle in a tin can.

"'It is nothing,' said one of the Predikants to the other in the same tongue that these Amahagger use. 'But when is he to be sacrificed? Soon, I hope, for I cannot sleep because of the noise he makes.'

"'When the edge of the sun appears, not before,' answered the other Predikant. 'Then the new queen will be brought out of the hut and this white man will be sacrificed to her.'

"'I think it is a pity to wait so long,' said the first Predikant, 'for never shall we sleep in peace until the red-hot pot is on his head.'

"'First the victory, then the feast,' answered the second Predikant, 'though he will not be so good to eat as that fat young woman who was with the new queen.'

"Then, Baas, they both smacked their lips and one of them went back towards the hut. But the other did not go back. No, he sat down on the ground and glowered at Baas Red-Beard upon the stone. More, he struck him on the face to make him quiet.

"Now, Baas, when I saw this and remembered that they had said that they had eaten Janee whom I liked although she was such a fool, the spirit in me grew so very angry and I thought that I would give this old *skellum* (*i.e.* rascal) of a Predikant a taste of sacrifice himself, after which I purposed to creep to the hut and see if I could get speech with the Lady Sad-Eyes, if she was there.

"So I wriggled up behind the Predikant as he sat glowering over Red-Beard, and stuck my knife into his back where I thought it would kill him at once. But it didn't, Baas, for he fell on to his face and began to make a noise like a wounded hyena before I could finish him. Then I heard a sound of shouts, and to save my life was obliged to run away into the mist, without loosing Red-Beard or seeing Lady Sad-Eyes. I ran very hard, Baas, making a wide circle to the left, and so at last got back here. That's all, Baas."

"And quite enough, too," I answered, "though if they did not see you, the death of the Medicine-man may frighten them. Poor Janee! Well, I hope to come even with those devils before they are three hours older."

Then I called up Umslopogaas and the Amahagger captains and told them the substance of the story, also that Hans had located the army, or part of it.

The end of it was that we made up our minds to attack at once; indeed I insisted on this, as I was determined if I could to save that unfortunate man, Robertson, who, from Hans' account, evidently was now quite mad and raving. So I fired the two shots as had been arranged and presently heard the sound of distant shoutings on the slope of the opposing ridge. A few minutes later we started, Umslopogaas and I leading the vanguard and the Amahagger captains following with the three remaining companies.

Now the reader, presuming the existence of such a person, will think that everything is sure to go right; that this cunning old fellow, Allan Quatermain, is going to surprise and wipe the floor with those Rezuites, who were already beguiled by the trick he had instructed Goroko to play. That after this he will rescue Robertson who doubtless shortly recovers his mind, also Inez with the greatest ease, in fact that everything will happen as it ought to do if this were a romance instead of a mere record of remarkable facts. But being the latter, as it happened, matters did not work out quite in this convenient way.

To begin with, when those Amahagger told me that the Rezuites never fought in the dark or before the sun was well up, either they lied or they were much mistaken, for at any rate on this occasion they did the exact contrary. All the while that we thought we were stalking them, they were stalking us. The Goroko manoeuvre had not deceived them in the least, since from their spies they knew its exact significance.

Here, I may add that those spies were in our own ranks, traitors, in short, who were really in the pay of Rezu and possibly belonged to his abominable faith, some of whom slipped away from time to time to the enemy to report our progress and plans, so far as they knew them.

Further, what Hans had stumbled on was a mere rear guard left around the place of sacrifice and the hut where Inez was confined. The real army he never found at all. That was divided into two bodies and hidden in bush to the right and left of the ridge which we were descending just at the spot where it joined the plain beneath, and into the jaws of these two armies we marched gaily.

Now that hypothetical reader will say, "Why didn't that silly old fool, Allan, think of all these things? Why didn't he remember that he was commanding a pack of savages with whom he had no real acquaintance, among whom there were sure to be traitors, especially as they were of the same blood as the Rezuites, and take precautions?"

Ah! my dear reader, I will only answer that I wish you had handled the job yourself, and enjoyed the opportunity of seeing what *you* could do in the circumstances. Do you suppose I didn't think of all these points? Of course I did. But have you ever heard of the difficulty of making silk purses out of sows' ears, or of turning a lot of gloomy and disagreeable barbarians whom you had never even drilled, into trustworthy and efficient soldiers ready to fight three times their own number and beat them?

Also I beg to observe that I did get through somehow, as you shall learn, which is more than you might have done, Mr. Wisdom, though I admit, not without help from another quarter. It is all very well for you to sit in your armchair and be sapient and turn up your learned nose, like the gentlemen who criticise plays and poems, an easy job compared to the writing of them. From all of which, however, you will understand that I am, to tell the truth, rather ashamed of what followed, since *qui s'excuse, s'accuse.*

As we slunk down that hill in the moonlight, a queer-looking crowd, I admit also that I felt very uncomfortable. To begin with I did not like that remark of the Medicine-man which Hans reported, to the effect that the feast must come after the victory, especially as he had said just before that Robertson was to be sacrificed as the sun rose, which would seem to suggest that the "victory" was planned to take place before that event.

While I was ruminating upon this subject, I looked round for Hans to cross-examine him as to the priest's exact words, only to find that he had slunk off somewhere. A few minutes later he reappeared running back towards us swiftly and, I noticed, taking shelter behind tree trunks and rocks as he came.

"Baas," he gasped, for he was out of breath, "be careful, those Rezu men are on either side ahead. I went forward and ran into them. They threw many spears at me. Look!" and he showed a slight cut on his arm from which blood was flowing.

Instantly I understood that we were ambushed and began to think very hard indeed. As it chanced we were passing across a large flat space upon the ridge, say seven or eight acres in extent, where the bush grew lightly, though owing to the soil being better, the trees were tall.

On the steep slope below this little plain it seemed to be denser and there it was, according to Hans, that the ambush was set. I halted my regiment and sent back messengers to the others that they were to halt also as they came up, on the pretext of giving them a rest before they were marshalled and we advanced to the battle.

Then I told Umslopogaas what Hans said and asked him to send out his Zulu soldier whom he could trust, to see if he could obtain confirmation of the report. This he did at once. Also I asked him what he thought should be done, supposing that it was true.

"Form the Amahagger into a ring or a square and await attack," he answered.

I nodded, for that was my own opinion, but replied, "If they were Zulus, the plan would be good. But how do we know that these men will stand?"

"We know nothing, Macumazahn, and therefore can only try. If they run it must be up-hill."

Then I called the captains and told them what was toward, which seemed to alarm them very much. Indeed one or two of them wanted to retreat at once, but I said I would shoot the first man who tried to do so. In the end they agreed to my plan and said that they would post their best soldiers above, at the top of the square, with the orders to stop any attempt at a flight up the mountain.

After this we formed up the square as best we could, arranging it in a rather rough, four-fold line. While we were doing this we heard some shouts below and presently the Zulu returned, who reported that all was as Hans had said and that Rezu's men were moving round us, having discovered, as he thought, that we had halted and escaped their ambush.

Still the attack did not develop at once, for the reason that the Rezu army was crawling up the steep flanks of the spur on either side of the level piece of ground, with a view of encircling us altogether, so as to make a clean sweep of our force. As a matter of fact, considered from our point of view, this was a most fortunate move, since thereby they stopped any attempt at a retreat on the part of our Amahagger, whose bolt-hole was now blocked.

When we had done all we could, we sat down, or at least I did, and waited. The night, I remember, was strangely still, only from the slopes on either side of our plateau came a kind of rustling sound which in fact was caused by the feet of Rezu's people, as they marched to surround us.

It ceased at last and the silence grew complete, so much so that I could hear the teeth of some of our tall Amahagger chattering with fear, a sound that gave me little confidence and caused Umslopogaas to remark that the hearts of these big men had never grown; they remained "as those of babies." I told the captains to pass the word down the ranks that those who stood might live, but those who fled would certainly die. Therefore if they wished to see their homes again they had better stand and fight like men. Otherwise most of them would be killed and the rest eaten by Rezu. This was done, and I observed that the message seemed to produce a steadying effect upon our ranks.

Suddenly all around us, from below, from above and on either side there broke a most awful roar which seemed to shape itself into the word, *Rezu*, and next minute also from above, below and either side, some ten thousand men poured forth upon our square.

In the moonlight they looked very terrible with their flowing white robes and great gleaming spears. Hans and I fired some shots, though for all the effect they produced, we might as well have pelted a breaker with pebbles. Then, as I thought that I should be more useful alive than dead, I retreated within the square, Umslopogaas, his Zulu, and Hans coming with me.

On the whole our Amahagger stood the attack better than I expected. They beat back the first rush with considerable loss to the enemy, also the second after a longer struggle. Then there was a pause during which we re-formed our ranks, dragging the wounded men into the square.

Scarcely had we done this when with another mighty shout of "Rezu!" the enemy attacked again—that was about an hour after the battle had begun. But now they had changed their tactics, for instead of trying to rush all sides of the square at once, they concentrated their efforts on the western front, that which faced towards the plain below.

On they came, and among them in the forefront of the battle, now and again I caught sight of a gigantic man, a huge creature who seemed to me to be seven feet high and big in proportion. I could not see him clearly because of the uncertain moonlight, but I noted his fierce aspect, also that he had an enormous beard, black streaked with grey, that flowed down to his middle, and that his hair hung in masses upon his shoulders.

"Rezu himself!" I shouted to Umslopogaas.

"Aye, Macumazahn, Rezu himself without doubt, and I rejoice to see him for he will be a worthy foe to fight. Look! he carries an axe as I do. Now I must save my strength for when we come face to face I shall need it all."

I thought that I would spare Umslopogaas this exertion and watched my opportunity to put a bullet through this giant. But I could never get one. Once when I had covered him an Amahagger rushed in front of my gun so that I could not shoot, and when a second chance came a little cloud floated over the face of the moon and made him invisible. After that I had other things to which to attend, since, as I expected would happen, the western face of our square gave, and yelling like devils, the enemy began to pour in through the gap.

A cold thrill went through me for I saw that the game was up. To re-form these undisciplined Amahagger was impossible; nothing was to be expected except panic, rout and slaughter. I cursed my folly for ever having had anything to do with the business, while Hans screamed to me in a thin voice that the only chance was for us three and the Zulu to bolt and hide in the bush.

I did not answer him because, apart from any nasty pride, the thing was impossible, for how could we get through those struggling masses of men which surrounded us on every side? No, my clock had struck, so I went on making a kind of mental sandwich of prayers and curses; prayers for my soul and forgiveness for my sins, and curses on the Amahagger and everything to do with them, especially Zikali and the woman called Ayesha, who, between them, had led me into this affair.

"Perhaps the Great Medicine of Zikali," piped Hans again as he fired a rifle at the advancing foe.

"Hang the Great Medicine," I shouted back, "and Ayesha with it. No wonder she declined to take a hand in this business."

As I spoke the words I saw old Billali, who not being a man of war was keeping as close to us as he could, go flat onto his venerable face, and reflected that he must have got a thrown spear through him. Casting a hurried glance at him to see if he were done for or only wounded, out of the corner of my eye I caught sight of something diaphanous which gleamed in the moonlight and reminded me of I knew not what at the moment.

I looked round quickly to see what it might be and lo! there, almost at my side was the veiled Ayesha herself, holding in her hand a little rod made of black wood inlaid with ivory not unlike a field marshal's baton, or a sceptre.

I never saw her come and to this day I do not know how she did so; she was just there and what is more she must have put luminous paint or something else on her robes, for they gleamed with a sort of faint, phosphorescent fire, which in the moonlight made her conspicuous all over the field of battle. Nor did she speak a single word, she only waved the rod, pointed with it towards the fierce hordes who were drawing near to us, killing as they came, and began to move forward with a gliding motion.

Now from every side there went up a roar of "*She-who-commands! She-who-commands!*" while the people of Rezu in front shouted "*Lulala! Lulala!* Fly, Lulala is upon us with the witchcrafts of the moon!"

She moved forward and by some strange impulse, for no order was given, we all began to move after her. Yes, the ranks that a minute before were beginning to give way to wild panic, became filled with a marvellous courage and moved after her.

The men of Rezu also, and I suppose with them Rezu himself, for I saw no more of him at that time, began to move uncommonly fast over the edge of the plateau towards the plain beneath. In fact they broke into flight and leaping over dead and dying, we rushed after them, always following the gleaming robe of Ayesha, who must have been an extremely agile person, since without any apparent exertion she held her place a few steps ahead of us.

There was another curious circumstance about this affair, namely, that terrified though they were, those Rezuites, after the first break, soon seemed to find it impossible to depart with speed. They kept turning round to look behind them at that following vision, as though they were so many of Lot's wives. Moreover, the same fate overtook many of them which fell upon that scriptural lady, since they appeared to become petrified and stood there quite still, like rabbits fascinated by a snake, until our people came up and killed them.

This slaying went on all down the last steep slope of the ridge, on which I suppose at least two-thirds of the army of Rezu must have perished, since our Amahagger showed themselves very handy men when it came to exterminating foes who were too terror-struck to fight, and, exhilarated by the occupation, gained courage every moment.

## CHAPTER 18

# The Slaying of Rezu

At last we were on the plain, the bemused remnant of Rezu's army still doubling before us like a mob of game pursued by wild dogs. Here we halted to re-form our ranks; it seemed to me, although still she spoke no word, that some order reached me from the gleaming Ayesha that I should do this. The business took twenty minutes or so, and then, numbering about two thousand five hundred strong, for the rest had fallen in the fight of the square, we advanced again.

Now there came that dusk which often precedes the rising of the sun, and through it I could see that the battle was not yet over, since gathered in front of us was still a force about equal to our own. Ayesha pointed towards it with her wand and we leapt forward to the attack. Here the men of Rezu stood awaiting us, for they seemed to overcome their terror with the approach of day.

The battle was fierce, a very strange battle in that dim, uncertain light, which scarcely showed us friend from foe. Indeed I am not sure that we should have won it, since Ayesha was no longer visible to give our Amahagger confidence, and as the courage of the Rezuites increased, so theirs seemed to lessen with the passing of the night.

Fortunately, however, just as the issue hung doubtful, there was a shout to our left and looking, I made out the tall shape of Goroko, the witch-doctor, with the other Zulu, followed by his two hundred and fifty men, and leaping on to the flank of the line of Rezu.

That settled the business. The enemy crumpled up and melted, and just then the first lights of dawn appeared in the sky. I looked about me for Ayesha, but she had gone, where to I knew not, though at the moment I feared that she must have been killed in the *mêlée*.

Then I gave up looking and thinking, since now or never was the time for action. Signalling and shouting to those hatchet-faced Amahagger to advance, accompanied by Umslopogaas with Goroko who had joined us, and Hans, I sprang forward to give them an example, which, to be just to them, they took.

"This is the mound on which Red-Beard should be," cried Hans as we faced a little slope.

I ran up it and through the gloom which precedes the actual dawn, saw a group of men gathered round something, as people collect about a street accident.

"Red-Beard on the stone. They are killing him," screeched Hans again.

It was so; at least several white-robed priests were bending over a prostrate figure with knives in their hands, while behind stood the huge fellow whom I took to be Rezu, staring towards the east as though he were waiting for the rim of the sun to appear before he gave some order. At that very moment it did appear, just a thin edge of bright light on the horizon, and he turned, shouting the order.

Too late! For we were on them. Umslopogaas cut down one of the priests with his axe, and the men about me dealt with the others, while Hans with a couple of sweeps of his long knife, severed the cords with which Robertson was tied.

The poor man who in the growing light I could see was raving mad, sprang up, calling out something in Scotch about "the deil." Seizing a great spear which had fallen from the hand of one of the priests, he rushed furiously at the giant who had given the order, and with a yell drove it at his heart. I saw the spear snap, from which I concluded that this man, whom rightly I took to be Rezu, wore some kind of armour.

Next instant the axe he held, a great weapon, flashed aloft and down went Robertson before its awful stroke, stone dead, for as we found out afterwards, he was cloven almost in two. At the sight of the death of my poor friend rage took hold of me. In my hand was a double-barrelled rifle, an Express loaded with hollow-pointed bullets. I covered the giant and let drive, first with one barrel and then with the other, and what is more, distinctly I heard both bullets strike upon him.

Yet he did not fall. He rocked a little, that is all, then turned and marched off towards a hut, that whereof Hans had told me, which stood about fifty yards away.

"Leave him to me," shouted Umslopogaas. "Steel cuts where bullets cannot pierce," and with a bound like to that of a buck, the great Zulu leapt away after him.

I think that Rezu meant to enter the hut for some purpose of his own, but Umslopogaas was too hard upon his tracks. At any rate he ran past it and down the other slope of the little hill on to the plain behind where the remnants of his army were trying to re-form. There in front of them the giant turned and stood at bay.

Umslopogaas halted also, waiting for us to come up, since, cunning old warrior as he was, he feared lest should he begin the fight before that happened, the horde of them would fall on him. Thirty seconds later we arrived and found him standing still with bent body, small shield advanced and the great axe raised as though in the act of striking, a wondrous picture outlined as it was against the swiftly rising-sun.

Some ten paces away stood the giant leaning on the axe he bore, which was not unlike to that with which woodmen fell big trees. He was an evil man to see and at this, my first full sight of him, I likened him in my mind to Goliath whom David overthrew. Huge he was and hairy, with deep-set, piercing eyes and a great hooked nose. His face seemed thin and ancient also, when with a motion of the great head, he tossed his long locks back from about it, but his limbs were those of a Hercules and his movements full of a youthful vigour. Moreover his aspect as a whole was that of a devil rather than of a man; indeed the sight of it sickened me.

"Let me shoot him," I cried to Umslopogaas, for I had reloaded the rifle as I ran.

"Nay, Watcher-by-Night," answered the Zulu without moving his head, "rifle has had its chance and failed. Now let us see what axe can do. If I cannot kill this man, I will be borne hence feet first who shall have made a long journey for nothing."

Then the giant began to talk in a low, rumbling voice that reverberated from the slope of the little hill behind us.

"Who are you?" he asked, speaking in the same tongue that the Amahagger use, "who dare to come face to face with Rezu? Black hound, do you not know that I cannot be slain who have lived a year for every week of your life's days, and set my foot upon the necks of men by thousands. Have you not seen the spear shatter and the iron balls melt upon my breast like rain-drops, and would you try to bring me down with that toy you carry? My army is defeated—I know it. But what matters that when I can get me more? Because the sacrifice was not completed and the white queen was not wed, therefore my army was defeated by the magic of Lulala, the White Witch who dwells in the tombs. But *I* am not defeated who cannot be slain until I show my back, and then only by a certain axe which long ago has rusted into dust."

Now of this long speech Umslopogaas understood nothing, so I answered for him, briefly enough, but to the point, for there flashed into my mind all Ayesha's tale about an axe.

"A certain axe!" I cried. "Aye, a certain axe! Well, look at that which is held by the Black One, the captain who is named Slaughterer, the ancient axe whose title is Chieftainess, because if so she wills, she takes the lives of all. Look at it well, Rezu, Giant and Wizard, and say whether it is not that which your forefather lost, that which is destined to bring you to your doom?"

Thus I spoke, very loudly that all might hear, slowly also, pausing between each word because I wished to give time for the light to strengthen, seeing as I did that the rays of the rising sun struck upon the face of the giant, whereas the eyes of Umslopogaas were less dazzled by it.

Rezu heard, and stared at the axe which Umslopogaas held aloft, causing it to quiver slightly by an imperceptible motion of his arm. As he stared I saw his hideous face change, and that on it for the first time gathered a look of something resembling fear. Also his followers behind him who were also studying the axe, began to murmur together.

For here I should say that as though by common consent the battle had been stayed; we no longer attacked and the enemy no longer ran. They, or whose who were left of them, stood still as though they felt that the real and ultimate issue of the fight depended upon the forthcoming duel between these two champions, though of that issue they had little doubt since, as I learned afterwards, they believed their king to be invulnerable.

For quite a while Rezu went on staring. Then he said aloud as if he were thinking to himself.

"It is like, very like. The horn haft is the same; the pointed gouge is the same; the blade shaped like the young moon is the same. Almost could I think that before me shook the ancient holy axe. Nay, the gods have taken that back long ago and this is but a trick of the witch, Lulala of the Caves."

Thus he spoke, but still for a moment hesitated.

"Umslopogaas," I said in the deep silence that followed, "hear me."

"I hear you," he answered without turning his head or moving his arms. "What counsel, Watcher-by-Night?"

"This, Slaughterer. Strike not at that man's face and breast, for there I think he is protected by witchcraft or by armour. Get behind him and strike at his back. Do you understand?"

"Nay, Macumazahn, I understand not. Yet I will do your bidding because you are wiser than I and utter no empty words. Now be still."

Then Umslopogaas threw the axe into the air and caught it as it fell, and as he did so began to chant his own praises Zulu fashion.

"Oho!" he said, "I am the child of the Lion, the Black-maned Lion, whose claws never loosened of their prey. I am the Wolf-king, he who hunted with the wolves upon the Witch-mountain with my brother, Bearer of the Club named Watcher-of-the-Fords, I am he who slew him called the Unconquered, Chief of the People of the Axe, he who bore the ancient Axe before me; I am he who smote the Halakazi tribe in their caves and won me Nada the Lily to wife. I am he who took to the King Dingaan a gift that he loved little, and afterward with Mopo, my foster-sire, hurled this Dingaan down to death. I am the Royal One, named Bulalio the Slaughterer, named Woodpecker, named Umhlopekazi the Captain, before whom never yet man has stood in fair and open fight. Now, thou Wizard Rezu, now thou Giant, now thou Ghost-man, come on against me and before the sun has risen by a hand's breadth, all those who watch shall see which of us is better at the game of war. Come on, then! Come on, for I say that my blood boils over and my feet grow cold. Come on, thou grinning dog, thou monster grown fat with eating the flesh of men, thou hook-beaked vulture, thou old, grey-whiskered wolf!"

Thus he changed in his fierce, boastful way, while his two remaining Zulus clapped their hands and sentence by sentence echoed his words, and Goroko, the witch-doctor, muttered incantations behind him.

While he sang thus Umslopogaas began to stir. First only his head and shoulders moved gently, swaying from side to side like a reed shaken in the wind or a snake about to strike. Then slowly he put out first one foot and next the other and drew them back again, as a dancer might do, tempting Rezu to attack.

But the giant would not, his shield held before him, he stood still and waited to see what this black warrior would do.

The snake struck. Umslopogaas darted in and let drive with the long axe. Rezu raised his shield above his head and caught the blow. From the clank it made I knew that this shield which seemed to be of hide, was lined with iron. Rezu smote back, but before the blow could fall the Zulu was out of his reach. This taught me how great was the giant's strength, for though the stroke was heavy, like the steel-hatted axe he bore, still when he saw that it had missed he checked the weapon in mid air, which only a mighty man could have done.

Umslopogaas saw these things also and changed his tactics. His axe was six or eight inches longer in the haft than that of Rezu, and therefore he could reach where Rezu could not, for the giant was short-armed. He twisted it round in his hand so that the moon-shaped blade was uppermost, and keeping it almost at full length, began to peck with the gouge-shaped point on the back at the head and arms of Rezu, that as I knew was a favourite trick of his in fight from which he won his name of "Woodpecker." Rezu defended his head with his shield as best he could against the sharp points of steel which flashed all about him.

Twice it seemed to me that the Zulu's pecks went home upon the giant's breast, but if so they did no harm. Either Rezu's thick beard, or armour beneath it stopped them from penetrating his body. Still he roared out as though with pain, or fury, or both, and growing mad, charged at Umslopogaas and smote with all his strength.

The Zulu caught the blow upon his shield, through which it shore as though the tough hide were paper. Stay the stroke it could not, yet it turned its direction, so that the falling axe slid past Umslopogaas's shoulder, doing him no hurt. Next instant, before Rezu could strike again, the Zulu threw the severed shield into his face and seizing the axe with both hands, leapt in and struck. It was a mighty blow, for I saw the rhinoceros-horn handle of the famous axe bend like a drawn bow, and it went home with a dull thud full upon Rezu's breast. He shook, but no more. Evidently the razor edge of *Inkosikaas* had failed to pierce. There was a sound as though a hollow tree had been smitten and some strands of the long beard, shorn off, fell to the ground, but that was all.

"*Tagati!* (bewitched)," cried the watching Zulus. "That stroke should have cut him in two!" while I thought to myself that this man knew how to make good armour.

Rezu laughed aloud, a bellowing kind of laugh, while Umslopogaas sprang back astonished.

"Is it thus!" he cried in Zulu. "Well, all wizards have some door by which their Spirit enters and departs. I must find the door, I must find the door!"

So he spoke and with springing movements tried to get past Rezu, first to the right and then to the left, all the while keeping out of reach. But Rezu ever turned and faced him, as he did so retreating step by step down the slope of the little hill and striking whenever he found a chance, but without avail, for always Umslopogaas was beyond his reach. Also the sunlight which now grew strong, dazzled him, or so I thought. Moreover he seemed to tire somewhat—or so I thought also.

At any rate he determined to make an end of the play, for with a swift motion, as Umslopogaas had done, he threw away his shield and grasping the iron handle of his axe with both hands, charged the Zulu like a bull. Umslopogaas leapt back out of reach. Then suddenly he turned and ran up the rise. Yes, Bulalio the Slaughterer ran!

A roar of mockery went up from the sun-worshippers behind, while our Amahagger laughed and Goroko and the two Zulus stared astonished and ashamed. Only I read his mind aright and wondered what guile he had conceived.

He ran, and Rezu ran after him, but never could he catch the swiftest-footed man in Zululand. To and fro he followed him, for Umslopogaas was taking a zigzag path towards the crest of the slope, till at length Rezu stopped breathless. But Umslopogaas still ran another twenty yards or so until he reached the top of the slope and there halted and wheeled round.

For ten seconds or more he stood drawing his breath in great gasps, and, looking at his face, I saw that it had become as the face of a wolf. His lips were drawn up into a terrible grin, showing the white teeth between; his cheeks seemed to have fallen in and his eyes glared, while the skin over the hole in his forehead beat up and down.

There he stood, gathering himself together for some mighty effort.

"Run on!" shouted the spectators. "Run back to Kôr, black dog!"

Umslopogaas knew that they were mocking him, but he took no heed, only bent down and rubbed his sweating hand in the grit of the dry earth. Then he straightened himself and charged down on Rezu.

I, Allan Quatermain, have seen many things in battle, but never before or since did I see aught like to this charge. It was swift as that of a lioness, so swift that the Zulu's feet scarcely seemed to touch the ground. On he sped like a thrown spear, till, when within about a dozen feet of Rezu who stood staring at him, he bent his frame almost double and leapt into the air.

Oh! what a leap was that. Surely he must have learnt it from the lion, or the spring-buck. High he rose and now I saw his purpose; it was to clear the tall shape of Rezu. Aye, and he cleared him with half a foot to spare, and as he passed above, smote downwards with the axe so that the blow fell upon the back of Rezu's head. Moreover it went home this time, for I saw the red blood stream and Rezu fell forward on his face. Umslopogaas landed far beyond him, ran a little way because he must, then wheeled round and charged again.

Rezu was rising, but before he gained his feet, the axe *Inkosikaas* thundered down where the neck joins the shoulder and sank in. Still, so great was his strength that Rezu found his feet and smote out wildly. But now his movements were slow and again Umslopogaas got behind him, smiting at his back. Once, twice, thrice, he smote, and at the third blow it seemed as though the massive spine were severed, for his weapon fell from Rezu's hand and slowly he sank down to the ground, and lay there, a huddled heap.

Believing that all was over I ran to where he lay with Umslopogaas standing over him, as it seemed to me, utterly exhausted, for he supported himself by the axe and tottered upon his feet. But Rezu was not yet dead. He opened his cavernous eyes and glared at the Zulu with a look of hellish hate.

"*Thou* hast not conquered me, Black One," he gasped. "It is thine axe which gave thee victory; the ancient, holy axe that once was mine until the woman stole it, yes, that and the craft of the Witch of the Caves who told thee to smite where the Spirit of Life which I feared to enter wholly, had not kissed my flesh, and there only left me mortal. Wolf of a black man, may we meet elsewhere and fight this fray again. Ah! would that I could get these hands about thy throat and take thee with me down into the Darkness. But Lulala wins if only for a while, since her fate, I think, shall be worse than mine. Ah! I see the magic beauty that she boasts turn to shameful——"

Here of a sudden life left him and throwing his great arms wide, a last breath passed bubbling from his lips.

As I stooped to examine the man's huge and hairy carcase that to me looked only half human, with a thunder of feet our Amahagger rushed down upon us and thrusting me aside, fell upon the body of their ancient foe like hounds upon a helpless fox, and with hands and spears and knives literally tore and hacked it limb from limb, till no semblance of humanity remained.

It was impossible to stop them; indeed I was too outworn with labours and emotions to make any such attempt. This I regret the more since I lost the opportunity of making an examination of the body of this troll-like man, and of ascertaining what kind of armour it was he wore beneath that great beard of his, which was strong enough to stop my bullets, and even the razor edge of the axe *Inkosikaas* driven with all the might of the arms of the Zulu, Bulalio. For when I looked again at the sickening sight the giant was but scattered fragments and the armour, whatever it might have been, was gone, rent to little pieces and carried off, doubtless, by the Amahagger, perhaps to be divided between them to serve as charms.

So of Rezu I know only that he was the hugest, most terrible-looking man I have ever seen, one too who carried his vast strength very late in life, since from the aspect of his countenance I imagine that he must have been nigh upon seventy years of age, though his supposed unnatural antiquity of course was nothing but a fable put about by the natives for their own purposes.

Presently Umslopogaas seemed to recover from the kind of faint into which he had fallen and opening his eyes, looked about him. The first person they fell on was old Billali who stood stroking his white beard and contemplating the scene with an air which was at once philosophic and satisfied. This seemed to anger Umslopogaas, for he cried, "I think it was you, ancient bag of words and sweeper of paths for the feet of the great, who made a mock of me but now, when you thought that I fled before the horns of yonder man-eating bull—" and he nodded towards the fragments of what once had been Rezu. "Find now his axe and though I am weak and weary, I will wash away the insult with your blood."

"What does this glorious black hero say, Watcher-by-Night?" asked Billali in his most courteous tones.

I told him word by word, whereon Billali lifted his hands in horror, turned and fled. Nor did I see him again until we arrived at Kôr.

* * * * * * * *

At the sight of the fall of their giant chief Rezu whom they believed to be invulnerable, his followers, who were watching the fray, set up a great wailing, a most mournful and uncanny noise to hear. Then, as I think did the hosts of the Philistines when David brought down Goliath by his admirable shot with a stone, they set out for their homes wherever these may have been, at an absolutely record pace and in the completest disarray.

Our Amahagger followed them for a while, but soon were left standing still. So they contented themselves with killing any wounded they could find and returned. I did not accompany them; indeed the battle being won, metaphorically I washed my hands of them, and in my thoughts consigned them to a certain locality as a people of whom it might well be said that manners they had none and their customs were simply beastly. Also, although fierce and cruel, these night-bats were not good fighting men and in short never did I wish to have to do with such another company.

Moreover, a very different matter pressed. The object of this business so far as I was concerned, had been to rescue poor Inez, since had it not been for her sake, never would I have consented to lead those Amahagger against their fellow blackguards, the Rezuites.

But where was Inez? If Hans had understood the medicine-man aright, she was, or had been, in the hut, where it was my earnest hope that she still remained, since otherwise the hunt must be continued. This at any rate was easy to discover. Calling Hans, who was amusing himself by taking long shots at the flying enemy, so that they might not forget him, as he said, and the Zulus, I walked up the slope to the hut, or rather booth of boughs, for it was quite twenty feet long by twelve or fifteen broad.

At its eastern end was a doorway or opening closed with a heavy curtain. Here I paused full of tremors, and listened, for to tell the truth I dreaded to draw that curtain, fearing what I might see within. Gathering up my courage at length I tore it aside and, a revolver in my hand, looked in. At first after the strong light without, for the sun was now well up, I could see nothing, since those green boughs and palm leaves were very closely woven. As my eyes grew accustomed to the gloom, however, I perceived a glittering object seated on a kind of throne at the end of the booth, while in a double row in front knelt six white-robed women who seemed to wear chains about their necks and carried large knives slung round their middles. On the floor between these women and the throne lay a dead man, a priest of some sort as I gathered from his garb, who still held a huge spear in his hand. So silent were the figure on the throne and those that knelt before it, that at first I thought that all of them must be dead.

"Lady Sad-Eyes," whispered Hans, "and her bride-women. Doubtless that old Predikant came to kill her when he saw that the battle was lost, but the bride-women killed him with their knives."

Here I may state that Hans' suppositions proved to be quite correct, which shows how quick and deductive was his mind. The figure on the throne was Inez; the priest in his disappointed rage *had* come to kill her, and the bride-women had killed *him* with their knives before he could do so.

I bade the Zulus tear down the curtain and pull away some of the end boughs, so as to let in more light. Then we advanced up the place, holding our pistols and spears in readiness. The kneeling women turned their heads to look at us and I saw that they were all young and handsome in their fashion, although fierce-faced. Also I saw their hands go to the knives they wore. I called to them to let these be and come out, and that if they did so they had nothing to fear. But if they understood, they did not heed my words.

On the contrary while Hans and I covered them with our pistols, fearing lest they should stab the person on the throne whom we took to be Inez, at some word from one of them, they bowed simultaneously towards her, then at another word, suddenly they drew the knives and plunged them to their own hearts!

It was a dreadful sight and one of which I never saw the like. Nor to this day do I know why the deed was done, unless perhaps the women were sworn to the service of the new queen and feared that if they failed to protect her, they would be doomed to some awful end. At any rate we got them out dead or dying, for their blows had been strong and true, and not one of them lived for more than a few minutes.

Then I advanced to the figure on the throne, or rather foot-stooled chair of black wood inlaid with ivory, which sat so silent and motionless that I was certain it was that of a dead woman, especially when I perceived that she was fastened to the chair with leather straps, which were sewn over with gold wire. Also she was veiled and, with one exception, made up, if I may use the term, exactly to resemble the lady Ayesha, even down to the two long plaits of black hair, each finished with some kind of pearl and to the sandaled feet.

The exception was that about her hung a great necklace of gold ornaments from which were suspended pendants also of gold representing the rayed disc of the sun in rude but bold and striking workmanship.

I went to her and having cut the straps, since I could not stop to untie their knots, lifted the veil.

Beneath it was Inez sure enough, and Inez living, for her breast rose and fell as she breathed, but Inez senseless. Her eyes were wide open, yet she was quite senseless. Probably she had been drugged, or perhaps some of the sights of horror which she saw, had taken away her mind. I confess that I was glad that this was so, who otherwise must have told her the dreadful story of her father's end.

We bore her out and away from that horrible place, apparently quite unhurt, and laid her under the shadow of a tree till a litter could be procured. I could do no more who knew not how to treat her state, and had no spirits with me to pour down her throat.

\* \* \* \* \* \* \* \*

This was the end of our long pursuit, and thus we rescued Inez, whom the Zulus called the Lady Sad-Eyes.

## CHAPTER 19

# The Spell

Of our return to Kôr I need say nothing, except that in due course we reached that interesting ruin. The journey was chiefly remarkable for one thing, that on this occasion, I imagine for the first and last time in his life, Umslopogaas consented to be carried in a litter, at least for part of the way. He was, as I have said, unwounded, for the axe of his mighty foe had never once so much as touched his skin. What he suffered from was shock, a kind of collapse, since, although few would have thought it, this great and utterly fearless warrior was at bottom a nervous, highly-strung man.

It is only the nervous that climb the highest points of anything, and this is true of fights as of all others. That fearful fray with Rezu had been a great strain on the Zulu. As he put it himself, "the wizard had sucked the strength" out of him, especially when he found that owing to his armour he could not harm him in front, and owing to his cunning could not get at him behind. Then it was that he conceived the desperate expedient of leaping over his head and smiting backwards as he leapt, a trick, he told me, that he had once played years before when he was young, in order to break a shield ring and reach one who stood in its centre.

In this great leap over Rezu's head Umslopogaas knew that he must succeed, or be slain, which in turn would mean my death and that of the others. For this reason he faced the shame of seeming to fly in order to gain the higher ground, whence alone he could gather the speed necessary to such a terrific spring.

Well, he made it and thereby conquered, and this was the end, but as he said, it had left him, "weak as a snake when it crawls out of its hole into the sun after the long winter sleep."

Of one thing, Umslopogaas added, he was thankful, namely that Rezu had never succeeded in getting his arms round him, since he was quite certain that if he had he would have broken him "as a baboon breaks a mealie-stalk." No strength, not even his, could have resisted the iron might of that huge, gorilla-like man.

I agreed with him who had noted Rezu's vast chest and swelling muscles, also the weight of the blows that he struck with the steel-hafted axe (which, by the way, when I sought for it, was missing, stolen, I suppose, by one of the Amahagger).

Whence did that strength come, I wondered, in one who from his face appeared to be old? Was there perchance, after all, some truth in the legend of Samson and did it dwell in that gigantic beard and those long locks of his? It was impossible to say and probably the man was but a Herculean freak, for that he was as strong as Hercules all the stories that I heard afterwards of his feats, left little room for doubt.

About one thing only was I certain in connection with him, namely, that the tales of his supernatural abilities were the merest humbug. He was simply one of the representatives of the family of "strong men," of whom examples are still to be seen doing marvellous feats all over the earth.

For the rest, he was dead and broken up by those Amahagger blood-hounds before I could examine him, or his body-armour either, and there was an end of him and his story. But when I looked at the corpse of poor Robertson, which I did as we buried it where he fell, and saw that though so large and thick-set, it was cleft almost in two by a single blow of Rezu's axe, I came to understand what the might of this savage must have been.

I say savage, but I am not sure that this is a right description of Rezu. Evidently he had a religion of a sort, also imagination, as was shown by the theft of the white woman to be his queen; by his veiling of her to resemble Ayesha whom he dreaded; by the intended propitiatory sacrifice; by the guard of women sworn to her service who slew the priest that tried to kill her, and afterwards committed suicide when they had failed in their office, and by other things. All this indicated something more than savagery, perhaps survivals from a forgotten civilisation, or perhaps native ability on the part of an individual ruler. I do not know and it matters nothing.

Rezu is dead and the world is well rid of him, and those who want to learn more of his people can go to study such as remain of them in their own habitat, which for my part I never wish to visit any more.

********

During our journey to Kôr poor Inez never stirred. Whenever I went to look at her in the litter, I found her lying there with her eyes open and a fixed stare upon her face which frightened me very much, since I began to fear lest she should die. However I could do nothing to help her, except urge the bearers to top speed. So swiftly did we travel down the hill and across the plain that we reached Kôr just as the sun was setting. As we crossed the moat I perceived old Billali coming to meet us. This he did with many bows, keeping an anxious eye upon the litter which he had learned contained Umslopogaas. Indeed his attitude and that of the Amahagger towards the two of us, and even Hans, thenceforward became almost abject, since after our victory over Rezu and his death beneath the axe, they looked upon us as half divine and treated us accordingly.

"O mighty General," he said, "She-who-commands bids me conduct the lady who is sick to the place that has been made ready for her, which is near your own so that you may watch over her if you will."

I wondered how Ayesha knew that Inez was sick, but being too tired to ask questions, merely bade him lead on. This he did, taking us to another ruined house next to our own quarters which had been swept, cleaned and furnished after a fashion, and moreover cleverly roofed in with mats, so that it was really quite comfortable. Here we found two middle-aged women of a very superior type, who, Billali informed me, were by trade nurses of the sick. Having seen her laid upon her bed, I committed Inez to their charge, since the case was not one that I dared to try to doctor myself, not knowing what drug of the few I possessed should be administered to her. Moreover Billali comforted me with the information that soon She-who-commands would visit her and "make her well again," as she could do.

I answered that I hoped so and went to our quarters where I found an excellent meal ready cooked and with it a stone flagon, of the contents of which Billali said we were all three to drink by the command of Ayesha, who declared that it would take away our weariness.

I tried the stuff, which was pale yellow in colour like sherry and, for aught I knew, might be poison, to find it most comforting, though it did not seem to be very strong to the taste. Certainly, too, its effects were wonderful, since presently all my great weariness fell from me like a discarded cloak, and I found myself with a splendid appetite and feeling better and stronger than I had done for years. In short that drink was a "cocktail" of the best, one of which I only wish I possessed the recipe, though Ayesha told me afterwards that it was distilled from quite harmless herbs and not in any sense a spirit.

Having discovered this, I gave some of it to Hans, also to Umslopogaas, who was with the wounded Zulus, who, we found, were progressing well towards complete recovery, and lastly to Goroko who also was worn out. On all of these the effect of that magical brew proved most satisfactory.

Then, having washed, I ate a splendid dinner, though in this respect Hans, who was seated on the ground nearby, far outpassed my finest efforts.

"Baas," he said, "things have gone very well with us when they might have gone very ill. The Baas Red-Beard is dead, which is a good thing, since a madman would have been difficult to look after, and a brain full of moonshine is a bad companion for any one. Oh! without doubt he is better dead, though your reverend father the Predikant will have a hard job looking after him there in the Place of Fires."

"Perhaps," I said with a sigh, "since it is better to be dead than to live a lunatic. But what I fear is that the lady his daughter will follow him."

"Oh, no! Baas," replied Hans cheerfully, "though I daresay that she will always be a little mad also, because you see it is in her blood and doubtless she has looked on dreadful things. But the Great Medicine will see to it that she does not die after we have taken so much trouble and gone into such big dangers to save her. That Great Medicine is very wonderful, Baas. First of all it makes you General over those Amahagger who without you would never have fought, as the Witch who ties up her head in a cloth knew well enough. Then it brings us safe through the battle and gives strength to Umslopogaas to kill the old man-eating giant."

"Why did it not give *me* strength to kill him, Hans? I let him have two Express bullets on his chest, which hurt him no more than a tap upon the horns with a dancing stick would hurt a bull-buffalo."

"Oh! Baas, perhaps you missed him, who because you hit things sometimes, think that you do so always."

Having waited to see if I would rise to this piece of insolence, which of course I did not, he went on by way of letting me down easily, "Or perhaps he wore very good armour under his beard, for I saw some of those Amahagger who pulled his hair off and cut him to pieces, go away with what looked like little bits of brass. Also the Great Medicine meant that he should be killed by Umslopogaas and not by you, since otherwise Umslopogaas would have been sad for the rest of his life, whereas now he will walk about the world as proud as a cock with two tails and crow all night as well as all day. Then, Baas, when Rezu broke the square and the Amahagger began to run, without doubt it was the Great Medicine which changed their hearts and made them brave again, so that they charged at the right moment when they saw it going forward on your breast, and instead of being eaten up, ate up the cannibals."

"Indeed! I thought that the Lady who dwells yonder had something to do with that business. Did you see her, Hans?"

"Oh, yes! I saw her, Baas, and I think that without doubt she lifted the cloth from over her head and when the people of Rezu saw how ugly was the face beneath, it did frighten them a little. But doubtless the Great Medicine put that thought into her also, for, Baas, what could a silly woman do in such a case? Did you ever know of a woman who was of any use in a battle, or for anything else except to nurse babies, and this one does not even do that, no doubt because being so hideous under that sheet, no man can be found to marry her."

Now I looked up by chance and in the light of the lamps saw Ayesha standing in the room, which she had entered through the open doorway, within six feet of Hans' back indeed.

"Be sure Baas," he went on, "that this bundle of rags is nothing but a common old cheat who frightens people by pretending to be a spook, as, if she dared to say that it was she who made those stinking Amahagger charge, and not the Great Medicine of the Opener-of-Roads, I would tell her to her face."

Now I was too paralysed to speak, and while I was reflecting that it was fortunate Ayesha did not understand Dutch, she moved a little so that one of the lamps behind her caused her shadow to fall on to the back of the squatting Hans and over it on to the floor beyond. He saw it and stared at the distorted shape of the hooded head, then slowly screwed his neck round and looked upwards behind him.

For a moment he went on staring as though he were frozen, then uttering a wild yell, he scrambled to his feet, bolted out of the house and vanished into the night.

"It seems, Allan," said Ayesha slowly, "that yonder yellow ape of yours is very bold at throwing sticks when the leopardess is not beneath the tree. But when she comes it is otherwise with him. Oh! make no excuse, for I know well that he was speaking ill things of me, because being curious, as apes are, he burns to learn what is behind my veil, and being simple, believes that no woman would hide her face unless its fashion were not pleasing to the nice taste of men."

Then, to my relief, she laughed a little, softly, which showed me that she had a sense of humour, and went on, "Well, let him be, for he is a good ape and courageous in his fashion, as he showed when he went out to spy upon the host of Rezu, and stabbed the murderer-priest by the stone of sacrifice."

"How can you know the words of Hans, Ayesha," I asked, "seeing that he spoke in a tongue which you have never learned?"

"Perchance I read faces, Allan."

"Or backs," I suggested, remembering that his was turned to her.

"Or backs, or voices, or hearts. It matters little which, since read I do. But have done with such childish talk and lead me to this maiden who has been snatched from the claws of Rezu and a fate that is worse than death. Do you understand, Allan, that ere the demon Rezu took her to wife, the plan was to sacrifice her own father to her and then eat him as the woman with her was eaten, and before her eyes? Now the father is dead, which is well, as I think the little yellow man said to you—nay, start not, I read it from his back—since had he lived whose brain was rotted, he would have raved till his death's day. Better, therefore, that he should die like a man fighting against a foe unconquerable by all save one. But she still lives."

"Aye, but mindless, Ayesha."

"Which, in great trouble such as she has passed, is a blessed state, O Allan. Bethink you, have there not been days, aye and months, in your own life when you would have rejoiced to sleep in mindlessness? And should we not, perchance, be happier, all of us, if like the beasts we could not remember, foreknow and understand? Oh! men talk of Heaven, but believe me, the real Heaven is one of dreamless sleep, since life and wakefulness, however high their scale and on whatever star, mean struggle, which being so oft mistaken, must breed sorrow—or remorse that spoils all. Come now."

So I preceded her to the next ruined house where we found Inez lying on the bed still clothed in her barbaric trappings, although the veil had been drawn off her face. There she lay, wide-eyed and still, while the women watched her. Ayesha looked at her a while, then said to me, "So they tricked her out to be Ayesha's mock and image, and in time accepted by those barbarians as my very self, and even set the seals of royalty on her," and she pointed to the gold discs stamped with the likeness of the sun. "Well, she is a fair maiden, white and gently bred, the first such that I have seen for many an age. Nor did she wish this trickery. Moreover she has taken no hurt; her soul has sunk deep into a sea of horror and that is all, whence doubtless it can be drawn again. Yet I think it best that for a while she should remember naught, lest her brain break, as did her father's, and therefore no net of mine shall drag her back to memory. Let that return gently in future days, and then of it not too much, for so shall all this terror become to her a void in which sad shapes move like shadows, and as shadows are soon forgot and gone, no more to be held than dreams by the awakening sense. Stand aside, Allan, and you women, leave us for a while."

I obeyed, and the women bowed and went. Then Ayesha drew up her veil, and knelt down by the bed of Inez, but in such a fashion that I could not see her face although I admit that I tried to do so. I could see, however, that she set her lips against those of Inez and as I gathered by her motions, seemed to breathe into her lips. Also she lifted her hands and placing one of them upon the heart of Inez, for a minute or more swayed the other from side to side above her eyes, pausing at times to touch her upon the forehead with her finger-tips.

Presently Inez stirred and sat up, whereon Ayesha took a vessel of milk which stood upon the floor and held it to her lips. Inez drank to the last drop, then sank on to the bed again. For a while longer Ayesha continued the motions of her hands, then let fall her veil and rose.

"Look, I have laid a spell upon her," she said, beckoning to me to draw near.

I did so and perceived that now the eyes of Inez were shut and that she seemed to be plunged in a deep and natural sleep.

"So she will remain for this night and that day which follows," said Ayesha, "and when she wakes it will be, I think, to believe herself once more a happy child. Not until she sees her home again will she find her womanhood, and then all this story will be forgotten by her. Of her father you must tell her that he died when you went out to hunt the river-beasts together, and if she seeks for certain others, that they have gone away. But I think that she will ask little more when she learns that he is dead, since I have laid that command upon her soul."

"Hypnotic suggestion," thought I to myself, "and I only hope to heaven that it will work."

Ayesha seemed to guess what was passing through my mind, for she nodded and said, "Have no fear, Allan, for I am what the black axe-bearer and the little yellow man called a 'witch' which means, as you who are instructed know, one who has knowledge of medicine and other things and who holds a key to some of the mysteries that lie hid in Nature."

"For instance," I suggested, "of how to transport yourself into a battle at the right moment, and out of it again—also at the right moment."

"Yes, Allan, since watching from afar, I saw that those Amahagger curs were about to flee and that I was needed there to hearten them and to put fear into the army of Rezu. So I came."

"But how did you come, Ayesha?"

She laughed as she answered, "Perhaps I did not come at all. Perhaps you only thought I came; since I seemed to be there the rest matters nothing."

As I still looked unconvinced she went on, "Oh! foolish man, seek not to learn of that which is too high for you. Yet listen. You in your ignorance suppose that the soul dwells within the body, do you not?"

I answered that I had always been under this impression.

"Yet, Allan, it is otherwise, for the body dwells within the soul."

"Like the pearl in an oyster," I suggested.

"Aye, in a sense, since the pearl which to you is beautiful, is to the oyster a sickness and a poison, and so is the body to the soul whose temple it troubles and defiles. Yet round it is the white and holy soul that ever seeks to bring the vile body to its own purity and colour, yet oft-times fails. Learn, Allan, that flesh and spirit are the deadliest foes joined together by a high decree that they may forget their hate and perfect each other, or failing, be separate to all eternity, the spirit going to its own place and the flesh to its corruption."

"A strange theory," I said.

"Aye, Allan, and one which is so new to you that never will you understand it. Yet it is true and I set it out for this reason. The soul of man, being at liberty and not cooped within his narrow breast, is in touch with that soul of the Universe, which men know as God Whom they call by many names. Therefore it has all knowledge and perhaps all power, and at times the body within it, if it be a wise body, can draw from this well of knowledge and abounding power. So at least can I. And now you will understand why I am so good a doctoress and how I came to appear in the battle, as you said, at the right time, and to leave it when my work was done."

"Oh! yes," I answered, "I quite understand. I thank you much for putting it so plainly."

She laughed a little, appreciating my jest, looked at the sleeping Inez, and said, "The fair body of this lady dwells in a large soul, I think, though one of a somewhat sombre hue, for souls have their colours, Allan, and stain that which is within them. She will never be a happy woman."

"The black people named her Sad-Eyes," I said.

"Is it so? Well, I name her Sad-Heart, though for such often there is joy at last. Meanwhile she will forget; yes, she will forget the worst and how narrow was the edge between her and the arms of Rezu."

"Just the width of the blade of the axe, *Inkosikaas*," I answered. "But tell me, Ayesha, why could not that axe cut and why did my bullets flatten or turn aside when these smote the breast of Rezu?"

"Because his front-armour was good, Allan, I suppose," she replied indifferently, "and on his back he wore none."

"Then why did you fill my ears with such a different tale about that horrible giant having drunk of a Cup of Life, and all the rest?" I asked with irritation.

"I have forgotten, Allan. Perhaps because the curious, such as you are, like to hear tales even stranger than their own, which in the days to be may become their own. Therefore you will be wise to believe only what I do, and of what I tell you, nothing."

"I don't," I exclaimed exasperated.

She laughed again and replied, "What need to say to me that which I know already? Yet perhaps in the future it may be different, since often by the alchemy of the mind the fables of our youth are changed into the facts of our age, and we come to believe in anything, as your little yellow man believes in some savage named Zikali, and those Amahagger believe in the talisman round your neck, and I who am the maddest of you all, believe in Love and Wisdom, and the black warrior, Umslopogaas, believes in the virtue of that great axe of his, rather than in those of his own courage and of the strength that wields it. Fools, every one of us, though perchance I am the greatest fool among them. Now take me to the warrior, Umslopogaas, whom I would thank, as I thank you, Allan, and the little yellow man, although he jeers at me with his sharp tongue, not knowing that if I were angered, with a breath I could cause him to cease to be."

"Then why did you not choose Rezu to cease to be, and his army also, Ayesha?"

"It seems that I have done these things through the axe of Umslopogaas and by the help of your generalship, Allan. Why then, waste my own strength when yours lay to my hand?"

"Because you had no power over Rezu, Ayesha, or so you told me."

"Have I not said that my words are snowflakes, meant to melt and leave no trace, hiding my thoughts as this veil hides my beauty? Yet as the beauty is beneath the veil, perchance there is truth beneath the words, though not that truth you think. So you are well answered, and for the rest, I wonder whether Rezu thought I had no power over him when yonder on the mountain spur he saw me float down upon his companies like a spirit of the night. Well, perchance some day I shall learn this and many other things."

I made no answer, since what was the use of arguing with a woman who told me frankly that all she said was false. So, although I longed to ask her why these Amahagger had such reverence for the talisman that Hans called the Great Medicine, since now I guessed that her first explanations concerning it were quite untrue, I held my tongue.

Yet as we went out of the house, by some coincidence she alluded to this very matter.

"I wish to tell you, Allan," she said, "why it was those Amahagger would not accept you as a General till their eyes had seen that which you wear upon your breast. Their tale of a legend of this very thing seemed that of savages or of their cunning priests, not to be believed by a wise man such as you are, like some others that you have heard in Kôr. Yet it has in it a grain of truth, for as it chanced a little while ago, about a hundred years ago, I think, the old wizard whose picture is cut upon the wood, came to visit her who held my place before me as ruler of this tribe—she was very like me and as I believe, my mother, Allan—because of her repute for wisdom.

"At that time I have heard there was a question of war between the worshippers of Lulala and the grandfather of Rezu. But this Zikali told the People of Lulala that they must not fight the People of Rezu until in a day to come a white man should visit Kôr and bring with him a piece of wood on which was cut the image of a dwarf like to that of Zikali himself. Then and not before they must fight and conquer the People of Rezu. Now this story came down among them and you who may have thought the first tale magical, will understand it in its simplicity: is it not so, you wise Allan?"

"Oh! yes," I answered, "except that I do not see how Zikali can have come here a hundred years ago, since men do not live as long, although he pretends to have done so."

"No, Allan, nor do I, but perhaps it was his father, or his grandfather who came, since being observant, you will have noted that if the parent is mis-formed, so often are the descendants; also that the pretence of wizardry at times comes down with the blood."

Again I made no answer for I saw that Ayesha was fooling me, and before she could exhaust that amusement we reached the place where Umslopogaas and his men were gathered round a camp fire. He sat silent, but Goroko with much animation was telling the story of the fight in picturesque and colourful language, or that part of it which he had seen, for the benefit of the two wounded men who took no share in it and who, lying on their blankets with heads thrust forward, were listening with eagerness to the entrancing tale.

Suddenly they caught sight of Ayesha, and those of the party who could stand sprang to their feet, while one and all they gave her the royal salute of *Bayéte*.

She waited till the sound had died away. Then she said, "I come to thank you and your men, O Wielder of the Axe, who have shown yourself very great in battle, and to say to you that my Spirit tells me that every one of you, yes, even those who are still sick, will come safe to your own land again and live out your years with honour."

Again they saluted at this pleasing intelligence, when I had translated it to them, for of course they knew no Arabic. Then she went on, "I am told, Umslopogaas, Son of the Lion, as a certain king was named in your land, that the fight you made against Rezu was a very great fight, and that such a leap as yours above his head when you smote him with the axe on the hinder parts where he wore no armour, and brought him to his death, has not been seen before, nor will be again."

I rendered the words, and Umslopogaas, preferring truth to modesty, replied emphatically that this was the case.

"Because of that fight and that leap," Ayesha went on, "as for other deeds that you have done and will do, my Spirit tells me that your name will live in story for many generations. Yet of what use is fame to the dead? Therefore I make you an offer. Bide here with me and you shall rule these Amahagger, and with them the remnant of the People of Rezu. Your cattle shall be countless and your wives the fairest in the land, and your children many, for I will lift a certain curse from off you so that no more shall you be childless. Do you accept, O Holder of the Axe?"

When he understood, Umslopogaas, after pondering a moment, asked if I meant to stay in this land and marry the white chieftainess who spoke such wise words and could appear and disappear in the battle at her will, and like a mountain-top hid her head in a cloud, which was his way of alluding to her veil.

I answered at once and with decision that I intended to do nothing of the sort and immediately regretted my words, since, although I spoke in Zulu, I suppose she read their meaning from my face. At any rate she understood the drift of them.

"Tell him, Allan," she said with a kind of icy politeness, "that you will not stop here and marry me, because if ever I chose a husband he would not be a little man at the doors of whose heart so many women's hands have knocked—yes, even those that are black—and not, I think, in vain. One, moreover, who holds himself so clever that he believes he has nothing left to learn, and in every flower of truth that is shown to him, however fair, smells only poison, and beneath, nurturing it, sees only the gross root of falsehood planted in corruption. Tell him these things, Allan, if it pleases you."

"It does not please me," I answered in a rage at her insults.

"Nor is it needful, Allan, since if I caught the meaning of that barbarous tongue you use aright, you have told him already. Well, let the jest pass, O man who least of all things desires to be Ayesha's husband, and whom Ayesha least of all things desires as her spouse, and ask the Axe-bearer nothing since I perceive that without you he will not stay at Kôr. Nor indeed is it fated that he should do so, for now my Spirit tells me what it hid from me when I spoke a moment gone, that this warrior shall die in a great fight far away and that between then and now much sorrow waits him who save that of one, knows not how to win the love of women. Let him say moreover what reward he desires since if I can give it to him, it shall be his."

Again I translated. Umslopogaas received her prophecies in stoical silence, and as I thought with indifference, and only said in reply, "The glory that I have won is my reward and the only boon I seek at this queen's hands is that if she can she should give me sight of a woman for whom my heart is hungry, and with it knowledge that this woman lives in that land whither I travel like all men."

When she heard these words Ayesha said, "True, I had forgotten. Your heart also is hungry, I think, Allan, for the vision of sundry faces that you see no more. Well, I will do my best, but since only faith fulfils itself, how can I who must strive to pierce the gates of darkness for one so unbelieving, know that they will open at my word? Come to me, both of you, at the sunset tomorrow."

Then as though to change the subject, she talked to me for a long while about Kôr, of which she told me a most interesting history, true or false, that I omit here.

At length, as though suddenly she had grown tired, waving her hand to show that the conversation was ended, Ayesha went to the wounded men and touched them each in turn.

"Now they will recover swiftly," she said, and leaving the place was gone into the darkness.

CHAPTER 20

# The Gate of Death

Before turning in I examined these wounded men for myself. The truth is that I was anxious to learn their exact condition in order that I might make an estimate as to when it would be possible for us to leave this valley or crater bottom of Kôr, of which I was heartily tired. Who could desire to stay in a place where he had not only been involved in a deal of hard, doubtful, and very dangerous fighting from which all personal interest was absent, but where also he was meshed in a perfect spider's web of bewilderment, and exposed to continual insult into the bargain?

For that is what it came to; this Ayesha took every opportunity to jeer at and affront me. And why? Just because I had conceived doubts, which somehow she discovered, of the amazing tales with which it had amused her to stuff me, as a farmer's wife does a turkey poult with meal pellets. How could she expect me, a man, after all, of some experience, to believe such lies, which, not half an hour before, in the coolest possible fashion she had herself admitted to be lies and nothing else, told for the mere pleasure of romancing?

The immortal Rezu, for instance, who had drunk of the Cup of Life or some such rubbish, now turned out to be nothing but a brawny savage descended from generations of chiefs also called Rezu. Moreover the immemorial Ayesha, who also had drunk of Cups of Life, and according to her first story, had lived in this place for thousands of years, had come here with a mother, who filled the same mystic role before her for the benefit of an extremely gloomy and disagreeable tribe of Semitic savages. Yet she was cross with me because I had not swallowed her crude and indigestible mixture of fable and philosophy without a moment's question.

At least I supposed that this was the reason, though another possible explanation did come into my mind. I had refused to be duly overcome by her charms, not because I was unimpressed, for who could be, having looked upon that blinding beauty even for a moment? but rather because, after sundry experiences, I had at last attained to some power of judgment and learned what it is best to leave alone. Perhaps this had annoyed her, especially as no white man seemed to have come her way for a long while and the fabulous Kallikrates had not put in his promised appearance.

Also it was unfortunate that in one way or another—how did she do it, I wondered—she had interpreted Umslopogaas' question to me about marrying her, and my compromising reply. Not that for one moment, as I saw very clearly, did she wish to marry me. But that fact, intuition suggested to my mind, did not the least prevent her from being angry because I shared her views upon this important subject.

Oh! the whole thing was a bore and the sooner I saw the last of that veiled lady and the interesting but wearisome ruins in which she dwelt, the better I should be pleased, although apparently I must trek homewards with a poor young woman who was out of her mind, leaving the bones of her unfortunate father behind me. I admitted to myself, however, that there were consolations in the fact that Providence had thus decreed, for Robertson since he gave up drink had not been a cheerful companion, and two mad people would really have been more than I could manage.

To return, for these reasons I examined the two wounded Zulus with considerable anxiety, only to discover another instance of the chicanery which it amused this Ayesha to play off upon me. For what did I find? That they were practically well. Their hurts, which had never been serious, had healed wonderfully in that pure air, as those of savages have a way of doing, and they told me themselves that they felt quite strong again. Yet with colossal impudence Ayesha had managed to suggest to my mind that she was going to work some remarkable cure upon them, who were already cured.

Well, it was of a piece with the rest of her conduct and there was nothing to do except go to bed, which I did with much gratitude that my resting place that night was not of another sort. The last thing I remember was wondering how on earth Ayesha appeared and disappeared in the course of that battle, a problem as to which I could find no solution, though, as in the case of the others, I was sure that one would occur to me in course of time.

I slept like a top, so soundly indeed that I think there was some kind of soporific in the pick-me-up which looked like sherry, especially as the others who had drunk of it also passed an excellent night.

About ten o'clock on the following morning I awoke feeling particularly well and quite as though I had been enjoying a week at the seaside instead of my recent adventures, which included an abominable battle and some agonising moments during which I thought that my number was up upon the board of Destiny.

I spent the most of that day lounging about, eating, talking over the details of the battle with Umslopogaas and the Zulus and smoking more than usual. (I forgot to say that these Amahagger grew some capital tobacco of which I had obtained a supply, although like most Africans, they only used it in the shape of snuff.) The truth was that after all my marvellings and acute anxieties, also mental and physical exertions, I felt like the housemaid who caused to be cut upon her tombstone that she had gone to a better land where her ambition was to do nothing "for ever and ever." I just wanted to be completely idle and vacuous-minded for at least a month, but as I knew that all I could expect in that line was a single bank holiday, like a City clerk on the spree, of it I determined to make the most.

The result was that before the evening I felt very bored indeed. I had gone to look at Inez, who was still fast asleep, as Ayesha said would be the case, but whose features seemed to have plumped up considerably. The reason of this I gathered from her Amahagger nurses, was that at certain intervals she had awakened sufficiently to swallow considerable quantities of milk, or rather cream, which I hoped would not make her ill. I had chatted with the wounded Zulus, who were now walking about, more bored even than I was myself, and heaping maledictions on their ancestral spirits because they had not been well enough to take part in the battle against Rezu.

I even took a little stroll to look for Hans, who had vanished in his mysterious fashion, but the afternoon was so hot and oppressive with coming thunder, that soon I came back again and fell into a variety of reflections that I need not detail.

While I was thus engaged and meditating, not without uneasiness, upon the ordeal that lay before me after sunset, for I felt sure that it would be an ordeal, Hans appeared and said that the Amahagger *impi* or army was gathered on that spot where I had been elected to the proud position of their General. He added that he believed—how he got this information I do not know—that the White Lady was going to hold a review of them and give them the rewards that they had earned in the battle.

Hearing this, Umslopogaas and the other Zulus said that they would like to see this review if I would accompany them. Although I did not want to go nor indeed desired ever to look at another Ama-hagger, I consented to save the trouble of argument, on condition that we should do so from a distance.

So, including the wounded men, we strolled off and presently came to the crumbled wall of the old city, beyond which lay the great moat now dry, that once had encircled it with water.

Here on the top of this wall we sat down where we could see without being seen, and observed the Amahagger companies, considerably reduced during the battle, being marshalled by their captains beneath us and about a couple of hundred yards away. Also we observed several groups of men under guard. These we took to be prisoners captured in the fight with Rezu, who, as Hans remarked with a smack of his lips, were probably awaiting sacrifice.

I said I hoped not and yawned, for really the afternoon was intensely hot and the weather most peculiar. The sun had vanished behind clouds, and vapours filled the still air, so dense that at times it grew almost dark; also when these cleared for brief intervals, the landscape in the grey, unholy light looked distorted and unnatural, as it does during an eclipse of the sun.

Goroko, the witch-doctor, stared round him, sniffed the air and then remarked ocularly that it was *wizard's weather* and that there were many spirits about. Upon my word I felt inclined to agree with him, for my feelings were very uncomfortable, but I only replied that if so, I should be obliged if he, as a professional, would be good enough to keep them off me. Of course I knew that electrical charges were about, which accounted for my sensations, and wished that I had never left the camp.

It was during one of these periods of dense gloom that Ayesha must have arrived upon the review ground. At least, when it lifted, there she was in her white garments, surrounded by women and guards, engaged apparently in making an oration, for although I could not hear a word, I could see by the motions of her arms that she was speaking.

Had she been the central figure in some stage scene, no limelights could have set her off to better advantage, than did those of the heavens above her. Suddenly, through the blanket of cloud, flowing from a hole in it that looked like an eye, came a blood-red ray which fell full upon her, so that she alone was fiercely visible whilst all around was gloom in which shapes moved dimly. Certainly she looked strange and even terrifying in that red ray which stained her robe till I who had but just come out of battle with its confused noise, began to think of *the garments rolled in blood* of which I often read in my favourite Old Testament. For crimson was she from head to foot; a tall shape of terror and of wrath.

The eye in heaven shut and the ray went out. Then came one of the spaces of grey light and in it I saw men being brought up, apparently from the groups of prisoners, under guard, and, to the number of a dozen or more, stood in a line before Ayesha.

Then I saw nothing more for a long while, because blackness seemed to flow in from every quarter of the heavens and to block out the scene beneath. At least after a pause of perhaps five minutes, during which the stillness was intense, the storm broke.

It was a very curious storm; in all my experience of African tempests I cannot recall one which it resembled. It began with the usual cold and wailing wind. This died away, and suddenly the whole arch of heaven was alive with little lightnings that seemed to strike horizontally, not downwards to the earth, weaving a web of fire upon the surface of the sky.

By the illumination of these lightnings which, but for the swiftness of their flashing and greater intensity, somewhat resembled a dense shower of shooting stars, I perceived that Ayesha was addressing the men that had been brought before her, who stood dejectedly in a long line with their heads bent, quite unattended, since their guards had fallen back.

"If I were going to receive a reward of cattle or wives, I should look happier than those moon-worshippers, Baas," remarked Hans reflectively.

"Perhaps it would depend," I answered, "upon what the cattle and wives were like. If the cattle had red-water and would bring disease into your herd, or wild bulls that would gore you, and the wives were skinny old widows with evil tongues, then I think you would look as do those men, Hans."

I don't quite know what made me speak thus, but I believe it was some sense of pending death or disaster, suggested, probably, by the ominous character of the setting provided by Nature to the curious drama of which we were witnesses.

"I never thought of that, Baas," commented Hans, "but it is true that all gifts are not good, especially witches' gifts."

As he spoke the little net-like lightnings died away, leaving behind them a gross darkness through which, far above us, the wind wailed again.

Then suddenly all the heaven was turned into one blaze of light, and by it I saw Ayesha standing tall and rigid with her hand pointed towards the line of men in front of her. The blaze went out, to be followed by blackness, and to return almost instantly in a yet fiercer blaze which seemed to fall earthwards in a torrent of fire that concentrated itself in a kind of flame-spout upon the spot where Ayesha stood.

Through that flame or rather in the heart of it, I saw Ayesha and the file of men in front of her, as the great King saw the prophets in the midst of the furnace that had been heated sevenfold. Only these men did not walk about in the fire; no, they fell backwards, while Ayesha alone remained upon her feet with outstretched hand.

Next came more blackness and crash upon crash of such thunder that the earth shook as it reverberated from the mountain cliffs. Never in my life did I hear such fearful thunder. It frightened the Zulus so much, that they fell upon their faces, except Goroko and Umslopogaas, whose pride kept them upon their feet, the former because he had a reputation to preserve as a "Heaven-herd," or Master of tempests.

I confess that I should have liked to follow their example, and lie down, being dreadfully afraid lest the lightning should strike me. But there—I did not.

At last the thunder died away and in the most mysterious fashion that violent tempest came to a sudden end, as does a storm upon the stage. No rain fell, which in itself was surprising enough and most unusual, but in place of it a garment of the completest calm descended upon the earth. By degrees, too, the darkness passed and the westering sun reappeared. Its rays fell upon the place where the Amahagger companies had stood, but now not one of them was to be seen.

They were all gone and Ayesha with them. So completely had they vanished away that I should have thought that we suffered from illusions, were it not for the line of dead men which lay there looking very small and lonesome on the *veld*; mere dots indeed at that distance.

We stared at each other and at them, and then Goroko said that he would like to inspect the bodies to learn whether lightning killed at Kôr as it did elsewhere, also whether it had smitten them altogether or leapt from man to man. This, as a professional "Heaven-herd," he declared he could tell from the marks upon these unfortunates.

As I was curious also and wanted to make a few observations, I consented. So with the exception of the wounded men, who I thought should avoid the exertion, we scrambled down the debris of the tumbled wall and across the open space beyond, reaching the scene of the tragedy without meeting or seeing anyone.

There lay the dead, eleven of them, in an exact line as they had stood. They were all upon their backs with widely-opened eyes and an expression of great fear frozen upon their faces. Some of these I recognised, as did Umslopogaas and Hans. They were soldiers or captains who had marched under me to attack Rezu, although until this moment I had not seen any of them after we began to descend the ridge where the battle took place.

"Baas," said Hans, "I believe that these were the traitors who slipped away and told Rezu of our plans so that he attacked us on the ridge, instead of our attacking him on the plain as we had arranged so nicely. At least they were none of them in the battle and afterwards I heard the Amahagger talking of some of them."

I remarked that if so the lightning had discriminated very well in this instance.

Meanwhile Goroko was examining the bodies one by one, and presently called out, "These doomed ones died not by lightning but by witchcraft. There is not a burn upon one of them, nor are their garments scorched."

I went to look and found that it was perfectly true; to all outward appearance the eleven were quite unmarked and unharmed. Except for their frightened air, they might have died a natural death in their sleep.

"Does lightning always scorch?" I asked Goroko.

"Always, Macumazahn," he answered, "that is, if he who has been struck is killed, as these are, and not only stunned. Moreover, most of yonder dead wear knives which should have melted or shattered with the sheaths burnt off them. Yet those knives are as though they had just left the smith's hammer and the whet-stone," and he drew some of them to show me.

Again it was quite true and here I may remark that my experience tallied with that of Goroko, since I have never seen anyone killed by lightning on whom or on whose clothing there was not some trace of its passage.

"*Ow!*" said Umslopogaas, "this is witchcraft, not Heaven-wrath. The place is enchanted. Let us get away lest we be smitten also who have not earned doom like those traitors."

"No need to fear," said Hans, "since with us is the Great Medicine of Zikali which can tie up the lightning as an old woman does a bundle of sticks."

Still I observed that for all his confidence, Hans himself was the first to depart and with considerable speed. So we went back to our camp without more conversation, since the Zulus were scared and I confess that myself I could not understand the matter, though no doubt it admitted of some quite simple explanation.

However that might be, this Kôr was a queer place with its legends, its sullen Amahagger and its mysterious queen, to whom at times, in spite of my inner conviction to the contrary, I was still inclined to attribute powers beyond those that are common even among very beautiful and able women.

This reflection reminded me that she had promised us a further exhibition of those powers and within an hour or two. Remembering this I began to regret that I had ever asked for any such manifestations, for who knew what these might or might not involve?

So much did I regret it that I determined, unless Ayesha sent for us, as she had said she would do, I would conveniently forget the appointment. Luckily Umslopogaas seemed to be of the same way of thinking; at any rate he went off to eat his evening meal without alluding to it at all. So I made up my mind that I would not bring the matter to his notice and having ascertained that Inez was still asleep, I followed his example and dined myself, though without any particular appetite.

As I finished the sun was setting in a perfectly clear sky, so as there was no sign of any messenger, I thought that I would go to bed early, leaving orders that I was not to be disturbed. But on this point my luck was lacking, for just as I had taken off my coat, Hans arrived and said that old Billali was without and had come to take me somewhere.

Well, there was nothing to do but to put it on again. Before I had finished this operation Billali himself arrived with undignified and unusual haste. I asked him what was the matter, and he answered inconsequently that the Black One, the slayer of Rezu, was at the door "with his axe."

"That generally accompanies him," I replied. Then, remembering the cause of Billali's alarm, I explained to him that he must not take too much notice of a few hasty words spoken by an essentially gentle-natured person whose nerve had given way beneath provocation and bodily effort. The old fellow bowed in assent and stroked his beard, but I noticed that while Umslopogaas was near, he clung to me like a shadow. Perhaps he thought that nervous attacks might be recurrent, like those of fever.

Outside the house I found Umslopogaas leaning on his axe and looking at the sky in which the last red rays of evening lingered.

"The sun has set, Macumazahn," he said, "and it is time to visit this white queen as she bade us, and to learn whether she can indeed lead us 'down below' where the dead are said to dwell."

So he had not forgotten, which was disconcerting. To cover up my own doubts I asked him with affected confidence and cheerfulness whether he was not afraid to risk this journey "down below," that is, to the Realm of Death.

"Why should I fear to tread a road that awaits the feet of all of us and at the gate of which we knock day by day, especially if we chance to live by war, as do you and I, Macumazahn?" he inquired with a quiet dignity, which made me feel ashamed.

"Why indeed?" I answered, adding to myself, "though I should much prefer any other highway."

After this we started without more words, I keeping up my spirits by reflecting that the whole business was nonsense and that there could be nothing to dread.

All too soon we passed the ruined archway and were admitted into Ayesha's presence in the usual fashion. As Billali, who remained outside of them, drew the curtains behind us, I observed, to my astonishment, that Hans had sneaked in after me, and squatted down quite close to them, apparently in the hope of being overlooked.

It seemed, as I gathered later, that somehow or other he had guessed, or become aware of the object of our visit, and that his burning curiosity had overcome his terror of the "White Witch." Or possibly he hoped to discover whether or not she were so ugly as he supposed her veil-hidden face to be. At any rate there he was, and if Ayesha noticed him, as I think she did, for I saw by the motion of her head, that she was looking in his direction, she made no remark.

For a while she sat still in her chair contemplating us both. Then she said, "How comes it that you are late? Those that seek their lost loves should run with eager feet, but yours have tarried."

I muttered some excuse to which she did not trouble to listen, for she went on, "I think, Allan, that your sandals, which should be winged like to those of the Roman Mercury, are weighted with the grey lead of fear. Well, it is not strange, since you have come to travel through the Gates of Death that are feared by all, even by Ayesha's self, for who knows what he may find beyond them? Ask the Axe-Bearer if he also is afraid."

I obeyed, rendering all that she had said into the Zulu idiom as best I could.

"Say to the Queen," answered Umslopogaas, when he understood, "that I fear nothing, except women's tongues. I am ready to pass the Gates of Death and, if need be, to come back no more. With the white people I know it is otherwise because of some dark teachings to which they listen, that tell of terrors to be, such as we who are black do not dread. Still, we believe that there are ghosts and that the spirits of our fathers live on and as it chances I would learn whether this is so, who above all things desire to met a certain ghost, for which reason I journeyed to this far land.

"Say these things to the white Queen, Macumazahn, and tell her that if she should send me to a place whence there is no return, I who do not love the world, shall not blame her overmuch, though it is true that I should have chosen to die in war. Now I have spoken."

When I had passed on all this speech to Ayesha, her comment on it was, "This black Captain has a spirit as brave as his body, but how is it with your spirit, Allan? Are you also prepared to risk so much? Learn that I can promise you nothing, save that when I loose the bonds of your mortality and send out your soul to wander in the depths of Death, as I believe that I can do, though even of this I am not certain— you must pass through a gate of terrors that may be closed behind you by a stronger arm than mine. Moreover, what you will find beyond it I do not know, since be sure of this, each of us has his own heaven or his own hell, or both, that soon or late he is doomed to travel. Now will you go forward, or go back? Make choice while there is still time."

At all this ominous talk I felt my heart shrivel like a fire-withered leaf, if I may use that figure, and my blood assume the temperature and consistency of ice-cream. Earnestly did I curse myself for having allowed my curiosity about matters which we are not meant to understand to bring me to the edge of such a choice. Swiftly I determined to temporise, which I did by asking Ayesha whether she would accompany me upon this eerie expedition.

She laughed a little as she answered, "Bethink you, Allan. Am I, whose face you have seen, a meet companion for a man who desires to visit the loves that once were his? What would they say or think, if they should see you hand in hand with such a one?"

"I don't know and don't care," I replied desperately, "but this is the kind of journey on which one requires a guide who knows the road. Cannot Umslopogaas go first and come back to tell me how it has fared with him?"

"If the brave and instructed white lord, panoplied in the world's last Faith, is not ashamed to throw the savage in his ignorance out like a feather to test the winds of hell and watch the while to learn whether these blow him back unscorched, or waft him into fires whence there is no return, perchance it might so be ordered, Allan. Ask him yourself, Allan, if he is willing to run this errand for your sake. Or perhaps the little yellow man——" and she paused.

At this point Hans, who having a smattering of Arabic understood something of our talk, could contain himself no longer.

"No, Baas," he broke in from his corner by the curtain, "not *me*. I don't care for hunting spooks, Baas, which leave no spoor that you can follow and are always behind when you think they are in front. Also there are too many of them waiting for me down there and how can I stand up to them until I am a spook myself and know their ways of fighting? Also if you should die when your spirit is away, I want to be left that I may bury you nicely."

"Be silent," I said in my sternest manner. Then, unable to bear more of Ayesha's mockery, for I felt that as usual she was mocking me, I added with all the dignity that I could command, "I am ready to make this journey through the gate of Death, Ayesha, if indeed you can show me the road. For one purpose and no other I came to Kôr, namely to learn, if so I might, whether those who have died upon the world, live on elsewhere. Now, what must I do?"

## Chapter 21

# The Lesson

"Yes," answered Ayesha, laughing very softly, "for that purpose alone, O truth-seeking Allan, whose curiosity is so fierce that the wide world cannot hold it, did you come to Kôr and not to seek wealth or new lands, or to fight more savages. No, not even to look upon a certain Ayesha, of whom the old wizard told you, though I think you have always loved to try to lift the veil that hides women's hearts, if not their faces. Yet it was I who brought you to Kôr for my own purposes, not your desire, nor Zikali's map and talisman, since had not the white lady who lies sick been stolen by Rezu, never would you have pursued the journey nor found the way hither."

"How could you have had anything to do with that business?" I asked testily, for my nerves were on edge and I said the first thing that came into my mind.

"That, Allan, is a question over which you will wonder for a long while either beneath or beyond the sun, as you will wonder concerning much that has to do with me, which your little mind, shut in its iron box of ignorance and pride, cannot understand today.

"For example, you have been wondering, I am sure, how the lightning killed those eleven men whose bodies you went to look on an hour or two ago, and left the rest untouched. Well, I will tell you at once that it was not lightning that killed them, although the strength within me was manifest to you in storm, but rather what that witch-doctor of your following called wizardry. Because they were traitors who betrayed your army to Rezu, I killed them with my wrath and by the wand of my power. Oh! you do not believe, yet perhaps ere long you will, since thus to fulfil your prayer I must also kill you—almost. That is the trouble, Allan. To kill you outright would be easy, but to kill you just enough to set your spirit free and yet leave one crevice of mortal life through which it can creep back again, that is most difficult; a thing that only I can do and even of myself I am not sure."

"Pray do not try the experiment——" I began thoroughly alarmed, but she cut me short.

"Disturb me no more, Allan, with the tremors and changes of your uncertain mind, lest you should work more evil than you think, and making mine uncertain also, spoil my skill. Nay, do not try to fly, for already the net has thrown itself about you and you cannot stir, who are bound like a little gilded wasp in the spider's web, or like birds beneath the eyes of basilisks."

This was true, for I found that, strive as I would, I could not move a limb or even an eyelid. I was frozen to that spot and there was nothing for it except to curse my folly and say my prayers.

All this while she went on talking, but of what she said I have not the faintest idea, because my remaining wits were absorbed in these much-needed implorations.

\*\*\*\*\*\*\*\*

Presently, of a sudden, I appeared to see Ayesha seated in a temple, for there were columns about her, and behind her was an altar on which a fire burned. All round her, too, were hooded snakes like to that which she wore about her middle, fashioned in gold. To these snakes she sang and they danced to her singing; yes, with flickering tongues they danced upon their tails! What the scene signified I cannot conceive, unless it meant that this mistress of magic was consulting her familiars.

Then that vision vanished and Ayesha's voice began to seem very far away and dreamy, also her wondrous beauty became visible to me through her veil, as though I had acquired a new sense that overcame the limitations of mortal sight. Even in this extremity I reflected it was well that the last thing I looked on should be something so glorious. No, not quite the last thing, for out of the corners of my eyes I saw that Umslopogaas from a sitting position had sunk on to his back and lay, apparently dead, with his axe still gripped tightly and held above his head, as though his arm had been turned to ice.

After this terrible things began to happen to me and I became aware that I was dying. A great wind seemed to catch me up and blow me to and fro, as a leaf is blown in the eddies of a winter gale. Enormous rushes of darkness flowed over me, to be succeeded by vivid bursts of brightness that dazzled like lightning. I fell off precipices and at the foot of them was caught by some fearful strength and tossed to the very skies.

From those skies I was hurled down again into a kind of whirl-pool of inky night, round which I spun perpetually, as it seemed for hours and hours. But worst of all was the awful loneliness from which I suffered. It seemed to me as though there were no other living thing in all the Universe and never had been and never would be any other living thing. I felt as though *I* were the Universe rushing solitary through space for ages upon ages in a frantic search for fellowship, and finding none.

Then something seemed to grip my throat and I knew that I had died—for the world floated away from beneath me.

Now fear and every mortal sensation left me, to be replaced by a new and spiritual terror. I, or rather my disembodied consciousness, seemed to come up for judgment, and the horror of it was that I appeared to be my own judge. There, a very embodiment of cold justice, my Spirit, grown luminous, sat upon a throne and to it, with dread and merciless particularity I set out all my misdeeds. It was as if some part of me remained mortal, for I could see my two eyes, my mouth and my hands, but nothing else—and strange enough they looked. From the eyes came tears, from the mouth flowed words and the hands were joined, as though in prayer to that throned and adamantine Spirit which was *me*.

It was as though this Spirit were asking how my body had served its purposes and advanced its mighty ends, and in reply—oh! what a miserable tale I had to tell. Fault upon fault, weakness upon weakness, sin upon sin; never before did I understand how black was my record. I tried to relieve the picture with some incidents of attempted good, but that Spirit would not hearken. It seemed to say that it had gathered up the good and knew it all. It was of the evil that it would learn, not of the good that had bettered it, but of the evil by which it had been harmed.

Hearing this there rose up in my consciousness some memory of what Ayesha had said; namely, that the body lived within the temple of the spirit which is oft defied, and not the spirit in the body.

\*\*\*\*\*\*\*\*

The story was told and I hearkened for the judgment, my own judgment on myself, which I knew would be accepted without question and registered for good or ill. But none came, since ere the balance sank this way or that, ere it could be uttered, I was swept afar.

Through Infinity I was swept, and as I fled faster than the light, the meaning of what I had seen came home to me. I knew, or seemed to know for the first time, that at the last *man must answer to himself,* or perhaps to a divine principle within himself, that out of his own free-will, through long aeons and by a million steps, he climbs or sinks to the heights or depths dormant in his nature; that from what he was, springs what he is, and what he is, engenders what he shall be for ever and aye.

Now I envisaged Immortality and splendid and awful was its face. It clasped me to its breast and in the vast circle of its arms I was upborne, I who knew myself to be without beginning and without end, and yet of the past and of the future knew nothing, save that these were full of mysteries.

As I went I encountered others, or overtook them, making the same journey. Robertson swept past me, and spoke, but in a tongue I could not understand. I noted that the madness had left his eyes and that his fine-cut features were calm and spiritual. The other wanderers I did not know.

\* \* \* \* \* \* \* \*

I came to a region of blinding light; the thought rose in me that I must have reached the sun, or a sun, though I felt no heat. I stood in a lovely, shining valley about which burned mountains of fire. There were huge trees in that valley, but they glowed like gold and their flowers and fruit were as though they had been fashioned of many-coloured flames.

The place was glorious beyond compare, but very strange to me and not to be described. I sat me down upon a boulder which burned like a ruby, whether with heat or colour I do not know, by the edge of a stream that flowed with what looked like fire and made a lovely music. I stooped down and drank of this water of flames and the scent and the taste of it were as those of the costliest wine.

There, beneath the spreading limbs of a fire-tree I sat, and examined the strange flowers that grew around, coloured like rich jewels and perfumed above imagining. There were birds also which might have been feathered with sapphires, rubies and amethysts, and their song was so sweet that I could have wept to hear it. The scene was wonderful and filled me with exaltation, for I thought of the land where it is promised that there shall be no more night.

People began to appear; men, women, and even children, though whence they came I could not see. They did not fly and they did not walk; they seemed to drift towards me, as unguided boats drift upon the tide. One and all they were very beautiful, but their beauty was not human although their shapes and faces resembled those of men and women made glorious. None were old, and except the children, none seemed very young; it was as though they had grown backwards or forwards to middle life and rested there at their very best.

Now came the marvel; all these uncounted people were known to me, though so far as my knowledge went I had never set eyes on most of them before. Yet I was aware that in some forgotten life or epoch I had been intimate with every one of them; also that it was the fact of my presence and the call of my sub-conscious mind which drew them to this spot. Yet that presence and that call were not visible or audible to them, who, I suppose, flowed down some stream of sympathy, why or whither they did not know. Had I been as they were perchance they would have seen me, as it was they saw nothing and I could not speak and tell them of my presence.

Some of this multitude, however, I knew well enough even when they had departed years and years ago. But about these I noted this, that every one of them was a man or a woman or a child for whom I had felt love or sympathy or friendship. Not one was a person whom I had disliked or whom I had no wish to see again. If they spoke at all I could not hear—or read—their speech, yet to a certain extent I could hear their thoughts.

Many of these were beyond the power of my appreciation on subjects which I had no knowledge, or that were too high for me, but some were of quite simple things such as concern us upon the earth, such as of friendship, or learning, or journeys made or to be made, or art, or literature, or the wonders of Nature, or of the fruits of the earth, as they knew them in this region.

This I noted too, that each separate thought seemed to be hallowed and enclosed in an atmosphere of prayer or heavenly aspiration, as a seed is enclosed in the heart of a flower, or a fruit in its odorous rind, and that this prayer or aspiration presently appeared to bear the thought away, whither I knew not. Moreover, all these thoughts, even of the humblest things, were beauteous and spiritual, nothing cruel or impure or even coarse was to be found among them: they radiated charity, purity and goodness.

Among them I perceived were none that had to do with our earth; this and its affairs seemed to be left far behind these thinkers, a truth that chilled my soul was alien to their company. Worse still, so far as I could discover, although I knew that all these bright ones had been near to me at some hour in the measurements of time and space, not one of their musings dwelt upon me or on aught with which I had to do.

Between me and them there was a great gulf fixed and a high wall built.

Oh, look! One came shining like a star, and from far away came another with dove-like eyes and beautiful exceedingly, and with this last a maiden, whose eyes were as hers who my own heart told me was her mother.

Well, I knew them both; they were those whom I had come to seek, the women who had been mind upon the earth, and at the sight of them my spirit thrilled. Surely they would discover me. Surely at least they would speak of me and feel my presence.

But, although they stayed within a pace or two of where I rested, alas! it was not so. They seemed to kiss and to exchange swift thoughts about many things, high things of which I will not write, and common things; yes, even of the shining robes they wore, but never a one of *me!* I strove to rise and go to them, but could not; I strove to speak and could not; I strove to throw out my thought to them and could not; it fell back upon my head like a stone hurled heavenward.

They were remote from me, utterly apart. I wept tears of bitterness that I should be so near and yet so far; a dull and jealous rage burned in my heart, and this they did seem to feel, or so I fancied; at any rate, apparently by mutual consent, they moved further from me as though something pained them. Yes, my love could not reach their perfected natures, but my anger hurt them.

As I sat chewing this root of bitterness, a man appeared, a very noble man, in whom I recognised my father grown younger and happier-looking, but still my father, with whom came others, men and women whom I knew to be my brothers and sisters who had died in youth far away in Oxfordshire. Joy leapt up in me, for I thought— these will surely know me and give me welcome, since, though here sex has lost its power, blood must still call to blood.

But it was not so. They spoke, or interchanged their thoughts, but not one of me. I read something that passed from my father to them. It was a speculation as to what had brought them all together there, and read also the answer hazarded, that perhaps it might be to give welcome to some unknown who was drawing near from below and would feel lonely and unfriended. Thereon my father replied that he did not see or feel this wanderer, and thought that it could not be so, since it was his mission to greet such on their coming.

Then in an instant all were gone and that lovely, glowing plain was empty, save for myself seated on the ruby-like stone, weeping tears of blood and shame and loss within my soul.

So I sat a long while, till presently I was aware of a new presence, a presence dusky and splendid and arrayed in rich barbaric robes. Straight she came towards me, like a thrown spear, and I knew her for a certain royal and savage woman who on earth was named Mameena, or "Wind-that-wailed." Moreover she divined me, though see me she could not.

"Art there, Watcher-in-the-Night, watching in the light?" she said or thought, I know not which, but the words came to me in the Zulu tongue.

"Aye," she went on, "I know that thou art there; from ten thousand leagues away I felt thy presence and broke from my own place to welcome thee, though I must pay for it with burning chains and bondage. How did those welcome thee whom thou camest out to seek? Did they clasp thee in their arms and press their kisses on thy brow? Or did they shrink away from thee because the smell of earth was on thy hands and lips?"

I seemed to answer that they did not appear to know that I was there.

"Aye, they did not know because their love is not enough, because they have grown too fine for love. But I, the sinner, I knew well, and here am I ready to suffer all for thee and to give thee place within this stormy heart of mine. Forget them, then, and come to rule with me who still am queen in my own house that thou shalt share. There we will live royally and when our hour comes, at least we shall have had our day."

Now before I could reply, some power seemed to seize this splendid creature and whirl her thence so that she departed, flashing these words from her mind to mine, "For a little while farewell, but remember always that Mameena, the Wailing Wind, being still as a sinful woman in a woman's love and of the earth, earthy, found thee, whom all the rest forgot. O Watcher-in-the-Night, watch in the night for me, for there thou shalt find me, the Child of Storm, again, and yet again."

She was gone and once more I sat in utter solitude upon that ruby stone, staring at the jewelled flowers and the glorious flaming trees and the lambent waters of the brook. What was the meaning of it all, I wondered, and why was I deserted by everyone save a single savage woman, and why had she a power to find me which was denied to all the rest? Well, she had given me an answer, because she was "as a sinful woman with a woman's love and of the earth, earthy," while with the rest it was otherwise. Oh! this was clear, that in the heavens man has no friend among the heavenly, save perhaps the greatest Friend of all Who understands both flesh and spirit.

Thus I mused in this burning world which was still so beautiful, this alien world into which I had thrust myself unwanted and unsought. And while I mused this happened. The fiery waters of the stream were disturbed by something and looking up I saw the cause.

A dog had plunged into them and was swimming towards me. At a glance I knew that dog on which my eyes had not fallen for decades. It was a mongrel, half spaniel and half bull-terrier, which for years had been the dear friend of my youth and died at last on the horns of a wounded wildebeeste that attacked me when I had fallen from my horse upon the *veld*. Boldly it tackled the maddened buck, thus giving me time to scramble to my rifle and shoot it, but not before the poor hound had yielded its life for mine, since presently it died disembowelled, but licking my hand and forgetful of its agonies. This dog, Smut by name, it was that swam or seemed to swim the brook of fire. It scrambled to the hither shore, it nosed the earth and ran to the ruby stone and stared about it whining and sniffing.

At last it seemed to see or feel me, for it stood upon its hind legs and licked my face, yelping with mad joy, as I could see though I heard nothing. Now I wept in earnest and bent down to hug and kiss the faithful beast, but this I could not do, since like myself it was only shadow.

Then suddenly all dissolved in a cataract of many-coloured flames and I fell down into an infinite gulf of blackness.

Surely Ayesha was talking to me! What did she say? What did she say? I could not catch her words, but I caught her laughter and knew that after her fashion she was making a mock of me. My eyelids were dragged down as though with heavy sleep; it was difficult to lift them. At last they were open and I saw Ayesha seated on her couch before me and—this I noted at once—with her lovely face unveiled. I looked about me, seeking Umslopogaas and Hans. But they were gone as I guessed they must be, since otherwise Ayesha would not have been unveiled. We were quite alone. She was addressing me and in a new fashion, since now she had abandoned the formal "you" and was using the more impressive and intimate "thou," much as is the manner of the French.

"Thou hast made thy journey, Allan," she said, "and what thou hast seen there thou shalt tell me presently. Yet from thy mien I gather this—that thou art glad to look upon flesh and blood again and, after the company of spirits, to find that of mortal woman. Come then and sit beside me and tell thy tale."

"Where are the others?" I asked as I rose slowly to obey, for my head swam and my feet seemed feeble.

"Gone, Allan, who as I think have had enough of ghosts, which is perhaps thy case also. Come, drink this and be a man once more. Drink it to me whose skill and power have brought thee safe from lands that human feet were never meant to tread," and taking a strange-shaped cup from a stool that stood beside her, she offered it to me.

I drank to the last drop, neither knowing nor caring whether it were wine or poison, since my heart seemed desperate at its failure and my spirit crushed beneath the weight of its great betrayal. I suppose it was the former, for the contents of that cup ran through my veins like fire and gave me back my courage and the joy of life.

I stepped to the dais and sat me down upon the couch, leaning against its rounded end so that I was almost face to face with Ayesha who had turned towards me, and thence could study her unveiled loveliness. For a while she said nothing, only eyed me up and down and smiled and smiled, as though she were waiting for that wine to do its work with me.

"Now that thou art a man again, Allan, tell me what thou didst see when thou wast more—or less—than man."

So I told her all, for some power within her seemed to draw the truth out of me. Nor did the tale appear to cause her much surprise.

"There is truth in thy dream," she said when I had finished; "a lesson also."

"Then it was all a dream?" I interrupted.

"Is not everything a dream, even life itself, Allan? If so, what can this be that thou hast seen, but a dream within a dream, and itself containing other dreams, as in the old days the ball fashioned by the eastern workers of ivory would oft be found to contain another ball, and this yet another and another and another, till at the inmost might be found a bead of gold, or perchance a jewel, which was the prize of him who could draw out ball from ball and leave them all unbroken. That search was difficult and rarely was the jewel come by, if at all, so that some said there was none, save in the maker's mind. Yes, I have seen a man go crazed with seeking and die with the mystery unsolved. How much harder, then, is it to come at the diamond of Truth which lies at the core of all our nest of dreams and without which to rest upon they could not be fashioned to seem realities?"

"But was it really a dream, and if so, what were the truth and the lesson?" I asked, determined not to allow her to bemuse or escape me with her metaphysical talk and illustrations.

"The first question has been answered, Allan, as well as I can answer, who am not the architect of this great globe of dreams, and as yet cannot clearly see the ineffable gem within, whose prisoned rays illuminate their substance, though so dimly that only those with the insight of a god can catch their glamour in the night of thought, since to most they are dark as glow-flies in the glare of noon."

"Then what are the truth and the lesson?" I persisted, perceiving that it was hopeless to extract from her an opinion as to the real nature of my experiences and that I must content myself with her deductions from them.

"Thou tellest me, Allan, that in thy dream or vision thou didst seem to appear before thyself seated on a throne and in that self to find thy judge. That is the Truth whereof I spoke, though how it found its way through the black and ignorant shell of one whose wit is so small, is more than I can guess, since I believed that it was revealed to me alone."

(Now I, Allan, thought to myself that I began to see the origin of all these fantasies and that for once Ayesha had made a slip. If she had a theory and I developed that same theory in a hypnotic condition, it was not difficult to guess its fount. However, I kept my mouth shut, and luckily for once she did not seem to read my mind, perhaps because she was too much occupied in spinning her smooth web of entangling words.)

"All men worship their own god," she went on, "and yet seem not to know that this god dwells within them and that of him they are a part. There he dwells and there they mould him to their own fashion, as the potter moulds his clay, though whatever the shape he seems to take beneath their fingers, still he remains the god infinite and unalterable. Still he is the Seeker and the Sought, the Prayer and its Fulfilment, the Love and the Hate, the Virtue and the Vice, since all these qualities the alchemy of his spirit turns into an ultimate and eternal Good. For the god is in all things and all things are in the god, whom men clothe with such diverse garments and whose countenance they hide beneath so many masks.

"In the tree flows the sap, yet what knows the great tree it nurtures of the sap? In the world's womb burns the fire that gives life, yet what of the fire knows the glorious earth it conceived and will destroy; in the heavens the great globes swing through space and rest not, yet what know they of the Strength that sent them spinning and in a time to come will stay their mighty motions, or turn them to another course? Therefore of everything this all-present god is judge, or rather, not one but many judges, since of each living creature he makes its own magistrate to deal out justice according to that creature's law which in the beginning the god established for it and decreed. Thus in the breast of everyone there is a rule and by that rule, at work through a countless chain of lives, in the end he shall be lifted up to Heaven, or bound about and cast down to Hell and death."

"You mean a conscience," I suggested rather feebly, for her thoughts and images overpowered me.

"Aye, a conscience, if thou wilt, and canst only understand that term, though it fits my theme but ill. This is my meaning, that consciences, as thou namest them, are many. I have one; thou, Allan, hast another; that black Axe-bearer has a third; the little yellow man a fourth, and so on through the tale of living things. For even a dog such as thou sawest has a conscience and—like thyself or I—must in the end be its own judge, because of the spark that comes to it from above, the same spark which in me burns as a great fire, and in thee as a smouldering ember of green wood."

"When *you* sit in judgment on yourself in a day to come, Ayesha," I could not help interpolating, "I trust that you will remember that humility did not shine among your virtues."

She smiled in her vivid way—only twice or thrice did I see her smile thus and then it was like a flash of summer lightning illumining a clouded sky, since for the most part her face was grave and even sombre.

"Well answered," she said. "Goad the patient ox enough and even it will grow fierce and paw the ground.

"Humility! What have I to do with it, O Allan? Let humility be the part of the humble-souled and lowly, but for those who reign as I do, and they are few indeed, let there be pride and the glory they have earned. Now I have told thee of the Truth thou sawest in thy vision and wouldst thou hear the Lesson?"

"Yes," I answered, "since I may as well be done with it at once, and doubtless it will be good for me."

"The Lesson, Allan, is one which thou preachest—humility. Vain man and foolish as thou art, thou didst desire to travel the Underworld in search of certain ones who once were all in all to thee—nay, not all in all since of them there were two or more—but at least much. Thus thou wouldst do because, as thou saidest, thou didst seek to know whether they still lived on beyond the gates of Blackness. Yes, thou saidest this, but what thou didst hope to learn in truth was whether they lived on in *thee* and for *thee* only. For thou, thou in thy vanity, didst picture these departed souls as doing naught in that Heaven they had won, save think of thee still burrowing on the earth, and, at times lightening thy labours with kisses from other lips than theirs."

"Never!" I exclaimed indignantly. "Never! it is not true."

"Then I pray pardon, Allan, who only judged of thee by others that were as men are made, and being such, not to be blamed if perchance from time to time, they turned to look on women, who alas! were as they are made. So at least it was when I knew the world, but mayhap since then its richest wine has turned to water, whereby I hope it has been bettered. At the least this was thy thought, that those women who had been thine for an hour, through all eternity could dream of naught else save thy perfections, and hope for naught else than to see thee at their sides through that eternity, or such part of thee as thou couldst spare to each of them. For thou didst forget that where they have gone there may be others even more peerless than thou art and more fit to hold a woman's love, which as we know on earth was ever changeful, and perhaps may so remain where it is certain that new lights must shine and new desires beckon. Dost understand me, Allan?"

"I think so," I answered with a groan. "I understand you to mean that worldly impressions soon wear out and that people who have departed to other spheres may there form new ties and forget the old."

"Yes, Allan, as do those who remain upon this earth, whence these others have departed. Do men and women still re-marry in the world, Allan, as in my day they were wont to do?"

"Of course—it is allowed."

"As many other things, or perchance this same thing, may be allowed elsewhere, for when there are so many habitations from which to choose, why should we always dwell in one of them, however strait the house or poor the prospect?"

Now understanding that I was symbolised by the "strait house" and the "poor prospect" I should have grown angry, had not a certain sense of humour come to my rescue, who remembered that after all Ayesha's satire was profoundly true. Why, beyond the earth, should anyone desire to remain unalterably tied to and inextricably wrapped up in such a personality as my own, especially if others of superior texture abounded about them? Now that I came to think of it, the thing was absurd and not to be the least expected in the midst of a thousand new and vivid interests. I had met with one more disillusionment, that was all.

"Dost understand, Allan," went on Ayesha, who evidently was determined that I should drink this cup to the last drop, "that these dwellers in the sun, or the far planet where thou hast been according to thy tale, saw thee not and knew naught of thee? It may chance therefore that at this time thou wast not in their minds which at others dream of thee continually. Or it may chance that they never dream of thee at all, having quite forgotten thee, as the weaned cub forgets its mother."

"At least there was one who seemed to remember," I exclaimed, for her poisoned mocking stung the words out of me, "one woman and—a dog."

"Aye, the savage, who being Nature's child, a sinner that departed hence by her own act" (how Ayesha knew this I cannot say, I never told her), "has not yet put on perfection and therefore still remembers him whose kiss was last upon her lips. But surely, Allan, it is not thy desire to pass from the gentle, ordered claspings of those white souls for the tumultuous arms of such a one as this. Still, let that be, for who knows what men will or will not do in jealousy and disappointed love? And the dog, it remembered also and even sought thee out, since dogs are more faithful and single-hearted than is mankind. There at least thou hast thy lesson, namely to grow more humble and never to think again that thou holdest all a woman's soul for aye, because once she was kind to thee for a little while on earth."

"Yes," I answered, jumping up in a rage, "as you say, I have my lesson, and more of it than I want. So by your leave, I will now bid you farewell, hoping that when it comes to be *your* turn to learn this lesson, or a worse, Ayesha, as I am sure it will one day, for something tells me so, you may enjoy it more than I have done."

# Chapter 22

# Ayesha's Farewell

Thus I spoke whose nerves were on edge after all that I had seen or, as even then I suspected, seemed to see. For how could I believe that these visions of mine had any higher origin than Ayesha's rather malicious imagination? Already I had formed my theory.

It was that she must be a hypnotist of power, who, after she had put a spell upon her subject, could project into his mind such fancies as she chose together with a selection of her own theories. Only two points remained obscure. The first was—how did she get the necessary information about the private affairs of a humble individual like myself, for these were not known even to Zikali with whom she seemed to be in some kind of correspondence, or to Hans, at any rate in such completeness?

I could but presume that in some mysterious way she drew them from, or rather excited them in my own mind and memory, so that I seemed to see those with whom once I had been intimate, with modifications and in surroundings that her intelligence had carefully prepared. It would not be difficult for a mind like hers familiar, as I gathered it was, with the ancient lore of the Greeks and the Egyptians, to create a kind of Hades and, by way of difference, to change it from one of shadow to one of intense illumination, and into it to plunge the consciousness of him upon whom she had laid her charm of sleep. I had seen nothing and heard nothing that she might not thus have moulded, always given that she had access to the needful clay of facts which I alone could furnish.

Granting this hypothesis, the second point was—what might be the object of her elaborate and most bitter jest? Well, I thought that I could guess. First, she wished to show her power, or rather to make me believe that she had power of a very unusual sort. Secondly, she owed Umslopogaas and myself a debt for our services in the war with

Rezu which we had been told would be repaid in this way. Thirdly, I had offended her in some fashion and she took her opportunity of settling the score. Also there was a fourth possibility—that really she considered herself a moral instructress and desired, as she said, to teach me a lesson by showing how futile were human hopes and vanities in respect to the departed and their affections.

Now I do not pretend that all this analysis of Ayesha's motives occurred to me at the moment of my interview with her; indeed, I only completed it later after much careful thought, when I found it sound and good. At that time, although I had inklings, I was too bewildered to form a just judgment.

Further, I was too angry and it was from this bow of my anger that I loosed a shaft at a venture as to some lesson which awaited *her*. Perhaps certain words spoken by the dying Rezu had shaped that shaft. Or perhaps some shadow of her advancing fate fell upon me.

The success of the shot, however, was remarkable. Evidently it pierced the joints of her harness, and indeed went home to Ayesha's heart. She turned pale; all the peach-bloom hues faded from her lovely face, her great eyes seemed to lessen and grow dull and her cheeks to fall in. Indeed, for a moment she looked old, very old, quite an aged woman. Moreover she wept, for I saw two big tears drop upon her white raiment and I was horrified.

"What has happened to you?" I said, or rather gasped.

"Naught," she answered, "save that thou hast hurt me sore. Dost thou not know, Allan, that it is cruel to prophesy ill to any, since such words feathered from Fate's own wing and barbed with venom, fester in the breast and mayhap bring about their own accomplishment. Most cruel of all is it when with them are repaid friendship and gentleness."

I reflected to myself—yes, friendship of the order that is called candid, and gentleness such as is hid in a cat's velvet paw, but contented myself with asking how it was that she who said she was so powerful, came to fear anything at all.

"Because as I have told thee, Allan, there is no armour that can turn the spear of Destiny which, when I heard those words of thine, it seemed to me, I know not why, was directed by thy hand. Look now on Rezu who thought himself unconquerable and yet was slain by the black Axe-bearer and whose bones tonight stay the famine of the jackals. Moreover I am accursed who sought to steal its servant from Heaven to be my love, and how know I when and where vengeance will fall at last? Indeed, it has fallen already on me, who through the long ages amid savages must mourn widowed and alone, but not all of it—oh! I think, not all."

245

Then she began to weep in good earnest, and watching her, for the first time I understood that this glorious creature who seemed to be so powerful, was after all one of the most miserable of women and as much a prey to loneliness, every sort of passion and apprehensive fear, as can be any common mortal. If, as she said, she had found the secret of life, which of course I did not believe, at least it was obvious that she had lost that of happiness.

She sobbed softly and wept and while she did so the loveliness, which had left her for a little while, returned to her like light to a grey and darkened sky. Oh, how beautiful she seemed with the abundant locks in disorder over her tear-stained face, how beautiful beyond imagining! My heart melted as I studied her; I could think of nothing else except her surpassing charm and glory.

"I pray you, do not weep," I said; "it hurts me and indeed I am sorry if I said anything to give you pain."

But she only shook that glorious hair further about her face and behind its veil wept on.

"You know, Ayesha," I continued, "you have said many hard things to me, making me the target of your bitter wit, therefore it is not strange that at last I answered you."

"And hast thou not deserved them, Allan?" she murmured in soft and broken tones from behind that veil of scented locks.

"Why?" I asked.

"Because from the beginning thou didst defy me, showing in thine every accent that thou heldest me a liar and one of no account in body or in spirit, one not worthy of thy kind look, or of those gentle words which once were my portion among men. Oh! thou hast dealt hardly with me and therefore perchance—I know not—I paid thee back with such poor weapons as a woman holds, though all the while I liked thee well."

Then again she fell to sobbing, swaying herself gently to and fro in her sweet sorrow.

It was too much. Not knowing what else to do to comfort her, I patted her ivory hand which lay upon the couch beside me, and as this appeared to have no effect, I kissed it, which she did not seem to resent. Then suddenly I remembered and let it fall.

She tossed back her hair from her face and fixing her big eyes on me, said gently enough, looking down at her hand, "What ails thee, Allan?"

"Oh, nothing," I answered; "only I remembered the story you told me about some man called Kallikrates."

She frowned.

"And what of Kallikrates, Allan? Is it not enough that for my sins, with tears, empty longings and repentance, I must wait for him through all the weary centuries? Must I also wear the chains of this Kallikrates, to whom I owe many a debt, when he is far away? Say, didst thou see him in that Heaven of thine, Allan, for there perchance he dwells?"

I shook my head and tried to think the thing out while all the time those wonderful eyes of hers seemed to draw the soul from me. It seemed to me that she bent forward and held up her face to me. Then I lost my reason and also bent forward. Yes, she made me mad, and, save her, I forgot all.

Swiftly she placed her hand upon my heart, saying, "Stay! What meanest thou? Dost love me, Allan?"

"I think so—that is—yes," I answered.

She sank back upon the couch away from me and began to laugh very softly.

"What words are these," she said, "that they pass thy lips so easily and so unmeant, perchance from long practice? Oh! Allan, I am astonished. Art thou the same man who some few days ago told me, and this unasked, that as soon wouldst thou think of courting the moon as of courting me? Art thou he who not a minute gone swore proudly that never had his heart and his lips wandered from certain angels whither they should not? And now, and now——?"

I coloured to my eyes and rose, muttering, "Let me be gone!"

"Nay, Allan, why? I see no mark here," and she held up her hand, scanning it carefully. "Thou art too much what thou wert before, except perhaps in thy soul, which is invisible," she added with a touch of malice. "Nor am I angry with thee; indeed, hadst thou not tried to charm away my woe, I should have thought but poorly of thee as a man. There let it rest and be forgotten—or remembered as thou wilt. Still, in answer to thy words concerning my Kallikrates, what of those adored ones that, according to thy tale, but now thou didst find again in a place of light? Because they seemed faithless, shouldst thou be faithless also? Shame on thee, thou fickle Allan!"

She paused, waiting for me to speak.

Well, I could not. I had nothing to say who was utterly disgraced and overwhelmed.

"Thou thinkest, Allan," she went on, "that I have cast my net about thee, and this is true. Learn wisdom from it, Allan, and never again defy a woman—that is, if she be fair, for then she is stronger than thou art, since Nature for its own purpose made her so. Whatever I have done by tears, that ancient artifice of my sex, as in other ways, is for thy instruction, Allan, that thou mayest benefit thereby."

Again I sprang up, uttering an English exclamation which I trust Ayesha did not understand, and again she motioned to me to be seated, saying, "Nay, leave me not yet since, even if the light fancy of a man that comes and goes like the evening wind and for a breath made me dear to thee, has passed away, there remains certain work which we must do together. Although, thinking of thyself alone, thou hast forgotten it, having been paid thine own fee, one is yet due to that old wizard in a far land who sent thee to visit Kôr and me, as indeed he has reminded me and within an hour."

This amazing statement aroused me from my personal and painful pre-occupation and caused me to stare at her blankly.

"Again thou disbelievest me," she said, with a little stamp. "Do so once more, Allan, and I swear I'll bring thee to grovel on the ground and kiss my foot and babble nonsense to a woman sworn to another man, such as never for all thy days thou shalt think of without a blush of shame."

"Oh! no," I broke in hurriedly, "I assure you that you are mistaken. I believe every word you have said, or say or will say; I do in truth."

"Now thou liest. Well, what is one more falsehood among so many? Let it pass."

"What, indeed?" I echoed in eager affirmation, "and as for Zikali's message——" and I paused.

"It was to recall to my mind that he desired to learn whether a certain great enterprise of his will succeed, the details of which he says thou canst tell me. Repeat them to me."

So, glad enough to get away from more dangerous topics, I narrated to her as briefly and clearly as I could, the history of the old witch-doctor's feud with the Royal House of Zululand. She listened, taking in every word, and said, "So now he yearns to know whether he will conquer or be conquered; and that is why he sent, or thinks that he sent thee on this journey, not for thy sake, Allan, but for his own. I cannot tell thee, for what have I do to with the finish of this petty business, which to him seems so large? Still, as I owe him a debt for luring the Axe-Bearer here to rid me of mine enemy, and thee to lighten my solitude for an hour by the burnishing of thy mind, I will try. Set that bowl before me, Allan," and she pointed to a marble tripod on which stood a basin half full of water, "and come, sit close by me and look into it, telling me what thou seest."

I obeyed her instructions and presently found myself with my head over the basin, staring into the water in the exact attitude of a person who is about to be shampooed.

"This seems rather foolish," I said abjectly, for at that moment I resembled the Queen of Sheba in one particular, if in no other, namely, that there was no more spirit in me. "What am I supposed to do? I see nothing at all."

"Look again," she said, and as she spoke the water grew clouded. Then on it appeared a picture. I saw the interior of a *Kaffir* hut dimly lighted by a single candle set in the neck of a bottle. To the left of the door of the hut was a bedstead and on it lay stretched a wasted and dying man, in whom, to my astonishment, I recognised Cetywayo, King of the Zulus. At the foot of the bed stood another man—myself grown older by many years, and leaning over the bed, apparently whispering into the dying man's ear, was a grotesque and malevolent figure which I knew to be that of Zikali, Opener-of-Roads, whose glowing eyes were fixed upon the terrified and tortured face of Cetywayo. All was as it happened afterwards, as I have written down in the book called *Finished*.

I described what I saw to Ayesha, and while I was doing so the picture vanished away, so that nothing remained save the clear water in the marble bowl. The story did not seem to interest her; indeed, she leaned back and yawned a little.

"Thy vision is good, Allan," she said indifferently, "and wide also, since thou canst see what passes in the sun or distant stars, and pictures of things to be in the water, to say nothing of other pictures in a woman's eyes, all within an hour. Well, this savage business concerns me not and of it I want to know no more. Yet it would appear that here the old wizard who is thy friend, has the answer that he desires. For there in the picture the king he hates lies dying while he hisses in his ear and thou dost watch the end. What more can he seek? Tell him it when ye meet, and tell him also it is my will that in future he should trouble me less, since I love not to be wakened from my sleep to listen to his half-instructed talk and savage vapourings. Indeed, he presumes too much. And now enough of him and his dark plots. Ye have your desires, all of you, and are paid in full."

"Over-paid, perhaps," I said with a sigh.

"Ah, Allan, I think that Lesson thou hast learned pleases thee but little. Well, be comforted for the thing is common. Hast never heard that there is but one morsel more bitter to the taste than desire denied, namely, desire fulfilled? Believe me that there can be no happiness for man until he attains a land where all desire is dead."

"That is what the Buddha preaches, Ayesha."

"Aye, I remember the doctrines of that wise man well, who without doubt had found a key to the gate of Truth, one key only, for, mark thou, Allan, there are many. Yet, man being man must know desires, since without them, robbed of ambitions, strivings, hopes, fears, aye and of life itself, the race must die, which is not the will of the Lord of Life who needs a nursery for his servant's souls, wherein his swords of Good and Ill shall shape them to his pattern. So it comes about, Allan, that what we think the worst is oft the best for us, and with that knowledge, if we are wise, let us assuage our bitterness and wipe away our tears."

"I have often thought that," I said.

"I doubt it not, Allan, since though it has pleased me to make a jest of thee, I know that thou hast thy share of wisdom, such little share as thou canst gather in thy few short years. I know, too, that thy heart is good and aspires high, and Friend—well, I find in thee a friend indeed, as I think not for the first time, nor certainly for the last. Mark, Allan, what I say, not a lover, but a *friend*, which is higher far. For when passion dies with the passing of the flesh, if there be no friendship what will remain save certain memories that, mayhap, are well forgot? Aye, how would those lovers meet elsewhere who were never more than lovers? With weariness, I hold, as they stared into each other's empty soul, or even with disgust.

"Therefore the wise will seek to turn those with whom Fate mates them into friends, since otherwise soon they will be lost for aye. More, if they are wiser still, having made them friends, they will suffer them to find lovers where they will. Good maxims, are they not? Yet hard to follow, or so, perchance, thou thinkest them—as I do."

\* \* \* \* \* \* \* \*

She grew silent and brooded a while, resting her chin upon her hand and staring down the hall. Thus the aspect of her face was different from any that I had seen it wear. No longer had it the allure of Aphrodite or the majesty of Hera; rather might it have been that of Athene herself. So wise it seemed, so calm, so full of experience and of foresight, that almost it frightened me.

What was this woman's true story, I wondered, what her real self, and what the sum of her gathered knowledge? Perhaps it was accident, or perhaps, again, she guessed my mind. At any rate her next words seemed in some sense an answer to these speculations. Lifting her eyes she contemplated me a while, then said, "My friend, we part to meet no more in thy life's day. Often thou wilt wonder concerning me, as to what in truth I am, and mayhap in the end thy judgment will be to write me down some false and beauteous wanderer who, rejected of the world or driven from it by her crimes, made choice to rule among savages, playing the part of Oracle to that little audience and telling strange tales to such few travellers as come her way. Perhaps, indeed, I do play this part among many others, and if so, thou wilt not judge me wrongly.

"Allan, in the old days, mariners who had sailed the northern seas, told me that therein amidst mist and storm float mountains of ice, shed from dizzy cliffs which are hid in darkness where no sun shines. They told me also that whereas above the ocean's breast appears but a blue and dazzling point, sunk beneath it is oft a whole frozen isle, invisible to man.

"Such am I, Allan. Of my being thou seest but one little peak glittering in light or crowned with storm, as heaven's moods sweep over it. But in the depths beneath are hid its white and broad foundations, hollowed by the seas of time to caverns and to palaces which my spirit doth inhabit. So picture me, therefore, as wise and fair, but with a soul unknown, and pray that in time to come thou mayest see it in its splendour.

"Hadst thou been other than thou art, I might have shown thee secrets, making clear to thee the parable of much that I have told thee in metaphor and varying fable, aye, and given thee great gifts of power and enduring days of which thou knowest nothing. But of those who visit shrines, O Allan, two things are required, worship and faith, since without these the oracles are dumb and the healing waters will not flow.

"Now I, Ayesha, am a shrine; yet to me thou broughtest no worship until I won it by a woman's trick, and in me thou hast no faith. Therefore for thee the oracle will not speak and the waters of deliverance will not flow. Yet I blame thee not, who art as thou wast made and the hard world has shaped thee.

"And so we part: Think not I am far from thee because thou seest me not in the days to come, since like that Isis whose majesty alone I still exercise on earth, I, whom men name Ayesha, am in all things. I tell thee that I am not One but Many and, being many, am both Here and Everywhere. When thou standest beneath the sky at night and lookest on the stars, remember that in them mine eyes behold thee; when the soft winds of evening blow, that my breath is on thy brow and when the thunder rolls, that there am I riding on the lightnings and rushing with the gale."

"Do you mean that you are the goddess Isis?" I asked, bewildered. "Because if so why did you tell me that you were but her priestess?"

"Have it as thou wilt, Allan. All sounds do not reach thine ears; all sights are not open to thy eyes and therefore thou art both half deaf and blind. Perchance now that her shrines are dust and her worship is forgot, some spark of the spirit of that immortal Lady whose chariot was the moon, lingers on the earth in this woman's shape of mine, though her essence dwells afar, and perchance her other name is Nature, my mother and thine, O Allan. At the least hath not the World a soul—and of that soul am I not mayhap a part, aye, and thou also? For the rest are not the priest and the Divine he bows to, oft the same?"

It was on my lips to answer, Yes, if the priest is a knave or a self-deceiver, but I did not.

"Farewell, Allan, and let Ayesha's benison go with thee. Safe shalt thou reach thy home, for all is prepared to take thee hence, and thy companions with thee. Safe shalt thou live for many a year, till thy time comes, and then, perchance, thou wilt find those whom thou hast lost more kind than they seemed to be tonight."

She paused awhile, then added, "Hearken unto my last word! As I have said, much that I have told thee may bear a double meaning, as is the way of parables, to be interpreted as thou wilt. Yet one thing is true. I love a certain man, in the old days named Kallikrates, to whom alone I am appointed by a divine decree, and I await him here. Oh, should-est thou find him in the world without, tell him that Ayesha awaits him and grows weary in the waiting. Nay, thou wilt never find him, since even if he be born again, by what token would he be known to thee? Therefore I charge thee, keep my secrets well, lest Ayesha's curse should fall on thee. While thou livest tell naught of me to the world thou knowest. Dost thou swear to keep my secrets, Allan?"

"I swear, Ayesha."

"I thank thee, Allan," she answered, and grew silent for a while.

At length Ayesha rose and drawing herself up to the full of her height, stood there majestic. Next she beckoned to me to come near, for I too had risen and left the dais.

I obeyed, and bending down she held her hands over me as though in blessing, then pointed towards the curtains which at this moment were drawn asunder, by whom I do not know.

I went and when I reached them, turned to look my last on her.

There she stood as I had left her, but now her eyes were fixed upon the ground and her face once more was brooding absently as though no such a man as I had ever been. It came into my mind that already she had forgotten me, the plaything of an hour, who had served her turn and been cast aside.

## CHAPTER 23

# What Umslopogaas Saw

Like one who drams I passed down the outer hall where stood the silent guards as statues might, and out through the archway. Here I paused for a moment, partly to calm my mind in the familiar surroundings of the night, and partly because I thought that I heard someone approaching me through the gloom, and in such a place where I might have many enemies, it was well to be prepared.

As it chanced, however, my imaginary assailant was only Hans, who emerged from some place where he had been hiding; a very disturbed and frightened Hans.

"Oh, Baas," he said in a low and shaky whisper, "I am glad to see you again, and standing on your feet, not being carried with them sticking straight in front of you as I expected."

"Why?" I asked.

"Oh, Baas, because of the things that happened in that place where the tall *vrouw* with her head tied up as though she had tooth-ache, sits like a spider in a web."

"Well, what happened, Hans?" I asked as we walked forward.

"This, Baas. The Doctoress talked and talked at you and Umslopogaas, and as she talked, your faces began to look as though you had drunk half a flask too much of the best gin, such as I wish I had some of here tonight, at once wise and foolish, and full and empty, Baas. Then you both rolled over and lay there quite dead, and whilst I was wondering what I should do and how I should get out your bodies to bury them, the Doctoress came down off her platform and bent, first over you and next over Umslopogaas, whispering into the ears of both of you. Then she took off a snake that looked as though it were made of gold with green eyes, which she wears about her middle beneath the long dish-cloth, Baas, and held it to your lips and next to those of Umslopogaas."

"Well, and what then, Hans?"

"After that all sorts of things came about, Baas, and I felt as though the whole house were travelling through the air, Baas, twice as fast as a bullet does from a rifle. Suddenly, too, the room became filled with fire so hot that it scorched me, and so bright that it made my eyes water, although they can look at the sun without winking. And, Baas, the fire was full of spooks which walked around; yes, I saw some of them standing on your head and stomach, Baas, also on that of Umslopogaas, whilst others went and talked to the white Doctoress as quietly as though they had met her in the market-place and wanted to sell her eggs or butter. Then, Baas, suddenly I saw your reverend father, the Predikant, who looked as though he were red-hot, as doubtless he is in the Place of Fires. I thought he came up to me, Baas, and said, 'Get out of this, Hans. This is no place for a good Hottentot like you, Hans, for here only the very best Christians can bear the heat for long.'

"That finished me, Baas. I just answered that I handed you, the Baas Allan his son, over to his care, hoping that he would see that you did not burn in that oven, whatever happened to Umslopogaas. Then I shut my eyes and mouth and held my nose, and wriggled beneath those curtains as a snake does, Baas, and ran down the hall and across the kraal-yard and through the archway out into the night, where I have been sitting cooling myself ever since, waiting for you to be carried away, Baas. And now you have come alive and with not even your hair burnt off, which shows how wonderful must be the Great Medicine of Zikali, Baas, since nothing else could have saved you in that fire, no, not even your reverend father, the Predikant."

"Hans," I said when he had finished, "you are a very wonderful fellow, for you can get drunk on nothing at all. Please remember, Hans, that you have been drunk tonight, yes, very drunk indeed, and never dare to repeat anything that you thought you saw while you were drunk."

"Yes, Baas, I understand that I was drunk and already have forgotten everything. But, Baas, there is still a bottle full of brandy and if I could have just one more tot I should forget *so* much better!"

By now we had reached our camp and here I found Umslopogaas sitting in the doorway and staring at the sky.

"Good-evening to you, Umslopogaas," I said in my most unconcerned manner, and waited.

"Good-evening, Watcher-by-Night, who I thought was lost in the night, since in the end the night is stronger than any of its watchers."

At this cryptic remark I looked bewildered but said nothing. At length Umslopogaas, whose nature, for a Zulu, was impulsive and lacking in the ordinary native patience, asked, "Did you make a journey this evening, Macumazahn, and if so, what did you see?"

"Did you have a dream this evening, Umslopogaas?" I inquired by way of answer, "and if so, what was it about? I thought that I saw you shut your eyes in the House of the White One yonder, doubtless because you were weary of talk which you did not understand."

"Aye, Macumazahn, as you suppose I grew weary of that talk which flowed from the lips of the White Witch like the music that comes from a little stream babbling over stones when the sun is hot, and being weary, I fell asleep and dreamed. What I dreamed does not much matter. It is enough to say that I felt as though I were thrown through the air like a stone cast from his sling by a boy who is set upon a stage to scare the birds out of a mealie garden. Further than any stone I went, aye, further than a shooting star, till I reached a wonderful place. It does not much matter what it was like either, and indeed I am already beginning to forget, but there I met everyone I have ever known. I met the Lion of the Zulus, the Black One, the Earth-Shaker, he who had a 'sister' named Baleka, which sister," here he dropped his voice and looked about him suspiciously, "bore a child, which child was fostered by one Mopo, that Mopo who afterwards slew the Black one with the Princes. Now, Macumazahn, I had a score to settle with this Black One, aye, even though our blood be much of the same colour, I had a score to settle with him, because of the slaying of this sister of his, Baleka, together with the Langeni tribe.[1] So I walked up to him and took him by the head-ring and spat in his face and bade him find a spear and shield, and meet me as man to man. Yes, I did this."

"And what happened then, Umslopogaas?" I said, when he paused in his narrative.

"Macumazahn, nothing happened at all. My hand seemed to go through his head-ring and the skull beneath, and to shut upon itself while he went on talking to someone else, a captain whom I recognised, yes, one Faku, whom in the days of Dingaan, the Black One's brother, I myself slew upon the Ghost-Mountain.

"Yes, Macumazahn, and Faku was telling him the tale of how I killed him and of the fight that I and my blood-brother and the wolves made, there on the knees of the old witch who sits aloft on the Ghost Mountain waiting for the world to die, for I could understand their talk, though mine went by them like the wind.

"Macumazahn, they passed away and there came others, Din-

---

1. For the history of Baleka, the mother of Umslopogaas, and Mopo, see the book called *Nada the Lily*.—Editor.

gaan among them, aye, Dingaan who also knows something of the Witch-Mountain, seeing that there Mopo and I hurled him to his death. With him also I would have had words, but it was the same story, only presently he caught sight of the Black One, yes, of Chaka whom he slew, stabbing him with the little red assegai, and turned and fled, because in that land I think he still fears Chaka, Macumazahn, or so the dream told.

"I went on and met others, men I had fought in my day, most of them, among them was Jikiza, he who ruled the People of the Axe before me whom I slew with his own axe. I lifted the axe and made me ready to fight again, but not one of them took any note of me. There they walked about, or sat drinking beer or taking snuff, but never a sup of the beer or a pinch of the snuff did they offer me, no, not even those among them whom I chanced not to have killed. So I left them and walked on, seeking for Mopo, my foster-father, and a certain man, my blood-brother, by whose side I hunted with the wolves, yes, for them, and for another."

"Well, and did you find them?" I asked.

"Mopo I found not, which makes me think, Macumazahn, that, as once you hinted to me, he whom I thought long dead, perchance still lingers on the earth. But the others I did find . . ." and he ceased, brooding.

Now I knew enough of Umslopogaas's history to be aware that he had loved this man and woman of whom he spoke more than any others on the earth. The "blood-brother," whose name he would not utter, by which he did not mean that he was his brother in blood but one with whom he had made a pact of eternal friendship by the interchange of blood or some such ceremony, according to report, had dwelt with him on the Witch-Mountain where legend told, though this I could scarcely believe, that they had hunted with a pack of hyenas. There, it said also, they fought a great fight with a band send out by Dingaan the king under the command of that Faku whom Umslopogaas had mentioned, in which fight the "Blood-Brother," wielder of a famous club known as Watcher-of-the-Fords, got his death after doing mighty deeds. There also, as I had heard, Nada the Lily, whose beauty was still famous in the land, died under circumstances strange as they were sad.

Naturally, remembering my own experiences, or rather what seemed to be my experiences, for already I had made up my mind that they were but a dream, I was most anxious to learn whether these two who had been so dear to this fierce Zulu, had recognised him.

"Well, and what did they say to you, Umslopogaas?" I asked.

"Macumazahn, they said nothing at all. Hearken! There stood this pair, or sometimes they moved to and fro; my brother, an even greater man than he used to be, with the wolf-skin girt about him and the club, Watcher-of-the-Fords, which he alone could wield, upon his shoulder, and Nada, grown lovelier even than she was of old, so lovely, Macumazahn, that my heart rose into my throat when I saw her and stopped my breath. Yes, Macumazahn, there they stood, or walked about arm in arm as lovers might, and looked into each other's eyes and talked of how they had known each other on the earth, for I could understand their words or thoughts, and how it was good to be at rest together where they were."

"You see, they were old friends, Umslopogaas," I said.

"Yes, Macumazahn, very old friends as I thought. So much so that they had never had a word to say of me who also was the old friend of both of them. Aye, my brother, whose name I am sworn not to speak, the woman-hater who vowed he loved nothing save me and the wolves, could smile into the face of Nada the Lily, Nada the bride of my youth, yet never a word of me, while she could smile back and tell him how great a warrior he had been and never a word of me whose deeds she was wont to praise, who saved her in the Halakazi caves and from Dingaan; no, never a word of me although I stood there staring at them."

"I suppose that they did not see you, Umslopogaas."

"That is so, Macumazahn; I am sure that they did not see me, for if they had they would not have been so much at ease. But I saw them and as they would not take heed when I shouted, I ran up calling to my brother to defend himself with his club. Then, as he still took no note, I lifted the axe *Inkosikaas*, making it circle in the light, and smote with all my strength."

"And what happened, Umslopogaas?"

"Only this, Macumazahn, that the axe went straight through my brother from the crown of his head to the groin, cutting him in two, and he just went on talking! Indeed, he did more, for stooping down he gathered a white lily-bloom which grew there and gave it to Nada, who smelt at it, smiled and thanked him, and then thrust it into her girdle, still thanking him all the while. Yes, she did this for I saw it with my eyes, Macumazahn."

Here the Zulu's voice broke and I think that he wept, for in the faint light I saw him draw his long hand across his eyes, whereon I took the opportunity to turn my back and light a pipe.

"Macumazahn," he went on presently, "it seems that madness took hold of me for a long while, for I shouted and raved at them, thinking that words and rage might hurt where good steel could not, and as I did so they faded away and disappeared, still smiling and talking, Nada smelling at the lily which, having a long stalk, rose up above her breast. After this I rushed away and suddenly met that savage king, Rezu, whom I slew a few days gone. At him I went with the axe, wondering whether he would put up a better fight this second time."

"And did he, Umslopogaas?"

"Nay, but I think he felt me for he turned and fled and when I tried to follow I could not see him. So I ran on and presently who should I find but Baleka, Baleka, Chaka's 'sister' who—repeat it not, Macumazahn—was my mother; and, Macumazahn, *she* saw me. Yes, though I was but little when last she looked on me who now am great and grim, she saw and knew me, for she floated up to me and smiled at me and seemed to press her lips upon my forehead, though I could feel no kiss, and to draw the soreness out of my heart. Then she, too, was gone and of a sudden I fell down through space, having, I suppose, stepped into some deep hole, or perchance a well.

"The next thing I knew was that I awoke in the house of the White Witch and saw you sleeping at my side and the Witch leaning back upon her bed and smiling at me through the thin blanket with which she covers herself up, for I could see the laughter in her eyes.

"Now I grew mad with her because of the things that I had seen in the Place of Dreams, and it came into my heart that it would be well to kill her that the world might be rid of her and her evil magic which can show lies to men. So, being distraught, I sprang up and lifted the axe and stepped towards her, whereon she rose and stood before me, laughing out loud. Then she said something in the tongue I cannot understand, and pointed with her finger, and lo! next moment it was as if giants had seized me and were whirling me away, till presently I found myself breathless but unharmed beyond the arch and—what does it all mean, Macumazahn?"

"Very little, as I think, Umslopogaas, except that this queen has powers to which those of Zikali are as nothing, and can cause visions to float before the eyes of men. For know that such things as you saw, I saw, and in them those whom I have loved also seemed to take no thought of me but only to be concerned with each other. Moreover when I awoke and told this to the queen who is called She-who-commands, she laughed at me as she did at you, and said that it was a good lesson for my pride who in that pride had believed that the dead only thought of the living. But I think that the lesson came from her who wished to humble us, Umslopogaas, and that it was her mind that shaped these visions which we saw."

"I think so too, Macumazahn, but how she knew of all the matters of your life and mine, I do not know, unless perchance Zikali told them to her, speaking in the night-watches as wizards can."

"Nay, Umslopogaas, I believe that by her magic she drew our stories out of our own hearts and then set them forth to us afresh, putting her own colour on them. Also it may be that she drew something from Hans, and from Goroko and the other Zulus with you, and thus paid us the fee that she had promised for our service, but in lung-sick oxen and barren cows, not in good cattle, Umslopogaas."

He nodded and said, "Though at the time I seemed to go mad and though I know that women are false and men must follow where they lead them, never will I believe that my brother, the woman-hater, and Nada are lovers in the land below and have there forgotten me, the comrade of one of them and the husband of the other. Moreover I hold, Macumazahn, that you and I have met with a just reward for our folly.

"We have sought to look through the bottom of the grave at things which the Great-Great in Heaven above did not mean that men should see, and now that we have seen we are unhappier than we were, since such dreams burn themselves upon the heart as a red-hot iron burns the hide of an ox, so that the hair will never grow again where it has been and the hide is marred.

"To you, Watcher-by-Night, I say, 'Content yourself with your watching and whatever it may bring to you in fame and wealth.' And to myself I say, 'Holder of the Axe, content yourself with the axe and what it may bring to you in fair fight and glory'; and to both of us I say, 'Let the Dead sleep unawakened until we go to join them, which surely will be soon enough.'"

"Good words, Umslopogaas, but they should have been spoken ere ever we set out on this journey."

"Not so, Macumazahn, since that journey we were fated to make to save one who lies yonder, the Lady Sad-Eyes, and, as they tell me, is well again. Also Zikali willed it, and who can resist the will of the Opener-of-Roads? So it is made and we have seen many strange things and won some glory and come to know how deep is the pool of our own foolishness, who thought that we could search out the secrets of Death, and there have only found those of a witch's mind and venom, reflected as in water. And now having discovered all these things I wish to be gone from this haunted land. When do we march, Macumazahn?"

"Tomorrow morning, I believe, if the Lady Sad-Eyes and the others are well enough, as She-who-commands says they will be."

"Good. Then I would sleep who am more weary than I was after I had killed Rezu in the battle on the mountain."

"Yes," I answered, "since it is harder to fight ghosts than men, and dreams, if they be bad, are more dreadful than deeds. Good-night, Umslopogaas."

\* \* \* \* \* \* \* \*

He went, and I too went to see how it fared with Inez. I found that she was fast asleep but in a quite different sleep to that into which Ayesha seemed to have plunged her. Now it was absolutely natural and looking at her lying there upon the bed, I thought how young and healthy was her appearance. The women in charge of her also told me that she had awakened at the hour appointed by She-who-commands, as it seemed, quite well and very hungry, although she appeared to be puzzled by her surroundings. After she had eaten, they added that she had "sung a song," which was probably a hymn, and prayed upon her knees, "making signs upon her breast" and then gone quietly to bed.

My anxiety relieved as regards Inez, I returned to my own quarters. Not feeling inclined for slumber, however, instead of turning in I sat at the doorway contemplating the beauty of the night while I watched the countless fireflies that seemed to dust the air with sparks of burning gold; also the great owls and other fowl that haunt the dark. These had come out in numbers from their hiding-places among the ruins and sailed to and fro like white-winged spirits, now seen and now lost in the gloom.

\* \* \* \* \* \* \* \*

While I sat thus many reflections came to me as to the extraordinary nature of my experiences during the past few days. Had any man ever known the like, I wondered? What could they mean and what could this marvellous woman Ayesha be? Was she perhaps a personification of Nature itself, as indeed to some extent all women are? Was she human at all, or was she some spirit symbolising a departed people, faith and civilisation, and haunting the ruins where once she reigned as queen? No, the idea was ridiculous, since such beings do not exist, though it was impossible to doubt that she possessed powers beyond those of common humanity, as she possessed beauty and fascination greater than are given to any other woman.

Of one thing I was certain, however, that the Shades I had seemed to visit had their being in the circle of her own imagination and intelligence. There Umslopogaas was right; we had seen no dead, we had only seen pictures and images that she drew and fashioned.

Why did she do this, I wondered. Perhaps to pretend to powers which she did not possess, perhaps out of sheer elfish mischief, or perhaps, as she asserted, just to teach us a lesson and to humble us in our own sight. Well, if so she had succeeded, for never did I feel so crushed and humiliated as at that moment.

I had seemed to descend, or ascend, into Hades, and there had only seen things that gave me little joy and did but serve to reopen old wounds. Then, on awaking, I had been bewitched; yes, fresh from those visions of the most dear dead, I had been bewitched by the overpowering magic of this woman's loveliness and charm, and made a fool of myself, only to be brought back to my senses by her triumphant mockery. Oh, I was humbled indeed, and yet the odd thing is that I could not feel angry with her, and what is more that, perhaps from vanity, I believed in her profession of friendship towards myself.

Well, the upshot of it was that, like Umslopogaas, more than anything else in the world did I desire to depart from this haunted Kôr and to bury all its recollections in such activities as fortune might bring to me. And yet, and yet it was well to have seen it and to have plucked the flower of such marvellous experience, nor, as I knew even then, could I ever inter the memory of Ayesha the wise, the perfect in all loveliness, and the half-divine in power.

********

When I awoke the next morning the sun was well up and after I had taken a swim in the old bath and dressed myself, I went to see how it fared with Inez. I found her sitting at the door of her house looking extremely well and with a radiant face. She was engaged in making a chain of some small and beautiful blue flowers of the iris tribe, of which quantities grew about, that she threaded together upon stalks of dry grass.

This chain, which was just finished, she threw over her head so that it hung down upon her white robe, for now she was dressed like an Arab woman though without the veil. I watched her unseen for a little while then came forward and spoke to her. She started at the sight of me and rose as though to run away; then, apparently reassured by my appearance, selected a particularly fine flower and offered it to me.

I saw at once that she did not know me in the least and thought that she had never seen me before, in short, that her mind had gone, exactly as Ayesha had said that it would do. By way of making conversation I asked her if she felt well. She replied, Oh, yes, she had never felt better, then added, "Daddy has gone on a long journey and will not be back for weeks and weeks."

An idea came to me and I answered, "Yes, Inez, but I am a friend of his and he has sent me to take you to a place where I hope that we shall find him. Only it is far away, so you also must make a long journey."

She clapped her hands and answered, "Oh, that will be nice, I do so love travelling, especially to find Daddy, who I expect will have my proper clothes with him, not these which, although they are very comfortable and pretty, seem different to what I used to wear. You look very nice too and I am sure that we shall be great friends, which I am glad of, for I have been rather lonely since my mother went to live with the saints in Heaven, because, you see, Daddy is so busy and so often away, that I do not see much of him."

Upon my word I could have wept when I heard her prattle on thus. It is so terribly unnatural, almost dreadful indeed, to listen to a full grown woman who talks in the accents and expresses the thoughts of a child. However, under all the circumstances I recognised that her calamity was merciful, and remembering that Ayesha had prophesied the recovery of her mind as well as its loss and how great seemed to be her powers in these directions, I took such comfort as I could.

Leaving her I went to see the two Zulus who had been wounded and found to my joy that they were now quite well and fit to travel, for here, too, Ayesha's prophecy had proved good. The other men also were completely rested and anxious to be gone like Umslopogaas and myself.

While I was eating my breakfast Hans announced the venerable Billali, who with a sweeping bow informed me that he had come to inquire when we should be ready to start, as he had received orders to see to all the necessary arrangements. I replied—within an hour, and he departed in a hurry.

But little after the appointed time he reappeared with a number of litters and their bearers, also with a bodyguard of twenty-five picked men, all of whom we recognised as brave fellows who had fought well in the battle. These men and the bearers old Billali harangued, telling them that they were to guide, carry and escort us to the other side of the great swamp, or further if we needed it, and that it was the word of She-who-commands that if so much as the smallest harm came to any one of us, even by accident, they should die every man of them "by the hot-pot," whatever that might be, for I was not sure of the significance of this horror.[2] Then he asked them if they understood. They replied with fervour that they understood perfectly and would lead and guard us as though we were their own mothers.

As a matter of fact they did, and I think would have done so independently of Ayesha's command, since they looked upon Umslopogaas and myself almost as gods and thought that we could destroy them all if we wished, as we had destroyed Rezu and his host.

I asked Billali if he were not coming with us, to which he replied, No, as She-who-commands had returned to her own place and he must follow her at once. I asked him again where her own place might be, to which he answered vaguely that it was everywhere and he stared first at the heavens and then at the earth as though she inhabited most of them, adding that generally it was "in the Caves," though what he meant by that I did not know. Then he said that he was very glad to have met us and that the sight of Umslopogaas killing Rezu was a spectacle that he would remember with pleasure all his life. Also he asked me for a present. I gave him a spare pencil that I possessed in a little German silver case, with which he was delighted. Thus I parted with old Billali, of whom I shall always think with a certain affection.

I noticed even then that he kept very clear indeed of Umslopogaas, thinking, I suppose, that he might take a last opportunity to fulfil his threats and introduce him to his terrible Axe.

---

2. For this see the book called *She*.—Editor.

## CHAPTER 24

# Umslopogaas Wears the Great Medicine

A little while later we started, some of us in litters, including the wounded Zulus, who I insisted should be carried for a day or two, and some on foot. Inez I caused to be borne immediately in front of myself so that I could keep an eye upon her. Moreover I put her in the especial charge of Hans, to whom fortunately she took a great fancy at once, perhaps because she remembered subconsciously that she knew him and that he had been kind to her, although when they met after her long sleep, as in my own case, she did not recognise him in the least.

Soon, however, they were again the fastest of friends, so much so that within a day or two the little Hottentot practically filled the place of a maid to her, attending to her every want and looking after her exactly as a nurse does after a child, with the result that it was quite touching to see how she came to depend upon him, her *monkey*, as she called him, and how fond he grew of her.

Once, indeed, there was trouble, since hearing a noise, I came up to find Hans bristling with fury and threatening to shoot one of the Zulus, who stupidly, or perhaps rudely, had knocked against the litter of Inez and nearly turned it over. For the rest, the Lady Sad-Eyes, as they called her, had for the time became the Lady Glad-Eyes, since she was merry as the day was long, laughing and singing and playing just as a healthy happy child should do.

Only once did I see her wretched and weep. It was when a kitten which she had insisted on bringing with her, sprang out of the litter and vanished into some bush where it could not be found. Even when she was soon consoled and dried her tears, when Hans explained to her in a mixture of bad English and worse Portuguese, that it had only run away because it wished to get back to its mother which it loved, and that it was cruel to separate it from its mother.

We made good progress and by the evening of the first day were over the crest of the cliff or volcano lip that encircles the great plain of Kôr, and descending rapidly to a sheltered spot on the outer slope where our camp was to be set for the night.

Not very far from this place, as I think I have mentioned, stood, and I suppose still stands, a very curious pinnacle of rock, which, doubtless being of some harder sort, had remained when, hundreds of thousands or millions of years before, the surrounding lava had been washed or had corroded away. This rock pillar was perhaps fifty feet high and as smooth as though it had been worked by man; indeed, I remembered having remarked to Hans, or Umslopogaas—I forget which—when we passed it on our inward journey, that there was a column which no monkey could climb.

As we went by it for the second time, the sun had already disappeared behind the western cliff, but a fierce ray from its sinking orb, struck upon a storm-cloud that hung over us, and thence was reflected in a glow of angry light of which the focus or centre seemed to fall upon the summit of this strange and obelisk-like pinnacle of rock.

At the moment I was out of my litter and walking with Umslopogaas at the end of the line, to make sure that no one straggled in the oncoming darkness. When we had passed the column by some forty or fifty yards, something caused Umslopogaas to turn and look back. He uttered an exclamation which made me follow his example, with the result that I saw a very wonderful thing. For there on the point of the pillar, like St. Simeon Stylites on his famous column, glowing in the sunset rays as though she were on fire, stood Ayesha herself!

It was a strange and in a way a glorious sight, for poised thus between earth and heaven, she looked like some glowing angel rather than a woman, standing as she seemed to do upon the darkness; since the shadows, save for the faintest outline, had swallowed up the column that supported her. Moreover, in the intense, rich light that was focussed on her, we could see every detail of her form and face, for she was unveiled, and even her large and tender eyes which gazed upwards emptily (at this moment they seemed very tender), yes, and the little gold studs that glittered on her sandals and the shine of the snake girdle she wore about her waist.

We stared and stared till I said inconsequently,"Learn, Umslopogaas, what a liar is that old Billali, who told me that She-who-commands had departed from Kôr to her own place."

"Perhaps this rock edge is her own place, if she be there at all, Macumazahn."

"If she be there," I answered angrily, for my nerves were at once thrilled and torn. "Speak not empty words, Umslopogaas, for where else can she be when we see her with our eyes?"

"Who am I that I should know the ways of witches who, like the winds, are able to go and come as they will? Can a woman run up a wall of rock like a lizard, Macumazahn?"

"Doubtless——" and I began some explanation which I have forgotten, when a passing cloud, or I know not what, cut off the light so that both the pinnacle and she who stood on it became invisible. A minute later it returned for a little while, and there was the point of the needle-shaped rock, but it was empty, as, save for the birds that rested on it, it had been since the beginning of the world.

Then Umslopogaas and I shook our heads and pursued our way in silence.

\* \* \* \* \* \* \* \*

This was the last that I saw of the glorious Ayesha, if indeed I did see her and not her ghost. Yet it is true that for all the first part of the journey, till we were through the great swamp in fact, from time to time I was conscious, or imagined that I was conscious of her presence. Moreover, once others saw her, or someone who might have been her. It happened thus.

We were in the centre of the great swamp and the trained guides who were leading came to a place where the path forked and were uncertain which road to take. Finally they fixed on the right-hand path and were preparing to follow it together with those who bore the litter of Inez, by the side of which Hans was walking as usual.

At this moment, as Hans told me, the guides went down upon their faces and he saw standing in front of them a white-veiled form who pointed to the left-hand path, and then seemed to be lost in the mist. Without a word the guides rose and followed this left-hand path. Hans stopped the litter till I came up when he told me what had happened, while Inez also began to chatter in her childish fashion about a "White Lady."

I had the curiosity to walk a little way along the right-hand path which they were about to take. Only a few yards further on I found myself sinking in a floating quagmire, from which I extricated myself with much difficulty but just in time for as I discovered afterwards by probing with a pole, the water beneath the matted reeds was deep. That night I questioned the guides upon the subject, but without result, for they pretended to have seen nothing and not to understand what I meant. Of neither of these incidents have I any explanation to offer, except that once contracted, it is as difficult to be rid of the habit of hallucinations as of any other.

********

It is not necessary that I should give all the details of our long homeward journey. So I will only say that having dismissed our bearers and escorts when we reached higher ground beyond the horrible swamp, keeping one litter for Inez in which the Zulus carried her when she was tired, we accomplished it in complete safety and having crossed the Zambezi, at last one evening reached the house called Strathmuir.

Here we found the wagon and oxen quite safe and were welcomed rapturously by my Zulu driver and the *voorlooper*, who had made up their minds that we were dead and were thinking of trekking homewards. Here also Thomaso greeted us, though I think that, like the Zulus, he was astonished at our safe return and indeed not overpleased to see us. I told him that Captain Robertson had been killed in a fight in which we had rescued his daughter from the cannibals who had carried her off (information which I cautioned him to keep to himself) but nothing else that I could help.

Also I warned the Zulus through Umslopogaas and Goroko, that no mention was to be made of our adventures, either then or afterwards, since if this were done the curse of the White Queen would fall on them and bring them to disaster and death. I added that the name of this queen and everything that was connected with her, or her doings, must be locked up in their own hearts. It must be like the name of dead kings, not to be spoken. Nor indeed did they ever speak it or tell the story of our search, because they were too much afraid both of Ayesha whom they believed to be the greatest of all witches, and of the axe of their captain, Umslopogaas.

Inez went to bed that night without seeming to recognise her old home, to all appearance just a mindless child as she had been ever since she awoke from her trance at Kôr. Next morning, however, Hans came to tell me that she was changed and that she wished to speak with me. I went, wondering, to find her in the sitting-room, dressed in European clothes which she had taken from where she kept them, and once more a reasoning woman.

"Mr. Quatermain," she said, "I suppose that I must have been ill, for the last thing I remember is going to sleep on the night after you started for the hippopotamus hunt. Where is my father? Did any harm come to him while he was hunting?"

"Alas!" I answered, lying boldly, for I feared lest the truth should take away her mind again, "it did. He was trampled upon by a hippopotamus bull, which charged him, and killed, and we were obliged to bury him where he died."

She bowed her head for a while and muttered some prayer for his soul, then looked at me keenly and said, "I do not think you are telling me everything, Mr. Quatermain, but something seems to say that this is because it is not well that I should learn everything."

"No," I answered, "you have been ill and out of your mind for quite a long while; something gave you a shock. I think that you learned of your father's death, which you have now forgotten, and were overcome with the news. Please trust to me and believe that if I keep anything back from you, it is because I think it best to do so for the present."

"I trust and I believe," she answered. "Now please leave me, but tell me first where are those women and their children?"

"After your father died they went away," I replied, lying once more.

She looked at me again but made no comment.

Then I left her.

\* \* \* \* \* \* \* \*

How much Inez ever learned of the true story of her adventures I do not know to this hour, though my opinion is that it was but little. To begin with, everyone, including Thomaso, was threatened with the direst consequences if he said a word to her on the subject; moreover in her way she was a wise woman, one who knew when it was best not to ask questions. She was aware that she had suffered from a fit of aberration or madness and that during this time her father had died and certain peculiar things had happened. There she was content to leave the business and she never again spoke to me upon the subject. Of this I was very glad, as how on earth could I have explained to her about Ayesha's prophecies as to her lapse into childishness and subsequent return to a normal state when she reached her home seeing that I did not understand them myself?

Once indeed she did inquire what had become of Janee to which I answered that she had died during her sickness. It was another lie, at any rate by implication, but I hold that there are occasions when it is righteous to lie. At least these particular falsehoods have never troubled my conscience.

Here I may as well finish the story of Inez, that is, as far as I can. As I have shown she was always a woman of melancholy and religious temperament, qualities that seemed to grow upon her after her return to health. Certainly the religion did, for continually she was engaged in prayer, a development with which heredity may have had something to do, since after he became a reformed character and grew unsettled in his mind, her father followed the same road.

On our return to civilisation, as it chanced, one of the first persons with whom she came in contact was a very earnest and excellent old priest of her own faith. The end of this intimacy was much what might have been expected. Very soon Inez determined to renounce the world, which I think never had any great attractions for her, and entered a sisterhood of an extremely strict Order in Natal, where, added to her many merits, her considerable possessions made her very welcome indeed.

Once in after years I saw her again when she expected before long to become the Mother-Superior of her convent. I found her very cheerful and she told me that her happiness was complete. Even then she did not ask me the true story of what had happened to her during that period when her mind was a blank. She said that she knew something had happened but that as she no longer felt any curiosity about earthly things, she did not wish to know the details. Again I rejoiced, for how could I tell the true tale and expect to be believed, even by the most confiding and simple-minded nun?

To return to more immediate events. When we had been at Strathmuir for a day or two and I thought that her mind was clear enough to judge of affairs, I told Inez that I must journey on to Natal, and asked her what she wished to do. Without a moment's hesitation she replied that she desired to come with me, as now that her father was dead nothing would induce her to continue to live at Strathmuir without friends, or indeed the consolations of religion.

Then she showed me a secret hiding-place cunningly devised in a sort of cellar under the sitting-room floor, where her father was accustomed to keep the spirits of which he consumed so great a quantity. In this hole beneath some bricks, we discovered a large sum in gold stored away, which Robertson had always told his daughter she would find there, in the event of anything happening to him. With the money were his will and securities, also certain mementos of his youth and some love-letters together with a prayer-book that his mother had given him.

These valuables, of which no one knew the existence except herself, we removed and then made our preparations for departure. They were simple; such articles of value as we could carry were packed into the wagon and the best of the cattle we drove with us. The place with the store and the rest of the stock were handed over to Thomaso on a half-profit agreement under arrangement that he should remit the share of Inez twice a year to a bank on the coast, where her father had an account. Whether or not he ever did this I am unable to say, but as no one wished to stop at Strathmuir, I could conceive no better plan because purchasers of property in that district did not exist.

As we trekked away one fine morning I asked Inez whether she was sorry to leave the place.

"No," she replied with energy, "my life there has been a hell and I never wish to see it again."

\* \* \* \* \* \* \* \*

Now it was after this, on the northern borders of Zululand, that Zikali's Great Medicine, as Hans called it, really played its chief part, for without it I think that we should have been killed, every one of us. I do not propose to set out the business in detail; it is too long and intricate. Suffice it to say, therefore, that it had to do with the plots of Umslopogaas against Cetywayo, which had been betrayed by his wife Monazi and her lover Lousta, both of whom I have mentioned earlier in this record. The result was that a watch for him was kept on all the frontiers, because it was guessed that sooner or later he would return to Zululand; also it had become known that he was travelling in my company.

So it came about that when my approach was reported by spies, a company was gathered under the command of a man connected with the Royal House, and by it we were surrounded. Before attacking, however, this captain sent men to me with the message that with me the King had no quarrel, although I was travelling in doubtful company, and that if I would deliver over to him Umslopogaas, Chief of the People of the Axe, and his followers, I might go whither I wished unharmed, taking my goods with me. Otherwise we should be attacked at once and killed every one of us, since it was not desired that any witnesses should be left of what happened to Umslopogaas. Having delivered this ultimatum and declined any argument as to its terms, the messengers retired, saying that they would return for my answer within half an hour.

When they were out of hearing Umslopogaas, who had listened to their words in grim silence, turned and spoke in such fashion as might have been expected of him.

"Macumazahn," he said, "now I come to the end of an unlucky

journey, though mayhap it is not so evil as it seems, since I who went out to seek the dead but to be filled by yonder White Witch with the meat of mocking shadows, am about to find the dead in the only way in which they can be found, namely by becoming of their number."

"It seems that this is the case with all of us, Umslopogaas."

"Not so, Macumazahn. That child of the King will give you safe-conduct. It is I and mine whose blood he seeks, as he has the right to do, since it is true that I would have raised rebellion against the King, I who wearied of my petty lot and knew that by blood his place was mine. In this quarrel you have no share, though you, whose heart is as white as your skin, are not minded to desert me. Moreover, even if you wished to fight, there is one in the wagon yonder whose life is not yours to give. The Lady Sad-Eyes is as a child in your arms and her you must bear to safety."

Now this argument was so unanswerable that I did not know what to say. So I only asked what he meant to do, as escape was impossible, seeing that we were surrounded on every side.

"Make a glorious end, Macumazahn," he said with a smile. "I will go out with those who cling to me, that is with all who remain of my men, since my fate must be theirs, and stand back to back on yonder mound and there wait till these dogs of the King come up against us. Watch a while, Macumazahn, and see how Umslopogaas, Bearer of the Axe, and the warriors of the Axe can fight and die."

Now I was silent for I knew not what to say. There we all stood silent, while minute by minute I watched the shadow creeping forward towards a mark that the head messenger had made with his spear upon the ground, for he had said that when it touched that mark he would return for his answer.

In this rather dreadful silence I heard a dry little cough, which I knew came from the throat of Hans, and to be his method of indicating that he had a remark to make.

"What is it?" I asked with irritation, for it was annoying to see him seated there on the ground fanning himself with the remains of a hat and staring vacantly at the sky.

"Nothing, Baas, or rather, only this, Baas: Those hyenas of Zulus are even more afraid of the Great Medicine than were the cannibals up north, since the maker of it is nearer to them, Baas. You remember, Baas, they knelt to it, as it were, when we were going out of Zululand."

"Well, what of it, now that we are going into Zululand?" I inquired sharply. "Do you want me to show it to them?"

"No, Baas. What is the use, seeing that they are ready to let you pass, also the Lady Sad-Eyes, and me and the cattle with the driver and *voorlooper*, which is better still, and all the other goods. So what have you to gain by showing them the medicine? But perchance if it were on the neck of Umslopogaas and *he* showed it to them and brought it to their minds that those who touch him who is in the shadow of Zikali's Great Medicine, or aught that is his, die within three moons in this way or in that—well, Baas, who knows?" and again he coughed drily and stared up at the sky.

I translated what Hans had said in Dutch to Umslopogaas, who remarked indifferently, "This little yellow man is well named Light-in-Darkness; at least the plan can be tried—if it fails there is always time to die."

So thinking that this was an occasion on which I might properly do so, for the first time I took off the talisman which I had worn for so long, and Umslopogaas put it over his head and hid it beneath his blanket.

\* \* \* \* \* \* \* \*

A little while later the messengers returned and this time the captain himself came with them, as he said to greet me, for I knew him slightly and once we had dealt together about some cattle. After a friendly chat he turned to the matter of Umslopogaas, explaining the case at some length. I said that I quite understood his position but that it was a *very* awkward thing to interfere with a man who was the actual wearer of the Great Medicine of Zikali itself. When the captain heard this his eyes almost started out of his head.

"The Great Medicine of the Opener-of-Roads!" he exclaimed. "Oh, now I understand why this Chief of the People of the Axe is unconquerable—such a wizard that no one is able to kill him."

"Yes," I replied, "and you remember, do you not, that he who offends the Great Medicine, or offers violence to him who wears it, dies horribly within three moons, he and his household and all those with him?"

"I have heard it," he said with a sickly smile.

"And now you are about to learn whether the tale is true," I added cheerfully.

Then he asked to see Umslopogaas alone.

I did not overhear their conversation, but the end of it was that Umslopogaas came and said in a loud voice so that no one could miss a single word, that as resistance was useless and he did not wish me, his friend, to be involved in any trouble, together with his men he had agreed to accompany this King's captain to the royal kraal where he had been guaranteed a fair trial as to certain false charges which had been brought against him. He added that the King's captain had sworn upon the Great Medicine of the Opener-of-Roads to give him safe conduct and attempt no mischief against him which, as was well known throughout the land, was an oath that could not be broken by anyone who wished to continue to look upon the sun.

I asked the captain if these things were so, also speaking in a loud voice. He replied, Yes, since his orders were to take Umslopogaas alive if he might. He was only to kill him if he would not come.

Afterwards, while pretending to give him certain articles out of the wagon, I had a few private words with Umslopogaas, who told me that the arrangement was that he should be allowed to escape at night with his people.

"Be sure of this, Macumazahn," he said, "that if I do not escape, neither will that captain, since I walk at his side and keep my axe, and at the first sign of treachery the axe will enter the house of that thick head of his and make friends with the brain inside.

"Macumazahn," he added, "we have made a strange journey together and seen such things as I did not think the world had to show. Also I have fought and killed Rezu in a mad battle of ghosts and men which alone was worth all the trouble of the journey. Now it has come to an end as everything must, and we part, but as I believe, not for always. I do not think that I shall die on this journey with the captain, though I do think that others will die at the end of it," he added grimly, a saying which at the time I did not understand.

"It comes into my heart, Macumazahn, that in yonder land of witches and wizards, the spirit of prophecy got caught in my *moocha* and crept into my bowels. Now that spirit tells me that we shall meet again in the after-years and stand together in a great fray which will be our last, as I believe that the White Witch said. Or perhaps the spirit lives in Zikali's Medicine which has gone down my throat and comes out of it in words. I cannot say, but I pray that it is a true spirit, since although you are white and I am black and you are small and I am big, and you are gentle and cunning, whereas I am fierce and as open as the blade of my own axe, yet I love you as well, Macumazahn, as though we were born of the same mother and had been brought up in the same kraal. Now that captain waits and grows doubtful of our talk, so farewell. I will return the Great Medicine to Zikali, if I live, and if I die he must send one of the ghosts that serve him, to fetch it from among my bones.

"Farewell to you also, Yellow Man," he went on to Hans, who had appeared, hovering about like a dog that is doubtful of its welcome;

"well are you named Light-in-Darkness, and glad am I to have met you, who have learned from you how a snake moves and strikes, and how a jackal thinks and avoids the snare. Yes, farewell, for the spirit within me does not tell me that you and I shall meet again."

Then he lifted the great axe, and gave me a formal salute, naming me "Chief and Father, Great Chief and Father, from of old" (*Baba! Koos y umcool! Koos y pagate!*), thereby acknowledging my superiority over him, a thing that he had never done before, and as he did, so did Goroko and the other Zulus, adding to their salute many titles of praise. In another minute he had gone with the King's captain, to whose side I noted he clung lovingly, his long, thin fingers playing about the horn handle of the axe that was named *Inkosikaas* and Groan-maker.

"I am glad we have seen the last of him and his axe, Baas," remarked Hans, spitting reflectively. "It is very well to sleep in the same hut with a tame lion sometimes, but after you have done so for many moons, you begin to wonder when you will wake up at night to find him pulling the blankets off you and combing your hair with his claws. Yes, I am very glad that this half-tame lion is gone, since sometimes I have thought that I should be obliged to poison it that we might sleep in peace. You know he called me a snake, Baas, and poison is a snake's only spear. Shall I tell the boys to *inspan* the oxen, Baas? I think the further we get from that King's captain and his men, the more comfortably shall we travel, especially now when we no longer have the Great Medicine to protect us."

"You suggested giving it to him, Hans," I said.

"Yes, Baas, I had rather that Umslopogaas went away with the Great Medicine, than that you kept the Great Medicine and he stopped with us here. Never travel with a traitor, Baas, at any rate in the land of the king whom he wishes to kill. Kings are very selfish people, Baas, and do not like being killed, especially by someone who wants to sit upon their stool and to take the royal salute. No one gives the royal salute to a dead king, Baas, however great he was before he died, and no one thinks the worse of a king who was a traitor before he became a king."

CHAPTER 25

# Allan Delivers the Message

Once more I sat in the Black Kloof face to face with old Zikali.

"So you have got back safely, Macumazahn," he said. "Well, I told you you would, did I not? As for what happened to you upon the journey, let it be, for now that I am old long stories tire me and I daresay that there is nothing wonderful about this one. Where is the charm I lent you? Give it back now that it has served its turn."

"I have not got it, Zikali. I passed it on to Umslopogaas of the Axe to save his life from the King's men."

"Oh! yes, so you did. I had forgotten. Here it is," and opening his robe of fur, he showed me the hideous little talisman hanging about his neck, then added, "Would you like a copy of it, Macumazahn, to keep as a memory? If so, I will carve one for you."

"No," I answered, "I should not. Has Umslopogaas been here?"

"Yes, he has been and gone again, which is one of the reasons why I do not wish to hear your tale a second time."

"Where to? The Town of the People of the Axe?"

"No, Macumazahn, he came thence, or so I understood, but thither he will return no more."

"Why not, Zikali?"

"Because after his fashion he made trouble there and left some dead behind him; one Lousta, I believe, whom he had appointed to sit on his stool as chief while he was away, and a woman called Monazi, who was his wife, or Lousta's wife, or the wife of both of them, I forget which. It is said that having heard stories of her—and the ears of jealousy are long, Macumazahn—he cut off this woman's head with a sweep of the axe and made Lousta fight him till he fell, which the fool did almost before he had lifted his shield. It served him right who should have made sure that Umslopogaas was dead before he wrapped himself in his blanket and took the woman to cook his porridge."

"Where has the Axe-bearer gone?" I asked without surprise, for this news did not astonish me.

"I neither know nor care, Macumazahn. To become a wanderer, I suppose. He will tell you the tale when you meet again in the after-days, as I understand he thinks that you will do.[1] Hearken! I have done with this lion's whelp, who is Chaka over again, but without Chaka's wit. Yes, he is just a fighting man with a long reach, a sure eye and the trick of handling an axe, and such are of little use to me who know too many of them. Thrice have I tried to make him till my garden, but each time he has broken the hoe, although the wage I promised him was a royal *kaross* and nothing less. So enough of Umslopogaas, the Woodpecker. Almost I wish that you had not lent him the charm, for then the King's men would have made an end of him, who knows too much and like some silly boaster, may shout out the truth when his axe is aloft and he is full of the beer of battle. For in battle he will live and in battle he will die, Macumazahn, as perhaps you may see one day."

"The fate of your friends does not trouble you over much, Open-er-of-Roads," I said with sarcasm.

"Not at all, Macumazahn, because I have none. The only friends of the old are those whom they can turn to their own ends, and if these fail them they find others."

"I understand, Zikali, and know now what to expect from you."

He laughed in his strange way and answered, "Aye, and it is good that you must expect, good in the future as in the past, for *you*, Macumazahn, who are brave in your own fashion, without being a fool like Umslopogaas, and, although you know it not, like some master-smith, forge my assegais out of the red ore I give you, tempering them in the blood of men, and yet keep your mind innocent and your hands clean. Friends like you are useful to such as I, Macumazahn, and must be well paid in those wares that please them."

The old wizard brooded for a space, while I reflected upon his amazing cynicism, which interested me in a way, for the extreme of unmorality is as fascinating to study as the extreme of virtue and often more so. Then jerking up his great head, he asked suddenly, "What message had the White Queen for me?"

"She said that you troubled her too much at night in dreams, Zikali."

"Aye, but if I cease to do so, ever she desires to know the reason

---

1. For the tale of this meeting see the book called *Allan Quatermain*.— Editor.

why, for I hear her asking me in the voices of the wind, or in the twittering of bats. After all, she is a woman, Macumazahn, and it must be dull sitting alone from year to year with naught to stay her appetite save the ashes of the past and dreams of the future, so dull that I wonder, having once meshed you in her web, how she found the heart to let you go before she had sucked out your life and spirit. I suppose that having made a mock of you and drained you dry, she was content to throw you aside like an empty gourd. Perchance, had she kept you at her side, you would have been a stone in her path in days to come. Perchance, Macumazahn, she waits for other travellers and would welcome them, or one of them alone, saying nothing of a certain Watcher-by-Night who has served her turn and vanished into the night.

"But what other message had the White Queen for the poor old savage witch-doctor whose talk wearies her so much in her haunted sleep?"

Then I told him of the picture that Ayesha had shown me in the water; the picture of a king dying in a hut and of two who watched his end.

Zikali listened intently to every word, then broke into a peal of his unholy laughter.

"*Oho-ho!*" he laughed, "so all goes well, though the road be long, since whatever this White One may have shown you in the fire of the heavens above, she could show you nothing but truth in the water of the earth below, for that is the law of our company of seers. You have worked well for me, Macumazahn, and you have had your fee, the fee of the vision of the dead which you desired above all mortal things."

"Aye," I answered indignantly, "a fee of bitter fruits whereof the juice burns and twists the mouth and the stones still stick fast within the gizzard. I tell you, Zikali, that she stuffed my heart with lies."

"I daresay, Macumazahn, I daresay, but they were very pretty lies, were they not? And after all I am sure that there was wisdom in them, as you will discover when you have thought them over for a score of years.

"Lies, lies, all is lies! But beyond the lie stands Truth, as the White Witch stands behind her veil. You drew the veil, Macumazahn, and saw that beneath which brought you to your knees. Why, it is a parable. Wander on through the Valley of Lies till at last it takes a turn, and, glittering in the sunshine, glittering like gold, you perceive the Mountain of everlasting Truth, sought of all men but found by few.

"Lies, lies, all is lies! Yet beyond I tell you, beauteous and eternal stands the Truth, Macumazahn. *Oho-ho! Oho-ho!* Fare you well, Watcher-by-Night, fare you well, Seeker after Truth. After the Night comes Dawn and after Death comes what—Macumazahn? Well, you will learn one day, for always the veil is lifted, at last, as the White Witch showed you yonder, Macumazahn."

# Wisdom's Daughter

# Dedication

In bygone years the books *She* and *Ayesha* were dedicated to Andrew Lang. Now, when he is dead, this, the last romance that will be written concerning "*She-Who-Must-Be-Obeyed*," is offered as a tribute to his beloved and honoured memory.
Ditchingham
1922

# Editor's Note

What was the greatest fault of Ayesha, *She-Who-Must-Be-Obeyed*? Surely a vanity so colossal that, to take one out of many examples, it persuaded her that her mother died after looking upon her, fearing lest, should she live, she might give birth to another child who was less fair.

At least, as her story shows, it was vanity, rather than love of the beauteous Greek, Kallikrates, that stained the hands of She with his innocent blood and, amongst other ills, brought upon her the fearful curse of deathlessness while still inhabiting a sphere where Death is lord of all. Had not Amenartas taunted her with the waning of her imperial beauty, eaten of the tooth of Time, never would she have disobeyed the command of her master, the Prophet Noot, and entered that Fire of Immortality which she was set to guard.

Thus it seems that by denial she would have escaped the net of many woes in which, perchance, she is still entangled and of Ayesha, Daughter of Wisdom yet Folly's Slave, there would have been no tale to tell and, from her parable of the eternal war of flesh and spirit there would have been no lesson to be learned. But Vanity—or was it Fate?—led her down another road.

*The Editor*

# Introductory

The manuscript of which the contents are printed here was discovered among the effects of the late L. Horace Holly, though not until some years after his death. It was in an envelope on which had been scribbled a direction that it should be forwarded to the present editor "at the appointed time," words that at first he did not understand. However, in due course it arrived without any accompanying note of explanation, so that to this hour he does not know by whom it was sent or where from, since the only postmark on the packet was London, W., and the address was typewritten.

When opened the package proved to contain two thick notebooks, bound in parchment, or rather scraped goat or sheepskin, and very roughly as though by an unskilled hand, perhaps in order to preserve them if exposed to hard usage or weather. The paper of these books is extremely thin and tough so that each of them contains a great number of sheets. It is not of European make, and its appearance suggests that it was manufactured in the East, perhaps in China.

There could be no doubt as to who had owned these notebooks, because on one of them, the first, written in red ink upon the parchment cover in block letters, appears the name of Mr. Holly himself. Also on its first pages are various memoranda of travel evidently made by him and no one else. After these follow sheet upon sheet of apparently indecipherable shorthand mixed up with tiny Arabic characters. This shorthand proved to belong to no known system, and though every effort was made to decipher it, for over two years it remained unread.

At length, when all attempts had been abandoned, almost by chance, it was shown to a great Oriental scholar, a friend of the Editor, who glanced at it and took it to bed with him. Next morning at breakfast he announced calmly that he had discovered the key and could read the stuff as easily as though it were a newspaper leader. It seemed that the writing was an ancient form of contracted Arabic, mixed in places with the Demotic of the Egyptians—a shorthand Arabic and a shorthand Demotic, difficult at first, but once the key was found easily decipherable by some six or eight living men, of whom, as it chanced, the learned scholar into whose hands it had thus fallen accidentally was one.

So it came about that with toil and cost and time, at length those two closely written volumes were transcribed in full and translated. For the rest, they speak for themselves. Let the reader judge of them.

There is but one thing to add. Although it is recorded in note-books that had been his property, clearly this manuscript was *not* written by Mr. Holly. For reasons which she explains it was written with the hand of *She* herself, during the period of her second incarnation when at last Leo found her in the mountains of Tibet, as is described in the book called "Ayesha."

## CHAPTER 1

# The Halls of Heaven

To the learned man, ugly of form and face but sound at heart, Holly by name, a citizen of a northern land whom at times I think that once I knew as Noot the Holy, that philosopher who was my master in a past which seems far to him and is forgot, but to me is but as yesterday, to this Holly, I say, I, who on earth am named Ayesha, daughter of Yarab the Arab chief, but who have many other titles here and elsewhere, have told certain stories of my past days and the part I played in them. Also I have told the same or other stories to my lord Kallikrates, the Greek, now named Leo Vincey, aforetimes a warrior after the habit of his race and his forefathers, who for religious reasons became a priest of Isis, the great goddess of Egypt and, once I believed, my mother in the spirit. Also I have told these or different tales to one Allan, a wandering hunter of beasts and a fighting man of good blood who visited me at Kor, though of this I said nothing to Holly or to my lord Kallikrates, now known as Leo or the Lion, because as to this Allan I held it wiser to be silent.

All these stories do not agree together, since often I spoke them as parables, or in order to tell to each that which he would wish to hear, or to hide my mind for my own purposes. Yet in every one of them lay hid something of the truth, a grain of gold in the ore of fable that might be found by him who had the skill and strength to seek.

Now my spirit moves me to interpret these parables and set down what I am and whence I came and certain of the things that I have seen and done, or at the least such of them as I am permitted to reveal by those mightier than I of whom I am the servant, as they in their turn are the servants of others yet mightier than themselves.

Here in these Asian caves I sit, the Hesea of the Mountain, the last priestess of the worship of Mother Isis upon earth, as aforetime I sat amid the ruins of Kor in Libya.

At Kor for two thousand years I watched and waited till at length reborn Kallikrates, whom unwittingly I slew in a rage of jealousy, came back to me where I had slain him. There, because of the curse that is on me and him, I lost him again, for in this very place, too, I was slain most horribly, slain by an excess of life wherewith I thought to make myself more beautiful even than I was and in striving to overfill the vase, shattered it to the vilest dust. Thus once more Fate made a mock of me; once more I lost Kallikrates whom it is my doom to desire in the flesh and to raise up in the spirit through time untold.

My soul passed out and on and here for a little while it found a home masked in the withered shape of an ancient priestess of my worship.

As was foredoomed my lord came back to me and saw the shining soul within that hideous shape and claimed it with a kiss, as I think the bravest deed and the most faithful that was ever done by man. In the magic of that kiss as also was foredoomed, my beauty great again before his eyes, so that once more I stand a glory upon earth. Now we are plighted, now, if all goes well, within a year we shall be wed, aye, within one short year after I have borne him back to Kor and unsealed the hidden Fire of Life and plunged him in its essence, giving to him my own gift of undying days.

And yet and yet—who knows the end? He presses me sore, and the starved woman part of me is passionate and weak and I may yield, and if his lips touch mine, who can say but that the fire within me will destroy him, the unfortified, and bring all my plans to dust and nothingness? I am great, set far above mortals, yet I play against forces I cannot see, that are greater than I, and it may please them to snatch the cup from my lips, and once more to overthrow me; for even though the blood of gods runs in him, as it runs in all of us, who can stand against their master, Doom, and its decrees? Therefore I, named Wisdom's Daughter, named Child of Isis, to-night am as full of fears as any mortal maid craving her lover beneath the moon and not knowing but that war, or chance, or the vile breath of sickness may have borne him away into that gulf where all things must be lost—until they are found again.

\* \* \* \* \* \* \* \*

From month to month Leo, my lord, hunts upon the mountain after the fashion of men, and I, Ayesha, brood within the caves after the fashion of women. Yes, I who am half a goddess still brood within the caves after the fashion of women who wait and watch. Holly, the instructed, who loves me, as all men must do, bides here with me in the caves and we talk together of ancient things whereof the world has lost count, for he is a learned man skilled in the tongues of Greece and Rome, and one who thinks and, perchance, remembers.

But yesterday he said to me that I who seemed to know the past and to whom doors were opened that cannot be entered by human feet, should write down what I know and have experienced, that in time to come the world may be the wiser.

This the fancy has taken me to do, though whether I can persevere to the end, I cannot say. He has given me that wherein I can write. 'Tis not the old papyrus, but it will serve, and I have pens of reed and can make ink of various colours, who in the bygone days was no mean scribe. Also I sleep but little, whose body, filled like a cup with life, needs small rest, and the long hours of the night pass wearily for me who lie and brood upon what has been and is to come, searching the darkness of the future with aching, fearful soul. Moreover, I am able to write in characters which, with all his learning, Holly cannot read, I who am not minded that he should know my thoughts and deeds and betray them to my lord whom they might cause to think the worse of me.

Why, then, should I write at all? For this reason: in certain matters I have foreknowledge and my spirit tells me that in a day to come, at the time appointed, some will guess the secret of my script and render it into tongues that all may read, so that when, soon or late, upon the circle of my eternal path, I pass hence to whence I came, and, like to the Fire-God in the caves of Kor am hid awhile, this record will remain my monument. Ah! there peeps out the mortal in me, for see! like any common man or woman I would not be forgot even among the passing dwellers in a petty world.

Now to my task.

* * * * * * * *

I have a vision of what chanced to my soul before it descended to dwell on earth, and with it I will begin. Maybe it is but a parable not to be strictly rendered, a token and a symbol rather than a truth. Yet of this I am sure that in it there is something of the truth, since otherwise why through the long centuries did it return to me again and yet again? Maybe Greece and Egypt had no gods save those they fashioned for themselves. Holly tells me, as did the Wanderer, Allan, who also had some smattering of knowledge, that Zeus and Aphrodite and Osiris and Horus and Ammon are now dethroned with all their company and lie in the dust like the shattered columns of their temples, the mock of men who talk of them as the fables of the early world, so that of all the divinities that I knew, He of the Jews, although changed of character and countenance, alone is worshipped and remains.

Doubtless it is so, yet while man lives, always there is God, though his shapes be many. Always there is the eternal Good, as in the dream the holy Noot named the ultimate Divine, and behold! it is called Ammon or otherwise. Always there is Evil and behold! it is called Set or Baal, or Moloch, or otherwise. Always the stained soul of man seeks redemption, and he who saves is called Osiris or otherwise. Always Nature endures and she is called Isis or otherwise. Always the great world that will not die strains and pulses to new life, and the Life-bringer is called Aphrodite, or otherwise. And so continually. Where man is, again I say, there was and is and will be God, or Good—the Spirit named by many names.

I go to my window-place in this cave-chamber and look out upon the stars shining countless in the frosty sky and lo! there I see God clad in one of the most glorious of His garments. I look at the moth flitting round my lamp or resting on the wall and, by the magic that is in it, summoning its mate from far, and lo! there I see God in another of His humbler garments. For God is in all things and everywhere, and from the great suns down, to Him who sent them forth and to Whom they return again, all that hath life must bow.

\*\*\*\*\*\*\*\*

This is the vision wherein I read a parable of eternal truths.

I, Ayesha, daughter of Yarab, not yet of the flesh, but above and beyond the flesh inhabited the halls of that great goddess of the earth, a minister of That which rules all the earth (Nature's self as now I know), who in Egypt was named Isis, Mother of Mysteries. *Child*, she named me, and *Messenger*, and in that dream or parable, as a child was I to her, for I drank of the cup of her wisdom and something of her greatness was in my soul.

The goddess sat brooding in her sanctuary where Spirits came and went bearing tidings from all lands or emptying at her feet the cups of offered prayer. About her fell her robes, blue as the sky, and over the robes hung down her hair dusky as the night, and beneath her bent brows shone her eyes like stars of the night. In her hand was the rod of power and the footstool at her feet was shaped like the round world. There, canopied with light, she sat upon an ebon seat and brooded while round her beat music like sea waves upon the shore, such music as is not known upon the earth.

I appeared. I stood before her, I abased myself, I bowed till my forehead lay upon the ground and my hair swept the dust of the ground. She touched me with her sceptre, bidding me arise.

"Speak, Child," she said. "What message dost thou bring from the shores of Nile? How goes my worship in the temples of Isis and are my servants faithful to my law?"

Then I made answer.

"O Mother divine, I have accomplished my embassy. Unseen, a spirit, I have wandered through the Land of Egypt. I have visited thy temples, I have hearkened to the councils of thy priests, I have watched thy worshippers and read their hearts. This is my report. Thy holy temples are empty; thy priests neglect thine altars; save a remnant who remain faithful, thy worshippers bow themselves before the shrines of another goddess."

"How is this goddess named, O Child of my love and wisdom?"

"She is named Aphrodite of the Greeks, a people who have flowed into Egypt, also other folk know her as Ashtoreth and Venus. Her sanctuary of sanctuaries is at Paphos in Cyprus, an island of the sea over against Egypt. She is the Queen of earthly love and love is the ritual of her worship, and she makes a mock of thee, O Mother, and of all the ancient gods, thy brothers and sisters, swearing that thy day and theirs is done and that she has risen from the sea to rule the world, and will rule it to the end. Here and there she reveals herself and conquers by her beauty, making all men to worship her and teaching all women to follow in her steps and beguile as she does, so that thy very priests turn to her and thy priestesses break from their vows and wanton with them."

"All of this I have learned, O Child, and more; yet it was my desire to hear it from thy lips that cannot lie, since in thee dwells my spirit. Hearken now! I am minded to be avenged upon these false Egyptians, and thou shalt be the sword of vengeance wherewith I will smite them, bringing their ancient glory to the dust and for ever setting the yoke of bondage on their necks. Aye, I am so minded and it shall be done, how, I will teach thee afterward. But first, as I have the power to do, I who under the Strength above me am regent of the ball of earth, will summon this Aphrodite to my presence here and now, and bid her speak out her heart to me.

"Hear me, Aphrodite, wherever thou art in earth or heaven. Aphrodite, I bid thee appear."

Then in vision the Mother rose from her throne. Standing before it, terrible to see, she beckoned with her sceptre, north and south and east and west, uttering the secret words of power. Thrice she beckoned and thrice she spoke the secret words, and waited.

********

There was a stir at the end of the great hall and a sound of singing. Behold! floating between the long lines of the flame-clad guardians of that hall, attended by her subject gods, her maenads and her maidens, a shape of naked loveliness, came Aphrodite of the Greeks. Veiled in her curling locks and roped about with gleaming pearls for necklace and for girdle, she stood before the throne and bowed to the Majesty it bore, then asked in a laughing voice of music,

"I have heard thy summons, Mother of Mysteries, and I am here. What wouldst thou of me, Isis, Queen of the World? How can the Sea-born whose name is Beauty and whose gift is Love, serve thee, Isis, Queen of the World?"

"Thus, thou who art shameless, thou born of the new gods and fashioned from the evil that is in the race of men—by lifting thy spell from off my worshippers. I know thy works. Drunken with desires they flock to thee in troops and for reward thou givest them the wages of their sin. Thou layest waste their homes; thou defilest their maidens, thou turnest men to beasts and makest a mock of them. Thy flowers fade; thy joys fill the mouth with ashes and those who drink of thy cup suck up poison in their souls. Thy fair flesh is a rottenness and thy perfumes are a stench and the incense of thine altars is the reek of hell. Therefore I command thee, go back to whence thou camest and leave the world in peace."

"Whither, then, should I go, Mother?" answered Aphrodite with her silvery laugh, "save into thy bosom, whence indeed I sprang, seeing that thou art Nature's self and I am thy child. Stern is thy law and sweet, yet without me thou wouldst have none over whom to rule. Aye, without me would no child be born and not even a flower would blow. Without me thou wouldst rule a wilderness with but the wisdom of which thou boastest to keep thee company. Hearken! We are at war and in that war I shall be conqueror, for I am eternal and all life is my slave, because my name is Life. Get thee to thy heavens, Isis, and rule there with Osiris, Lord of Death, but leave me the living. Soon their day is done and they pass beyond my spells into thy dominion. There treat them as thou wilt and be content, for then I have no more need of them, nor they of me. Why of a sudden art thou so wrath with me, whom thou hast known from the beginning? Is it because I take new names and set up my altars in thine own Egypt, altars wreathed with flowers, leaving all desolate thine where prayers are mumbled from starved hearts and cold hands make the offering of denial? Come now, Mother Isis, let us play a game and let Egypt be the stake. Thou hast the vantage there, seeing that for aeons it has bowed to thy laws and thy yoke has been upon its neck."

"What, then, O Aphrodite, dost thou promise Egypt to which I and those who rule with me have given greatness, wisdom, and hope beyond the grave?"

"None of these high things, Mother. My gifts are love and joy; sweet love and joy in which for a little while all fears are forgot. Small gains thou mayest think, looking backward to the past and onward to the future, thou whose eyes are upon eternity. Yet they shall prevail. Isis, in Egypt thy day is done; there, as elsewhere, thy sceptre falls."

"If so, Wanton, with it falls Egypt that henceforth shall be the world's slave. When conqueror after conqueror sets his foot upon her neck, then let her think on Isis whom she has forsaken, and wailing, fill her soul with thy swine's food. Lo! I depart, leaving my curse on Egypt. Have thy little day till before the Judgment seat we settle our account. No more will I listen to thy falsehoods and thy blasphemies. Till then, Wanton, look on my majesty no more."

* * * * * * * *

So in that vision spoke the Mother and was gone. With her, flashing like lightnings, went the flame-clad guardians that attend the goddess, leaving the great place empty save for Aphrodite and her throng, and for the soul of me, Ayesha, who watched and hearkened, wondering. The Paphian looked around and laughed, then glided to the vacant throne and seating herself thereon, laughed again, till the music of her mockery echoing from pillar to pillar, filled all the temple's halls.

"It is an omen," she cried. "What Isis leaves I take; henceforth her seat and power are mine. See now my ministers, I queen it here, though I wear no vulture cap or symbols of the moon, whose brow is better graced by these abundant locks and whose sceptre is a flower whereof the odours make men mad. Yes, I queen it here as everywhere, though in this solemn melancholy fane I lack a subject."

She glanced about her till her glorious, roving eyes fell upon that spirit which was I.

"Come hither, thou," she said, "and do me homage."

Now in my dream I, that spirit who in the world am named Ayesha, came and stood before her, saying,

"Nay, I am the child of Isis and to her I bow alone."

"Thinkest thou so?" she answered, smiling and looking me up and down. "Well, I have another mind. It seems to me that soon thou wilt

293

descend from this sad realm to the joyous fields of earth, that there thou mayest fulfil a certain purpose, for such is the fate decreed for thee. Now, I, Aphrodite, add to that fate and lighten it. Look behind thee, Spirit that shall be woman!"

I turned and looked, there to behold a shape of beauty that I knew for Man. So beautiful was he that my breast rose and the life in me stood still. He smiled at me and I smiled back at him. Then he was gone, leaving his picture stamped upon my soul.

"This is what I add to that tragic fate of thine, O Spirit that shall be woman. Take him, the man appointed to thee, who from the beginning was always thine, and as perchance thou hast done before, in his kiss forget thy Mother Isis and thy crown of woes."

\* \* \* \* \* \* \* \*

Thus this vision ends, and though now I, Ayesha, have learned that Isis, as we knew and named her in the ancient time, is but a symbol of that eternal holiness which is set above all heavens and all earths, I say again that, as I believe, in its parable is hid something of the changeless truth.

CHAPTER 2

# Noot the Prophet Comes to Ozal

Such is the vision, such the dream that has haunted me through the centuries, and brooding over it from age to age, I, Ayesha, doubt not that in its substance it is true, though its trappings may be fancy-wrought. At least this I know, that my spirit is the child of immortal Wisdom, such as once men believed that Isis held, as my undying shape is born of the beauty that is fabled Aphrodite's gift. At least it is certain that even before I dipped me in the Fire of Life, the most of learning and all human loveliness were mine. I know also that it was my mission to bring Egypt to the dust, and did I not bring it to the dust, smiting to its heart through proud Sidon, and Cyprus, Aphrodite's home? And have I not for these deeds borne Aphrodite's curse, as, because of Aphrodite's yoke laid upon my helpless neck, I have borne and bear the curse of Isis, I whose destiny it is thus at once to be the instrument and sport of rival powers whose battle-ground is the heart of every one of us.

Alas! were my tale known, the world in its haste might judge me hardly and think that I, who by burning its Phoenician props over-turned an ancient empire, am cruel-natured, or that because I sought the love of a certain man and in my anger slew him when he turned from me, which in truth I did not desire to do, that I am wanton and ungoverned. Yet these things are not so, seeing that it was Fate, not I, that gave Egypt to the Persian dog (whom in his turn I overthrew) and made of its people slaves, and my flesh, not I, which after I had tasted of the Fire that is Nature's Soul, cursed me with passion and its fruits, perchance because I hated it and would never bow myself to it wholly, I who followed after purity, desiring not man's love but Wisdom's gifts and a crown of spiritual gold.

Moreover, I had earthly and righteous warrant to bring about Si-don's fall and through it that of Egypt, seeing that their kings would have put me to utter shame and robbed my father of his life, as shall be told. So, too, I had the warrant of a woman's heart to worship the man I sought and for the death I brought upon him in my jealous madness my soul has paid full measure in remorse and tears. Still, since justice is hard to come by here on the earth, or even in the heaven above, I know that some would judge me harshly and must bear it with the rest. Even Holly, and at times my Lord Leo who once was named Kallikrates, have cherished such thoughts, though their lips dare not utter them, for I read it in their minds which to me are as an open book. Therefore never shall Holly, nor my lord either, look upon this written truth, lest therefrom they might distil some poison of mistrustful doubt, for it is sure that all men stain the whiteness of pure verity to the colour of their twisted minds. Therefore, too, I write it in tongues and symbols that they do not understand, which yet shall be deciphered in their season.

As I taught Holly long ago in the caves of Kor, and truly, though afterward for some forgotten reason of my own or to give him food for thought, I may perhaps have changed my tale, puzzling him with stories of great Alexander and the rest, by my mortal birth I am an Arabian of the purest and most noble blood, born in Yaman the Happy and in the sweet city of Ozal. My father was named Yarab after the great ancestor of our race, and I, his only child, was named Ayesha after my highborn mother. Of her, whom I never knew, for she was gathered to the bosom of whatever god she worshipped but one moon from my birth, this is said.

At first she would not look upon me, being angered because I was not a son, but at length at my father's pleading she was prevailed upon to command that I should be brought to her. When she saw how fair a babe Heaven had given her, such a babe as had not been known or told of among our people, she was amazed and put up a prayer that she might die. This, those who knew her declared, she did for two reasons:—first because, foreseeing my greatness, she desired that I alone should hold my father's heart and that of all our tribe, and secondly because she feared lest, should she live, she might bear other children whom she would hate when she compared them to my perfectness.

So it came about as, amongst others, my father told me often, that her prayer was granted and having kissed and blessed me, for a while she entered into rest.

This is the true story of her end, not the other, which those who envied me put about in after days, that owing to certain revelations which came to her at the time of my birth, as to the deeds which I was doomed to do and the loves and hates which I was doomed to earn, my mother thought it better to ask death from her gods rather than to continue in a life which she must live out at my side. This tale, my father often swore to me when I asked him of it, was as false as the changeful pictures which are seen at sunset on the desert, and sometimes at noonday also.

For the rest this beloved father of mine took no other wife while I was yet a child, fearing lest for her own sake, or her children's, she should be jealous and maltreat me, and afterward when I became a maiden, because I would not suffer that another woman should share the rule of his household with me. As I showed to him, he had servants in plenty and these should be enough, to which he bowed his head and answered that without doubt my will was that of God.

Thus it came about that I grew up with my noble father, his adviser and his strength, and through him, or rather with him, ruled all his great tribe, who always worshipped me. Be it admitted that from the first, or at least from the time that I came to womanhood, I brought him trouble as well as blessing, though through no fault of my own, but because of the beauty with which, as in those days I believed, Isis, or Aphrodite, or both of them, had endowed me for their own divine purposes. Very soon this beauty of mine, also my wit and knowledge, were noised abroad through all Arabia, so that princes came from far to court me, and afterward quarrelled and fought, for, being gentle-hearted, I said a kind word to every one of them and left them to reason out which was the kindest.

This, for the most part, they did with spears and arrows after the fashion of violent and insensate men, so that there was much fighting on my account, which made my father some enemies, because the people of certain of the princes who were killed swore that I had promised myself in marriage to them. This, however, I had never done, who desired to marry no man that I might become a slave, cooped up in a fortress to bear children that I did not desire with some jealous tyrant for their father. Nay, being higher-hearted than any of my time, already I sought to rule the world, and if I must have any lover, to choose one whom I wished, and, when I wished, to have done with him.

But at that time I asked no lover who myself was in love—with wisdom. Knowledge, I saw, was strength, and if I would rule, first I must learn. Therefore I studied deeply, taking for masters all the wisest in Arabia who were proud to teach Ayesha the Beautiful, daughter and heiress of Yarab the great chief who could call ten thousand spears to his standards, all of his own tribe; and ten thousand more sworn to us but not of our blood.

I learned of the stars, a deep learning this that taught my soul its littleness, though it is true that while I studied I wondered, as still I wonder now, in which of them I was destined to rule when my day on earth was done. For always from the beginning I knew that wherever I am, there I must be the first and reign.

Perchance I had learned this aforetime in the halls of Isis who then to me had seemed so great, though afterward contemplating those stars in the silence of the desert night, I came to understand that even the Universal Mother, as men named her in those far days, was herself but small, one who must fight for sovereignty with Aphrodite and other gods.

Holly has told me much of what the astronomers in these latter years have won of Nature's secrets: of how they number and weigh the stars, and measure to a mile their infinite distance from the earth, and how assuredly that each of them, even the farthest, is a sun as great or greater than our own, round which revolve worlds unseen. He has been astonished also, and affected to disbelieve, when I answered him, that we of Arabia guessed all these things over two thousand years ago, and indeed knew some of them. Yet, so it was.

Thus communing with greatness, my soul grew ever greater.

Moreover, I sought other and deeper lore. There wandered a certain strange man to our town, Ozal, where my father kept his court, if so it may be called, that is when we were not camping with our great herds in the desert, as we did at certain seasons of the year after the rains had caused the wilderness to throw up herbage. This man, named Noot, was always aged and white-haired, ugly to look on, with a curious wrinkled face of the colour of parchment, much such a face as that of Holly will be should he attain to his years. Indeed in this and other ways he was so like to Holly that often I think that in him dwells something of Noot's spirit now returned again to earth, as that of Kallikrates has returned to Leo.

Now this Noot, who came to Egypt none knew whence, for by birth he was not Egyptian, had been the high-priest of Isis and *Kher-heb* or Chief Magician in Egypt, one who had much power on earth and still more beyond the earth, since he was in touch with things divine. Moreover, he was an honest magician and told the truth even to the kings, as the gods and his wisdom showed it to him, and this was the cause of his downfall, for woe betide those who tell the truth to kings or to any who wield the sceptre of their might. On a certain day

298

Nectanebes, the first of that name, the Pharaoh of Egypt whom others called Nekht-nebf, after a victory he had gained over the Persians, was filled with pride and took counsel with Noot, his Chief Magician, bidding Noot search out the future and tell him of glories to come to Egypt and to the Royal House, after he had been gathered to Osiris, that thereon he might feed his soul.

Noot answered that it was wiser to leave the future to care for itself and to satisfy his heart with the present and its joys and greatness.

Then the Pharaoh grew wrath and bade him fulfil his command.

So Noot bowed and went, and alone in some tomb or sanctuary drew the circles, uttered the words of power, and called upon the gods he served to show him such things as should befall to Egypt and to Pharaoh's House.

The magic sleep fell upon him and in it appeared the Spirit of Truth and spoke to him dreadful words of fate and doom. These she bade him deliver to Pharaoh, but when they were spoken to fly for his life's sake from Egypt and seek out a maiden called Ayesha, the daughter of Yarab, the Sheik of Ozal, and with her take refuge since she was an appointed instrument of Heaven. Moreover, this spirit commanded him to consult the maiden Ayesha in everything and impart to her all his gathered learning and the very secrets of the gods that had been revealed to him, that to any other it would be death to speak.

Now in the morning Noot went into the presence of Pharaoh who rejoiced to see him, and cried,

"Be welcome, *Kherheb*, the first of all magicians, you that men say were born beyond the earth, you in whom lives the spirit of Maat, goddess of Truth. Tell me now what the gods have revealed to you as to the glories they prepare for the ancient land of Egypt, and the House of me the Pharaoh who have made her great again, driving out the dogs of Persians!"

"Life! Blood! Strength! O Pharaoh!" answered Noot, saluting in the ancient form. "I have heard the word of Pharaoh who commanded me against my counsel to make divination and to seek to learn of the future from the gods. Behold! the gods hearkened. Behold! by the mouth of Maat, Lady of Truth, the goddess of the land where I was born, they spoke to me in the silence of the night. Thus they spoke. 'Say to Nectanebes who impiously dares to lift the veil of Time, that because he has fought for Egypt against the Barbarians who worship other gods, it is granted to him to die in his bed which shall chance ere long. Say that after him shall come a usurper whom the Barbarians shall defeat, so that he dies a slave in the land of Persia. Say that after him the son of Pharaoh shall wear the Double Crown and be called by the name of Pharaoh, the last of the true Blood of Egypt who shall ever sit upon its throne. Say that this son of his is accursed because he is in league with evil spirits and has worked apostasy, putting about his neck the chain of Aphrodite of the Greeks and the chains of Baal and of Moloch which never can be broken. Therefore, though he make many false offerings, yet is he accursed and the Barbarians shall overcome him, so that he flees away, nor shall all his magic be a shield to him. Because of him Egypt shall fall and her cities shall be burned and her children slaughtered and her temples desecrated, and never more shall one of her pure and ancient blood hold her sceptre.' Such is the oracle that the gods have commanded me to speak, O Pharaoh."

Now when Nectanebes heard these awful decrees of Fate upon him and upon his son, he trembled and rent his robes. Then rage took him and he reviled Noot the Prophet, calling him a liar and a traitor, and saying that he would make an end of him and his prophecies together. But because they were alone together within a chamber, before he could summon guards to kill him, Noot, helped of Heaven, fled away out of the palace and as darkness was falling, mingled with the throng and could not be found by the soldiers who sought him.

Ere daylight he was far from the city and, disguised, escaped from Egypt, bringing with him only his *Kherheb's* staff of power, also the ancient sacred books of spells or words of strength that were hidden in his robes. With these he brought, moreover, a little ancient image of Isis which he made use of in his divination and prayed before by day and night.

*  *  *  *  *  *  *  *

Thus it came about awhile later, one eve when I, the young maiden Ayesha, stood alone in the desert communing with my soul and drawing wisdom from the stars, that there appeared before me a withered, ancient man who, when he saw me, knelt down and bowed to me. I looked on him and asked,

"Why, aged One, do you kneel to me who am but a mortal?"

"Are you indeed a mortal?" he asked. "Methought that I who am the head-priest of Isis saw in you the goddess come to earth, and indeed, Lady, I seem to see the holy blood of Isis coursing in your veins."

"It is true, Priest, that of this goddess whom my mother worshipped I have dreams and memories and that sometimes she seems to speak with me in sleep, yet I tell you that I am but a mortal, the daughter of Yarab the far-famed," I answered to him.

"Then you are that maiden whom I am commanded to seek, she who is named Ayesha. Know, Lady, that great is your destiny, greater than that of any kind, and that it is revealed to me that you will become immortal."

"All who believe in the gods trust to find the pearl, Immortality, beneath Death's waters, O Priest."

"Yes, Lady, but the immortality that is foretold for you is different and begins upon the earth, and I confess that I understand it not, though perhaps it may be an immortality of fame."

"Nor I, Priest. But meanwhile, what would you of me?"

"Shelter and food, Lady."

"And what can you offer for these, Priest?"

"Learning, Lady."

"That I think I have already."

"Nay, Lady Ayesha, not such learning as I can give; the knowledge of the secrets of the gods; spells that will sway the hearts of kings, magic that will show things afar and call ghosts from the grave, power that will set him who wields it upon the pinnacle of worship——"

"Stay!" I broke in. "You are old and ugly! you are tired, your foot bleeds, you seek protection, and it seems to me that you need food. How comes it that one who can command so much lore and power is in want of such things as these that the humblest peasant does not lack, and must seek to purchase them with flatteries?"

When he heard these words, of a sudden the aspect of that old man changed. To me his shrunken body seemed to swell, his face grew fierce and set, and a strange light shone in his deep eyes.

"Maiden," he said in another voice, "I perceive that you are in truth in need of such a teacher as I am. Had you the inner wisdom, you would not judge by the outward appearance and you would know that ofttimes the gods bring misfortunes upon those they love in order that thereby they may work their ends. Beauty is yours, wit is yours, and a great destiny awaits you, though with it, as I think, great sorrow. Yet one thing is lacking to you—humility—and that you must learn beneath the rods of destiny. But of these matters we will talk afterward. Meanwhile, as you say, I need food and shelter, which are necessary to all while still they labour in the flesh. Lead me to your father!"

********

Without more talk though not without fear, I guided this strange wanderer to our tents, for at the time we were camping in the desert, and into the presence of my father, Yarab, who gave him hospitality after the Arab fashion, but save for the common words of courtesy, held no converse with him that night.

On the following morning before we struck our camp, however, they had much speech together, and at the end of it I was summoned to the great tent.

"Daughter," said my father, pointing to the wanderer who was sitting cross-legged on a carpet before him after the fashion of an Egyptian scribe, "I have questioned this learned man, our guest. I discover from him that he is the First Magician of Egypt, the head-priest also of the greatest goddess of that land, she whom your mother worshipped. At least, he says he was these things—but now, having quarrelled with Pharaoh, that he is nothing but a beggar, which is a strange state for a magician. Also, according to his tale, Pharaoh seeks his life, as he declares, because of certain prophecies that he made to him concerning the fate of Egypt and of Pharaoh's House. It seems that he desires to abide here with us and to impart his wisdom to you, which wisdom, it is evident, has brought him to an evil case. Now I ask you, as one gifted with discretion beyond your years, what answer shall I return to him? If I keep this Noot here, for that he tells me, is his name, though of his race and country he will say nothing, perchance Pharaoh, whose arm is long, will come to seek him and bring war upon us, and if I sent him away, perchance I turn my back upon a messenger from the gods. What then shall I do?"

"Ask him, my Father; seeing that one who prophesies evil to the Pharaoh to his own ruin must be a truthful man."

Then my father stroked his long beard, being perplexed, and inquired of the wanderer whether he should keep him or send him away.

Noot replied that he thought that my father would do well to send him away, but better to keep him. He said that he had no revelation on the matter, though if it were wished he would seek one, but he believed that although his presence might bring trouble, from his dismissal would come yet worse trouble. He added that in a vision he had been commanded by the goddess Isis to find out a certain Lady Ayesha and become her instructor in mysteries that the purposes of Heaven might be fulfilled, and that it was ill to flout goddesses whose arms were even longer than those of Pharaoh.

Now for the second time my father who did nothing great or small without my counsel, asked my judgment on the matter after I had heard the words of Noot. I pondered, remembering what the wanderer had promised to me in the desert, namely, knowledge and the secrets of the gods, also spells that would sway the hearts of kings, with the gifts of magic and of power. At length I answered,

"To what end is all this empty talk, my Father? Has not this stranger eaten of your bread and salt and is it the custom of our people to drive away from their doors for no fault those to whom they have given hospitality?"

"True," said my father. "If he were to be sent hence, it should have been done at once. Abide in my shadow, Noot, and pray your gods to bring a blessing on me."

\* \* \* \* \* \* \* \*

So Noot, the priest and prophet, remained with us and from the first day of his coming, opened out to my eager eyes all the scrolls of his secret lore. Still it is true that he brought to my father, not blessing but death, as shall be told, though this did not come for many moons.

Meanwhile he taught and I learned, for his knowledge flowed into my soul like a river into the desert and filled its thirsty sand with life. Of all that I learned from him, because of the oaths I swore, even now it is not lawful that I should write, but it is true that in those years of study I grew near to the gods and wrested many a secret from the clenched hands of Nature.

Moreover, though as yet I did not take the vows, I became a votary of Isis, as Noot, her high-priest, had authority to make me, and one of the inner circle. Yes, I determined even then that I would forswear marriage and all fleshly joys and make to Isis the offering of my life, while she through her priest vowed to me in return such power and wisdom as had scarce been given to any woman before me.

Thus the time went by till at length fell the blow and I—for all my wisdom—never heard Aphrodite laughing behind her veil. Nor indeed did Noot, but then he was an old man, who, as I drew out of him, save those of his mother, had not once touched a woman's lips. All learning was his, but it seemed that in his search for it there were some things he had passed by. At least so I believed, or rather half-believed, at this time, but as I learned afterward, there are matters upon which even the most holy think it no shame to lie, since in the end Noot confessed to me that in his youth he had been as are other men. Also I think that he heard the laughter of Aphrodite, though I did not. However these things may be, as I was to discover afterward, Mother Isis is a stern mistress to whoever looks the other way.

Also, although Noot told me much, he hid more. Not for many a year was I to learn that he was a citizen of the ancient, ruined land of

Kor, and the only one who knew the fearful mystery it hid, which in a far day to come he was commanded to reveal to me, Ayesha, and to no other man or woman. Nor did he tell me that it was the purpose of Heaven that under her other shape and name of Truth I should again establish the worship of Isis in that land and once more make of it a queen of the world. Yet these things were so and therefore was he sent to me and for no other reason. Therefore was he commanded to reveal the doom of Egypt to Nectanebes, that this Pharaoh in his wrath might drive him, a wanderer, to our tents at Ozal there to dwell for years and instruct me, the chosen, in all things that I must learn, so that when at last the appointed hour dawned, I might be fitted for my mighty task.

********

But all this while Aphrodite laughed on behind her veil!

## Chapter 3

# The Battle and the Flight

In the end trouble came upon us thus. As I have said already, my beauty was the talk of men throughout Arabia, and of women also, who were jealous of it, since those who travelled in caravans bore its fame from tribe to tribe and those who sailed upon the sea took up the report and carried it to distant shores. But now to this tale was added another, namely that the wearer of so much loveliness was also a vessel into which the gods had poured all their wisdom, so that there were few marvels which she could not work and little or nothing that she did not know. It was added, truly enough, that the channel through which this wisdom flowed into her heart was a certain Noot who aforetime had been *Kherheb* in Egypt and high-priest of Isis.

Presently this tale, carried by the mariners, came to the ears of the Pharaoh Nectanebes in his city of Sais, who knew well enough that Noot was the prophet whom he had driven from the land and whom by now he desired to have back again, for his inspired counsel's sake.

The end of it was that the Pharaoh sent an embassy to my father, Yarab, demanding that I should be given to him or to his son, the young Nectanebes, I know not which, in marriage, and that Noot should return to Egypt as my guardian, and there be reinstated in all his offices.

My father answered, speaking with my voice, that least of anything did I desire to become one of the women of Pharaoh, a man already near the grave, or even of Pharaoh's son, I who was a free-born Arabian, and that as for Noot, his head felt safer on his shoulders in Ozal where he was an honoured guest, than it would at Pharaoh's court.

These words Nectanebes took ill, so ill indeed that, for this and other reasons of policy, he sent an army to invade Yaman the Happy, and to capture me and kill Noot, or drag him away to Egypt in chains. Of all these plans we had warnings, partly through the priests of Isis in Egypt who still acknowledged Noot as their head, although another had been raised up in his place and filled his office, and partly through dreams and revelations that came to him from Heaven. Therefore we made ready and gathered in great strength to fight against Pharaoh.

At length his hosts came, borne for the most part in ships of Cyprus and of Sidon whereof at that time the kings were his allies, or rather vassals.

They landed upon a plain by the seashore and watching from our hills beyond, we suffered them to land. But that night, or rather just before the following dawn when their camp was still unfortified, we poured down upon them from our hills. Great was the fray! for they fought well. I led the horsemen of our tribe in this, my first battle, and by the light of the rising sun charged again and yet again into the heart of the hosts of Pharaoh, having no fear since I knew well that none could harm me.

There was a certain company of Greeks, two thousand of them perhaps, who served Pharaoh, and in the centre of them was his general, which company stood firm when the others fled. Thrice we attacked it with the horsemen and thrice were beaten back. Then my father came to my aid with his picked kinsmen mounted upon camels. Again we charged and this time broke through. Those about Pharaoh's general saw me and strove to make me captive, hoping to carry me back to him, whatever happened to the host. They surrounded me, one caught the bridle of my horse. Him I slew with a javelin, but others snatched at me. Then I cried to Isis and I think that she clothed me in some garment of her majesty, since foes well away in front of me, calling out—

"This is a goddess, not a woman!"

Yet I was cut off, ringed round by them, for all my companions were slain or driven back.

They pressed in on me to take me living, till I was hedged in with a ring of swords. My father appeared mounted on his swift white dromedary that was called Desert Wind, followed by others. They broke through the ring, and there was a fierce fight. My father fell, pierced by the spear of the general of the Egyptians. I saw it and, filled with madness, I charged at that general and drove my javelin through his throat, so that he fell also. Then a cry went up and the host of Pharaoh melted away, flying for the ships. Some gained them, but the most remained dead upon the shore or were taken captive.

Thus ended that battle and such was the answer that we of Ozal sent to Pharaoh Nectanebes. Therefore it was also that because of the death of my beloved father at their hands I hated Egypt, and not only

Egypt but Cyprus and Sidon in whose ships her hosts had been borne to attack us, yes, and swore to be avenged upon them all, which oath I kept to the full.

Now my father being dead, I, the daughter of Yarab, became ruler of our tribe in his place with Noot for my counsellor. For certain years I ruled it well. Yet troubles arose—in this fashion. By now the fame of my glory and loveliness had spread through all the earth, so that, more even than before, I was beset with demands for my hand from chiefs and kings who went well-nigh mad when I refused them. In the end, being brothers in their grief because I would have none of them, I whom they called by the names of Hathor and Aphrodite and other goddesses famed for beauty according to their separate worships, they made a great conspiracy together and sent envoys bearing a message. This was the message:—

That unless my people would give me up so that my husband might be chosen from among their number by the casting of lots, they would join their armies together and fall upon us and kill out our tribe so that not one remained to look upon the sun, save myself alone, who should then be the reward of him who could take me.

Now when I heard this I was filled with rage and having caused those messengers to be scourged before me, sent them back to their masters bearing my defiance. But when they were gone, the elders of the tribe came to me and said through their spokesman,

"O Daughter of Yarab, O Ayesha the Wise and Lovely, we adore you as one beyond price. Yet it is true that we love our wives and children and desire to live, not to die. How can we who are but few stand against so many kings? We pray you, therefore, Ayesha, to choose one of them to be your husband, for then because of jealousy doubtless they will destroy each other and we, your servants, shall be left in peace. Or if you will not marry, then we pray you to hide your beauty elsewhere for a while, so that the kings do not come to seek it here."

I hearkened and was angry because of the cowardice of this people who set their own welfare about my will and refused to fight with those who threatened me. Still, being politic, I hid my mind and said that I would consider and give them an answer on the third day. Then I took counsel of Noot and together we made divinations and prayed to the gods, but most of all to Isis.

The end of it was that before the dawn on the second day a small caravan of five camels might have been seen, had there been any to watch, leaving the city of Ozal and heading for the sea.

On the first of those camels sat an old merchant. On the second his wife or his daughter, or his woman, heavily veiled. On the three others was his merchandise. Woven carpets it seemed to be, though if opened, those carpets would have proved to be filled with a very great treasure in gold and pearls and sapphires and other gems, which for generations had been gathered together by my father, Yarab, and those who went before him out of the profits of their trade and of their flocks and herds, and hid away against the time of need.

That merchant was Noot the priest and prophet, and that woman was I—Ayesha. That treasure was mine and the camels were led by certain men who had served my father and now served me, being sworn to me by secret oaths that might not be broken.

We gained the sea and took ship to Egypt in a vessel that I had caused to be prepared. Yes, before we were missed the coast of Arabia was behind us, since I had given it out that I had gone to a secret place to consider of my answer to the elders of the people. As I heard afterward, when it was known that I had turned my back on them, there were woe and lamentations in every household of the tribe. Understanding what they had lost the men among them beat their breasts and wept, though it is said that some of the women rejoiced, because I outshone them all and they were jealous of me.

Afterward the kings and chiefs of whom I have spoken descended upon them to seek me, whereupon my people swore that I had been changed into a goddess and gone up into heaven. Some believed this, declaring that they had always held me to be more than mortal, but others of a coarser, common mind declared that I had been hidden away, and falling on the tribe, dispersed it, seizing many and selling them into slavery.

Thus then did the children of Yarab pay the price of their treachery to me, though I have heard that afterward once more they became a great people under the rule of some baseborn grandson of my father, and worshipped me as a guardian goddess from generation to generation, having come to believe that I was not a woman, but a spirit whom the gods sent to dwell with them for a while.

* * * * * * * *

So Noot and I came safely to Naukratis, a Grecian city upon the Canopic mouth of the Nile, and there abode disguised as a merchant and his daughter trading in precious stones and other costly wares, and thus adding to my wealth, though of this there was little need, since already it was great.

It was here that for the first time I went veiled in the Eastern fashion, in order to hide my beauty from the eyes of men.

Under cover of this trade I and Noot lived for two years or more while I studied the lore and language of the Egyptians, learning to read their picture-writing which the Greeks call hieroglyphs, and mastering their history. Also I perfected myself in the Grecian tongue and read the works of their great writers as well as those of the Romans. Moreover, I learned other things, since at the beginning of the year Nectanebes, the Pharaoh who had sought me in marriage, being now dead, and Egypt for a while in the hands of the usurper Zehir, who some say was his son born of a concubine, we travelled up the Nile disguised and came to the ancient city of Thebes. This we did slowly, stopping at every great town, where we received the hospitality of the head priests of the various gods, Ammon, Ptah, and the rest, since to these priests Noot by secret signs revealed himself. Indeed the news of our coming was passed on before us so that always we found some waiting to welcome us who, once within the temple walls, were treated like the greatest, although we were garbed as humble travellers. All of these priests we found full of rage, both because the gods of the Greeks, and even of the Persians and Sidonians, were being set above their own, and still more for the reason that their revenues were seized and used to pay Grecian mercenaries, so that they who had been very rich were now poor and the gods lacked their offerings, nor could their holy temples be repaired.

Of all these things I took note whose heart was set upon one thing only,—to bring about the fall of the Egyptians and their allies that had slain my father whom I loved, as indeed I was fated to do. Therefore by a word here and a word there I blew the anger that smouldered in them to flame, hinting of rebellion and the setting up of a new dynasty in Egypt, of which at that time I thought to be the first, a priestess-queen, *Isis-come-to-Earth*. Of this plan I hinted also through the mouth of Noot, nor was it ill received, since already those priests to whom he had told my history and the revelations that had come to him concerning me, looked on me as something more than woman. Could a mortal maid, they asked, have so much beauty and so much learning; was I not in truth a goddess clothed in woman's flesh?

Only on the road I purposed to tread there was this stumbling block, that each of those high-priests desired that he himself, or at least one who worshipped *his* god, were it Ammon or Osiris or Ptah, or Khonsu, should be the Pharaoh of that new dynasty. For they were jealous each of the other and could not agree together, as is common among rival priests.

We passed on to Thebes where I saw the wonders of the mighty temples which stood there reared by a hundred kings, which Holly tells me now are but ruins, though the great hall of columns among which I used to wander still stands in part. Also I crossed the Nile and visited the tombs of the Pharaohs.

Standing beneath the moon in that desolate Valley of Dead Kings, for the first time, I think I came to know all the littleness of Life and of the vanities of earth. Life, I saw, was but a dream; its ambitions and its joys were naught but dust. Those kings and those queens, some of them had been very great in their day; the people worshipped them as gods and when they stretched out their sceptres, the world trembled. And now what were they? But names, if so much as a name remained of them.

I saw a great queen whose tomb some while before had been broken into by robbers, Persians or Greeks I was told. They had unrolled her mummy and stripped her of her royal ornaments and there she lay, she in whom had centred all the world's pomp, a little black and withered thing, grinning at us from the dust, like a dead ape, a sight so strange and unhuman that the priest who guided us, a coarse fellow, broke into laughter. I remembered that laugh and afterward paid him back for it, though he never knew whence his misfortune came.

I, Ayesha, have many sins to my count and at that time was full of faults, as perchance still I am to-day. Thus I was proud of my beauty and my genius which were given to me above any other woman; passionate and revengeful, too, and led on by ambitions. Yet this I swear by all the gods of all the heavens, that ever in my secret self I have set the spirit above the flesh and desired to attain to another glory than that of earth. From the flesh came my sins, because it was begotten of other flesh and the flesh is sin incarnate. Yet my soul sins not, because it comes from that which is sinless and, its tasks accomplished here, laden with knowledge and purified by suffering, to this holy fount at last it shall return again. At the least such are my faith and hope.

So it came about that there in the Valley of Dead Kings I swore myself to the worship of God (since all the gods are one God) and to use the world as a ladder whereby I might climb nearer to His throne.

Thus I swore with old Noot for witness, noting that he shook his wise head and smiled a little at the oath. For if I forgot Aphrodite and the flesh, he remembered them, or perchance he to whom the Future spoke already guessed something of my fate which it was not lawful that he should tell. Also at that time I knew nothing of that everlasting King of Fire who dwells in majesty beneath the rocks of Kor, nor of his evil gifts. Least of all did I know that Noot himself was by inheritance and appointment the guardian of the Fire.

From Thebes we passed up Nile to Philae on the Isle of Elephantine, where Mother Isis had her holy sanctuary, and Nectanebes, the first of that name, he who had sought me as a wife and now was not long dead, had begun to build a temple of surpassing beauty to the goddess, which temple was completed in my time by his son, the second Nectanebes, he with whom I had to do and brought to nothingness.

Here I abode a year making final preparations utterly to vow myself to the goddess. I kept the fasts, I purified my heart, I passed the trials and at length alone I seemed to die and descended into the gulf of death and fled through the Halls of Death pursued by terrors, till I saw, or dreamed I saw, the goddess in her glory and fell swooning at her feet. More I may not say, even now that over two thousand years have passed since that holy hour of fears and victory, save this one thing which indeed has come to pass. When I arose from that swoon certain words were written on my mind, though whether the goddess whom I seemed to see or some spirit spoke them to me I do not know. These were the words:—

"Far to the south in this land of Libya beyond the region of Punt, is an ancient city, whence my worship came ere Egypt had a people. Thither, Daughter of Isis, shalt thou bear it back and there shalt thou blow upon it with thy breath and keep alive the holy spark that at last is doomed to die upon the earth amidst those snows which as yet no southern foot has trod. There, Daughter, in that fallen and deserted land, my prophet Noot shall welcome thee. There shall he guard the Door of Life which of mortal women thou alone shalt pass. There shalt thou stain thy hands with blood, and there in solitude amidst the tombs, with tears from thy repentant eyes, shalt thou wash thy sin away. Yet of the seed that thou sowest in fire in the womb of the world, thou shalt reap the harvest upon the mountain tops amidst the snows."

Such were the words branded upon my memory when I awoke from the swoon after the night of trial. Later I repeated them to Noot, my Master, praying him to read their meaning, which either he could not or would not do. He said, however, it was true that far to the south there stood a great city, now a ruin sparsely peopled, whence came the first forefathers of the Egyptians thousands of years before the pyramids were built. He said also that he knew the road to that city by sea and by land, though how he knew it he would not tell. Nor would he interpret the rest of those dream words. Yet, when I harassed him with questions he said carelessly, as one who hazards a guess, that perchance the goddess meant that it would be my lot after its fall or corruption in Egypt, to bear back her worship to this its earlier home and there establish a great nation of her servants. As to the "Door of Life" that I alone could pass, of which he was named the Guardian, and the "northern snows," he declared that he knew not what was meant by them, but doubtless these things would be made clear in their season.

So he spoke somewhat lightly, like one who humours a frightened child, as though he would make me think that I had but dreamed a dream. This indeed I came to believe, as is the fashion of mankind concerning things that they cannot see or handle, however real those things may appear in the hour of their experience. For these in the end always we write down as dreams, such as haunt us by the thousand in our sleep.

Yet now that two thousand years have gone by, I know that this dream was true. For is there not a city called Kor and was I not there doomed to find the Door of Life whereof Noot was guardian? And did I not sin there and from generation to generation wash the blood from off my hands with tears of bitterest repentance, and afterward expiate that sin in loss and shame and agony? And lastly do I not reap that harvest of tears upon the mountain tops amidst the northern snows whither the spirit bore me, still holding in those hands the embers of the worship of that regnant Good who to us of the ancient world was known as the Universal Mother to whom I swore myself in Philae's temples?

But enough of these things now; let them be spoken of in their season.

## CHAPTER 4

# The Kiss of Fate

There came a man to Philae. Watching from a pylon top whither I had gone to pray alone, I saw him land upon the island and from far off noted that he was a godlike man, clad in armour such as the Greeks used, over which was thrown a common cloak, hooded as though to disguise him; one who had the air of a warrior. At a distance from the temple gate he halted and looked upward as though something drew his glance to me standing high above him upon the pylon top. I could not see his face because of the shadow thrown by the great walls behind which the sun was sinking, but doubtless he could see me well enough, whose shape was outlined against the veil of golden light that must have touched me with its glory, though, as that light was behind me, my face also would be hidden from him. At least he stood a little while as though amazed, staring upward steadily, then bowed his head and passed into the temple, followed by men bearing burdens.

Some pilgrim to the shrine, I thought to myself, then turned my mind to other matters, remembering that with men I had no more to do. Thus for the first time here in the body, all unknowing, I looked upon Kallikrates and he looked on me, but often afterward I have thought that there was a veiled lesson or a parable in the fashion of this meeting.

For did I not stand far above him, clothed in the glory of heaven's gold, and did he not stand far beneath in the gloom of the shadows that lay upon the lowly earth, so that between us there was a space unclimbable? And has it not been ever thus throughout the centuries, for am I not still upon the pylon top clad in the splendour of the spirit, and is he not still far beneath me wrapped with the shadows of the flesh? And since as yet the secret of the pylon stair is hidden from him, must I not descend to earth if we would meet, leaving the light and my pride of place that I may walk humbly with him in the shadow?

And is it not often so between those that love, that one is set far above the other, though still this rope of love draws them together, uplifting the one, or dragging down the other?

The man passed into the temple and that night I heard he was a Grecian captain of high blood, one who though young had seen much service in the wars and done great deeds, Kallikrates by name, who had come to seek the counsel of the goddess, bringing precious gifts of gold and Eastern silks, the spoil of battles in which he had fought.

I asked why such an one sought the wisdom of Isis, and was told that it was because his heart was troubled. It seemed that he had been dwelling at Pharaoh's court as a captain of the Grecian guard, and that there he had quarrelled with and slain one who was a brother to him, if indeed he were not his very brother. This ill deed, it was said, preyed upon his soul and drove him into the arms of Mother Isis, seeking for pardon and that comfort which he could not find at the hand of any of the gods of the Greeks.

Again I asked idly enough why this Kallikrates had killed his familiar friend or his brother, whichever it might be. The answer was—because of some highly placed maiden whom both of them loved, so that they fought from jealousy, after the fashion of men. For this reason the life of Kallikrates was held to be forfeit according to the stern military law of the Grecian soldiers, and he must fly. Also the deed had tarnished that great lady's name; also his heart was broken with remorse and hither he came to pray Isis to mend it of her mercy, he who had forsaken the world.

The tale moved me a little, but again I cast it from my mind, for are not such things common among men? Always the story is the same: two men and a woman, or two women and a man, and bloodshed and remorse and memories which will not die and the cry for pardon that is so hard to find.

Yes, I cast it from my mind, saying lightly—oh! those evil-omened words—that doubtless his own blood in a day to come would pay for that which he had spilt.

******** 

For a while, some months indeed, this Grecian Kallikrates vanished from my sight and even from my thoughts, save when, from time to time, I heard of him as studying the Mysteries among the priests, having, it was said, determined to renounce the world and be sworn to the service of the goddess. Noot told me that he was very earnest in this design and made great progress in the faith, which pleased the priests who desired above all things to convert those that served Grecian gods with whom the deities of Egypt, and above all Isis, were at war. Therefore they hastened his preparation so that as soon as might be he should be bound to the Heavenly Queen by bonds that could not be loosed.

At length his fasts and instruction were completed; his trials had been passed and the hour came when he must make his last confession to the goddess and swear the awful oaths to her very self.

Now since Isis did not descend to earth to stand face to face with every neophyte, it was necessary in this great ceremony that one filled with her spirit should take her place and as may be guessed, that one was I, Ayesha the Arab. To speak truth, in all Egypt, because of my beauty, my learning, and the grace that was given to me, there was none so fitting to wear her mantle as myself. Indeed afterward this was acknowledged when, with a single voice, the Colleges of her servants throughout the land, men and women together, promoted me to be her high-priestess, and gave me, who aforetime among them was known by the title of Wisdom's Daughter, the new name of *Isis-Come-To-Earth*, or in shorter words, *The Isis*. For my own name of Ayesha I kept hid lest it should be discovered that I was that chieftainess, the child of Yarab, who had defeated the army of Nectanebes.

Therefore at a certain hour of the night, draped in the holy robes, wearing on my brow the vulture cap and the bent symbol of the moon, holding in my hand the *sistrum* and the cross of Life, I was conducted to the pillared sanctuary and seated alone upon the throne of blackest marble, with the round symbol of the world for my footstool.

Thus, having learned my part and the ancient hallowed words that I must say, I sat awhile wondering in my heart whether Isis herself could be more glorious or more fair. So indeed did the priests and priestesses who saw me thus arrayed and bent the knee to me as though I were the very goddess, which in truth many of the humbler among them half believed.

Thus I sat in the moonlight that flowed from the unroofed hall beyond, while the carven gods watched me with their quiet eyes.

At length I heard the sound of footsteps whereon there came a priestess and flung over me the white veil of innocence sewn with golden stars that until the appointed moment must hide Isis from her worshipper. The priestess withdrew and, wrapped in the dark, hooded robe that signified the stained flesh about to be cast away, which hid all of him so that his face could not be seen, came that tall neophyte led by two priests who held his right hand and his left. I noted those hands because they were so white against the blackness of the robe, and even by the moonlight saw that they were beautiful, long and thin and shapely, though the palm of one, the right, was somewhat broadened as though by long handling of the tools of war.

The priests led him to the entrance of the shrine and in hushed whispers bade him kneel upon a footstool and make his sacrifice and confession to the goddess as he had been taught to do. Then they departed leaving us alone.

There followed silence which at length I broke, whispering,

"Who is this that comes to visit the Mother in her earthly shrine and what is his prayer to the Queen of Heaven and Earth?"

Though I spoke so gently and so low, perhaps because of their very sweetness, my words seemed to frighten him, or perhaps he believed that he stood in the very presence of the goddess; at least he answered in a voice that trembled,

"O holy Queen adored, in the world I was named Kallikrates the comely. But the priests, O Queen, have given me a new name, and it is, *Lover-of-Isis.*"

"And what have you to say to Isis, O Lover-of-Isis?"

"O Queen eternal, I have to tell my sins and ask her pardon for them, I who have passed the Trials and am accepted by her servants. If it is granted, then to her I must make the oath, binding myself eternally to love and serve her, her and no other in heaven or on earth."

"Set out those sins, O Lover-of-Isis, that my Majesty may judge of them, whether they can be forgiven or are beyond forgiveness," I answered in the words of the appointed ritual.

Then he began and told a tale that made me redden behind my veil, for all of it had to do with women, and never before had I learned what wantons those Greeks could be. Also he told of men whom he had slain in war, one of them in the battle against my tribe, in which strangely enough it seemed he had fought as a lad, for this man was a great warrior. Of these killings, however, I took no account, because they had been of those who were the enemies of himself or of his cause.

In stern silence I listened, noting that save for these matters of light love and fightings, the man seemed innocent enough, for in his story there was naught of baseness or of betrayal. Moreover, it seemed that he was one in whom the spirit had striven against the flesh, and who, however much his feet were tangled in the poisonous snares of earth, from time to time had set his eyes on Heaven.

At length he paused and I asked of him,

"Is the black count finished? Tell now the truth and dare to hold nothing back from the goddess who notes all."

"Nay, O Queen," he answered, "the worst is yet to come. I came to Egypt as a captain of the Grecian guard that watches the House of Pharaoh at Sais. With me came another man, my half-brother, for our father was the same, with whom I was brought up and loved as never I loved any other man, and who loved me. He was a glorious warrior, though some held that I was more handsome in my person, Tisisthenes by name, that in my Grecian tongue in which I speak means the Avenger. Thus he was called because my father, whose first-born he was, desired that he might grow up to work vengeance upon the Persians who slew his father named like myself, Kallikrates, the most beauteous Spartan that was ever born. Foully they slew him before the battle of Plataea, whilst he was aiding the great Pausanius to make sacrifice to the gods. This Tisisthenes my brother I killed with my own hand."

"For what cause did you kill him?"

"There was a royal maiden at that court, one fairer than any woman has been, is, or will be—ask not her name, O Mother, though doubtless it is known to you already. This lady both of us saw at the same time and by the decree of Aphrodite both of us loved. As it chanced it was I who won her favour, not my brother. We were spied upon; the tale was told; trouble fell upon that royal maiden who, when she should be old enough, was sworn in marriage to a distant king. To save her name she made denial, as we must do. She swore there was naught between her and me, and to prove it turned her face from me and toward my brother. I came upon them together in a garden. She had plucked a flower which she gave to him and he kissed the hand that held the flower. She saw me and fled away. I, maddened with jealousy, smote my beloved brother in the face and forced him to fight with me. We fought. He guarded himself but ill, as though he cared nothing of the end of that fray. I cut him down. He lay before me dying, but ere he died, he spoke:

"'This is a very evil business,' he said. 'Know Kallikrates, my most beloved brother, that what you saw in the garden between that royal maid and myself was but a plot to save you both, since thereby I purposed to take on to my own head the weight of your transgression against the law of this land, because she prayed it and it was my wish. This I have done, and for this reason I suffered you to slay me, though during that fight twice I could have pierced you, because you were blinded with rage and forgot your swordsmanship. Now it will be said that you found me pursuing this royal maiden and rightly slew me according to your duty and that it was I who loved her and not you, as has been commonly reported. Yet in truth I love her well and am glad to die because it was to you that her heart turned and not to me; also because thereby I save both her and you. Yet, Kallikrates, my brother, the gods give me wisdom and foresight in this the hour of my death, and I say that you will do well to have done with this lady and all women, and to seek rest in the bosom of the gods, since, if you do not, great trouble will come upon you, and through this same curse of jealousy such a death as mine shall be yours also. Now let us who are the victims of Fate kiss each other on the brow as we used to do when we were children, playing together in the happy fields of Greece, from whom death was yet a long way off, forgiving each other all and hoping that we may meet once more in the region of the Shades.'

"So we embraced, and my brother Tisisthenes gave up his spirit in my arms and looking on him I wished that I were dead in his place. Then as I turned to go the soldiers of our company found me and seeing that I had slain my brother, would have brought me to trial, not because we had fought together, but because he was my superior in rank and therefore I who, being under his command, drew sword on him, by the law of the Greeks, must die. Yet before I could be put upon my trial, some of those who loved me and guessed the truth of the business thrust me out of our camp disguised, with all the treasure that I had won in war, bidding me hide myself awhile till the matter was forgotten. O Queen, I did not desire to go; nay, I desired to stay and to pay the price of my sin. But they would not have it so. I think indeed that there were others behind, great ones of Egypt, moving in this matter; at least I was thrust forth, all being made easy for me, and all eyes growing blind."

Again he paused, and I, Ayesha, clothed as the goddess, asked,

"And what did you then, you who could slay you brother for the sake of a woman?"

"Then, Divine One, I fled up Nile, where, because of the trouble that was in the land, Pharaoh's arm could not reach me, nor the arm of the commander of the Greeks. Tarrying not and without speech with that high maiden who was the cause of my sin, I fled up Nile."

"Why did you fly up Nile and not back to your own people, O most sinful man?"

"Because my heart is broken, Queen, and I desired to seek the mercy of Isis whose law I had learned already and to become her priest. I knew that those who bow themselves to her may look no more on woman, but thenceforth must live virgin to the death, and it was my will to look no more on woman, since woman had stained my hands with a brother's blood, and therefore I hated her."

Now I, Ayesha, asked,

"What gods did you worship before your heart was turned to Isis, Queen of Heaven?"

"I worshipped the gods of Greece and first among them Aphrodite, Lady of Love."

"Who has paid you well for your service, making of you a murderer of one of your own blood who, before she blinded your eyes, was more to you than any on the earth. Do you then renounce this wanton Aphrodite?"

"Aye, Queen, I renounce her for ever. Never more will I offer at her altars or look on woman in the way of love. If I may have pardon for my sins, here and now I vow myself to Isis as her faithful priest and servant. Here and now I blot the name of Aphrodite from my heart; yea, I reject her gifts and tread down all her memories beneath my aspiring feet that at last shall bear my soul to peace."

Thus the man spoke in a quivering and earnest voice, and was silent. Yes, deep silence reigned in that holy place, whilst I, Ayesha, although it is true that as a woman I misdoubted me of such rash oaths, as the minister of the goddess, prepared myself to grant pardon to this seeker in the hallowed, immemorial words, and to open to his troubled heart the doors of purity and rest eternal.

Then suddenly in that silence clearly I heard the sound of silvern laughter, soft, sweet laughter that seemed to come from the skies above and though it was so low to fill the shrine and all the hall beyond. I looked about me but could see naught. It would seem, too, that the Greek heard also, for he turned his head and looked behind him, then once more let it fall upon his hands.

Whence came that sound? Could it be that she of Paphos——? Nay, it was impossible, and not thus would I be turned from my office, I who was clothed with the robe and for that hour wielded the might of Isis.

"Hearken, O man, in the world named Kallikrates," I said. "On behalf of Isis, the All-Mother, goddess of virtue and of wisdom, speaking with her voice, hearing with her ears, and filled with her soul, I wash you clean of all your sins and accept you as her priest, promising you light burdens on the earth and beyond the earth great rewards for ever. First swear the oath that may not be broken, and then draw near that I may kiss you on the brow, accepting you as the slave and lover of Isis, from this day until the moon, her heavenly throne, shall crumble into nothingness."

Having spoken thus, letting the words fall one by one, slowly as the tears of the penitent fell upon the ground, I uttered the oath, the form of which even now I must not write.

It was a dreadful oath covering all things, and binding him who took it to Isis alone, an oath that if it were forgot wrought upon the traitor the agelong doom of death in this world and woe in the worlds to come, till by slow steps, with pierced heart and bleeding feet, the holy height from which he had fallen should be climbed again.

At length it was finished and he said faintly,

"I swear! With fear and trembling still I swear!"

Then I beckoned to him with the *sistrum* of which the little shaken bells make a faint compelling music that already he had learned to follow, and he came and kneeled before me. There I laid the Cross of Life upon his head and gave him blessing, laid it upon his lips and gave him wisdom, laid it upon his heart and gave him existence for thousands upon thousands of years. All these things I did in the name and with the strength of Isis the Mother.

Came the last rite, the greeting of the Mother to her child new-born in spirit, the rite of the Kiss of welcome. At that moment supreme a light fell on me from above: perchance it came from Heaven, perchance it was an art of the watching priests; I do not know. At least it fell upon me illumining my glittering robes and jewelled headdress with a soft splendour in the darkness of that shrine. At that moment, too, at a touch my veil fell down, so that the moonlight struck full upon my face making it mystical and lovely in the frame of my flowing hair.

The priest new-ordained lifted his bent head that I might consecrate his brow with the Kiss of welcome, and his hood fell back. The moonlight shone on his face also, his beautiful face like to that of a sculptured Grecian god, shapely, fine-featured, large-eyed, and crowned with little golden curls—for as yet he was unshorn; yes, a face more beautiful than that which I had seen on any man, set above a warrior's tall and sinewy form.

By Isis! I knew this face; it was that which had haunted me from childhood, that which often I had seen in a dream of halls beyond the earth, that of a man who in this dream had been sworn to me to complete my womanhood. Oh! I could not doubt, it was the same, the very same, and looking on it, the curse of Aphrodite fell upon me and for the first time I knew the madness of our mortal flesh. Yea, my being was rent and shattered like a cedar beneath the lightning stroke; I was smitten through and through. I, the priestess of Isis, proud and pure, was as lost as any village maid within her lover's arms.

The man, too! He saw me and his aspect changed; the holy fervour went out of his eyes and into them entered something more human, something more fateful. It was as though he, too, remembered—I know not what.

With a mighty effort of the will, aware that the eyes of the goddess and perchance of her priests also were upon me, I conquered myself and with beating heart and heaving breast bent down to touch his brow with the Kiss of ceremony. Yet, I know not how—I know not if the fault were his or mine or perchance of both of us—it was his *lips* I touched, not his brow, just touched them and no more.

It was nothing, or at any rate but a little thing, in one instant come and gone, and yet to me it was all. For in that touch I broke my holy vows, and he, new-sworn to the worship of the goddess, broke his, yes, in the very act of sacrifice. What drove us to it? I do not know, but once again I thought I heard that low, triumphant laughter, and it came into my mind that we were the sport of an indomitable power greater than ourselves and all the oaths that mortals swear to gods or men.

I waved my sceptre. The new-made priest arose, bowed and withdrew, I wondering of whom he was the priest—of Isis or of Aphrodite. The singing of a distant choir broke out upon the silence, the *heirophants* came and led him away to be of their company till his death: the ceremony was ended. My attendants, arrayed as the goddesses Hathor and Nut, conducted me from the shrine. I was unrobed of my sacred panoplies and once more from a goddess became a woman, and as a woman I sought my couch and wept and wept.

For had I not at the first temptation in my heart broken the law and betrayed the trust of her who, as then I believed, is and was and shall be; her whose veil no mortal man had lifted, the Mother of the sun and all its stars?

## CHAPTER 5

# The Summons

None knew my fault. Yet I knew, and what is known to one soul is known to all souls, since one is all and all are one. Moreover, it was known to That which begets souls, That from which they come and to which they return again, again to come, as Plato, the great philosopher, who died before my day, has taught us in his writings. Also it was known to that accursed priest who was the cause and partner of my crime. I was overcome; I was eaten up with shame, I who thought myself purer than the mountain snows, as indeed I was and, in the flesh, to this hour have remained.

Soon I could no longer bear my torment. To Noot I went, Noot the high-priest, my counsellor and master, and in a secret place kneeling on my knees, there I told him all.

He hearkened with a little smile upon his withered face, then answered,

"Daughter, in your honesty you do but reveal that which I knew—how I knew it matters not. And now take comfort, since the blame is not altogether yours, or even that of this new-made priest, whose foot was caught in the same snare. You worship Isis, as I do, but what is Isis whom we portray on earth as a woman glorious above all women? Is she not Nature's self, the universal Mother, the Supreme in whom all gods and goddesses have a part? She wars on Aphrodite, it is true, yet does not that mean that in verity she wars upon herself? And are we not as Isis is, not one but many poured into a single mould, for do we not all war upon ourselves? Believe me, Daughter, the human heart is a great battleground where the higher and the lower parts of us fight with spiritual spears and arrows, till one side or the other wins victory and hoists the banner of good or evil, or Isis or of Set. Only out of a struggle comes perfectness; that which has never struggled is a dead creature from whom little may be hoped. The ore must be melted in the fire and lo! the most of it is dross, refuse to be thrown away. Had it never known the fire, there could be no pure gold to adorn the brows of Heaven, nor even copper and iron to shape the swords of men. Rejoice, then, that you have felt the hurt of fire."

"Master," I answered, "Lord of Wisdom to whom alone Ayesha bows the knee, your words are true and comfortable, yet bethink you, and if it is permitted, interpret me this riddle. I dreamed a dream of the time before my earthly days—you know it well for I have told it to you. I dreamed of a place in Heaven and of two goddesses matched against each other and of a command that was laid upon me to bring woe upon those who had deserted the one and turned to the other. Now if they were parts of a single whole, why should this command be laid upon me?"

"Daughter, in your dream you were ordained to be a Sword of Vengeance, not because the Egyptians turned from one part of the holy Unity to another part of that Unity, but because they have become corrupt and faithless, worshipping no gods save themselves and following after that which is low, not that which is high. Such is my answer, yet of the truth or the falsehood of that dream I say nothing. Perchance it was but a dream."

"Perchance, Master. Yet in that dream, true or false, I saw a face, and lo! a few nights gone I, draped as Isis in the shrine, I saw that face again and knew it; knew also that with it my fate is intertwined. What of this?"

"Daughter, who are we that we should read the mysteries of Fate, we who know not whence we come nor whither we go, nor what we have been, nor why we are? It may be that you have some mission toward the spirit that is clothed in the flesh of yonder man. It may be that you are destined to uplift that spirit, and in so doing yourself to be trodden down. If so, I say that in the end you shall rise again and bear him upward with you."

He paused, and I knelt silent, pondering the prophecy, for such I knew it well to be. Then again he spoke,

"You heard a laughter in the shrine, yet there was no laughter save that of the evil in your own heart, mocking and triumphant. Such laughter mayhap you will often hear, but while you can hear it and repent, be not dismayed. When the ears of the soul grow deaf then utter loss is near; while they are open, hope remains. Those who still strive can never wholly fall. Fate rules us every one, yet within the circle of that Fate power is given to us to work out our redemption. I have finished. Ask me no more."

"What punishment, Master?" I asked.

"Daughter, this. For a while look no more upon that man. I say for a while, since with you I hold that his destiny and yours are intertwined. I have a command for you: that presently you accompany me hence to lands beyond the seas. Now, go rest, and in rest find forgetfulness."

So I went, wondering yet comforted, though I knew well that Noot the Holy had not told me all, no, nor yet the half of what he knew. For often those to whom the gods give vision are forbid to speak it, lest, as in the old Hebrew parable, men should eat of the tree of knowledge and grow like to them. Or perchance they cannot speak it, since it comes to them in a tongue which may not be rendered in the words that the passer-by would understand. So indeed it is with me to-day.

\*\*\*\*\*\*\*\*

Thus it came about that soon I and my master, Noot, left Philae and as before travelled the Nile disguised. Never since then have my eyes looked upon that island and its holy fane which Holly, who has visited it, tells me is now a ruin with stark, Hathor-headed columns standing here and there amongst the tumbled stones. He says, moreover, that his people who rule the land to-day purpose to sink it beneath the Nile that the lands below may be enriched and multiplied. Herein I see an allegory; the temples of Isis are drowned and the learning they held is lost in order that more food may grow to feed the common and the ignorant. Yet to what end, seeing that if there is more food, more men will come to eat it, all of them common and ignorant, while Isis and her wisdom are swallowed in the slime. Thus has it ever been in Egypt, and doubtless elsewhere, for such is Nature's law. Food breeds multitudes and where carrion is, there are flies, while in the deserts both are lacking. Yet I think that the deserts and the few that wander on them beneath the sun and stars are nearer far to God.

Once more disguised as merchants, I and Noot, my master, took ship and visited far lands to see their state and gather wisdom. We visited Rome, then breaking her shackles and rising to her greatness. They were a great people, those Romans that Noot out of his foresight told me would one day rule the world. Or perhaps it was I who told Noot, judging them by their qualities; I am not sure. At least I loved them not, because of their rude natures, their lack of arts and their love of power and gain. Therefore when I had studied their language and their politics I passed on.

We came to Greece and tarried there awhile, studying philosophies and other things. The Greeks I did love, because they were beautiful and called forth beauty from all they touched. Also they were brave who defied the Persian might and had they but stood together, might have queened it on the earth. But they would not, for ever State tore out the throat of State, so that in the end all were undone and overwhelmed by a multitude of commoner folk who held Greece before them, for such was their destiny. Moreover, they worshipped gods made like themselves, with all the faults of men grown greater and more vile, and told fables concerning them fit to please children, which I thought strange in a people that could produce such philosophers and poets. Yet those gods had come down to them from their fathers, and it is hard to shake off the yoke of gods until some greater god appears and breaks it with the hammer of war.

Here in Greece it was that I posed to its most famous sculptor for a statue of Aphrodite, or rather it was as a mould of perfect Womanhood that I posed, desiring that this sculptor, who pleased me, should have one flawless model to copy in his future work, for which he blessed me, naming that statue "Beauty's Self." Yet when I visited him a while afterward I found that he had changed this name to Aphrodite.

I was angered who did not desire that my loveliness should be accredited to mine enemy and that of Isis whom I served, and asked him why this had been done.

He answered, humbly enough, because of a dream in which the Paphian had appeared to him and threatened him with blindness unless he gave her own name to so divine a face and form. Moreover, being in the thrall of superstition he prayed me, even with tears, that thus it might remain, since otherwise he must break that statue and as he thought, be blinded as well. So out of pity I let him have his way and even gave him my hand to kiss in token of forgiveness.

Thus it comes about that Aphrodite unashamed throughout the ages has taken the tribute of a million eyes, clothed in a borrowed loveliness. So be it, since what she has stolen is but a fraction of the truth. No sculptor, however great, can mould the perfect out of frozen stone.

From Greece, still disguised as a merchant and his daughter, we wandered to Jerusalem, feigning to trade in pearls and gems, since there I would study the religion of the Jews whereof I had heard so much. The "City of Peace" it was called among the Egyptians of old times, or so they interpreted its name, but never found I one in which there was less of peace. Fierce-faced were those Jews and quarrelsome; revengeful too and ever waging war, public and private, upon one another. A peculiar people, as they name themselves, full of hate, particularly of the stranger within their gates. To trade with them was scarcely possible, because he who sold them wares was always left the loser, though for this I who sought their philosophy, not their gold, cared nothing.

So I turned myself to the study of their faith, and found that God, as they interpreted Him, was well-nigh as fierce as were his worshippers. Yet this I will say, that He was one God, not many, and a true God also, since otherwise how could his prophets have written so gloriously concerning Him? Moreover, it was their belief that He would come to earth and lead them to the conquest of the world. This, Holly tells me, has chanced though not in the shape they hoped, since the King who came would have led them but to the conquest of the evil that is in the hearts of men and to the knowledge of a life to be, in which they had small faith. Therefore they persecuted and slew Him as a malefactor after their cruel fashion, and what is now accepted by millions, so says Holly, they still reject.

I preached to them, for my heart burned in me at the sight of their sacrifices. Yes, I preached to them against the shedding of blood, telling them of a higher philosophy of gentleness and mercy. For a while they listened, then took up stones and stoned me, so that had I and Noot not been protected by Heaven, we should have been slain. After this affront I turned my back upon Jerusalem and its hook-nosed, fierce-eyed people, and went to Cyprus where I debated with the lewd priests of Aphrodite at Paphos. Thence I got me back to Egypt whence I had been absent many years.

At Naukratis priests of Isis who knew of our coming, how I cannot tell, perchance Noot had told them by messenger, or in a dream as he could do, met us and conducted us up the Nile to the temple of Isis at Memphis. Here we were received in state in the great hall of the temple and lo! at the head of those who welcomed us was the Greek Kallikrates, now by his holiness and zeal risen high in the service of the goddess.

When I saw him, beauteous as of old, my heart stood still and the blood rushed to my brow.

Yet I gave no sign, treating him as a stranger on whom my eyes had never fallen until that hour. He for his part stared at me with a puzzled air, then shook his head as one does who sees a face that he believes he has met in dream and yet is doubtful. For be it remembered, this man had looked on me but once, when robed as Isis I received him into the company of her priests at Philae, and then but for a moment in the light of the moon. Perchance he still thought that it was the goddess herself whom he saw thus and not a mortal. At the least he did not know that I, the beauteous prophetess who came to Memphis after wanderings through the world, was the same as she who had sat upon the throne of Isis at Philae and whom by chance he had kissed upon the lips. Mayhap even he did not remember the kiss, or if he remembered, set it down as part of the ceremonial. Thus, if I knew him but too well, to him I was a stranger.

I bethought me of flight, knowing in my heart that to me this man was as the fabled sword that hung above the head of Damocles, though what harm I had to fear from him, I did not know.

Again I sought the counsel of Noot who smiled and answered,

"Have I not told you, Daughter, that perils must be faced since those from which we flee will be swift to overtake us? If Destiny has brought you and this man together, be certain that it is for its own purposes. Surely you have learned your lesson and steeled your soul against all fleshly vanities."

"Yes, my Father," I answered proudly, "I have learned my lesson and steeled my soul. Moreover, your thought is my thought, nor will I turn my back on any man. Here I bide, defying woman's weakness and all the wiles of evil gods."

"Well spoken," answered Noot, and blessed me in the ancient words. Yet as he did so I noticed that he sighed and shook his head.

* * * * * * * *

For many a moon, I know not how many who, having all time at my command, seem to have lost its petty count, I remained there in the temple at Memphis of which soon I became the prophetess and the head of the priestesses. Ere long the fame of my divinations spread far and wide, so that from all the land those who sought wisdom or knowledge of the future would come to consult me, bringing great gifts to the goddess, though not one gem or piece of gold did Noot and I keep for ourselves, who indeed had no need of such common dross.

So I sat in a carven chair in the sanctuary, my diviner's bowl at my side, and uttered dark sayings like to those of the famous oracles of the Greeks at Delphi, many of which fulfilled themselves. For in truth, I think that there was a spirit in me—whether it came from the Heavens or elsewhere I do not know—which enabled me to read much that was passing upon the earth and even sometimes that which had not yet happened upon the earth. So the renown of the Lady Isis spread till I became a power in the land. Moreover, thus

I learned many things, for those who consult an oracle, like those who seek the help of a physician, lay bare their souls, keeping no secret back.

Now at this time Egypt and all the countries round seethed with war like a pot boiling on the flames. For years Egypt had beaten off the attacks of the Persians, but now the Pharaoh Nectanebes, the second of that name who then sat upon the throne, the last native king who reigned upon the Nile, was threatened by Artaxerxes, that one of this accursed race who as named Ochus. This Persian Ochus had gathered a mighty force to subdue Egypt, hundreds of thousands of men, tens of thousands of horsemen, hundreds of *triremes* and of transport ships.

The last act of the tragedy had begun of which the end was to be the crushing of Egypt who never more should know a Pharaoh of her own blood and choosing. Of all these things I learned through those who came to consult the oracle of Isis, and much did I talk of them with Noot.

Now of myself during these long years of quiet and preparation for great events, I will say that the things of earth behind me, I grew nearer to the Divine, and in the night time I communed with my soul which seemed to have become a part of that which is above the world. The Greek, Kallikrates, I saw continually, but no word passed between us save such as had to do with matters of our faith and of the worship of Isis in whose service he now stood high. Never did we interchange a touch or a look of love. He was apart from me and I from him. And yet always in my heart I feared this man, this beautiful man, the warrior who had become a priest, for some prescience told me that he would bring disaster on my head, or I should bring it upon his, I knew not which.

So there we sat in the sanctuary, Noot the wise and aged, who yet never seemed to change, Kallikrates the priest, and I, and alone or together gave counsel to kings and captains, or uttered oracles. Clear seemed our sky and free from trouble, yet on the far horizon in my spirit I discerned the tempest clouds arising, the terrible clouds in which the lightnings played like the swords of Destiny that in a day to come were doomed to overwhelm and pierce us through.

Nectanebes the second, the Pharaoh, came to his palace at Memphis to gather troops from Upper Egypt and made great offerings to the gods, seeking their favour in the coming war. Now I saw him for the first time, a gray-haired, fat, heavy-jowled man, bald-headed, large-nosed, with great eyes like to those of an ox. Such as Nectanebes, the magician, the consorter with familiar spirits, named the Destroyer, a title which the gods who hated him must have given him in irony since himself he was doomed to be destroyed. But one good thing can I say of this Nectanebes, that he was a lover of the arts and raised glorious buildings to the gods. Learning that I, the high-priestess, had dwelt at Philae, he came to consult me as to the beautiful temple with the Hathor-headed columns which he built there and through my counsel it was made perfect, for I drew its plans, or at least those of its adornments. Holly tells me that even as a ruin, although so small, there is no lovelier building in all Egypt.

Now this Pharaoh thought me a Greek and did not know that I was an Arab and the daughter of him of Ozal in Yaman, whom his father, the first Nectanebes, had brought to his death because once long ago I had been refused as a wife to himself or to this son of his who now had succeeded him. Of these things doubtless he remembered little or nothing, since that was one of the smallest of Egypt's wars. But I, I remembered and swore that in payment for my father's blood I would bring his accursed House to ruin. Always also I received him veiled since I did not desire that he should look upon my beauty and inquire concerning my history; therefore, as a prophetess had a right to do, I received the Pharaoh veiled.

Often he came to visit me because he had learned that I was a mistress of Magic and he who practised magic much hoped that I would teach him secrets he did not know, and show him how to lay spells upon his enemies. This indeed I did, but the secrets that I taught him were evil and the spells were spears that when he threw them would fall back upon his head.

So the scene was set, and at length came the summons to begin the play with the watching world for audience.

A writing sealed with Pharaoh's seal was brought to the temple of Isis, commanding Noot the high-priest and me, Ayesha, who now was named *Oracle-of-Isis*, and the Greek Kallikrates, Chief of the Ceremonies, whose office it was to assist me in my divinations, to attend the court of Pharaoh and there declare to him the future of the war as it should be revealed to us by the great goddess whom we served. At first we refused to go, whereon there came another message which said that if we continued to refuse, we should be brought. The Pharaoh wished to offer no affront to Isis, the messenger declared, but the matter was urgent, as great things hung upon the revelations which we alone could make, and some of the kings and generals who were gathered in the temple as allies of Nectanebes, being the worshippers of other gods, could not set foot in the holy shrine of Isis.

Then, there being no help for it, we answered that we would come that very night at the rising of the moon.

Hastily consulting together we planned the words of an oracle, double-edged words that yet prophesied good to Nectanebes and encouraged him to war; for thus we believed we should most quickly bring about his downfall.

Yet as those words were never spoken I will not write them down.

## CHAPTER 6

# The Divination

Accompanied by the priests and priestesses of Isis clad in their robes and chanting the holy songs, I was borne veiled to the palace of the Pharaoh in a litter, with its curtains drawn. On my right hand walked Noot the high-priest, white-bearded, venerable; and on my left the Greek Kallikrates, Master of the Rites.

Thus we came to the palace of which the outer courts were filled with Grecian soldiers of the guard, some of whom in past years Kallikrates had once commanded, although as a shaven priest of Isis, disguised in his white robes, they knew him no more. These men stared at us, ready to mock and yet afraid, as did Phoenicians, Sidonians, men of Cyprus, and others who were gathered in the courts as though awaiting some great event.

In an outer hall a captain of the guard bade our escort of priests and priestesses to await our return, but we three, that is I, Ayesha, Noot, and Kallikrates, were summoned to the small banqueting chamber where Nectanebes with a few of the most highly placed of his guests sat at their feast. Among these were the King of Sidon, two more kings from Cyprus, three Grecian generals, some great nobles of Egypt, and others. Also certain royal ladies were present, and among them one who instantly drew my eyes to her. She was younger than I—perchance there may have been ten years between us, tall, slender, and lovely in her dark fashion, with a strong, quiet face and large brooding eyes, soft as a deer's and rather blue than black in colour.

Suddenly as we entered I, who note all, saw these eyes grow frightened like to those of one who sees some spirit returned from the halls of Death; saw also the rich-hued face turn pale, then grow red again as the blood flowed back; saw the breast heave beneath the jewelled robes, so sharply that a flower fell from them, and the lips of coral part as though to utter some remembered name.

Wondering what had thus disturbed this beauteous royalty since I, being veiled, it could not have been the vision of myself, I glanced round and perceived that Kallikrates, who was on my left, but a little behind me, had become pale as a dead man and stood like one frozen into stone.

"Who is that royal woman?" I whispered to Noot through my veil, for royal I knew her to be by the *Uraeus* circlet she wore upon her raven hair.

"Pharaoh's daughter, Amenartas," he whispered back, "whom the Greeks call *The Maiden* because she will take no man in marriage."

Then I remembered a certain confession that once I had heard sitting on the throne of the goddess Isis at Philae, of how the penitent had loved a girl of the royal House of Egypt, and for her sake killed his own dear brother; remembered also that this penitent was none other than the priest Kallikrates. Now I understood all, and though Kallikrates was naught to me save a fellow servant of the goddess, I hated that Amenartas and became aware that between her and me there was war unending, though how and why I knew not.

Next I looked at a man clad in kingly robes who sat on Pharaoh's right. He was a large man of about five and forty years of age with dark, handsome face and shifting eyes; one with a jovial aspect which yet I felt to be but a mask covering a heart full of evil schemes. From his purple robe sewn with pearls and the style of his attire and head-dress I guessed that this must be Tenes the Phoenician, King of the city of Sidon that was reported the wealthiest in the world, which city, having revolted, had joined Egypt in its war against the Persians. Instantly I weighed that man in the balance of my mind and wrote him down as an ambitious rogue who was also a coward and, as I judged from the many charms he wore, full of superstition.

The others I had no time to study for at once the Pharaoh began to speak.

"Greeting, Prophetess," he said, rising from his chair and bowing to us, or rather to me, "Greeting, High-priest of Isis, Queen of Heaven, Mistress of the World; greeting also, Priest, Master of the Rites of Isis. Pharaoh thanks you all for thus promptly answering to his summons, since this night Egypt needs your wisdom more perchance than ever before in all the ages of its history."

"Be pleased, O Pharaoh, to set out what you desire of us, the servants of the eternal goddess," said Noot.

"This, High-priest: that you should declare the future to us. Hearken! As you know, the great war has begun. The mighty Tenes here, King of Sidon, my ally, by the help of the Greeks I sent him, has defeated the Persians and against these Cyprus also is in revolt. But now Artaxerxes Ochus has seized the throne of Persia, having murdered all who stood between it and him, with the help of Bagoas the eunuch, his counsellor and general. He has raised a countless host and is pouring down upon Sidon and upon Egypt. Therefore we would learn how the war shall go and to what gods we must sacrifice to secure the victory."

"O Pharaoh," answered Noot, "in bygone years when your father sat upon the throne and I was the *Kherheb*, yes, the first magician of Egypt, he asked me such questions as these, and having prayed to my goddess, I answered him in the words that she commanded. None heard these words save your father himself, for he and I were alone together. Yet there was that in them which made him wroth so that he sought to kill me, and to save my life I fled out of Egypt, going whither the goddess led me. Afterward I was called back to Egypt where once more I an high-priest of Isis though the office of *Kherheb* is filled by another. How know I, Pharaoh, if I obey you as I obeyed your father, and again the goddess should utter prophecies which are not pleasing to the ears of kings, that once more my life may not be sought in payment?"

"I swear, High-priest," answered Nectanebes eagerly, "that whatever may be revealed by the goddess, you shall take no harm. I swear it by the name and throne of the holy Isis, to whom I will make great gifts, and all this company are witnesses of the oath. If it be broken, may the curse of Isis and of all the gods of Egypt fall upon the head of me and mine. Draw nigh now that I may touch you with my sceptre, thereby forgiving all that you have said or shall say against me or my House, and restoring to you your office of *Kherheb* of Egypt, whereof my father, who to-day is gathered in Osiris, robbed you."

So Noot drew near and Pharaoh touched him with his sceptre, a cedar wand surmounted with a little golden image of Horus, which he always carried because of his throne-name which signified "*Horus-of-Gold*." Moreover, he re-created him *Kherheb* and in token of it set upon his shoulders the gold chain from his own neck, and swore to him his place and power for life and the gift of an alabaster coffin wherein to lie after life was done. This sarcophagus, however, Noot refused, saying darkly that it was fated that he should sleep his last sleep far away from Egypt. Then he, Noot, drew back and as he went I saw Pharaoh's daughter rise and whisper awhile in her father's ear. He listened and nodded. Then he said,

"Come hither, priest who is named *Lover-of-Isis* and Master of her rites, the royal Lady of Egypt says to me that in bygone days when she was scarce a woman, she thinks that before you were a priest, you held some command amongst the Greeks of my guard, as from your stature and bearing I can well believe. She says also that if her memory serves her, you slew some man in a quarrel and for this reason fled away and sought refuge with Isis. If such things happened I have forgotten them, nor do I ask concerning them. Let them lie. Yet, lest you should be afraid that old tales may be told against you or vengeance wrought upon you, come hither also and receive pardon for the past, and protection and advancement for the future and with these a gift from Pharaoh."

Now I marvelled at this lady's foresight and cunning which showed her how to take advantage of Pharaoh's mood and safeguard one who once had loved her, all of which told me that she must be a wise woman as well as beauteous. Also it told me that the worship of this man had been pleasing to her. Then Kallikrates drew near and was touched with the sceptre. Moreover, Pharaoh spoke to him in like words that he had spoken to Noot, pardoning him all and promising him much. Moreover, in token of his favour he gave him a gold cup of Grecian workmanship having two handles, that was chased about with the story of the loves of Aphrodite and Adonis, and bordered with a wreath of those anemones which were fabled to have sprung from his blood. This glorious, flower-like cup from which the guests, when we entered, were pledging themselves in wine of Cyprus, Pharaoh lifted from the board and sent to Kallikrates, a great gift which made it clear to me how deeply he desired to propitiate the goddess in the persons of her servants.

Lastly the private scribe was commanded to write down these decrees that he had spoken, which he did forthwith, sealing them with Pharaoh's seal and giving one copy to Noot whilst keeping the other to be filed among the records.

Thus Noot and Kallikrates were protected from all things, but to me, the Prophetess, nothing was said, as I thought for two reasons, first because I was known to Pharaoh, who as I have told, had often consulted me upon matters of magic, and secondly because as the "voice of the goddess" I was holy and above reward or punishment at the hands of man. Thus I thought, with how much truth shall be seen.

The gifts were received, the papyrus had been hidden away in the robe of Noot, and there was silence in the chamber. To me, Ayesha, this heavy silence was full of omen. My soul, made keen and fine with ceaseless contemplation of things that are above the earth, in that silence seemed to hear the breath of the watching gods of Egypt. To me it was as though they had gathered there to listen to the fate of this their ancient home on earth. Yes, I felt them about me; or at the least I felt a spirit stirring.

The company at the table drank no more wine and ceased from speech. They sat still staring in front of them and notwithstanding the glitter of the ornaments that proclaimed their royalty or rule, to me they were as dead men in a tomb. Only the Princess of Egypt, Amenartas, seemed to be alive and outside the circle of this doom, for I noted that her splendid eyes sought the face, the perfect, carven face of the priest Kallikrates and that though he stood with folded arms and gazed fixedly upon the ground, he knew it, for now and again covertly he glanced back at her.

At length one of those guests could bear no more, and spoke. He was a close-lipped, war-worn Grecian general who afterward I learned was named Kleinios of Cos, the commander of Pharaoh's mercenary forces.

"By Zeus!" he cried, "are we men or are we stones, or are we shades in Hades? Let these diviners divine, and have done, for I would get me to my wine again."

"Aye," broke in Tenes, King of Sidon. "Bid them divine, Pharaoh, since we have much to agree upon ere I sail at dawn."

Then all the company cried, *"Divine! Divine!"* save Amenartas only, who searched the face of Kallikrates with her eyes, as though she would learn what lay behind its cold and priestly mask.

"So be it," said Noot, "but first I pray Pharaoh to bid all mean men depart."

Pharaoh waved his sceptre and the butlers and attendants bowed and went. Then Noot motioned to Kallikrates, who thereon shook the *sistrum* that he bore, and in his rich, low voice, uttered a chant to the goddess, that which was used to summon her presence.

He ended his chant and Noot began to pray.

"Hear me, thy prophet, O thou who wast and art and shalt be, thou in whose bosom is locked all the wisdom of heaven and earth," he prayed. "These kings and great ones desire knowledge, declare it unto them according to thy will. They desire truth—let them learn the truth in such fashion as thou shalt decree."

Then he was silent. None spoke, yet it seemed that a command came to the three of us, for suddenly Noot looked at the priest Kallikrates, a very strange look. Next the priest Kallikrates, rising from his knees, laid down the *sistrum* and taking the beautiful cup that Pharaoh had given him, went to the table and washed it with pure water from a silver ewer, then filled it to the brim from the ewer and brought it to me, Ayesha. Now I knew that I was commanded to gaze into that cup and to say what things I saw.

So I set it on the ground in front of me and kneeling, threw my veil over it and gazed into the water in the shallow golden cup.

For a little while I saw nothing, till presently a face formed in the water, the face of the royal lady, Amenartas, which stared up at me out of the cup. Yes, it stared hard and seemed to threaten me, for in its eyes were hate and vengeance. Then another face came and covered it, the face of Kallikrates the priest, and in its eyes were trouble and desire.

Now I knew that the goddess Isis, or perchance another, she of the Greeks, spoke to me of matters that had to do with myself and not with the fate of Egypt. In my heart I prayed to the Queen of Heaven to rid me of these visions, though to give me others I did not pray her, since it was my design to speak certain politic words which we had prepared.

Yet other visions came unsought, for some spirit possessed me, a spirit of truth and destiny. They were many and all of them terrible. I saw battlefields; I saw men fall in thousands, I saw cities in flames. I saw that false-eyed king, Tenes, dead. I saw the General, Kleinios of Cos, also dead, lying on a heap of Grecian slain. I saw the Pharaoh Nectanebes flying up Nile upon a boat—I knew it was Nile because the current rippled against the prow of his ship, I saw him seized by black savages and throttled with a rope till his tongue hung out and the great round eyes started from his head. I saw the temples of Egypt burning and a fierce-faced, drunken king hacking at the statues of the gods with a Persian sword and butchering the priests upon the altar. Then I saw no more but a voice called in my ears.

"Death to Egypt! Death and desolation! Death to her king, death to her priests, death to her gods! Finished, finished, all is finished!"

I cast the bowl from me. It overset but lo! there flowed from it not water but blood, or dark-hued wine, staining the white marble of the pavement. I stared at it! All stared at this god-sent horror!

"A trick!" cried the Princess Amenartas. "She has coloured the water behind the shelter of her veil."

The others too, especially the Greeks, took up the cry, echoing,

"A trick, a brazen trick!"

Only I noted that Pharaoh was silent, Pharaoh who knew that Ayesha, named *Isis-come-to-Earth*, did not deal in tricks; Pharaoh who himself practised magic and had seen such omens sent by Set. Lo! Pharaoh looked afraid and spoke no word, only glared with his great eyes at the stain upon the marble.

"What answer did the goddess give to your prayer, prophetess," asked Amenartas, sneering at me.

"This answer, royal Lady of Egypt," and I pointed to the marble, "the answer of blood."

"Blood! Whose blood? That of the Persians?"

"Nay, Lady, that of many who sit at this feast and who ere long shall sit at the table of Osiris, and of thousands who cling to them. Yet be comforted, Lady, not your blood. I think that you have much mischief to work ere you sit also at the table of Osiris, or mayhap at that of Set," I added, giving thrust for thrust.

"Declare then their names, Seeress."

"Nay, I declare them not. Go, seek them for yourself, Lady, or let Pharaoh your father seek, for is he not a magician? though what god gives him vision I do not know. You name me cheat, or rather you name the goddess cheat. Therefore the goddess is dumb and her prophetess is dumb."

"Aye, I name you cheat," she cried, who in her heart was mad with fear, "and cheat you are. Now let this temple hag who hides her hideousness behind a silken screen unveil that we may see her as she is, and let her be searched and the vase of dye be taken from her bosom or her robes."

"Aye, let her be searched," shouted the guests who were also afraid.

"No need to search, high lords," I said in a quavering voice, as though I too were overcome with fear. "I will obey the Princess. I will unveil, yet I beseech you all, make not a mock of me when you see me as I am. Once I was perchance as fair as that royal Lady who commands, but years of abstinence and the sleepless search for wisdom mar the features and wither the frame. Moreover, time touches the locks, such of them as remain to me, since these too grow thin with age. Yet I will unveil and the vase of precious dye shall be the prize of him who first can snatch it from my bosom or my robe."

"Aye," said one of them, it was the king Tenes, "and in payment for her trick we will make her drink what remains of it to give colour to her poor old carcase."

"Aye," I answered, "and I will drink what remains of it for I think the stuff is harmless. Oh! be not angry because a poor conjurer plays her tricks."

Now Noot stared at me as though he were about to speak. Then

337

his face changed like to that of a man who of a sudden receives a command that others cannot hear. He let fall his eyes, remaining silent, and I, watching, knew that it was the will of the goddess, or at least Noot's will, that I should unveil.

I glanced at the priest Kallikrates but he stood still, looking like Apollo's self frozen into stone.

During this play I had loosened the fastenings of my veil and hood and now of a sudden I cast them from me, revealing myself clad as Isis, that is in little save a transparent, clinging robe fastened about my middle. On my breast, hanging from a chain of pearls, were her holy symbols carved in gems and gold, and on my head her vulture cap beneath which my tresses hung almost to my feet, having the golden feathers of the cap adorned with sapphires and with rubies and the *uraeus* rising from it fashioned of glittering diamonds.

Aye, I unveiled and stood before them, my arms folded upon the jewelled girdle beneath my breast.

"Behold! Kings and Lords," I said, "the temple hag stands before you in such poor shape as it has pleased the gods to fashion her. Now let him who can see it, come, take the vase that hides this unveiled trickster's dye."

For a moment there was silence while those brutal men devoured my white loveliness with their eyes, taking count of every beauty of my perfect face and form. Amenartas stared at me and her ruddy cheeks went pale; yes, even the coral faded from her rich lips. Then from between those lips there burst these words:

"This is not a woman! This is the very goddess. Beware of her, ye men, for she is terrible."

"Nay, nay," I answered humbly, "I am but a poor mortal, not even royal like to yourself, Lady—but a poor mortal with some wits and wisdom, though perchance Isis for a while to your sight has touched me with her splendour. Come, take the vase ere I veil myself again."

Then those men went mad, all save Pharaoh, who sat brooding.

"Goddess or woman," they cried, "give her to us who henceforward can never look upon the beauty of another."

King Tenes rose, his coarse face afire and his shifting eyes fixed upon me greedily.

"By Baal and Ashtoreth!" he cried, "goddess or woman, never have I seen such an one as this prophetess of Isis. Hearken, Pharaoh, before the feast we disputed together concerning a great sum of gold and in the end it was confessed by you that it was due to me in aid of my costs of war although, so you said, it could not be found in Egypt save by raiding the rich treasury of Isis. Perchance the goddess learned of this design of yours and by way of answer sent us an evil oracle. I know not, but this I do know, that she sent you also a means to pay the debt without cost to yourself or the robbing of her sacred treasury. Give me this fair priestess to comfort me with her wisdom and otherwise"—here the company laughed coarsely—"and I will talk no more of the matter of that gold."

Pharaoh listened without raising his head, then looked on me with rolling eyes and answered:

"Which would anger the goddess most, King Tenes—to lose her gold or her prophetess?"

"The former as I think, Pharaoh, seeing that gold is scarce, and prophetesses—true or false—are many. Give her to me, I say."

"I cannot for my oath's sake, King Tenes."

"You swore an oath to yonder high-priest and to yonder man, who looks like a Grecian god clad in a priest's robe and is called Master-of-the-Rites, but to this lady you swore none."

"I swore the oath to Isis, King Tenes, and if I break it doubtless she will be avenged upon me. Go your way; the gold shall follow you to the last ounce, but the prophetess is not mine to give."

Now Tenes stared at me again and I, who hated him with all my soul, gave him back his stare with interest, though this did but seem to inflame him the more. Then he turned on Pharaoh furiously and answered in a cold voice,

"Hear me, Pharaoh. It is but a small matter, yet my mind is set upon this woman who knows the heart of the gods and can pour their wisdom into my ears. Therefore make your choice:

"In Sidon there are two factions of almost equal strength. One of them says 'Make an alliance with Egypt and fight the Persian Ochus whom already you have defeated once.' The other says 'Make an alliance with Ochus and as reward in a day to come sit on Pharaoh's throne!' I have taken the first counsel as you know. Yet it is not too late to change that counsel for a second which perchance would prove the wiser, if there be aught in yonder divination," and he pointed to the blood-stain upon the marble floor. Then he went on:

"Moreover, I have my captains about me at this board and those that serve me without with all my fleet, and therefore should it be changed I need not fear to tell you so and to your face. So I say to you that if you will not please me in this small matter, presently my ambassadors go forth to Susa with a message for the ear of Ochus to which it would rejoice you to listen, seeing that without the strong aid of Sidon and her fleets Egypt cannot conquer in this war."

Thus Tenes spoke and laid his hand upon the pommel of his short Phoenician sword.

Now the face of the Pharaoh, bearded thus in his own city and at his own board, grew red with rage and I saw that he was about to answer this outland king, defying him as many of the great monarchs who filled his throne before him would have done. But ere he could speak his royal daughter Amenartas whispered in his ear and although I could not hear her words, I read their purport in her face. They were—"Tenes speaks truth. Without Sidon you cannot stand against the Persians and Egypt is lost. Let the woman go. Isis, understanding, will forgive, who otherwise must see the Persian Holy Fire burning on her altars."

Pharaoh heard and the anger written in his eyes was changed to trouble. Rolling them in his fashion he looked on Noot and said to him as one who asks a question,

"I swore an oath to you, *Kherheb*, and to yonder priest, but to the prophetess I swore no oath and perchance Egypt's fate hangs upon this business."

The old high-priest paused awhile like a man who awaits a message. If so, it seemed to come, for presently he answered in a quiet voice, "Pharaoh is right; Egypt's fate hangs upon this business; also Pharaoh's fate; also that of King Tenes and many others. The only fate which is not touched, whether it be finished in this way or in that, is the fate of yonder seeress who is named *Isis-Come-To-Earth*, since the goddess will protect her own. Settle the matter as you will, Pharaoh. Only settle it swiftly, because under our rule it is time that I and my company who wait without should return to the temple to make our nightly prayer and offerings to the goddess, the Queen of all the earth, the Queen of Pharaoh and of Egypt; the Queen of the King of Sidon, and in the end the Queen also of Artaxerxes Ochus, the Persian, as one day surely he shall learn."

Thus spoke Noot unconcernedly and hearing him, I laughed, for now I was sure that I had nothing to fear from Tenes or any other man upon the earth. Therefore I laughed, which that company thought strange in one who was about to be borne away a slave, and bade Kallikrates give me my veil and hood, also the cloak that I had thrown off when I entered the banqueting hall.

He obeyed, and while he was assisting me to cover up my beauty in the folds of that veil, I noted that alone among all the men here present, this beauty did not seem to stir him at all. Had he been clothing a marble statue or an ivory image of the goddess, as every day it was his duty to do at sunrise, anointing it with perfumes and garlanding it with flowers, he could not have been less moved. Or perhaps so truly had the priest in him overcome the man that he had learned to cloak all the feelings of a man. Or perhaps it was because that royal Amenartas watched his every movement with her eyes. I know not, but this I do know, that his calm angered me and it came into my mind that were I not the head-priestess of Isis and sworn to her, there should be a different tale to tell. Yes, even in that moment of destiny this came into my mind, which shows that in my soul I had not forgotten the meeting of our lips in yonder shrine at Philae. At least I have often thought so since, I, who have had much time for thought.

"Priestess, you are mine," cried King Tenes in triumph. "Make ready to sail with me for Sidon within an hour."

"Do you think that I am yours, King Tenes?" I asked in a musing voice as I fastened the folds of my veil and arranged the hood. "If so, I hold otherwise. I hold that I, Ayesha, a free-born lady of the ancient Arab blood, am not the slave of any Phoenician who for a little while chances to be a king, but of her who is the Queen of kings, Isis the Mother. Nay, Tenes, I am more, I am Isis herself, *Isis-Come-To-Earth*. It seems that go with you I must, since such is the will of the goddess, but, Phoenician, take heed. Should you dare to befoul me even with a touch, I tell you that I have strength at my command and that ere long Sidon shall lack a king and Set shall gain a subject. For your own sake therefore and for that of Sidon, think again and let me be!"

Now the great jaws of Tenes fell and he stared at me open-mouthed.

"Yet you shall go with me," he muttered thickly, "and for the rest Ashtoreth rules in Sidon, not Isis, for know that there are two Queens of Heaven."

"Aye, Tenes, a false queen and a true, and let the false beware of the true."

Then I turned to Nectanebes and said,

"Is it still your command, O Pharaoh, that I accompany this ally of yours to Sidon? Bethink you ere you answer, since much hangs upon your words."

"Yea, Priestess, it must be so. I have spoken and my decree is recorded. The fate of Egypt is more than that of any priestess and doubtless King Tenes will treat you well. If not, you say that you have strength to defend yourself against him."

Now as I answered, I laughed lightly and the sound of my laughter was like the tinkle of falling silver.

"So be it, Pharaoh. To me it is nothing; indeed I would see Sidon, the glorious city, while she still is Sidon, home of merchants, mistress of the seas. Still ere I go, shall I tell you something, Pharaoh, of what was shewn to me in yonder bowl before its water was turned to blood—by dye from that vase which none of you has found? If I remember right, for as you who practise magic, know, Pharaoh, such visions fade quickly like dreams at dawn—I say that if I remember right, it had to do with the fate of a great king. Have you ever seen a king, O Pharaoh, when in place of the chain of royalty a collar of rope is set about his throat and drawn hard till the tongue is thrust from the royal mouth and the royal eyes start from their sockets? Nay? Then shall I draw his picture? Perchance in days to come you would know it again?"

"Witch, accursed witch!" shouted Pharaoh. "Take her, Tenes, and begone, though sooner would I nurture a viper in my bosom," and rising from the board, he turned and fled away.

Again I laughed as I answered,

"I must go, but it seems that Pharaoh has gone first. Royal Amenartas, watch the good god, your father, for I think that he is too superstitious and that which men believe fulfils itself upon them."

Then I went to Noot and spoke with him—few words for already the guards were advancing upon me.

"Fear nothing, Daughter," he said, "you are safe."

"I know that I am safe, Master, yet be ready to come to my aid when I call, as my spirit tells me that call I shall."

He bent his head and the guards came up. As I went I glanced at the priest Kallikrates, who taking no note of me or of my fate, still stood staring at the royal Amenartas like a statue cut in stone, while she stared back at him.

## CHAPTER 7

# The Quelling of the Storm

They set me on board a great ship, on the prow of which were images of certain gods of the Phoenicians, called by the Greeks *Pataeci*, not unlike to that which the Egyptians worshipped by the name of Bes, before which images burned fire. There was a royal cabin in that ship which was given to me, and with it splendid robes and furnishings of gold for my table.

At dawn we cast off from the quay of the white-walled city while thousands of the worshippers of Isis who learned that I was being taken from them, stood upon the quay and wailed, crying that the *Mouth-of-Isis* was sent away to slavery and that where her "Mouth" went, there the goddess would follow, leaving vengeance to fall upon their heads. For that the head-priestess of Isis should be given into the hands of barbarians and their foreign gods was such a crime as had not been known in Egypt.

Therefore they wailed, prophesying evil, and I stood upon the stern alone in my white robes, veiled, and hearkened to them, for none dared to come near to me. Yes, I hearkened and blessed them with my hands, whereat they knelt and wailed the more.

When at last we had passed down the Nile and were out upon the great sea, sailing swiftly for Sidon over quiet waters, I, Ayesha, having taken counsel of the goddess and of my woman's craft, sent for King Tenes, who was also on board the ship, and received him in his own cabin that had been given up to me.

For my heart was black with rage against him, and against Nectanebes, Pharaoh of Egypt, who had betrayed me, and in my heart I swore that I would destroy them both. Yes, there I, the captive, sat and received the captor king in his own cabin, purposing his doom, though how this was to be accomplished as yet I did not know.

"O King," I said, "I, your slave who, when not a slave, was high-priestess of Isis in Egypt and her seeress, into whose breast the goddess poured her wisdom and her secrets, as indeed still she does, would speak with you, and since I could not come to you among so many men, have prayed your Majesty to come to me. What would you do with me, King Tenes, since it has pleased you to force Pharaoh to give me into your keeping? Is it an oracle that you desire concerning your fate or that of your country in the war? If so, I will———"

"Nay, Priestess," he broke in hurriedly, "of your oracles I and others have had enough. They are bitter bread for daily food. Keep them, I pray you, to nurture your own soul."

"What would you of me then, King Tenes, that you have been at such pains to steal me away from Egypt, even threatening Pharaoh to break your solemn pact with him if he did not give me to your hands, me, the snared bird, who by chance was left out of his oath to the high-priest and Isis's officer, the Greek."

"Lady Ayesha," blurted out Tenes, "that I have learned to be by birth, daughter of Yarab, once ruler of Ozal, upon whom, with the Egyptians, I made war in the past and brought to his death, because of *you*, Lady, tell me, you who are wise, what would any man of you who had beheld your beauty as I saw it some nights gone?"

"Man, being man, that is, a ravening beast fashioned like a god in shape but not in soul, would make me his prey, Tenes. Such at least was the desire of the first Nectanebes whom you aided with the ships of Sidon to destroy my father, and of many since his time."

"Good. Well, I who am a man and something more, being not a god indeed, but a great king, would make you my prey, as you say, for to tell truth, having once looked on you I see no other woman in the whole world."

Now I threw back my veil and studied him with my eyes.

"So you would take me for your queen, Tenes? Indeed I guessed as much. But what would your other queen, for doubtless you have one, say to this, O King?"

"My queen!" he said in an astonished voice, "my queen?"

"Surely, Tenes, you would scarcely dare to proffer less than queenship to such a one as I?"

"May be not. Well, let us say that I would make you my queen, since in Sidon it is not difficult to be rid of others of whom one may be weary; that is, it is not difficult to a king who also is high-priest of Baal and of Ashtoreth. Yes, yes, I am sure that I would make you my queen. I will offer it to you in writing if you desire."

"Aye, I do desire it, King, and that there may be no faults or traps in it, I myself will draw up the writing for you to sign. Only I doubt much whether I shall accept the offer if it is made."

"Why not, Lady? Is it a small thing to be Queen of Sidon?"

"For Ayesha, daughter of Yarab, high-priestess and prophetess of Isis, the wisest and most beauteous woman in the world, one who has never turned to look on man, it is a very small thing indeed, King Tenes. It is so small a thing that I will not deign to accept that proffered crown of yours, unless——"

"Unless what, Lady?"

"Unless it is made larger, King, so large and wide that she who wears it holds rule over all the earth."

"By Baal, Ashtoreth, and Moloch, all three of them, what mean you, Woman?"

"What I say, Man. I mean that when you are monarch, not of Sidon only, but of Egypt, Cyprus, Persia, and all the East, then perchance I will marry you, unless my fancy changes, as it may do, but certainly not before."

"Surely you are mad," he gasped. "How can I gather all these diadems upon a single brow? It is impossible."

"Aye, for you it is impossible, King Tenes, but for me it is possible. I can gather them and set them on your brow and on my own, I who have within me all the wisdom of the earth and much of the strength of Heaven. Understand that if I desire it and you follow my counsel, I can crown you emperor of the world, no less, but the question is, do I desire it and will you follow my counsel?"

"Lady, I swear that you are mad, unless in truth you are a goddess as they say in Egypt."

"Perchance I am somewhat of a goddess, and being so, marvel whether for any reward that can be given I shall debase myself by taking such a one as you to husband, King Tenes. Now, first, look on me well and answer whether you do indeed desire me and are ready to win me through toil and danger, or whether you will let me be. For know, Tenes, that though I seem to be your captive, you cannot snare me or do me violence. Lay but a finger on me against my will, and it shall be your death, since I have those to aid me whom you cannot see. Now look—and answer."

He looked, devouring me with his greedy eyes, then said,

"Of a truth I desire you more than anything on the earth, and since I may not do so otherwise, for I perceive that you are too strong for me, will take you at your own price. Yea, even if I must wait for years, still I will take you. Now tell me, most beauteous and most wise, what I must do, and swear to me that when I am king of all things you will wed me."

"Aye, Tenes, I swear that when you are king of all things I will wed you," I answered gently, laughing in my heart as I remembered that the first and last of all things, the greatest of all things, is—Death. "Hearken. You shall bring me to Sidon, not as a captive but as a strange goddess who has come to aid you and your people, and with honour shall you receive me in Sidon, causing your priests and priestesses to offer me worship and incense."

"And if so, what then?"

"Then, when I have studied your people and your preparations for war, we will take counsel together and I will show you how you may prevail. Tell me, Tenes, do you love Pharaoh Nectanebes?"

"Nay, Lady, I hate him who asks too much and gives too little, as I hated his father before him. Still we sleep in the same bed and prop up the same wall, and if one of us ceases to support the wall, the Persians will push it down on both."

"I understand. Yet even so it comes into my mind that perchance you would have been safer had you been pushing at the wall with the Persian Ochus and not holding it up with the Egyptian Nectanebes."

He glanced at me with his shifting eyes and answered,

"I have had that thought, as you know well, but having rebelled against Ochus, defeated his satraps, and slain thousands of his soldiers, or rather those of his father, if I climb the wall I might find spears waiting for me on the farther side. Lady, it is too late."

"Yes, King Tenes, perhaps it is too late; I will consider of the matter in your interest and my own. But first send me papyrus and writing tools that I may set down our pact. When you have approved and signed it, then I will consider of this and other matters, and not before. For the while, farewell."

He rose and went unwillingly enough and when I was alone in the cabin I laughed in my heart. This fish had been easy to hook, but he was a large fish and strong, and I must beware lest he pull me into the deep sea where both might drown together. Moreover, the man was hateful to me, more so even than that ox-eyed, heavy-jowled Pharaoh, and his presence seemed to poison the air I breathed. Yet if I entered into this pact with him doubtless I must breathe it often, which vexed me who shrank from men and their desires, and above all from this man. Yet he had done me wrong and insult; he had helped the Egyptians to make war upon my people and he had taken me as a slave, me, Ayesha, thinking to make of me his woman, and cost what it might, I would pay him back as I would pay back Nectanebes who sold me.

The papyrus was brought to me by a slave and on it I wrote such a contract as I think was never signed by a king before. It was brief and ran thus:—

"Ayesha, daughter of Yarab, high-priestess of Isis, prophetess of Isis, known in Heaven and among her servants as *Isis-Come-To-Earth*, and *Child of Wisdom*, to Tenes, King of Sidon.

"When you, Tenes, are king not only of Sidon but of Egypt, Cyprus, Persia, and the East, as I can make you, if you obey me in all things, then I, Ayesha, vow myself to you as your sole wife and queen. But if, ere this dignity is mine and yours, you dare even to touch my robe, then in the name of Isis and speaking with the voice of Isis, I, Ayesha, vow to you shame and death in the world and after it all the torments of hell and the jaws of the Devourer that await the judgment of Truth on perjured souls beyond the Sun.

"Accepted and sealed by Ayesha, daughter of Yarab and by Tenes, King of Sidon."

Having copied this writing, I sent it to Tenes by the slave that he might study it. Awhile later he asked audience of me, and entering, said in a thick voice that only a madman would set his seal to such words.

I looked at him and answered that it was nothing to me whether he sealed or did not seal them; indeed that considering all, I should be better pleased if he let the bargain be.

He stared at me and rage took hold of him who was inflamed with wine.

"Who are you," he said, "that dare to talk thus to Tenes the King? You are but a woman clad in the robes of a priestess who pretend to powers you have not. Why should I not take you and have done?"

Now I mocked him, answering,

"Because I think you love to sit upon a throne better than to lie in a grave, Tenes, even in a king's coffin. Still, as you desire to know more particularly, I will put your question to the goddess, who is not far from me even on this ship, and to-morrow when the sun is up I will pass on her words to you—that is, if you live to look upon to-morrow's sun, King Tenes," I added, staring him in the eyes.

These words seemed to sober him, for he turned pale and left the cabin, making a sign to avert the evil eye, but as I noted, taking the writing with him. Yet me he left perplexed and afraid, for my heart was not so bold as my mouth!

\* \* \* \* \* \* \* \*

Now that night, whether by chance or by the will of Heaven, a great tempest sprang up suddenly. The captain of the *trireme*, a Greek or a half-Greek of Naukratis, Philo by name, whom now upon this ship I met for the first time, came himself to warn me, and to make sure that all was fast in my cabin. He was a quick-brained man, very active in his body and pleasant-faced, with a brown, pointed beard, who had seen some five and thirty years upon the earth. I had made inquiries concerning him from a certain slave who attended me, and was told that although he pretended to timidity, this Philo was in truth a great warrior and one of the best handlers of a bow upon the mouths of the Nile, since that which he aimed at he always hit, even if it were a fowl in flight. Moreover, he was a very good seaman and, it was said, faithful to those he served and a worshipper of the gods.

"If so," I answered to that old slave, "how comes it that this Philo, instead of a humble captain, is not the first general or admiral amongst the Greeks, as a man of such quality should be?"

"Because, divine Lady, of certain faults," answered the slave, "such faults as have made of me what I am instead of the Count of a Nome upon the Nile as I should have been. This Philo has always thought more of the welfare of others than of his own, which is a very evil weakness; also he has loved women too much, which is a worse."

"Vile sins indeed," I said, "more particularly the second. The wise always think of themselves first, and the holy never love more than one woman, and her not too much, which perhaps is why the wise and the holy are so hateful and so dull. Bring this Philo to me; he is one whom I should wish to know."

In the end Philo came, though whether because my message had reached him, or because of the advancing storm, I am not certain. At least he came, and as he bowed before me, made a certain secret sign whereby I knew that he was a worshipper of Isis, and one of high degree, though not of the highest, since when I tried him with that sign he could not answer. Still his rank in our great company was enough, and thenceforward we spoke to each other under the seal of the goddess, or as our phrase went in those days "within the shadow of her wings," as brother and sister might, or rather as mother and son.

That is, we did this after I had proved him further and brought to his mind the fate of those who betray the goddess and her ministers upon earth.

This Philo told me in few words, that although the *trireme* was

348

Egyptian and named *Hapi* after the god of Nile, for this voyage she was under charter to Tenes and for the most part manned with Sidonians, also with low fellows from Cyprus and the coast-ports. These like the Phoenician guards of Tenes, of whom there were fifty on the vessel, worshipped other gods than those of Egypt, that is, such of them as worshipped any gods at all.

Many of these men, Philo said warningly, murmured because a priestess of Isis was on board their ship, which they thought would anger the Phoenician gods of whom the images had been set upon the prow, as might lawfully be done when a vessel was hired by Tyre or Sidon.

I answered laughing that as he and I knew, Isis could hold her own against Baal, Astarte, and all their company. Then, changing my mien, I asked him suddenly what he meant.

"Only this, Holy one," he answered: "That if by chance the ship came into danger—and I like not the signs of the sky and the moaning of the black north wind with rocks not two leagues away upon our lee, then I say if this ship came into danger, as might chance this very night, for here gales grow suddenly—well, Holy one, you might be in danger also. In such cases, Holy one, sometimes the Phoenicians demand a sacrifice to the *Cabiri*, the great gods of the sea whom we do not worship."

"Is it so?" I answered coldly. "Then tell them that those who demand sacrifices often furnish the victims. Have no fear, my brother-in-the-goddess. But if trouble comes, call on me to help you."

Then I stretched out to him the *sistrum* that was part of my ornaments of office in which I had been brought aboard that ship, and he kissed it with his lips and went about his business.

Scarce had he gone when the black north wind began to blow. It blew fearfully, rising hour by hour and even minute by minute, till the gale was terrible. The rowers could no longer row, for the great seas broke their oars, of which the handles struck them, hurling them backward from the benches, and the sail they tried to hoist upon the mast was torn away and went flapping down the wind like a wounded gull. Thus continually the *Hapi* was driven in toward the coast of Syria where, still some miles away, the moonlight when it broke out between the clouds showed the white surf of breakers foaming on the iron rocks of Carmel.

Toward midnight the tall mast snapped in two like a rotten stick and went overboard, carrying with it certain men and crushing others. Then terror took hold of all the company upon this ship, so that they began to cry aloud who believed that black death was upon them.

Now one shouted,

"We are bewitched! At this season there should be no such gale, it is against nature."

Another answered,

"Little wonder that we are bewitched when you carry with us a sorceress of Egypt, one who hates our gods, wherefore they are angry."

This they said because they had heard the tale of the water turned to blood, also of the oracles I was wont to utter in the temple at Memphis. For in that city dwelt many Phoenicians who were great talkers and lovers of strange tales, though now, Holly tells me all their race is silent for ever and the only tales they hear are those of Gehenna.

Then arose another shout from many throats,

"Sacrifice the witch to the gods of the Sea. Throw her into the sea that they may take her and we may live to look upon to-morrow's sun!"

Next there was a rush toward the afterpart of the *trireme* where I was in the cabin. In the waist of the ship appeared the captain, Philo, as I saw watching from between the curtains, and with him a number of the crew who were Egyptians and faithful to him, perhaps six in all, not more. In his hands Philo held a bow, and a drawn short-sword was thrust through his belt.

He shouted to the mob of madmen to stand back, but they would not, and led by one of the guards of Tenes, crept forward. Philo knelt, resting his back against a water-cask, waiting till the ship steadied herself a little on the crest of a wave. Then he drew the bow and shot. Very well and straight did he shoot, for the arrow pierced that leader of the guard of Tenes from breast to back, so that he fell down dead. Seeing this, the others grew afraid and stayed where they were, clinging to the bulwarks of the ship or whatever they could grasp with their hands.

Tenes appeared among them. They shouted to him and he shouted back to them, but what they said I could not hear because of the howling of the wind.

Philo crept into the cabin and his face was very heavy.

"Holy one," he said, "make ready to join Isis in the heavens. Fearing for his own life, that dog of a Sidonian king has consented to your sacrifice and I am come to die with you."

"The goddess thanks you, O great-hearted man, and I, her servant, thank you also," I said, smiling at him. "Yet have no fear, since my spirit tells me that neither I nor you shall die this night. Help me now and let us go forth and talk with these hissing snakes of Sidon."

"But what will you say to them, Holy one?"

"The goddess will teach me what to say," I answered, who in truth did not know what I should say. All I knew was that some spirit moved me to go forth and to talk with them.

So we went, I leaning upon Philo as it was hard to stand upon my feet, and came to the stump of the broken mast in the midst of the hollow ship, all the mob of the crew drawing back before me. Here with one arm I clung to the mast, and beckoned to them with the other in which I held the *sistrum* of our worship. They drew near, Tenes among them, his face covered by a cloak.

"Hearken!" I cried. "I learn that you would offer me, the Prophetess of Isis, as a sacrifice to your gods. Fools! Is not Isis greater than your gods? O Queen of Heaven! send a sign to show that thou art greater than these foreign gods!"

So I spoke and stared upward at the moon, for the wind had torn away my veil, and waited.

A great billow came and struck the forepart of the ship, burying it deep in green water. As she rose I saw two dark forms fly from her high-tossed prow and a voice cried,

"The guardian images have gone and the sacred fire is quenched!"

"Aye," I answered, "they are gone where you shall go, every one of you, if you dare to touch me. Know that I do not fear for my own life which cannot be taken from me, but for your lives I fear, and for Sidon, which presently shall lack a king—if you dare to touch me. Be silent now and though you deserve it not, I will pray Isis to save you."

Then gaping on me standing there like one inspired, as indeed I think I was, they were struck to silence and through the roaring gale and flying foam I prayed to Heaven to preserve that ship and those she bore from the grinding rocks on which the surf beat not a mile away.

A marvel happened, whether because the tempest had grown weary of its raging, or because That which hears the prayers of men had accepted my prayer for its own purposes, to this hour I know not. At least the marvel happened, for although the sea still beat and rushed, wave following wave, like white-maned, countless charging steeds, of a sudden the gale died down and there was calm between sky and sea.

"It has pleased the great goddess to hearken to me and to save your lives, yes, even the lives of you who would have murdered her priestess," I said in a quiet voice. "Now get you to your oars and row as never you rowed before, if you would hold the ship off yonder rocks."

They gasped. They stared with open mouths! One said,

"*Thou* art the goddess; *thou* art the very goddess! Pardon us, pardon us, thy slaves, O Queen of Heaven!"

Then they rushed to their oars and with toil and danger drew the *Hapi* past the promontory of Carmel where the water boiled upon the rocks, and out into the deep sea beyond.

"What did I say to you, Philo?" I said, as he led me back to the cabin.

He made no answer, only lifting the hem of my garment, he pressed it to his brow.

## CHAPTER 8

# The King of Sidon

Next morning the sun came up in a sky of perfect blue and the *Hapi*, driven forward by the oars, since her mast was gone, passed northward over a quiet sea. Not a league away upon our right, gleaming like gold, were the roofs of the glorious city of Tyre, set like a queen upon her island throne, Tyre that as yet did not dream of evil days when her marble palaces should melt in flame and her merchant princes and citizens lie butchered by the thousand in her streets; Tyre the wanton, the beauteous, the wealthy, who sucked riches from all the lands.

Seeing our shattered state, a boat manned by red-capped seamen came out from the Egyptian harbour to learn if we needed help. But Philo shouted back to its officer that, save for the loss of a mast and some men, we had taken no harm in the gale and hoped ere night to be safe in Sidon.

So the boat returned and we rowed on.

By midday we caught sight of the towers of Sidon and within three more hours, the sea being calm, had dropped anchor in the southern harbour.

\* \* \* \* \* \* \* \*

Now after we left Tyre Tenes the King came to visit me in my cabin. At the sight of him my gorge rose for I remembered that this dog of a Sidonian had consented to the demand of the sailors that I should be hurled into the deep as a sacrifice to his god. Yet I restrained my soul and received him smiling and unveiled.

"Hail, King Tenes," I said, "Isis has been very merciful to you in answer to my prayer; for know that never again did I think to look upon you living."

"You are great, Lady," he answered, staring at me with frightened yet devouring eyes. "I think that you are as great as that Isis whom you serve, if indeed you are not that Isis come to earth, as they name you in Egypt. Isis I know not who worship Ashtoreth, she who is also styled Tanith and Baaltis, and like your Isis, is an acknowledged Queen of Heaven, but you I know, and your power, for did you not cause the terrible tempest to cease last night and save us all from death upon the rocks of Carmel?"

"Aye, I did this, Tenes, having strength given to me, whence it matters not. It is strange to think, is it not?"—here I bent forward and stared him in the eyes—"that on board this ship there are men so cowardly and so evil that they took counsel to cast me to the deep as a sacrifice to their gods, and that had they done so, though me, had they known it, they could not harm, they themselves, every one of them, would have been that sacrifice?"

Now he writhed and turned colour beneath my glance, but answered, "Is it so, Lady? Name me those men and they shall be slain."

"Aye, King Tenes, without doubt they shall be slain, every one of them, since Isis does not forget a threat of murder against her priestess. Yet I name them not. Where is the need when already those names are written on the tablets of Heaven? Let them be till Fate finds them, since I would not have you in your rage stain your hands with their vile blood. But what would you with me, King?"

"You know well," he answered thickly. "I worship you. I am mad with love of you. When I saw you standing by the broken mast and making prayer, even then upon the edge of doom, my heart melted for you. I say that there is a raging fire in my breast that only you can quench," and he made as though he would fall upon his knees before me.

I motioned to him to remain seated, and answered,

"I remember, King, that you spoke in this same fashion before the storm and that, half in jest, I wrote certain terms upon which I would become your queen, namely, when you could give me rule over all the earth. Wisely, perhaps, to these terms you would not set your seal; indeed you asked me why you should not take me to be your toy, and to that question an answer came to you last night when the ship wallowed water-logged and on her lee you saw the billows spouting on the rocks of Carmel. Also the goddess has told me more of what would chance to you should you dare to lift a hand against her priestess. I tell you that it is horrible, so horrible that I spare you, since if you heard it, you would tremble. What need to talk of such a crime when such a judgment would follow hard upon its heels? So have done, Tenes, and learn that it is my pleasure to return to Egypt in this ship."

"Nay, nay!" he cried, "I cannot part with you; sooner would I lose my crown. I tell you that if I lost sight of you and hope of you, I should go mad——"

"Which perchance you may do yet, Tenes," I replied laughing, "if indeed you are not already mad after the fashion of tyrants who for the first time are robbed of that which they desire. You have my commands, so have done. I would speak with Philo the captain as to when he can be ready to sail for Nile."

"Hearken, Lady, hearken!" he said thickly. "I have the writing here. I will sign it in your presence if you swear to abide by it."

"Is it so? Well, Tenes, I do not change my word. When you can crown me Queen of Phoenicia, Egypt, Persia, and the rest, as I can show you how to do, then I will take you for husband and reign as your sole wife. But until then never shall you dare so much as to touch me. Now I am weary, who last night slept so ill. Do you wish to seal the writing, for if so it shall be done before a witness whose life and welfare henceforth shall be as sacred to you as my own."

"Aye, aye, I will seal, I will seal," he said.

Then I clapped my hands and the slave who waited without appeared. I bade him summon Philo, the captain of the ship, and to bring wax. Presently Philo came and I told him what was needed of him. More, demanding the papyrus from Tenes, I read it to both of them, Philo listening with a stony stare of amazement. Then the wax was spread upon the papyrus and Tenes sealed it with his seal, which was a cylinder of lapis lazuli having images of gods upon it after the old Babylonian fashion. Also, beneath my own, he wrote his name in Phoenician letters which I could not read. Then Philo as witness wrote his, for being half a Greek, he knew this art, and sealed it with his seal, a scarab cut in cornelian by no mean artist, doubtless a Grecian, which scarab, he said, he had taken many years before from the finger of one whom he killed in battle. When I looked at what it left upon the wax, I laughed, for behold the device was that of a Diana, or perchance a nymph, shooting with an arrow a brute-faced faun that had surprised her at the bath. To my mind the face of that faun or satyr was very like to the face of Tenes, and Philo thought it also for I saw him glance from one to the other, and heard him mutter, "An omen! An omen!" beneath his breath in the Egyptian tongue which Tenes did not understand.

When the roll was signed Tenes would have taken it, but I answered,

"Nay, on that day when its conditions are fulfilled it shall be yours. But till then it is mine."

Still I promised to give him a copy of the writing, and with this he was, or feigned to be, content.

When Philo had gone Tenes asked me how he was to become ruler of the world and thus to win me.

I answered that I would tell him later in Sidon after I had thought and prayed. But one thing he must swear, namely, to listen to no counsels save my own, since otherwise he might lose me and with me all. He did so by his gods, being at that time so bemused that he would have sworn anything if thereby he might keep near to me. Moreover, he told me that it was his purpose to set me in a palace near his own, or perchance in a part of his own, that there he might visit me daily and learn my counsels.

I bowed my head and said, the more often the better, so long as he came for counsel and no more. Then I dismissed him and he went like any slave.

When he had gone once more I summoned Philo and, "under the wings of the goddess," that is, under an oath of secrecy to break which is death, I told him, my brother-in-Isis, the meaning of this play, namely that I would be avenged upon Tenes who had affronted me and the goddess, who also, in his cowardice, had proposed to sacrifice me in the deep, an offering to his false divinities. Moreover, I gave him that copy of the writing which I had made and, his charter being fulfilled, bade him get back to Egypt as soon as might be and deliver it to Noot, the high-priest of Isis, and with it all this story.

There at Memphis I bade him bide, having a great ship, this one or another, ready, manned with brave men, all of them followers of Isis, with whom Noot would furnish him, also with the moneys needful to hire or buy that ship. There he was to wait till my word came. How it would come I did not know as yet. Perchance this would be by messenger, or perchance I should talk with the spirit of Noot, by means at the command of those initiated in the highest mysteries of the goddess. At least when my word came he must sail at once and come to me at Sidon.

These things he swore to do. Moreover, I wrote a letter which afterward I gave to him to deliver to Noot.

We cast anchor in the harbour, hoisting the royal standard of Tenes as best we could on a tall pole at the prow. At once gilded barges, on board of which were generals and priests, put off from the quay, and watching from my cabin, I saw Tenes talk earnestly with these notables who from time to time glanced toward where I was hidden. Then a messenger came to pray me to be pleased to abide on board the ship till preparation had been made to receive me, a matter to which the king departed to attend. So I stayed there and spoke with Philo about many things, learning from him much concerning the Sidonians, their wealth and their strength in war.

Two hours later a barge arrived, the royal barge, I think, for it was glorious with silks and gold and the rowers wore blazoned uniforms. On board this barge was Tenes himself and with him, among others, priests who wore tall caps, also some priestesses. The king came and bowing, led me to a carpeted ladder by which I descended into the barge. As I went down its steps I said with a laugh,

"If some had won their way last night, O King, I should have left this ship in a very different fashion. Well, I forgive them, poor fools and cowards, but whether the goddess whom I serve will forgive them is another matter"—words at which I saw him wince.

Before I went also I stepped aside and again spoke to Philo who stood near the head of the ladder, cap in hand. That speech was short yet sufficient, being of but two words,

"Remember everything."

"To the death! Child of Wisdom," he answered.

"What says the mariner?" asked Tenes suspiciously.

"Naught, O King. That is, he only prays me to intercede with the goddess lest the fate of those who would have harmed me on this ship should overtake him also who is its captain."

Again Tenes winced and again I smiled.

We were rowed ashore, and there upon the quay waited a chariot drawn by milk-white horses in which chariot I was seated, splendidly apparelled men leading the horses. In front of me went the king in another chariot and behind followed an escort of guards.

Thus we proceeded through the glorious streets of Sidon and being moved thereto, I lifted my veil and stood up in the chariot as though I would see these better. Already the fame of my coming had spread abroad, so that those streets and the flat roofs of the houses were crowded with thousands of the people. These, when they saw my beauty, gasped with wonder and cried in their own tongue,

"No woman! No woman! A goddess indeed!"

Yet I thought that I heard others answer,

"Aye, a false goddess sent to Sidon to be her ruin."

True words indeed, though, as I think, inspired by hate and jealousy rather than from on high.

We came to a great and noble square, the Holy Place it was called, round which stood statues of those whom the Sidonians worshipped,

Baal, Ashtoreth, and the rest of their daemons. Moreover, with its back to the temple stood a huge and hideous god of brass, who in front of him, upon great hands which seemed to be discoloured with fire, held a curved tray whereof the inner edge rested on an opening in the belly of the figure. I asked of one who walked by the chariot what was the name of this god. He answered,

"Dagon whom some call Moloch, to whom the firstborn are sacrificed by fire. See, the priests are storing the hollow place beneath with wood. Soon, doubtless, there will be a great offering."

Thenceforward I hated this people, for what could one born in Arabia and a servant of Isis, the holy and gentle, think of a race that offered sacrifice of those born of them to a daemon? Yes, I looked on their faces, keen, handsome, and cruel, and hated them, one and all.

We came to the door of the palace where slaves ran forward, assisting me from the chariot. By it stood Tenes surrounded with glittering nobles and white-robed priests who stared at me doubtfully.

"Be pleased to enter my house, Lady, fearing nothing, for there you shall be well lodged and given of the best that Sidon has to offer," said Tenes.

"I thank you," I answered, bowing and letting fall my veil, "and I doubt it not, for what less than her best could Sidon give to the Daughter of Isis, the Queen of Heaven?"

Yes, thus I answered proudly, I who played a great game and staked all upon a throw.

"Here we have another Queen of Heaven and she is not named Isis," I heard one of the dark-browed priests mutter to a companion, thinking that I did not understand his words.

They led me into a glorious dwelling wherein were chambers more splendid than any that I had seen in my journeys through the Eastern world. Gold and gems were everywhere and on the walls hung priceless trappings dyed with the Tyrian purple of that costly sort to use which is the prerogative of kings. The very carpets on the floors shone like silk and were woven to things of beauty, while the lamps seemed to be hollowed from great gems.

"Who lodges in this place?" I asked of a slave when I was alone.

"Who but the Queen Beltis, divine one," answered the slave, bowing low before me.

"Where then is the Queen Beltis? I see her not."

"Nay, divine one, she visits her father at Jerusalem, whence she should return shortly. Indeed, the King has issued orders that other chambers should be prepared for her against her coming."

"Is it so?" I replied indifferently, but within my heart I wondered what this queen would say when she came to find her place inhabited by a stranger and a rival.

Then to the sound of sweet music I ate from services of gold and drank out of jewelled cups, and afterward, being weary, who had rested little on that ship and was tempest-tossed, laid me down to sleep in a soft and scented bed guarded by women and by eunuchs.

"Easy enough," thought I to myself, "would it be for these to murder me, one unfriended and alone in a strange land," and because of this for a little felt afraid who at that time was but as other mortals are. On the ship I had feared nothing, for there was Philo, a brother of my faith, and with him some others who could be trusted. But here I was but as a lamb ringed round with wolves. Moreover, besides the wolves there was a lion, the king-brute Tenes, who sought to snare me, and whom I knew for a liar, not to be trusted whatever he might swear.

Yes, for a little while, perhaps for the first time in my life, and certainly for the last, that is, where my body was at stake, I felt somewhat afraid, so much so that I went to a window-place to watch the rising of the moon and to make my prayer to Isis of whom it was the symbol, that she would be pleased to protect me in this city whither by her will I had wandered.

This window looked out upon that flame-lit square which was called the Holy Place. There I noted that thousands of those of Sidon were gathered, some of them staring up at the palace to which it was known I had been taken, pointing and talking. The most of them, however, wandered round the great brazen statue, that hideous, devil-faced thing whereof I have written, and when they could, caught one of the priests by the arm and put questions to him.

Among these, I noticed, were many women, some of whom from their mien seemed to be noble, whose faces were strange to see. Defiant they were, yet in a way proud, as might be the faces of those about to do some great deed. Moreover, many of these women led or carried children, which little ones they showed to the priests who smiled horribly and nodded approval, patting the children on the arm and even kissing them.

One lady, after her son had received such a kiss, wailed aloud and, clasping him to her breast, turned and fled away, whereon the priest cursed her and the other women shouted "Shame!" then strove to cover up the misery that peeped out of their eyes by singing some fierce song in honour of their gods.

Studying this scene, presently the meaning of it came home to me.

Those children were doomed to be sacrificed to the brazen Dagon or Moloch whereof I remembered having heard in Jerusalem as a devil to whom the firstborn were passed through the fire. Yes, and these the mothers had brought them there that they might look upon the god and grow accustomed to the sight of him.

Oh! it was horrible, and my heart chilled at the thought of such iniquity. What reward from Heaven, I marvelled, for a people who practised such a faith?

As I marvelled an answer seemed to come to me. The sun had sunk but there were heavy clouds in the sky above upon which struck its departing rays. Thence they were reflected on to the city and chiefly upon this Holy Place, as it was called, and the brazen image that sat there before the temple. Yes, from those clouds came red light that filled the air and the city beneath and the Holy Place, as it were with a mist of blood. It was as though everything were dyed with blood, and in the midst, ringed round with torches, glowed Moloch, a god of blood!

Then I knew that Sidon was doomed to be drowned in blood; that such was the decree of Heaven and that I, Ayesha, was the instrument appointed to loose this spear of death upon her beauteous, sinful breast. I shivered at the thought, I who love not cruelty or to spend the lives of men, though it was true that I would kill Tenes. Yet what was I but the lightning in the hands of Fate, and can the lightning choose where it will strike? Must it not fall whither it is drawn? To this end had I been sent to earth, namely that I might bring woe upon false Egypt and the peoples who clung to her.

Such was the burden of that dream by which my sleep was haunted, such too the command of Heaven which again and again Noot the prophet had whispered in my ear. I must destroy Egypt, or rather her apostate priests and rulers, and afterward once more build up the worship of Isis in some far land that should be revealed to me. Such was my mission, whereof it was decreed that I should fulfil the first part and because of my sin leave the rest undone.

Holly the learned tells me that the new faith he follows, to which I will not listen who am weary of religions and their changeful march toward a changeless end, writes it down that free will is given to man, that he is able to choose this path and reject the other; that he is the master of his own soul which he can guide here or there as the horseman guides his steed or Philo steered his ship.

And yet he read to me from the writings of one of the great apostles of that faith, a certain holy one named Paulus, words which declared that man is predestined ere he was born to eternal life or eternal death, to the glory of the light or the unfathomed dark. To me these doctrines seem to war one upon the other, though for aught I knew both may be true, seeing that within the circle of the starry spheres and the vast soul of That which made them, there is room for a multitude of truths whereof the shadows falling upon the gross earth take a thousand shapes of error.

Moreover, I hold that whatever is, is true because it is, and that men do but tangle themselves in seeming differences that are only varying lights darting from the eternal eyes of Truth. On all hearts shine those eyes, but none beholds them as his brother does, for to each they burn as a separate torch of different-coloured flame. Therefore it is that men worship many gods not knowing that these are the same God whose hands hold all things.

Thus I sum up the matter. At least through the millions of the ages and the multitudes of lives man may attain to freedom if his face be set that way of his own desire. Yet in his little hour on the earth, that falsely he believes his all, looking from birth to death and the blackness that bounds them both, he is not free but a part of Strengths that are greater than his own. Have I, Ayesha, been free, I who chose the holy path and fell from it into Nature's gulfs? Did I desire to fall? Did I not desire to climb that steep road to the heights of Heaven and sit enthroned upon the topmost snows of purity and peace? And yet another Might hurled me thence and now it is my fate to climb again; by slow and painful steps to climb eternally.

But of these things I will speak in their season, telling what is the price those pay who seek to overleap the bounds that hem us in and to match their pettiness against divine decree.

These in the midst of the red light that filled Sidon like a bowl with blood and shone on me and all; on me, the priestess, on the brazen Dagon towering up against me, on fantastic, lamp-lit, temples and palaces, on the great place about which they stood and the fierce-faced multitude that wandered on its marble pavements, there in the window-opening I knelt me down and prayed, lifting my face to the pure heavens above. To Isis did I pray, as an idolater prays to an image in a cave, because Isis was my symbol, or rather to That which is as far above Isis as Isis was above me. For I prayed to the Soul of that Universe whereof my eyes could see a part in the arching skies, and of this Soul what was Isis but one golden thread in a glittering garment that wraps the majesty of God? And what then was I and what were those fierce-faced worshippers of Dagon?

Oh! in that hour of dedication, for such I felt it to be, these truths came home to my heart as never they had done before. And this was the sum of them, that I and all I could see and know were but as impalpable grains of dust, not sufficient to cause the delicately hung balance wherein the wilfulness of the world is poised against the decrees of the immortal Law to vary by a hair's breadth. Still I prayed and because that which is small yet contains that which is smaller, and the smaller finds a god in the small, as the small does in the great, from that prayer I won comfort.

My prayer finished I laid me down to rest in the golden bed of Beltis, the queen into whose place I had been thrust, bethinking me how many and near were the dangers by which I was surrounded. That brute king desired me for a prey and here in his palace I lay in the hollow of his hand. He had the key to all my doors; the servants who stood about them were his creatures whom at a nod he could send to death. I was a stranger in a strange land, utterly unfriended, for Philo was far off upon his ship; there was nothing between me and him save the impalpable veil of fear which I had woven between us by the strength of my spirit. I was a prize to be taken, unarmoured, without javelin or arrow to protect me, with nothing, nothing save that veil of fear. If he chose to break through it, daring my curse and that of my goddess, he could do so. Then the curse would fall indeed, but it would be too late to save me, and I the proud and pure, must pass hence defiled, as pass I would. Still trusting to the goddess, or rather to the part of her which dwelt in me, or to That which was above us both, I laid me down and slept.

********

At midnight I awoke. The light of the moon flowing through the window-places flooded the splendid chamber, catching on the cornices of gold, the polished mirrors and the silver vessels. The door opened and through it wrapped in a dark cloak came Tenes. Though his face was hidden I knew him by his heavy shape and shambling step. He crept toward me like a wolf upon a sleeping lamb. There I lay in the golden bed illumined by the moon, and watched through the web of my outstretched hair, my hand upon the dagger that was buckled to my girdle. He drew near, he bent over me breathing heavily, and his eyes devoured my beauty. Still I feigned sleep and watched him, while my fingers closed upon the handle of the dagger. He unbuckled his cloak, revealing his hook-nosed visage, and a draught of wind seemed to catch it, for it flapped and fell from his shoulders, though I felt no wind. He stooped as though to lift it, and it would seem came face to face with I know not what. Perchance it was the goddess invisible to me. Perchance it was some picture of his own death to come. I cannot say. At least his shifting eyes sank in till they seemed to vanish beneath the hairy brows, and his fat cheeks grew pallid as though the blood were draining from them by a mortal wound. Words came hissing from his thick lips and they were,

"Horrible! Horrible! She is indeed divine, for gods and ghosts protect her! Horrible! Death walks the air!"

\* \* \* \* \* \* \* \*

Then he reeled from the room dragging the cloak after him, and knowing that I had no more to fear, I returned thanks to the guardian spirits and slept sweetly. The danger that I dreaded had drawn near and passed—to return no more.

## CHAPTER 9

# Dagon Takes His Sacrifice

The sun arose on Sidon and drove away the terrors of the dark. I too arose and was led to the bath by slaves. Then those slaves clothed me in the silks of Cyprus, over which I threw a new veil bordered with the purple of Tyre. More, they brought me gifts from the King, priceless jewels, pearls with rubies and sapphires set in gold. Those I laid aside who would not wear his gems. Then, in another chamber, I ate as before of meats delicately served by bowing maidens. Scarce had I finished my meal of fish from the sea and fruit and snow-cooled water drunk from a crystal cup, when a eunuch came saying the King Tenes craved audience of me.

"Let him enter," I answered.

Presently he stood before me, making salutation, and asked me with feigned carelessness whether I had rested well.

"Aye, great King," I answered, "well enough, save for a single, very vivid dream. I dreamed that Set, the god of Evil, rose out of the darkness of hell wearing the shape of a man whose face I could not see, and that this fiend would have seized me and dragged me down into the pit of hell. I was afraid, and while I lay as one in a net, there came to me a vision of the divine Isis who said,

"'Where is thy faith, Daughter? If I saved thee on the ship, giving thee the lives of all her company, cannot I save thee now and always? Fiends shall not harm thee, nor men; swords shall not pierce thee nor fires burn, and if any would lay hands on thee, on them I give thee power to call down my vengeance and to cast them to the jaws of the Devourer who, awaiting evil-doers, watches ever in the black depth of death.'

"Then in my dreams the Mother whispered into the ears of that fiend shaped like a man, and passing her hand before his eyes, showed him certain visions, though what these were I know not. At the least they caused him to wail aloud with terror, also to my sight to fall as from a precipice and, like some foul vulture pierced by an archer's shaft, go whirling down, down, and down, into gulfs that had no bottom. It was a very evil dream, King Tenes, and yet sweet, because it told me that though I should journey to the ends of the earth, still I shall not pass out of the shelter of the circling arms of Isis."

"Evil indeed, Lady," he said hoarsely, biting his lips to still the quaver in his voice. "Yet it ended well, so what of dreams?"

"Very well, O King—for me. And as for dreams, I, who by gifts and training am skilled in their interpretations, hold that for the most part they are a shadow of the Truth. I know that certainly no harm can come to me in your palace over which one day I must rule, or in your city where I am a guest. Yet doubtless some peril of the spirit did threaten me last night, and by the help of Heaven was brought to nothing."

"Doubtless, doubtless! though of such matters *I* know nothing, who deal with the things of earth, not with those of Heaven. But, Lady, I came to tell you that this day there is a great sacrifice on the Holy Place yonder, and that from these windows you will be able to watch it well. It is to propitiate our gods that they may well give us victory in the war against the Persians."

"Is it so, King? But where are the victims? I see no kine, nor sheep, nor doves, such as are offered in Rome and in Jerusalem, or even flowers and fruit such as in Egypt we lay upon our gentler altars."

"Nay, Lady; here we make more costly offerings, tithing our own blood. Yes, here Moloch claims the fruit of our bodies, taking them to his purifying fires so that their innocent breath may rise as a sweet savour to the nostrils of the devouring and protecting gods."

"Do you, perchance, mean children, King?"

"Aye, Lady, children, many children, and among these to-day one of my own, a son of a certain Beltis who is of my household. He is a child of promise, yet I grudge him not to the god if thereby my people may be benefited."

"And does this Beltis not grudge him, King?"

"I know not," he answered sullenly. "She is a woman of the royal House of Israel and is absent on a journey. Therefore I know not, and when she returns the boy will have joined the gods and it will be too late for her to make trouble concerning him, should she be so minded."

Now horror took hold of me, Ayesha, and my soul sickened.

"King Tenes," I said, "bethink you of that mother's heart and, I pray you, spare this child."

"How can I, Lady? Must not the king bear that yoke which is laid upon the necks of his people? If I spare him, would not the mothers of Sidon whose young have passed into the fire spit at me and curse me—aye, and tear me to pieces if they might? Nay, he must die with the rest. The priests have so decreed."

"On your head be it, King," I said and choked in my loathing of him. Then a thought took me, and I cried to those who were gathered about the door of the chamber, captains of the guard, eunuchs, slaves, scribes, and a priest or two, "Come hither, ye of Sidon, and hearken to the words of her who in Egypt is named *Oracle-of-Isis*."

They came, drawn by wonder, or perchance because my strength compelled them.

"Take note of my words and record them," I said, while they stared on me. "Take note and forget it not, that I, the daughter of Isis, have made prayer to King Tenes of Sidon, that he will spare the life of his son and the son of a lady named Beltis, and that he has refused my prayer. Ye have heard me. It is enough. Go!"

They went, looking at each other, the scribes, as I saw, writing down what I had said upon their tablets. Tenes also stared at me curiously.

"You are an Arab by birth, born of an Egyptian mother, and wholly Egyptian in your faith and mind, though the Arab courage still strikes through these qualities," he said. "Therefore I forgive you who do not understand our customs. Yet, know, Lady, that those of Sidon whom it pleases you to call as witnesses will think you mad."

"Doubtless, Tenes, before all is done, those of Sidon will think many things of me, as you will also. But what will this lady Beltis think?"

"I neither know nor care who weary of Beltis and her moods," he answered, scowling. "Beauteous one, I sent you jewels. Why do you not wear them?"

"The daughter of Isis wears no jewels save those the goddess gives her, King. Yet yours shall go to enrich her shrines when I return to Egypt, and in her name I thank you for them, bounteous King."

"Aye, when you return to Egypt. But how can you return if you bide here as my wife?"

"If I bide here as your wife, then I shall bide as the Queen of Egypt as is written in our bond, and from time to time the Queen of Egypt must visit her dominions, King, and give thanks to the goddess for her advancement. Do you understand?"

"I understand that you are a very strange woman, so strange that I would I had never set eyes on you and your accursed beauty," he answered in a rage.

"What! So soon?" I said, laughing. "That this should be so in the beginning makes me wonder what you will wish in the end. Why not take your eyes off me and have done, King Tenes?"

"Because I cannot. Because I am bewitched," he answered furiously, and rising left me, while I laughed and laughed.

He departed and I went to the window-place to breathe air free from the poison of his presence. There I saw that the Holy Place beneath was already filled with tens of thousands of the Sidonians. I saw, moreover, that priests were engaged in lighting fire at the foot of the great brazen image of Dagon, which fire seemed to burn within the image, since smoke poured out far above from an opening in his head. Moreover, by degrees the copper plates of which its vast and hideous bulk was built up grew red with heat, so that the upper part of it became one glowing furnace.

White-robed priests, gathered in troops, began to offer prayers and celebrate rites of which I did not know the meaning. They bowed themselves to the image, they gashed their arms with knives and catching the blood that fell from them in shallow shells of the sea, cast it into the fire. Orators made speeches, prophets uttered prophecies. Bands of fair women appeared naked to the middle and having their breasts gilded, who danced wildly before the god.

Then suddenly there was a great silence and from the mouth of some gateway that I could not see, because it lay almost beneath the balconies of the palace, appeared the King Tenes clad in gorgeous, sacerdotal robes, those, I think, of the high-priest of Baal. With him was a woman who led by the hand a little boy who perhaps had seen three summers, dressed in white with a garland of flowers about his neck. Tenes bowed to the glowing image and cried in a loud voice,

"People of Sidon, I the King make sacrifice of my son to Dagon the great god, that Dagon may be propitiated and Sidon may conquer in this war. O Dagon, take my son that his spirit may pass through the flames and be gathered to thy spirit and that thine appetite may feed upon his blood."

At these words a great and joyous shout went up from the tens of thousands of people, and in the midst of the shout Tenes bent down and kissed his son, which was the only kindly, human thing that ever I saw him do. The child, affrighted, clung to his robes, but the woman at his side snatched the boy away and ran with him, struggling, to a priest who stood by the foot of a little iron ladder of which the top rested against the outstretched giant hands of the glowing image.

The priest took the child from the woman, holding him aloft that the multitude might see him and know him for the very son of the king. Oh! never shall I forget the look upon that child's face as he was thus held aloft in the hands of the brutal priest who stood upon the lower rungs of the ladder. He had ceased to scream, but his ruddy cheeks were blanched, his black eyes seemed to start from his head, and his little hands grasped emptily at the air or were lifted up to heaven, which indeed was near to him, as though in supplication for deliverance from the cruelty of man.

The priest climbed the ladder, bearing the child, and I noted a kind of metal covering upon his breast and head, set there to shield him from the heat of the fiery idol.

He reached the platform of the outstretched hands. The child's fingers clung to his garments, but he tore them free and with a cry of triumph let fall the little body into the hollow of the hot hands. Then, to drown the victim's cries, priests standing below began to play upon instruments of music, as they played, singing some hymn to the god. I saw the little arms tossed aloft above the edge of the hollow of the brazen hands. Then I saw those arms lift themselves, feebly for the last time, and that poor, tortured, innocent babe rolled slowly into the red abyss beneath, while the savage multitude screamed its delight to heaven.

This royal sacrifice was accomplished, yet it was but the first of many, for woman after woman brought her child, or sometimes it was a man who brought it, and babe after babe was thrown upon the red-hot hands and rolled thence into the flames beneath. All the while the priests played upon their instruments and sang their songs while the shameless priestesses, and others, those with the gilded breasts, danced lewdly, tossing up their white arms, and the thousands of the people of Sidon, filled with the lust of blood, roared aloud in their drunken joy, and the poor mothers, now that the deed was done, crept thence, laughing and crying both together, back to their desolated homes, there to stare at the cots emptied into "the bosom of the god."

At length I could bear no more of this scene of hell, and departing to my sleeping-chamber, caused women to draw curtains over the window-places and having dismissed them, sat myself down and thought.

A great rage filled me, Ayesha, who have ever loved children—will a day come when I shall nurse one upon my breast, I wonder, and if so in what star will it be born?—and a mighty hate of those accursed Sidonians. All pity left my heart, even for the young who would grow up to be as were those who begat them. These sharks and tigers loved blood. Good. They should be filled with blood, their own blood. All of them were guilty, all, all were murderers. Hearken to their horrible re-joicings! Old men and maidens, young men and matrons, the toothless crone and the budding girl, the great lords and ladies, the toilers on the deep and the traders of the city, the bond and the free, from the king down to the meanest slave, all of them screamed with hideous rejoicing as babe after babe was swallowed by the glowing gorge of the daemon they named a god. Therefore I vowed by Isis that all of them should pay the price of this innocent blood and go down to find their god in hell. Yes, I swore it by the Mother and by my own outraged soul!

* * * * * * * *

The next day Beltis came. The King Tenes was in my outer cham-ber fawning on me and watching me out of his crafty eyes, as I saw through the veil that I had let fall over my face, and my flesh crept at the sight of him. Trained though I was and wise though I was, who knew well that the hour had not come to strike, scarce could I bear him near me who longed to drive my dagger through his lying throat. Yet I sat still and listened to his flattery and answered him with double-edged and mocking words of which he could not read the meaning. He told me that already the great sacrifice had borne good fruit, since tidings had come of a new victory over the vanguard of the Persians, in which five thousand of the men of Ochus had perished.

I answered that I doubted not it would bear yet better fruit, then asked him how many of his folk dwelt in Sidon.

He answered, some sixty thousand.

"Then, O King," I said, "I who am filled with the spirit of the Mother, make a prophecy to you, I prophesy that in reward of the piety of this people of yours who do not grudge their own children to the gods, the gods will take sixty thousand lives from among the wicked of the earth who worship fire—as I am told these Persians do."

"That is a good saying, Lady," he said, rubbing his fat hands, "though it is true that some might say that we Sidonians also worship fire, or rather Moloch whose belly is filled with flame as we saw yesterday."

Now while we were speaking and this brute bemused was talking thus almost at hazard, for his mind was set on me only, I noted that those who attended him slipped from the place, taking with them the waiting women and closing the carven doors behind them, so that he and I were now alone. Guessing that this was done by order, I knew that I must prepare for some outburst of the man's passion and took counsel with myself. What it was does not matter because of that which followed.

369

Already he had begun, for the words, "O most beauteous!" had passed his lips when the door burst open and through it came a noble-looking woman. She was tall, dark, and handsome with swift-glancing, tragic eyes, as I knew at once, a Jewess, since I had seen others like her in Jerusalem. She glanced at me as though wondering what my veil hid, and advancing, stood before Tenes. He had not heard her come or seen her, his mind being full of other matters and his back toward the doorway. At the sound of her feet he turned and, coming face to face with her, stepped backward three paces with a frightened face and uttering some Phoenician curse.

"Have you returned so soon, Beltis?" he asked. "What has brought you here before the appointed time?"

"My heart, O Tenes, king and husband. Yonder in Jerusalem a prophet of Jehovah said words to me that caused me to return and swiftly. Tell me, Tenes, where is our son? On my path to this chamber I passed through those where he should be and found him not. All I found was his nurse weeping; aye, so choked with tears that she could not answer my question. Where is our son, Tenes?"

Now he cast his eyes about him like one who finds himself in a snare, and answered thickly,

"Alas! Lady, the gods have taken our son."

She gasped and clasped her hands upon her heart, saying, or rather moaning,

"How did they take him, Husband?"

He looked through the window-place at the hideous brazen image dulled with heat and blackened by smoke; he looked at the lady with the white face and the terrible eyes. Then he strove to speak, but as it seemed, could not, for the mumbled words choked each other in his throat.

"Answer!" she said coldly, but he could not, or would not answer.

Then my spirit moving me, I played a part in this ineffable tragedy. Yes, I, Ayesha, threw back my veil, saying,

"Queen, if it pleases you to listen I will tell you how your son died."

She looked at me wondering, and asked like one who dreams,

"Is this a woman or a goddess, or perchance a spirit? Speak on, woman, or goddess, or spirit."

"Queen," I said, "look through the window-place and tell me what you see."

"I see the image of Dagon, the brazen image towering to the housetops, blackened with fire and staring at me with empty eyes, and beyond it the temple and above it Heaven."

"Queen, yesterday I looked from this window-place and saw that image of Dagon, only then from those empty eyes came flame. Also I saw King Tenes lead out a beauteous, black-eyed boy of three summers or so, which boy he declared to be his son. This boy he gave to a woman, although the child clung wailing to his robe. The woman gave him to a priest. The priest climbed a ladder—look, there it stands—and laid him upon the red-hot hands of the idol whence he rolled amidst the plaudits of the people into a womb of fire, to be perchance reborn in Heaven."

Beltis heard and as she heard her face seemed to freeze into a mask of ice. Then she stared at Tenes and asked almost in a whisper,

"Are these things so, O dog of a Sidonian, that like a dog can devour your own flesh?"

"The god claimed him," he mumbled, "and like others I must give when the god claims, that victory may crown our arms. Who can deny the god? Rejoice, O mother, that he has been pleased to accept that which was born of you."

So he mumbled on as priests patter to their idols, till at length in that cold silence his voice died away.

Then Beltis the Queen began to hiss a curse at him, such a curse as, save once only, I have never heard come from the lips of woman. In the Name of Jehovah, God of the Jews, she cursed him, calling down woe and desolation upon his head, consigning him to death in blood and appointing Gehenna, as she named hell, as a resting-place for his soul, where devils fashioned as children should tear him eternally with hooks of flame. Yes, she cursed him living and dead, but always in that low, whispering voice, that inhuman voice which did not seem to come from the throat of woman, such a voice as the gods or spirits use when from time to time they speak to their servants in the inmost sanctuaries.

He cowered before her. Once even he sank to his knees, holding his hands above his head as though to ward off her words of evil omen. Then, as she would not cease, he sprang up, shouting,

"You also shall be a sacrifice, you worshipper of the God of the Jews. Dagon is greater than the God of the Jews. Be you a sacrifice to him, O Sorceress of Israel!"

He drew the sword at his side and shook it. She did not stir, only with her hands she tore open the robes upon her breast, saying,

"Smite on, dog of a Sidonian, and complete the circle of your crimes. Where the son went, there let the mother follow!"

Now in madness, or in rage, or in terror, he lifted the sword and was about to do the deed, when I stepped between him and her.

Loosing the veil I wore I threw it over her head, and turning, said to Tenes, "Now, King, touch her who is hid in the veil of Isis if you dare. Of Isis I think you have learned something on a certain ship when the breakers called for you off Carmel, yes, of Isis and her prophetess. Know then that she who could save can also slay, and give you over to such dreams as came to you, Tenes, at midnight in a bed in yonder room. Aye, she can slay, and swiftly. Strike then through the Veil of Isis and learn whether her prophetess speaks truth."

He looked at me; he looked at Beltis standing still and ghostlike beneath the veil. Then he cast down the sword and fled.

When he had gone I went to the door and shot its bolt. I returned, I lifted the veil from about that queen.

"Who and what are you?" she asked, "that can brave Tenes in his palace and save one whom he would slay, though for that I thank you not. So little do I thank you that——" And she stooped to grasp the sword.

Moving swiftly as a swallow flies, I flitted between her and it. Before her fingers could touch it, I had snatched it away who understood her purpose.

"Be seated, Lady, and listen," I said.

She sank into a chair and, resting her head upon her hand, regarded me with a cold and curious look.

"Queen," I went on, "I am one whom Heaven has sent to this land to destroy Tenes and the Sidonians."

"Then I welcome you, Stranger. Speak on."

So briefly I told her all my tale, and in proof of it read to her the writing in which I promised myself to Tenes when he could crown me queen of the world.

"So you desire my place and this man?"

"Aye," I answered, "as much, or as little, as life desires death. Study the conditions. Can he crown me queen of all the earth, and under them until he does so, can he take me? Do you not understand that I would lead the fool on to his ruin?"

She nodded her head.

"Then will you not help me?"

"Aye, Lady, but how?"

"I will show you how," and bending forward, I whispered in her ear.

"It is good," she said when I had finished. "By Jehovah my God, and by the blood of my son, with you I stand or fall, and when all is done take Tenes if you will."

## CHAPTER 10

# The Vengeance of Beltis

So it came about that this queen, whose name I learned was Elishe-ba among her own people, the Hebrews, Beltis being a title given to her in Sidon, and I dwelt together in the palace of Tenes. Leave me she dared not, nor would I suffer it who knew that then certainly she would be murdered, while with me she was safe because Tenes dared not touch one whom I sheltered, being afraid of me; one, moreover, over whom I had placed the veil of Isis. For the rest she was glad to stay with me whom soon she learned to love, especially after she had learned how I pleaded for her son's life.

I, too, was glad that she should do so, both because she was a companion to my loneliness and a protection, since Tenes could not persecute me with his passion in her presence, and because she had those who loved her in Sidon, certain Hebrews through whom we learned much. Yet we were in a strange case, the queen who reigned and the queen to whom her place was promised, dwelling together like sisters, and both sworn to destroy him who was her husband and who desired to be mine.

For we made a pact together, she swearing by Jehovah and I by Isis, that we would neither rest nor stay till we saw Tenes dead and his Si-donians with him. Oh! if I hated him and these, she, the robbed moth-er, hated them worse, so deeply indeed that if only she might come by vengeance she cared nothing for her life. She was a fierce-natured woman, such as those of the Hebrews often are, and all her heart's love had been given to this boy, her only child, whom Tenes butchered at the bidding of the priests and because of his superstitions.

From the beginning this Beltis or Elisheba had hated the Sidoni-ans and Tenes, to whom she was given in a marriage of policy by the rulers of Jerusalem because of her beauty and her royal blood, and now to her they were but as wild beasts and snakes to be destroyed.

Yet she was clever also and played her part well, feigning sorrow for the wild words she spoke in the hour of her agony and with it obedience to the wishes of the King. She even told him in my presence that when the time came she would be willing that I should take her crown and she but a second place, or if it pleased him better, that she would return to her own people. This, however, he did not desire, since he feared lest the disgrace of so great a lady should bring the wrath of Jerusalem upon him, or even cause the Hebrews to join his enemies.

So well did she play that part, indeed, making it appear that her spirit was crushed and that she was one from whom there was nothing to fear, that soon Tenes came to believe that this was so, and in order to please me he suffered her to dwell on there in peace.

\*\*\*\*\*\*\*\*

Now I have to tell of the war and of the end of Sidon. First I should say, however, that before he sailed for Egypt, after the *Hapi* had been fitted with a new mast of cedar, I caused Philo to be summoned to the palace by the help of those Jews who were the friends of Beltis. He was brought to my presence with two merchants, disguised as one of their company, and, while Beltis made pretence to chaffer with them for their costly goods, I spoke with him apart.

I told him to get him to Memphis as quickly as he might, and there make all ready as we had agreed, awaiting my message. How this would reach him, or Noot, or both of them, I did not know. It might be by writing, or by messenger who would bear certain tokens, or it might be otherwise. At least when it came he must sail at once, and arriving off the port of Sidon, every night after the setting of the sun and before its rising, must light a flare of green fire at his masthead, causing it to burn for the fourth part of an hour, so that I might be sure that the ship which signal led was his and no other. Then in this way or in that I would find means to come aboard that vessel, and the rest was in the hands of the gods.

These things he vowed to do and departed safely with the merchants, nor did Tenes ever learn that Philo had visited the palace.

Meanwhile Tenes was making mighty preparations for the war. He dug a triple ditch about Sidon and heightened its walls. He hired ten thousand Grecian mercenaries and armed the citizens. By help of the Greeks he drove the Persian vanguard out of Phoenicia, and for a while all went well for him and Egypt. At length came the news that the vast army of Ochus was rolling down on Sidon, together with three hundred *triremes* and five hundred transports; such an army as Phoenicia had never seen.

One morning Tenes came to my chamber and told of the march of Ochus, Beltis withdrawing herself. He was in a very evil case, for he trembled and even forgot to say sweet words or to devour me with his eyes after his fashion. I asked him why his hand shook and his lips were pale, he, who as a warrior king, should be rejoicing at the prospect of battle. He answered because of a dream he had dreamed, in which he seemed to see himself defeated by the Persians and cast down living from the wall of the city. Then he added these words:

"You, Lady, promised to show me how to conquer the world. Do so, I pray you, for I say that my heart is afraid and I know not how I shall stand against Ochus."

Now I laughed at him and answered,

"So at last you come to me for counsel, Tenes, who for days have been wondering for how long you would be content to take that of Mentor of Rhodes and of the King of Cyprus. Well, what would you learn?"

"I would learn how I may defeat the Persians, Lady, the Persians who pour upon us like a flood through a broken wall."

"I do not know, Tenes. To me it seems impossible. I think that dream of yours is coming true, Tenes, that is——" And I ceased.

"What, then, must I do, Lady? What is your meaning?"

"I mean that you are mad to fight Ochus."

"But I am fighting Ochus."

"Those who have been enemies may become friends, King Tenes. Have I not told you that you would be safer as the ally of Ochus than as his foe? What is Egypt to you that you should destroy yourself to save Nectanebes?"

"Egypt may be little, Lady, but Sidon is much. The Sidonians are pledged to this war and the hand of Ochus might be heavy on them."

Again I laughed and answered,

"Which is dearer to a man, his own life or those of others? Fight and die if you will, O King; or make peace and perchance let others die if you will, O King. They say that Ochus is generous and knows how to reward those who serve him."

"Do you mean that I should make a pact with him and betray my people?" he asked hoarsely.

"Aye, my words may be so read. Hearken. You have great ambitions. You would win the world—and me. My wisdom tells me that only thus can you win the world—and me. Continue this war, and very soon you will lose me and all that you command of Earth shall be such small part of it as hides your bones. Now make your choice and trouble me no more, who in truth find little joy in timid hearts that fear to take hold of opportunity. Therefore, follow your counsel or my own, I care not which who would be gone back to Egypt to seek a higher destiny than that of consort to a conquered slave."

"Whatever I may lose, you I cannot lose," he said slowly. "Also your mind is mine. This Persian is too strong for me, and on Egypt I cannot lean too hard lest it break beneath me. These Sidonians, also, are rebellious and murmur against me. I think that they would kill me if they dared, who now call me Child-murderer because I gave my son in sacrifice to please the priests."

"Mayhap, King," I answered carelessly, "since mobs are fickle. I repeat that the wise man and he who would be great does not think of others but of himself."

"I will consult with my General, Mentor the Greek, for he is far-sighted," he said, and left me.

"The poison works," I thought to myself as I watched him go. Then I called Beltis and told her all that had passed between her lord and me. She listened and asked,

"Why do you lead Tenes down this road, Ayesha?"

"Because of the pit at the end of it," I answered. "Have not your spies told us that this Ochus is implacable? He will make a pact with Tenes and then he will destroy him. Such at least is the counsel that comes to me from Heaven, which he has angered, as I think."

"Then I pray that Tenes may follow it, Ayesha, so long as it hurls him down to hell, and the Sidonians with him."

As it chanced he did, for it was of a sort that his false heart loved. The rest may be told in few words. Tenes sent his minister, Thessalion, another crafty fellow, to make a treaty with Ochus. These were the terms of this treaty: That he, Tenes, should surrender Sidon and in payment receive the royalty of Egypt after it had been conquered, and of all Phoenicia also, and with it that of Cyprus. Ochus swore these gifts to him and continued his advance. When he reached a certain spot, he halted. Then Tenes, as he had undertaken to do, led out a hundred of the chief citizens of Sidon to a Council of the States of Phoenicia, or so he said.

Howbeit, presently they found themselves in the camp of Ochus who butchered them to the last man, all save Tenes himself, who returned to Sidon with a tale of an ambush from which he had escaped.

Then it was I saw that the end drew near, and in a ship, which not Tenes, but the captains of the Sidonians sent to Nectanebes at Memphis to pray for more aid, I caused a faithful Jew to sail, one sworn to the service of Beltis, who carried with him hidden in the hollow sole of his sandal a letter addressed to Noot and to Philo, praying that Philo would sail at once and do all those things that had been agreed upon between us. Also night by night I sent out my spirit, or rather my thought, to seek the spirit of Noot, as he had taught me to do, and it seemed to me that answers came from Noot telling me that he read my thought and would do those things which I desired.

The chief men of the Sidonians held a council in the great hall of the palace. Hidden behind curtains in a gallery of the hall, Beltis and I saw and heard all that passed at this council, over which Tenes presided as King. Bitter was the talk of those lords, for doubts were abroad. They thought it very strange that Tenes alone should have escaped from that ambush. Yet like the liar that he was, he cozened them with false tales, showing them also that the gods of the Sidonians had preserved his life, that he in his turn might preserve theirs. Yes, he said this and other things, he the knave and traitor, who already plotted to destroy them all.

At this council the Sidonians took a desperate road. Day by day many were escaping from the city by sea and otherwise. Already nigh a third of the people had gone, and among them some thousands of the best soldiers, so that the captains saw that soon the great city would be left with few to defend her. Therefore they came to this resolve—to burn all their ships so that no more could flee upon them, and to set watches at the gates and round the walls with orders to slay any who might attempt flight by land.

Fearing for his life, Tenes consented to these deeds, swearing that he desired but one thing, to conquer or to die with the citizens of Sidon.

So it came about that soon the darkness was made as light as day by the flames which sprang from over a hundred vessels of war besides a multitude of smaller ships, while the Sidonians, watching them burn from the roofs of their houses, beat their breasts and moaned. For now they knew they were cut off and must conquer or perish.

The ships of Ochus watched the port of Sidon, though somewhat carelessly because it was known to him that its harbours were empty, and the vast army of Ochus rolled down in countless hosts upon its walls.

Hour by hour spies came in with terrible reports, causing the hearts of the Sidonians to melt with fear. For now they understood that all hope of victory was gone and that they were doomed, though as yet they did not know that it was their king who had betrayed them.

Another council was held, at which Beltis and I watched as before, and there it was agreed that the city should throw itself upon the mercy of Ochus. Tenes affected to protest and at last to allow himself to be overruled, as I, to whom he came day by day for guidance, put it into his black heart to do. Heralds were sent to the camp of Ochus, offering to surrender upon honourable terms, and while they were absent bloody sacrifices of children and others were made to Dagon and his company in the Holy Place before the temple, till its pavements ran red with blood. For thus these cruel folk hoped to propitiate Heaven and to win mercy from Ochus.

The heralds returned bearing the word of Ochus. He said that if five hundred of the chief citizens came out unarmed and made submission to him, he would grant their prayer and spare Sidon; but if they did not, that he would pull it stone from stone and slaughter all who lived within its walls. Also one of the Persian ambassadors who accompanied them brought a secret letter for Tenes. This letter Tenes, who by now did nothing without my counsel, read to me.

It was brief. This was its substance:

If he would put Sidon into his hands, Ochus swore to Tenes by his most solemn Persian oaths advancement greater than he had ever dreamed; and to Mentor the Rhodian and the general of the Grecian and Egyptian Mercenaries, he swore a vast sum in gold and one of the first commands in the Persian army. If Tenes would not do this, then Ochus proposed to make peace with Sidon for a while but afterward to destroy it. To Tenes himself, however, he promised death at the hands of the Sidonians themselves, to whom all his treachery should be revealed. Lastly an answer was demanded without delay.

"What shall I say to Ochus, Lady?" asked Tenes of me.

"I know not," I answered. "Honour would seem to demand that you should lay down your life and save Sidon and her citizens, if only for a while. Yet, O King, what is honour? How will honour help you when you have been torn to pieces by the maddened mob upon yonder Holy Place, and your spirit has gone to Baal, or wherever the spirits of those sacrificed to Moloch may go. Will this empty honour give you that great advancement of which the Persian speaks, which doubtless will carry with it the rule of Phoenicia and of Egypt, and perchance also that of the East? For Ochus being mortal, Tenes, once you have brought him to his death, as I can show you how to do, who is fitter than yourself to fill his throne? Lastly, will death with honour bring me whom you desire to your side, King Tenes? I have spoken, now judge," and lifting my veil, I sat and smiled at him.

"It is not safe," he said. "All hangs on Mentor and the Greeks. Unless they join in the plot the Sidonians will fight to the last with their aid, and when they discover my traffic with Ochus they will slay me. And if I fly to Ochus and the Sidonians fight, then mayhap he will slay me as one who has helped him nothing. But if Mentor joins us, then we can open the gates to the Persians and ourselves go out safe to reap our reward."

"There speaks a great man," I said, "one who is fore-sighted, one not tied by petty scruples; there speaks such a one as I would take to be my lord. Aye, there speaks a man fit to rule the world, to whom the great advancement the Persian promises is but the first rung in the ladder of glorious triumph—that ladder which reaches to the very stars. Already these Sidonians hate you, Tenes. I saw them mutter when you passed among them yesterday; aye, and one laid his hand upon his dagger, but another checked him, having a look in his eyes that seemed to say—'Not yet.' If once they learn the truth, Tenes, perchance soon you also will lie on the altar of sacrifice and be cast living into the fiery jaws of Dagon, where your son went before you, Tenes. Why do you not send for Mentor and search his mind?"

So Mentor was sent for, and meanwhile I gave Tenes my hand to kiss. Yes, I even suffered this that I might fix him the more firmly on my hook.

Mentor came. He was a burly Greek, a great soldier with a keen brain behind his laughing eyes; one who loved gold and wine and women, and for these and high place and generalship was ready to sell his sword to whoever bid the most.

Tenes set out the matter to him very craftily and showed him the writing of Ochus. He listened, then asked,

"And what does this veiled Daughter of Isis think? I remember hearing in Egypt where she was held the first of Oracles and named Child of Wisdom, that her prophecies never fail to fulfil themselves."

"The Daughter of Isis thinks that among the Persians Mentor will grow tall, but that here among the Sidonians he will be felled like a forest tree and go to feed a mighty fire, such a fire as consumed the fleets of Sidon awhile ago."

Thus I answered, and when Mentor heard my words, he laughed and said that he was of the same mind, which without doubt was true, for afterward I learned that he had already been in treaty with Ochus.

So he and Tenes struck hands upon their bargain, the most infamous perhaps that was ever made by men, since it gave to slaughter forty thousand or more who trusted to them.

Thus was signed the doom of an accursed people, that doom which I was destined to bring upon their heads, and thus was Tenes sent down the road to hell. Only Mentor prospered greatly for a while in the service of the Persians, and what was the end of him I do not know. After all, he was but one of many who flit from master to master as advantage leads them. Doubtless long ago the world has forgotten him, his Grecian cunning, his generalship, and his treachery.

The five hundred went out to the Persian camp to plead with Ochus, bearing palm branches in their hands; yea, they went with light hearts, for Tenes had told them that certainly their prayer would be granted and that he knew this from the lips of Ochus himself. Led by the priesthoods of the various gods—oh! how it rejoiced me to see those vile and cruel priests in that company!—they went, but not one of them returned again, for Ochus received them with mockeries and reviling, and to make sport for himself and his soldiers, told them to run back to Sidon. Then he loosed his horsemen on them and slew them with swords and javelins and set their heads on stakes around the walls.

When the Sidonians knew and saw, they went mad with rage and terror. They gathered themselves by thousands in the Holy Place, and had it not been for Mentor and his Greeks, would have stormed the palace, for now they were sure that Tenes had betrayed them. Indeed Beltis had made the truth of this treachery known through the Hebrews who served her. Also they clamoured that I, Ayesha, should be led forth and sacrificed, saying that it was the presence of a priestess of Isis in the city which had caused their gods to desert them. For a little while I was afraid, who remembered what had chanced upon the ship *Hapi* when Tenes would have suffered me to be thrown to the deep to satisfy the superstition of the sailors. Therefore thinking it best to be bold, I sent for Tenes and said to him,

"If by evil chance I should be slain, O King, then know that I have it from the goddess whom I serve that you with whose lot mine is intertwined will die within an hour. I, Tenes, am the bright star of your fortunes, and if I set, farewell to them and you."

"I know it," he answered, "as I know that without you I can never rise to be king of the world. Therefore I will defend you to the last; also, beauteous one, I desire you for my wife. Yet," he added, "some might think that this star of your wisdom has hitherto led my feet into dark and evil places," and he looked at me doubtfully.

"Fear nothing," I answered. "'Tis ever darkest before the dawn and out of evil arises good. Great glory awaits you, Tenes, or rather great glory awaits both of us. History will embalm your name, Tenes." But to myself I thought that it was the Persians who would embalm his body, unless indeed they cast it to the dogs!

Now every evening after sundown it was my custom to walk upon the flat roof of the palace and look out over the ocean which, also for reasons of my own, rising early, I did before the dawn. That night while I walked I put up my prayers to Heaven, for though I played so bold a game, its odds seemed to be gathering against me. Doubtless, as it deserved, this hateful Sidon would fall, but when its walls were crashing down, with what should I protect my head? I did not know. Yet it is true that never did I lose faith. Always I knew that I was the instrument of that Strength which directs the fate of men and nations, that what I did was because I was driven and commanded so to do for reasons that were dark to me; moreover, that I was not an instrument to be broken and thrown aside. Nay, however strait the path and however great the perils that beset it, I was sure that I should walk it with safety, because it was fated that I should do so, though whither it would lead me I could not tell in those days when I was but as other women are. Still I put up my prayer to Heaven and scanned the horizon with my eyes.

Lo! far away beyond the lights of the watching *triremes* of Ochus, so far that it seemed almost set upon the surface of the sea, burned a faint green fire. For the fourth part of an hour it burned, and went out. Then I knew that my words had reached Egypt, whether in the writing or by the swift path of the spirit, and that Noot or Philo had come to save me.

Before the dawn once more I climbed to the roof of the palace, and behold! far away again the green fire burned upon the bosom of the deep, telling me that out yonder the great *trireme* waited for my coming. Aye, but how was I to come?

Tenes the vile and Mentor the venal played their parts well. They opened the gates of the outmost wall which the Greeks held, and let in the Persians whom these Greeks greeted as brothers, having at times served under them in the past. The Sidonians saw and knew that the dice had fallen against them; knew too that they were loaded dice.

They gathered in the Holy Place and raved for the blood of Tenes who cowered behind a curtain and hearkened to them. Beltis and I, playing our parts, came to comfort him.

"Be brave!" I said gently. "The road to the kingship of the world is steep and difficult. Yet when the peak is gained, how glorious, O Conqueror, will be the prospect spread out before your eyes."

"It is steep and difficult," he muttered, wiping his brow with the fringe of his broidered robe.

Had he been seen the look which Beltis cast upon him, standing behind him with folded arms and humble air, perchance he would have thought it steeper still.

"Let us talk," I said, "for the end draws near. What is your plan? How will you and we, your queens, escape from this city?"

"All is prepared," he answered. "At the King's wharf, to which a covered way runs from the palace, in the house where the royal boats are moored, is my own barge that, being thus secured, escaped burning with the ships. In this barge, which is manned with Greeks to whom a great reward is promised and who wait in the boathouse day and night, we will row from the harbour for a hidden land and be escorted thence to the encampment of the Great King. Yet perchance it may be wiser that I should be with Mentor to welcome Ochus when he enters to take peaceful possession of the city. If so, Daughter of Isis, you will do well to leave it by yourself, or with the lady Beltis if she wishes to accompany you, and to meet me in the camp of Ochus."

"Perhaps that would be better," I answered, "since it might not be thought seemly that the great King Tenes should slip away to his ally by night. Nay, let him rather march out as a monarch should. Only then we must have authority to act as occasion may direct."

"Aye, Lady, take this ring," and slipping the royal signet from his finger he gave it to me. "It will be obeyed by all who see it; moreover, I will issue certain orders. So long as we meet again at last, we whose fates are intertwined, it matters not by what separate roads we travel."

"It matters not at all, my lord Tenes," I answered as swiftly as I hid away the signet.

It was just then, at the hour of sunset, that Mentor entered the chamber. No longer was he gay and light-hearted; indeed his brows were bent and his eyes full of trouble.

"By Zeus!" he said, "a dreadful thing has happened. In their despair these Sidonians of yours, King Tenes, have taken counsel together. They have determined that rather than fall into the hands of Ochus, they will burn the city and with it themselves and their wives and children. Yes, uttering the curse of all the gods upon you, thus they have determined. Look, the fires begin!"

We went to the window-places and gazing from them, saw desperate men rushing to and fro with lighted torches of cedar wood in their hands, while other men drove mobs of screaming women and children into the houses, yes, and into the temples, and shut the doors upon them. Here and there, too, from the roofs of these houses rose wisps of smoke that soon were mingled with flame. East and west and north and south, through the great city of Sidon arose that smoke and flame. Everywhere also mobs of the people whose courage failed them and who did not desire to die thus were rushing toward the gates and into the camp of the Greeks. In this fashion, I believe, that from ten to twenty thousand of the inhabitants of Sidon escaped, though afterwards Ochus the cruel slew many of them and enslaved the rest.

I looked, I saw, and my heart melted within me. Hateful as were these insolent, bloodstained folk, I grieved that I should have had any hand in bringing their reward upon them. After all, they were brave and would have fought to the end, who now made expiation by a great self-sacrifice, which was also brave. Oh! if I could I would have lifted that doom from off them. Then I remembered that it was not I who did these things, but Fate which made of me its instrument; remembered also that only thus could I escape the foul hands of Tenes.

I turned to look upon that traitor. He trembled, and trembling tried to seem brave; he laughed, and in the midst of his laughter burst into tears.

"Behold the fate of those who would have slain their king! Truly the gods are just," he said. "Now let us fly to the great Ochus and receive from him his royal welcome and reward. Truly the gods are just!"

He turned about seeking for Mentor, but Mentor had gone. There remained in that chamber only Beltis the Queen, he, and I, Ayesha. Beltis glided to the door and made it fast. Then she came to Tenes and before he guessed her purpose, snatched the gold-hilted sword from his belt. She stood before him with fierce white face and blazing eyes.

"Truly the gods are just," she repeated in a low and terrible voice. "Fool, do you not know what welcome Ochus will give you yonder and what rewards? Hearken! That false Greek, Mentor, told me of these but now, for pitying my lot, he offered me his love and to take me to safety. After I had refused him, he went his way while you stared from the window-place."

"What words are these, Woman?" gasped Tenes. "Ochus is my ally; Ochus will greet me well who have served him well. Let us be going."

"Ochus will greet you thus, O Tenes; I have it from the mouth of Mentor who has it from Ochus himself. Slowly he will cause you, a king, to be beaten to death with rods, which is the fate the Persians give to slaves and traitors. Then he will stuff your body with spices and tie it to the masthead of his ship, that when presently he sails for Egypt it may be a warning to Nectanebes the Pharaoh whom also you have betrayed."

"It is a lie, it is a lie!" shouted Tenes. "Daughter of Isis, tell this mad woman that it is a lie."

I stood still, answering nothing, and Beltis went on,

"Tenes, Fate is upon you. Will you meet it less bravely than the meanest of the thousands of this people whom you have given to doom? Take my last counsel and leap from yonder window, that you who have lived a coward and a traitor may at last die a man."

He gnashed his teeth, he stared about him. He even went to the window-place and looked out as though he would brave the deed.

"I dare not," he muttered, "I dare not. The gods are just; they will save me who sacrificed my son to them."

Then he knelt down in the window-place and began to pray to Moloch whose brazen image showed redly in the gathering gloom.

"Take your sword, Tenes, if you dare not leap, and make an end," said the cold voice of the fierce-faced Hebrew lady who stood behind him, whilst I, Ayesha, watched all this play as a spirit might that is afar from the affairs of earth, wondering how it would end.

But Tenes only answered,

"Nay, sharp steel is worse than steep air. I would live, not die. The gods are just, the gods are just!"

Then he went on praying to Moloch.

Queen Beltis grasped the handle of the short sword with both her hands and with all her strength drove it down between the broad shoulders of Tenes.

"Aye, dog of a Sidonian," she cried, "the gods are very just, or at the least my God is just, and here—child-slayer—is the justice!"

Tenes screamed aloud, then struggled to his feet and stood striking at the air, the short sword still fixed in his back, a dreadful sight to behold.

"Would you murder me, Jewess?" he babbled, and staggered after her, still beating at the air with his clenched fist.

"Nay," she answered, ever retreating before him, "I would but give you your due, or some of it. Go, garner the rest in Gehenna's deep, O butcher of children and traitor blacker than the world has ever seen. Die, hound! Die, lurking jackal who would have mumbled the bones of greatness left by the full-fed Persian lion. Die, slaughterer of the son that sprang from us, and go meet his spirit in the world below, telling him that Elisheba his mother, a woman of the royal house of Israel, the Queen whom you had rejected, sent you thither. Die, while the city, the great City of the Seas, burns with the fires that your treachery has lighted and the cries of its tortured citizens ring in your ears. Pass with them to Gehenna and there strike your account, having their fire-shrivelled souls for witnesses and Moloch and Baal and Ashtoreth for judges and for company. Die, dog, die! and while your brain darkens, remember to the last that it was Elisheba, the robbed mother, who gave you to drink of the cup of death."

So she reviled, ever flitting before him, while he staggered slowly after her round the great chamber. At length he could no more and fell at my feet, grasping my robe,

"Daughter of Isis," he babbled, "whom I desired and would have made my queen, save me! Is this the great advancement that you swore to me?"

"Aye, mighty Tenes," I answered, "since death is the greatest of all advancements. In death be king of Phoenicia, of Egypt, and of all the East, since surely there you will stand above all thrones, powers, and dominions. In death all things will be yours, O traitor Tenes, who would have done violence to the daughter of Isis, everything save Ayesha's self, who here bids you farewell, vile Tenes."

\* \* \* \* \* \* \* \*

Then, wailing and moaning, he died, and thus robbed Ochus of his vengeance upon a tool of which he had no further need.

## CHAPTER 11

# The Escape From Sidon

All was over and done. Within that royal chamber was silence, though without the flames roared and the cries of the Sidonians went up to Heaven. I, Ayesha, and Beltis the Queen, faced each other in the gloom and between us lay the body of Tenes, on whose white, distorted face flickered the light of the fires that burned without.

"What now, Queen?" I said.

"Death, I think," she answered in a quiet voice, for all her rage seemed to have left her. "Why cheat his jaws of their richest morsel?"

"I have still work to do, my hour has not yet come, Queen."

"Aye, I forgot. Follow me, Daughter of Isis; Beltis does not forsake those who have served her. Look your last upon this carrion that hoped to call you wife, and follow me."

As we passed from that chamber I glanced through the window and saw that, although darkness now had fallen, the Holy Place beneath was bright as noon with the flames of the burning temple, and that in them the vast graven image of Moloch glowed as it had done upon the day of sacrifice when the child of Beltis was swallowed in its red-hot jaws. There it sat hideous; grinning as though in unholy triumph over this greatest of all sacrifices.

Then suddenly a pinnacle from the temple fell upon it, grinding it to powder. This was the end of Moloch, since, although Sidon, as I have learned, was rebuilt in the after years, never more was sacrifice made to that devil within its walls. This at least I, Ayesha, brought to pass—the end of the worship of Moloch at Sidon.

We passed through my sleeping-chamber, and as we went I seized the cabinet of priceless gems that Tenes from time to time had heaped upon me, since these were sworn to Isis and no goddess loves to be robbed of her offerings. At the back of the chamber was a passage leading to a door by which a lighted lamp had been set in readiness.

At this door stood a man whom I knew for one of the Jewish servants sworn to the service of Beltis.

"You are late, royal Lady," he exclaimed. "So late that I was about to flee, for look, the palace burns beneath us," and he pointed to little wreaths of smoke that forced themselves up between the boards of the flooring of the bedchamber that we had passed.

"Late, but not too late," she answered. "The King detained us and has gone another way. You have his orders and here is his ring," and she pointed to the royal signet upon my hand. "Obey it and lead on."

The man held up the lantern and glanced at the ring. Then he bowed and beckoned to us to follow him.

We went down passages, long passages with many turnings, and at length came to another door which he opened with a key. Passing it, we found ourselves in a vaulted place beneath which was water, where floated the royal barge, the same in which I had been rowed to the shore of Sidon. Oarsmen sat waiting within this barge, and guarding it were two Grecian soldiers, who commanded us to halt.

"This boat awaits King Tenes," said one of them, "and none else may enter it."

"I am the Queen," answered Beltis.

"With whom I hear the King has quarrelled," broke in the Greek with a sneer. "Queen or no, Lady, you cannot enter that boat without the King, or an order under his signet."

Then I held up my hand, saying,

"Here is the signet itself. Let us pass."

He stared at it by the light of the lamp, then said something to the other Greek and very doubtfully they obeyed. It was certain that these guards standing in that vaulted place did not know what was passing in the city. Moreover, I think it had come into their minds to rob us, or worse. At the least this is sure, that unless we could have killed those two Greeks, without the signet never should have we have won to the boat.

We went on twelve paces or so and reached the barge, which was manned with sailors who wore the uniform of the King's bodyguard, men who knew the Queen and saluted her by raising their oars. Beltis motioned first to me and afterward to the Jew who had been our guide from the palace, to enter the barge, then suddenly she said to the steersman who commanded the sailors,

"Go now whither this lady shall direct you, and know that if harm comes to her your lives shall pay the price of it, for she is no woman, but a goddess whom Death obeys."

Now I stared at her and asked,

"Do you not come also, Queen Beltis?"

"Nay," she whispered. "I choose another road to safety. Fear not for me, I will tell you all when we meet again. For a while farewell, Child of Wisdom and my friend. May the gods with whom you commune be your shield upon earth and receive you when you leave the earth, you who strove to save a certain one and cast your mantle over Beltis when a sword that now is set in another's heart was at her own. Give way, sailors," she cried, "and if you would look once more upon the sun, obey."

Then with her own hands she thrust at the stern of the boat, causing it to move into the channel. Next moment Beltis had shrunk back into the darkness and was gone.

Now I would have returned to seek for her, but the Jew at my side called out,

"Give way! Give way and question not the word of the Queen who doubtless has work elsewhere. Be swift; doom is behind you."

For a moment they hesitated, then bent them to their oars while I wondered what might be the meaning of the part that Beltis played. Did she perchance plan some trap for me? I did not know, but this I knew, that behind was the burning city, whereas in front lay the open sea. Whatever its perils I would face the sea, trusting to destiny to be my guide. As for Beltis, doubtless she took some other road to freedom. Mayhap after all she would shelter with Mentor, or Ochus had promised her deliverance in payment for the blood of Tenes.

So I sat silent, and presently the channel took a turn; the swinging water-gates that hid its mouth were thrust open with an oar by a man who stood at the barge's prow, and we passed into the southern harbour.

Yes, out of the darkness we passed into a blaze of light, and out of the silence into a hideous tumult of sound. For all around us the city burned furiously and from it rose one horrible wail of woe.

The rowers saw and understood who until now had known nothing in the silence of the secret harbour cave. They hung upon their oars. Then they brought round the barge's prow seeing to return into the cave, but could not because those doors had swung to behind them and, having locked themselves by some device, could only be opened from within. Nor indeed could I tell where these were since they seemed to form part of the harbour wall.

The helmsman looked back and from side to side at the hell of fire which raged behind and around him. He looked at the jutting pier upon our right and noted that already its timbers were ablaze. Then he looked in front and cried,

"Now I see why the Queen left us! Well, there is but one chance. Onward to the open sea."

"Aye," I echoed, "onward to the open sea. Here you must die; there I will lead you to safety. I swear it by the Queen of Heaven."

"'Tis well to talk," said one, "but how shall we gain the sea? Look, the Persians are barring the harbour mouth and slaying those who strive to escape."

It was true. Many of the miserable inhabitants of Sidon had found boats of this sort or of that, or even were swimming upon logs or barrels. For these the Persians or those in their pay waited at the mouth of the harbour and with mocking words and laughter butchered them as they came. Yes, from their smaller ships they slew them with spears and arrows or by throwing stones that drove out the bottoms of the boats.

"Keep in the shadow of the jetty," I said, "where the wind-driven smoke hangs thick and near which the *triremes* dare not come because of the rocks whereon it is built, and row, row fast."

They heard and obeyed. On we went beneath an arching canopy of smoke laced with bursts of flame from the kindling timbers, till at length we reached the head of the jetty on which stood a wooden tower where a light burned at night to be a guide to mariners entering the harbour. Here we waited a while, clinging to one of the piers, for although the wind was rising, in this sheltered place the sea remained calm.

Rowing across the head of the jetty was a Persian *trireme*, and until she had gone by we dared not attempt the sea. At length she passed, leisurely, and our chance came. At a muttered word the oarsmen gave way with all their strength and we shot clear of the mole into the open deep. As we did so, I looked back and perceived behind and above me a sight that after more than two thousand years still haunts me in my sleep.

Upon the end of this timber-crested mole, as I have said, there was a wooden tower from which in times of peace a beacon burned. Now this tower was blazing like the pierway behind it and no beacon shone there. Only where it should be stood a woman on whose face the strong light beat, since the wind swept away the smoke and revealed her like a statue on a column that rises above mist. I looked at this shape and this face and saw that they were those of Beltis the Queen of Sidon. How she had come there, I do not know, but I think that she had run along the burning mole before it was too late, being well acquainted with the path, and had climbed the stairway of the tower, that from its crest she might look her last upon Sidon and on life.

There at least she stood, royal-looking, silent, with her arms crossed upon her breast, while the purple cloak that marked her rank floated behind her like a banner on the breeze.

She saw the barge that bore us shoot out of the gloom and reek into the deep sea. I know that she saw because she stretched out her arm as though to bless us. Then she turned and lifted her hands towards the burning city as though to curse it. Lastly, once more she folded her arms upon her breast and stood motionless, her white face raised to the heavens.

Thus she remained while one might count an hundred, till suddenly the timbers of the tower, gnawed through by the flames, fell in and she vanished in a roaring gulf of fire.

Such was the end of that great and ill-fated woman, the royal Beltis, Queen of Sidon, whom, mayhap in expiation of sin done in another star, the gods gave to the arms of perchance the vilest man that ever lived upon the earth. Greatly she died, a sacrifice, as her son had been a sacrifice, but not before she had wrought a fitting vengeance upon the murderer of her child and the betrayer of his people. Moloch, god of fire, took her as he took them all, but now she was beyond the reach of Moloch, Moloch who was but molten metal, an offering to himself.

In the great flame of the fallen tower the *trireme* that bore the banner of Ochus saw our boat escaping out to sea and put about to pursue it.

"Row on!" I cried, "row into the darkness," and knowing that their lives hung on the issue, since, as we had already seen, the Persians spared none whom they overtook in the boats but drove the *triremes* over them, shooting any who swam with arrows, those sailors rowed sturdily. Yet our progress was but slow and that of the three-banked ship behind us fast; moreover, the fires of burning Sidon lit up the sea for miles.

Could we reach the darkness before we were overtaken? We came to its edge with the great *trireme* not a hundred paces from our stern— so near indeed that the soldiers on board of her began to shoot at us, though in the gathering gloom and because of the rolling platform on which they stood, their shafts went wide. She was right upon us; her hull had vanished in the shadows but the light from the fires still gleamed upon her gilded masthead, while her great oars beat the sea with a sound like thunder.

"Put about," I cried, "or she will sink us."

Very skilfully the steersman obeyed so that we doubled like a hunted hare and the Persian shot past us. Then once more we turned and rowed on into the night. When it wrapped us round, the sailors, exhausted, rested on their oars. Again we heard the thunder of the great slave-manned sweeps, and again the brazen prow of the tall ship, cruel, enormous, hung almost over us. Only by an ell or two did the broad blades of the oars miss us, the eddies that they made causing our little craft to rock dangerously. But this time that huge sea-hound was blinded by the darkness and not seeing us, nor hearing anything, for we sat silent as the grave, she rushed upon her way, and for a time we saw her no more.

All was quiet upon the breast of ocean. Far off burned Sidon like a gigantic beacon fire, but there came to us no whisper of her agony. Yes, all was quiet, save for the sighing of the night wind that, to my strange fancy, seemed like to such a sound as might be made by the rush of ten thousand spirits passing from the cruel earth upward to the peace above. Slowly the wearied oarsmen drove the boat still farther out to sea; then their captain said,

"Whither away, Lady? It is in my mind to change our course and run for the coast northward, where perchance there are no Persians."

"Nay," I answered, "we stay where we are, I search for a ship."

"Mayhap we shall find one," he said with a hoarse laugh, "a ship of the fleet of Ochus."

They began to dispute as to what course they should take.

"Obey me," I said, "or obey me not, as you will. Only then I, who have the counsel of the gods, tell you that save I only, by sunrise tomorrow everyone of you will be dead."

They whispered together, for my words frightened them. At length the captain spoke, saying,

"The great Queen Beltis who is gone told us that this woman is a goddess and that what she commanded, that we must do. Let us remember the words of the great Queen Beltis who is dead and doubtless watches us from the sky."

So this danger passed also, and all that night we floated, keeping the boat's stern to burning Sidon while the most of the oarsmen slept in their places. So weary were they that not even the horror behind them and the loss of their kinsfolk, or even their own fears, could hold them back from sleep.

But I, Ayesha, did not sleep; nay, I watched and thought. If Philo had fled away, or if his ship had been sunk, what then? Then all was finished. Nay, not so, since it could not be that I should die with but half my task accomplished. I was friendless among strange men, yet in my breast there dwelt the greatest of friends, that spirit whose name is Fate. I threw out my soul to my master Noot the Seer, and lo! it seemed to me that his soul answered, saying,

"Fear nothing, Daughter of Isis, for the wings of Isis shadow thee."

It drew near to the dawn; I knew it by the stars which I was wont to watch and by the smell of the air. I rose in my seat and stared into the darkness. Behold! not four furlongs from our prow suddenly there sprang into life a fire of green flame.

"Awake," I cried, "and row on swiftly, for if you would you live you must reach the ship upon which yonder fire burns before the breaking of dawn."

They obeyed, wondering, who knew not what this fire might mean. We sped forward, and as the first light gleamed saw almost above us the bulk of the great *trireme* named *Hapi*.

"Hail her!" I cried, and the captain did so. One appeared by her bulwark rail, holding a lantern. Its light shone upon his face and I saw that it was that of Philo the Greek.

"Ye are saved," I said quietly, "for yonder is the vessel that awaits me."

"Of a truth this is a goddess!" muttered the captain of the barge.

Now Philo saw us in the growing light, and cried to us to come swiftly, pointing to something which he could discover but we could not. We were alongside, eager hands dragged us from the boat. We were aboard, I still carrying the casket of jewels though at the time I did not know I held it fast. Philo bowed the knee to me as to one divine, at which our oarsmen stared. Then he shouted a command and again pointed behind us.

Lo! there, scarce two bowshots away, was the great Persian ship which we had escaped in the gloom of the night. Our oars struck the water, we leapt forward like an unleashed hound, and after us came the *trireme* like a lion springing on the hound. *Trireme* have I called her? Nay, as we saw now, she was a *quinquereme*, one of the new five-banked ships built by Ochus, a mighty monster. For a little while she hesitated as though wondering whether to attack or let us be. Then as the light strengthened the eyes of her watchmen caught sight of our abandoned boat and by its gilding and emblems knew it for the royal barge of Tenes.

A great shout arose, a shout of

"The King escapes. The King and Queen Beltis escape. After them!"

Then the *quinquereme* leapt forward in pursuit. Because of her bulk she was slow in gathering speed and we who had the start of her drew away quickly, especially after a shift of wind which seemed to miss the *Holy Fire*, for so Philo, who knew her, said the Persian was named, filled our great sail.

Seeing this and hoping that our danger was past, I went to that same captain which had been mine when as the captive of Tenes I sailed upon this ship, which seemed to be just as I had left it. This I did without speech to Philo, save a word to commend to his care the Jew and those others who had been my companions upon the barge.

For now that all was over, it seemed to me as though I must rest or die; moreover, I was foul with travel and needed food. This indeed I found ready upon a table which caused me to wonder, though dully, which I did even more when I saw clean woman's garments such as I was accustomed to use spread out upon the cabin couch. So I cleansed and clothed myself and ate a little, drinking some wine, which I did rarely, then lay down upon the couch and for a space, perhaps, slept as though I were dead.

I woke, I knew not why who could have slumbered on for hours, yet feeling as though the most of my weariness had rolled off me. The place was very dim for the curtained door was shut and at first I could see nothing. Presently, however, I became aware that I was not alone in the cabin. For as my eyes grew accustomed to such light as reached it, I discovered the shape of a man, an old, white-bearded man, kneeling at its far end as though in prayer, and wondered whether I dreamed, for what could such a one be doing here? Soon indeed I was sure that I dreamed, since this shape was that of the high-priest Noot, my Master, whom I supposed to be far away in Egypt. Or perchance Noot was dead and this was his spirit that visited me in my sleep. Spirit or dream or man, words came from the lips of that vision spoken in the very voice of Noot; such words as these,

"O Mother Isis, and Thou without a name whom Isis and all the gods serve and obey, I thank ye that ye have been pleased to bring this maiden in safety through her appointed tasks, throwing over her the shield of a strength divine. I thank ye that ye have led her back to me, her father in the spirit, that defilement has not touched her, that fire has not burned her, that water has not drowned her, and that the foeman's spears have not pierced her heart. I pray ye, O Mother Isis and O Thou without a name in the hollow of whose hand lie the world and all that live thereon, that as has been the beginning, so may be the end, and that this chosen woman may return safe to whence she came, there to accomplish those tasks that she was created to fulfil."

Thus that voice prayed on, the holy, well-remembered voice, till at length I brought its supplications to an end, saying,

"Tell me, Noot my father, why do you still fear in this hour of deliverance?"

He rose, he came to me, and drawing aside a curtain on a little window-plate, scanned me with kind and gentle eyes. Then he took my outstretched hand, kissed it, and answered,

"Alas! there is still much to fear, O my daughter, but of that you shall learn presently. First tell me the story of what has chanced to you since we parted."

Briefly, omitting much, I told him that tale.

"It is as my spirit showed me," he said when I had finished. "Heaven has not deceived its servant. Your messenger reached us, Daughter, but had he died upon the road it would have mattered little, since long ere he had set foot in Egypt my soul had heard your soul and made all things ready. Yet last night, when Sidon burned, I confess that my faith failed me and this soul of mine shook with fear. Indeed an hour after sunset I thought that your ghost passed me, crying that all was done."

"Perchance it was the ghost of Beltis that passed. But of these things we will talk afterward. I see fear in your eyes. Of what are you afraid?"

"Rise and look through that window-place, Daughter."

I did so and behold! but a little distance away the great *quinquereme* named the *Holy Fire* sped upon our track, so fast that her five banks of oars lashed the sea to foam.

"Father divine," said a voice without, a voice that I seemed to know, "I have words to say."

"Enter and speak," answered Noot.

The door was opened and the curtain drawn, admitting a rush of sunlight. Lo! there before me stood a warrior clad in such armour as the Greeks wear and, thus attired, the most beautiful and glorious-looking man that ever my eyes beheld.

It was *Kallikrates, Kallikrates himself*, only now in place of the priest's robe his great form was clad in bronze; in place of a chaplet a helm was on his head and in place of the *sistrum* his hand gripped a sword hilt. Yes, it was Kallikrates, he whose lips in past days had met mine in the holy shrine, but as he had been before he had vowed himself to Isis because of a certain crime. For now again he was a man and a captain of men, not one who with bent brows and humble mien from hour to hour mutters prayers to an unseen divinity.

Oh! I will tell truth. When I saw him thus I liked him well. Yes, though for long he had been nothing to me save a fellow servant of the goddess, once more I was thrilled with a cup of that same wine which I had seemed to drink when our lips met far away in Egypt;

once again that fire which I had stamped to ashes beneath my feet sprang to life and scorched my heart.

Mayhap it was his beauty, as great perhaps as that of any man who ever lived, or mayhap it was the light of battle that shone in his gray eyes which thus stirred the woman in me. At least I who had sickened at the sight of Tenes and all other men, I who had given myself to higher things and, rejecting the flesh, followed the spirit only, was stirred like any common maid who finds her lover at the moonrise. Moreover, Noot, who could read hearts and above all my heart, noted it for I saw him smile and heard him sigh.

Perchance Kallikrates also noted something, for the colour came to his brows—I saw it redden beneath the plumed helm of bronze, and he dropped those bold and beautiful eyes. More, he sank upon his knee, saluting me with the secret sign and saying,

"Pardon, Child of Wisdom, High-priestess of the Queen of Heaven, that once again, if only for a little while, I have put on the harness which I used to wear. It is done to save you, Child of Wisdom. It is done by command."

"Aye," said Noot, "it is the command of Her we serve that this priest should lift sword on behalf of Her and us, her slaves."

I bowed my head, but answered—naught.

## Chapter 12

# The Sea Battle

The great Persian ship was on us. Strive as we would, we could not escape her. She raced upon our beam not a spear's cast away. I stood upon the high poop of the *Hapi* and saw it all, for the old Arab blood was on fire in me, as it had been when I charged in the battle where my father fell, and I would play no woman's part. Moreover, my spirit told me that I had not escaped from the hands of Tenes and out of the burning hell of Sidon, to die there upon the sea.

Standing thus upon the poop by the side of Philo the cunning captain, I noted this strange thing, that no arrow was shot and no spear thrown from the Persian's decks. She raced alongside us, that was all. I looked at Philo, a question in my eyes, and he answered the question briefly between his set lips.

"They think the King and Queen are aboard and would take us living. Hark! They shout to us to surrender."

Again I looked at him, wondering what he would do.

He issued an order and presently our speed slackened so that we fell a little behind the Persian. He issued another order and we leapt forward again under a changed helm. Now I saw that he was minded to ram the *Holy Fire*. The Persian saw it also and sheered off. We ran alongside of her, shipping our oars as we came on that side which was nearest to her. But the Persian had no time to ship hers. Our sharp prow caught her fivefold line of sweeps, smashing the most of them as though they were but twigs, and casting the rowers in a broken, tumbled heap within her deep hold.

"That was worthy of Philo," I said, but he, ever a humble man, as are all masters of their trade, shook his head and answered,

"Nay, Lady, I missed my mark and now we must pay for it. Ah! I thought so."

As he spoke, from sundry places on the *Holy Fire* grapnels flew out which caught in the rails, ropes and rowing benches of the *Hapi*, binding the two ships together.

"They are about to board us," said Philo. "Now, Lady, pray to Mother Isis to give us aid."

Then he blew two blasts upon his whistle. Instantly rose up upon our deck a band of men, nigh a hundred of them, perhaps, clad in armour and captained by the Greek, Kallikrates. Also behind these I saw the crew of the royal barge, armed with such weapons as they could find, and the sailors of the *Hapi*.

The Persians thrust out boards or ladders from one ship to the other, across which their boarders, most of them Greeks, came in swarms. The fighting began and it was very fierce. Our men cut down many of the foe and drowned others by casting off the boards and ladders, so that those on them fell into the sea. Still a great number of them won on board of us, and oh! fierce was that fray. Always in the thickest of it I saw Kallikrates towering a head above the others, and who now would have dreamed that he was a priest of Isis? For he smote and smote and man after man went down before him, while as his sword rose and fell he shouted out some old Greek battle cry, such as once his fathers used.

On a space of deck ringed round with dead and dying, he came face to face with the captain of the boarders, a great and burly man, also, as I think, a Greek. They fought terribly, whilst others paused to watch that fray which Homer might have sung. Kallikrates was down and my heart stood still. Nay, he was up again but his bronze sword had broken on the foeman's mail.

That foeman had an axe; he swung it up to make an end. Kallikrates, rushing beneath it, seized him in his arms and they wrestled there upon the slippery deck. The ship lurched; together they staggered to the bulwarks. The foeman loosed one arm and drew a dagger; with it he smote Kallikrates again and again. Kallikrates bent, and with his freed hand seized the man beneath the knee. By a mighty effort he lifted him to the bulwark's edge and there they clung awhile. Then Kallikrates with that same freed hand smote the other on the brow. Thrice he smote and his blows were as those of a hammer falling on an anvil.

The grip of the captain of the boarders loosened and his head hung back. Once more Kallikrates smote and behold! his foe rolled down and was crushed to powder between the swelling sides of the two great ships as they ground one against the other, while the servants of Isis cheered and the sullen Persian hordes gave back.

I caught sight of Philo thrusting his way along the bulwarks. He held an axe in his hand but he was not fighting. Nay, he avoided those who fought. Once indeed he stood still and gave an order, noting, as I had done, that of a sudden the wind had begun to blow. Certain sailors who heard this order ran to the mast and I saw the great sail rising slowly.

Meanwhile Philo slipped along those bulwarks, taking cover beneath them like a jackal beneath a wall. But whenever he came to one of the grapnels he stopped and smote it with his axe, severing the rope that held it. Three of them did he sever thus, so that the prows of the vessels swung apart.

Now the great sail was up and filled. The *Hapi* forged ahead, dragging round the stern of the *Holy Fire* by those grapnels that remained. The Persians understood and grew frightened. Those who were still alive upon our decks rushed to the planks and ladders, but few gained them, for Kallikrates and the men of Isis were on their heels. They were cut down; they fell from the sliding planks and ladders, or they leapt into the sea and for the most part drowned there. Very soon not one of them was left upon our deck.

The grapnels were torn away, or the ropes broke. We were free. Yet the Persian was not beaten, for she was full of men of whom those who had been killed were but a tithe.

She, too, hoisted her sail and thrust out fresh sweeps to continue the pursuit. Her captain, standing on her prow, roared out,

"Dogs of Egyptians, I'll hang you yet."

Philo heard and took up his bow. Now we were sweeping across the bow of the *Holy Fire*; mayhap it was a hundred paces away. Philo aimed and shot. So truly did he shoot that his arrow struck the Persian captain beneath his helm and down he went.

His fall seemed to bewilder the crew of the *Holy Fire*. They hung upon their oars shouting at each other, as though they knew not what to do. Then their sail began to rise and I saw that they were putting about.

Philo at my side laughed, a hard little laugh.

"Mother Isis is good to us," he said. "See, the hunter has become the hunted!"

Then he gave orders and we came round so that our great sail taken aback flapped against the mast.

"Down with the sail and row," he shouted, "row as never ye rowed before!"

Those at the sweeps obeyed. Oh! it was splendid to see them bending their broad backs and tugging at the oars till these also bent like bows in the water. Here was no slave work, for they were servants of Isis and free men, every one of them. Philo rushed to the steering gear and with the aid of another man took charge of it himself. We leapt forward like a panther on its prey. The *Holy Fire* saw and strove to escape. Too late, too late! For presently the sharp prow of the *Hapi* crashed into her side with such a shock that all who stood upon the deck were thrown down, I among them. I struggled to my feet again and heard Philo screaming,

"Back water! Back! lest she take us with her."

We backed. Slowly the prow appeared again from where it was buried three paces deep in the foeman's flank.

The *Holy Fire* reeled over; the water rushed in through the gap. Crippled and helpless she wallowed; aye, she began to sink. From her swarming decks went up a yell of terror and dismay. Still the water rushed in with an ever-gathering flood and still she sank and sank. Men threw up their arms, praying for mercy; men sprang into the sea. Then suddenly the *Holy Fire* reared her glittering prow into the air and stern foremost vanished into the deep. It was finished!

The Persians swam about us, or clung to wreckage, praying to be taken aboard. But we rowed on coming to the wind again. I know not how it is in the world to-day, but then in time of war there was little mercy. Egypt alone was merciful because age had mellowed her and because of her gentle worship of her gentle gods. But now Egypt was fighting for her life against the Persian. So we rowed on, and those barbarians were abandoned to drown and in the world below seek the warmth of the Fire they worshipped.

Philo left the helm and came to where I stood. I noted that he was white and shaken and called to one to bring him wine. He drank of it thankfully, not forgetting first to pour a libation at my feet, or rather at those of the goddess to whom I was so near.

"Bravely done!" I said. "You understand your trade, Philo."

"Not so ill, Lady, though it might have been better. Had I been at the helm we should have rammed that swarming hulk before the boarding and saved some lives. Well, Set has her now and Ochus lacks his finest ship."

"It might have been far otherwise," I said.

"Aye, Lady. Had I commanded the *Holy Fire* it would have been otherwise, for she had two oars and three men to our one, but her captain was wanting in sea-craft, and when my arrow found him, there was none to take his place. They should have swept us with their boarders, but that all Greek captain called Kallikrates, who they tell me was once a priest, handled his soldiers well. He is a gallant man and I grieve that we are like to lose him."

"Why?" I asked.

"Oh! because in his fight with a fellow whom he flung over the bulwarks, he took a knife-thrust in the vitals, which they think will be mortal. See, they are bearing him to my cabin," and he pointed to Kallikrates being carried forward by four men—a sight that stirred my heart.

Then Philo was summoned away, for it seemed that when the *Hapi* rammed, she sprang a leak and the carpenters called Philo to consult with them as to how it might be stopped.

When they had gone I followed after Kallikrates and found him laid in Philo's cabin. They had taken off his armour and the leech, an Egyptian, was cleaning a cut in his thigh whence the blood ran down his ivory skin.

"Is it mortal?" I asked.

"I know not, Lady," answered the leech, "I cannot tell the depth of the thrust. Pray Isis for him, for he has lost much blood."

Now I who was skilled in medicine and in the treatment of wounds which I had learned from a great master in my youth among the Arabs, helped that physician as best I might, staunching the blood flow and stitching up the cut with silk before we bandaged it.

Moreover, taking from my hand a charmed and ancient amulet that gave health and had the power, so it was said, to cause the sick or wounded to recover, I set it on the finger of Kallikrates that it might cure him. This amulet was a ring of brown stone on which were graven certain hieroglyphics that meant *Royal Son of the Sun*. He who gave it to me told me that it had been worn by that greatest of all healers and magicians, Khaemuas, the eldest son of the mighty Rameses. Once only did I see this ring again as shall be told. Then of it I lost sight and knowledge till, after more than two thousand years, I beheld it on the hand of Holly in the caves of Kor.

As I worked thus the pain of the needle awoke Kallikrates from his swoon. He opened his eyes, looked up and saw me, then muttered in Greek so low that only I who was bending over him heard his words. They were:

"I thank thee, Beloved. I thank thee and the gods who have granted that like my forefathers I should die no priest, but a soldier and a man. Yea, I thank thee, *O royal and beautiful Amenartas*."

Then he swooned again and I left him quickly, having learned that it was of the Egyptian he dreamed, and doubtless that it was for the sake of this same Egyptian that he had changed his sacred robe for mail, yes, the Egyptian Amenartas for whom he had mistaken me, Ayesha, in the wandering of his weakness.

Well, why not? What had I to do with him or any man? Yet of a sudden I grew weary of the world and almost wished that the *Holy Fire* had rammed the *Hapi* and not the *Hapi* the *Holy Fire*.

Yonder behind us a thousand men were now at peace beneath the sea. Being overwrought with all that I had endured and seen, almost I could have wished that I, too, was at peace beneath the sea, sleeping for ever, or perchance to wake again nursed in the holy arms of Isis.

\* \* \* \* \* \* \* \*

In the cabin sat my master, the prophet Noot, staring through the open doorway at the infinite blue of heaven above, as I knew that he had done during all that fearsome fight.

He smiled when he saw me and asked,

"Whence come you, Daughter, and why do your eyes shine like stars?"

"I come from the sight of the death of men, my Father, and my eyes shine with the light of battle."

"With other lights also, I think, Daughter. O Ayesha, beauty is yours, wisdom is yours, and you are filled with spirit like a cup with wine. But what of the cup? What of the cup? I fear me that those fair feet of yours have far to travel before they reach their home."

"What is their home, Father?"

"Do you not know it after these many years of learning? Hearken. I will tell you. Your home is God, not this god or that god called by a hundred names, but the God beyond the gods. Doubtless you will love and you will hate, as you have loved and hated. And doubtless you are destined to draw up what you love and to come to peace with what you hate. Yet know that above all mortal loves there is another love in which they must be both lost and found. God is the end of man, O Ayesha, God or—death. All sin, all stumble on the path, but only those who continue on that path or who, having lost it, with tears and broken hearts seek it again and, like the Sisyphus of fable, thrust before them their frozen load of fleshly error, till at length it melts in the light that shines above; only those, I say, attain to the eternal peace."

So solemnly did he speak, uttering the slow words one by one, and so deep and holy was the lesson that they hid, that I, Ayesha, grew afraid.

"What have you seen and what do you know, my Father?" I asked humbly.

"Daughter, I have seen you yonder in Sidon rejoicing in vengeance for vengeance's sake; aye, glad when the vile hound who would have gripped you, gasped out his life before your eyes. You did not slay him, Ayesha, but it was your counsel that gave cunning to the thought that planned and strength to the arm that dealt the blow."

"It was so fated, O my father, and otherwise——"

"Yes, it was so fated; yet you should not have rejoiced in the hour of your triumph. Nay, you should have sorrowed as the gods sorrow when they fulfil the decrees of Destiny. Again I have seen you burning with the flame of battle, your heart filled with songs of victory when Philo's skill and the Grecian courage of Kallikrates sent those mad brutes of Persians to their account. And lastly unless I dream——What did you but now in Philo's cabin, Daughter?"

"I tended a wounded man, my Father, as I have the skill to do. Also I gave him an amulet which it is said has virtue to heal the sick."

"Aye, that was right and kind and the just reward of courage. Did he thank you, Daughter? I thought that in the quiet I heard thanks come from his lips."

"Nay," I answered sullenly, "his mind wandered and he thanked—another woman who was not there."

Again Noot smiled a little, and answered,

"Was it so? Then let her name be. Yet remember that from such wanderings of a mind distraught ofttimes springs the truth, like water from a shattered rock. Oh! Daughter, Daughter, if this man forgets his vows, must you do the same? For him there is excuse who is a soldier—can we doubt it who have looked upon his deeds today? He became a priest for love's sake, and the shed blood which it brought. But for you there is none—at least none upon the earth," he added hastily. "I pray you, therefore, let this man be, for if you do not, my gift of wisdom tells me that you will bring much trouble on your head and his. Why will you seek after vanity? Is it because in the pride of your beauty you cannot bear that another should be preferred before you and that a fruit which it is not lawful for you to pluck, should fall into some other woman's lap? I say to you, Daughter, that this beauty is your curse, because to it you demand obedience night and day, although of it you should think nothing, remembering its end. You are too proud, you are too puffed up. Look upon the stars and learn to be humble, lest you should be humbled by that which is stronger."

"I am still a woman, Father, a woman whose mission it is to love and to bear babes."

"Then learn to love that which is above and let the babes you bear be those of wisdom and good works. Is it your part to suckle sinners like any hedge-side troll, you to whom the heavens stretch out their hands? Is it for you in whose breast springs the tree of life to root it up and in its place to sow the seed of a woman's common arts, that by their aid you may snatch her lover from a rival? Because he sins, if sin he does, should you cease from being holy? Where is your greatness? Where are your purity and pride? I pray to you, beloved daughter of my spirit, swear to me by Heaven which we serve, that with this man you will have no more to do. Twice have you sinned—once in the sanctuary yonder at Philae when his kiss met yours, and now again not an hour gone upon this ship, when your heart was torn with jealous rage because the name of another woman escaped from lips that you thought were about to shape your own. Twice have you sinned and twice has the goddess turned her head and shut her eyes. But if for a third time you should walk into this pit dug of your own hands, then know that escape will be hard indeed. I tell you"—here his face and his low voice hardened—"I tell you that from age to age shall you strive unceasingly to wash the stain of blood from off those hands and that all your breath shall become a sigh and your every heart-beat shall be an agony. Swear then, swear!"

I looked at his eyes and saw that they were alight and unearthly, yes, that some spirit shining from within caused them to glow like alabaster lamps. I looked at the thin hand which he stretched out toward me and saw that it trembled in his passion.

I looked and was moved to obey. Yet ere I did so I asked,

"Were *you* ever young, my Father? Did *you* ever suffer from this eternal curse which Nature lays on men and women because she would not die? Did *you* ever take the bribe of sweet madness with which she baits her hook? Or, as once I think you told me in bygone years, were you always holy and apart?"

He covered his eyes with those thin hands, then answered,

"I was young. I suffered from that curse. Whatever I may have said to you in the past when you were but a child, I gorged that bait, not once but many times, and I have paid the price. Because I have paid it to my ruin, I pray you whom I love not to empty your heart of its purest virgin gold and fill the void with pain and penitence. Easy is it to fall, Daughter, but hard, very hard to rise again. Will you not swear?"

"Aye," I answered, "I swear by Isis and by your spirit, O Purified."

"You swear," he said, whispering, "but will you keep the oath? I wonder, aye, I wonder greatly, will you keep that oath, O high-hearted woman whose blood runs with so red and strong a stream?"

Then bending forward he kissed me on the brow, and rising left me.

\*\*\*\*\*\*\*\*

Kallikrates did not die. Under the care of that cunning leech or of something above the leech, Death was cheated of him, since it seemed that the knife-thrust had not reached his vitals, or at least had not pierced them beyond repair. Still he was sick for a long while, for his whole body was drained of blood, so that had he been older, or less vigorous, Osiris would have taken him. Or perchance not in vain had I set upon his finger that scarab-talisman once charmed by Khaemuas. I visited him no more, and thus it was not until we were passing up the Nile and drew near to Memphis that I saw him again. Then, very pale and wasted, yet to my fancy more pleasing than he had been, since now his face had grown spiritual and his eyes were those of one that had looked close into those of Death, he was carried in a bed on to the deck. There I spoke with him, thanking him in the name of the goddess for the great deeds that he had done. He smiled and his white face took a little tinge of red as he answered,

"I fear me, O Mouth-of-Isis, that it was not of the goddess that I thought in that fray, but rather of the joy of battle which I, a priest, had never hoped to feel again. Nay, nor was it for the goddess that I smote as best I could, since in the extremities of war the gates of heaven, which are then in truth so near, seem very far away, but rather that after all which you had passed, you, with the rest of us, might not fall into the hands of the heathen fire-worshippers."

Now I smiled back, for the words, if false, were courteous, and replied that doubtless also he, who was still young, desired to go on living.

"Nay," he answered earnestly, "I think that I desire to die rather than to live, and to pass hence as often my forefathers have done, sword in hand and helm on head. Life is no boon to a shaven priest, Lady, one who by his vows is cut off from all its joys."

"What is a man's joy in life?" I asked.

"Look at yourself in a mirror, Lady, and you will learn," he answered, and there was that in his voice which caused me to wonder whether it was possible after all that the wrong name came from his lips in the wanderings of his mind.

For then I did not know that a man may love two women and at the same time; one with his spirit and the other with his flesh, since through all things runs this war between the spirit and the flesh. The spirit of Kallikrates was always mine, having been given to me from the beginning, but with his flesh it was otherwise, and perchance while he is in the flesh it will so remain.

Before we reached Memphis a signal was made for us to anchor. Then a barge, flying the standard of Pharaoh, came off to us from the shore. On board of it was Nectanebes himself and with him his daughter, the Princess of Egypt, the lady Amenartas; also certain councillors and Grecian captains in his service.

The Pharaoh and the others came aboard to learn tidings of what had chanced at Sidon, and were received by Philo and by Noot. Presently they demanded to be led to me and I met them on the deck outside my cabin, noting that the eyes of Nectanebes were troubled and that his fat cheeks had fallen in.

"So you are returned to us, Oracle-of-Isis," he said in a hesitating voice, scanning my form, for my face he could not see because it was veiled.

"I am returned, O Pharaoh," I answered, bowing before his Majesty. "It has pleased Her whom I serve to deliver me out of the hands of King Tenes of Sidon, to whom Pharaoh offered me as a gift."

"Aye, I remember. It was at that feast when the water in the cup you held turned to blood. Well, if all I hear is true, there has been blood enough out yonder."

"Yes, Pharaoh, the Sidonian sea runs red with it. Tenes, Egypt's ally, surrendered the city to Ochus the Persian, thinking to find great advancement, which he won by death, whereon the Sidonians burned themselves in their houses with their wives and children. So it comes about that all Phoenicia is in the hands of Ochus who advances upon Egypt with a mighty host."

"The gods have deserted me!" moaned Nectanebes, waving his arms.

"Aye, Pharaoh," I answered in a cold voice, "for the gods are very jealous and seldom forgive those who forsake them and betray their servants into the hands of enemies that hate them."

He understood and answered in a low, babbling voice,

"Be not angry with me, Oracle-of-Isis, for what else could I do? That Sidonian dog, whom may Set devour eternally, was mad for you. Always I mistrusted him and I was sure that if I refused you to him, he would make his peace with Ochus and bite me in the back, as indeed he threatened at the feast. Also I knew well that Mother Isis would protect you from all harm at his hands, which it seems that she has done."

Now when I heard these words rage filled me and I answered,

"Aye, Pharaoh, Mother Isis has done this and more. Have you heard how your poison worked? Nay? Then I will tell you. Having sacrificed her only son to Dagon, Tenes would have put away Beltis, his queen, to give her place to me. Mad with hate, Beltis led him into the arms of the Persian and afterward when his treachery was accomplished, slew him with her own hand, for I saw the deed. And now, Pharaoh, Sidon has fallen and with it all Phoenicia, and soon, Pharaoh, Egypt will follow Sidon. Aye, I, the Oracle, tell you that because you were pleased to throw the high-priestess of Isis into the arms of Tenes as though she were some singing woman of whom you had wearied, these things have come about. Therefore too soon there will no longer be a Pharaoh in Egypt and the Persian will take the Land of Nile and defile the altars of its gods."

He heard. He trembled. He had naught to say. But there was another who heard also. As I had noted, the Princess Amenartas, when she came on to the ship, went straight to where Kallikrates lay upon a couch beneath an awning on the deck, and there talked with him earnestly. What they said I could not hear for they spoke together beneath their breath. But their faces I could see, and watching them I grew sure that the Greek had made no error of a mind distraught when he spoke this royal lady's name as I tended his wounds. For those faces were the faces of lovers who met after long separation and the passing of great dangers.

Leaving Kallikrates this Amenartas had returned to her father and stood at his side listening to our talk. Now she broke in fiercely,

"Surely, Priestess, you were ever a bird of evil omen croaking of disaster. You fly to Sidon and lo! Sidon burns, yet you escape with wings unscorched. Now you flit back to Egypt and again wail of woe like a night owl of the desert. How is it, O *Isis-come-to-Earth*, as it pleases you to call yourself, that you alone escape from Sidon and return here to curdle the blood of men with prophecies such as those you uttered at the feast when by a trick you turned the water into blood? Have you perchance made friends with Ochus?"

"Ask it of Philo the captain of this ship, Lady," I answered in a quiet voice. "Or stay. Ask it of yonder priest which perchance will please you better, the Grecian who in the world was named Kallikrates. Ask them how I showed friendship to Ochus by so working through the strength of Isis and their skill and valour that the Persian's finest ship of war with a multitude of his sailors and fighting men lies to-day at the bottom of the deep."

"Perchance because a captain was skilled and a certain priest, or soldier, was brave, that ship is sunk with all she bore, but not, I think, through you or your prayers, O Oracle. I say to you, Pharaoh, my father, that if I held your sceptre I would send this *Isis-Come-To-Earth* to seek Isis in Heaven ere she bring more sorrows on us and Egypt."

"Nay, nay," muttered Nectanebes, rolling his big eyes, "speak not so madly, Daughter, lest the Mother should hear and once more smite me. Hearken. Last night I, who have skill, consulted my spirit, the Daemon who obeys me. He came, he spoke. I heard him with my ears. Yes, he spoke of this prophetess. He said that she drew near to Memphis on a ship. He said that she was great, almost a goddess, that she must be cherished, that to you and me she would be a shelter from the storm, that in her is the power of One who sits above. O Oracle, O *Isis-come-to-Earth*, O Wisdom's Daughter, forgive the wild words of this royal child of mine who is distraught with fear, and know that, to the last, Pharaoh is your friend and your protector."

"As mayhap, if this Daemon of yours speaks truth, before all is done I shall be the protector of Pharaoh and of the Princess of Egypt whom it pleases to revile me," I replied.

Then bowing to him I turned and sought my cabin.

## CHAPTER 13

# The Shame of Pharaoh

When Pharaoh and his daughter had gone, though I did not see them go, I bade farewell to Philo, thanking him much and, in reward for all he had done, calling down on him the blessing of the goddess which he received upon his bended knees. Moreover, when he had risen from them he swore himself to my service, saying that while he lived he would come even from the ends of the earth to do my will. Also he showed me how I might call him by certain secret ways.

So we bade farewell for a while, nor did I let him go empty-handed, since from those jewels that Tenes had heaped upon me, which almost by accident I had preserved in my flight, I took certain of great value and gave them to him as a gift from the goddess. Thus we parted though, as both of us were sure, not for the last time.

So soon as our coming was known the priests and priestesses of Isis flocked to the quay in solemn procession to receive Noot, their high-priest, and me their high-priestess, which they did with sacred ceremony and holy chants. By them we were escorted through the streets of Memphis to the temple of Isis accompanied by many of the crew of the *Hapi* that were of our brotherhood. Among them I missed one.

"Where is the priest Kallikrates?" I asked of Noot.

He smiled and answered,

"I think that he has been taken to the palace of Pharaoh to be nursed until he recovers from his wounds. Perchance for a while he is minded, or it is decreed that he should continue to play a warrior's part. Yet fear not, Daughter; those upon whose brow Isis has laid her hands, in life or death must return to her at last. They are hawks upon a string which, though it stretches, cannot be broken."

"Aye," I answered, "in life or death," and asked no more of this Kallikrates.

In the midst of the rejoicings of the city at our safe return, we came to the temple and made sacrifice. There it was that I set the jewels of Tenes, all save those that I had given to Philo, upon the alabaster statue of the goddess in her inmost shrine that only I and Noot might enter, and there too by signs and wonders she signified to me her acceptance of the offering. For here while we stood alone before the effigy of the goddess in that holy place, a trance fell upon Noot and in his trance he spoke to me with the voice of Isis and out of her infinite heart. This was the divine message that came to me through the lips of Noot:

"Daughter, I, thy mother, know of all that thou hast passed and of all that thou must pass. Though the barbarian come and the gods of Egypt are thrown down and ruin smites the land and thou seemest to be left alone, abide thou here till my word bids thee to depart. By myself and That of which under the name of Isis I am a minister, I swear that no harm shall befall thee or that place where thou art, or those of my servants who remain with thee. Therefore await my commands with patience, doing such things as I inspire thee to do, that thou mayest bring the vengeance of the gods upon those dogs who desecrate their shrines."

Thus spoke Noot in his trance, not knowing what he had said until I told him afterward. He listened earnestly and bade me obey.

"Even if I be taken from you for a while, as it comes to me will happen—perchance I learned it in my swoon, Daughter—and you are left unfriended and alone, still I pray you to obey. If so, think not that I am dead, who do but return to my own place and land, but wait until my message comes. Then obey that also though I know not what it will be."

Thus he spoke solemnly and I bowed my head and hid his words within my heart——

* * * * * * *

The war began, Egypt's last war for life. Nectanebes as the Pharaoh, inspired by his evil Daemon, thrust aside his captains and declared himself General in Chief of his armies, he who had scarce the wit or the courage to command the guard of a harem. At first that Daemon served him well, since at Barathra, as the gulfs are named which make the Sirbonian bog, the Persians were trapped and lost many thousands of their men who sank through the sand into the marshes and there were drowned or speared. But their numbers were uncountable and the rest came on. Pelusium was besieged and for a while held its own against the giant Nicostratus of Argos, a man as strong as Hercules who, like Hercules, clothed himself in a lion's skin and for a weapon bore a great club. The Grecian captain, Kleinios of Cos, he who had been present at the feast when I was given over to Tenes and whom in my vision at that feast I had seen dead, lying upon a heap of slain, attacked Nicostratus and after a mighty fight was defeated, Kleinios and five thousand men of those who were with him being slain. Thus was my vision fulfilled.

Then his Daemon departed from Nectanebes taking his heart with him, for of a sudden Pharaoh ceased to be a man and, becoming a coward, fled back to Memphis, leaving his fleet, his cities, and their garrisons to their fates.

Rumour ran fast; it told of the fall of city after city, some stormed, some bribed to surrender; it told that Ochus had sworn to burn Memphis and after it Thebes; also to seize Nectanebes and roast him living upon the altar in the great temple of Ptah here at Memphis, or otherwise to make him fight with the bull Apis after the beast had been driven mad by fiery darts. It told that the Egyptians, enraged at the desertion of their armies by Pharaoh, would themselves seize him and give him up to Ochus as a peace-offering. Crowds gathered and rushed through the streets of Memphis calling imprecations on his name, or clustered like bees round the altars of the gods, praying for help in their despair, yes, round the neglected altars of the gods of Egypt.

Then of a sudden came Amenartas, flying to the temple of Isis for sanctuary, since it was reported that Ochus had said that the shrines of Isis he would spare alone, because she was the Mother of all things and her throne was the moon and her husband was Osiris-Ra, who was the Father of fire which he worshipped; also because a certain priestess of the goddess had done him great service in the war, words that caused me to wonder.

So this royal priestess came and put on the veil of a novice that it might protect her should Ochus take the city. But though this veil changed her face and form to the eyes of men, her heart it did not change.

A little later came Kallikrates from the war in the Delta where I learned that he had done great things, fighting bravely. Indeed he told me himself that he had fought the giant Nicostratus in single combat and wounded him, though the matter was not pressed to an end, since others rushed up and separated them. He said that he was a very terrible man, and that when that huge club of his wavered above him, for the first time in his life he felt afraid. Notwithstanding he ran in beneath the club and stabbed Nicostratus in the shoulder.

Thus it happened that all being lost in war and his service at an end, Kallikrates the captain once more became Kallikrates the priest and again put on the robes of Isis. Therefore in that temple, serving together before its altars were Amenartas, Princess of Egypt, and Kallikrates, priest of Isis.

Often I, Ayesha, seated in my chair of state as first of that holy company, save the aged Noot alone, watched them from beneath my veil while they anointed the statue of the goddess or joined in the sacred chants and hymns of praise. As I watched I noted this—that always they drew near together as though some strength compelled them; that always their glances thrown from the corners of their eyes, met and turned away and met again, and that always, if occasion served, the robe of the one brushed the robe of the other, or the hand of the one touched the hand of the other. These things I noted in silence, wondering what judgment the goddess would call down upon this beauteous pair who dared thus to violate her sanctuary with their earthly passion. Oh! much I wondered, though little did I guess what it would be and by whose hand it was destined to fall upon them.

Lastly came Nectanebes himself, his great eyes full of terror and his fat frame wasted with woe and sleeplessness. He sought audience of me.

"O Prophetess," he said, "all is lost! Ochus Artaxerxes has his foot upon my neck. I fly, seeking shelter beneath the wings of Isis, seeking shelter from you, O *Isis-come-to-earth*. Help me, Daughter divine, for my Daemon has deserted me, or if he comes at all it is but to jibber and to mock."

"Strange words from Pharaoh," I answered in a voice of scorn, "very strange words from Pharaoh who gave this same prophetess to be the woman of a vile, Baal-serving king; from Pharaoh who has deserted his army, his country, and his gods, and now seeks only to save his treasure and his life."

"Reproach me not," he moaned, "Fate has been too strong for me, as perchance one day it may be too strong for you also. At first all went well. In the bygone years I conquered the Persian; I built temples to the gods. Then of a sudden Fortune hid her face and now—and now!"

"Aye, O fallen Pharaoh," I answered, "and why did Fortune hide her face? I will tell it, to whom it has been revealed. It was because although you built temples to the gods, you were false to the gods. In secret, following the counsel of that Daemon of yours, you made bloody sacrifice to devils, to Baal, to Ashtoreth, and to Aphrodite of the Greeks. Nay, do not start and deny, for I know all. Lastly, to crown your crimes, you gave me, the high-prophetess of Isis, to the base,

411

red-handed Tenes, one who offered his own son to idols. What has chanced to Tenes who took me, and say, what shall chance to him who sold me, O Nectanebes no more a Pharaoh?"

Now I thought that surely he would kill me and cared not if he did. For my heart was sore—oh! because of many things my heart was sore. But like a beaten cur he only cowered at my feet, praying me to pardon him, praying me to cease from beating him with my tongue, praying me to counsel him. I listened and pity took hold of me, who was ever tender-minded though a lover of justice and a hater of traitors.

"Hearken," I said at last. "If Ochus finds you here, O fallen Pharaoh, first he will make a mock of you and then he will torture you to death. I have heard what he will do. He will bring you to his judgment seat and lay you bound upon your back and grind his sandals upon your face. Then he will force you to sacrifice to the fire that he worships and one by one to spit upon the effigies of the gods of Egypt. Lastly, either he will cause the holy bull Apis to gore you to death, or he will bind you upon the altar in the temple of Ptah and there slowly with torments bring you to your end."

Now when Nectanebes heard these things, he wept and I thought that he would swoon away.

"Hearken," I said again, "I will show you a road whereby although defeated and disgraced you may yet win glory that shall be told of from age to age. Summon the people while there is yet time. Go to the temple of Ammon, King of the gods of Egypt. Stand before the shrine of Ammon and make confession of your sins in the ears of all. Then, there in the sight of all, slay yourself, praying Ammon and all the gods to accept your life as an offering and to spare Egypt and the people upon whose head you, the hated of the gods, have brought all these woes. So can you cause the Persian and the world to marvel and say that though accursed, still you were great, and so perchance you shall turn away the wrath of heaven from apostate Egypt."

A flash of pride shone in his eyes that had been empty of light and filled with tears. He lifted his head stiffly as though still it felt the weight of the great earrings of state, the golden *uraeus*, and the double crown. For a moment he looked as once he had done at Sais reviewing his triumphant army after his first victory over the Persians and drinking in the incense of its shouts, yes, he looked as great Thotmes and the proud Rameses might have done in their day, a Pharaoh, the king of all the world he knew.

"It would be well to die thus," he murmured, "it would be very well, and then, perhaps, the gods I have betrayed would forgive me, the old, old gods to whom thirty dynasties of recorded kings have bowed the knee, and those who went before them for unnumbered generations. Yes, then perhaps that great company of Pharaohs would not turn their backs on me or spit at me when I join them at the table of Osiris. But, Prophetess"—here his face fell in again and his crab-like eyes projected and rolled, while his voice sank to a whisper, "Prophetess, *I dare not.*"

"Why, Nectanebes?"

"Because—oh! because years ago I struck a bargain with a certain Power of the Under-world, a daemon if you will, at least some spirit of evil that comes I know not whence and dwells I know not where, which became manifest to me. It promised me glory and success if I would sacrifice to it—nay, I will not tell what I sacrificed, but once I had a son, yes, like Tenes I had a son———"

Here I, Ayesha, shivered, then motioned to him to speak on.

"This was the bargain, that though to please the people I might build temples to the gods, by certain means I must defile them in their shrines. Aye, and I did defile them, and when the priest dressed me, the Pharaoh, in the trappings of those gods according to custom, by thought and word and deed I blasphemed them. Yet one divinity remained outside the pact because my Daemon warned me that she was too strong for him and must not be offended," and he paused.

"Was she perchance named Isis?" I asked.

"Aye, prophetess, she was named Isis and therefore I never polluted her shrine and therefore to her alone in my heart I offered prayer. So all went well and I gathered great armies and vast wealth, I hired Greeks by thousands to fight for me, I made alliances with many kings and was sure that again I should defeat the Persians and be the master of the world. Then came the evil hour of that accursed feast at which you, the Mouth of Isis, were summoned to prophesy and, moved by some madness, you unveiled your beauty before Tenes, and I, forgetting whose minister you were, gave you to Tenes, thereby outraging Isis in your person."

"Did I not warn you, Nectanebes, and did not the holy Noot warn you?"

"Aye, you warned me, but in my need I took the risk, or I forgot. From that moment all went ill and ruin, like a giant before whom none may stand, has hunted me by night and day."

"Yes, Nectanebes, and Isis is the name of that giant."

"I made error upon error," he went on. "I trusted to Tenes and Tenes betrayed me. My Daemon counselled me to thrust aside the

Grecian generals and take command of the armies, and at first there was victory, then came defeat. It might have been retrieved, but of a sudden my courage failed me. It fell like a temple of which the foundations have been washed out by hidden waters. It crashed down; in a moment its proud pylons, its tall columns, its massive, honourable walls blazoned with the records of glorious deeds, fell to a shapeless heap hidden in the dust of shame. I am undone. I am what you see, a loathsome worm, a wounded worm wriggling in the black slime of despair, I who was Pharaoh."

Again pity touched me, Ayesha, and I answered,

"There still remains the road that I have pointed out. While we live, however black our record, repentance is always possible, since otherwise there would be no hope for man the sinner. Moreover, repentance, if it be true, brings amendment in its train, and this god-born pair struggling upward, hand in hand, over cruel rocks, through swamps and streams, through brakes and briars, blinded with tears and the gross darkness of despair, at length see the sweet shape of Forgiveness shining before them like a holy dawn such as never gleams upon this world. Hearken, therefore, to one who speaks not with her own voice, or out of the foolishness of her own weak flesh, but as she is commanded of a spirit that is within her. Go to the temple of Ammon and there in the presence of the people make confession of your sins and fall, a sacrifice, upon your sword. Self-murder is a sin, but occasions come when to live on is a greater sin, since it is better to die for others than to cherish breath that poisons them."

"To die! There you speak it, Prophetess. I say again that I dare not die. When I die I pass to the Daemon. This was the pact: that for my life he should give me success and glory and that in return after death, I should surrender him my soul."

"Is it so?" I answered. "Well, the bargain is ancient, as old as the world, I think; one also that every human being in his degree seals or refuses to seal in this way or in that. Still my counsel holds. This Daemon of yours has broken his oath, for where now are the success and glory, Nectanebes? Therefore he cannot claim the fulfilment of your own."

"Nay, Prophetess," he answered in a wailing voice, "he has *not* broken it. From the first he told me that I must work no harm to Isis the Mother, since the Queen of Heaven was more powerful than all the denizens of hell, and that if once it were spoken, her Word of Strength would pierce and shrivel him like a red-hot sword and cutting his web of spells, would bring his oaths to nothingness and me with them. And now the web is cut, and I the painted insect that it meshed, fall from it to where the hell-born spider sits in his hole. Prophetess, I have seen him with these eyes, I have seen his orbs of fire, I have seen his snout and fangs like to those of a crocodile, I have seen his great hairy arms and the searching talons stretched out to grip me, and I tell you that I dare not die to be cast into the jaws of the Devourer and burn eternally in his belly of flames. Show me how to save my life, so that I may continue to look upon the sun. Oh! because you are a tender woman and charitable, though I have sinned against you, show me how to save my life."

Now hearing this creature plead with me thus, this coward who at the last did not dare go face the indignant gods like a man, saying, as a great soul should, "I have deeply erred, O ye Gods; I repent, pardon me of your nobility, or slay my soul and make an end," my pity left me and its place was filled with scorn and loathing.

"Those who would live when the Persian dogs are on their heels, must fly fast and far, Nectanebes; they must fly like the deer of the desert on whom the hunters close. The road up Nile is empty, Nectanebes; as yet there are no Persians there. As you would not die, take it and live."

"Aye," he said as the thought went home, "why not? I have still a vast treasure; for many years I have hoarded against misfortune, for who can put all his trust in any Daemon? With it I can buy friends in the south; with it I may found another empire among the Ethiopians or those of Punt. Why should I not fly, Prophetess?"

"I know not," I answered, "save that Death is always fast and untiring and in the end wears down the swiftest runner."

This I said darkly for at that moment there came into my mind a vision that once I had seen of a certain servile slave, aforetime a Pharaoh, that same royal slave who grovelled before me; yea, a vision of him throttling in a rope while black men mocked him. Yet of that I said nothing, only added,

"If it should please you to go south, Nectanebes, would it please you also to take with you that royal and beautiful lady, Amenartas your daughter, aforetime Princess of Egypt?"

"Nay," he answered sharply, "since hour by hour she scourges me with her tongue because I am fallen. Let her abide here under the veil of Isis. Yet why do you ask this, Prophetess?"

"Because of Isis. Because, as I think, this lady of the royal blood makes play with a certain priest who is sworn to Isis, and the goddess does not love that her vowed servitors should desert her for the sake of mortal woman."

"What priest?" he asked dully.

"A Greek who is named Kallikrates."

"I know him, Prophetess. A very beauteous man, like to their own Apollo; a brave one too who did good service yonder in the marshes, fighting the giant general whom he wounded. Also I remember that in the past he was a captain of my guard before he became a priest and that there was trouble concerning him, though what trouble I forget, save that Amenartas pleaded for him. Well, if he has offended you, there are still those who do my will. Send for him, and if it pleases you, he shall be killed. I give you his life. Yes, his blood shall flow at your feet. Indeed I will command it at once, since you tell me he has shamed the goddess or angered you, her priestess," and he opened his hands to clap them, summoning the messengers of death.

I saw, I thrust my arm between so that they struck not upon each other, but upon my soft flesh, making no sound.

"Nay," I said, "this warrior-priest is a good servant of the Queen Isis, one, moreover, who fought for me, her prophetess, upon the seas. He shall not die for so small a matter. Yet I pray you, Nectanebes, take with you the royal princess Amenartas, when you fly south with your treasure."

"Aye," he answered wearily, "as it is your desire I'll take her if she will come, though if so there will be small rest for me."

Then he went, bowing to me humbly, and this was my farewell to Nectanebes, the last Pharaoh of Egypt. I watched him go and wondered whether I had done well in forbidding him to kill Kallikrates. It came into my mind that the death of this man would save me much trouble. Why should he not die as others did who had sinned against the goddess? An answer rose within me. It was that he had sinned, not only against the goddess, but also against me—and this by preferring another woman before me.

Was I then so feeble that I could not hold my own against another woman should I choose to do so? Nay. Yet my trouble was that I did not choose.

Now I saw the truth. My rebellious flesh desired that which my spirit rejected. My spirit was far from this man, yet my flesh would have him near. Aye, my flesh said: "Let him be slain rather than another should take him," while my spirit answered, "What has he to do with one whose soul is set upon things above? Let him go his way, and go you yours. Above all, be not stained with his blood."

So I let him go, not knowing that it was written in the books of Fate that I *must* be stained with his blood, steeped in it to the eyes. Aye,

I saved him from the sword of Nectanebes and let him go, determining to think of him no more.

Yet as it chanced Fate played me an evil trick in this matter. On the morrow, or the next day, I sat in the gloom of the outer sanctuary praying to the goddess to ease me of my sore heart, for alas! strive as I would to hide it, that heart was sore. There came a white-robed priest, Kallikrates himself, but changed indeed from that glorious Grecian warrior who had beat back the boarders on the *Hapi*, or who had fought in single combat with the giant Nicostratus. For now the little golden curls were shaven from his head and he was pale with the thin diet of the fruits of the earth and pure water which alone might pass the lips of those who were sworn to Isis, enough indeed for me who touched no other food, or such a one as the aged Noot, but not for a great-framed man bred to the trade of arms. Moreover, his face was troubled as though with some struggle of the soul.

He passed me unseen and going to the statue of the goddess, knelt down before it and prayed earnestly, perhaps for help and blessing. Rising at length, once more he passed me and I saw that his gray eyes were full of tears and longed to comfort him. Also I saw that still he carried on his hand that ring talisman which I had set there upon the ship *Hapi*, that it might perchance defend him from the evil influences which desire and compass the death of men.

He went out across the pillared court toward the cloister at its end. From this cloister appeared a woman, the dark and beauteous Amenartas herself. This was easy to see since, I know not why, she had put off the veil of Isis and was gloriously attired in the robes of a princess—scanty enough I thought them, for they left bare much of her loveliness—while on her dark and abundant hair shone a golden circlet from which rose the royal *uraeus*, and on her arms and bosom sparkled jewels and necklaces.

They meet by plan, thought I to myself. But it was not so, for seeing her, Kallikrates started and turned to fly; also he covered his eyes with his hand as though to hide her beauty from him. She lifted her face like one who pleads, yes, and when he would not hearken, caught him by the hand and drew him into the shadow of the cloister.

There they remained a long while, for at this hour the place was deserted by all. At length they appeared again on the edge of the shadow and I saw that her arms were about him and that her head rested on his breast. They separated. She vanished into the shadows and went her way, while he walked to and fro across the court, muttering to himself like a man who knows not what he does.

I came from my place and met him, saying,

"Surely you are troubled, Priest. Can it be that the goddess refuses your prayers? Or is it perchance that you weary of them and would still play the part of a warrior of warriors as you did on the galley *Hapi*, or but the other day yonder in the northern marshes? If so, it is too late, Priest, for Egypt is fallen and all is lost. That is, unless, like Mentor and many of your race, you would sell your sword to Ochus Artaxerxes."

"Aye, Prophetess," he answered, "Egypt is lost which, being a Greek, should not trouble me over much, and I too am lost, I, the driven of an evil fate."

"Speak on it if it pleases you. Or be silent if it pleases you, O Priest. What the prophetess hears, she tells only to the Mother."

Then I turned and went back into the shadow of the shrine where I leaned against a pillar—I remember that on it was sculptured the scene of Thoth weighing hearts before Osiris. Here I waited, wondering whether he would follow me or go his ways.

For a while he stood hesitating, but at length he followed me.

"Prophetess," he said hoarsely, "I speak under the veil of Isis, knowing that such confessions cannot be revealed. Yet it is hard to speak, since the matter has to do with woman, aye, and with yourself, most holy Prophetess."

"In Isis I have no self," I answered.

"Prophetess, in bygone years, as I think you know, I learned to love a royal maiden, one set far above me, and it seems that she loved me. That passion brought a brother's blood upon my hands, as you also know. I fled to the goddess, seeking peace and forgiveness. For in me I think there are two selves, the self of my body and the self of my soul."

"As in most that breathe beneath the sun," I answered, sighing.

"I was bred a soldier, one who came from a race of soldiers, men of high blood and good to look upon, as once I was, though in this garb few would guess it."

"I have seen you wearing war-harness and can guess," I answered, smiling a little.

"That soldier-self, Prophetess, was as are others of the breed. I drank and I revelled, I bowed the knee to Aphrodite, loving women and for an hour being loved. I fought, not without honour. Then seeking advancement, with my brother I entered the service of Pharaoh, and of that story doubtless you know the rest."

I bowed my head and he went on,

"I came to Philae, I made confession, I took the first vows. At

418

night and alone I was led to the sanctuary, there to see the vision of the goddess. I saw that vision glowing in the darkened shrine, and oh! it was glorious."

Here I started and watched him narrowly, wondering how much he knew or guessed.

"Something took hold of me, Prophetess, for now I beheld her whom all my soul adored, her with whom it would be united. It was as though a memory came to me from afar, a memory and a promise. That Power which took hold of me caused me to bend my head as though to kiss the vision and thereby pledge my soul to the divine. The vision also bent its head and our lips met, and lo! hers were like to those of mortal woman, yet sweeter far."

"The Mother is mistress of all shapes, Priest. Yet think not that she forgets the pledge that thus it pleased her to accept. From that moment you were sworn to her, and doubtless in a day to come, in this form or in that, she will claim you—should you remain true to her, O Priest."

"The years passed," he went on, "and true I remained. Fate brought me here to Memphis and in this temple I saw you, holy Prophetess, and learned to worship you from afar, not with the body, but with the spirit; since to me you were and are what the vulgar call you, *Isis-Come-To-Earth*, and the sight of you ever put me in mind, as it does to-day, of that divine vision whose lips met mine in the shrine at Philae. Perchance you never knew it, but thus with my spirit I worshipped you."

Now I, Ayesha, remained silent, leaning against the pillar, for weakness took hold of me who felt as though I were about to fall. Yet—and let the vengeful gods write this to my honour—yet I made him no sign that I was she who had played the part of Isis in the sanctuary.

"It is well," I said presently, "and doubtless at the appointed hour the goddess will thank you. But what then is your trouble, Priest? To love a goddess with the spirit is no crime."

"Aye, Prophetess. But what if he who loves the goddess with his spirit and is sworn to her alone for ever in a vow of perpetual chastity, should love a woman with his flesh and thus betray both heaven and his own soul?"

"Then, Priest," I answered, speaking very low, "I fear that he is one whose hope of forgiveness is but small. Yet for those who repent and deny, there is pardon. Only they must deny, they must deny while there is still time."

"Easy to say and hard to do," he answered, "at least for him who has to deal with one that will not be denied; with one who holds his heart in the hollow of her hand and crushes it; with one whose eyes are like star-beacons to which the wanderer must fly; with one whose breath is as roses and whose lips are as honey; with one who can drive the desires of man as a racer drives his chariot; with one to whom oaths also have been sworn, such oaths as the youth swears to the maid in the first madness of the flesh, decreed by those who made it. Goddesses are far away, but woman is near; moreover, among men there is a law which even a prophetess may understand, which says that oaths vowed with the lips may not be broken to benefit the vower's soul."

"These are ancient arguments," I answered; "from age to age they echo from the roofs of the temples of Aphrodite and of Ashtoreth, but Isis knows them not. The flesh is given to mankind that its wearers may learn to scorn and trample it; the spirit is given to mankind that its holders may learn to rise upon its wings. Woe to those who choose the flesh and reject the spirit. Repentance is still possible, and after it comes amendment and after amendment, forgiveness."

He brooded awhile, then said,

"Prophetess, I repent who above all things desire at the end—that end which again and again I have sought in battle wherever it has passed me by—to be united with the goddess, shaped like the divine one whom I saw at the shrine of Philae. Yes, with her and with no other. But how can I amend who am a lion in a net, a net woven of woman's hair?"

Now I searched him with my eyes and learned that although so sore beset, this man spoke nothing but the truth. Then I answered,

"The wise bird flies the snare which it sees spread in its sight. To-morrow at the dawn Noot the Holy sails north to meet certain ambassadors of the Persians and if he can make terms, to ransom the temples of Isis from the rage of Ochus. Will you go with him, breathing no word of his purpose or of yours? If so, perchance thus at last you shall find that goddess whose lips met yours at Philae, here—or otherwhere."

He thought awhile, then muttered,

"It is hard, very hard, yet I will go; I who would satisfy my soul and not my flesh."

********

As he spoke a tall priestess flitted past us, passing from shadow into shadow, but thinking that she was one of those whose duty it was to watch the inner shrine at this hour, I took no note of her. Nor did Kallikrates, lost in his own thoughts, so much as see her.

## CHAPTER 14

# The Beguiling of Bagoas

That night Noot my master came to bid farewell to me.

"I go north as I have been commanded—as to how the command came, let that be—hoping thereby to preserve the temples of our worship and those who serve in them. I know not if I shall return, or when, and therefore, Daughter of my spirit, it grieves me to part from you in these troublous times. Yet the command said that you must not accompany me but bide here. For your comfort, learn two things: first, that no harm shall come to you, as I have told you before; and secondly, though that hour be far away, even in the flesh we shall meet again. Wait then till my word comes to you."

I bowed my head in obedience and asked whether he was unattended.

"Nay, Daughter," he answered. "I take with me certain of our fellowship, and among them that Greek Kallikrates who has asked leave to accompany me. Being a man of war, as you have seen, he may perchance prove of service upon such a mission. How he learned that I was going I cannot say," he added, looking at me curiously.

"I told him. Ask no more, Master."

"There is little need, I think," he answered, smiling. "It may please you to learn," he added bitterly, "that the traitor who was Pharaoh, flies up Nile to-morrow ere the dawn. Already they lade his ship with the chests of Egypt's treasure, many of them, that should have gone to pay his soldiers and strengthen his allies."

"May the counting of them comfort him in his honourable exile among the Ethiopians! Yet, my Master, I think that he will need to count quickly, unless it pleased the gods to send a false vision to me when I prophesied in the palace yonder, ere this shameless Nectanebes gave the Daughter of Isis to Tenes the Sidonian."

"If so, Ayesha, the gods sent a false vision to me also. How will he face them, I wonder, with the blood of Egypt on his hands, and with what voice will he tell them of their desecrated shrines?"

"I know not, Master, yet it was written that because of her apostasies and sins Egypt must fall. Can the gods, then, be wroth with their own instrument?"

Noot pondered awhile, shaking his head, then answered,

"Go ask that question of the Sphinx who sits yonder in the sand by the pyramids of the ancient kings brooding, as the legend says, over the secrets of earth and heaven. Or," he added slowly, "when your own days are done, Ayesha, ask it of your soul. Perchance then some god will make clear the riddle of the world below, but here on earth it cannot be answered, since he who could read it would know all things and be himself a god. Sin must come, and to sin, sinners are necessary. But to what sin is necessary, I do not know, unless it be that from it good is born at last. At least the sinner can plead that he is but an arrow on the bow of Destiny and that the arrow must fly where the shooter aims, even though it drinks innocent blood, widows women, and makes children fatherless."

"Mayhap, my Master, it will be answered to this arrow that it fashioned itself to deal out death; that it grew the wood and forged the barb and bound upon its shaft the feathers of desire; which wood, had it chosen otherwise, here or elsewhere might have flourished—a tree bearing fruits—or as seasoned wood, shaped itself to be a staff to lean upon or a rod of justice in the hands of kings."

"You are wise, Ayesha, nor have I instructed you in vain," he replied with a gentle smile. "Yet I repeat, when for the last time you watch the sun sink and your soul prepares to follow it over the edge of the world, then again propound to it this riddle and hear the answer of that invisible Sphinx which broods in the heaven above, on the earth below, and in the breast of every child it bears."

Thus he spoke and waved his hand, making an end of that debate. Nor have I ever forgotten it, or his words, and now when sometimes I feel or hope soon I, even I, the half-immortal, may see the sun sink for the last time, once more, as Noot commanded, I ask this riddle of the Sphinx that broods within my instructed spirit, and wait its answer. For alas and alas! how am I better than Nectanebes? He betrayed the gods. Have I not betrayed the gods who were nearer to me than ever they came to his coarse and gluttonous soul? He shed blood to satisfy his rage and lust. Have I not shed blood and shall I not perchance shed more of it before all is done, when my unconquerable appetites are on me and there is a dear prize that I would win? He fled with the treasures of Egypt to waste them in the desert sand. Have I not fled with the treasures that were given me—with the jewelled crowns of my wisdom, with the golden talents of my heaped-up learning, with the alabaster vessel of my beauty, with the perfumes of my power and my eloquence—that drilled, ordered, and massed together, and added to the greatest gift of all, my length of undying days, might have re-formed the world and led it into peace?

Have I, Ayesha, not fled with all these countless splendours clasped upon my breast, and buried them in the wilderness, as did Nectanebes with Egypt's wealth, before the barbarians slew him? Have I not done these things because of a great desire and because, robbed of that desire, the world I should have guided was gall to my tongue and gravel to my teeth? Yet was I to blame? Was not that blind man I loved to blame who could not see with his darkened, fleshy eyes the glory that lay within his grasp and thus stirred my soul to madness? Was not the woman to blame also who darkened those eyes of his by arts the evil gods had given her?

Oh! I know not. Perchance they too can put up a tale before the Judgment Seat which I shall find it hard to answer, for they too are as they were made, or as they made themselves, shaping their own arrows from the wood of circumstance that grew I know not where. And now my desire has drawn near to me again; it gleams, a glittering fruit, upon the Tree of Life, and I stretch out my hand to pluck it. Yes, I stand on tiptoe and almost reach it with my finger-tips. Yet what if it prove a corruption? What if it crumble into dust, rotted by the great sun of my spirit, withered at the fingering of my undying hand?

Oh! my lord hunts upon the mountain after the fashion of men, and Atene, once named Amenartas, sits in her dark beauty in the City of the Plains and, as aforetime, plots my ruin and her fleshly theft. Who knows the end? But there within my soul broods the Sphinx smiling its immortal smile and to it soon or late I must put that question to which Noot, the holy and half divine, could give no answer—or would not if he could.

\* \* \* \* \* \* \* \*

"What of the royal Princess, Amenartas?" I asked. "Know, Master, that I grow weary of this woman."

"Aye, Daughter, these temple courts are wide, but not wide enough for both of you. Take comfort, she sails to-morrow."

"North?" I asked.

"Nay, south with her father, Nectabenes. Or so she tells me, saying that his fortune shall be her own and that together they will reign or fall."

"It is well," I answered.

Then we talked of humble matters that had to do with the shrine of the goddess and of the hiding away of her treasures lest the Persians should take them. When all was finished, Noot rose, blessed me, calling on the Powers above to protect me, and went his ways in the ship *Hapi* which he had purchased to bring it to my aid at Sidon, nor did I guess that for years I should see him no more. Yet I think he knew it well.

\*\*\*\*\*\*\*\*

Like a mighty river in its flood the Persian hosts poured down on Memphis. As such a torrent sweeps away the village and the humble homestead, drowns the cattle, twists out the palm trees by their roots, covers the corn with slime, floods cities, palaces, and temples, chokes the breath from their inhabitants and strews the kind earth with the corpses of those that tilled it, so did Ochus and his barbarians to Egypt. Rapine and massacre, flames of fire and misery marked their path. Men were butchered by the thousand, the aged and women who were no longer fair were driven into the desert to starve. Yes, it was the sport of those Persians to drive them like game to where there was no water, and then watch them die of thirst beneath the burning sun. Only the young women were spared to be concubines or slaves, and the flower of the children to be put to vile purposes. The cities and the temples were pillaged, their citizens tortured to drag from them the secret of the hiding-places of treasure, the priests were forced to sacrifice to the god of fire and to spit upon their own or die, the priestesses were burned or defiled, or both.

So pitiful was the case of Egypt that although I knew that by her sins and faithlessness she had brought these woes upon herself, I who by my work at Sidon had become one of the appointed ministers of her destruction, my heart wept for her and I prayed the avenging gods to hold their hands. Also I prayed them to give Ochus to drink of his own cup and to make of me the butler who mixed his wine. Nor did I pray in vain.

Thus the red Ochus came at length to Memphis, the white-walled city, the ancient, the holy, and filled its streets with horror, till they were spread thick with dead and one wail of woe went up to heaven. Yet he did not burn the place, perchance because our prayers availed and the gods relented, perchance because he wished to keep it to be the seat of his majesty. Only here as elsewhere he sacked the temples and wrought sacrilege.

From the pylon top of the temple of Isis that overlooked the courts of that of Ptah and the gilded stable of the bull Apis, with my own eyes I saw the Persians, for in this business the Greeks would have no hand, drag out the sacred beast whom they held to be a god of the Egyptians, though in truth he was but the emblem of the god, or rather of the generating power that is in Nature, and butcher it with jeers and mockery. More, their scullions came and cooked the sacred flesh after which, at tables spread in the inner court, Ochus and his captains ate it, forcing the priests of Ptah to "taste of their own god" and to drink of the liquor in which it had been seethed. They were cowards, those priests, or surely they would have found means to mix the broth with poison.

After the feast, when all the revellers were drunk with wine, a great jackass was brought and, the statue of the god having been thrown out of it, was stabled in the sanctuary.

Such were some of the things that were done in Memphis and indeed throughout Egypt, for as Apis was served, so was the holy ram of Mendes. Moreover, other things were done too shameful to record.

Now all this while I sat in the temple of Isis awaiting what might befall. I will not say that I was unafraid, because I was afraid. Yet within me was that proud spirit which forbade me to show my fear. Moreover, within me also burned a certain fire of faith whereof the light was my guide in the darkness of despair. The holy Noot, my Master, had told me that I and those with me should take no harm, and I would not doubt my Master. Moreover, when I prayed at night, a voice from heaven speaking in my heart seemed to command me to be brave, since there fought for me and mine those whom I could not see.

So there I sat quite alone with none to counsel me and none to help me, giving courage as best I could to those poor priests and priestesses, my fellow servants of the goddess. The worship of the temple went on as before, each morn the statue of the Mother was decked and dressed, the perfumes were poured, the offerings were made, the processions wound round the courts preceded by the singers and the shakers of the *sistrum*, while at night the holy hymns were chanted to the stars.

The Persians came to know of these things and gathered at the gates, amazed.

"Who are these," they asked, "who have no fear?"

But we answered nothing though death stared us in the face.

The matter reached the ears of Ochus and stirred his wonder, so that in the end he came in person to visit the temple. I received him in the great hall, veiled and seated in a chair of state that was set at the foot of a statue of the goddess. With him were sundry of his great lords dressed in silks and perfumed, also the general Mentor, whom I had known at Sidon where he played traitor, deserting with his Greeks to the Persians. Further there was present Bagoas the eunuch and first councillor of the King of kings, who commanded his army also; like all these unfortunates, a fat, shrill-voiced man with a smooth and furtive manner, who waved his long hands to and fro when he spoke.

Now this Bagoas was by birth Egyptian; so I had heard, and my first sight of him confirmed the tale. Yes, without doubt by birth he was an Egyptian of the small-boned, large-eyed, round-headed type that had descended from the ancient blood, as I knew by the statues of many that I have seen taken from the earliest tombs before it became the custom to embalm the dead. I noted this, and at once a thought came to me.

Would an Egyptian desire to see the sanctuary of Isis and her priests desecrated and destroyed? Perchance he did not worship Ptah or Apis, or other of the gods, but all born upon the Nile venerated Mother Isis, the Queen of Heaven, and bowed to her sovereignty. That was a faith which where'er they wandered and upon whatever altars they burned incense, they never could forget, because through a hundred generations it came down to them with their blood. Yet who knew? This Bagoas, it was said, was a cunning fellow steeped in murder, who from his crimes had reaped a rich reward, and such an one, looking only to his day of glory, might forget even Isis and the wrath to come.

Ochus, loose-lipped, cruel-faced, and weary-eyed, wearing a look of pride that yet was full of haunting terrors, such as are ever the companions of murderers who know that in a day unborn surely themselves they will be murdered, stood before me. I, rising from my chair, made obeisance to the King of kings—and had he but known it, cast the curse of Isis at him from beneath my veil.

"What is this?" he asked, speaking in Greek, in the thick voice of one who has drunk well at the feast, and pointing at me with his sceptre. "Is it one of those wrapped bodies that we drag from the tombs, such as we used for the cooking of the god Apis, broiling him with his own worshippers? Nay, for it moves and talks and seems to have the shape of a woman. Bagoas, strip that veiled thing naked, that we may see whether it be a woman, and if so, of what favour."

Now when I, Ayesha, heard this, at once all my courage came back to me, as ever it does when peril gets me by the throat. At once I laid my plan, which was short and simple.

If that eunuch so much as advanced to lay a finger on me, I would draw the knife that hung to my girdle, the curved, razor-edged Arab knife that had been my father's, and thrusting him aside, I would spring past him and strike it through the heart of yonder King of kings, sending him to sum up his account with Isis. Then if there were time, I would serve Bagoas in the same way, and afterward, if must be, use the knife upon myself. Better thus than that I should be shamed before these barbarians.

I spoke no word and my face was hid, yet I think that out of my soul sprang something which warned these two of their danger. Or perchance it was my guardian spirit that warned them. At the least Bagoas went down upon his knees and bowed till his forehead touched the ground.

"O King of kings," he said, "I pray thee command not thy slave to do this deed. Yonder lady is the prophetess of Isis, Queen of all gods, Queen of Heaven and Earth, and to touch her with an unhallowed hand is a sacrilege that brings death in this world and in that to come everlasting torment."

Now Ochus laughed brutally, then turned and asked,

"What do you say, Mentor, who are a Greek and know no more of the gods of Egypt than I do? Is there any reason why we should not strip this veiled priestess and discover what she is like beneath those wrappings?"

Now Mentor rubbed his brow and answered,

"Since I am asked, O King of kings, one does come into my mind. Do you remember Tenes, King of the Sidonians? He took this same prophetess as a gift from Nectanebes, and also wished to strip her in his fashion. Well, Tenes came to a very bad end, and so did Nectanebes who gave her to him, or is in the way of it. Therefore, O King of kings, were I in your place I should advise that she remain veiled, who perhaps after all is but an ugly old woman. I have known little of Isis, still she is a goddess with a great name and perchance it is scarcely worth while to risk her wrath to look at the wrinkled flesh of an ugly old woman. One never knows, O King of kings, and I have seen so much of it of late that I come to learn that death, with the curse of Heaven thrown in, is a bad business."

Thus spoke Mentor in his bluff, rambling, soldier talk, that yet was so full of Grecian cunning, and Ochus, appearing suddenly to grow sober, listened to him.

"I seem to remember," Ochus said, "that this same priestess served me well yonder at Sidon, giving the Phoenician dog, Tenes, counsel that led him down to ruin. So at least the tale runs. Therefore, not because of the Egyptian goddess whom I despise," and he spat on the statue of Isis, an act at which I saw Bagoas shiver, "or for the reasons that you fools give, but because by design or chance, I know not which, she served me well at Sidon, let her continue to wear her veil. I command also that this temple, which is beautiful in its fashion, shall not be burned or harmed, and that those who serve it may continue to dwell there and carry on their mad worship as it pleases them, provided that they stay within its walls and do not attempt to stir up the people by pageantry in the streets. In token thereof I stretch out my sceptre," and he held the ivory-headed wand he carried toward me.

Bagoas whispered to me that I must touch it, so I thrust my arm between the folds of my veil and did so, though next instant I remembered that it would have been wiser to grasp the wand from beneath the veil.

At once Ochus noted the beauty of that arm and exclaimed with a laugh,

"By the holy fire! yonder hand and wrist are not those of an ugly old woman, such as was spoken of by you slaves, but rather those of one who is still young and fair. Had I seen them but a moment gone, surely she would have been stripped. Indeed——"

"I have touched the sceptre of the Great King," I broke in coldly. "Once the sceptre has been touched the decree of the Great King may not be altered."

"Wise also," said Ochus, "for she knows our Persian laws. Well, she is right. The sceptre has been touched, and what has been said cannot be changed. See now, all of you who are ignorant, how good a shield is wisdom. Come, Mentor, let us be going to make sport with those young priestesses of Ammon who, not being wise, but only pretty, await us in the palace. It will be a merry night. Bagoas, bide you here, lest you should be shocked," and he laughed brutally, "also to inquire whether this heavenly harlot called Isis decks herself with jewels, for if so, as to them I swore no oath. Farewell, Priestess. Continue to be wise and to wear a veil, because of the rest of you is as shapely as your hand, who knows but that some night when wine has drowned all promises, I, or others, might cause you to be stripped at last."

Then he turned and went, followed by his foul company. Only Bagoas remained behind as he had been bidden.

When the doors had closed and by the shouts from without the walls I knew that the Persians were gone, I said to Bagoas, who was alone with me in the place,

"Tell me, Egyptian, cradled beneath the wings of Isis, are you not afraid?" and I turned my head, glancing at the vile stain upon the alabaster statue.

"Aye, Prophetess," he answered, "I am afraid, as much afraid as you were but now."

"Fool!" I mocked back at him, "I was not afraid. Ere ever a hand had been laid upon me by you, you would have been dead, and that king whom you serve would have been dead also—ask me not how—and by now your souls would be writhing beneath the hooks of the Tormentors of the Under-world. Have you not heard of the curse of Isis, Eunuch, and do you think that your pomp and power can protect you from her swift sword? Now, *now*, should I but breathe one prayer to her, she can slay you if she wills."

He quaked, he fell on his knees; yes, this murderer of kings fell upon his knees before me, one veiled woman in a shrine, imploring me to spare him and to protect him from the wrath of Heaven. For in his soul Bagoas was still Egyptian, and the blood of his forefathers who had worshipped Isis for a thousand years still ran strong in him. Moreover, he feared me, the priestess whose fame he knew as he knew the fate of those who had offended me.

"Forgiveness! Protection! Methinks these must be most dearly bought, Bagoas. Are you one of those who have eaten the flesh of Apis and dragged the virgins of Ammon from their sanctuary? Are you one of those who have stabled an ass in the temple of Ptah, have burned the ancient fanes and have butchered the priests upon their altars?"

"Alas! I am," he said, beating his breast, "but not of my own will. What I did I must do, or die."

"It may be so. Make your own peace with those gods if you can. I have little to do with them who serve the Supreme Mother. But for her what atonement?" and again I glanced at the foul stain upon the alabaster of the image.

"That is what I need to be told. What atonement, Prophetess? I will swear that there are no jewels here; that the Mother is decked only with flowers and perfumes. I will guard this shrine so that never again a Persian sets foot within its walls. I will cause any who offend you, Prophetess, to die secretly and at once. Is it enough?"

"Nay, nor by a hundredth part. You would spare the ceremonial trappings of the Mother, but where is the vengeance upon him who defiled her with his spittle? You would protect the priestess, but where is vengeance upon him who would have stripped her stark to be his sport and that of his barbarians? If that is all you have to offer, Bagoas, take the Mother's curse and that of her Oracle, and get you down to hell." Here Bagoas lifted his hand as though to protect his head and began to protest, but without heeding him I went on,

"Hurry not, linger as long as you will upon the road. Deck yourself like a woman with broidered robes, perfume yourself with scents; set chains about your neck and jewels upon your fingers. Pander to the lusts you cannot share and take your pay in gold and provinces. Poison those you hate and from pure children wring out their lives, because these stand between you and the fruit of some new fantasy. Glut yourself with the swine's food of earth, swell yourself out with the marsh-gas of power, and then, Bagoas, die! die! one year, ten years, fifty years hence, and get you down to hell and look upon the awful eyes of the goddess you have shamed, of her whom your forefathers worshipped from the beginning, and wait the coming of her priestess, that with every merciless particular she may lay the count against you from the pavement of the Judgment Hall."

"What, then, shall I do? What shall I do to save my soul? Know, Priestess, that I who am maimed in my body would save my soul, and that all these gauds you count are but gall and ashes to me; for having nought else to gain—being robbed of wives and children I needs must seek them and thus drug the spirit that is within me. Oh! it is something—being what I am, that I should feel the necks of all these great ones writhing beneath my foot. Yes," here his voice dropped to a whisper, "even that of the King of kings himself, who forgets that there were other Kings of kings before him. Tell me— what must I do?"

Secretly I drew the curved knife at my girdle; secretly and unwincing, unseen of him, I gashed my arm—oh! I cut deep, for I can see the mark to-day, though this fair flesh of mine once seemed to perish in the immortal fire, but to re-arise elsewhere. The blood from a severed vein leaped forth and stained my veil, a little mark at first which grew and grew, till it cried of murder. The man's eyes fastened themselves upon the prodigy, for so he thought it; then he asked,

"Blood! *Whose* blood?"

"Perchance that of the wounded goddess. Perchance that of a shamed priestess. What does it matter, Bagoas?"

"Blood," he went on, "for what does the blood ask?"

"Perchance it cries to Heaven for vengeance; perchance it demands to be washed away with other blood, Bagoas. Who am I that I should interpret parables?"

Now he understood, and struggling from his knees, bent forward whispering in my ear. Yes, the priceless jewels that hung from his pointed golden cap jingled against my ear.

"I understand," he said, "and be sure it shall be done. But not yet. It cannot be yet. Still I swear that it shall be done when the hour is ripe. I hate him! I say that I hate him who while he showers gifts upon me with his hands, mocks me with his tongue, and who, when by my wit I win victories for him, jeers at the soldiers who are led by one who is neither man nor woman. Yes, I hate him who, knowing that I am of Egypt, forces me to desecrate their shrines and to butcher those who serve them. Oh! I swear that it shall be done in its season."

"By what, O Bagoas?"

"By this, Prophetess," and seizing the dripping veil he rubbed that which stained it upon his lips and brow, "I swear by the blood of Isis, or of her Priestess and Oracle in whom Isis is, that I will neither rest nor stay till I bring Ochus Artaxerxes to his doom. Years may go by, but still I will bring him to his doom—at a price."

"What price?" I asked.

"That of absolution, Priestess, which is yours to give."

"Aye, it is mine to give or to withhold. Yet I give it not until Ochus lies dead, and by your hand. Then I call it down from Heaven—not before."

"At least protect me till that hour, O Daughter of the Queen of Heaven."

From the necklace I wore beneath my veil I loosed a certain charm of power, the secret symbol of the Queen herself, worked cunningly in jasper, and known only to the initiate. This I breathed upon and blessed.

"Take it," I said, "and wear it on your heart. It shall protect you from all ills while your heart is true. But if once that heart turns from its purpose, then this holy token shall bring all ills upon you, here and hereafter, Bagoas. For then upon your doomed head shall fall the curse of the goddess that even now hangs suspended over it, as in the Grecian fable the sword of Damocles hangs by its single hair. Take it and be gone, to return no more till you come to tell me that Ochus Artaxerxes treads that same road upon which he has set so many feet."

Bagoas took the talisman and pressed it on his brow, as though it had been the very signet of the King of kings, and hid it away about him. Then he prostrated himself before me, who sat upon a greater throne, that of the Queen of queens, prostrated himself till his forehead touched the ground beneath my feet. Then rising, without another word, Bagoas withdrew himself with humble obeisances till he reached the doors where he vanished from my sight.

\* \* \* \* \* \* \* \*

When the man had gone I, Ayesha, laughed aloud, I who had played a great game and won it.

Yes, I laughed aloud; then, having purified the statue of the goddess and burnt incense before it, I went upon my knees and returned my humble thanks to that just Heaven of which I was the minister.

CHAPTER 15

# The Plot and the Voice

The weary years went by. Ochus returned to Persia, bearing his spoils with him and leaving one Sabaco, a brutal fellow, to rule Egypt and wring tribute from her.

All this while I, Ayesha, sat alone, quite alone, in the temple of Isis at Memphis whose walls I never left, for the command of Ochus was obeyed and whatever happened to those of other gods, the shrine of Isis was left inviolate. Here, then, surrounded by a dwindling company of priests and priestesses, I remained, as Noot, my Master, had commanded me to do, awaiting a word that never came, and carrying on the ceremonies of the temple in such humble fashion as our poverty allowed.

What did I through all that slow and heavy time? I dreamed, I communed with Heaven above, I studied the ancient lore of Egypt and of other lands, growing ever wiser and full of knowledge as a new-filled jar with perfume or with wine. Yet of what use was this knowledge to me? As it seemed, of none. Yet it was not so, since my heart fed on it like a bee upon its winter store of honey, and without it I should have died, as the bee must die. Moreover, now I understand that this space of waiting was a preparation for those long centuries which afterward I was doomed to pass in the tombs of Kor. It was a training and a discipline of the soul.

Thus forgotten of the world I brooded and endured, I who had thought to rule the world.

So moon added itself to moon, and, still filled with a divine patience, I abode within those temple walls till the appointed hour, which I knew would dawn at last. Of Nectanebes I heard nothing; he had vanished away—I doubted not to the doom which I had foreseen. Of Amenartas, his daughter, I heard nothing, she also had vanished away, as I supposed with him. Of Kallikrates, the soldier priest, I heard nothing. Doubtless he was dead and that beauty of his had turned to evil-odoured dust as my own must do, a thought from which I shrank.

Much I wondered why this man alone upon the earth should have stirred my soul and awakened the longings of my woman's flesh. I knew not, unless it was agreed that when the gates were passed I should meet him in a world that lies beyond, if such there were. For from the beginning I was sure that it had been laid upon me to lift up his spirit to the level of my own, perchance because in some far-off star or state I had sinned against it and him and dragged them down.

Indeed is not this the common lot of the great, that with toil and tears and bitter disappointment they must strive to draw the spirits of others to that high peak upon which themselves they stand? And amongst all the sins of our vile condition, is there one blacker than to cast back some soul that struggles toward the pure and good into the seething depths of ill?

Thus in those days I thought of that lost Kallikrates, whose lips alone had touched my own. I thought, too, with a sad wonderment, how strange it was that I to whose feet men had crept by scores, I the most beautiful of women and the most learned, had been rejected, or at the least turned from by this man, the favourer of another, who although she was fair and bold of heart, still shone with a smaller light, as does the pale moon when compared with the glory of the sun.

Indeed, now that all was over and done, as I believed, and that nought remained of these fires of folly save a pinch of burnt-out ash, I smiled to myself as I remembered them. Yet to tell truth, I smiled sadly, who here alone at the dear feast of love which, to a woman, means more than all other feasts, had been served with the cups of defeat and shame by the grinning varlet, Destiny. Yet I was well served, for what had I, Wisdom's Daughter, the vowed to eternal glory, to do with such matters of our common flesh?

Oh! I was glad to have done with the gray-eyed Kallikrates, who could wield a sword so manly-well in battle, and yet, when remorse took hold of him, could pray with the best of priests. Now at least once more I was the mistress of my own soul with leisure to shape it to the likeness of the gods and, in those days of holy contemplation, truly its wings beat against their bars, struggling to be free. Would that they had burst them, but Fate had built that cage too strong.

* * * * * * * *

At length news came to me, for Isis still had eyes and ears in Egypt and all that these saw or heard I learned, news that Ochus, grown timid or weary in his Persian palace, had determined once more to drink the waters of the Nile, or perchance to check the accounts of his satrap Sabaco whose sum of tribute had fallen off of late.

So he came with all his Eastern pomp and at last took up his abode in the palace of Memphis within two bowshots of the temple where I dwelt. The people received him with rejoicings; it was pitiful to see them decking themselves and the streets with flowers, spreading branches of palm for him to tread on, and flying banners from the lofty tops of the fire-scorched pylons—slaves welcoming their torturer and tyrant and grinning to hide the terror in their hearts. He came, and there was festival throughout the great town as though Osiris had returned to earth, accompanied by all the lesser gods.

Only in the temple of Isis there was none. No palm leaves decked its stark and ancient walls, no bonfires burned within its courts, and no lanterns hung in its window-places. Not thus would I, Ayesha, bow the knee to Baal or sacrifice to Moloch, though it is true that some of my servants looked askance when I forbade it and asked who would protect us from the wrath of the King of kings because of this neglect of his command.

"The goddess will protect us," I answered, "or if she does not, I will," and sent them to their tasks.

On the second night after the coming of Ochus, Bagoas waited on me and I commanded that he should enter, but alone. So his Eastern rabble of gorgeous servitors was turned back from the gates and he came in unattended, splendid in gold-embroidered silk and jewels. Where he had left me, there I received him, seated veiled in the chair of state before the alabaster statue of the goddess, at the entrance to the outer sanctuary that overlooked the great hall.

"Hail! Bagoas," I said, "how goes it with you? Has that amulet of power which I gave to you protected you from harm?"

"Prophetess," he answered, bowing, "it has protected me. It has lifted me up so that now, save for the King of kings, my master most august," he added with a sneer in every word, "I am now the greatest one in the whole world. I give life, I decree death. I lift up, I cast down; satraps and councillors crawl about my feet; generals beg my favour; gold is showered upon me. Yea, I might build my house of gold. There is nought left for me to desire beneath the sun."

"Except certain things to which, thanks to the cruelty of the King of kings, or those who went before him, you cannot attain? For example, children to inherit all this glory and all this gold, Bagoas, although you live among so many of those who might be mothers."

He heard, and his face, that I noted had grown thinner and more fierce since last I saw him, became like to that of the devil.

"Prophetess," he hissed, "surely you are one who knows how to pour acid into an open wound."

"That thereby it may be cleansed, Bagoas."

"Yet your words are true," he went on, unheeding. "All this splendour, all this wealth and power I would give, and gladly, to be as my fathers were before me, gently bred but humble owners of a patch of land between Thebes and Philae. There they sat for a score of generations with their women and their children. But where, thanks to the Persians, are *my* woman and *my* children? In the western cliff yonder there is a sepulchre. In the chapel of that sepulchre above the coffins of those who lie beneath is an image of him who dug it. He lived some fourteen hundred years ago in the days of Aahmes, he who won back Egypt from the Hyksos kings, the invaders who held it as the Persians do to-day. For he was one of the captains of the troops of Aahmes who, when he conquered, gave him that patch of land in guerdon for his service."

Here Bagoas paused like to one overwhelmed by unhappy memories, then continued,

"From age to age, Prophetess, it has been the custom for the children of the children of this soldier upon a certain day to make offerings to that statue, wherein, as we hold, dwells the *Ka* of him whose face and form it pictures; to set a golden crown, that of Osiris, upon its head, to wind a golden chain about its neck; to give it food, to give it flowers. Such is the sacred duty, from generation to generation, of the descendants of that captain who served Aahmes and helped to free Egypt from the barbarian foe. Myself I have fulfilled that duty, aye, when Ochus the Destroyer first came to Memphis, I travelled up Nile and placed the crown upon the head and wound the chain about the neck, and offered the flowers and the food. But, Prophetess, of this blood I am the last, for because of my beauty as a child the Persian seized me and made of me a dry tree, so that never again will there be one to make offering in the tomb of my forefather, the captain of Aahmes, or to read the story of his deeds that fourteen hundred years ago, while yet living, he caused to be recorded upon his funeral tablet."

I heard and laughed.

"A common tale," I said, "a very common tale in Egypt to-day, the Egypt of the Persians, as doubtless it was long ago in the Egypt of the Hyksos. But this ancestor of yours was a man who smote, or helped to smite, the Hyksos and lived to write his glorious deeds on stone to be an example to those who came after him. Well, the story is finished, is it not? Indeed I wonder that the glorious Bagoas, slave of the Persian, Bagoas with his pomp and pleasures, thinks fit to waste time upon the tale of a forgotten warrior who in his hour struck for freedom. What are the flowers and the humble scents which for more than a thousand years have been offered to the spirit of that warrior, but now can never be offered again since there are none of his blood left to bring them, compared to the priceless balms, the jewels and the gold, that daily are poured upon the feet of Bagoas, the Chief Eunuch and Counsellor of the King of kings, who, did he know of those holy ones that sleep in the tomb of the race of Bagoas, doubtless would drag them out and cause Bagoas, the last of its blood, to fire them, that he might see a merry blaze? That would be a good sport for the King of kings, to force the great Bagoas to burn his ancestors and on their bones to cook a royal meal, as he forced the priests of Ptah to broil Apis for his feast."

The mighty Bagoas heard and understood me, as I could see well, for at every word he winced like a high-bred steed beneath the whip.

"Cease," he said hoarsely, "cease! I can bear no more. Why do you rub sand into my eyes, Prophetess?"

"To clear away their rheum that they may see the better, Bagoas. But let us be done with the tale of that honourable, long-lost ancestor of yours to whose spirit no more offerings will be made, and tell me of the wonders of the great estate of you in whom runs his blood, the last drops of it, that soon will be sucked up in the sands of Death. Seal that sepulchre, Bagoas, but first set it in another writing, graven on a tablet of emerald or gold, telling how he who hallowed it was by the gods given the glory of being the far forefather of Bagoas, Chief Eunuch of the King of kings, Ochus, who burned the shrines of that forefather's gods."

"Cease, cease!" he moaned. "The hour is at hand."

"What hour, Bagoas?"

"The hour of vengeance which I swore to Isis."

"Does the Egyptian worshipper of the Persian holy Fire remember his vows to Isis? Be plain, Bagoas."

"Hearken, Prophetess. During all these years I have been seeking opportunity. Now of a sudden I see it to my hand. A thought came to me whilst you talked of the captain of Aahmes to whom no more of his blood can make offerings."

"Speak it, then, Bagoas."

"Prophetess, the King of kings is wrath with you, because alone of all the great places in Memphis, on the temple of Isis no welcoming banners hang to greet him at his royal coming and because no priest or priestess of Isis spread flowers before his conquering feet. So wrath is he that, were it not for his oath, which he fears to break, he would pull this sanctuary stone from stone, slaughter its priests, and give its priestesses to the soldiers."

"Is it so?" I asked indifferently.

"Aye, Prophetess. But by that oath you are saved, for ever I keep it before his mind and warn him of the fate of those who do violence to the Queen of Heaven. Only this morning I did this while he stood staring at these unbannered walls and muttered vengeance."

"And what said he then, Bagoas?"

"He laughed and answered that he would do the goddess not violence, but honour, thus. On the third night from this, the night of full moon, he will make a great feast in the inner court of this temple. At that feast the King of kings and his women will sit upon a platform laid over the coffins of the royalties of Egypt dragged from their sepulchres, so that its kings and queens may be beneath his feet. This platform will be supported by the statues of the gods of Egypt which once they worshipped. In front of it will burn the holy Fire of Persia and that fire will be fed with the mortal remnants of priests and priestesses of these Egyptian gods. Ochus the king will be clad in the robes of Osiris, and at the end of the feast from behind her consecrated statue, that before which we sit, the goddess herself, dressed in the robes of Isis and wearing the holy emblems upon her head, will appear veiled, led by priestesses or by royal Persian women. *You* will be that goddess, Prophetess."

"And then?" I asked.

"Then you will be brought up on to the platform and there this new Osiris will unveil you, embracing you as his wife in welcome before all that company. This he will do to make a mock of you because he believes you to be an ancient woman who goes veiled to hide her baldness and her wrinkles, for so the rumour runs among the Persians."

Now when I, Ayesha, heard these terrible words and my heart understood the height and depth of the sacrilege which this mad king would dare and all that it might mean to me, I trembled; yes, the bones seemed to melt within me so that almost I fell from the throne whereon I sat. Yet gathering up my strength I asked,

"Is this all, Bagoas?"

"Nay. At that feast, Prophetess, I myself as Vizier and the head of the world under him, must serve Ochus as his cup-bearer. While the priests of Osiris and the priestesses of Isis sing the ancient chants of the awakening of Osiris from the tomb and of his reunion with Isis the Wife Divine, it will be my part to hand the jewelled goblet filled with the holy wine to Osiris-Ochus, King of Heaven and Earth. From it he will drink the marriage-draught, and having drunk, will pour the dregs of the goblet upon your feet, or for aught I know will cast them in your face. Nay, I forgot. First the Persian women of the royal household will strip the coverings from you that Osiris may see his long-lost bride and the company may have sport, jeering at her withered age."

"And if she should prove to remain unwithered, if even she should chance to be passing fair, what then, Bagoas?"

"Then perchance, Prophetess, it is in the mind of Ochus to add Isis to the number of his queens, thinking thus to gain the favour of the Egyptians, if not of their gods. Oh! Prophetess, you are very wise, as all know, yet once your foot slipped—or rather your hand slipped, when in bygone days you stretched it out to touch the sceptre of the King of kings. Ochus has often spoken of the beauty of that hand and arm, and of how, more than all things, he desired to see the face above them and the form of which they are a part. Perchance, Prophetess, that is why he plans all this mummery."

"And if I refuse to act this play, what then, Bagoas?"

"Then since the command is lawful and designed to honour the goddess, the Great King's oath is at an end. Then the temple of Isis will be sacked and burned like others, then her priests will be murdered unless they make offerings to the holy Fire, and her priestesses be en-slaved or find a home in the soldiers' tents or Persian households."

"Bagoas," I said, rising and standing over him, "know that the Curse of Isis hovers about your head. Show me a path out of this trouble or you die—not to-morrow or next year, but at once. How, it matters not, still you die; and for the rest, are the Sidonians the only ones who can fire their temples and perish in them?"

He cringed before me after the fashion of his unhappy kind, then answered,

"I waited for such words, Prophetess, and had I not been prepared against them, never would I have entered these gates alone. Did I not tell you that at this feast I shall be the King's cup-bearer? Now," he went on in a whisper, "I add that his own physician, who is in my pay, will mix the marriage wine, that his life is in the hollow of my hand; that the guards and captains are my servants; that the great lords are sworn to me, and that the hour for which I have waited through long years has come at last. Lady, you are not the only one who desires vengeance upon Ochus."

"Fine words," I said. "But how know I that they will be fulfilled? In Egypt Bagoas is called the King's Liar."

"I swear it by Isis, and if I fail you, may the Devourer take my soul."

"And I, who am her Mouth and Oracle, swear by Isis that if you fail me I will take your blood. Aye, though I die, a thousand will live on to avenge me, and the dagger or the shaft of one of them shall reach your heart at last. Or if they miss their aim then the goddess herself will smite."

"I know it, Prophetess, and I will not fail. After drinking of that cup sleep will fall upon the King of kings; yes, the new Osiris will return to his tomb and sleep sound, but *not in the arms of Isis*."

Then for a while there was silence between us, till at length I motioned to him to begone.

********

The night of the feast came and all was prepared. I did not trust Bagoas and therefore I made a plan, a splendid and terrible plan. I determined to offer all those feasters, yes, the King of kings with his women, his generals, his chamberlains, his councillors, and his company, as one vast sacrifice to the outraged gods of Egypt, and with them if need were, myself and my servants, to guide them upon the road to hell.

Beneath that hall of the temple which Ochus had appointed for the feast was a vast vault for the storage of oil and fuel against times of want or tumult. This vault, as it chanced, was full to the roof, since in those troublous days I never knew from moon to moon when the place might be besieged. Also in it was much prepared papyrus with many written rolls that for centuries had been hidden there, great weight of bitumen such as the embalmers use, a stack of coffins prepared by the living to receive their bodies at the end; and lastly hundreds of bundles of dried reeds that served to strew the courts. What more was needed, save to open the air shafts to the hall above that the flames might find full play, and to set in the vault one who could be trusted with a lamp of which the light was hidden, commanded at a certain signal to cast it among the oil-soaked reeds and fly?

As it chanced such an instrument was to my hand, an old, fierce-hearted woman in whom ran royal blood, for that hard on seventy years had served as priestess of this temple.

That very night I summoned the priests and priestesses who re-mained and in the sanctuary under the wings of Isis, I told them all: told them how I purposed to sweep this human dirt of Persians with the red bosom of destruction out of the company of the living over the edge of the world into the Avenger's everlasting jaws.

This band of the faithful hearkened and bowed their cowled heads. Then the first of them, an old priest, asked,

"Is it decreed that we must eat fire with these swine? If so, we are ready."

"Nay," I answered, "the secret passage that runs from the back of the sanctuary of the ruined temple of Osiris will be unbarred, that passage by which in the old days the holy effigy of Osiris was brought at the great festival of the Resurrection to be laid upon the breast of Isis. By this passage at the first sign of fire, you must flee, as I will if I may. But if I come not you will know that the goddess has called me. At the water-steps of the temple of Osiris boats will be waiting manned by brothers of our faith. In the darkness and the tumult, those boats will pass down Nile to the secret shrine that is called *Isis-Among-the-Reeds*, where once, the legend tells, the goddess found the heart of Osiris hidden there by Typhon, the shrine upon the isle that none dare visit, no, not even the Persians, because it is guarded by the ghosts of the dead, or by spirits sent from the Under-world fashioned like flames of fire. Thither fly, and there lie hid until the word of Isis comes to you, as come it will."

Again they bowed their cowled heads in the gloomy sanctuary lit by a single lamp. Then the old priest said,

"Great is the deed that we shall do, and worthy. Surely the song of it shall echo through all the courts of Heaven and the gods themselves shall crown our brows with splendour. Yet ere it is decreed, O Proph-etess inspired, let us seek a sign from the Queen immortal that such is her command."

"Aye," I answered, "let us seek a sign."

So there in the half darkness we chanted the mystic ritual, hand in hand before the goddess we chanted it, bowing and swaying, weeping and praying, demanding that a sign be given to us who were prepared to die that her splendour might shone forth as a star.

Yet no sign came.

"O Oracle inspired," said the old priest, "it is not enough. Yet in your heart are locked the unutterable Words, the Words of Power, the Words of the Opening of the Mouth Divine, that may not be spoken save at the last extreme. Are not these words known to you, the Oracle inspired?"

"They are known to me," I answered. "From Noot I had them under the Seven Oaths when I was ordained prophetess; yea, under the Seven Curses if those words should be used unworthily, the seven dreadful curses, deer-footed, snake-headed, lion-maned with red fire, that shall hunt the betrayer's soul from star to star, till the black vault of space falls in and buries Time. Kneel now and bow your heads and stop your ears till they be spoken. Then open your ears and hearken."

They knelt in a double row and I, I the Oracle, clothed in the might of my Queen, I dared to draw near to her holy effigy gleaming white above us in the darkness of the shrine. Yes, this I dared, not knowing what would chance. I took the jewelled *sistrum* of my office; I laid it upon the lips of the goddess, I shook it till it chimed before her face, I clasped her feet and kissed them.

Then I rose and into her ear I whispered the dreadful Words of Power, which even now, after so many ages, I dare not so much as shape in the halls of memory. I whispered them and returning to my company of kneeling worshippers, I motioned to them to unstop their ears and folding my arms upon my breast, I waited with downcast eyes.

Presently there was a stir in the sanctuary as of bearing wings; a cold air blew upon us; then a voice spoke, the very voice of Noot my Master, Noot, the holy priest of priests. Said the voice:

*"Fulfil! It is decreed. Fulfil and fear not!"*

"Ye have heard," I said.

"We have heard," they answered.

"Whose voice did ye hear?" I asked.

"The voice of Noot, the holy priest of priests who has gone from us," they answered.

"Is it enough?" I asked.

"It is enough," they answered.

\*\*\*\*\*\*\*\*

Then I departed rejoicing, who knew by this sign that Noot, who spoke with his human voice, still lived upon the earth, and that through him it had pleased Heaven to utter its decree.

## CHAPTER 16

# The Feast of the King of Kings

It was the night of the great feast. All day long artificers by scores had toiled in the court of the temple. All down its length tables had been set up and by them couches and benches upon which hundreds of the feasters would lie or sit according to their degree. Near to the head of the court a platform had been built, of which the foundation beams were supported by the statues of gods dragged from a score of temples where they had stood in solemn peace for ages. Yes, there were Ptah, Ammon, Osiris, Mut, Khonsu, Hathor, Maat, Thoth, Ra, Horus, and the rest, bearing on their sacred brows and headdresses the eating-table of a heathen horde. But they bore more than this, since around and between them and the platform upon which stood this table were laid the coffins of long-dead kings or queens, and other great ones, torn, it was said, from the pyramids or their surrounding tombs. Dark with the dust of ages there they lay, some of them uncovered, so as to reveal the grim shapes that slept within.

Above these again was placed the wide platform carpeted with purple cloth of Tyre, and on it stood the board and gilded furniture of the feast. Here, too, was a golden throne at the back of which was a peacock fan of jewels, while to its front was set a table fashioned of black wood inlaid with ivory, and around it other smaller thrones and tables. These were the seats of the King of kings and some of his favoured women.

Nor was this all, for in an outer court but within the pylon gates, cooks and scullions had built fires whereon they dressed meats, and butlers set out their store of wines. Never before within the memory of man had so strange and rich a feast been seen in Egypt as that which was now preparing in the courts of Isis, to defile which with the smell of flesh was a sacrilege and the eating of it there an abomination.

When the sun had turned toward the west came Bagoas with other

443

eunuchs and chamberlains, and being admitted to the inner courts, summoned our company and issued his commands as to the ceremonial that we must keep. We hearkened meekly, saying that we were the slaves of the King of kings, we and our goddess together, and in all things would obey his words.

Then they went away, but as he passed me, affecting to stumble, he whispered in my ear,

"Be not afraid, Prophetess. All is well and the end shall be good."

"I am not afraid, Eunuch," I answered, "who know that all is well and that the end will be good."

* * * * * * * *

The night fell; great flares of light set upon stands of bronze were lit adown the hall, and with them countless lamps placed at intervals along the tables. The feasters gathered; they came by scores and hundreds; Persian lords in their rich robes, generals and captains in their armour, merchants of many lands, Egyptian apostates, and I know not who besides, men, all of them, whom it pleased the King of kings to honour. They were marshalled in their appointed places by the stewards and butlers, and there waited in silence, or speaking only in low voices.

From behind the curtains of the outer sanctuary I and my company watched it all. These were clad in their festal garments of white, garlanded with flowers. But I, according to command, wore the glorious robes of Isis beneath my veil, and on my head the vulture cap of Isis, the golden *Uraeus*, the earrings and the crescent of the moon. Moreover, about my bosom were hung the sacred necklaces and the other jewelled emblems of the goddess, while in my hands I held the *sistrum* and the Cross of Life.

Trumpets blew announcing the advent of the King of kings. Up the long hall he marched, clad in the mummy wrappings of Osiris, somewhat widened at the feet so that he might walk in them, wearing on his head the tall feathered crown and holding in his hands the Crook of Dominion and the Scourge of Rule. His chamberlains and great officials led him by a stairway to the platform that was built above the bodies of ancient kings, where was set a tiny altar upon which burned the Holy Persian Fire. There for a while he stood in pride, waving the scourge with which he flogged the world, while all that company fell upon their faces and adored him as a god, after which they lay still as corpses in the grave.

It was strange to see them lying on their faces like dead men, who indeed soon were to be dead, every one of them, and adoring this

444

human image, this dressed-up doll, fashioned in their own likeness, to be the plaything of the gods and about to be broken by them and cast upon the rubbish heap of time.

I, Ayesha, watching through the veil and alive with that spirit which in the hour of great events comes to such as I am, thought it very strange; so strange that I could have laughed. For there in this mime, this puppet king upon the platform, with the tame tiger, Bagoas, that was about to tear out his throat, crouching at his feet, I saw the very type of all grandeur that is built of clay and not of spirit, since assuredly there is one grandeur of the earth and another of the spirit. Whether by the poison of Bagoas or by the fire of Isis, yonder man who stood triumphing over the mighty monarchs that lay coffined beneath his feet, like a wind-filled toad upon a consecrated altar, was about to die and then what of his triumph and what of his pomp?

His cup of blood was full, and when the blast of doom overturned it into the sands of Death, what tongues would it take, I wondered, in which to urge a million trembling accusations against his trembling soul? Lastly, what mocking devil had persuaded him to don the robes of Osiris, that in them he might do insult to Isis who, whate'er she may not be, at least under her royal name of Nature is the mighty vassal of the Most High, forgetting that Osiris is the god of Death and that Isis-Nature ever avenges herself upon those who violate her laws? Little wonder then that I who laughed but seldom in those days did so in my heart, while my eyes took their fill of the tinselled panoply of this lost madman.

Ochus-Osiris waved his sceptre, and the seeming dead who lay around him, as they had been drilled to do by those who planned this play, came to life in a grim mockery of ghosts called from the grave. They rose up and each, according to his degree, took his place at this Table of Osiris brought to earth.

The feast went on; they ate much; they drank more, till their brains were bemused with wine and scarce could they stand upon their feet. At length the climax came; the coping-stone was set upon this black pyramid of mortal sin against the spirit of Divinity.

Ochus rose, waving the Crook of Dominion.

"Osiris is risen again in Egypt!" he cried. "Let his wife, the divine Isis, be brought forth that he may drink with her the cup of marriage and embrace her as her husband."

Thereon that ribald company shouted,

"Yea, the god Osiris is risen again in Egypt. Bring out Queen Isis. Bring her out, that we may see her drink with him and be kissed!"

Guards summoned us. We came forth from the curtained sanctuary, white-robed in simple state. Singing the ancient hymn of Reunion to the music of harps and of shaken *sistra*, our company came forth into the great hall, I at the head of them. We walked into the hall, a solemn troop at whom the drunken feasters forgot to mock; indeed some of them bowed their heads as though in awe. We came to the dais that was supported by the statues of the gods of Egypt and platformed with her ancient royalties, and here we halted. Guards led me up a stairway so that I stood upon the platform, facing Ochus-Osiris. He spoke, saying, mockingly,

"Hail! Queen of Heaven. Behold Osiris re-arisen on the Nile has found you at last. Unveil, Queen of Heaven, that he may look upon your glory, for as goddesses do not grow old, doubtless you are glorious."

At these words of insult the company broke into coarse laughter. I waited till it had died away, then answered,

"O King wrapped in the robes of a greater king, yea, in the robes of Death, have you not heard that it is very dangerous to draw the veil of Isis, that none, indeed, has drawn it and lived? You think me but a woman, but know that here in the shrine of Isis, aye, here in her holy House which you desecrate with revellings and with the flesh of butchered beasts, I, her Prophetess and Oracle, am the very goddess and clothed with her divinity. I pray you, therefore, think again ere you bid me to draw my veil."

For a moment he seemed to grow afraid, as did that company, for they were silent. Then rage took hold of him who was full of wine and pride.

"What?" he shouted. "Am I, the King of the world, to be defied and threatened by an old hag who calls herself a priestess, or a goddess, or both? Woman, once before I listened to your prayer and left you wrapped in that rag, but now when I come both as your king and as your god, why I claim the privilege of the god. Off with that veil or I will bid my women strip you stark."

Again the silence fell, and for a little while I looked about me. I looked at the feasters illumined by the strong flares of the essence of bitumen; I looked at the blue heaven above in which the great moon floated royally; I turned and looked at the white statue of the goddess showing faint and pure between the curtains in the darkness of the distant shrine beyond. Then I lifted my head and prayed aloud, saying,

"O Thou, that from thy moon-throne watchest all things passing on the earth, O Thou, great Spirit of the world whom men name Isis, Thou that canst spare; Thou that canst avenge; Thou that knowest both life and death; Thou that rulest hearts and destinies; Thou to whose equal sight the king is as the slave, since both kings and slaves are but dust beneath thine immortal feet, hear me, thy priestess and thine Oracle. Thou knowest my strait and that of these thy servants over whom I rule beneath thee. Protect me and them, if thou wilt, or if thou wilt not, then take us to thyself. I ask nothing of thee; I seek not to turn the chariot wheels of Fate; judge thou of my cause who with thy judgment am content. In thine hands hang the scales of doom and the great worlds are thy weights. Who then am I that I should seek to press upon thy balances? Judge now between me, O Mother Isis, and this death-attired king who mocks thee, the Queen of Heaven, in mocking me, thy servitor on earth."

"Have done, woman!" mocked Ochus. "Cease your whimperings to a goddess sitting in the moon, for she is far away from you—and unveil. Bagoas, give me the Marriage Cup, that I may drink to this new wife of mine who thinks herself divine."

Bagoas beckoned and a dark-faced, black-bearded man whom I knew for the king's physician came forward with a golden goblet on which were vile carvings of the loves of satyrs. This he tasted, or effected to taste, with much ceremony, and as he did so, though save I none noted it, let fall the poison into the wine. Then with humble steps, lifting the cup thrice, lowering it again thrice, doubtless to mix the venom with the wine, he came to the Presence and kneeling, presented the goblet to his master, the King of kings, the King of the world.

"Now," said the drink-besotted Ochus as he grasped the goblet, "now, Priestess, will you unveil or must I call the women?"

"It is not needful," I answered. "Yet, O most glorious monarch, yet, O conqueror of all things, first I would add one word. Even a king so great that he dares to clothe himself in the raiment of the Lord of Death perchance may err from time to time. Thus, Mighty One, do you err when you say that Isis is far from me, for Isis is here and *I am Isis.*"

Then at a word two priestesses sprang to my side and loosed me of my veil. It fell to the ground and there I stood before them clad in all the splendid pomp of Isis, beautiful as Isis, with the terrible eyes of Isis, and holding in my hands the emblems of Isis and the sceptre with which Isis ruled the world.

They saw, and from that crowded hall there went up a sigh of wonder—or was it of fear? Ochus saw also; his eyes started, his mouth opened.

"By the holy Fire!" he muttered, "here is one worth wedding, be she goddess or woman."

"Then drink the cup, O Ochus-Osiris, and take her, be she goddess or woman," I answered, pointing at him with the Cross of Life.

He drank, he drank deep, and forgetting to offer the wine to me, loosed the goblet from his hand so that it fell upon the little altar where burned the holy Fire, extinguishing it, and thence rolled from the platform to the ground. I glanced at Bagoas and read in his eyes such a look as I had never seen upon the face of man. Oh! it was cruel, that look—cruel yet triumphant, this cold stare of the victim who had become a conqueror. All hell was in that look.

The feasters murmured at the omen of the death of the Fire, but that draught seemed to sober Ochus, who took no heed of it. The wildness left his eyes; they grew cunning as those of a merchant. Merchant-like he appraised my loveliness seen through the gauzy wrappings such as are used to deck the painted effigy of the goddess.

"I look before I take," he said. "'Twas good to win Egypt; it will be better to win you, O Divine in flesh if not in spirit. Now I understand why in the past you would not suffer me to draw your veil."

Thus he spoke slowly, savouring the words upon his tongue as his greedy eyes savoured my beauty. Then he rose to pass the small altar and advance upon me.

In that fierce moment of time I considered all. It came into my mind that Bagoas had tricked me; that his cup lacked poison, or at least that the plan had failed, and that if I was to be saved it must be by myself. Yet I paused ere I did that which would cause the death of hundreds.

"Stay!" I said to him. "Lay no finger on me lest you shall call the curse of Isis upon your head."

"Nay," he answered, "it is the blessing of Isis that I am about to call upon my lips, O most Beautiful, O Loveliness incarnate!"

He came on. He was past the marble altar. His fierce, bestial face glared into mine and he gripped me; his hot arm was about me, he dragged me to his embrace, while all the beasts of his company shouted in vile joy.

I let fall the *sistrum* that I held. The moment of mercy had gone by. That shout had sealed the doom of all those dogs and satyrs. It was the signal!

By the arts known to us instantly the command was passed on to her who waited below. Instantly this fierce-souled destroyer was at her work with lamp and torch. Never did lover run so swiftly to her lover's side as she did from pile to pile, firing the oil, firing the reeds.

Now that brute-king had me! He pressed his hot kisses upon my breast, upon my lips. I stood still. I struggled not. I stood like the statue of the goddess. This cold calm of mine seemed to frighten him.

"Are you woman?" he asked, hesitating.

"Nay," I hissed back, "I am Isis. Woe to them who lay hands upon Isis!"

He unloosed. He stood staring at me, and as he stared I saw his face change.

"What is in your eyes?" he asked. "All the devils in Egypt are looking out of your eyes."

"Nay," I answered, "all the devils of hell look out of my eyes. Isis commands the devils of hell and unchains them, O death-clothed king."

"What do you mean? What do you mean?" he asked.

"That you will learn presently—in hell. Therefore bid farewell to the world, O Corpse of a king!"

He glowered at me. He swayed to and fro. Then suddenly down he went like one pierced through the heart with an arrow. There he lay upon his back across the altar staring up at the moon.

"Isis is in the moon!" he cried. "She threatens me from the moon. Persians, be afraid of Isis the Moon-dweller. Bagoas! Physician! Physician! Bagoas! protect me from Isis. She is wringing my heart with her hands. Witch! Witch! loose my heart from your hands."

Thus he wailed in a horrible voice and these were his last words, for having spoken them he lifted his head, glaring about him with a twisted mouth, then let it fall heavily, rolled to the platform, and was still.

Bagoas and the physician ran to him.

"The Curse of Isis has fallen upon the King of kings," cried Bagoas.

"He who bestrode the world is dead, smitten by Isis of the Egyptians!" cried the physician.

From the royal women and all that company there went up a wail of:

"Ochus is dead! Artaxerxes is dead! The King of kings is dead!"

Bagoas and the physician, helped by the wailing women of Ochus, lifted the body. They carried it from the platform, they bore it down the hall, they vanished with it into the darkness, and presently in the utter silence I heard the gates of the courts and the outer gates of the pylon clang behind them and the clashing of the bolts as they were shot by the guards of the gates.

Still for awhile the silence held, for all were like dead men with terror. Then a voice cried,

"The witch has killed the king with her kiss! Slay her. Tear her to pieces. Slay her and her company!"

The spell-bound mob began to stir; I heard swords rattling in their scabbards. They rose like waves on a quiet sea, and like a wave began to flow toward the platform on which I now stood alone. I stooped down, lifted the *sistrum* from the platform, and held it toward them.

"Be warned!" I cried. "Stay still lest the Curse of Isis fall on you also."

"Witch! Witch! Witch!" they screamed, hesitating awhile, and again swayed forward.

I waved my arm, and as though in answer to it from the grating of stone beyond the platform suddenly arose dense smoke followed by bursts of flame. I waved it a second time, and from the gratings at the end of the hall arose smoke followed by bursts of flame. They looked, they saw, they understood.

"The Curse of Isis!" they screamed. "The Curse of Isis is upon us! Fire rises from hell."

"Nay," I answered, "fire falls from Heaven sent by the outraged gods!"

Now between me and them flared a fence of flame which the boldest dared not face. They paused, one hurled a sword at me which passed above my head. Then they turned, flying for the gateways of the hall, and there were met by another fence of flame. Some of the boldest leapt through it only to find that the gates were shut and that the terror-stricken guards had fled. They rushed back, burning, yea, their silken robes and their oil-anointed hair turned them, yet living, into torches. Now they took another counsel. They dragged the tables together, piling them each on each and striving thus to climb the walls of the hall. This, perhaps, they might have done, some of them, had not every man pulled down his neighbour, so that they fell in tumbled heaps upon the stone flooring where the life was trampled out of them.

I turned and behind the veil of smoke fled from the platform, none seeing me, back behind the hangings that hid the outer sanctuary, where all the company of Isis was gathered, save only that fierce old priestess who yet with lamp and torch lit fire upon fire in the vaults beneath and, at last, doubtless, passed to Heaven on the chariot wheels of flame.

Here my servants stripped off my sacred trappings, wrapping me in dark garments and a hooded cloak. While they did so I looked back. The hall was filled with spouts of fire. The platform upon which Ochus had feasted was burning and the royal dead beneath blazed merrily. Only the stone gods by whom it was upborne still stared silent and dreadful through the vesture of smoke and fire, emblems of vengeance and eternal doom.

I could see no more but above the roaring flames I heard the mad screams of those trapped feasters who had come to see their king make a mock of Isis and her priestess, and these were terrible to hear. Then the floor gave way and down they went into the furnace pit beneath. Yes, they who worshipped fire were devoured of their own god.

******** 

Thus did I, Ayesha, Child-of-Wisdom, daughter of Yarab according to the flesh, work the vengeance of Heaven upon the Persians and their King of kings. By fire I wrought it, I whose path ever was and ever shall be marked by fire; I, Ayesha, who grew undying in the breath of fire and who, in the caverns of Kor, clasped it to my breast and was wedded to its secret Soul.

## CHAPTER 17

# The Flight and the Summons

We gained the hidden passage, bearing with us the treasures and the holy books of the Sanctuary that to this day lie buried in the caves of Kor. We came safely to the ruined temple of Osiris that the Persians had destroyed, and through it to the water-gate where the boats waited. None noting us, we embarked upon the boats, and glided away down Nile. If any saw us pass, they thought us country-folk, or perchance Egyptians who fled from the Persians in Memphis. But I think that none did see us, since all eyes were bent upon the flaming temple of Isis and all ears were filled with the rumours that fled from mouth to mouth, telling that the goddess had descended in fire and made an end of the tyrant Ochus, his generals, his councillors, and his court.

Thus did I bid farewell to white-walled Memphis which never again my eyes should see, though often my spirit shows it to me in visions of the night, and often I seem to hear the last wild agony of those upon whom I executed the decree of Heaven.

What happened afterward? Of that I know little, though rumours which Philo brought in the later years told me that Bagoas and the physician let fall or flung away the corpse of Ochus. These rumours said that it was found devoured by cats and jackals, so that had it not been for the rent Osiris wrappings, none would have known that here lay all that was left of the King of kings who desolated Egypt and made her a widow. They told also that Bagoas set Arses, the son of Ochus, upon the throne of Persia, and later poisoned him and all his children save one. Then it seems that he made Darius king, and this Darius Codamannus, knowing that Bagoas would poison him also, smote the first, forcing him to drink of the drugged cup that he had given to so many.

Such, it appears, was the end of Bagoas whom I used as the artist

452

uses a tool, harnessing him to the chariot of my wrath and, like the *Erinnyes* of the Greeks, making of him a sword wherewith I, or Heaven working through me, stabbed Persia to the heart, as through Tenes I had stabbed Sidon and through Sidon, Egypt. For such were the dooms that I was commanded to bring about. Thus Bagoas walked the road down which, aforetime, he drove his victims, and save for an evil name that echoes through the ages, this was the end of him and all his crimes.

Ere dawn our company came to the great reed-bed and through it by channels known only to our pilots, reached the secret shrine named *Isis-Among-the-Reeds*, where all had been made ready for our coming by the priests who watched there. Worn out, as well I might be, I laid me down and slept in a tiny cell, fearing no harm, since I knew surely that none would come to me or to those with me. Why I knew it I cannot say, but it was so. I knew further that I had done with Egypt; my work there was finished; henceforth we were divorced.

All that day I slept and through most of the night which followed, lulled by the whispering of the tall, surrounding reeds. I suppose that it must have been during those night hours that I dreamed a strange dream. In it I stood upon the desert, a vast waste of sand bordered in the distance by the Nile. I was alone in this desert save for the sun that sank in the west and the moon that rose in the east, and between them, shone upon by sun and moon, by Ra and by Isis, crouched a mighty Sphinx of stone with a woman's breasts and head, which Sphinx I knew was Egypt. There she sat, immemorial, unchanging, stern, beautiful, and stared with brooding eyes toward the east whence morn by morn arose the sun.

Appeared before her, one by one, each adorned with its own sacred emblems, all the gods of Egypt, a grim, fantastic crowd such as a brain distraught might fashion in its madness. Beast-headed and human-shaped, human-headed and beast-shaped; dogs and hawks, crocodiles and owls; swamp-birds, bulls, rams, and swollen-bellied dwarfs, came this rout of gods and bowed before the stern and beauteous Sphinx that wore a woman's head.

The Sphinx opened its mouth and spoke.

"What would ye of me who have sheltered you for long?" it asked.

One shaped like a man but from whose shoulders rose the beaked head of an ibis crowned with a crescent moon on which stood a feather, and holding in his hand the palette of a scribe; he whom the Egyptians named Thoth the Measurer, the Recorder, stood forward and made answer.

"We would bid thee farewell, Mother Egypt, our shelterer for thousands upon thousands of years. Out of thy mud we were created, into thy mud we return again."

"Is it so?" answered the Sphinx. "Well, what of it? Your short day is done. Yet tell me, who gave you these monstrous shapes and who named you gods?"

"The priests gave them to us and the priests named us gods," answered the ibis-headed man. "Now the priests are slain and we perish with the priests, because we are but gods made of thy mud, O Egypt."

"Then get you gone back into the mud, ye gods of mud. But first tell me, where is my Spirit that in the beginning, when the world was young, I sent forth that it might be a Soul divine to rule Egypt and the world?"

"We know not," answered Thoth the Recorder. "Ask it of the priests who made us. Perchance they have hidden it away. Farewell, O Egypt, farewell, O Sphinx, farewell, farewell!"

"Farewell!" echoed all that monstrous throng and then faded miserably away.

There was silence and with it solitude; the Sphinx stared at Nothingness and Nothingness stared at the Sphinx, and I, the watcher, watched. At length out of the nothingness arose something, and its shape was the shape of woman. It stood before the Sphinx and said,

"Behold me! I am thy lost spirit, but thou, O Egypt, didst not create me, for I created thee by a divine command. I am she whom men know as Isis here upon the Nile, but whom all the world, and all the worlds beyond the world know as Nature, the visible garment of the Almighty God. Gone are those fantasies, man-nurtured and priest-conceived. Yet I remain and thou remainest, aye, and though we be called by many names in the infinite days to come as we have been called in the infinite days that are gone, ever shall we remain until this little floating globe of earth ceases from its journeyings and melts back into that from which it came, the infinite arms of the infinite God."

Then the human-headed Sphinx rose from the rock whereon it had laid from the beginning. It reared its giant bulk, it went upon its knees and bowed to the woman-shape, the tiny woman-shape that was Isis, that was Nature, that was the Executrix of God. Thrice it bowed—and vanished.

The Spirit was left and I, Ayesha, was left. The Spirit turned and looked on me and lo! to my sight it was shaped as I am shaped. Sadly it looked, with grieving eyes, but never a word it spoke.

"Mother. My mother," I called, "speak to me, my mother!"

But never a word it answered, only it pointed to the skies and suddenly was gone. Then I, Ayesha, I stood alone in the immeasurable desert looking at the setting sun, looking at the rising moon, looking at the evening star that shone between, and wept and wept and wept because of my loneliness. For what company is there for a human soul in sun and moon and evening star when the spirit that formed it and them has departed, leaving them to gaze one upon the other, voiceless in the void?

\* \* \* \* \* \* \* \*

Such was my dream upon which I have pondered from year to year, asking an answer to its riddle from sun and moon and evening star, and finding none. Only the spirit can interpret its own problems, and to me, because of my sins, because, like the gods of Egypt I am fashioned of mud that veils my soul's dim lamp within, as yet that spirit is choked and dumb. Still, one day the Nile of death that I have dammed from me for so long will burst its barriers and wash away the mud. Then the lamp will shine out again; then the spirit will come and refresh it with its holy oil and breathe upon it with its breath, and in that breath perchance I shall understand my dream and learn the answer to its riddle.

Indeed already Time lays its foundations bare, for does not Holly tell me that for nigh upon two thousand years her gods have been dead in Egypt? For awhile they lingered on beneath the Greeks and Romans, changed masks of what once they were; for awhile their effigies were still painted upon the coffins of her people. Then the star of a new Faith rose, a bright and holy star, and in its beams they withered and crumbled into dust. Only the old Sphinx remains staring at the Nile and mayhap in the silence of the night holds commune with Isis the Mother, telling of dead kings and wars forgot, for being Nature's self, Isis alone can never die although from age to age her vestments change.

Yea, when I, Ayesha, fired the hall and burned those foul Persian feasters, with them I slew the gods of Egypt, and their sad and solemn statues stared a farewell to me through that wavering wall of flame. Nay, it was not I who did it, nor was it I who brought its doom on Sidon and his death on Ochus, but Destiny that used me as its sword, as I used Bagoas, me, Fate's doom-driven daughter.

\* \* \* \* \* \* \* \*

When I awoke it was still dark save for the light of the sinking moon, and in the night-wind, with a faint continual voice, the tall reeds whispered their prayer to Heaven. For though we know it not, all that has life must pray or die. From the great star rushing through space on its eternal journey to the humblest flower nestling beneath a stone, everything must pray, for prayer is the blood of the spirit that is in them and if that blood freezes, then they are resolved to matter that cannot grow and, knowing neither hope nor fear, is lost in the blind gulf of darkness.

I hearkened to those whispering reeds telling of the mysteries below to the mysteries above, and on the wings of their sweet petitions, sent up my own to Heaven.

For in truth I was troubled and knew not what to do. Here I could not bide for long, since surely, soon or late the Persians would seek me out and surely Bagoas, to cover his own crimes, would slay me as the destroyer of his king. This did not affright me who was weary of the world with all its horrors and in a mood to walk the gate of death, hoping that beyond it I might find a better. But there were those with me, my fellow servants to whom I had sworn safety and who put their faith in me, as though in truth I were the goddess herself, and if I died, certainly they would die also.

Therefore I must save them if I could. Yet how? I had no ship in which to flee from Egypt, and if it were to hand, whither should I fly now that all the earth was Persian? Oh! that Noot were here to counsel me. That he lived somewhere I was sure, since had not his voice spoken in the shrine and this by no priestly trick, for when I put up that prayer for guidance, I knew not how it would be answered or by whom, or if indeed it would but fall upon the deaf ears of the winds, and like a dead leaf, in their breath be blown away and lost.

Yes, he still lived, yet how could I know that it was here he lived? Mayhap he spoke from far beyond this stormy air of earth. Even so he who had counselled me once might counsel me again.

"O whispering reeds," I cried in my heart, "with all your million tongues, pray east and west and north and south, that Ayesha in her need may be helped of the wisdom of the holy Noot."

Yes, thus I prayed like a little, bewildered child who sees God in a cloud and thinks that flowers open for her joy and that the great Pleiades look down from the sky and love her. Yes, toil and grief and terror had made me like a little child.

Well, it is to such, rather than to the proud and learned, the rulers of the earth and the challengers of Heaven, that answers oftenest come and with them knowledge of the truth. At least to me, emptied of strength and wisdom and in that weak hour, forgetful even of my beauty, my great deeds, and the lore that I had won, swiftly there came an answer.

Of a sudden, at the first blush of dawn upon night's pale cheek, a priestess stood by my pallet,

"Awake, O *Isis-come-to-Earth*," she said, bowing. "A man stands without who would have speech with you. He came here in a boat and when he was challenged answered with all the signs, aye, and even spoke the secret words known to few, those words that open the sanctuary's door. The priests questioned him of his business. He answered that he could tell it only to her who bore the jewelled *sistrum*, to her who veiled her head with cloud like a mountain-top, to that Prophetess who in all shrines is known as Child-of-Wisdom, but who among men was named Ayesha, Daughter of Yarab."

Doubting me of this man and scenting treachery, I caused that instructed priestess to repeat one by one the mystical words that he had spoken. At last she uttered a certain syllable of which even she did not know the meaning. But I knew it and knew also who had its custody.

Filled with a great hope I rose and wrapped myself in a dark garment.

"Lead me to this man," I said, "but first make sure that three priests stand round him with drawn swords."

She went and presently returned again, saying that the man awaited me in the fore-court of the little temple, guarded as I had bidden. To this court I followed her. It was but a small place, like to a large room. I entered it from the sanctuary to the west. Through the eastern door poured the first rays of the rising sun, that struck upon a man who stood waiting in the centre of the court, guarded by three priests with lifted swords.

I could not see his face, though perhaps even beneath my cowl he could see mine upon which those rays also struck. At least I saw him start, then fall to his knees, raising his hand in salute with a quick and curious motion. It was enough. I knew him at once. This man was Philo and no other. With a word I bade the armed priests leave us and the priestess who had accompanied me bide in the shadow. Then I went forward, saying,

"Rise, Philo, for whom I have looked so long that I began to think you were no more to be found beneath the sun. Whence come you, Philo, and for what purpose?"

"O Prophetess, O adored, O Lady divine," he answered in a voice of joy, "I, your slave in the flesh and your fellow servant in the goddess, greet you whom never I hoped to see again after all that has passed in Egypt. Suffer that I may kiss your hand and thereby learn that you are still a woman and not a ghost."

I stretched out my hand and reverently he touched it with his lips.

"Now tell your tale, friend Philo," I said. "Whence come you, most welcome Philo, and by what magic do you find me here?"

"I come from far to the south, Prophetess, out of an ancient land of which you shall learn afterward. For three moons have I struggled over difficult seas driven by contrary winds, to reach the mouths of Nile and to find you, if still you lived."

"And who sent you, friend Philo?"

"A certain Master who is known to both of us, he sent me."

"Is he perchance named Noot?" I asked in a low voice, "and if so, did you sail hither over mortal seas, or over those through which Ra travels in the Under-world?"

This I said wondering, for it came into my mind that he who knelt before me might perchance be not a man but a shadow sent to summon me to the halls of Osiris.

"Mortal seas I sailed; those of the Under-world still await my prow, O Wisdom's Daughter. Here is the proof of it," and drawing a roll from his bosom, with it he touched his brow in token of reverence, then gave it to me.

I broke the seals, I opened that roll, and by the light of the rising sun I read. It ran thus:

"From Noot, the son of Noot, the high-priest, the guardian of Secrets, to Ayesha, Child of Isis, Wisdom's Daughter, the Instructed, the Oracle: Thus saith Noot.

"I live, I do not sleep in my eternal house. My spirit shows me that which passes upon the Nile. I know that you have obeyed my commands which I gave to you before we parted in the bygone years, O my begotten in the goddess. I know that you have waited patiently in faith through many tribulations. I know also that this writing will find you in an hour of great peril when for the second time you have escaped from fire, leaving behind you the ashes of your foes. Come to me now and at once, Philo the beloved brother and the consecrated *sistrum* that is the sceptre of your office being your guides. Philo shall lead you; through all dangers the *sistrum* shall be your shield. I write no more.

"Obey, Mouth of Isis, bringing with you those that are left to the service of the goddess. Read the seal of Noot, high-priest and prophet, and tarry not."

I read and hid away the roll. Then I asked,

"Upon what wings do we fly to Noot who is so far from us, friend Philo?"

"Upon those of a ship that is known to you, Prophetess, the ship named *Hapi*, upon which already you have passed many perils. She lies yonder fully manned in the outer fringe of this sea of reeds."

"How did you find those reeds, and how did you know that I was hidden among them?" I asked curiously.

"Noot marked them on a chart he gave me and told me that in them, where, as the story runs, Isis discovered the heart of Osiris, there I should find the child of Isis. Prophetess, inquire no more."

I heard and returned thanks in my heart. Truly what I whispered to the whispering reeds had been borne to the ears of Heaven.

The *trireme Hapi*, with her mast struck, lay hidden in shallow water midst beds of tall bulrushes and papyrus plants, into which Philo had worked her by the moonlight. All that day we laboured lading her with the treasures of the temple of Isis and those of the secret shrine, which were many, for during these times of trouble much gold and priceless furnishing of precious metals had been hidden here among the reeds. Also with them were some of the most ancient and hallowed statues of the goddess fashioned in gold and ivory and alabaster stone.

All of these together with my own great wealth of jewels and other gear were borne in boats to the *Hapi* and stored within her hold where they lay hid beneath much merchandise that Philo had purchased at the ports of Nile. Hither he had come disguised as a merchant from the south, having his ship laden with the produce of Punt such as ivory and rare woods. These he sold at the ports where he gathered tidings of all that passed in Egypt, and having purchased other goods in place of them, passed unsuspected up the Nile to the secret Isle of Reeds where Noot had bidden him to make inquiry for me at the time of full moon in this very month. It was not difficult for him to find this isle as it seemed that, being an initiate of Isis, once in bygone days he had visited it on the business of the goddess.

While we were at this work we saw boats full of Persian soldiers pass down Nile, as though they searched for someone, and toward the evening saw them return up Nile again, heading for Memphis. I knew for whom they sought and noted that they did so very idly, since all believed that I and my company had perished with the Persians in the burning temple.

At nightfall I gathered the priests and priestesses, in all they were thirty and three in number, and spoke to them, saying,

"Here in Egypt we who are the servants of the goddess can stay no more. The gods of Khem are fallen, their shrines are desolate, and death by sword and fire, or by the torturer's hooks, is the lot of those that worship them. Noot, the high-priest, the Master, the Prophet, summons us from afar, bidding us bear the worship of the goddess to new lands that lie I know not where. Philo, our brother, is his messenger and here is the message written in this roll; read it if you will. I, the Oracle and Prophetess, obey the summons; this very night I sail setting my course for seas unknown, and trusting to the goddess to be my guide, mayhap into the gates of death. Noot the high-priest bids you to accompany me. Yet I give you choice. Bide on here if you will and live out your lives disguised as scribes or peasants, for in the temples you can no longer find a home. Mayhap thus you shall escape the vengeance of the Persians. Or come with me if you will, knowing that I promise you nothing. Let each speak as the Spirit directs the heart within."

They consulted together; then one by one they said that it was their mind to be of my company since they held it better to die with me and pass pure to the arms of the goddess rather than to live on defiled, or perchance to perish miserably beneath the stripes of the executioners, having first been forced to do sacrifice to the Persian god of Fire. So man by man and woman by woman they swore the oath that might be broken by those who would escape the jaws of the Devourer, and in token kissed the holy *sistrum* that I held to the lips of each. Then for the last time we celebrated the rites of Isis in a temple of Isis on the Nile and with weeping and with woe sang the psalm of farewell, such as is chanted over the dead of our fellowship.

This done we went to the boats and were rowed on board the *Hapi*.

When the moon was bright the mariners, fierce, foreign men most of them, such as I had never seen before, who wore great earrings of gold and had rings thrust through their noses, poled the vessel out from among the reeds into the deep waters of the Nile. Here they hoisted the mast and set the sails which presently filled before the strong wind blowing from the upper land, and bore us forward swiftly.

Passing out of the Nile by a little-used mouth, as we could do now that the river was in flood, we entered the canal that joins the seas, which canal the old Pharaohs dug and the Persians had caused to be cleared of drifting sand. By it, though not easily, for in places it was both narrow and shallow, at length we came safely into the Red Sea and bade farewell to Egypt. None hindered us on this journey, and, having crossed the lakes, only once did we stay at a little unravaged town at the far mouth of the canal, to buy bread, fresh fish, and meat wherewith to stock our ship.

This town we found to be full of rumours, for the news of the death of Ochus had reached it and many tales were told of the manner of his end. That which these coast-dwellers favoured was that Set the god had appeared in person at a feast, and seizing Ochus, had set him upon a winged Apis, that very Apis bull which he had sacrificed and eaten, and borne him away to hell. At this fable I smiled, though indeed in it there was a seed of truth, since without doubt, if there be a hell, the blood-soaked Ochus was its inhabitant that day.

* * * * * * * *

Now of all that journey I, who grow weary of writing, will omit the story. Most marvellously it prospered, so much so that I think, unseen by us, spirits from the Under-world must have stood upon our prow. From day to day a strong and steady wind blowing from the north drove us forward swiftly. No storm smote us nor did we strike upon any rock, and when we made land for water, either it was uninhabited, or the folk who dwelt there, strange barbarous folk, were friendly.

So the time went by creeping from moon to moon and ever we sailed on southward. Nor was the time unhappy, since there I sat in that same cabin which had been mine when Pharaoh gave me as a bribe to Tenes and that therefore was familiar to me, having something of the aspect of a home. Indeed with a certain taste of acid pleasure, from time to time I recalled all that had happened to me upon this ship and in that very cabin. For instance where I had wrung the writing from the passion-maddened Tenes; where he had stood and knelt; where his shadow had struck upon the cedar walls. There, too, in the wood was an arrow hole, which arrow should have drunk my life.

Then in the waist of the ship was the place where the boarders from the *Holy Fire* had won aboard, whence Kallikrates, the Grecian captain turned *heirophant*, had beat them back so gallantly. Aft, also, was the shelter where I had visited him and dressed his wounds that were almost to the death. Here I placed upon his finger the charmed scarab ring of Khaemuas, the Magician, whereon were cut symbols with a secret meaning, though they seemed to read only as "Son of Ra," that this ring might raise him from the darkness of death, as Osiris rose and as Ra rises from the Under-world.

Here, too, it was that I heard him mistake me for another woman and to that woman give his thanks, thus opening my eyes to all the folly of my heart. Years ago these things had chanced to me, and now when

461

they were dead things, I say that I could dream of them with that soft grief which is like to the tenderness of eve after the promise of the morning and the burning noonday heat have become but memories buried beneath the dust of time. Yet it is true that now and again those memories renewed their life, especially within the shrines of sleep.

Oh! it was all so long ago. Had not Philo's beard, that I remembered brown and rich, since then grown gray, and were not his curling locks thinned upon his temples? And I who then was young, had I not grown to middle-age, though still I remained more lovely than any other woman in the world, and was not my soul burdened with much learning, and had not the sorrows I had passed pierced it with a thousand spears? Now, too, doubtless Kallikrates was dead, and all the dreams to which he alone among men had given birth within me had gone wherever dreams may go, perchance to be lost in the vast unknown, or perchance after the change called death, there to be found again?

Yet I, I wandered forward on my path, Fate-driven as of old, to what end I knew not and did not greatly care to know. For now it seemed my part was played; the world and its stirrings were left behind me and the last shreds of my web must be spun of poor stuff in petty, unknown places, where I should patter prayers beneath an alien sky till it pleased death to enfold me in its wings and bear me to the depths of its enormous habitations.

Well, so let it be, since, as I have said, I was weary of the world; its toils, its bloody issues, and its perpetual strivings to grasp that which man or woman may not hold—except in dreams.

With Philo I talked much, but always of the past; of those things which we had experienced together, or of other events of his earlier, adventurous life, or of my own. A most pleasant companion was this Philo, of a shrewd wit and some learning also, a brave citizen of the world who had seen much, and yet one who revered the gods, whatever the gods might be, and had thoughts of that which lies beyond the world, whatever this may be. But of the present or of what had happened to him since he sailed away with Noot, my Master, when Ochus invaded Egypt, and least of all of the future and whither we went or why, I did not talk at all.

For when these matters came to my lips, as they did even before we were clear of Nile, Philo made a certain sign to me which being interpreted meant that he was under an oath, a very solemn oath, not to speak of any of them, which oath I respected, as indeed I was bound to do. Therefore I asked no more and sailed on careless as a child that recks not of what is to come and from whom death is still very far away.

CHAPTER 18

# The Tale of Philo

Once more it was a night of full moon. As we had done for many days we were sailing before that steady wind along the coast of Libya, having this upon our right hand, and upon our left, at a distance, a line of rocky reef upon which breakers fell continually.

It was a very splendid moon that turned the sea to silver and lit up the palm-grown shore almost as brightly as does the sun. I sat upon the deck near to my cabin and by me stood Philo watching that shore intently.

"For what do you seek, Philo? Are you in fear of sunken rocks?"

"Nay, Child of Isis, yet it is true that I seek a certain rock which by my reckoning should now be in sight. Ah!"

Then suddenly he ran forward and shouted an order. Men leapt up and sprang to the ropes while the rowers began to get out the sweeps. As they did this the *Hapi* came round so that her bow pointed to the shore and the great sail sank to the deck. Then the long oars bit into the water and drove us shoreward.

Philo returned.

"Look, Lady," he said. "Now that the moon has risen higher you can see well," and he pointed to a headland in front of us.

Following his outstretched hand with my eyes I perceived a great rock many cubits in height and carven on the crest of it a head far larger than that of the huge Sphinx in Egypt. Or perchance it was not carved; perchance Nature had fashioned it thus. At least there it stood and will stand, a terrible and hideous thing, having the likeness of an Ethiopian's head gazing eternally across the sea.

"What is it?" I asked.

"Lady, it is the Guardian of the Gate of the land whither we go. Legend tells that it is shaped to the likeness of the first king of that land who lived thousands upon thousands of years before the pyramids were built; also that his bones lie in it, or at least, that it is haunted by his spirit. For this reason none dare to touch and much less to climb yonder monstrous rock."

Then he left me to see to the matters of the ship, because, as he said in going, the entrance to the place was strait and dangerous. But I sat on alone upon the deck watching this strange new sight.

Within an hour, rowing carefully, we entered the mouth of a river, having the rock shaped like to a Negro's head upon our right. Then it was that I saw something which put me in mind of Philo's tale about an ancient king. For there, unless I dreamed, upon the very point of the skull of the effigy, of a sudden I perceived a tall form clad in armour which shone silvery bright in the moon's rays. It leaned upon a great spear, and when we were opposite to it, straightened itself and bent forward as though to stare at our ship beneath. Next, thrice it lifted the spear in salutation; thrice it bowed, as I thought in obeisance to me, and having done so, threw its arms wide and was gone.

Afterward I asked Philo if he also had seen this thing.

"Nay," he answered in a doubtful voice as though the matter were one of which he did not wish to talk, adding,

"It is not the custom of mariners to study that head in the moonlight, because the story goes that if they do and chance to see some such ghost as that you tell of, it casts a spear toward them, who then are doomed to die within the year. Yet at you, Child of Isis, he cast no spear, only bowed and gave the salute of kings, or so you tell me. Therefore doubtless neither you nor any of us, your companions, are marked for death."

I smiled and said that I whose wraith was in touch with Heaven feared not the wrath of any ancient king, nor did we speak more of this matter. Yet in the after ages it came into my mind that there was truth in this story and that this long-dead king appeared thus to give greeting to her who was destined to rule his land through many generations; also that perchance he was not dead at all, but, having drunk of a certain Cup of Life of which I was to learn, lived eternally there upon the rock.

I laid me down and slept, and when I woke in the bright morning it was to find that we had passed from that river into a canal dug by man which, though deep, was too narrow for the sweeps to work. Therefore the *Hapi* must be pushed along with poles and towed by ropes dragged at by the mariners from a path that ran upon the bank.

For three days we travelled thus making but slow progress, since the toil of dragging so large a ship was great, and at night we tied up to the bank, as boats do upon the Nile. All this while we saw no habitation though certain ruins we did see. Indeed that country was very desolate and full of great swamps that were tenanted by wild beasts, the haunt of owls and bitterns, where lions roared and serpents crept, great serpents such as I had never seen.

At length at noon on the fourth day we came to a lake where the canal ended, which lake once had been a harbour, for we saw stone quays where still were tied some boats that seemed to be little used. Here Philo said that we must disembark and travel on by land. So we left the *Hapi*, sadly enough for my part, because those were happy, quiet days that I had spent on board of her, veritable oases in the storm-swept desert of my life.

Scarcely had we set foot upon the land when appeared, I knew not whence, a company of men, handsome, hook-nosed, sombre men, such as I had seen among the crew upon the *Hapi*. These men, though so fierce in appearance, were not barbarians, for they wore linen garments that gave to them the aspect of priests. Moreover, their leaders could speak Arabic in its most ancient form, which, having studied it, as it chanced, I knew. With this army, who bore bows and spears, came a multitude of folk of a baser sort that carried litters, or burdens, also a guard of great fellows that Philo told me were my especial escort. Now my patience failed so that I turned upon Philo saying,

"Hitherto, Friend, I have trusted myself to you, because it seemed decreed that I should do so. Now tell me, I pray you, what means this journey over countless leagues of sea into a land untrod, and whither go I in the fellowship of these barbarians? Because you brought me a certain writing in an acceptable hour, I gave myself into your keeping, nor did I even ask any revelation from the goddess or seek to solve the mystery by spells. Yet, now I ask and, as the Prophetess of Isis, demand the truth of you, her humbler servant."

"Lady divine," answered Philo, bowing himself before me, "what I have withheld is by command, the command of a very great one, of none less than Noot the aged and holy. You go to an old land that is yet new to find Noot, your master and mine."

"In the flesh or in the spirit?" I asked.

"In the flesh, Prophetess, if still he lives, as these men say, and see, I accompany you, I whom in the past you have found faithful. If I fail you, let my life pay forfeit, and for the rest, ask it of the holy Noot."

"It is enough," I said. "Lead on."

We entered the litters; we laded the bearers with the treasures of Isis and with my own peculiar wealth, and having placed the ship *Hapi* under guard, marched into the unknown like to some great caravan of merchants. For days we marched, following a broad road that was broken down in places, over plains and through vast swamps, and at night sleeping in caves or covered by tents which we brought with us.

This was a strange journey that I made surrounded by that host of hook-nosed, silent, ghost-like men, who, as I noted, loved the night better than they did the day. Almost might I have thought that they had been sent from Hades to conduct us to those gates from which for mortals there is no return. My fellowship of the priests and priestesses grew afraid and clustered round me at night, praying to be led back to familiar lands and faces.

I answered them that what I dared they must dare also, and that the goddess was as near to us here as she had been in Egypt, nor could death be closer to us than it was in Egypt. Yea, I bade them have faith, since without faith we could not be at peace one hour who, lacking it, must be overwhelmed with terrors, even with the walls of citadels.

They hearkened, bowing their heads and saying that whatever else they might doubt, they trusted themselves to me.

So we went on, passing through a country where more of these half-savage men that I learned were called *Amahagger* dwelt in villages surrounded by their cattle, or by colonies in caves. At last there arose before us a mighty mountain whose towering cliffs had the appearance of a wall so vast that the eye could not compass it. By a gorge we penetrated that mountain and found within it an enormous, fertile plain, and on the plain a city larger than Memphis or than Thebes, but a city half in ruins.

Passing over a great bridge spanning a wide moat once filled with water that now here and there was dry, we entered the walls of that city and by a street broader than any I had ever seen, bordered by many noble, broken houses, though some of these seemed still to be inhabited, came to a glorious temple like to those of Egypt, only greater, and with taller columns. Across its grass-grown courts, that were set one within another, we were carried to some inner sanctuary. Here we descended from the litters and were led to sculptured chambers that seemed to have been made ready to receive us, where we cleansed ourselves of the dust of travel and ate. Then came Philo, who conducted me to a little lamp-lit hall, for now the night had fallen, where was a chair of state such as high-priests used, in which at his bidding I sat myself.

I think that being weary with travel, I must have slept in that chair, since I dreamed or seemed to dream that I received worship such as is given to a queen, or even to a goddess. Heralds hailed me, voices sang to me, even spirits appeared in troops to talk to me, the spirits of those who thousands of years before had departed from the earth. They told me strange stories of the past and of the future; tales of a fallen people, of a worship and a glory that had gone by and been swallowed in the gulfs of Time. Then gathering in a multitude they seemed to hail me, crying,

"Welcome, appointed Queen! Build thou up that which has fallen. Discover thou that which is lost. Thine is the strength, thine the opportunity, yet beware of the temptations, beware of the flesh, lest the flesh should overcome the spirit and by its fall add ruin unto ruin, the ruin of the soul to the ruin of the body."

I awoke from my vision and saw Philo standing before me.

"Hearken, Philo," I said. "Of these mysteries I can bear no more. The time has come when you must speak, or face my wrath. Why have I been brought hither to this strange and distant land where it seems that I must dwell in a place of ruins?"

"Because the holy Noot so commanded, O Child of Wisdom," he answered. "Was it not set down in the writing I gave you at the Isle of Reeds upon the Nile?"

"Where then is the holy Noot?" I asked. "Here I see him not. Is he dead?"

"I do not think that he is dead, Lady. Yet to the world he is dead. He has become a hermit, one who dwells in a cave in a perilous place not very far from this city. To-morrow I will bring you to him, if that be your will. So only can you see him who now for years has never left that cave, or so I think, save to fetch the food which is prepared for him."

"A strange tale, Philo, though that Noot should become a hermit does not amaze me, since such was ever his desire. Now tell me how he came hither, and you with him?"

"Lady, you will remember that in the bygone years when Nectanebes, he who was Pharaoh, fled up Nile, the holy Noot embarked upon my ship, the *Hapi*, to sail to the northern cities, that there he might treat with the Persians for the ransom of those temples of Egypt that remained unravished."

"I remember, Philo. What chanced to you upon that journey?"

"This, Lady: that we were very nearly slain, every one of us, for whom the Persians had set a trap, thinking to snare Noot and his company and torture him till he revealed where the treasures of the temples of Isis were hid away. Nevertheless, because I am a good sail-or and because that warrior priest, Kallikrates, was brave, we escaped into the canal which is called the *Road of Rameses* and so at last out to sea, for to return up Nile was impossible. Then Noot commanded that I should sail on southerly upon a course he seemed to know well enough; or perchance the goddess taught it to him; I cannot say. At least I obeyed, so that in the end we reached that harbour which is guarded by a rock carved to the likeness of an Ethiopian's head, and thence travelled to this place, still guided by the wisdom of Noot who knew the road."

"And Kallikrates? What became of Kallikrates—who it seems was with you?" I asked in an indifferent voice, though my heart burned to hear his answer.

"Lady, so far as it is known to me this is the story of Kallikrates and the Princess Amenartas."

"The Princess Amenartas! By all the gods, what is your meaning, Philo? She went up Nile with Nectanebes her father, he who was Pharaoh."

"Nay, Lady, she went down Nile with Kallikrates, or perhaps with Noot, or perhaps with herself alone. I do not know with whom she hid since I never saw her, nor learned that she was aboard my ship until we were two days' journey out to sea and the coasts of Egypt were far behind us."

"Is it so?" I asked coldly, though I was filled with bitter anger. "And what did the holy Noot when he found that this woman was aboard his vessel?"

"Lady, he did nothing except look on her somewhat doubtfully."

"And what did the priest Kallikrates? Did he strive to be rid of her?"

"Nay, Lady, and indeed that would have been impossible, unless he had thrown her overboard. He did nothing except talk with her—that is, so far as I saw."

"Well, then, Philo, where is she now, and where is Kallikrates? I do not see him in this place."

"Lady, I cannot tell you, but I think it probable that they are dead and in the fellowship of Osiris. When we had been some weeks at sea we were driven by storm to an island off the coast under the lee of which we took shelter, a very fertile and beautiful island, peopled by a kindly folk. After we had sailed again from that island it was discovered that the priest Kallikrates and the Royal Princess Amenartas were missing from the ship, nor because of the strong wind that blew us forward was it possible for us to return to seek for them. I made inquiry of the matter and the sailors told me that they had been fishing together and that a shark which took their bait pulled them both into the sea; in which case doubtless they were drowned."

"And did you believe that story, Philo?"

"Nay, Lady. I understood at once that it was one which the sailors had been bribed to tell. Myself I think that they went to the island in one of the boats of the people who dwell there; perhaps because they could no longer bear the cold eyes of Noot fixed upon them, or perhaps to gather fruit, for which those who have been long upon water often conceive a great desire. But," he added simply, "I do not know why they should have done this seeing that the island-dwellers brought us plenty of fruits in their boats."

"Doubtless they preferred to pluck them fresh with their own hands, Philo."

"Perhaps, Lady, or perhaps they wished to stay awhile upon that island. At least I noted that the Princess took her garments and her jewels with her, which she could scarcely have done if the shark had dragged her into the sea."

"Are you so sure, Philo, that she did not leave some of those jewels behind—in *your* keeping, Philo? It is very strange to me that the Princess Amenartas could have come aboard your ship and have left your ship, and you know nothing."

Now Philo looked up innocently and said,

"Surely it is lawful for a captain to receive faring money from his passengers, and that I admit I did. But I do not understand why the Child of Wisdom is so wrath because a Greek and a great lady were by chance left together upon an island where, for aught I know, one or other of them may have had friends."

"Am I not the guardian of the honour of the goddess?" I answered. "And do you not know that under our law Kallikrates was sworn to her alone?"

"If so, Prophetess, doubtless that captain, or that priest, remembers his oath and deals with this princess as though she were his sister or his mother. At the least the goddess can guard her own honour, so why should you fret your soul concerning it, Prophetess? Lastly, it is probable that by now both of them are dead and have made all things clear to Isis in the heavenly halls."

Thus he prattled on, adding lie to lie as only a Greek can do. I listened until I could bear no more. Then I said but one word. It was "Begone!"

He went humbly, yet as I thought, smiling.

Oh! now I saw it all. Noot had made a plot to remove Kallikrates far from me, so that I might never look upon him again. Philo knew of this plot, and through him Amenartas knew it also. Unknown to Noot she bribed Philo to hide her upon his ship till they were far from land, though whether the plan was known to Kallikrates I could not say, nor did it greatly matter. Then the rest followed. Amenartas appeared upon the ship and cast her net about Kallikrates who had sworn to have done with her, and the end can be guessed. Noot was wrath with them, so wrath that when the chance came they fled away, purposing to stay upon that island until they could find a ship to take them back to Egypt or elsewhere. Thus, I was sure, ran the story, and, as it proved afterward, I was right.

Well, they were gone and as I hoped, dead, since only death could cover up such a sin, and for my part I was glad that I had done with Kallikrates and his light-of-love. And yet there, seated on the couch of state, I wept—because of the outrage done to Isis whom I served. Or was it for myself that I wept? I cannot say, I only know that my tears were bitter. Also I was very lonely in this strange and desolate place. Because Noot had commanded it, sending for me from afar, and what he commanded, that I must obey. Where, then, was Noot, who, Philo swore, still lived? Why had he not appeared to greet me? I covered my eyes with my hands and threw out my soul to Noot, saying,

"Come to me, O Noot. Come to me, my beloved Master."

Lo! a voice, a well-remembered voice answered.

"Daughter, I am here."

I let fall my hand. I gazed with my tear-stained eyes, and behold! before me, white-robed, gold-filleted, snowy-bearded, grown very ancient and ethereal, stood the prophet and high-priest, my Master. For a moment I thought that it was his spirit which I saw. Then he moved, and I heard his white robes rustle, and knew that there stood Noot himself whom I had travelled so many thousand leagues to find.

I rose; I ran to him; I seized his thin hand and kissed it, while he, murmuring, "My Daughter, at last, at last!" leaned forward and with his lips touched me on the brow.

"Far away your summons reached me in an hour of peril," I said. "Behold! I obeyed, I came. In faith I came, asking no questions, and I am here in safety, for I think the goddess herself was with me on that journey. Tell me all, O Noot. What is this place? How were you brought to it and why have you called me to you?"

"Hearken, Daughter," he said, seating himself beside me on the throne-like couch. "This city is named Kor. Once she was queen of the world, as after her, Babylon, Thebes, Tyre, and Athens are, or have been queens. From Kor thousands of years ago in the black, lost ages Egypt was peopled, as were other lands. In those dim days by another title her citizens worshipped Isis, Queen of Heaven, only they named her *Truth* whom in Egypt you know as Maat. Then apostasy arose and many of this great people, abandoning the pure and gentle worship of Isis wrapped in the veil of Truth, under the name of Rezu, a fierce sun-daemon, set up another god to whom they made human sacrifices, as the Sidonians did to Moloch. Yea, they sacrificed men, women, and children by thousands, and even learned to eat their flesh, first as a sacred rite, and afterward to satisfy their appetites. Heaven saw and grew wrath; Heaven smote the people with a mighty pestilence, so that they perished and perished till few were left. Thus Kor fell by the sword of God as, for like cause, fell Sidon."

"Of all this afterward," I answered impatiently. "Tell me first, how came you here? Long years ago you sailed down Nile to treat with the Persians for the ransom of the temples of Egypt, a mission in which it seems you failed, my Father."

"Aye, Ayesha, I failed. It was but a trap, since those false-hearted Fire-worshippers thought to take me captive and hold my life in gage against all the treasures of Isis. By the cunning and seamanship of Philo and the courage of a priest named Kallikrates, whom you may still remember after all these years," here he glanced at me sharply, "I escaped when a gang of them disguised as envoys strove to snare me. But the road up Nile being barred, we were forced to fly south, and down Pharaoh's Great Ditch, till at length, after many wanderings and adventures, we came to this land, as it was fated that I should do. You will remember, Daughter, that I told you I believed that we were parting for a long while, although I believed also that we should meet again in the flesh."

"I remember well," I answered, "also that I swore to come to you at the appointed hour."

"I came to this land," went on Noot, "but Kallikrates, the Greek captain who was a priest of Isis, never reached it. He was lost on the way."

"With another, my Father. But now I have heard that story from Philo."

"With another who caused him to break his vows. Be sure, Daughter, that I knew nothing of her plot or that she was hidden aboard the ship, though perchance Philo knew. The goddess hid it from me, doubtless for her own purposes."

"Are this pair dead, or do they still live, my Father?"

"I cannot say; that also is hidden from me. Better for them if they are dead, since soon or late for such sacrilege vengeance will fall upon the head of one, if not of both of them. Peace be to them. May they be forgiven! At least as I think they loved each other much and, since love is very strong, all who have ever loved where they ought not should have pity on them," and again his questioning eyes played upon my face.

## CHAPTER 19

# The Hermitage of Noot

"Tell me of what has passed in Egypt since Ochus conquered and Nectanebes fled away. Does Ochus still live, Daughter?" asked Noot after a pause during which both of us had sat staring at the ground.

"Nay, Father, Ochus is dead and by my hand, or through it," and I told him all that story of the burning of the temple of Isis at my command and of the Persians who defiled it.

"A great deed such as you alone could have planned," he muttered, "but terrible, terrible!"

"Then your soul must bear its burden, Prophet, since it was your voice that we heard in the sanctuary, when in our extreme we prayed for guidance, and it told us to go forward. There are those with me who can bear witness that they heard your very voice, as I do."

"Mayhap, Daughter. It is true that on a certain day not so many moons ago, I seemed to hear you calling to heaven in great trouble and danger, also that by direction which came I know not whence, I answered in my spirit that you must 'fulfil and fear not.' What you were to fulfil I did not know, though it came to my mind that the business had something to do with the burning of a temple."

"As it had indeed. Well, I fulfilled, as Ochus Artaxerxes with some hundreds of his Persian ravagers can testify before all the gods until the end of time, for those dogs at least have ceased to pollute the earth and to-day are enriching hell. There let them lie with Tenes and Nectanebes also, if in truth he has joined them, and many another false priest and king. Afterward we will talk of them and all their deeds of shame. But first tell me why I am here. For what end did you summon me from Egypt. Was it to save me from death?"

"Nay, Ayesha, from more than that. Why should I wish to hold you back from the great boon of death in which so soon I must have joined you? I summoned you because I was commanded so to do, that now when Isis has passed from Egypt, you should cause her worship to re-arise at Kor which was her ancient home. It is willed that here you should abide and once more build up this people and make it great by the help of the Queen of Heaven who then will lead it on to triumph and to glory."

"That is a mighty task, Prophet. Still perchance with your aid it may be done if the gods give me life and wisdom."

He shook his head and answered,

"Look not to my aid, for at length my day is finished. Has not Philo told you that I mix no more with matters of the world, I who for years past have dwelt a hermit in a terrible place, sheltered only by a cave and lost in the contemplation of holy things?"

"No, Father, he has told me little or nothing—by your will, or so he said," I replied, amazed.

"Yet it is so; moreover, presently I must return to that prison whence I came, there to await the change called death. I have played my part, but your work still remains to do; Philo will aid you in it."

"Why do you live in that place, Father, leaving me without the guidance of your wisdom?"

"Because there I guard a great secret, that was revealed to me long ago, it matters not how, the greatest secret in the whole world—that of how men may escape death and live on eternally upon the earth."

Now I stared at him, thinking that age and abstinence had made him mad. Then, to test the matter, I asked,

"If it be so great a secret, why do you tell it to me, Master?"

"Because I must. Because I know well that if I do not, you would discover it for yourself, and being unwarned, would fall into the trap, and still living beneath the sun, dare to clothe yourself with this garment of immortality. It was for this reason that until twice the command had come to me, I would not summon you to Kor."

Now a new thought thrilled my soul. If this strange tale were true; if indeed here on earth there could be found such a door leading to the divine, why should I not pass it, and become as are the gods? Only I did not believe that it was true.

"Surely you have dreamed in your loneliness, my Father," I said. "But know that if you did not dream, if it were true, I, Ayesha, should be minded to wear that robe of life eternal. Why not, O Prophet?"

"Because, Ayesha, the man or woman who dared to eat of this fruit forbidden to their race here on earth, where death is decreed for all, would be a man or woman who dared to enter into hell."

"I think otherwise, Prophet Noot, I think that this man or woman would enter into glory and become the ruler of the world," I answered, and as I spoke the words my eyes flashed and my breast heaved.

"Not so, Ayesha, since from that fatal peak of pride Heaven will beat back all human feet. Oh, hearken to me and purge your soul of the madness of this desire by which I see already it is possessed. It was laid upon me to reveal this secret to you, which I think was given me for that very purpose, so that you might show your greatness by rejecting it, the deadliest bribe that the god of Ill ever offered to mortal woman."

"Or perchance by accepting it, Master!"

"Nay, nay! Bethink you. Is the world a fit place for the undying? Moreover, this secret that I guard is but the world's spirit, not that of immortality; the hidden force from which our earth draws its strength, but which will perish with the earth, as it must do upon a day still hidden in the deeps of time. The drinker of that cup therefore would become, not eternal, but long-lived only, destined to perish at last with this passing star. For him death would not be destroyed, it would only be delayed, waiting ever to snare him in the end. Meanwhile he must endure desolate and alone, watching the generations pass one by one to their appointed rest; while, filled perchance with fearful appetites which he must know eternally and yet remain unsatisfied, he stands but as a frozen rock upon the plain, wearing a human shape, yet alien to mortality, though still torn by its ambitions, its loves, its hates, its hopes, its fears, and waiting terrified for that predestined moment when this globe shall crumble and death shall devour it and him.

"I am old, I am feeble, my hour is well nigh done, I pass to my repose in Heaven. Ayesha, I have no strength to stay your feet, if you elect to drink this cup my weak hand cannot dash it from your lips. Yet as one who has taught and loved you, as one to whom the gods have given great wisdom, I pray you to thrust aside this great temptation. As our faith teaches truly, already your spirit is immortal and has its home prepared above. Desire not, therefore, to perpetuate your flesh, since if you do, Ayesha, I tell you that you will become but as a painted mummy in a tomb, simulating life, yet dead and cold within. Swear to me, Daughter, that you will lock this knowledge in your heart and thrust the poison from your lips."

"You speak wisely," I answered, "aye, as one inspired by the truth, and though I take no oaths, it is my purpose to do your will. Yet, Father, what is this secret? Having told me so much, tell all, lest I should go to discover it for myself."

"Daughter, near to this ancient city, amid the mountain cliffs, deep in the bowels of the rocks burns a travelling fire which is the very soul of the world, the flaming heart that gives it life. Yet this fire is no fire, but rather the essence of existence, and he who bathes in it will be filled with that essence and endure while it endures."

"Perchance such a one might be destroyed by that fire," I answered doubtfully.

"Daughter, I would that I could leave you thinking thus, for then a great fear would pass from me. But we who are the chief servants of Isis dare not hide the truth from one another, since to do so is to break our oaths. Moreover, in this matter I do not speak with my own voice, but with that of a Strength which is greater than I, to whom now I stand so near that almost it and I are one. Therefore to your eyes I must withdraw all veils, showing you what is, as it is, and not as I would have it be. Yonder fire will not destroy the mortal who finds the courage to stand in its raging path; it will give him life, and with it such strength, such beauty, and such wisdom as have never been the lot of man born of woman. Also it will give him such passions, such despairs, such un-ending woes as hitherto no mortal heart has known.

"There is the truth. Ask me not how it comes into my keeping and what that voice may be which is speaking it through my lips. A minute gone this truth was mine alone, or perchance mine and one other's. Now it is yours also, and being yours, I pray to that Divine from which we come and whither we return again, that it may give you strength and the true wisdom, knowing all, to reject all, and turning aside from this glittering guerdon of enduring life, patiently to walk your human path to the end appointed to our human feet."

"Will you show me this fire, Prophet?"

"Aye, if you will, for so I am commanded," he answered faintly; "yet why look upon that which must excite desire?"

Then weariness overcame him and he sank down swooning, so that had I not caught him, he would have fallen.

\* \* \* \* \* \* \* \*

Noot abode three days at Kor and talked with me of many things, but at that time of the wonderful Secret of Life he spoke no more. As though by consent both of us let that matter lie awhile. For the rest there was much to say. I told him everything that had passed in Egypt and the outer world since long years before he had left me to sail down Nile, never to return. I told him how I had obeyed his last commands to the letter, and surrounded though I was by foes, had preserved the worship of Isis in her temple from season to season, celebrating her festivals in their appointed course, though I never dared to leave its walls.

"So, Ayesha," he said when I had done, "while I have been a hermit here at Kor, you have been a hermit at Memphis. Well, each of us has served the goddess as best might be, so may she reward us both according to our deserts, which doubtless are but small. And now my task is finished, but yours lies before you, seeing that you still have strength, even if your youth has gone."

"Yes," I answered somewhat bitterly, "mid-age has overtaken me, my youth has passed in the service of Heaven, and what has Heaven given to me after all my wars and strivings? Just this—that in a savage, desolate land among ruins and barbarians I must begin anew. I must restore a faith decayed, collect those barbarians into armies and order them, enact laws and cause them to be obeyed, fight battles, till lands, build ships and carry on commerce, collect revenues and spend them wisely, labour without cease day by day, finding but little rest at night because of the troubles that await the morrow. I must be at once a high-priestess, an oracle, a general, a law-giver, a judge, an architect, a land-tiller and a queen beneath an alien sky; without counsel, without friends, without love, without children to tend me in my age or to pile the earth upon my bones. Such is the lot that the goddess has given to her priestess Ayesha in payment of all her strivings."

Thus I spoke bitterly enough, but Noot answered with a gentle smile,

"At least, Daughter, it might have been more evil. You have a planning and a thoughtful mind and here you can shape all things afresh to your desire. You love power and here you will be absolute, a very queen, you who cannot brook denial. Here there will be none to say you nay. You hate rivals who would rule alone. Here they will be lacking. You desire to remain celibate who are wed to the spirit. Here no more kings or others will come to trouble you, plotting to win your beauty. It has ever been your wish to commune with Nature and that Divine from which it springs; here in this deserted place is Nature's very home and in solitude the Divine draws near to empty souls.

"Truly you should be thankful, therefore, whose prayers have been fulfilled, who have attained to all you sought, whose ambitions are satisfied and who in the holy calm and the healthful weariness that follows upon long-continued labours, at last when your task is done, will sink gently to the grave to seek their reward elsewhere. Soon, very soon, you will be as I am and when that day comes there will be an empty hermitage yonder where in darkness and in contemplation you can patiently await the end and those new endeavours which, after it, may be appointed to you elsewhere. For be sure of this, Ayesha—all existence is a ladder up which painfully and with many slips we must climb step by step."

"And when we reach the top, what then, Master?"

"I do not know, Daughter, but I do know that if we fall to the bottom, all those steps must be climbed again, only this time the rungs of the ladder will be wreathed with thorns."

"It seems that yonder hermitage of yours is no home of joy, my Father."

"Nay, Daughter. It is a home of grief and repentance. The joy lies beyond. Such are the philosophy of life and the teachings of all religion. Be sorrowful and afterward you will rejoice. Rejoice and afterward you will be sorrowful."

"A sad philosophy, Prophet, and such lessons as slaves learn beneath the whip."

"Aye, Ayesha, but one that must be endured, as, if they could speak, Tenes and Ochus and Nectanebes would tell you to-day."

So he droned on who grew weak and senile, having become but the dry shell of a man, whence the sap had withered, like to a sterile nut indeed, from which, if it were sown, no shoot would spring. At length wearying of his melancholy talk, I fell to the thought of that Fire of Life raging in its eternal vigour beneath his hermitage, which, as he swore, would give unending beauty, youth, glory, and dominion to him who could find faith and courage to dare its terrors.

\* \* \* \* \* \* \* \*

On the following day I accompanied Noot back to his hermitage for the quiet of which he seemed to yearn, so much so indeed that even for my sake whom he loved more than anything on earth and in whose fellowship he delighted, he would not be separated from it for another hour.

It was a rough journey that we made borne in litters to the foot of the great precipice which surrounds the plain of Kor like to a measureless wall chiselled by Titans at the shaping of the world. We climbed up a cleft in that wall and entered a hidden fold of rock, invisible from below. Following this fold we came to the mouth of a cave. Here I noted that food was set in plenty by the dwellers in this land who revered Noot as a prophet and thus supplied him with his sustenance. Here also were torches which were lit by those who accompanied us to give us light upon our journey through the cave that was long and rough. At length we came to its end to find before us a terrible chasm. Thousands of feet above us was a line of blue sky and beneath lay a gulf of darkness. Out into this chasm down which winds raved and howled, ran a giant spur of rock of which the end was lost in darkness. I looked at it doubtfully and said,

"Where then is your habitation, Noot, and by what road is it reached?"

"It lies yonder in the darkness, Daughter," he answered, smiling, "and this is the road that those who would visit me must travel," and he pointed to the spur of rock that trembled in the roaring gale, adding, "To my feet it is familiar; moreover, I know that on it as elsewhere I am protected from harm. But if you fear to walk such a path, turn back while there is still time. Perhaps it would be better that you should turn back."

Now I looked at the trembling rock and then I looked at Noot, my Master.

"What," thought I to myself, "shall I, Ayesha, who dread neither man nor devil, be afraid to follow where this frail old priest can lead? Never will I blench from peril though in it lies my death."

So I stared him in the face and answered,

"To the task, Father, and swiftly, for here the wind blows chill. I go first; Philo, follow me close."

Now Philo, who was my companion upon this adventure, glanced at me with questioning eyes, but being a brave man and one who as a sailor was accustomed to perilous heights, said nothing.

For a moment Noot paused, looking upward, perchance to pray or perchance for other reasons. Then having asked Philo how long it was to the time of sunset and been answered that it lacked between the half and the fourth part of an hour before Ra sank behind the western cliff, he started, walking boldly down the spur. I followed next, and last came Philo.

Very terrible was that journey in the uncertain light which as we progressed into the gulf grew ever fainter, till at last we were wrapped about with gloom. Moreover, always the spur of rock narrowed, and the raving gusts of wind which blew about that hideous gorge buffeted us more fiercely.

Still we went on leaning our weight against them, and as we went a kind of exaltation seized me, as it does always in moments of great danger, so that my heart grew bold and feared no more. I would match myself against these elemental strengths as I had matched myself against those of hostile and desiring kings, and conquer them. Or perchance it was the breath from the divine fire that burned below that already had entered into me. I cannot say, but this I remember, that before I had reached the point of that fearful rock I was filled with a wild joy and could laugh at Philo crawling after me with hesitating steps and breathing prayers now to Isis and now to the Grecian gods that he had worshipped as a child.

At length we came to the end of that long needle which thrust itself thus into the dark stuff of space, and as we did so all light went out of the sky above, leaving us plunged in blackness. I seated myself upon the throbbing point of rock, clinging to Philo who had done likewise, and cried into the ear of Noot, kneeling at our side.

"What now? Show us and be swift, lest we should be thrown from this place like stones from a sling."

"Hold fast and wait," answered Noot.

We did so, grasping the roughness of the rock with our hands. Then suddenly a marvel happened, since from somewhere, I know not whence and have never learned, a fierce red ray of light, cast doubtless by the setting sun, struck us through some hole in the opposing cliffs. Aye, it struck like a blazing sword, showing all things that could be seen. They were these: ourselves crouched upon that point of rock; infinite space beneath us, infinite space above reaching up to a single star that shone upon the sky, and we three hemmed in by two black precipices. Moreover, they showed, not four paces from the point, a huge trembling stone that was joined to that fearsome spar by a little bridge of wood laid from the one to the other by the hand of man, which bridge rose and fell and rocked as the great stone trembled on its farther side.

"Follow me swiftly before the light dies," cried Noot as he stepped across this bridge and, reaching the crest of the trembling stone, stood there like a ghost illumined with fire; like also to that figure which I had seen watching from the brow of the Ethiopian's head when we entered the harbour from the sea.

I obeyed and joined him, and after me came Philo.

By the last rays of that fleeting light we descended a rough stairway cut on the farther side of the Trembling Stone and of a sudden found ourselves in shelter. Light sprang up and I saw that it was held in the hand of a dwarf, a curious, solemn dwarf. Whence this creature came and who he was I do not know, but I think that he must have been a spirit, some gnome from the Under-world appointed by the Powers which ruled in that dark place to attend to the wants of the holy Noot, their Master and mine.

This I noted at least, and so did Philo, that we could never see this creature's face. Even when he moved about us, always it seemed to be hidden either by shadows or something that hung in front of it like a veil. Yet man, or gnome, or ghost, he was a good servant, since in that hermit's cave, or rather caves, for there were several of them, joined one to the other, all things were made ready. Thus a fire burned, food was prepared upon a table, and in the inner caves beds were spread, each in a little separate chamber.

The outer cave also was furnished in a fashion and I noted that in a niche stood the small statue of Isis which I remembered well, since wherever Noot my Master went in the past years when we journeyed together, that statue went with him and now still it was his companion. Indeed the tale was that it could speak and gave him counsel in all hours of doubt and trouble, and that from this enchanted thing he gathered his great wisdom. Whether or no this tale were true, I do not know, since I never heard it utter words, nor would Noot tell me when I asked him. Yet it is true that it was his custom to pray to it; also that it was very ancient and valued by him more than all the gold and jewels on the earth. Now it stood here, as it had done in my Father's house at Ozal, as it had done at Philae in his chamber, at Memphis, on the ship *Hapi* and elsewhere when we journeyed together throughout the world, and it was strange to me to behold its familiar face again in this dreadful habitation.

"Eat," said Noot, "then sleep, for you are weary."

Philo and I did as he commanded. We ate, we laid ourselves down upon the beds in the inner caves, and slept. The last thing that my eyes saw before slumber closed them was Noot my Master, now become more of a spirit than a man, kneeling in solemn prayer before the hallowed effigy of Isis.

I know not for how long we slept, but it must have been many hours, for when we woke it was to see that dwarf whose face was always hidden, setting another meal upon the table in the outer cave. There, too, by the lamplight, I perceived Noot still praying to the statue of Isis as though he had never risen from his knees, which perchance he had not done who no longer was as are other men. It was a strange sight in that dreadful place and one that affrighted Philo, as he told me, and left me not unmoved, who felt that here we stood upon the edge of mortal things.

I went to him, and seeing me come, he rose from his knees to greet me, asking me whether I had rested well.

"Neither well nor ill," I answered. "I slept, yet my sleep was full of dreams, very strange dreams that boded I know not what. They told me both of the past and of the future, and the burden of them was that I seemed to see myself living alone from generation to generation in caves as you do to-day."

"May the gods defend you from such a fate, Daughter," he answered as though the thought disturbed him.

"They have not defended you, Father. Oh! how can you bear to dwell in the darkness of this dreadful place round which the winds howl eternally, companioned only by your thoughts and a dwarf who never speaks? How did you find it, how came you here, and what put into your mind the thought of choosing this burrow for a hermitage? Tell me truly, who as yet, I think, have hidden half the truth even from me, for I am devoured with wonder and would understand."

"Hearken, Ayesha. When first we met in Arabia, I was already very old, was I not, I who now long have passed the tale of man's allotted days? Before that time for many years I had been a head-priest and prophet of Isis in Egypt, also the chief Magician of that land. Yet I was not born an Egyptian nor did my eyes so much as look upon the Nile until I had counted over sixty summers."

"Where then were you born, Father?"

"Here in Kor. I am the last descendant of the king-priests who ruled in Kor before the great apostasy and the falling of the Sword of God. To the holy men who were my fathers had descended their knowledge of that secret of secrets whereof I have spoken to you, and ever it was their custom when age took a hold of them to withdraw into this living sepulchre and there as guardians of the Fire, to await the end. Also under many oaths each of them passed on to his descendants the knowledge of the secret.

"Thus, Daughter, it came into my keeping, for my grandsire told my father, and my father whispered it to me. Then, while my grandsire still lived, the goddess for her own ends of which now I think I see the purpose, called me from this desolate land away to Egypt, there to serve her as I have done. Again she called me to Arabia that there you might be given into my keeping, as you were for certain years. A third time she called me back to Kor, whither I came with Philo. Here I found my grandsire dead and his son, my father, dead after him, leaving the hermitage of the Watcher of the Fire untenanted. Therefore setting Philo to command the savage tribes who dwell around the ruins of haunted Kor, hither I came, as for generations my forbears have done, to fill the office that they filled, and—to die."

"Forgetting me upon whose head you left a heavy burden, my Father in Isis," I said bitterly.

"Nay, Ayesha, I forgot you not, who knew well that at the appointed time we should meet once more, as meet we have. Always in my prayers I have watched over you and many of your troubles and dangers have been made known to me in dreams. It was in a dream that I heard you calling for guidance, and sent the answer that was commanded. Aye, and before that already I had despatched Philo to Egypt to bring you to me, as also I was commanded. And now you stand here before me in my hermitage and I tell you all these things because last night I learned, while I prayed and you were lost in sleep, that we shall speak no more together. My hour is at hand and since I have no child of my body, to you, my child in the Spirit, I pass on the great secret as to you already I have passed on my high office and my wisdom. When the breath has left me, Ayesha, then to you will descend the guardianship of the Fire, and here, doubtless, when age has overtaken you, you also will end your days."

"Is it so?" I asked, dismayed, staring around me at the rocky walls and listening to the tempest that raged eternally without.

"Aye, Ayesha, it is so, since that is the high duty laid upon your soul, whereby it shall find wings to fly to Heaven. Know that no Guardian of the Fire enters into the Fire. He watches it—no more—and if it is threatened he seals it for ever from the sight of man. Listen, I will tell you how," and leaning forward he whispered certain words into my ear and showed me certain hidden things.

I heard, I saw, I bowed my head. Then I asked,

"And if the Guardian of the Fire entered into the Fire, what then, Watcher of the Fire?"

"Daughter, I know not," he answered, horror-struck. "But then I think the Fire would become *his* guardian, a terrible guardian that at the last would also be the destroyer of its false servant. More I cannot tell, because though some have breathed its essence, none of them has dared this deed."

"Two nights ago you told me, O Noot, that this fire gives youth and beauty and uncounted days to those who bathe therein. If none has ever entered it, how know you this?"

"Because it is so, Ayesha. Moreover, I did not say that none had ever entered it. Perchance there are beings now known to the world as gods or daemons, who, by accident rather than design, have tasted of this cup. Perchance that shape you saw standing on the Ethiopian's head, in some bygone age stood for an instant in its path. At least I repeat that it is so. Believe or disbelieve me as you will, but ask me no more, and above all do not venture to solve the mystery in your mortal flesh."

"At least, Prophet, let me look upon that which I must guard," I said.

"Aye, you shall look," he answered. "It is for that reason that I have brought you here, Priestess and Daughter of Wisdom, for having looked, I do not think that you will desire to bathe in that red flame. Eat now and make ready."

## CHAPTER 20

# The Coming of Kallikrates

Awhile later we left the cave, Noot, Philo, and I, each of us bearing a lighted lamp. Clad in a dark cloak Noot led the way, his lamp in one hand and in the other a long staff such as herdsmen use upon the mountain side. Strange enough he seemed thus arrayed, with his thin, transparent face, his eyes grown large and luminous from staring at the darkness, and his long white beard showing like snow against the black texture of the cloak; more of a spirit than a man indeed, or like Charon leading shadows of the dead to that boat in which all—aye, even I, Ayesha—must embark at last. Never shall I forget his aspect as he searched for and found the stair that led to the rock-strewn slope which stretched downward for a furlong or more to the narrow passage at its end, through which presently we travelled into the infernal halls beyond.

Great were those halls or caverns; so great that we light-bearers were but as ants creeping through their vastness, so great that we could see neither their walls nor roof.

We passed through two of them, our footfalls echoing in their fearful silence, and came to a passage.

"Bide here," said Noot to Philo, "and await us, since it is not lawful for you to look upon that which lies beyond. If perchance we should not return within three hours so nearly as you can measure them, which may happen since we go to where there is danger for mankind, win your way back to the world and say that the gods have taken Noot the Prophet and Ayesha the High-Priestess to be of their company."

So Philo, out of whose eyes all the Grecian joyousness had fled, sat himself down upon a rock to wait, as I could see unwillingly enough, for he loved this adventure little and was troubled for the safety of me whom he loved much.

"Fear not," I whispered to him, "the hour is still far in which Ayesha must fall a ripe fruit from the Tree of Life."

"I pray so, Child of Isis," he answered, "since surely we have entered into Hades where I would not be left without so much as a fellow shade to comfort me. Yet beware! for I know not whither that old ghost is leading you," and he glanced at the tall shape of Noot striding into the tunnel in which this cave ended, the lamp held above his head.

I followed after him, also holding my lamp aloft, though presently it became needless since now the darkness of that hole grew alive with rosy light. On like a swift shadow glided Noot, and I followed him into the heart of the light, into a place, too, where thunder was imprisoned, like winds in the bag of Aeolus, aye, a place filled with glories and with roarings, though whence these came I could not guess.

We entered yet another cavern, not so very large in size and carpeted with fine white sand.

It was empty save for one thing. On the sand lay a withered shape, a hideous little shape that once had been man or woman. Whose it was and how it came there I never learned, since in the marvel of all that followed and afterward I forgot to ask it of Noot, if indeed he could have told me. Perchance some seeker of the Fire who lived a thousand or ten thousand years before had perished of terror at the sight of it, or perchance for his or her impiety that seeker had been sacrificed by gods or men. Yet even then I thought it dreadful and ominous that the first sight my eyes beheld in this terrible place should be this shrivelled, long-haired lump of death lying there in eternal solitude, while in front of and around it played the fierce essences of Life eternal.

This cavern was filled with a light like to that of some tempestuous Libyan dawn. Also it was filled with a muttering, thunderous sound, such sound as is caused by the iron wheels of a thousand chariots rushing to battle adown a rocky way. The light multiplied and was stabbed through as though by many coloured *levins* flashing hither and thither; the thunders gathered to an awful roar; those unearthly chariots were rolling down upon us.

"To your knees," cried Noot in my ear. "The Fire comes, the god is passing by!"

I knelt; my hand rested by chance upon that little shrivelled form, and lo! at my touch it crumbled into dust. It had been, it was not; the grinning twisted face was gone; nothing remained of it save a lock or two of curling hair—surely it must have been a woman's hair. Then the marvel happened. Before me appeared a turning column of glorious, many-coloured brightness, that roared and bellowed like a million maddened bulls. To my eyes it seemed to take the shape of a mighty man, and in its glowing crest I saw green eyes of emerald like to those of tigers, which eyes fixed themselves upon me. Arms it had also, blood-red, splendid arms that stretched themselves towards me as though to clasp me to that burning breast. It was terrible and yet it was most beauteous. Never until I saw it had I known beauty, no not even in the dawn or in the sunset, or in the sight of the wild shock of battle.

This mighty god of Life seemed to call to the life within me, like a king to his subject, like a master to his slave; I longed to lose myself in that embrace of fire. Half I rose from my knees. Noot caught me by the arm.

"Enter not!" he cried sternly, and again I sank down and hid my face upon the sand.

How long I lay there I do not know, for exaltation seized me and made my senses drunk, so that I could take no count of time. It may have been for a minute or an hour; I say I do not know. When I looked up again, the Fire had gone by, the god was hidden in his secret sanctuary, though still the cavern glowed with rosy light.

* * * * * * * *

Noot drew me from that place. Without we found Philo pale-lipped and trembling, and together, slowly and with labour, we climbed our upward course back to the hermitage beneath the swaying stone. Here we rested in silence until at last Noot drew me aside and spoke.

"Ayesha," he said, "you have seen as it was decreed that you must see. In that burning presence temptation took hold of you, so sharp a hold that had I not been there, perchance you would have yielded, forgetting my warnings and my prayers. Now I beseech you, guard the Fire in the days to come, but look on it no more for ever, since although in other matters you are so strong, in this I feel you frail. While I live indeed never again shall you behold it with your eyes, since first I will call upon the goddess to cut your thread of life and take you to herself."

I bowed my head but made no answer, nor did he ask for any.

What happened then? Oh! I remember that we ate of food that was made ready doubtless by the gnome-like dwarf whom I saw no more. After this Noot looked from the door of his hermitage and called to us to come swiftly, since the moment of sunset that brought with it the falling ray was at hand and the bridge must be crossed and the narrowest of the stone spur travelled ere it departed. Holding lighted lanterns in our hands, he led us to the crest of the Trembling Stone whereon the timbers of the bridge creaked and swayed. Here he clasped me in his arms, blessing me and bidding me farewell, and though he said it not, I was certain that in his mind, as at the moment I did in mine, he believed that our spirits parted for ever upon this earth; yes, believed it so surely that tears coursed down his pale cheeks.

Then suddenly the sword-like ray of fire stabbed the darkness and by it I and Philo crossed the bridge and while it endured clambered swiftly along the spur of which, I know not why, all fear had left me.

As that ray began to fade I turned my head to look my last on Noot. There in the heart of it he stood, clothed as it were with fire, as our faith tells are the messengers of Isis, Queen of Heaven. Yes, there he stood with clasped hands and uplifted eyes like to one lost in prayer. Then the ray went out like a blown lamp and the darkness fell and swallowed him.

We gained the plain in safety and through the night were borne back to Kor. The litter swayed; the slaves whose shoulders bent beneath the pole sang their low, weird chant inviting to sleep, but its messengers would not touch my eyelids with their rod of slumber. I could not sleep whose soul burned with a fierce wakefulness. Oh! what was this wonder that I had seen? The very fount of Life that, hidden from mankind, burns in the womb of the world! But if it were this, why did Noot speak of it as though it were a fount of Death? Why did he forbid me to taste its cup? Perhaps because not Life but Death inhabited that flame, as the little withered thing which had crumbled at my touch, that once had been man or woman—woman, as I think—hinted to the mind.

I knew not, but what I did know was that henceforth I was plighted to this god of Fire and that in some day to come I must feel his burning marriage kiss upon my brow.

********

When we came to Kor at the sunrise I beckoned Philo to me and made to him the sign of silence, which being initiated, he knew well, so that neither then nor at any other time should any word concerning these mysteries pass his lips. Nor indeed could it do so as he had not looked upon the greatest of them and only from afar had listened to the thunder of the wheeling flame.

Then with a new energy, as though inspired by the breath of that fiery god, I got me to my common daily task of rebuilding a perished faith and people. Let that business be. Why should I speak of it, since Destiny decreed that I must shape my work of water or of drifting sand, not of rock or fired clay. Oh! Fate, why didst thou fool me thus? Oh, Love the Destroyer, why didst thou make of me thy tool, and with me thus bring Isis and her worship to the dust?

*********

How long afterward was it that Kallikrates came? But a little while, I think, though to one who has lived over two thousand years Time loses its measure and significance.

I had sent Philo to the coast, purposing to prepare for the opening up of trade and converse with the outer world. For in this rich place, when its wild people were brought beneath my yoke, who already looked upon me as one half divine, as the spirit of their ancient goddess indeed, sent back to them from Heaven, I knew that we could produce much that the teeming tribes of Libya would seek and buy. One night he returned and was at once admitted to my presence. He told me of all that he had done, or failed to do, and I praised him, then made the signal of dismissal. He hesitated a while, then said,

"Child of Isis, be pleased to learn that I have not returned alone."

"That I know already, Philo, since there were many in your company."

"Be it understood, Child of Isis, that I have brought back with me some with whom I did not set forth."

"Doubtless envoys from the peoples of the coast," I answered indifferently.

"Nay," he replied, "travellers who have wandered long among those peoples and whom I found shipwrecked and in a desperate state. Travellers from Egypt."

"From Egypt! How many, Philo?"

"Nine in all, Prophetess, though the most of them are servants."

"Good, Philo. It will please me who must dwell so much alone to talk with strangers from Egypt. They may have news of what passes on the Nile. Give them hospitality such as we can command, and all they need, and to-morrow, after the morning ceremonies, bring them to me. To-night it is too late and doubtless they are weary."

Again he hesitated, then bowed, and went, leaving me wondering, for there was that in his manner which I thought strange. Still, having spoken my commands, I would not alter them. Yet as I laid me down to sleep terror took hold of me; yes, a terror of I knew not what. I felt that evil overshadowed me with its black wings; that I was about to

489

look upon something or someone I did not desire to see; that a doom unknown had meshed me so that I lay helpless like a gladiator over whom the net-thrower has cast his web and who lies struggling vainly, the trident at his throat. Thus often does advancing peril cast its cold shadow upon our mortal hearts which shiver at the touch of that they feel but cannot discern.

I thought that perchance I was about to die, that already Death gripped me with his clasp of ice; that in the dark recesses of the chamber where I lay already some murderer fingered the dagger which should pierce my breast, as well might happen in this wild land among man-eating savages upon whose necks I had set my heel. Again I thought that the spirits of the ancient dead whose place I occupied, were hunting me, demanding that I should give them back their own, the rule I had usurped.

Next I remembered Tenes transfixed by the sword of vengeance and knowing now that mine was the hand that drove it, and Ochus Artaxerxes when the poison began to burn his vitals as presently the fire would burn his company, guessing at the last that I, the outraged priestess, had brewed the cup and lit the fire. Yea, all these memories gathered round me, rising like black clouds upon my sky of life and threatening its eclipse, I who was terrified of I knew not what.

Lastly there came into my mind this tale of Philo's of shipwrecked strangers whom he had rescued and led hither to be comforted. Who were these strangers, I wondered? Assassins perchance, hid under a disguise of want and desolation, men who sought to kill me and free my spirit with their dagger-points, that it might no longer watch them here on earth. Yet, and this was marvellous, showing how blind are the eyes of our mortal flesh, never did the thought come to me that those strangers might be Kallikrates the Greek and Amenartas, aforetime Royal Princess of Egypt, she whom her desire and hate had made my foe.

I slept at last, though feverishly, only to wake when the high sun was flooding the temple court with its fierce summer rays. I rose, and since the day was one of ceremony and festival, was arrayed by my women in the queenly garments of the high-priestess of Isis and hung about with the sacred jewels and emblems of my rank.

Thus splendidly attired, I was led to my seat of state that I had caused to be placed in the inmost pillared court before a wondrous veiled statue of Truth standing on the world, which some god-gifted artist of old Kor had fashioned in the forgotten days. Here we celebrated our service with pomp and ritual, as once we were wont to do in Egypt, though alas! the *heirophants* and the singers were few in number. So was the outer congregation of half-converted worshippers creeping back from the blackness of their barbarous rites to the holy fellowship of the goddess.

The office was ended, the ringing of the *sistrum* had ceased, the blessing was given and with it the absolution of offences.

The worshippers had dispersed, save here and there one who remained to pray. I too was about to depart when Philo came, saying, humbly and hastily like one who desires to be done with an unwelcome task, that those wanderers of whom he had spoken waited upon my pleasure.

"Admit them," I answered, wondering within myself upon whom I was about to look. Malefactors perchance, I thought, who had fled from justice into far lands, or merchants driven southward by the gales, or humble seamen escaped from some sunk ship.

They came, a little knot of them, winding in and out between the great columns of the ruined temple, advancing through the shadows. Idly I noted, as they passed an open space where fell a stronger light, that the two who walked first had a noble air, different from that of those who followed after them. Then once more the shadows veiled them, whence presently they emerged before me, seated beneath the statue, and stood there, the sun's rays pouring down upon them.

I glanced at them and saw that they were man and woman, perfect man and very beauteous woman. Then I lifted my head and looked them fully in the face, only to sink back terrified, amazed, overwhelmed! Did I dream? Had some mocking spirit tricked my eyes, or were those that stood before me Kallikrates, the Grecian warrior-priest, and Amenartas, the Royal Princess of Egypt?

Lifting my hand to hide my face, I studied them beneath its shade. Oh! who could be mistaken? There before me, splendid in beauty as of old, stood the god-like Kallikrates and at his side, dark, magnificent and as yet untouched by time, or perchance protected from its ravages by arts she learned from her side, Nectanebes the sorcerer, was the imperial Amenartas. For a moment I kept silence, gathering up my strength, ordering my spirit. Then still holding my hand before my face, I spoke coldly as though without concern, saying,

"Whence come you, noble strangers? What are your names and why do you seek the hospitality of the Queen of this ruined land of Kor?"

Bold as ever, it was Amenartas who answered me, not Kallikrates, who stood staring about him as men do when they are uneasy in their minds or wearied with ceremonies.

491

"We are wanderers, Priestess, in station neither mean nor great; traders, to tell the truth, from the far north, who having suffered ship-wreck and many other things at length were rescued of this servant of yours who led us here," and she pointed to Philo standing near by with a stupid smile upon his face.

"By race we are Phoenicians called———" and she gave some name that I forget. "As to the rest, being in extremity, for those over whom we ruled rebelled against us and cast us out, we ask shelter from you until Fortune smiles upon us again, who of late has dealt us naught but frowns."

"It is granted, Lady. But tell me, what are you to each other? Broth-er and sister, perchance?"

"Aye, Priestess, brother and sister, as you have rightly guessed, see-ing that our names are one name."

"That is strange, Lady; indeed I think that you throw mud upon your father or your mother, or both, since how could these have be-gotten one dark, a high-born daughter of the Nile, and another fair as Apollo and having Grecian Apollo's face and mien? Again, how comes it that the sister of a Phoenician merchant binds up her locks with the circlet of Egyptian royalty?" And I pointed to the *uraeus*-twisted band of gold upon her brow.

"Blood plays strange tricks, Priestess, searching out now the like-ness of one ancestor, and now of another, so that ofttimes one child is born dark and the other fair. As for the ornament, I bought it in trade from an Arab merchant, not knowing whence it came or its signifi-cance," she began to answer unabashed, when of a sudden Kallikrates checked her, muttering,

"Have done!" Then addressing me, he said,

"O Queen and Priestess, take no heed of this lady's words, since of late, because of our misfortunes, we have been forced to tell many strange tales according to the conditions of the hour. We are not Phoe-nicians born of one House; we are by blood Greek and Egyptian, and by relation not brother and sister, but man and wife."

Now when I heard these words my heart stood still who hoped that Isis and their oaths might have held this pair apart. Yet I answered calmly,

"Is it so, Wanderer? Tell me then, of what faith are you twain and by whom were you wed? Did some minister of Zeus join your hands, or did you stand together before Hathor's altars?"

Then while he searched for some answer that he could not find, I went on, laughing a little,

"Perchance, O noble pair, you were not wed at all. Perchance you are not husband and wife but only lover and lover mated after Nature's fashion!"

He hung his head, confused, and even the bold eyes of Amenartas were troubled.

Now I could bear no more.

"O Grecian Kallikrates," I said, "aforetime captain of Pharaoh's guard, aforetime priest of Isis, and O Amenartas, daughter of Nectanebes, by birth Royal Prince of Egypt, why do you waste words, hoping to fool one who cannot be deceived? Doubtless you have bribed yonder Philo to hide the truth, as once you bribed him to hide a certain lady upon his ship and to set the two of you ashore upon a certain island."

"If so, he has betrayed us," stammered Kallikrates, the red blood rising to his brow.

"Nay, he has not betrayed you, being one who ever keeps faith with those who pay him well. Is it not so, Philo my servant?"

I waited for an answer, but none came, for Philo had gone. Then I continued,

"Nay, Philo did not betray you, nor was it needed. Royal Amenartas, whence had you that scarab ring upon your hand?"

"It was my lord's gift to me," she answered.

"Then tell me, Kallikrates, whence had you the ring, also if there be graven on its bezel in the Egyptian writing, signs that mean 'Royal Son of the Sun'?"

"Those signs are cut upon the ring, O Queen, which in bygone years was given to me as a talisman by a certain divine priestess whom I saved in battle, that its virtues might recover me of wounds which I received in the battle. This, as I was told afterward, it had the power to do because that ring was blessed, having been fashioned like to one which Isis the Mother set as her love gift upon the hand of dead Osiris ere she breathed his soul into him again. Or perchance it was the very same that Osiris left upon the earth when he passed to Heaven; I know not."

Thus he spoke, stumbling at the words like an ill-bred mule upon a stony path till, wearying of the tale, I broke in,

"Therefore, O Kallikrates, you in your turn gave the enchanted amulet to a woman you desired, or who desired you, hoping that its virtues might consecrate your unhallowed union. O priest forsworn, how did you dare this sacrilege—to set upon your lover's hand the ring, the very ring of Isis that once great Khaemuas wore, given to you by the Prophetess of Isis to lift you from the gates of death."

Then bending forward so that the shadow of the statue behind no longer hid me, I uncovered my face and looked him in the eyes.

"I thought it!" he said, "though who could have dreamed that here in this ruin——? It is the Oracle and the Prophetess. It is the Child of Isis, the Daughter of Wisdom herself whose voice I knew again through all her feigning," and he fell to the ground so that his brow was pressed upon its stones, muttering,

"Slay me, Queen, and have done, but spare this lady and send her back to her own land, since the sin is mine, not hers, who was no priestess."

Now Amenartas stared at me with her bold eyes, then cried with a hard laugh,

"Be not so sure, my Lord, for this is scarcely possible. Well do I remember looking upon her who was called *Isis-Come-To-Earth* in the bygone days, especially at a certain feast that Pharaoh gave when she unveiled to show herself to Tenes, King of Sidon, who afterward took her as his slave. But that seeress was a very fair woman, although perchance even then somewhat faded, or so I who but a little while before had bade farewell to childhood, judged of her. Therefore this ruler of ruins can scarcely be the same, seeing that none could name her fair. Look, she is old and withered, her neck has fallen in, her shape is flattened.

"The seeress I remember had a lovely mouth of coral, but this lady's lips are thin and pale; also she had large and beauteous eyes, but those of this lady are small and almost colourless. Moreover, they are ringed beneath with lines of black, such as are common to aged virgin priestesses who have never known the love of man, though of it, perchance, their holy souls still dream even in the midst of their customary, bead-checked prayers, while, like those of slaves, their knees harden upon the stones.

"Nay, my Lord, although time works strange changes in those who have passed the meridian of their days, this priestess who hides her gray hairs beneath the vulture cap of her persuasion can scarcely be the same as the glowing pythoness upon whom once we looked in Pharaoh's halls and who, as I recall, then looked much on you."

Now I listened to this vulgar venom, the common outpouring of a small-natured, jealous heart, and smiled. Yet it is true, for in these lines I write nothing which is not the truth, that some of those poisoned shafts went home. I knew well that all the beauty that once I had was no longer mine; that the passing of the years, that care and abstinence and the turning of my heart from things mortal to those divine, added to the weight of rule and wisdom and avengement which Destiny had laid upon my brow, had robbed me of my bloom and that imperial loveliness which once enthralled the world. Also it was true that Amenartas was still a child when I was a woman grown and therefore had Nature's vantage of me, which indeed must increase from moon to moon.

Still I smiled, and as I smiled a great thought smote me, sowing a seed of daring in the kind soil of my breast where thenceforth it was doomed to grow, to blossom, and in an unborn hour of fulfilment to bear its fearful fruit. Oh! if I have sinned against high Heaven and the commands of its minister, my guide, the holy Noot, let the recording gods remember that it was the whip of this woman's bitter tongue which drove me to the deed.

Now very gently I spoke, saying,

"Rise, Kallikrates, such words as you have heard spoken of one who once was set above you in her office can scarcely be pleasing to your ears, nor will I answer them. I know well that in them there is something of the truth and I am proud that it has been granted to me to make sacrifice to the Queen of Heaven whom I adore of such small gifts of the flesh and comeliness as once were mine. It is but another offering which I heap upon her altar, one of many.

"Yet, Kallikrates, though as I think you can no longer bow the knee before that Majesty as once you did, I pray you, if you can, to hold this lady's lips from pouring scorn upon her, as she does upon me, her priestess. I pray you to bring it to her memory that once, clad in her veil of Isis, she also worshipped at that shrine, aye, that in a time of peril, often there, she and you and I have sent up our pure petitions, though not in the 'customary bead-checked prayers' of which she speaks. Yes, bring it to her memory that though the temple of Memphis has been given to the flames, Mother Isis hears and watches not in Egypt, but in Heaven, and that though she will be slow to wrath, yet she still can smite. Now, Kallikrates, go rest you, taking your love with you, and afterward we will talk alone since, although I can forgive, I am not minded to be stoned with such words as angry women of the people throw at their rivals in the marketplace."

## CHAPTER 21

# The Truth and the Temptation

Not that day but on the morrow Kallikrates asked audience of me. Learning that he was alone, I received him in my private chamber and bade him be seated. He obeyed, and for awhile I watched him, the light from the window-place falling upon his golden head and upon his shining armour, battered with storm and war. For now he was clad in his soldier's garb, perchance the very same that years ago he had worn on board the *Hapi*, and thus attired looked like a king of men.

"The lady Amenartas is somewhat sick after all our journeyings," he said, "I think that the disorder which is common on the coast lands has fallen upon her, since her face is flushed and her hands are hot. Therefore she cannot await upon you, Prophetess. Yet she bids me thank you for your hospitality, and say that she asks your pardon for any bitter words she may have spoken yesterday, since these sprang, not from her heart, but from a fever burning in her blood."

"It is granted. I know this sickness though myself I have been protected from it, and will send her medicine and with it a skilled woman to wait upon her. Bid her not to fear; it is seldom dangerous. Now, my guest Kallikrates, if it pleases you, let me hear your story; you must have much to tell since we parted in the sanctuary at Memphis. Then, you will remember, your purpose was to accompany the holy Noot upon his mission, because you thought it best for reasons of your own to depart from Memphis for a while. Yet I think it was in your mind to go alone, not accompanied by that royal lady who is your companion."

"This is true, Prophetess," he answered heavily, "nor did I know that the lady of whom you speak was aboard the *Hapi* until, to escape capture at the hands of the Persians, we had fled from the Nile out toward the open sea."

"I understand, Kallikrates, nor can it be denied that Fate dealt hardly, or perchance I should say kindly, with you when it caused the lady Amenartas to embark in error upon the ship *Hapi*, which sailed down Nile, instead of that of her father, Nectanebes, which set its course for Thebes and Ethiopia."

"Mock me not, Child of Wisdom. As the lady Amenartas would tell you to your face, she knew well enough upon what ship she sailed, though I knew nothing who believed that I had said farewell to her for ever. Aye, abandoning her hope of royalty and all else, and taking every risk, she embarked upon the *Hapi*, setting some other woman tricked out to her likeness to fill her place awhile among the company of Nectanebes."

"That at least was bold, and I love courage, Kallikrates. Yet—what was her purpose?"

"Is that a question that you should ask me, Lady, who know well that great-hearted women will dare much for love?"

"Whether I should ask or not, at least I have the answer to my question, Kallikrates. Of a truth you should love and honour one who for your sake abandoned all to win what she thought more than all, even at the cost of her own shame and the ruin of your soul."

"I do love and honour her," he answered hoarsely. "When she was still a child I loved her and because of that love I slew my brother, believing that on reaching womanhood she had come to favour him, which, it seems, she did only to draw me closer to her."

"It would appear, Kallikrates, that this lady brings no good fortune to your race, since first she works the death of one of you, making a murderer of his own brother, and then of that brother fashions an apostate to his faith, yea, a traitor accursed from God and man."

"It is so," he said humbly. "Yet she loves me much, so much that whether I will it or not, I must love her, since if the woman loves enough what can the man do but follow on the path she leads? Tell me, Prophetess, you who are wise, had you been a man and sat in my place there upon the ship *Hapi*, which is a narrow prison, what would you have done, being a man I say—as I am?"

"Perhaps just what you did, Kallikrates, and therefore have become accursed, as you are, Kallikrates, seeing that the lady was sweet and loving, and that man must remain man however great the oaths he has sworn to goddesses who do not throw their arms about him or kiss him on the lips."

"Once I thought that a goddess did kiss me on the lips, Oracle of Isis, and the memory of that kiss is sweet and holy."

"Is it so?" I answered. "Well, since, you are no more of our communion, I may tell you now that in the shrine at Philae *I* played the part of the goddess and gave that ceremonial kiss."

Now he stared at me, reddening, then muttered,

"Always I guessed it who could not quite believe that a goddess would kiss so sweetly," and again he started like one who would ask a question that his lips do not dare to frame.

I remained silent, watching him, till presently he broke out,

"You tell me that I am accursed, Priestess. Tell me also why Isis is so wrath with me?"

"Did you not swear yourself to her alone and break your oath, Kallikrates? Do you not know that if women can be jealous, goddesses who are set far above them can be more greatly so of those who are bound to them in the mystic marriage? Have you not heard that to turn from them to a daughter of man is to offer them the most terrible of all insults?"

"Isis herself was wed to Osiris, Prophetess, and I have heard of priests and priestesses who served her who were also wed."

"Perchance, Kallikrates, after absolution given by one upon whom authority is conferred to strain vows for some high end. But who gave you authority to marry, you, who indeed are not married but only a woman's lover? Did you mayhap seek it from the holy Noot aboard the ship *Hapi*?"

"Nay," he answered, "that thought never came to me. Or if it came I believed that he would but heap curses upon me, or mayhap call down the vengeance of Isis upon another. You have heard, Prophetess, of what fate sometimes awaits those who tempt the feet of priests or priestesses from the strait path of their vows."

"Aye, Kallikrates, they die by fire, or they starve, or they perish shut up in some narrow, airless hole; each worship works its own vengeance for that unmeasured crime. Yet you were foolish not to make your prayer of Noot, by whom alone it could be granted, since who knows what he would have answered."

"Is it too late?" he asked eagerly. "For every sin there is forgiveness, why not for mine? Only who could grant it; since now I know not where to look for Noot, if indeed he lives."

"For every sin there is forgiveness, Kallikrates, but only at a price. First the sin itself must be laid upon the altar as a sacrifice. For dead sins there may be forgiveness; for those that live and are continued there is none, but only stripe added to stripe and remorse piled upon remorse. As for Noot it chances that he does live and not so far away. Would you lay your case before him and hear his judgment?"

"I do not know," he answered slowly. "Hearken, Child of Wisdom. I am in a strange strait. I love this lady with my body and am bound to her, but it is not so with my spirit. Our souls, I think, are far apart. Oh! bear me witness that my heart is set on higher things; it would sail into far seas unvisited of man, but always there is this anchor of the flesh chaining it to its native shore. Amenartas does not think thus, she loves to lie bound in life's pleasant harbour, or to wander to its green banks, wafted thither by the fitful breath of common things, there to deck her brow with the wreath of passion.

"'Let Heaven be!' she says, 'here is the happy earth beneath our feet, and round us murmur the waters of delight and I am very beautiful and I love you well. If there be gods and they are vengeful, at least their hour is not yet. This moment is ours to enjoy and to our lips it holds a glorious cup. If all the wine be drunk and the cup is shattered, at least there will remain with us their memories. What are these gods whom you seek so madly? What do they give to man save many curses—deaths and separations, sicknesses and sorrows, adding to these promises of woe to follow when they have worked their worst on earth? Are there any gods save those that man fashions from his own terrors? man who will not be content with Nature's food, but needs must sour it with an alien poison, and even when the sun shines round him, shivers in some cold shadow that superstition casts upon his heart.'

"Thus she reasons, and such ever were her arguments."

"Tell me, Kallikrates, has any child been born to you?"

"Aye, one, a very lovely child; he died of hardships that caused his mother's milk to fail."

"And when the royal Amenartas looked upon him dead, did she still reason in this fashion, saying that there are no gods and for man there is no hope beyond the grave?"

"Not altogether, since she cursed the gods, and who curse that in which they do not believe? Also I remember that she wept and prayed those gods to give him back to her while his little heart still beat, and like a moth new-crept from its chrysalis, he yet hung to the edge of the world, drying his soul's crinkled wings in the dawning lights of Heaven. But afterward she forgot and made sacrifice to her familiar Spirit, asking it to send her another child, which prayer she tells me is in the way of fulfilment."

"So Amenartas practices magic like her father Nectanebes?"

"Aye, Lady, and it would seem not without avail, though of this matter of dealing with daemons I neither know nor want to know anything. I think it comes to her with her Egyptian blood, also that the Pharaoh taught her these arts in her childhood, and what is learnt then is never quite forgotten. At least I know that when we have been in trouble or in danger during our long wanderings, with secret rites upon which I do not pry, she calls upon some Familiar and that thereafter, in this way or in that, our pathway has been straightened. Indeed she did this just before Philo found us starving."

"As the path of your babe was straightened from this world to the next, Kallikrates; as the devious path of Pharaoh Nectabenes was straightened to a road which led from the throne of Egypt—but pray the lady Amenartas to ask of her daemon whither it led, since here my wisdom fails me and I am not sure. Well, we have spoken long and so stands the case, one that might puzzle Thoth himself. Is it your pleasure, Kallikrates, to visit the divine Noot and take his counsel upon all these matters? I think that he alone upon the earth can give you guidance in them. Yet do as you will."

Kallikrates thought a while brooding, then he answered,

"Yes, it is my pleasure. When Amenartas is recovered of her sickness, we will go."

"The holy Noot is very ancient and the royal Amenartas may be sick for a long while. Therefore might it be wise to go at once, Kallikrates."

"Nay, Prophetess, I cannot. Amenartas has strange fancies and will not be left alone; she thinks that she may be poisoned; indeed that already she has tasted poison."

"Then let her make richer sacrifices to her daemon and pray him to protect her. Certainly they will not be without avail since I can swear that here in Kor no poison shall pass her lips, nor any harm come to her—save perchance from those gods whom she denies. Farewell, Kallikrates."

He bowed to me humbly and turned to go, then after a step or two came back and said,

"The gods! The gods! who for you and me in their sum are one god, Isis, Queen of Heaven. Tell me now, I pray you that are named Wisdom's Daughter, who and what is Isis?"

I thought a while since the question was a great one, a problem that as yet I had never tried to solve in words. Then I answered,

"By my soul I do not know. East and west and north and south, men in their millions worship this god or that. Yet is there one among them who save in dreams or ecstasies has ever seen his god, or if he tries to fashion him out before his mortal eyes, can do more than carve some effigy of wood or stone?"

Then I pointed to the veiled statue of Truth behind me, saying,

"Lo! there is Isis, a beauteous thing with a hidden face ruling o'er the world. She is one of Divinity's thousand forms. Aye, she is its essence, frozen to the shape we know in this world's icy air, and having a countenance chiselled differently from age to age by the changeful thought of man. She lives in every soul, yet in no two souls is she the same. She is not, yet eternally she is. Invisible, intangible; ever pursued and ever fleeing; never seen and never handled, yet she answers prayer and her throne is not in the high heavens but in the heart of every creature that draws the breath of life. One day we shall behold her and not know her. Yet she will know us. Such is Isis: formless, yet in every form; dead, yet living in all that breathes; a priest-bred fantasy, yet the one great truth."

"If Isis be thus, what of the world's other gods?"

"They all are Isis and Isis is them all. The thousand gods men worship are but one god wearing many faces. Or rather they are two gods, the god of good and the god of evil; Horus and Typhon who war continually for the souls of things created by that Divine, unseen, unknown yet eternally existent, who reigns beyond the stars alone in fearful glory and from his nameless habitation looks down both on gods and men, the puppets of his hands; on the rolling worlds that bear them, on the seas of space between and on the infusing spirit whose operation is the breath of life. So it was in the beginning, is now and shall be eternally. At least, Kallikrates, thus I have been taught by the wisdom of Noot my Master, and following his path, thus my searching soul has learned. Again farewell."

He looked at me muttering,

"Child of Isis, oh! well-named Child of Isis, and Wisdom's Daughter!" and there was awe in his eyes and voice.

Now as ever he is afraid of me, I thought to myself, and how can a man come to love that of which he is afraid, since love and fear are opposites and there is no bridge between them. Oh! why did I speak to him of these high things which as yet his spirit can scarce weigh or understand? Perhaps because I am so lonely and having naught into which I can pour my mind, no vase of gold and alabaster, my deep o'erflowing thought must fill the first coarse cup of clay that chance offers to my hand, like to the storing of priceless wine in some tarry bottle which it will burst.

Surely I should learn a lesson from yonder Amenartas, who knows well how to deal with such a one as he; one who still stands at thought's beginnings, looking dismayed at the steep upward path studded with sharp stones, wreathed in cruel thorns, strewn with quicksands and with pitfalls, and bordered by precipices from whose gulfs there is no return, that path which his feet long to tread yet dare not, lacking any guide.

She leads him by a different road, the road of mortal passion, bidding him to cease from staring at the stars; bidding him weave crowns of its heavy-scented flowers to set upon her brow and his. She prattles to him of daily doings, of the joy of yesterday and the promise of to-morrow, aye, even of the food he eats. And all the time she twists the spells her father taught her to strong ropes of charm, purposing by these to tie him to her everlastingly. Aye, like a gilded spider, that black-browed, bounteous-breasted witch meshes him in her magic web, binding him fast and yet more fast, till at length he lies there staring at her stirless as a mummy in its wrappings.

Thus I mused, clothing my musings finely yet knowing in my heart that what prompted them was the vilest of all causes and the most common, naught indeed but the jealousy of one woman of another. For now I knew the truth, it could no more be hidden, no longer could I blind my eyes, for it had come home to me while he told me his sad story. I loved this man; yes, and had always loved him since first I looked upon him far away at Philae, or certainly since, veiled in the wrappings of the goddess, I had yielded to Nature's promptings and kissed him upon the lips.

Oh! I had beaten down that truth, I had buried it deep, but now it arose like a ghost from the grave and frightened me with its stern, immortal eyes. I loved this man and must always love him and no other, and he—he feared yet adored me, as some high spirit is adored at its appearing—but love me he did not who was set so far above him.

Yes, I was jealous, if the great can be truly jealous of that which is small, for though we were wide apart as continent from continent, yet we both were women desirous of one man. With my spirit I was not jealous, for that I knew must conquer in the end, being so strong, so armoured against all the shafts of mortal change. Yet with my flesh I was jealous. He told me Amenartas had borne a son to him; that she hoped to bear another son, and—I too yearned to be the mother of his son. For is it not true that by a fixed unchanging law, whereas the man loves the woman for herself, the woman loves the man most of all because he may become the father of her child, and thus by the marvel of creation, even in the dust preserve her from perpetual death?

So, so, let me think. I loved this man and would take him for myself and would lift him up and would make him my equal, if that could ever be, and would teach him glorious things, and would show him the secret light that burned within my heart, and would guide him onward by the rays of my own peculiar star. How could it be brought about? Yonder woman, wrapped round with the twice-dipped Tyrian purple of kings, which purple, be it admitted, she wore well enough although now she lacked a throne whereon to drape it, thought in her folly that I had poisoned or would poison her. Yes, she knew Ayesha so little that she believed that like a Persian eunuch she would stoop to call deadly venom to her aid and thereby rid her of a rival. Never! If I could not win by my own strength in a fair fight for favour, then let me fail, who deserved defeat. Were her life so utterly in my hands that I could destroy it with a wish, that wish would never form itself within my mind, and certainly never shape itself to deeds.

What then could be done? She was right. I began to grow old; Time's acid was gnawing at me so that my beauty was no more what it had been. Aye, I grew spare and old, while on her still shone the full glory of her womanhood. *If I would conquer I must cease from growing old!*

The Fire of Life! Ah! that Fire of Life which gave, it was said, the gift of undying days and of perfect youth and loveliness such as Aphrodite herself might envy. Who said so? Noot the Master who knew all things. Yet Noot had never entered into that fire, therefore how did he know, unless it were by revelation? At least he had forbidden me to taste its cup, perhaps because he was sure that it would slay me whom he desired to be his successor and to establish here a great kingdom whereof the people should accept Isis as their god.

Still the story might be true, for otherwise why did Noot sit in that melancholy hermitage watching the pathway to the Fire? There had been other tales of the same sort told in the world. Thus the old Chaldean legend spoke of a Tree of Life that grew in a certain garden whence the parents of mankind were driven lest they should eat of it and become immortal, which legend was expounded to me more fully by the Jewish rabbis in Jerusalem, and afterward by Holly the learned man. Therefore it seemed that there was a Tree of Life, or a Fire of Life, jealously guarded of the gods lest the children of men should become their equals. And I, I knew where that Tree grew, or rather where that Fire burned. Yet Noot forbade it to me, and could I disobey Noot my Master, Noot the half divine? Well, Noot was very old and near his end, and when he died, I, by his own appointment, should be the guardian of the Fire, and may not a guardian taste of that he guards?

The gods decreed otherwise, he said. Mayhap, but what if in this matter where I had so much to gain, I chose to match myself against the gods? If the gods give knowledge, can they be wrath with those who use it? Yet if they are wrath—well, let them be wrath and set their worst against my best. Sometimes I grew weary of the gods and all the fantastical decrees which they—or their priests—heaped upon the heads of the sufferers of this earth. Were not life's curse and death's doom enough to satisfy their appetites, that they must load the toilful days between with so much of the lead of misery, denying this, denying that; strewing the path of men with spikes and crowning their heads with thorns?

If Noot's tale were true, what then? I should enter the Fire, I should emerge ever-glorious, beauteous beyond imagining, and ever young, having left death far behind me. I should need but to wait a while until Amenartas died, and when she was dead, or having grown weary of dull life in an ancient place, had departed to seek some other. Nay, for then in the first case Kallikrates also would be dead or ancient, and in the second, certainly she would take him with her.

Ah! now I had it; if I entered the Fire and came forth unharmed, Kallikrates must enter it after me, for then we should be fitly mated, even if we must wait until a little pinch of the sand of time had run out from between our fingers. Yet supposing that Amenartas chose to enter it also, as being so fond of magic and so determined to cling to that which she had won, perchance she might do, would my case be bettered? The play would be set upon a larger stage, that is all. Well, should I not be the Guardian of the Fire and would it not be in my hand to determine who should taste or who should be denied its glories? Let that matter decide itself when the hour came, since the decision would be such as I and not as Amenartas willed.

Here then was my plan. And yet—one thought more. What if the Fire slew? If so, had I found life so sweet that I should be afraid to die, as in any case within some few years die I must? Let me take my chance of death who was ready to fade away into a land where Kallikrates and Amenartas and all earthly miseries and all baulked desires and ambitions, and all hopes and fears and sufferings must be forgot. Only would they be forgot? Perchance there they might be remembered and pierce the soul eternally with an even keener edge. Noot believed that we were made of an immortal stuff, and so at heart did I. It must be risked. What is life but a long risk, and why should we fear to add to its tremendous count? I at least did not fear.

\* \* \* \* \* \* \* \*

So all was summed up and balanced. Yet from my reckoning I left out the largest charge, that which Fate makes against those who play at dice with the Unknown. The gods may smile at courage and pass a venture by, but who can tell how blind Fate will avenge the forcing of his rule decreed and the rape of knowledge from his secret store?

This problem I forgot, I who was doomed to learn its answer.

## CHAPTER 22

# Beware!

The days went by and it was not long before Amenartas recovered from her sickness, long at least before she would appear out of the lodging, the best at our command, which had been given to her. It was an ancient, ruined house near to the temple, that doubtless once had been a splendid place inhabited by forgotten nobles of old Kor. There were gardens round it, or rather what had been gardens, for now these were much overgrown, and in their shelter Amenartas hid herself and wandered, never leaving them to visit me.

Yet Kallikrates came often, though being unshriven and thrust out of our community by his own act, he did not share in the worship of the goddess. Often I would see him as our procession wound in and out of the columns of the great unroofed temple hall, standing afar off and gazing at it wistfully. Aye, and once when it passed near to him, I saw too, that there were tears upon his face, noting which my heart sorrowed for him who was an outcast for a woman's sake.

When these ceremonies were ended he would visit me in my chambers where we talked long and of many things. I asked him why the Princess Amenartas, who it seemed was recovered of her fever since now she could wander in her garden ground, laid no offering on the altar of the goddess. He answered,

"Because she will have naught to do with the gods of Egypt who, she says, if they are at all, have ever been the enemies of her House and have dragged her father, the Pharaoh Nectanebes, from his throne and hurled him forth, a discrowned fugitive, to perish amidst strangers."

"Upon those who follow after spells and affront the gods, the gods will be avenged, Kallikrates. For every sin there is forgiveness, save for that of the denial of Divinity, and of the setting of Evil in its place to be propitiated by the arts of sorcerers. Moreover, did not this Nectanebes offer deadly insult to the Queen of Heaven when he gave me, her servant and seeress, to be a slave to Tenes, the worshipper of her worst of foes, Baal and Ashtoreth and Moloch, that Tenes from whose grip you helped to save me, Kallikrates?"

"It is so," he answered sadly.

"And now," I went on, "the daughter follows in the father's steps. Oh! I am sure that yonder she spells out her charms, aiming her enchantments at my heart, whence they fall back harmless, as the bone-tipped arrows of wild men fall from a shield of Syrian bronze."

He hung his head who knew well that my words were true, and muttered,

"Alas! she loves you not, Lady, who from the first hour that she set eyes upon you, as often she has told me, feared and hated you, because, she says, her spirit warns and has ever warned her that you will bring disaster upon her head and call up Death to keep her company."

"At least he would be a better guest, Kallikrates, than the daemon that, like her father, she harbours in her breast. Oh! unhappy man, my heart bleeds for you, who are linked to this poisoned loveliness that divorces you from hope and charity; to this royal infidel who in the end will bind your spirit's wings and drag you down into her own darkness. For your soul's sake I pray you, Kallikrates, seek out the holy Noot, confess your sins and hear his counsel, since this matter is beyond my strength and I have none to give. Seek him soon, nay, at once, ere perchance it be too late, for I learn that he grows feeble."

"That is my great desire, Priestess, yet how can I, who know not where to find him?"

"I will be your guide, Kallikrates. When the sun rises on the second day from now we will march to visit Noot in his secret dwelling."

"I will be ready," he answered and left me.

On the morrow he came again and we spoke together of the state of Kor and of my plans for bettering it; also of certain savages who threatened us from without, man-eating tribes that it seemed were descended from the apostates who rejecting the worship of Truth or Lulala, as Isis was named by them in those times, had adopted that of a devil that, as they declared, inhabited the sun or some ill-omened star.

Kallikrates listened, he who at bottom was ever a soldier, for the tale awoke all his general's craft and courage. As a great captain does, he balanced the reasons for or against defence, for or against attack. He questioned me as to the numbers of my people and of their foes, as to their arms, and many other matters that have to do with war. Then having learned all that I could tell him, he set out the plan which he judged to be the best in our conditions, talking of it long and eagerly, he who for a while had forgot his woes. I listened to him, watching his bright and splendid face which seemed as that of the Sun-god of the Greeks. Speaking a word here and a word there, I listened, thinking to myself the while that if only he and I, he with his skill and courage and I with my wisdom, could guide the destinies of Kor, before our day was done we would drive them like the chariots of a conquering king from Egypt's borders to these of the uttermost southern seas, setting nation after nation beneath our feet, and building up such an empire as Libya had never known.

What had I dreamed? To Egypt's borders? Why should we stop at her borders? Why should we not hurl forth the foul Persian swarms and be crowned monarchs of the world at Susa and at Thebes? Yet it would take time, and life is short, and yonder, not so far away, burned the Fire of Immortality, and I, I held the key to its prison house, or soon should hold it when Noot had sought his rest. Almost these burning thoughts, these high ambitions, in whose fulfilment lay the seeds of peace attained through war and the promise of the welfare of the earth, burst from my lips in a torrent of hot words which I knew well would set his soul aflame. But I, Ayesha, refrained myself from myself, I wrapped myself in silence, I said to myself, "Wait, wait, the ripe hour has not dawned."

He rose to depart, then turned and said,

"At the sunrise I will be here, or rather," he added doubtfully, "we will be here, since Amenartas desires to accompany us upon this journey to visit the holy Noot."

"By whom I trust she will be well received, seeing the manner in which she parted from him upon the ship *Hapi*. Well, so be it; I rejoice to learn that the royal Amenartas again finds herself prepared to travel. Yet remind her, Kallikrates, that the road we go is rough and dangerous."

"She shall be told, yet it will serve little, since who can turn Amenartas from her ends? Not I, be sure; nor could her father before me, nor any living man."

"Nay, nor any god, Kallikrates, since the ends she follows are those of neither man nor god, but of something that stands beyond them both, as was the case of Pharaoh Nectanebes who begot her. Each of us shoots at his chosen mark, Kallikrates, you at yours, I at mine, and Amenartas at her own; therefore what right have we to judge of one another's archery? Let her come to visit Noot and I pray that she may return the happier."

Next morning ere the dawn I stood at the temple porch awaiting Philo and the litters. Came Amenartas cloaked heavily, for the air was cold, yet splendid even in those wrappings.

"Greeting, Wisdom's Child," she said, bowing in her courtlike fashion. "I learn that you and my husband would make some strange journey, and therefore, as a wife should, I accompany him."

"That is so, royal Lady, though I knew not that you were wed to the lord Kallikrates."

"What is marriage?" she asked. "Is it certain words mumbled before an altar and a priest, a thing of witnessed ceremony, or is it the union of the heart and flesh according to Nature's custom and decree? But let that pass. Where my lord goes, there I accompany him."

"None forbids you, O Lady of Egypt."

"True, Prophetess. Yet my own heart forbids me. Know that but last night I was haunted by a very evil dream. It seemed to me that my father Nectanebes stood before in a sable robe that was shot through with threads of fire. He spoke to me saying: 'Daughter, beware of that witch who goes on a dreadful quest, taking with her one who is dear to you. At the end of that quest lies Doom for her, for him, for you, though each of these dooms be different!'"

"It may be so, Princess," I answered coldly. "Then accompany me not and keep Kallikrates at your side."

"That I cannot do," she said in a sullen voice, "since now for the first time he will not listen to my pleading and crosses my will. You have laid your charm upon him as on others in the past, and where you lead, he follows."

"Mayhap as a slave follows one who can show him where he may loose his chains! But let us not bandy words, royal Amenartas. I depart. Follow if you will, or bide behind, one or both of you. See, here comes Kallikrates; agree together as it pleases you."

She turned and met him in the ruins of the ancient pylon, where they debated together in words I could not hear. Once she seemed to conquer, for both of them walked a little way toward their own home. Then Kallikrates swung round upon his heel and came back to me who stood by the litters. She hesitated awhile, ah! what mighty issues hung upon this trembling of the balance of her mind, but in the end she followed him.

After this, without more speech we entered the litters and began our journey.

As we went across the misty plain it came home to me, as many a time it has done during the long centuries that followed, how often the great depends upon the little. Another bitter word from Amenartas, a trifle less of courage in Kallikrates, and how differently would Fate have fashioned the destinies of every one of us. For be it remembered that the choice lay with these two; I did naught save wait upon their wills. Had they so desired, never need they have entered those litters. Alone I should have departed; alone I should have looked upon the Fire and drunk of that Cup of Life, or perchance, as is probable, I should have left it untasted and gone down my way to death after the common fashion of mankind. But it was not so decreed; of their own desire they took the path to doom, though perchance that desire was shaped by some Strength above their own.

******** 

We reached the precipice and climbed it, Amenartas, Kallikrates, Philo and I. We passed the cave by the light of lanterns, and we came to the trembling spur of rock that reaches out like a great needle thrust through the robe of darkness. When they looked upon it, Kallikrates and Amenartas shivered and drew back, seeing which I rejoiced, for it is true that at the moment I found no more heart for this adventure.

"Stay where you are," I cried, "and wait. I go to visit the holy Noot. I will return again, and if I return not within a round of the sun, then make your way back to Kor and there abide. Or if it pleases you, seek the coast-land and the harbour of the Ethiopian's Head and depart with the help of Philo, if he still lives, or if not, otherwise. Farewell! I go."

"Nay," cried Kallikrates, "whither you lead, Prophetess, thither I follow."

"If so," said Amenartas, laughing in her royal fashion, "you will not follow alone. What! Shall I not dare that which my lord can dare? Is this the first peril in which we twain have stood side by side? If it be the last, what of it?"

So we started down the spur, Philo coming at the end of our line, and though with many hazards, for once the brain of Amenartas swam so that almost she fell, reached its point in safety. Here we waited crouched upon the rough rock and clinging to it with our hands, lest its quick throbbing should hurl us into the gulf, or the fierce gusts should sweep us away like autumn leaves.

At length at the appointed moment the sword-like sunset ray appeared, striking full upon us and showing that the frail bridge of boards was still in the place, for it swayed and moved like the deck of a ship at sea.

"Be bold and follow," I cried, "since he who hesitates is doomed," and instantly I stepped across that perilous plank and took my stand upon the swaying stone beyond.

For a moment Kallikrates stood doubtful, as well he might, but Amenartas pushed past him and with a laugh crossed it as though she would teach me that I was not the only one to whom the gods had given courage. I caught her by the hand. Then Kallikrates followed because he must, and she caught him by the hand and after him Philo, the seaman, calmly enough, so that now all four of us stood together on the stone.

"Glad enough am I to be here, Prophetess," cried Kallikrates, though in that wailing wind his voice reached me only as a whisper. "Yet, I know not why, it comes into my mind that I go upon my last journey."

I made no answer because his fateful words chilled my heart and choked my voice; only I looked at his face and noted that it was white as ice even in the red light of the ray and that his large eyes shone as though with the fires of fever.

Taking Kallikrates by the hand and motioning to Philo to do like-wise with Amenartas, I led him to the little rough-hewn stair. By this stair we descended into the sheltered place that was in front of the hermitage of Noot and rejoiced was I to find myself and the others out of the reach of those raging winds and to see that lights burned within the cave beyond.

"Bide here, all of you," I said. "I will enter the cave and prepare the holy Noot for your coming."

I entered the place thinking to find that strange dwarf who was Noot's servant, but nowhere could he be seen. Yet I was sure that he must be near, since on the rough rock were set food and wooden plat-ters, four platters as though awaiting four guests. I thought to myself that doubtless the Master had seen us creeping down the spur, or per-chance his spirit had warned him of our coming—who could say?

I gazed about me to find Noot, and at length in the deep shadow, out of reach of the lamp's rays, I perceived him kneeling before that image of Isis whereof I have told, and wrapt in earnest prayer. I drew near and waited a while who did not dare to break in upon his ori-sons. Still he did not stir or look up. So quiet was he that he might have been carved in ivory. I bent forward, examining his face. Lo! his eyes were fixed and open and his jaw had fallen.

Noot was *dead!*

"My Master, my most beloved Master! Too late, too late!" I moaned, and bending down kissed him on his brow of ice.

Then I began to think and swiftly. Had he not warned me when I bade him farewell a while before that we spoke together for the last time? Where was my faith who had forgotten that the prophecies of Noot were always true? So he had gone to his rest in the bosom of Osiris, and on me had fallen his mantle. I, Ayesha, was the guardian of the Fire of Life, whereof alone I knew the secrets and held the key! The knowledge struck me like a blow; I trembled and sank to the ground. I think that for a little while I swooned and in that swoon strange dreams took hold of me, half-remembered dreams, dreams not to be written.

* * * * * * * *

Presently I rose and going to the doorway summoned the others, who stood there huddled together like sheep before a storm.

"Enter," I said, and they obeyed. "Now be seated and eat," I went on, pointing to the table on which the food was ready.

"Where is the master of the feast, Prophetess? Where is the holy Noot whom we have walked this fearful road to see?" asked Kallikrates, staring about him.

"Yonder," I answered, pointing to the depths of the shadow, "yonder—dead and cold. You tarried too long at Kor, Kallikrates. Now you must seek his counsel and his absolution at another table—that of Osiris."

Thus I spoke, for something inspired the words, yet ere they had left my lips I could have bitten out the tongue that shaped them. Was *this* the place to talk of the Table of Osiris to the man I loved?

They went to that dark nook where the little sacred statue looked down upon its quiet worshipper. They stared in silence; they returned, Philo muttering prayers, Kallikrates wringing his hands, for he had loved and honoured Noot above any man that lived. Also—I read the question in his mind—to whom now should he confess his sins? Who now could loose their burden?

Only Amenartas pondered a space; then she spoke with a slow and meaningful smile, saying,

"Perchance, my lord, it is as well that this old high-priest has come to discover whether he dreamed true dreams for so many years upon the earth. I know not what you would have said to him, yet I can guess that it boded but little good to me, your wife, for so I am, whatever yonder priestess may tell you, who also bodes little good either to me

512

or to you, my lord Kallikrates. Well, he is dead and even Wisdom's Daughter there cannot bring him back to life. So let us rest a while and eat, and then return by that dread road which we have trodden, ere our strength and spirit fail us."

"That you may not do, Princess Amenartas, until the sunset comes again and once more the red ray shows us where to set our feet, for to attempt it sooner is to die," I answered, and went on:

"Hearken. By the death of this holy man, or half-god, I have become the keeper of a certain treasure over which he watched. It is hidden deep in the bowels of the earth beneath us. I must go to visit it and see that it is safe. This I shall do presently. Bide you here, if you will, till I return, and if I return not, wait till the ray strikes upon the point of rock, cross the bridge, climb the spur, and flee whither you will. Philo can guide you."

"Not so, Child of Isis," said Philo. "My oath and duty are to you, not to this pair. Whither you go, I follow to the end."

"I follow also," said Kallikrates, "who would not be left in this darksome place companied by death."

"Yet it might be wiser, Kallikrates," I answered, "since who can escape that company of death of which you speak?" for again dreadful and ominous words rushed unbidden from my heart.

"I care not. I go," he said almost sullenly.

"Then I go also," broke in Amenartas. "This Prophetess doubtless is wise and holy, yet I may be pardoned if I choose to share her fellowship with you upon a road unknown. Perchance it has another gate elsewhere that I might never find," she added in bitter jest.

Oh! had this fool but known that her coarse stabs at me did but harden the heart which she sought to pierce, and drive it whither she did not desire.

"As you will," I answered. "Now eat and rest till the hour of departure comes and I summon you."

So they ate, if not much, though for my own part I touched no food, and laid them down in the inner cave as best they might, and there slept, or did not sleep. But I, I watched the hours away by the dead shell of the holy Noot, striving to commune with his spirit which I knew to be near to me. Yet it gave no answer to all my questions. Or at least there came one only which again and again seemed to shape itself to a single word,

"*Beware!*"

Strange, thought I to myself, that the prophet Noot my Master, who loved me better than any other living upon the earth, and knew the most of my lonely, wayward heart, now that he was justified and made perfect, as doubtless he must be, if such a lot can be attained by man, should find no more to say to me than this one word, which indeed while in the flesh often he had said before. Therefore it seemed that in the flesh and out of it his counsel was the same; one certainly that I should take.

What did it mean? That I should look no more upon the Fire; that I should rise up and get me back to Kor and there play such parts as I could compass, and wither and grow old and die, nurturing perchance the children of Kallikrates and Amenartas, should they seek the Shades before me; or, growing weary of barbarians and ruins, flee away from Kor to find the fellowship of instructed men.

That is what this counsel meant. Well, what did that of my own heart promise me? Perhaps a swift death and after it punishment in some dim land beyond, because I had disobeyed the shadowy cautionings of the holy Noot and dared to make trial of a new Strength, against which as yet no man had matched himself. Or perhaps a glory greater than any man had ever dreamed, and a power far above that of emperors and a life longer than that of mountains. Also more—more, the love that I desired, to me a greater guerdon than all these boons added together and multiplied by the snowflakes upon Lebanon or the sands of the seashore. Surely, come what might of it, I would take my own counsel and let the other be.

The hour came; although I saw it not, I knew that it was that of dawn in the world without. I arose, I summoned the others; we departed down that darksome path of which I have written, climbing from rock to rock in the bowels of the earth by the dim light of the lanterns which we bore.

We came to the outer cavern; we passed the passage and reached the second cavern, halting at the mouth of another passage through which at intervals shot flickerings of light, and from time to time sounds as of muttering thunder reached our ears.

"The treasure on which I would look lies yonder. Bide ye here," I said.

"Nay," answered Kallikrates, "now as before I follow."

"Where my lord goes there go I also," said Amenartas.

Only Philo, the cautious Greek, bowed his head and answered,

"I obey. I bide here. If I am needed, summon me, O Child of Isis."

"Good," I cried, who at that moment thought little of Philo and his fate, though it is true that, cunning as he might be, I loved him well.

Then I went on and with me went Kallikrates and Amenartas.

## CHAPTER 23

# The Doom of the Fire

We stood in the third cave that was carpeted with white sand and alive with rosy light. Making a dark stain upon that snowy sand was a black patch of dust. I knew it again; when last I had seen it, it bore the withered shape of one long dead. The rolling many-coloured fire approached from afar; its muttering grew to a roar, its roar grew to such a thunder as shakes the mountain peaks and splits the walls of citadels. It appeared, blazing with a thousand lights; for a while it hovered, twisting like a spun top. Then it departed upon its eternal round in the unknown entrails of the earth, and the tumult sank to silence.

Kallikrates, terrified, flung himself upon his face; even the proud Amenartas fell to her knees, covering her eyes with her hands; only I stood erect and laughed, I who knew that I was betrothed to that fire and that it ill became the bride-to-be to shrink from her promised lord.

Kallikrates rose, asking,

"Where is the treasure which you seek, Prophetess? If it be hidden here, in this awful house of a living god, look on it swiftly, and let us begone. I, a mortal man, am terrified."

"As well you may be," broke in Amenartas, "since such wizardries as these have not been told of in the earth. I say it, who know something of wizardries, and like my father have stood face to face with spirits summoned from the Under-world, giving them word for word of power."

"My treasure lies in the red heart of yonder raging flame, and presently I go to pluck it thence," I answered in a quiet voice. "Whether I shall return I do not know. Perchance I shall abide in the fire and be borne away upon its wings. Stay if you will, or if you will, while there is yet time, depart, but trouble me no more with words, who must steel my soul to its last trial."

They stared at me, both of them, and remained silent.

For a space I stood still pondering. It seemed to me that I was the plaything of two great Strengths that dragged me forward, that dragged me back. The spirit of the Fire cried,

"Come, O Divine! Come, be made perfect, and queen it in this red heart of mine. Come, drink of that full cup of mysteries which no mortal lips have drained. Come, see those things that are hidden from mortal eyes. Come, taste of joys wherewith no mortal heart has ever throbbed. Haste, haste to the fiery bridal and in the glory of my kiss learn what delight can be. Oh! doubt no more but take Faith by the hand and let her lead thee home. Doubt no more! Be brave, lay down mortality: put on the spirit and as a spirit sit enthroned beyond the touch of time and with immortal eyes, robed in eternal majesty, watch the generations pass, marching with sad feet from darkness into darkness. Behold there he stands who is appointed to thee, who was thine from the beginning, who shall be thine until the end of ends. Thy new-born loveliness shall chain him fast and he shall grow drunken in the breath of thy perfumed sighs who for ever and for ever and for ever shall be thy very own, turning the winter of thy widowed heart to summer of perpetual joy."

Thus spake the spirit of the Flame, but to it there answered another spirit that wore the shape of Noot, yea, of Noot grown stern and terrible.

"Turn back, O Wisdom's Daughter, ere thou art wrapped in the robe of madness and repentance comes too late," it seemed to say. "Always the tempter tempts and when bribe after bribe is scorned, at last he pours his richest jewels at the feet of her whom he would win. Woe, woe to her who, charmed of their false glitter, clasps them upon brow and breast, for there they shall change to scorpions and through the living flesh gnaw to the brain and heart within. Departing, have I not set thee to watch the Fire and wilt thou steal the Fire, therewith to make thyself a god? Do so and this I swear to thee: that the godhead which thou shalt put on will be that of hell. Thy love shall be snatched away; undying, through all the earth, through all the stars, thou shalt follow after him and never find, or, if thou findest, it will be but to lose again. Dost thou dare to wrest thy destiny out of the hand of Fate and fashion it to thy desire with the instrument of thy blind and petty will? Do so, and daemons shall possess it that from age to age shall drive thee on, torn by the furies of remorse, choked with bitter, unavailing tears, frozen by the icy blasts of sorrow; desolate, alone, unfriended, till at last thou standest before the Judgment-seat hearkening with bowed head to a doom that can never be undone. Daughter of Wisdom, art thou sunk so low that thou wilt forget thine oaths and break thy trust to rob another woman of her lover?"

Those visions passed and I grasped denial's robes. I would not do this thing. I would live out my life upon the earth, I would die—oh! might it be soon—to pass to whatever place had been prepared for me, or to sink into the deep abysm of that rich and boundless sleep which no dreams haunt.

Aye! renouncing joy and renounced of hope, already I turned to go and climb my upward path back to the bitter world.

Then, from far, far away came the faint music of the chant of the advancing god of Fire. Low and sweet it sang at first, soft as a mother's lullaby, and lo! I dreamed of a happy childhood's day. It swelled and grew and now I had entered into womanhood and strange, uncomprehended longings companioned me. It took a fiercer note and I bethought me of the beating of the hoofs of horses as, mounted on my crested stallion, I rushed across the desert like the wind. Louder yet, and behold! once more I was in the battle at my father's side; behind me the wild tribesmen surged and shouted; in front of me my foes were beaten down to death. Ah! bright flashed my javelin, ah! free flowed my hair among the flapping pennons. "The Daughter of Yarab! Follow the daughter of Yarab!" cried the thousands of my kin, and on we went, like sun-loosed snows down mountains, on upon the marshalled host beneath. We broke them, for who could stand before the Daughter of Yarab and her kin? We trampled them, Egyptian and Syrian and Mede and the men from Chittim's Isle; down they went before that wild charge, and see! my bright spear was red.

Deeper yet and more solemn grew that mighty music. Now I was alone in the wilderness beneath the stars, and from the stars knowledge and beauty fell upon my heart like dew. Now I was a ruler of men, and kings who would be my lovers bent at my feet and were the puppets of my hands. I cast them down and broke them; I saw Sidon go up in flames and filled my soul with vengeance. Hark! It is the footstep of the goddess, the Queen of Heaven sets her kiss upon my brow; she names me Daughter, her Appointed. Knowledge is mine, out of my lips flow prophecies, a spirit guides my feet. I, I hold my own against the Persian, when all else have fled I cast him from his throne. I give his pomp to the tongues of Fire. Oh! how they cry, those mockers of Egypt's gods, as I watch them scorch and perish.

I am lonely. Where is my love? I wend toward the grave and none are born of me. I seek my love. "There stands my love—not far away, but at thy side. Take him, take him, take him!" Thus said the Fire.

Now its voice is the voice of trumpets that blare and echo around the hills. They call, those trumpets call: "Where is the captain of our hosts? Where is our Queen? Come forth, O Queen, crowned with wisdom, diademed with power, holding in thine hand the gift of days. No longer would we be left leaderless, we who would march to victory and hold the world in thrall."

The King of Fire is at hand. He opens the gateways of the dark. Behind him march the legions: he comes with splendour, he comes with glory, he comes to take his bride. "Unrobe, unrobe! Prepare thyself, O Bride! The King of Fire calls!"

I unloosed my garments, I unbound my hair that covered me like to a sable robe.

"Art mad?" cried the Greek, Kallikrates, wringing his hands.

"Art mad?" echoed the royal Amenartas with a slow smile as she waited to see mine end.

"Nay, I am wise," I answered back, "I who weary of tame days and common things, I who seek death or triumph."

I ran. I stood in the pathway of the Fire. It saw; it stretched out its arms to me. Lo! it wrapped me round and in my ears I heard the shoutings of the stars.

Oh! what was this? I did not burn. The blood of the gods flowed through my veins. The soul within me became as a lighted torch. The Fire possessed me, I was the Fire's and in a dread communion the Fire was mine. By that lit torch of my heart I saw many visions; veils rolled up before my eyes revealing glory after glory, glories that cannot be told. Death shrank away from before my feet; pale and ashamed he shrank away. Pain departed, weakness was done. I stood the Queen of all things human.

Lo! mirrored in that Fire as in water I saw myself, a shape of loveliness celestial. Could this form be the form of woman? Could those orbs divine be a woman's eyes?

Then a great silence and in the silence a silvery tinkling sound that I knew well—the sound of the laughter of Aphrodite!

The pillar of flame had rolled away, its thousand blinding lights had ceased to shine, and there I stood triumphant, conquering, never to be conquered. I came forth speaking with a voice of music, knowing that I had inherited another soul. What now to me was Isis or any other goddess, to me who stood victorious, the equal of them all? Oh! I saw now that Isis was but Nature and henceforth Nature was my slave. I thought no more of sin or of repentance, I who from this day forth would fashion my own laws and be to myself a judge. That which I desired, that I would take. That which was hateful to me that would I cast away. Yea! I was Nature's very self. I felt all her springs stirring in my blood; it glowed with the heats of all her summers. I was kind with the kindness of her fruitful autumns; I was terrible with her winter wrath.

Look! There stood the man whom I desired. Somewhat coarse and poor he seemed to me; I smelt death upon him. To be my mate he must be my equal; he too must taste of the Fire; then we would talk of love. As he was, my love was not for him, nay, it would destroy him as the lightning blasts.

"Look on me, Kallikrates," I cried, "and tell me, in all your days have you seen aught so fair?"

"Fair, yes, fair!" he gasped, "but terrible in beauty. No woman, no woman! A very spirit. Oh! let me shut mine eyes. Let me flee!"

"Be still and wait," I answered, "for soon I shall show you how they may be opened. Look on me, Daughter of Pharaoh, and tell me, has that stamp of age of which you spoke to me not long ago departed from my face and form, or is it yet apparent?"

"I look," she answered, still bold, "and I see before me no child of man, but a very witch! Away from us, accursed witch! Clothe yourself, shameless one, and begone, or let us begone, leaving you to commune with your witch's fire."

I cast my robes around me and oh! they hung royally. Then once more I turned to Kallikrates, considering him. As I looked I became aware that a great change had fallen upon me. I was no longer the Ayesha of old days. That Ayesha had been spirit-driven; her soul aspired to the heavens; it glistened with the dews of purity. True, I had loved this man, little at the first, and more a hundred times after Noot had suffered me to look upon the Fire, since with the sight and the sound and the odours of it the great change began.

That Ayesha was one who dreamed of heavenly things; one with whom prayer was a constant habit of the mind; yes, all her thoughts were mixed with the leaven of prayer, so that the humblest deed and the most common of imaginings were by it sanctified! She knew that here was not her home, but that far away and out of sight, beyond the seas and mountains of the world, her everlasting house rose white and stately and that with her earthly toil and sufferings she built it stone by stone, filling its halls and porticoes with ivory statues of the gods, making it pure with clouds of incense that their perfected souls brooding on her soul drew from it, as at dawn the sun draws mist from rivers.

With grief and toil, with bleeding feet; buffeted by the winds of circumstance, wet with the rain of tears, washed by the waters of repentance, she climbed the stony upward path that led to the Peak of Peace. She believed in she knew not what, for always to her those gods were man-shaped symbols. Still day and night she struggled on, lit by the rays of the lamp of faith, sure that in the end the veils would be withdrawn and that she would look upon the Face Divine and hear its voice of welcome. She was obedient to the Law; she knew that time was not her own and that of every moment she must give account. Aye, she was in the way of holiness and before her shone the golden guerdons of redemption.

But now. What was Ayesha now when she had known the embrace of the Spirit of Fire, when she had dared the deed and wrung the secret from his burning heart? Aye, when on the earth she had attained to immortality, since even then a voice cried in her ears:

"Behold! thou shalt not die. Behold while the world lives, with it thou shalt live also, because thou hast drunk of the wine of Earth's primeval Soul that cannot be spilled until its mighty fabric is dissolved into the nothingness whence it sprang!"

What was she now? She was that very Earth. She was that Soul poured into the white vase of a woman's form; aye, she was its essence. Its lightnings and its hurricanes lay chained within her, ready to leap out when she was wrath, and who could abide before their strength? She knew all Earth's glory as alone it swung through space, kissed of the light of the Sun its father, or dreaming in the arms of darkness. The planets were her sisters, the bright, blazing stars acknowledged her as kin. Aye; with this mother-world she symbolled she was numbered among the multitude of that hierarchy of heaven.

Nor was this all, for in her reigned and glowed every power and passion of the Earth. Thenceforth all things were at her command, but, like that Earth, *she was alone and could no more speak with Heaven!*.

In a flash, in a twinkling, all this mighty truth came home to me, and with it other truths. I did not doubt, I did not dream, I knew, I knew, I *knew!*

There stood the man and I would take him. He was wed according to Nature's law, and now I owned no other. But what of that? The wine that I desired I would drink. I would mate me as the wild things mated, by strength and capture, since I was very strong and who could stand against my might? I, the reborn Ayesha, had commanded. It should be done.

\* \* \* \* \* \* \* \*

"Kallikrates," I said in my new voice of honeyed sweetness, "behold your spouse, one of whom you need not be ashamed. Make ready, Kallikrates. Go stand in the path of the Fire when it returns, and then let us hence to reign eternally."

"What, Witch," cried Amenartas, "would you rob me of my lord? It shall not be. If you are mighty, so am I, although I remain a woman. Kallikrates, look on me, your wife, she who has borne your child, that lost child who binds us yet with bonds that may not be broken. Have done with this fair daemon ere she enchant you. Away! Away from this haunted, mocking hell."

"I come. Surely I come," said Kallikrates, glancing at me fearfully. "I am afraid of her, and of that fire I will have none. Surely it is Set himself wrapped about with flames."

"Nay, you go not, Kallikrates. Let Amenartas go if she desires. Here you abide with me until all is accomplished. I command, and when I command, you must obey."

He wheeled about; he flung himself into the arms of Amenartas. They closed around him and held him fast. Then I threw out my will. Saying nothing I laid my strength upon him, so that he was dragged from out those arms and with slow steps drew near to me, as the bird draws near to the snake that charms it with its baleful eyes. Amenartas leaped between us and from her lips flowed words in torrents.

All she said I do not know; it is forgot; but very sore she pleaded and very bitterly she wept. Yet my heart, new steeled in yonder fire, felt no pity for her. An hour past I should have bade him go his way and to look upon my face no more, but now it was otherwise. I was cruel, cruel as Death, King of the world. The wild beast does not spare its rival, neither would I.

Still I drew him with my strength; still Amenartas clung and pleaded, till at last madness took hold of that tormented man. He raved, he cursed us both, he cursed himself who had left the quiet halls of Isis, who had spurned the love divine to seek the arms of woman. He prayed to Isis to be pitiful, to forgive, to receive his soul and shrive it.

Then suddenly from his belt he snatched his short Grecian sword and stabbed at his own heart.

Swift as a snake that strikes, or a falcon stooping at its prey, I sprang. I seized his arm, I dragged it back, and such might was there in my grasp, aye, the might of Hercules himself, that the sword flew far, and the strong man who held it reeled round and round and fell.

We stood aghast, thinking that he was sped. Yet he rose, the red blood running from his beast, and in a quiet voice, a little laugh upon his lips, said to Amenartas, not to me,

"Fear nothing, Wife. Alas! it is but a cut—skin deep, no more."

"Then let the fire heal it, O Kallikrates. Make ready to enter the fire that must soon retravel its circling path," I answered.

"Nay, nay, Husband," cried Amenartas. "By that blood of yours, the blood that flowed in our dead son and flows in that of the child to be, I adjure you turn from this witch and temptress and break her enchanted bonds."

"By our dead son," he repeated after her in a strange and heavy voice. "With what holier words could you conjure, O my wife? With that name of power I am new-armoured. Daughter of Wisdom, I reject your proffered gifts, nor will I enter your charmed fire though it should give to me eternal strength and gloriousness, and with these your shining beauty and your love. Child of the gods, farewell! I go to seek peace and pardon if it may be found. Yes, pardon for you and me, and for Amenartas, the mother of my child. Daughter of Wisdom, fare you well for ever!"

I heard and it seemed to me that I stood alone in the midst of a great silence while those cruel words, divorcing me from hope, fell one by one upon me like ice-drops from the sky, cutting to brain and heart and freezing me to stone. Then of a sudden rage possessed me, such rage as Nature knows in her fiercest moods, and I spoke as it gave me words, saying,

"I call down death upon thee, Kallikrates the Greek. Death be thy portion and the grave thy home. Because thou hast rejected me, because thou hast offered me insult to my face, it is my will that thou mayest die; it is my desire that thy name be blotted out from the roll of Life. Die, then, Kallikrates, that thine eyes may torment me no more and that I may learn to mock thy memory."

Thus I spoke those words of doom in my madness, though what conceived them in my heart I do not know. There they sprang up suddenly at the touch of the wand of Evil, such evil as until now I had never dreamed. Lo! in a moment they fulfilled themselves. There before my eyes that man *died*, smitten of the dominion over Death that was the Fire's fatal gift to me, as now, all unprepared, instantly I learned. Yes, the first service that I made of my dread majesty was to hurl that awful doom at the heart of the man I loved.

He died! Kallikrates died there before our eyes. Yet being dead, still he stood upon his feet and spoke, though even then I knew that it was not he who spoke, but some spirit possessing his flesh. His lips did not move, his eyes were glassed, his voice was not the voice of Kallikrates, nay, nor the voice of mortal man. Yet he spoke, or seemed to speak, and these were the words he said,

"Woman, known on earth as Ayesha, daughter of Yarab, but in the Under-world by many another name, hearken to thy fate. Here, where thou hast betrayed thy trust, here where thou didst slay the man of thy desire, here through long ages shalt thou abide undying, until in the fullness of time he returns to thee, O Ayesha, in lonely bitterness shalt thou abide; tears shall be thy drink and remorse thy bread. The power that thou didst crave shall be but a blunted, unused sword within thine hand. Thy kingdom shall be a desolation, thy subjects barbarians, and from century to century thy companions shall be the dead."

The voice ceased and I answered it, asking,

"And when the returning tide of Time bears this man back to me, what then, O Spirit? Is all hope passed from me, O Spirit?"

* * * * * * * *

No answer came, but that which had been Kallikrates sank in a huddled heap upon the sand.

## CHAPTER 24

# The Counsel of Philo

Roaring like a whirlwind, shouting triumphantly, once more the wheel of fire rolled on its tremendous course. I watched it come, I watched it go, while in it I thought I saw grinning, elf-like faces that gibbered at me and thrust out tongues of derision. It departed on its secret journey through the bowels of the world. Its thunder sank to mutterings, its mutterings to silence, while I said to my heart that could I be sure that it would slay, I would cast myself beneath its chariot wheels.

To what purpose? Since then, as I believed in those days, in the flames I should find but added life—I who could not die.

It was gone. Naught remained save the cave carpeted with white sand and the rosy light playing on the body of the dead Kallikrates. Nay, Amenartas remained also, and I became aware that she was cursing me by all her gods, or rather by those who had been her gods before she turned her face from them, seeking the counsel of familiar spirits.

Bravely she cursed and long, calling down upon my head every evil that can be found in heaven above or earth beneath; she who did not know that this was needless, for already the winged Furies had made it their resting-place and before they could be uttered all her imprecations were fulfilled.

"Have done!" I said when at length she grew weak and weary, "and let us summon Philo to help us bear this noble clay to some fitting sepulchre."

"Nay, Witch," she answered, "use your magic on me also, if you can. Slay the wife as you have slain the husband, and here let us rest eternally. What tomb can be better for both of us than that which saw our murder."

"Have done!" I repeated. "You know well that I have no desire to kill you and that it was my madness, not my will, that brought doom on Kallikrates, whom we loved; I who had not learned that hence-forth my spirit is a bow winged with deadly shafts."

I went down the cave and through the passage that lay beyond and from its mouth called to Philo to follow me.

He came, and perceiving my new loveliness as I stood awaiting him in the rosy light, fell to the ground, kissing my feet and the hem of my robe, and muttering,

"O *Isis-come-to-Earth*! O Queen divine!"

"Rise up and follow me," I said, and led him to where lay Kallikrates, by whom knelt the widowed Amenartas weeping bitterly.

"Overwhelmed with the sight of glory, alas! this lord has slain himself," I said, and pointed to the wound in the dead man's breast whence still the blood oozed drop by drop.

"Nay, this witch slew him," moaned Amenartas, but if Philo heard her words, he took no heed of them.

Then at my command the three of us lifted Kallikrates and bore him thence up the difficult ways, which never could we have done had I not discovered that now in my woman's shape that seemed so frail and weak was hid unmeasured strength.

So through the caves and up the winding slopes and stairs we bore the dead Kallikrates, bringing him back to the hermitage of Noot but a little before the hour of sunset. Here I commanded Amenartas and Philo to eat and drink, though myself I needed neither food nor wine. While they did so, aided of this new strength of mine, I lifted the body of Noot from where it knelt and laid it down, crossing the hands upon the breast, and having covered it with a robe, left him to his last sleep.

These things finished, we carried Kallikrates to the crest of the Swaying Stone, and waited the coming of the ray. Suddenly it shone out, and in its fierce light we dared the shifting bridge. Beneath a weight which it was ill designed to bear, the frail thing broke just as Amenartas and Philo, bearing the feet of the dead man, had found footing upon the point of the spur beyond. It seemed that I should have fallen, yet I fell not, who, I know not how, found myself at their side still supporting Kallikrates in my arms.

Then it was that first I learned that as I was protected from the gnawings of the tooth of Time so also I was armoured against all the strokes of chance. This indeed became very clear to me in the after days. Thus once when the roof of a cave fell upon me and others they were slain but I remained unbruised, and again, when a deadly snake bit me, its poison harmed me not at all. But what of these things which are not worthy to be chronicled, seeing that if I could die, in the passing of two thousand years and more, what men call mishap must long since have brought me to my end.

We bore Kallikrates down the spur and through the cavern whence it springs, till at length we found the litters waiting for us, and in one of these we laid his quiet form.

Thus at length we came back to Kor at the hour of the dawn.

Again we lifted up the corpse of Kallikrates and carried it to the chamber where I slept. A thought came to me.

"Philo," I said, "did you not tell me that among those who serve us in this temple are certain aged medicine-men who declare that knowledge of the arts whereby the people of old Kor preserved their dead from corruption has come down to them, which arts they still practise from time to time?"

"It is so, O Queen," for so he named me now. "There are three of them."

"Good. Summon them, Philo, and bid them bring with them their instruments and spices."

Awhile later the three appeared, very aged, cunning-looking men who had upon their hawk-nosed faces the stamp of high and ancient blood. I pointed to the body of Kallikrates and asked,

"Are ye able to hold back this holy flesh from the foul fingers of decay?"

"If he be not more than forty hours dead," answered one of them, "we can do so in such fashion that when five thousand years have passed it will seem as it does at this hour, O Queen."

"Then to your office, Slaves, and know that if ye do as ye have promised ye shall receive great reward. But if ye lie to me, ye die."

"We do not lie, O Queen," he said.

Forthwith they set a fire outside the chamber and thereon set a large earthen pot. In this pot, mixed with water, they placed dried leaves of a certain shrub, in shape long and narrow, and boiled them to a broth, whereof the pungent colour seemed to fill all the air about. While the pot was boiling they took the corpse of Kallikrates, and, having washed it, brushed it everywhere with some secret stuff that gave to it the aspect of white and shining marble. Then they brought a funnel of clay with a curved point, and having opened the great artery of the throat, inserted the point into the artery.

This done, they stood the stiff corpse on its feet and while two of them held it thus, the third brought the pot into which they poured stuff that looked like glass when it is molten, mixing all together with a rod of stone. Then he set a ladder, perhaps four paces in length, against the wall, and carrying the pot, climbed to the top of it, whence slowly he poured the brew into the funnel beneath so that its weight forced it through all the dead man's veins. When the most of it was gone he descended and the three of them finished their work in some way that I did not stay to watch, for the sight of this grim preparation for the tomb and the scent of these spicy drugs overcame me.

At length they summoned me and showed me Kallikrates lying like to one in a deep sleep, calm and beautiful as he had been in life.

"O Queen," said their spokesman, "by to-morrow at the sunrise the flesh of this man will be as marble, and so everlastingly remain. Then bear him where you will, but till then let him rest untouched."

I bade that they should be rewarded, and they went their ways. But first I asked them where the inhabitants of old Kor were wont to lay their royal dead. They answered that it was in the great caves at a little distance across the plain, and I commanded that on the morrow they should guide me thither, bearing the body of Kallikrates.

Philo came and said that the priests and priestesses of Isis would have speech with me and that they were gathered in the inmost court of the great temple before the veiled statue of the goddess Truth. I bade him lead on, but he wavered a little and said,

"O Queen, there is trouble. The royal lady, Amenartas, has told a tale in the ears of those priests and priestesses. She has sworn to them that you are not a woman but a daemon; aye, a witch risen from the Under-world, and that you murdered the lord Kallikrates because he would not give himself to you. Also she swore that you strove to murder her who, being protected by the magic which her father Nectanebes, the great wizard, taught her, was too strong for you and therefore escaped alive."

"As to the last, she lies," I answered carelessly.

We came to the inmost court. It was the hour of sunset and the place was filled with glowing light. I took my seat upon the throne-like chair beneath the statue and the light beat full upon me, a glory on a glory.

The priests and priestesses who were standing still with folded arms and bowed heads looked up and saw me. A murmur of astonishment rose from them and I heard one say to the other,

"The Princess has told us truth."

At first I did not understand; then I remembered that I was no long as mortal women are, but rather, as my mirror told me, an incarnate splendour, a very goddess to the sight.

"Speak," I said, and they shook at the new rich note of power in my voice, as leaves vibrate at the sudden swell of music.

The first of the priests, a large man of middle age, Rames by name, stood forward and fixing his round eyes upon my face, said,

"O Prophetess, O Daughter of Wisdom, O *Isis-come-to-Earth*, we know not what to say, since we have heard that you have changed your shape, now as is evident to us. Prophetess, you are not the same high-priestess who ruled over us in the temple at Memphis and whom we followed to this desolate land. Some magic has been at work with you."

"If so," I answered, "is it an evil magic? Tell me, Rames, am I changed for better or for worse?"

"You are beautiful," he answered, "so beautiful that madness must take all men who look on you. But, Prophetess, your loveliness is not such as mortal woman wears. Nay, it is such as Typhon might give to one who had sold her soul to him. Also, there is more. We learn that you murdered the Greek Kallikrates, who once was of our fellowship, because he refused his love to you; yes, that you, the high-priestess of Isis, murdered a man because he turned from your arms to those of his wife, the royal Amenartas, and that if you could, you would have murdered her also."

"Who tells this tale?" I asked slowly.

"The Princess herself," Rames answered. "See, she is here. Let her speak."

Amenartas appeared from among the throng, and cried,

"It is true, it is most true. Here before the statue of Truth herself, I swear it in the face of Heaven and to all the listening earth. There is a wound on the breast of my dead lord, Kallikrates. Ask yonder witch how that wound came there. Clothed only in her hair, she entered into a fire, a fire of hell. She came forth beautiful with a beauty that is not human. She called my lord to embrace her. Yes, this shameless one, she named herself his spouse. This she did before the eyes of his own wife and in the hearing of her ears. She bade him enter the Fire of Hell, and when he would not, when he turned to seek refuge in my arms, she sent him down the path of death by her words of power. She said:

"'I call down death upon thee, Kallikrates. Death be thy portion and the grave thine home. Die, Kallikrates, that thy face may torment me no more and that I may learn to mock thy memory.'

"These were her very words. Let her deny them if she can. I say, moreover, that always she has desired to lead astray the lord Kallikrates, and that when she could not do so of her woman's strength, then she made a pact with Typhon and strove to mesh him in her magic, but strove in vain. Therefore she slew him in her rage."

When the priests and priestesses heard these words they turned pale and trembled. Then they called me to answer. But I said,

"I answer not. Who are you that I should render account to you of what I have or have not done? Think what you will and do what you will, I answer not, save this, that what has chanced, has chanced by the decree of Fate who sits above all gods and goddesses, throned beyond heaven's remotest star."

They drew apart, they talked together. Then Rames came forward and, still staring at me, said:

"Whether you yet serve Isis, O Ayesha, daughter of Yarab, we do not know. But we who are her children, sworn to her obedience for which we have suffered many things, reject you from your place of rule in which you were set above us by the holy Noot, whom we learn has passed to the keeping of Osiris. No more are you our high-priestess, Ayesha, or Evil Spirit, and no longer shall you stand with us before the altars of the Queen of Heaven."

"Be it as you will," I answered. "Go and leave me to make mine own peace with Isis, who now and henceforward am her equal, I who have learned what Isis is, and been clothed with that same majesty. I see that you believe me to blaspheme; the horror upon your faces tells me so. Yet I do not; here in the shadow of Truth—if it were but known, the only goddess—I speak with the voice of Truth. Farewell. I wish you good fortune, and in all things will aid you if I can. Tell me, Philo, do you desert me like these others?"

"Nay, O Queen," he answered, "we are old comrades, you and I, who have gone through too much together to separate at last. I am a Greek who entered into the company of Isis chiefly after I met you, fair Daughter of Wisdom, and noted the deeds you did upon the ship *Hapi*, and to be short—whatever road you take is a good road for me. I know not whether you slew this Kallikrates, or whether he slew himself with his own sword, of which I noted the mark upon him, but if you offered him your love and he refused it then I hold that he deserved to die.

"For the rest, I am a merchant who take my gain where I can find it, and I know that you pay well. Therefore I follow your banner to the end, whether it lead me to the Heaven of Isis or to the Hades of my forefathers, where doubtless I shall meet Achilles and Hector and Odysseus and many another gallant seafaring warrior of whom our

Homer sings. That place whither you wend is home enough for me, for in your palace I shall always find a chamber, and on your ship of state I shall always stand upon the poop, however far the voyage."

Thus spoke that gay and cunning Greek, hiding the loyalty of his heart beneath his jesting words, and truly in that hour of deserted loneliness my gratitude went out toward him, as still it does to-day and will do for evermore. For though Philo would take a bribe where he could find it, as is the way of those who serve Fortune and must earn bread, still he was ever loyal to those he loved, and he loved me in that high fashion which is born of long service and of fellowship. When at length I come into my great inheritance, and rule otherwhere—as rule I shall—my first care shall be to reward Philo as he deserves, although once or more he did fill his pouch with the gold of Amenartas, or so I believe.

Yet at this time I only smiled at him and asked,

"These things being done, what of the Princess of Egypt? Let her speak her desire that I may fulfil it, if I can."

"It is simple," answered Amenartas, "that I may be rid of you, no less and no more. I would go hence to bear my child and to rear him to wreak vengeance on you for his father's blood, O Witch of the Under-world, and until I die, to work and pray that the Furies may be your bedfellows, O murderess and thief of love."

"Let these things befall as they are fated," I answered very quietly. "The stage of doom is set and on it throughout the ages until the play ends at last, we, the puppets of Destiny, must act our appointed parts to a consummation that we cannot foresee. But how will it end, Lady Amenartas? You know not; nor do I, though already some master's hand has writ the last scene upon his roll. Philo, it is my command that you lead Pharaoh's child to the coast, or wherever she would go, that thence she may find her way to Greece or Egypt as Fortune may direct her. That done, return and make report to me. Farewell, Amenartas."

"Fare ill, Witch," she cried. "We part, but as I think, to meet again elsewhere, seeing that between you and me there is a score to settle."

"Aye," I answered gently enough. "Yet boast not, Amenartas, and be not too sure of anything, since when at length that sum is added up, who knows on which side the balance will be struck."

"At least I know that the count will be long and that murder is a heavy weight in any scale," she answered.

Then she went; they all went and left me alone brooding there upon the chair of state, in which I sat for the last time. The darkness closed about me, then came the twilight of the rising moon in whose soft rays I saw the figure of a man creeping toward me as a thief creeps.

"Who comes?" I asked.

"Beauteous Queen," answered a thick voice, "it is I, Rames, the priest."

"Speak on, Rames."

"O most fair among women, if indeed you may be named woman, hear me. Those fools of priests and priestesses have thrown you from your place."

"So you told me but now, Rames, nor can they be blamed."

"So I told you because I must, not of my own will, and that which is done, cannot be undone. You are cast out and here in Kor the worship of Isis is at an end, since who is there that can fill your throne? Yet, hearken, hearken! I cling to you, I worship you. I desire you to be my wife, O most lovely. Here together we will rule in Kor and you shall be its Queen and goddess, and I will be its Captain. It is most wise that you should consent, O Lady divine."

"Why is it wise, Rames?"

"Because, Lady, I can protect you. You know the sentence that goes out against those who break the rule of Isis. I say that it is already uttered against you. I say that those bigots seek to murder you. But if you take me as husband, then we will be beforehand with them and kill or drive them away. Yea, now that you are lonely and deserted, I shall be your sure shield."

I heard and laughed aloud, and I think that this madman interpreted that laugh in a strange fashion. At least he threw himself upon me. He seized my hand and lifted it toward his lips, though by those lips it was never touched. For now rage took hold of me, such rage as had possessed my soul in the cave of the Fire of Life; rage and the desire of destruction, that with other evil gifts had come to me in the breath of the Fire.

"Accursed one!" I cried, "vile and insolent thief! Do you dare to touch me with your hand? Away with you to Set! Let the world know you no more!"

As the words passed my lips it seemed to me that from some strength within a withering flame leapt out of me and smote that man as the lightning smites. At the least he lifted his hands to his head; he reeled back, he fell, he groaned—he died.

Looking at him lying there in the moonlight, still and bereft of life, at the last I came to know full surely that henceforward I could slay with a thought, that I was the Lady of Death, and that such wrath as others express in words went forth from me with all the might of Heaven; moreover, that now this wrath rose suddenly and swiftly in me, easy to unchain, hard to hold. Yea, I was both a fury and a terror whom no man might cross or vex if he would continue to look upon the sun.

Philo came. He stared at me and at the dead Rames, then questioned me with his eyes.

"He would have laid hands on me, Philo, and I slew him," I said.

"Then what he has earned, he has been paid," answered Philo. "Yet, Queen, how did you slay him? I see no bruise or wound."

"By a power that has come to me, Philo. I desired him dead and he died. That is all the tale."

"A strange and a terrible power, Queen. Often when we are angry we wish that this one or that were dead—yet that they should forthwith die—! Henceforth you must watch your moods well, Daughter of Wisdom, since otherwise I think that you and I will soon be parted for, as I know, at times you are angry with me, and when next that chances I shall be sped."

"Aye, Philo, so I have learned. I must watch my moods very well. Yet fear nothing, since never could I wish you dead."

"Are you sure, Ayesha? Hearken. What was the crime of this poor wretch? Was it not that he, who hitherto had been a virtuous man, a good and earnest priest who never turned to look at woman, of a sudden went mad for love of you, and in his madness urged his suit—well, as men do when they have lost hold of the reins of reason, whereon you slew him? Now if men must die for such a crime, who is there that would live to grow old? I think that all of them would soon be driven to dwell in such a hermitage as that wherein the holy Noot sleeps to-night. Is it not true? I ask you who know the world."

"It is true," I answered.

"If so, Lady, I would ask another question. What was it that sent this man mad? Was it not the sight of such beauty as has never yet been known upon the earth? Which beauty, Ayesha, if I look upon it much longer, I think will send me mad also, or any other man. Daughter of Wisdom, such loveliness as you wear to-day is the greatest curse that the gods can grant to a woman, because being above Nature, all Nature must obey its might. Daughter of Wisdom, henceforward you must veil your face from the eyes of men, or become the murderess of more ill-fated ones."

"It seems that this is so," I answered heavily. "I have desired beauty and beauty has come to me, but however great, all gifts are not good."

"So I have heard philosophers preach in Greece, Lady, yet never did I know one of them to turn his back on any gift. Ayesha, hide those eyes of yours, hide them swiftly. While Rames lies there dead, love is frightened, but once his clay is gone, who knows? But I forgot, I came to warn you that a certain decree has been uttered against you, the same, Queen, that you have uttered against Rames, also to protect you, if I can."

Now I laughed outright.

"Foolish man," I said, "do you not yet understand that I cannot be killed or even harmed?"

"Ye Gods!" said Philo, holding up his hands in amazement. Then he was silent.

* * * * * * * *

That night I slept by the cold shape of Kallikrates and oh! it was the most fearful of all nights that ever I passed upon the earth. Evil, very evil were the dreams that came to me, if dreams they were. In them it seemed that Noot spoke with me. Nay, not Noot, but a flickering tongue of fire which I knew to be the spirit of Noot. Naught could I see save that burning tongue, and from it came terrible words.

"Daughter," it said, "you have cast my counsels to the winds, you have betrayed your trust, you have broken my commands that I gave to you out of the wisdom that was given to me. You have entered the Fire that you were set to watch. You have been embraced by the Fire and received its gifts. Behold the first fruits of them. The man whom you would have taken lies dead at your side, and yonder in the temple court another lies dead also, who was good until your hell-granted beauty made him evil. The worship of Isis is destroyed in this land that now nevermore will become a nation great and strong and pure. The heart of Amenartas is broken, yet she will live on to beget avengers, one of whom will overtake you at the appointed time. In loneliness, in remorse, in utter desolation you must endure till the Fire dies that cannot die while the world is; seeking yet never finding, or finding but to lose again. Henceforth you are an alien to the kindly race of men, a beauteous terror that all must desire and yet all fear and hate. Ever that which you seek will flit before you like a wandering star which you may never overtake, and in following it you will bring death to thousands. Daughter, you are accursed."

"Is there then no redemption?" I asked of Noot in my dream.

"Aye, Ayesha, when the world is redeemed, then perchance you may find your part in that great forgiveness. Hearken. There is a vision which throughout your life has haunted you. In that vision Aphrodite and the evil gods, those gods that she had led into Egypt to destroy its higher faith, were summoned before the throne of Isis. In it also a fate and a command were laid upon you—that you should war against those gods and bring its punishment on Egypt that received and welcomed them."

"It is but a fantasy," I answered. "Now I know that there are no evil gods; there lives no Aphrodite; even no Isis."

"Daughter, you err. True, there is no Isis who was shaped only by the faith of earth and in the dreams of men. Yet there is that which they name Isis, as the highest that they know and can fashion in their thought. There is the eternal Good and that Good is God. Throughout the countless ages man, warring against Nature, has lifted up his heart till almost he seems to look upon the face of that almighty, regnant Good. Thus it was with you, Daughter, and now wither have you wended? You have fled down the backward path. You have undone all, you have gone back to Nature. Henceforth you are Nature's self, shining with her false and passing beauty, inspired with her law of death, you who once drew near to the new law of Life that awaited you beyond the grave, which now you may not seek."

"Whate'er I did, I did for Love and Love shall save me," I seemed to answer in my agony.

"Aye, Ayesha, doubtless in the end Love will save you, as it saves all things that without its grace must perish everlastingly. Yet for you that salvation is now far away, and ere it can be found, one by one you must conquer those passions that found you in the Fire. You who sought undying beauty, must see your fair body more hideous and more horrible than the leper of the streets. You who are filled with rage and strength must grow gentle as a dove and weak as a little child. By suffering you must learn to soothe the sufferings of others. By expiation you must atone your crimes, by faith once more you must lift up your soul. By the knowledge you shall win you must come to understand your own blind pettiness through time untold. Ayesha, this is your doom."

Such was the substance of that dream and when I awoke from it, oh! how bitterly I wept. For now I understood. I was fallen—fallen! All that I had gathered through the long years of prayer and abstinence and service had been reft from me, and I who stood near to joy had sunk into a hell of unending sorrow. There was no Isis, so I had dreamed Noot to say, and so my new knowledge told me. Yet there was the eternal Good which in Egypt men knew as Isis, and in other lands by many a different name, and from that Good I was excommunicate.

Now like my savage ancestors of a million years before, I was but a part of Nature as we see her upon the earth and feel her in our blood and—this was the most dreadful of my punishments—my wisdom and my lost faith had become rules by which I could mete out the measure of my fall, for ignorance can smile at that which to knowledge is a hell. All Nature's gifts were mine; all her beauty, all her desires, all her fierceness, all her hates, and one by one, through countless time I must weed her every evil growth from the garden of my poisoned soul. The curse with which she was accursed had smitten me also, and in the end her death would be my death. Such was the doom that I had brought upon my head when I had listened to the calling of that god of Fire.

Oh! looking upon the cold corpse of Kallikrates and feeling the primeval passions surging in my breast, little wonder that I, the rejected of Heaven, wept as still I weep to-day.

For such is the lot of those who trample on all good as they run to seize the glittering gauds that the tempter spreads before their lusting eyes. Perchance Noot never broke his holy rest to speak to me in dreams; perchance it was the strength in my own soul that spoke to my heart, as that strength of which now I knew the power, in the old days wrought marvels that then I believed to be done by the invisible hand of Isis. At least the lesson taught is true.

CHAPTER 25

# In Undying Loneliness

Ere the dawn, guided by those old embalmers and bearing with me the dead Kallikrates, I departed from that hateful Kor. As I think, none saw me go, for, forgetful of their promised vengeance, the priests and priestesses were gathered trembling about the corpse of Rames in the inmost court of the Temple of Truth, though it is true that I felt the baleful eyes of Amenartas watching me. Or perhaps it was her pursuing hate I felt, and not her eyes.

Veiled so that no man might look upon my deadly beauty, I crossed the plain and came to the vast cave-sepulchres. Here those old embalmers lit lamps and showed me a deep and empty tomb. It had two shelves or niches, on one of which I laid my dead, choosing the other to be my couch. Thus then I took up my abode in the Sepulchres of Kor that for some two thousand years were to be my home.

* * * * * * * *

At my command Philo led the royal Amenartas from the haunted land of Kor, and returning three moons later, told me, truly or not, that she had passed the swamps and departed on a wandering ship, sailing north, whither he knew not. I asked him no more who did not desire to learn of her words and curses, though as it chanced this I must do after long ages had gone by. Some of the priests and priestesses went with her. Others remained in Kor and, if they were young enough, took wives or husbands and ruled there. Indeed, the last of their descendants whom I could trace before their blood was utterly swallowed up in that of the barbarians, died after five hundred years or more had passed away.

Philo, too, lived on at Kor, making trading journeys to the coast and along it in his ship and grew rich and, after a fashion, great. For Philo would never leave me whom he loved, though no more would

536

he look upon my unveiled face. At length, very old, he died in my arms, he who would have none of the Fire and its gifts. When his breath left him, for the first time since that night at Kor, I wept. For now I was quite alone.

While he lay dying he prayed me to unveil, saying that now, when no harm could come of it, he would look upon my face once more. I did so and he studied me long and earnestly with his hollow eyes.

"You are wondrous beautiful," he said, "nor during these past forty years or more, since last I beheld you unveiled in the sanctuary of the Temple of Truth, has your loveliness lessened by one wit. Indeed, I think that it has gathered. What is the meaning of this, fair Daughter of Wisdom?"

"It means what I have told you before, Philo, that I do not die until the world dies, although I may change and seem to pass away."

"Yet I die. Do we then part for ever?" he asked.

"Nay, I think not, Philo, for at last Death overtakes everything and in its hallways we may meet again. Moreover, the world lives long and to it, ere its end, you may return once, or often, and if so, perchance you will be drawn to me."

"I trust so, O Wisdom's Daughter. They call you witch, and doubtless such you are, who can slay with a glance, whom age does not touch, and whom Death scorns. Yet, witch or woman, or both, there lives none, no, not even wife or child, whom I so desire to meet hereafter."

So Philo died, and since those medicine-men who had embalmed Kallikrates now were dead also, leaving behind them none who had knowledge of their art, I buried him unpreserved in the great sepulchres.

Awhile ago the fancy took me to go to look upon him, but alas! after the passing of some sixteen hundred years, save for the skull, his naked bones had crumbled into dust.

\* \* \* \* \* \* \*

What more is there to tell? All died and came again in their children: generation after generation of them did I watch arise, flourish in their wild fashion, and go their way down the path of Death. I ruled those barbarians, if rule it can be called. They were my slaves who feared me as a spirit, and I was kind to them, but if they angered me, then I slew them, for thus only could they be held in a due subjection even to one that they believed to be an ancient goddess whom their forefathers worshipped, Lulala by name, whose throne was in the moon.

For these Amahagger were a terrible people, barbarians who loved the night because their deeds were evil, and who, if strangers wandered among them, slew them by the setting of red-hot pots upon their heads, and afterward ate their flesh. Yet among them were some of a nobler sort, descended, as I think, either from the unmixed blood of the ancients of old Kor, or perchance from those priests and priestesses of Isis who had been my companions. Such a one was a certain Billali whom my lord Leo and Holly knew. But for the most part they were hook-nosed, treacherous, dark-haunting savages, and as such they must be handled.

In the course of those long ages, to divert myself in my loneliness and for the purposes of study, I reared certain of these savages up to this and that. I stunted them to dwarfs, I bred them to giants. Musicians of a kind I made of some of them, though to do so took ten of their generations. Then I grew weary of the game and all these variants died back into the common stock; that fundamental type to which, if left alone, every species that springs on earth returns in time, and this more quickly than might be thought. The last breed that I created, or caused to create itself, was one of mutes evolved from a faithful strain who had served me well, since I found these mutes more docile and less wearisome than the rest.

But enough of that people with which I have done for ever.

What did I do through all those awful ages? At first, as I found I had the power, I threw my watching eyes across the world, and learned all that happened there. Thus I saw the battles of Alexander, his conquests and his death, and the rise of the Ptolemies in Egypt; also many other things in the countries with which I have had to do. But soon I tired of it all.

Men arose of whom I knew nothing. Peoples changed, and ever the play repeated itself afresh, though with new actors. I had naught in common with them and their petty aims and passions, I who watched as a god might watch those that served him not, or as an idle child watches the labours of colony after colony of ants. Yea, I tired of them and took no more heed of what they did or did not do upon their short journey to that forgetfulness wherewith the dust of Time would bury them. I was dead to the world, and the world was dead to me.

In the ages that followed I sent out my soul to seek kindred souls and found some with whom I communed, though they never knew who it was that talked to them. With wise men throughout the earth I held this converse, and from them gathered knowledge, giving them in return something of my wisdom, which doubtless they presented to the generations as their own. If so, the world was the gainer, and if Truth comes, what matters it whence it comes?

I did more. I sought out the dead in their habitations beyond the stars, aye, and found not a few of them. Always they were eager to learn of the world and in return paid me with the coin of their unearthly lore. They told me of those other worlds and I made acquaintance with their princes and their rulers: I gathered up the broken fragments from the feasts that were spread upon these alien tables and drank of the dregs of their new wine. But, and here was a mystery, here was the grief: never once could I grasp the robe of any whom I had known upon the earth. I found not my father, I found not Noot, I found not Kallikrates, I found not Philo, I found not Beltis or Amenartas. In all that countless multitude I discovered no single soul to whom my mortal lips had spoken in its little day. Of friend or foe I found not one. Perchance all them were still asleep and resting in their sleep.

I looked into the secrets of Nature and they opened themselves to me like flowers beneath the sun. I inhaled their perfume, I admired their beauty, so that at length little was hid from me. I learned how to turn clay to gold and how to harness the lightning to my service, aye, and many another thing. Yet what was the use of all of it to me, the dweller in a tomb?

Knowledge, the lord, is a barren grant unless it can also be a servant; aye, a slave at command to work good for man.

For the rest, what could I do? Without the caves I sowed the seed of trees. I watched them spring, I watched them grow to saplings and, in the slow progression of the centuries, swell to great timbers with far-reaching arms beneath whose shade I rested. Thus they stood for many a hundred years. Then for many another hundred they decayed, grew hollow, rotted to dust and fell, their long day done at last. And I, I sowed me others.

To mark the passage of those years lest I should lose count of them, in a certain cavern I laid me stones, a stone for every one as from the hand of Time it fell ripe into the bosom of Eternity. As on their rosaries, here and there, priests set larger beads to mark the tale of their completed prayers, so when ten years had gone I set a larger stone, and when a hundred had passed by, one larger yet and white in colour, while the thousandth year I marked with a little pyramid, two of which now stand in the Caves of Kor. It was a good plan whereby I could reckon easily, only some of the softer stones that lay near to the mouth of that cavern where sun and rain could reach them at length crumbled into sand.

Why did I stay at Kor? Why did I not wander forth through the world? Because I *could not*, because of the curse that had been laid upon me, that here I must wait until Kallikrates came again, as come I knew he would. Therefore no captive ever was more chained and fettered in his dungeon than I, Ayesha, by that compelling curse in the Sepulchres of Kor, where night by night I laid me down to rest in the cold company of the dead. From time to time, once in a generation mayhap, I would lift the cloths that covered him and look upon his pale beauty (for those old embalmers did not lie), and kiss his brow of ice and weep and weep. Then once more I laid the shroud, or a new shroud, upon him and went my weary way.

Oh! it is terrible in this world where all is change, where even the stones grow old and die to re-form again, to be the one thing that changeth not for ever. Yet, that was my lot, such was the gift of the Fire-lord whom I had wedded and embraced. There I sat in my eternal beauty which I was doomed to hide, lest brute men should be maddened at the sight of it, so that I must slay them with the lightning of my will. There I brooded, gathering to my breast all that wisdom of Mother Nature of whom now I was a part, all the useless wisdom whose weight at length clogged my sense and cramped my soul. There I sat, eaten of desire for one dead and burning with jealous hate of that woman who had borne his child and who, as I knew well, wandered with him, greater than I perhaps and still more fair, in some Elysium that even my spirit could not reach, taking the place that I might fulfil, if only I could attain to the boon of death which is everlastingly denied to me, until the old world itself shall die. There, I say, I sat while the slow fire of the torturer Time, burning in my breast, ate its path through all my being, till the hot soul within me turned to the bitter ash of hopelessness.

Oh! why did he not come? Why did he not come? Surely the circle must be complete and the time fulfilled. Surely he must be weary of those unknown heavenly fields and of the coarse love of Egypt's Lady. Surely he would come and soon. Only then, what if here, as there, she still companioned him?

At length one came, and when I learned of it my heart flamed up with hope as a torch flames in these dark caves. Alas! it was not he. So soon as my eyes fell on him afar, I knew it, yonder in the temple of Kor whither I had gone upon the matters of some petty savage trouble, such as had arisen thrice since the days of Philo. I saw and grew sick with hope destroyed, so sick that had he but known it, this little, wizened wanderer at that moment stood near to the world's edge. Yet afterward I came to like him well, perchance because he reminded me so much of Philo that once or twice almost I thought——But let this matter be.

He was a strange man, that wanderer; very shrewd, but one who believed nothing which he could not see or touch or handle. Thus when I told him tales concerning myself and my length of days and why I sat at Kor in beauty, yet like one who is dead in a desert, openly he mocked at them, which angered me. Not all of these were true, be it admitted, because, being a part of Nature as I am, how can I always speak the truth?

Nature shows many faces to those who court her; Nature has desert-fantasies wherewith the traveller is oft deceived, thinking he sees that which he does not see, though in some shape or form of a surety it exists elsewhere. Nature also keeps her secrets close and ever instructs in parables that yet hold the seed of perfect verity.

So, being a part of Nature's self, did I with that wanderer, as indeed I do to this day with Holly the learned, who followed after him. Yet here the example has its flaw, for this man who was called Watcher-in-the-Night, a name that fitted him well enough, did not court me, as her watchers court Nature the beautiful. Nay, he turned his back upon me saying he was not one who loved, moth-like, to singe his wings in a flame, however bright; I think because often he had singed them already.

Still, I found this so strange that almost I began to wonder whether once more my beauty was on the wane and whether it needed longer to be hidden beneath a veil, or whether perchance men had grown wiser than they used to be. Therefore, once for a little moment I put out my strength and brought him to his knees and having taught him certain lessons, I laughed at him and let him go. Yet be it said that I held and hold him dear, and look onward to the day when we shall meet again, as perchance we have met in those that are long past. So enough of this brave and honest man, gently born also, and instructed in his fashion. Doubtless he died many years ago.

I tire of this long, sad task; let the end of my tale be short.

*********

At last, at last, came Kallikrates reborn, lacking memories, changed in spirit, and yet in face and form the very same. Holly brought him hither, or he brought Holly, because of an ancient, lying screed that Amenartas wrote upon a sherd, which from age to age had passed down in his race, urging some descendant of her blood to find me out and slay me, for this Egyptian fool thought that I could be slain.

He came, and by Heaven! I knew not that he was here until the crabbed Holly led me to the couch whereon he lay fever-stricken and at the very point of death. By my arts I dragged him back from between those doors of doom, that almost once again had closed behind him, and afterward, revealing to him my beauty and my burning love, caused him to worship me. Yet, mark! He came not alone; as I feared would chance, something of Amenartas prisoned in a savage woman's breast came with him, and already he was her lover.

I slew that woman who was obstinate and would not leave him; though the deed grieved me, I slew her because I must. It mattered little, for soon she was forgot, and I held him fast.

Of the rest little need be said, for Holly knows it all and tells me that he has written it in a book. Because I might not wed with mortal man I led Kallikrates, he who now was known as Leo, down the perilous ways to that hid cavern where ever the bright Spirit of Life, clad in flame and thunder, marches on his endless round. Behold! as it had been over two thousand years before, so it was now. Again Kallikrates feared to enter the flames and, putting on majesty, to become undying king of all the world. Aye, even though the prize of my glory lay to his hand, his flesh shrank from the Fire.

Therefore that he might learn courage, once more I gave myself to the embrace of the god, and lo! this time he slew me. Yes, in utter shame and hideousness before my lover's eyes, there I died, or rather seemed to die; an ancient, shrivelled, ape-like thing. Yet dying, my unconquered spirit gave me strength to mutter in his ear that I should come again and once more be beautiful.

Nay, I did not die. Far away again I became incarnate in this distant Asian land, which after all is my own, since in a part of it first I saw the light. Here in this cavern-monastery where still lingers some shadow of the worship of the moon and of the great Principle that in the old days was named Isis, Queen of Heaven, once more I was clothed with mortal flesh.

The years went by, but two or three of them, and I found the power to search out Kallikrates, or Leo Vincey, still living on the earth, and in a vision showed him the mountains that I inhabit. He was faithful. Yes, like Holly he was faithful, and together they followed that vision. For twice ten years they searched, and then at last they found me. They passed the perils and the tests; Kallikrates, or Leo Vincey, escaped the web spun by the Queen Atene, she in whom Amenartas once more shows herself upon the earth. They endured the appointed trials. Aye, when I unveiled before him on the mountain peak, my Love, my eternal Love, my doom and my desire, found strength and faith to kiss my hideous, withered brow. Then was that faith rewarded. Then before his very eyes I changed into the flower of all beauty, into the glory of all power, and he worshipped, worshipped, worshipped!

*********

Now soon we shall be wed. Now soon the curse shall fall from us, like to a severed chain. Now soon my sin will be forgiven, and side by side we shall tread the endless path of splendour, no longer two but one, that path which leads through perfect joy—oh! whither does it lead? Even to-day I know not.

But this cannot be yet awhile. First he must bathe him in the Fire, since mortal man may not mix with my immortality and live as man. For while this world endures—have I not said it?—I who have drunk of the very Cup of its Spirit, aye, twice drunk deep, must also endure, and I think the world is still far away from the gates of Death. Aye, though I change a thousand times, still I shall be the same in other shapes, and though I seem to vanish, yet I must appear again.

Where I go, also, thither Kallikrates must follow me, or I must follow him, since he and I are one, and on me is laid the burden of the uplifting of the soul of him whose body once I slew.

And yet, and yet—oh! he is still human and death dogs the heels of man. As I write a horror seizes me. Aye, my hand trembles on the scroll and my spirit quakes. What if some chance, some sickness, some fate should strike him down, leaving me once more desolate and divorced, so that elsewhere all this dark tragedy must be played afresh?

Away with that hell-born thought! There are no gods and, Fate, I defy thee who am myself a Fate and thine equal. I will conquer thee, O Fate; thou shalt not conquer me. There is naught but that eternal Good whereof the fiery tongue which was the soul of Noot spoke, or seemed to speak, to me in my haunted sleep at Kor, and to that Good I, Ayesha, make my prayer.

Lo! I have suffered. Lo! I have paid the count to its last coin. Lo! I have endured. Through the long ages I have sown in tears, and my hour of harvest is at hand; aye, the night of sorrow dies, and already on the peak of heavenly Peace shines the dawn of joy. . . . My lord hunts upon the mountain after the fashion of men, and I brood within the caves after the fashion of women. . . .

". . . Holly, Holly! Awake! Look yonder! What is this? I seem to see my lord struggling on the snow and the spotted beast has him by the throat—"

\* \* \* \* \* \* \* \*

Here ends Ayesha's manuscript. Its last words are almost illegible and are written by one whose agitation was evidently great; indeed their appearance suggests that they were set down in some half-automatic fashion while the writer's mind was occupied with other matters. With them Ayesha ends her tale of which in outline the rest is to be found elsewhere—in the book that is named after her. Suddenly she appears to have tired of her task. Perhaps, heralded and induced by the incident of the snow-leopard that went near to ending the life of Leo Vincey, the presage of terrible woes to come, to which she alludes and not obscurely, paralyzed Ayesha's mind or filled it with forebodings that rendered her incapable of further effort of the kind, or at least unwilling to endure its labour, of which, it is clear, already she was wearying.

*Editor*

LEONAUR

# ALSO FROM LEONAUR
## AVAILABLE IN SOFTCOVER OR HARDCOVER WITH DUST JACKET

**TROS OF SAMOTHRACE 1: WOLVES OF THE TIBER** *by Talbot Mundy*—When his ship is taken and his crew slaughtered Tros of Samothrace is captured by Imperial Rome.

**TROS OF SAMOTHRACE 2: DRAGONS OF THE NORTH** *by Talbot Mundy*—Tros of Samothrace burns for vengeance and has declared himself the implacable enemy of Rome.

**TROS OF SAMOTHRACE 3: SERPENT OF THE WAVES** *by Talbot Mundy*—Tros, his allies and the forces of Rome have drawn apart to prepare for the conflict to come.

**TROS OF SAMOTHRACE 4: CITY OF THE EAGLES** *by Talbot Mundy*—As Tros of Samothrace continues in his attempts to confound Caesar's plans for the invasion of Britain, he journeys to the Eternal City to seek the aid of its great leaders—and Caesar's opponents—Cato, Pompey and the Vestal Virgins themselves!

**TROS OF SAMOTHRACE 5: CLEOPATRA** *by Talbot Mundy*—Cleopatra—Queen of Egypt—is a formidable character ever ready to play the game of intrigue, betrayal and shifting loyalties to suit her own objectives. Blood will surely be spilt and once again Tros finds himself inexorably caught up in monumental events that threaten his life and those he loves.

**TROS OF SAMOTHRACE 6: THE PURPLE PIRATE** *by Talbot Mundy*—The epic saga of the ancient world—Tros of Samothrace—draws to a conclusion in this sixth—and final—volume. Julius Caesar has been assassinated and Queen Cleopatra of Egypt finds herself in a perilous position and desperate for allies to secure her power.

**THE ILLUSTRATED & COMPLETE BRIGADIER GERARD** *by Sir Arthur Conan Doyle*—These are the adventures of Conan Doyle's incomparable French hero-the finest swordsman in the Light Cavalry-Etienne Gerard. Arranged for the first time in historical chronological order, his many enthusiasts can now properly appreciate his colourful career as he fights, loves and blunders his way through the Napoleonic epoch-from his earliest adventure as a young blade determined to reach his lady love despite the unwelcome attention of her fathers bull-through many campaigns and special missions-to the bloody field of Waterloo, the downfall of his beloved Emperor and beyond. This is the complete collection of these classic stories. What makes this edition exceptional is the inclusion of nearly 140 illustrations-mostly by the famed military artist William Barnes Wollen-which accurately portray the spirit of the stories and the uniforms and scenes of the events they portray.

LEONAUR

# ALSO FROM LEONAUR

**AVAILABLE IN SOFTCOVER OR HARDCOVER WITH DUST JACKET**

**GARRETT P. SERVISS' SCIENCE FICTION** *by Garrett P. Serviss*—Three Interplanetary Adventures including the unauthorised sequel to H. G. Wells' *War of the Worlds*--*Edison's Conquest of Mars, A Columbus of Space, The Moon Metal.*

**JUNK DAY** by *Arthur Sellings*—". . . . his finest novel was his last, *Junk Day*, a post-holocaust tale set in the ruins of his native London and peopled with engrossing character types . . . . perhaps grimmer than his previous work but pointedly more energetic." *The Encyclopedia of Science Fiction.*

**KIPLING'S SCIENCE FICTION** by *Rudyard Kipling*—Science Fiction & Fantasy stories by a Master Storyteller including 'As East As A,B,C' 'With The Night Mail'.

**THE COLLECTED SCIENCE FICTION AND FANTASY OF STANLEY G. WEINBAUM: THE BLACK HEART** by *Stanley G. Weinbaum*—Classic Strange Tales Including: the Complete Novel The Dark Other, Plus Proteus Island and Others Stories included in this Volume The Dark Other (novel) Proteus Island The Adaptive Ultimate Pymalion's Spectacles.

**THE COLLECTED SCIENCE FICTION AND FANTASY OF STANLEY G. WEINBAUM: STRANGE GENIUS** by *Stanley G. Weinbaum*—Classic Tales of the Human Mind at Work Including the Complete Novel The New Adam, the 'van Manderpootz' Stories and Others Stories included in this Volume The New Adam (novel) The Brink of Infinity The Circle of Zero Graph The Worlds of If The Ideal The Point of View.

**THE COLLECTED SCIENCE FICTION AND FANTASY OF STANLEY G. WEINBAUM OTHER EARTHS** by *Stanley G. Weinbaum*—Classic Futuristic Tales Including: Dawn of Flame & its Sequel The Black Flame, plus The Revolution of 1960 & Others.

**THE COLLECTED SCIENCE FICTION AND FANTASY OF STANLEY G. WEINBAUM INTERPLANETARY ODYSSEYS** by *Stanley G. Weinbaum*—Classic Tales of Interplanetary Adventure Including: A Martian Odyssey, its Sequel Valley of Dreams, the Complete 'Ham' Hammond Stories and Others Stories included in this Volume Mars A Martian Odyssey Valley of Dreams Venus Parasite Planet The Lotus Eaters Uranus The Planet of Doubt Titan Flight on Titan Pluto The Red Peri Io The Mad Moon Europa Redemption Cairn Ganymede Tidal Moon.

**SUPERNATURAL BUCHAN** by *John Buchan*—Stories of Ancient Spirits, Uncanny Places & Strange Creatures.